# RIGHTEOUS
# INDIGNATION

*by*

## Virginia C. Foley

## 2000

# Copyright © 2000 by Virginia C. Foley

*ISBN 0-7414-0505-9*

*Published by:*
**Buy Books on the web.com**
*519 West Lancaster Avenue*
*Haverford, PA 19041-1413*
*Info@buybooksontheweb.com*
*www.buybooksontheweb.com*
*Toll-free (877) BUY BOOK*
*Local Phone (610) 520-2500*
*Fax (610) 519-0261*

*Printed in the United States of America*
*Printed on Recycled Paper*
*Published October-2000*

For Hacksaw—

Life was always an
adventure, which he lived to
the fullest.
Till we meet again . . .

To Mom—thanks for your encouragement and starting me off in life as a lover of books.

To Melinda and Judy—I would have been lost without your editing skills and support. Thanks for helping me to believe that I had a story worth telling.

Man is unjust, but God is just; and finally justice triumphs.
- Henry Wadsworth Longfellow, *Evangeline*, 1847.

What other dungeon is so dark as one's own heart! What jailer so inexorable as one's self!
- Nathaniel Hawthorne, *The House of the Seven Gables*, 1851.

# CHAPTER 1

Cain sat in the small town police station, feeling tired and miserable. It had been a long day. He and three of his friends, including his closest friend, Scott Jacobs, had spent the warm, summer day in Lake Geneva boating and swimming and having a good time. It was the summer before his senior year in high school, and it was the first day he had had off from the grocery store where he worked in over a week. It felt good to cut loose and have good, clean fun. Then how did they end up here?

He thought back a few hours. They had made a final stop at a drug store before starting for home. If only they hadn't. It was Mike who had noticed the parking meter was loose in the ground and had put it in his car while the others were in the store. Mike had said it would make a great conversation piece for his room. Who were they to argue? It was his car and his wild idea. Not one of them had stopped to think that they were stealing city property, let alone the fact that it had money in it. How dumb could a bunch of honor students be? Then Greg had to go and stick his feet out the open window as they drove along the highway on the way home. That had drawn the policeman's attention. It didn't take him long to spot the stolen meter. The next thing they knew, they were following the police car to the station and calling home.

So, there he was—seventeen, ready to begin his senior year in high school, and a criminal. His stomach did a turn. He'd always been prone to mischief—more so than any of his four brothers or his sister—but he'd never been brought in by the police before. He was nervous and frightened. He didn't want a police record. What if he had to go to jail?

"What's the matter?" Scott asked him. "You haven't said a word in the past ten minutes."

"I keep thinking," he answered. "What a mess."

"It's not that bad," said Mike who was a year older than the rest of them and always seemed to know more. "They haven't booked us or anything. If they were serious, they would've done that first thing. They're just trying to scare us. We didn't do anything that wrong."

"I like the way you say *we*," said Scott. "You're the idiot who picked that thing up. The rest of us are only guilty by association!"

"Okay, okay," shrugged Mike. "You'll see, though, you're not in as much trouble as you think."

"I'll let my dad be the judge of that," sighed Cain.

Just then the door of the small holding room opened as if by prophecy and a policeman appeared.

"Cain Farrell," he said officially, "follow me."

Cain looked at his three friends and swallowed the lump in his throat. Scott winked at him. As Cain got up and followed the policeman out, he saw his parents waiting for him. He was relieved to see them, but he was mortified and dreaded their reaction. He was their second

1

youngest child, and none of them had ever been involved with the police before. His father, usually a reasonable and understanding man, looked at him sternly. His mother, who was his greatest ally and source of support, gave him a sad look as she fought the urge to run to him and hug him.

The policeman explained the situation to them. He told them that the police viewed the whole thing as unpremeditated and, though foolish, innocent fun. There would be no charges filed, but each of them would be fined $75 to pay for replacement of the meter and released to his parents. Will Farrell paid his son's fine, thanked the policemen, and left with his family.

"Dad," said Cain as they walked out toward the car.

"Don't say anything," said Will sternly. "Just get in the car. We'll talk when we get home."

Dejectedly, Cain got in the back seat of the car and tried not to think of his father's quiet anger. The long drive home was unnaturally quiet. Nobody spoke. After a while, Cain closed his eyes and slept through the uncomfortable calm before the storm. The next thing he was aware of was his mother's gentle touch as she coaxed him awake. He rolled his head toward her and opened his eyes.

"We're home, darling," she said.

He thought about how beautiful his mother was. He loved the hint of the Irish brogue that refused to be chased away, even after over twenty-five years of living in America. Moments later, reality dawned as he fully awoke and remembered the trouble he was in.

"I'll meet you upstairs in about two minutes," said Will as they walked into the large Victorian house.

Without a word, Cain went straight up to the room he shared with his identical twin, Matt, and their younger brother, Jim. He was happy to find the room empty. He sat on his bed, anxiously awaiting his father's arrival, which was prompt. Will closed the door after he entered.

"What seems to be your problem?" the father asked and then continued without waiting for an answer. "You're an honor student, a star athlete, newly elected president of the Student Council for next year, but you don't seem to have one shred of commonsense! Haven't your mother and I taught you anything?!"

"I was in the store," said Cain offering an explanation. "When I came out, Mike already had it in his car."

"You didn't know it was there?"

"Yeah, I knew. But he was taking it for himself. I didn't have anything to do with it—none of the rest of us did."

"Did you explain that to the police?"

"We explained how it happened and that none of us meant to steal anything—not even Mike."

"Did the police fine you any less than they did him? Did they just take him in and let the rest of you go?"

"No."

"Does that tell you anything about the wisdom of sticking around when things are not quite right and trouble could be brewing— even if you're not directly involved? I've told you and your brothers and sister that I didn't care what time it was or how far away you were, you could call me if you had to walk away from a bad situation, and I'd come and get you. You never had to stick around where trouble could be going down because you had no other way home. Do you remember that?"

"Yes," answered Cain staring ashamedly at the floor.

"Then I can only assume that you got caught today because you just plain weren't thinking! Come on, Cain, you know right and wrong, and taking something that isn't yours is wrong. So is being with someone else who's taking something that isn't his! You're just lucky you ran into a very understanding police force. And this whole fiasco cost me $75!"

"I'll pay you back when I get paid on Monday."

"You're damn right you will! In fact, you'll pay me back double—$75 in cash and $75 from your hide. Are you working tomorrow?"

"No, not until Monday."

"Well, I own your ass between now and Monday. I'll pay you $5 an hour to work off the second $75. Fifteen hours of hard labor and $75 cash. Then we'll call it even. The garage needs to be cleaned, as does the basement, and I have a number of other odd jobs that will keep you so busy this weekend that you won't have time for social life of any kind—not even a phone call. Every privilege or means of socializing has just been taken from you. No TV, phone, radio, **nothing**. You work your ass off all day, and then after dinner, you can sit up in your room until you go to bed. Maybe after two days of that, you'll think the next time you're confronted with a problem. You can start the sitting-in-the-room end of your punishment right now."

"I was supposed to go to a party with Joanne tomorrow night," said Cain still reeling from his father's harsh words.

"You got it right, son, you were supposed to go. Now you'll be cooling your ass right here."

"Can I call her so she knows?"

"I'll give you ten minutes. I'll see you in the morning at 8:00 sharp. Set your alarm." Without another word, Will left the room, firmly closing the door.

"Right," Cain said repressing the urge to slam his fist into the wall.

Picking up the phone, he punched in Joanne's number. As he listened to the other line ring, he tried to remember when he last ate.

"Hello," said Joanne in a cheery voice.

"It's me, Jo."

"Cain! I thought you were going to stop over when you got home. I've been waiting for you. I was just about to call . . ."

"I know," he interrupted. "I had planned on it, but there's been a problem."

"What?' she asked as the merriment left her voice. "Are you all right?"

"Yeah, I'm fine, but I can't come over."

"Cain, it's Friday night."

"I'm painfully aware of what night it is. I'm dead, or I may as well be. I've been seriously and unconditionally grounded for the entire weekend. I'm afraid that means the party tomorrow night, too. I'm sorry. This is the only call I'm allowed to make or receive. Every prisoner's allowed one call."

"Now what'd you get yourself into?"

He sighed miserably and told her the whole story.

"It was just one of those dumb things," he reasoned.

"Sometimes you're such a kid," she complained. "What's wrong with you?"

"I don't know," he answered meekly. "Don't be mad at me. My dad's mad enough for three people, and when my grandfather finds out, he'll give me hell, too. He sometimes thinks that just because he lives with us, he's entitled to chew my ass too."

"I'm sorry, Cain, but you bring it on yourself. Darn it, I was looking forward to that party. Why don't you do yourself a favor and start hanging out with Matt more often. He's the one that got all the commonsense when you two were conceived. There was a slip-up there somewhere. I guess it's too much to hope that after seventeen years, a little of it might rub off on you. I don't know why I love you so much."

"Ouch, that hurt. Have you forgotten my great body? And I'm handsome, witty, and intelligent!"

"So is Matt. And he has the same great body."

"Matt's going out with Alexis."

"I know, but if he wasn't, I'd drop you on your beautiful ass and pick up with him. He doesn't get into half the trouble you do."

"Boy, you really know how to hit below the waist. And after all I've been through today . . . I thought I could count on you."

He was smiling, and she knew it. That made her even more determined to scold him further.

"You're not taking this very seriously! I'm a year younger than you and twice as mature!"

"I'm taking it seriously," he argued. "It's just that I'm not a terribly serious person. Life's too short. I don't want to waste it being serious and boringly mature. Come on now, I have a long hard weekend ahead of me, and I have to hang up in a few minutes. Say something nice to me."

"I can't think of anything right now."

"Sure you can. Stop pouting and think about how much you're going to miss me. Think about me—after over a week I finally got three days off from work. I spent part of one in the police station, and the other two I'm going to spend being my father's slave! He's going to stand over me with a whip and work my poor ass from dusk till dawn—both days!

"Poor baby," she smiled.

"I'll make this up to you, Jo, I swear," he said becoming serious again. "I'm really sorry about the party."

"Maybe I'll call Paul Blakely and see if he wants to take me," she teased. "He's been waiting for you and me to break up."

"Come on, Joanne," said Cain not the least bit amused. "Don't do this to me! I have to miss the party, too. I'm joking around, but none of this is easy on me. I'm just trying to make the best of it. Don't make me sit around worrying if you're with someone else. I love you, Jo. Go to the party; just don't have too good a time."

"I'm sorry," she said sincerely. "You know I could never have fun with anyone but you. I was just kidding about Paul."

"That's more like it," he said as she felt the warmth of his smile travel through the telephone line.

"It's just lucky for you that you're so incredibly gorgeous, or I'd send you on your way in a minute!"

"We'll do something Monday night after work when I'm a free man again, okay?"

"A free **boy**, Cain," she corrected, "You've yet to prove yourself a man to me."

"You won't let me prove to you that I'm a man," he answered slyly.

"Let's don't get into that age-old argument again, or we'll end up in another fight. Sex has nothing to do with it! I'm talking about emotional maturity—and in that respect, I think you'll always be a little boy! But I'm crazy about you, anyway. I just can't help myself. If fact, if I could see you right now, I'd probably be melted all over your floor. There, is that something nice to send you off on your long weekend of hard labor?"

"Yeah," he smiled warmly. "I'll miss you. I'm crazy about you, too. I'd better go. You're not too mad at me, are you?"

"It's just the biggest party of the summer, but, no, I can never be mad at you for more than five or ten seconds at a time. I love you. Don't work too hard."

"I'll try not to. I love you, too. I'll talk to you Monday—I'll call during my break at work."

He hung up the phone and flopped on his bed. It wasn't long before his younger brother Jim came into the room they shared. Cain immediately rolled over on his side with his back to his brother.

Jim was fourteen, and the only one of Cain's siblings that he didn't get along with. There was a definite personality clash between the two brothers, and neither took much delight in the other's company.

"Nice going, Ace," said Jim. "You're getting into the big time, aren't you—the police and all?"

"Shut up," said Cain to the wall.

"I hope it was worth getting your wings clipped for the weekend," continued Jim foolishly. "I know I wouldn't want to be the one to clean out the garage. What a disaster area! And I was supposed to help Dad with the basement, but now I'm off the hook. I have to thank you for that. Grandpa said if it was up to him, he'd beat your ass with a belt on top of it. Boy, I'd sure like to see that!"

"Well Grandpa can go to hell," said Cain rolling to his back and leering at his brother. "And if you don't shut the hell up, I'm going to knock you cold!"

"Whoa, I'm scared," taunted Jim.

"Get lost, James," said Matt entering the room.

He grabbed Jim by the collar and aimed him at the door.

"Hey!" protested Jim. "This is my room, too!"

"No kidding," teased Matt. "Hey, Cain, this is his room, too."

"Couldn't be," said Cain rolling back toward the wall. "We don't allow no fairies in here."

"Go," whispered Matt motioning Jim toward the door. "I'm trying to save your life here. If he gets out of that bed, you're dead."

Jim considered the facts and wisely left; Cain was a good bit larger than he was. Matt went over and sat down on his own bed.

"You sure have lousy luck," he said to Cain. "Whatever possessed Mike to rip off that thing, anyway?"

"I don't know, and I don't really want to talk about it any more. I feel stupid enough."

"Steer clear of Grandpa, will you?" warned Matt. "He's on his high horse again. He's down there ranting and raving about how Dad's being too easy on you. Just let him talk. Don't go mixing in."

"I don't mix in with him," scowled Cain as he turned to look at his twin. "He comes after me."

"And you always try to get in the last word. If he says anything to you, just keep your mouth shut. Don't antagonize him."

As if Matt had been sent to prepare his way, Robert Farrell appeared at the door. Cain looked up at his accusing grandfather.

"You're damned lucky I'm not your father," said the eldest Farrell. "By God, if I was, I'd take a leather strap to your backside! And I guarantee you, you'd think twice before you stepped out of line again. You're a hell-raiser, Cain. A dance with the devil is all that makes you happy. Someone had better put a stop to your recklessness before it's too late. But your father won't listen to me. No one will. Tell me, do you plan these things to embarrass your family?"

6

"No sir," said Cain keeping a lid on his seething temper.

"You could've fooled me," mumbled Robert as he walked out and went to his own room.

Cain blasted the doorway his grandfather had just vacated with a lethal stare and gave the absent, old man the finger.

"Now, now," teased Matt. "Have some respect. And you might want to thank God he's not your father!"

"What the hell is his problem, anyway? He's always on my back about something or other. He never bothers with any of the rest of you."

"Maybe he just doesn't like hell-raisers!" smiled Matt. "Ignore him. It isn't worth the trouble you can get."

"Yeah, well, it hurts the way he talks to me."

"Well, it'll hurt even more if he beats your ass one day."

"Let him try!" said Cain angrily. "Who does he think he is, anyway?"

"Just stay out of his way. I gotta go. I have a date."

"It's late."

"I know. Alexis had to work. We have a couple of hours, so we thought we'd go get something to eat."

"Oh," moaned Cain, "don't mention food to me. I'm starving."

"You didn't have dinner?"

"No, and Dad was way too mad for me to remind him of that."

"I'll bring you a doggy bag."

"Better not. Jim will probably be up here when you get home, and he'd love nothing better then to tattle. I'm not sure if I'm starving as part of my punishment or if Dad was so worked up he overlooked it. The fact that Mom hasn't been up her with a feast fit for a king makes me feel it wasn't an oversight. Besides, I plan to be blissfully unconscious by the time you get back. I don't want to deal with this day any more."

"Okay. Then I'll see you in the morning."

As Matt left the room, Cain looked over at the clock. "Late" was relative. 9:15 was late for a teenage date but early for a healthy, active seventeen-year-old who had to stay in his room with virtually nothing to do. After staring at the ceiling for a few minutes, he decided he might as well go to bed. He didn't want to have to face his sister and his two other brothers when they got home. There would be time for that tomorrow. And there was no telling when Jim would come back up. He definitely didn't want another encounter with him.

Getting up and stretching to his full height, he walked over to the window and looked out. The night was clear and starry. It was difficult to remember the fun part of the day any longer. It seemed remote and almost like a vague dream. With a long, cleansing sigh, he stripped off his clothes and got in bed, covering up with only a sheet.

As he went down for breakfast in the morning, he could smell bacon cooking. He had planned to fix himself a bowl of cold cereal and about a half a loaf of toast. His mood lightened as he thought of his mother. She was the best. Although she always supported his father when it came to discipline, Cain knew where her heart was. She was beautiful, tender, and loving, and he knew he could always count on her.

"How come you're up already?" he asked as he kissed her cheek.

"I know some of the plans your father has for you today," she smiled, "and I figured you could use a good, hearty breakfast."

"That bad, huhn?"

"You'll live," she assured him as she put a plate of bacon and French toast in front of him. "I figure you must be pretty hungry. Unless they serve dinner in police lock-ups these days."

"They don't, and I am beyond hungry. Thanks, Mom."

"I'll keep cooking, and you just tell me when you're finally full. Did you sleep well? I came up to say good night to you, but you were already sound asleep."

"Yeah, I turned in early. There wasn't much use in staying up. And I did sleep well. I didn't hear a thing—not even Jim when he came to bed, and usually turns the light on and crashes around the room like a mad bull."

"He can be a bit abrasive, can't he?" smiled Nora.

"I can think of better words to describe him, but he's your son, so we'll leave it at abrasive. Actually, he's a spoiled brat, Mom."

"Well, you were the youngest for three years until he came along. I don't think you escaped completely unscathed."

"All right, all right, we're all a little spoiled. Who wouldn't be with you for a mom? Look at this breakfast."

"Well, we don't want our prisoners dropping like flies out there in the hot sun because of lack of nourishment!"

Cain smiled at her as his face lit up.

"You have a way of making things seem bearable," he said. "I don't feel so stupid when I'm with you."

"Stupid?!" she said as if the thought was from outer space. "You? You are anything but stupid. You and Matt are right there at the top of your class."

"You know what I mean, Ma. Sometimes stupid has nothing to do with IQ, as Dad so aptly pointed out last night. I've been thinking about something Joanne said to me last night when I called her to break our date for tonight."

"And what would that be?" she asked lovingly as she sat down next to him.

"She said I have no commonsense," he said looking up at his mother for some reassurance. "She said Matt got it all. Could that happen? He is pretty levelheaded and responsible. He seems to be able to avoid some of the problems that I get caught up in. I mean, when it comes to grades, he's good, but I'm better. He has to work harder, and he still doesn't do quite as well as I do. Then doesn't it stand to reason that Joanne has a point?"

"Well, it's possible, I guess, but you're forgetting one thing. You're a pretty together person when you have to be. It isn't just a quirk that you've been voted in to so many leadership roles. Your classmates and your teachers have been putting their confidence in you for years now. If you weren't responsible and sensible, they would've dropped you a long time ago. The same with baseball and anything else you partake in. You have a certain charisma that none of my other children quite has; but even more important, you have character. A pretty face and a strong, handsome body aren't enough to have gotten you as far as you've gone. People see through that kind of thing before too long. That might get you through your younger years, but they would've caught on to you by now. Most people know the real thing when they see it. You're fortunate enough to have the dynamite good looks, the intelligence, the character, and the drive to make you outstanding—but you're not perfect. Nobody is. Commonsense might be something you have to work on. The trouble with being such a fine, all-around person that you are is that people come to expect too much from you. They want you to be Superman. And when you show them you're human, they're disappointed. That's where Joanne's at. You're more spirited and out-going than Matt is. That's why you get into more mischief. And, you don't always think until it's too late . . . but that doesn't mean you're irresponsible and have no commonsense. There are times, however, when your lack of thinking is serious enough that it has to be punished—so that you learn the next time. You have the right to be human, but you also have to accept the responsibility for that right and pay whatever consequences are demanded as a result of it."

"I don't know what I'd do without you," he smiled.

"Nor I without you." She patted his cheek and got up and began fussing around the kitchen.

As Cain turned his head, he locked in on his father entering the kitchen. The smile faded from his face.

"Good morning," said Will, more business-like than friendly.

"Hi, Dad," answered Cain as he looked down at his plate to finish the last of his breakfast.

Will walked over to him and taking a hold of his chin, he raised the twin's face so that he could see it better. He squinted down at his son. Cain looked at him puzzledly.

"Just checking," Will explained. "I keep hoping that as you and Matt get older, you'll start looking less alike, but the opposite seems to be happening. I just wanted to be sure that if I'm going to be kicking ass today, I have the right ass." A trace of a grin covered his face.

"You have the right one," said Cain without a smile. "Where do you want me to start?"

"You'd better start with the lawn," said Will. "It needs to be mowed, front and back. You'd better get it done before it gets too hot. It's supposed to be a scorcher today. And you can go from there right to the garage."

Cain picked up his dishes and carried them to the sink. After he thanked his mother and kissed her cheek, he walked out the back door.

Nora turned and looked at her husband.

"Oh-oh," said Will. "I know that look anywhere. I'm in trouble."

"No, it's just that I think you're being a little hard on him. That business with the police wasn't even really his fault."

"I knew we'd end up on different sides of this issue before it was over. He has a way of getting through to you and winning you over."

"That's not true," insisted Nora. "It's just that I think making him pay back the fine and even grounding him for the weekend is punishment enough. You don't have to make him work so hard when it's so ungodly hot out."

"My father tells me I'm too easy on him. He thinks he should get a beating on top of everything else. Then you tell me I'm being too hard on him. The way I see it, I'm the middle-of-the-road, which is probably the best course. Unless of course, you and my father want to fight over who's going to discipline him. I'll bow out and let one of you play the bad guy. He has to learn, Nora; and a little hard work won't hurt him. And don't you dare be running out there coddling him every half-hour, undoing all the good I'm trying to instill."

"I won't. But this is going to be a very long weekend for me, too."


Halfway through the lawn, Cain stopped and took off his shirt and threw it on the back steps. Then he reached in his back pocket and pulled out a bandanna. Rolling it up, he tied it around his forehead. He looked quite dashing as the girl next-door and her friend spied on him through the curtains and giggled.

The Farrell house was busy. Cain watched as friends came to call and his brothers all took off for parks and beaches, each thanking him for taking over the chores that had been theirs that weekend. Without acknowledging any of them, he grudgingly went on with his work.

He finished with the grass and bagged the clippings, storing it behind the garage. The sun was shining full force by then, and it promised to be an exceptionally hot and humid day. As he went to the hose for a drink, his friend Mike drove up into the driveway.

"Cain?" he asked with uncertainty. Nobody ever knew for sure which twin was which, especially when they were not side by side.

"Yeah. Hi," said Cain running the water from the hose on the back of his neck. "What's up?"

"There are a bunch of us headed for the beach. How 'bout it?"

"Can't," answered Cain. "I'm Number One on the shit list around here this weekend after yesterday. I'm not out here working my ass off because I'm a nice guy."

"Your folks were mad?"

"You could say that. Yours weren't, I suppose."

"Not really. They said it was a dumb thing to do and asked me if I'd learned my lesson. That was pretty much it."

"Christ," sighed Cain as he pushed the lawnmower toward the garage to put it away. "You lucked out. It's going to be weeks before I'm out of the doghouse. And you'd better get out of here before I get in even more trouble. I'm being held incommunicado."

"Go ask your dad," coaxed Mike as he followed Cain to the garage. "He'll let you go. Then we'll go pick up Greg and Scott and forget all about that ugly, little experience."

Cain got the push broom out of the garage and began sweeping the driveway as he spoke. He wasn't about to take a chance and stop even for a minute.

"Let me explain something to you," he said. "I have four brothers and a sister. We usually all share these chores on the weekends. This week they all got off because I'm doing everything by myself. No radio, no TV, no phone, no nothing. It's just work, eat, and sit in my room for the weekend. So you see, there is no way in hell I'm going in there to ask him if I can go to the beach with you."

"What about Marta's party tonight? You're surely not going to miss that?"

"Have you been listening to me, or what? I'm grounded, man. In the shit house. My dad is pissed as hell. I'm not going anywhere till Monday. All because you had to have that damn parking meter, and because I was too stupid to stop you. Now will you get lost before I get my ass kicked again. I'm not supposed to be socializing."

"But Marta's party. We've been waiting weeks for this. Hey, maybe Matt could spell you for a while for the party anyway. You'd at least get to go for a while."

"Do you think we haven't thought of that one? Even tried it once or twice?" snarled Cain pushing even more ferociously at the grass clippings on the driveway. "Not this time, Mike. Now get out of here before I hit you with this broom!"

"Okay. I'm going. I'll see you Monday, I guess. And don't worry, I won't let Joanne get lonely at the party tonight!" Cain shot him a deadly, unamused look. "I was just kidding, okay? I'm going. Bye."

Cain leaned on the broom and frowned miserably as he watched his friend get into his beat-up old car and drive away. Then with a sigh, he squinted up at the house. There was his father, arms crossed at his chest, monitoring him reproachfully from the window.

"Shit," he mumbled under his breath then quickly got back to work.

Just as he was returning from the garage after putting the broom away, he spotted the family dog, a large Irish Setter, squatting in the middle of the lawn.

"You stupid dog!" screamed Cain humorlessly as he fell against the garage for support. "I just cleaned all that crap up before I mowed the lawn!"

He sighed in frustration and went back for the bag and a hand shovel. As he scooped up the mess, the playful dog jumped on him and licked his face, almost knocking him over.

"You think you're clever, don't you?" said Cain trying to hold him at bay so he could finish the job. "Well, I got news for you—if you were half as smart as you think you are, you'd learn to use the toilet like the rest of us!"

He worked non-stop throughout the morning, pausing only occasionally for a drink from the hose. Will kept a close eye on him and was satisfied that things were getting accomplished.

"It's nearly 1:00," said Nora as Will turned from the window. "He's been at it since 8:00 without a break. You're the boss, but can't I make him a lunch and call him in to cool off for a while?"

Will went to the back door.

"Put your shirt on and come in for lunch," he said still sounding sterner than Cain would have liked.

Happy for the break, he dropped what he was doing and ran for his shirt, putting it on as he took the back stairs two at a time. The air conditioning felt heavenly as he went to the kitchen sink and washed his hands and face.

"What'd Mike want?" asked Will.

Cain's heart skipped a beat.

"He wanted me to go to the beach with him."

"What'd his parents say about yesterday?"

"Not much, I guess," shrugged Cain.

"He didn't get punished?"

"No," answered Cain wishing they'd change the subject. He sat down at the table, and his mother put a plate with a hearty sandwich and some potato chips down in front of him.

"I suppose now you really think I over-reacted?"

"Why are you putting words in my mouth?" frowned Cain. "I'm not complaining."

"I just thought maybe you were thinking it," answered Will defensively.

"Well, I'm not. Okay? I was wrong. You're right. End of discussion." He boldly looked his father straight in the eye. Feeling his bravado deserting him, he quickly changed the subject. "How much longer do I have to work today?"

"Let's see," figured Will. "You've put in five hours so far. Three more today, and seven tomorrow."

Cain sighed mournfully at the thought and bit into his sandwich. His mother smiled affectionately behind his back where he couldn't see her. She wanted to give him a hug of encouragement, but she didn't dare. Will would never approve, and this was his show.

A while later, Cain was out painting the fence when Matt came home. He put his bike in the garage and then walked over to see Cain.

"You look like you're straight out of the pages of Mark Twain," grinned Matt.

"Well, in that case, grab a brush! This is boring as hell. I wish he'd at least let me have a radio. The time is going by painfully slow. I'll tell you this—I'm going to college and getting a degree or two. This manual labor is definitely not for me!"

"But look what good shape you'd be in!"

"Right. What'd you do today?"

"Alexis and I went down to the beach, but she wanted to come home to do her hair and her nails and all that for the party tonight." As soon as he had said the word, Matt regretted mentioning the party. "I'm sorry you can't go."

"Screw the damn party!" said Cain bitterly as he moved to the next board of the fence. "You'd better quit talking to me, or we'll both be in trouble. He's been watching me like a hawk."

No sooner had he gotten the words out of his mouth than Will appeared at the door.

"Matthew," he called, "come in the house."

"I told you . . . Matthew."

"Boy, he really is on your case, isn't he?"

"I think he's trying to prove something to Grandpa. Go on in. I have about another hour to go here, and then I'll be finished for today. I'll talk to you then."

At about 4:15, Will came out to inspect the fence. Cain continued painting, but kept one eye on his father.

"It's looking pretty good," said Will approvingly. "Call it a day. You can finish this up tomorrow after Church. It'll take a good couple of hours, and then you can work on the basement. At least it'll be cool down there."

"Okay," said Cain forlornly as he stood up. "Dad, I thought that maybe since I have all this work to do, I could miss Mass tomorrow."

"Well, you thought wrong. You can start again first thing **after** Church. Be sure you get all of this stuff cleaned up before you come in."

"I will."

Will walked into the house. Nora had been standing in the window watching.

"I almost wish he would argue with me or be snotty or something. He's being so damned good about the whole thing that he's beginning to make **me** feel guilty."

"That's his temperament," said Nora. "He's easy going."

"As long as you don't make him angry," said Will remembering numerous temper tantrums.

"He doesn't get angry that often," defended Nora. She put her arms around her husband and hugged him. "Let him go to the party. It's a big affair. Even Sean and his friends are going. He's worked so hard today without even so much as a grumble."

"I can't, Nora," scowled Will. "I can't go back on this now. He won't die because he missed that party."

A while later Cain came in looking spent. There was a mixture of dirt, perspiration, and paint on his face and upper body.

"Here," said Nora handing him a frosty glass. "I fixed you a Coke. Sit down and cool off."

"Thanks," he said taking the glass from her and sitting down at the large kitchen table. He wiped his face with his wadded shirt that he had in his hand. "I'm sorry I don't have this on, but I think it's dirtier than I am."

"We can make an exception," smiled Nora. "Tired?"

"Yeah, a little. I want to go take a shower, but I probably have to wait in line behind everyone getting ready to go out tonight." He smiled through the sweat and grit on his face. "I feel like Cinderella."

"I'm sorry, sweetheart. I wish you didn't have to miss the party."

"It's my own fault. I just wish this stupid party was over. Sounds like sour grapes, doesn't it?"

"A little, but I understand how you feel. Everybody has plans for dinner tonight except you and Dad and me. I have some beautiful steaks in the refrigerator. After everyone's gone and you've had a chance to shower, I'll send Dad out to cook them on the grill. We'll let him do some work for a change. I'm in the process of putting together a salad, and there's some good bread that Dan brought home from the bakery. Sound good?"

"Sounds great."

Just then his eighteen-year-old brother, Sean, came into the kitchen with a towel wrapped around his midsection. His hair was still dripping from the shower.

"Cain, can I borrow the blue shirt you got from Molly for your birthday?"

"Yeah. It's in my closet."

"Thanks," said Sean as he turned and hurried back upstairs.

"That's what I was gonna wear to the party. At least my shirt gets to go."

"Go hurry your brothers in the shower," his mother said with a smile. "You'll feel better after you clean up."

He sat for a few minutes and finished his drink. Then he took her advice and went up to shower.

When he came back down, his parents were out in the yard and everyone else was gone. He felt cleaner and more relaxed again, but his heart was still heavy. The more he tried to tell himself that it wasn't such a big deal that he was missing the party, the more he hurt because he was missing it. Then in an effort to occupy his mind, he quickly paged through the morning paper which he hadn't had time for before, and then he began setting the table.

"Aren't you a dear," said Nora as she walked into the kitchen. "I was just coming in to do that."

"No problem," said Cain soberly.

"Why don't you take these steaks out to your father, and I'll get the bread ready?"

He took the steaks from her and started for the door. She called to him and he turned.

"There'll be other parties, honey."

"I know," he said forcing a smile.

He was quiet during dinner, but he ate heartily. In spite of attempts made by both his parents, he would not be drawn into conversation. He was too preoccupied thinking about the party that was just getting underway. It had been bad enough before, but now that the time was here, it was almost unbearable for him.

"I'm going upstairs now," he said as he took his plate to the dishwasher.

"You don't have to go up so soon," said Will relenting on his hard stand. "You've worked hard today. Relax and watch TV with us for a while."

"No. Thanks anyway. I'm going to 7:30 Mass in the morning, so is it all right if I start working at 9:00?"

"Of course," said Will somewhat disarmed. "That'll be fine."

"Then I'll see you in the morning."

Upstairs, Cain sat at his desk and read for a while. It was hard for him to stay focused though, and he was growing tired. In spite of the early hour, he opted to go to bed. The darkness of the room felt refreshing, and his pillow and mattress cradled his exhausted body. The cool sheets soothed his bare skin. It was a night for sleeping in the nude, and the pleasant tactile sensations helped ease him into a deep, restful sleep. At last, he had escaped the agony of thinking about the party he was missing.

When Jim came home at 11:00, he thoughtlessly turned on their bedroom light in his usual irritating manner. Cain stirred and moaned.

Then he fumbled for his pillow and flip-flopped it from under his head to over it in an effort to block out the light. The maneuver was successful, and without having fully regained consciousness, he was sound asleep again. Jim shook his head and went on crashing about the room.

It was 1:00 A.M. when Matt got home. Drastically contrasting Jim, Matt quietly entered their room and began getting ready for bed. There was no intrusive light and no inconsiderate noise, but Cain woke almost immediately. It was as if his subconscious mind had sat up and waited for Matt to return, and then it quickly awakened the rest of his body.

"How was the party?" he asked in a hushed voice that was heavy with sleep.

"Hi," said Matt coming over to sit on Cain's bed. "The party was okay."

"Hey," complained Cain, "this is me you're talking to. How was it **really**? I want to know it all."

Matt sighed.

"Okay. It was great. Just what you'd expect. God, those people are rich! There was more food than I've ever seen in one place in my whole life! And a live band. Everyone was asking about you."

"Was Joanne there?"

"For a while. She said she really wasn't having much fun without you, so she left early?"

"By herself?"

"Yes. Nothing for you to worry about."

"Who else was there?"

"Everybody. When Marta Dempsey throws a party everybody who's anybody is invited. Scott, Greg, and Mike were there. They evidently didn't catch the hell you did over the Lake Geneva incident."

"Will you two shut up!" complained Jim raising his head from his pillow. "You woke me up for God's sake!"

"Get f . . ." snarled Cain getting riled.

"Relax," interrupted Matt putting a hand on Cain's forearm. "We'll talk more tomorrow."

After Matt went to bed, Cain lay awake for the longest time. He had had just enough sleep to make him feel wide-awake. Thoughts of Joanne and her perfume filled his mind. At least now the party was over. There was a small amount of comfort in that for him.

He cursed his alarm when it went off at 6:30. He awoke feeling groggy and unrested. The whole house was asleep except for him, and that did nothing to spark his enthusiasm. At least he wouldn't have to elbow his way into the bathroom.

A short time later he was down in the kitchen with a glass of orange juice, paging through the morning paper when his older sister, Molly, came down.

"Matt?" she asked.

"Cain," he answered without looking up.

"What are you doing up, cutie?" she smiled as she poured herself some orange juice. "I'm not used to seeing you much before noon."

"I'm still in hot water with Dad. I have a full day ahead of me."

"Not more work?"

"'Fraid so."

"He was kind of hard on you, don't you think?"

"He has high standards," shrugged Cain. "I respect him for that. Some of my friends have parents that are all talk and that's about all. Dad's not like that. He expects a lot from us, and it upsets him if we fall short. All I have to do is live through today, and I've got it made! And speaking of being up early, what's with you? You working?"

"Yep. I was just going to fix myself some breakfast. How about some eggs?"

"No thanks," he said taking a container of yogurt from the refrigerator. "I'll just have this, and then I'm off to Church."

"How do you eat that stuff," frowned Molly.

"With a spoon!" smiled Cain with a wink.

Later that morning, he was out in the yard painting the fence when his grandfather came out and stood over him. Cain knew that the old man and Jim were cut from the same mold, and he avoided both of them whenever possible. Therefore, he continued painting and paid little attention to his observer.

"Have you learned anything from all of this?" Robert asked. "Or is that too much to hope for?"

No answer. In fact, Cain didn't acknowledge his grandfather's presence in any way.

"I'm talking to you, Cain Farrell!"

"I understand that, but I have nothing to say to you about this matter. I don't want to be disrespectful, Grandpa, but this is none of your business."

"You carry my surname. What you do reflects back on me. That gives me no interest in the matter?"

"Okay," said Cain stopping for the first time and looking up at his grandfather, "let's get this over with. What do you want from me? An apology? Okay, I'm sorry. I really am. I didn't set out to get in trouble. It was just one of those things."

"Just one of those things?!"

"Yes! It just happened. What do you think—I go out looking for trouble?"

"As a matter of fact, that's exactly what I think. It seems to me you thrive on it."

"Well that's bullshit!"

"Don't get insolent with me!"

Cain sighed and rubbed his face.

"I didn't mean to be."

"Yeah, well, I still think a good beating would put you in the right frame of mind! Your father doesn't know how to get your attention!" Robert stormed off back into the house.

Cain moaned in frustration. There was no pleasing the old man. He wasn't even sure at that point that the beating his grandfather kept harping about would pacify him, but Cain wasn't about to offer his hide to prove his point.

Minutes later Will came out with a stern expression on his face. Cain didn't even have to wait for the tirade to begin to know what was on his father's mind. He sat back on his heels and waited.

"What on earth is your problem?" Will demanded. "Why do you have to insist on antagonizing your grandfather?"

"Me?! Antagonize him?! I was minding my own business, and he came out and started in on me! Dad, he's never happy unless he's rubbing my nose in something. I try to sit still for that, but it's not easy."

"I understand that, but you don't have to sass him back."

"I didn't!!"

"He's inside ranting and raving about your smart mouth. And you and I both know you have one."

Cain raised his hands in the air and let them drop on his lap.

"Dad . . ."

"Go inside and apologize to him."

Cain turned on his father angrily. His face was flushed with emotion, and the storm in his eyes was definitely brewing.

"No!"

"What?!!" asked Will not used to the defiance.

"I won't," confirmed Cain. "He started it, and I didn't sass him. I told him I was sorry for the trouble I caused up in Lake Geneva, and that was a stretch. I won't apologize for something he imagines I've done."

"Then you'll work an extra hour this afternoon. You don't defy me and get away with it."

Cain looked up miserably at his father. Angry, frustrated tears threatened.

"Dad, don't make me do this. I swear to you, I was perfectly civil to him."

"I'm not making you do anything. The choice is yours."

Will turned on his heel and walked away, cursing himself as he did. He realized that this whole scenario had taken a different turn than he had planned, but he couldn't rescind his ultimatum. Reluctantly, he continued his firm pace into the house.

Cain was on the verge of an emotional, tearful breakdown. He was plain tired of working off his punishment while everyone else, including the guys he had gotten in trouble with, was off enjoying

18

himself. And he still had a lot of work time ahead of him without adding another hour. He readily admitted to feeling sorry for himself, but he also felt he had good reason. He was growing tired of trying to love his cantankerous grandfather.

Angry, frustrated tears burned behind his eyelids as he fought valiantly to hold them back. He didn't need to add tears to his humiliating position. He wiped his lips with the back of his hand as he neared the decision to go in and apologize to his grandfather. What choice did he have?

He stood up and took a few deep breaths to try and bring his emotions under control. He fought the feeling that he was selling himself out in trade for one less hour of work. He didn't want to think about it at all; he just wanted to get it over with. Kicking a small mound of dirt to smithereens against the garage, he walked toward the house. When he walked into the kitchen, his parents, his oldest brother, Dan, and his grandfather were all sitting at the table. They all looked over at him as reluctant tears welled in his eyes and pride welled in his throat. He stood stubbornly silent for a moment as he fought desperately to keep the tears and his pride in their places.

"Grandpa," he finally said with great difficulty, " . . . I'm . . . I'm sorry I talked back to you out in the yard. I didn't mean to."

"You most certainly did," said Robert making a difficult situation nearly impossible.

"No," insisted Cain as his throat tightened and his chest heaved. A tear broke loose and rolled down his cheek, leaving a trail through the dirt and perspiration on his face. "I'm tired. I didn't mean it. I'm sorry."

"Fine," said Robert less than forgivingly. "Now quit wasting your father's time and get back to work!"

Cain stood with a firm grip on his wild temper, which was kicking up inside him. With his teeth clenched against an angry outburst, he shifted his eyes till they met his father's. *Are you satisfied?* Will dropped his gaze breaking contact with his son's pleading eyes. Then he nodded, giving him silent permission to leave. Cain wasted no time putting distance between himself and the humiliating situation.

As soon as he got out the door and closed it behind him, he broke down into angry, convulsive sobs. He put his hand over his mouth to hold back the outburst. After a number of deep breaths to bring himself under control, he went back to the fence and began painting.

Inside, his family sat in uncomfortable silence. Without a word Robert left the room. Dan started to get up to follow Cain, but Will took his arm and held him in place.

"I'll take care of this," the father announced.

He walked out into the yard and saw Cain back at the fence. As he stood back for a minute and just watched his son, he searched carefully for the right words. Tentatively he walked up to Cain and crouched down next to him. Realizing he was there, Cain quickly reached up and wiped tears from his face.

"It's all right to cry," said Will gently. No response. "Now it's my turn. I'm sorry for putting you through that. I should have known better. You see, fathers aren't perfect either."

"It's okay," said Cain vacantly as he continued to paint the fence. "It's over. I didn't expect anything more than what happened."

"Well, I just wanted you to know I'm sorry for compromising you that way. It wasn't right of me."

"I know he's your father," said Cain still not turning away from his painting, "but I sure do have a hard time loving him sometimes. Actually, all the time. I don't even like to be in the same room with him. And, Dad," he turned and stared his father tearfully in the eye, "I don't start it."

"I understand," said Will. "Come on, take time out, and I'll take you out for lunch. We'll get a burger or something."

"Thanks, but I'm not stopping for lunch. I just want to get finished. If I don't stop, I can be through by 4:00."

"I won't charge the time against you," coaxed Will. "It'll be my way of making up for the dirty trick I just pulled on you. Come on, how can you pass up a free meal on my time?!"

Cain stubbornly continued painting without commenting. After a minute, he looked straight up at the blazing, summer sky and exhaled through his mouth.

"I can still be through by 4:00?"

"Absolutely," smiled Will.

"I'm a mess."

"Of course I would expect that you would need a few minutes to wash up and put on a clean shirt."

"You don't have to do this."

"Oh, I know," said Will trying to act formal. "I'm the boss. I can do whatever I want."

Cain stared at him for a minute and then couldn't resist a smile.

"Thanks, Dad."

The afternoon was long and tedious, but not as bad as Cain had feared. Once the fence was finished, he went down to work on the basement. Will helped him, and together they did a major overhaul of the large cluttered cellar. Will did most of the delegating while Cain was in charge of moving the garbage out, sweeping, and reorganizing. Nora watched him sympathetically as he made numerous trips up and down the stairs carting heavy loads out behind the garage, but she resisted the urge to mother him. Time had buffered the raw emotions of his encounter with Robert, and he once again began smiling and joking in his light-hearted way.

They finished a little before 4:00, and Will released him from his obligation. When he went upstairs, he took a can of Coke from the refrigerator and sat down at the kitchen table.

"Finished?" Nora asked.

"Yeah," he smiled. His face was dirty and sweat-streaked. "I'm going to be so good for the rest of my life. I swear! I don't ever want to spend another weekend like this. I'm gonna eat dinner and go straight to bed, so I can rest up for work tomorrow!"

Nora laughed. "You've spent two very full and strenuous days, but you're young and strong and I'm sure you'll survive."

"I'm not quite as convinced as you, but I'll take your word for it. I'm going up to shower."

"Good idea. You have plenty of time before dinner, and a shower will probably do wonders for you."

# CHAPTER 2

Summer was coming to an all-too-swift end. It had been a hot, sunny season—one of those that young people love and try to hold on to for as long as possible. Cain was no exception. As he began preparing for his senior year in high school, he continued to get the most out of the last golden days of summer. Early one morning, he called Joanne.

"What time is it?" she asked sleepily.

"I don't know," he said with distraction. "About 8:30, I guess. I'm coming to pick you up."

"What?! Have you lost your mind, Cain?"

"I don't think so. Summer's coming to an end. There's still a lot to do. Let's do some of it."

"Like what?"

"I don't know. I was going to ask you what you wanted to do."

"Then I have to answer, sleep. That's what I want to do. I want to sleep-in these last few days, and 8:30 doesn't really measure up to sleeping-in."

"Come on, don't waste the day sleeping. I don't have to work, and Sean said I could use his scooter. I'll be over in about an hour. That should give you time to get up and get ready."

"Cain . . . "

"I'll see you about 9:30."

Before she had a chance to protest, he hung up.

As he rode to Joanne's on the motor scooter, he felt the warm air rushing passed him much the same way the summer was hastening toward a close. But he didn't care. He liked school and being productive; but even more important, he was in love so all the world seemed right.

As he pulled up in the driveway, Joanne ran out of her house and jumped on the back of the scooter. She squeezed him tightly around the waist as they breezed through the streets. There was nothing she liked better than being close to him, smelling his cologne and feeling his body pulsing and breathing within her grasp.

They parked the scooter and walked aimlessly, talking and window-shopping. Occasionally, they'd linger at a window to further admire its contents.

"One day I'll buy you that bracelet," said Cain indicating a silver and turquoise bracelet that Joanne couldn't seem to take her eyes off of.

"It is lovely, isn't it?" She sighed with a smile. "But don't worry, I won't hold you to it. Look at the price. It's very expensive."

"No matter," shrugged Cain. "A major league first baseman can make enough to buy you that bracelet and a lot more."

"I hope that dream comes true for you," she said looking up at him with adoration beaming all over her face. "But then all the lady fans will make such a fuss over you, you'll probably forget all about me."

"Never!" insisted Cain adamantly. "No matter what. You're the most important thing in the entire world to me. I know I could never even love anyone else, let alone ever forget about you. I mean that, Jo. There'll never be anyone else. You feel the same, don't you?"

"Of course, I do. I was only kidding. If anyone ever tried to take you away from me, I'd scratch her eyes out. I wonder what it would be like to be married to a big league ball player?"

"Give me a few years, and we'll find out," he smiled. "This isn't just one of those things that kids fantasize about. I'm gonna do it. I'm gonna make the big leagues. I've never wanted anything so bad. I'm gonna work my ass off to make it happen."

"You'll do it," she said as they began to walk again. "You're good; you're very good. My dad says you're the best high school player he's ever seen. But about working your ass off . . . try not to. It's your best asset."

He shoved her playfully as they walked on and got lost in each other.

At lunchtime they bought hot dogs and a drink and sat down by the lake.

"What is it about the beach that enchants you so?" she asked him breaking into his spellbinding gaze.

"I don't know," he smiled turning to look at her. "Have I been ignoring you?"

"No, you just get that faraway look in your eye, and I can't help wondering."

"It's just so . . . vast . . . Lake Michigan, that is. From here you can't see to the other side, and it seems to go on forever. It's beautiful. I could sit here for hours. It clears my mind and enables me to get a whole new outlook. Kind of like clearing the cobwebs."

"And what cobwebs do you have?"

"Everyone has cobwebs that need clearing every now and then."

"But you? Mr. 'A' Student, Mr. Athlete, Mr. School Politician, Mr. Angel-eyes-gorgeous-hunk, Mr. Personality."

"Where did all of that come from?" he frowned.

"You're all of that and more."

"Well, in your eyes, maybe. But seriously, don't you ever feel the need to just get away and clear your head?"

"Yes, but I don't have as much going for me as you do."

"Come on, Joanne, cut the crap."

"It's not crap," she insisted. "Do you know how many girls would swoop you up if I looked away for even a minute. And there's not one guy at school, except maybe Matt, who wouldn't trade places with you. Now go ahead, tell me about your cobwebs."

"My grandpa," he said bringing an end to her playful smile.

She took a deep breath. "Oh."

She knew about his relationship or, better stated, his lack of a relationship with his grandfather, and she knew how much it disturbed him. But she had no idea that was where this scenario was leading. She regretted she had pressed the issue. The magic was gone from his face, and she deemed herself responsible.

"Okay," she conceded. "My blunder. Can we move on?"

"You think that I'm some sort of a superhuman or something," he said keeping the issue alive. "It's not true, Jo. I'm mortal—quite mortal. Don't treat me like I'm up on a pedestal above everyone else. I'm not like that."

"I was kidding."

"But you always do that to me. You make me out to be someone I'm not. To listen to you, I sound like some sort of superficial window-dressing."

"Okay, I'm sorry. I really didn't mean for this to turn into such a serious conversation. I know who you are, and superficial is never a word I would use to describe you. Now come on, smile and let's get back to having fun on one of the last days of our vacation. Unless of course, you want to talk about your grandfather."

"No, that is definitely one subject I don't want to talk about."

"You're not going to sulk, are you?"

He looked at her intently, and then a wide grin crossed his face.

"No. Not today. But we'd better start heading home before traffic gets too bad."

Cain's vacation ended a few days early because of a heavy work schedule. On his last free day, he and his friends made a last trip to the beach for a marathon day in the sun. It didn't take long for others to join them, and soon they had a serious coed volleyball tournament in progress. There were plenty of laughs and good times as everyone put the impending school year out of his or her mind and concentrated getting the most out of the day.

"So where did you say Joanne is today?" asked Scott as they stopped for some lunch.

"Shopping with her mom. Some school clothes or something."

"I'm surprised you're here."

"Why shouldn't I be?"

"Joanne keeps pretty close reins."

"What?"

"I know you two have been going together for quite a while now, but it seems more and more lately I see less and less of you."

"Wow," smiled Cain. "Are we having a crisis here? Do I detect a note of 'three's a crowd'?"

"No," scowled Scott. "It's just that she takes up a lot of your time lately, and she'd be pissed as hell if she knew these girls were hanging out with us all day."

"Where did you get that from? She wouldn't care."

"She's not real happy with you hanging out with the guys—especially after Lake Geneva. And it doesn't take a prodigy to see she's as jealous as hell. Ninety-five percent of the girls here on the beach are drooling all over themselves, and the other five percent are blind. If Matt was here too, we'd probably have to resuscitate them all! That's Joanne's cup of tea, but only when she's around to let everyone know that you're hers. Then she loves having girls ogle you. It makes her feel important or something."

"I don't get it. Why has this never come up before?"

"I don't know," moaned Scott, "and I'm beginning to be real sorry that I brought it up now. Let's forget it, huhn?"

It was late when Cain got home. He was on his way up to take a shower when Matt stopped him in the hall.

"Joanne called a while ago," Matt announced. "She sounded pretty hot. She said you could call back up to midnight."

"What was she mad about?"

"Beats me. She doesn't share those things with me, thank God."

When he got her on the line, she was obviously still annoyed and wasted no time getting to the point.

"Where've you been?" she asked suspiciously.

"At the beach with Scott and some of the others. You knew I was going there. What is this?"

"Who were the girls, Cain? I thought you were going with the guys."

"I did. We met some girls there. Played a few games."

"What kind of games?" Her question was definitely rhetorical and condemning.

"Wait a minute. Let's back up a little here. What are you trying to say? And how do you know about the girls in the first place?"

"You weren't going to tell me about them? I found out though, didn't I?"

"Joanne."

"I was there, Cain. At the beach. My mom dropped me off to meet you; but before she left, I spotted you rolling in the sand with some beach bunny."

"What?!" He was enraged and incredulous at the same time. "Beach bunny! We were playing volleyball. You don't know what you're talking about. Why didn't you come over?"

"Cain, I was mortified. I just wanted to go home. Who was she?"

"I don't believe you. I don't even know who you're talking about. There were a lot of girls there, and we were all having fun together. You could have joined us. I wasn't trying to hide anything."

"I'm sorry," she disagreed. "It looked bad. I hope none of my friends were there and saw that."

"All I have to say is if I was having as much fun with someone as you say I was, I think I'll go try to find out who it was because this is absolutely no fun."

In an incensed rage, he slammed the phone down. When the phone rang seconds later, Cain purposely didn't pick it up. A minute or two later, Matt came into their room.

"That was Joanne," he said.

"I figured."

"She thought I was you and started letting me have it. I finally convinced her that she had the wrong guy. Her tirade plus the fact that you didn't answer the phone was enough for me to know that you didn't want to talk to her. I said you were in the shower. She knew I was lying, but what could she do?"

"Thanks."

"She said to call her."

"Yeah."


The next morning Cain got up and got dressed for work. As he stood in front of his mirror tying his tie, he could think of nothing but Joanne. He was hopelessly in love with her. Even at his tender age, he knew that no one else would ever do. How could she ever doubt that?

"What's wrong with him?" Nora asked Matt after Cain had left for work. "I asked him, but he kind of shrugged me off."

"I guess he should really tell you himself, but he's fighting with Joanne."

"He's too young to be having girl trouble," frowned Nora.

"He's in love, Mom."

"So are you."

"Not like Cain. I really wouldn't be surprised if he and Joanne get married some day. Then he'll really have his hands full. Are you ready for that?"

"She's a nice girl."

"Well, they may as well get married," he smiled, "she already has a ring in his nose!"


While Cain was at work stocking shelves, he suddenly looked up to see Joanne standing next to him. His mind raced as he tried to find the right mixture of humble pie and righteous indignation.

"Did Matt tell you I called?"

"Yeah, he did. I just really didn't have any more to say."

"So . . . where are we?"

"I don't know, Joanne. I guess that's up to you. You're the one who was upset."

"And you don't care?"

"No, I care. I care a lot. But I'm confused. I don't know what I did wrong."

She took a deep breath and angrily bit on her lip, carefully considering her next move.

"Look," he said before she could go on, "I'm due for my lunch break. Can we go outside and talk this over?"

"All right," she sighed.

Once they were outside, he situated himself at a picnic table across from her. He had already decided that he was going to take control of the conversation and let fate take care of the rest. He wasn't the type to snivel and crawl on bended knee—especially when he felt he had done nothing to warrant it. If Joanne was hoping for remorse and supplication, she was about to be sorely disappointed.

"I don't understand your anger," he started out, " and therefore, I'm having a hard time dealing with it. I didn't sleep half the night because I'm confused, angry, and hurt. Jo, you knew what I was planning to do yesterday. I asked you to come along. You can't expect me to never be around other girls when you're not around. What am I supposed to do, leave if a girl comes around and I'm not with you? Walk away from the fun and live like a monk until you're back to watch me? I don't need to be watched, Joanne. I love you. That should be enough. I understand love, and I know that love is true. We've been going together since junior high. Don't you know me by now?"

Again she didn't speak right away, but the anger was fading from her face. She hated it when he turned out to be right and she was wrong. She wasn't good at apologies.

"All right," she sighed. "I'm sorry. I just didn't like the way it looked."

"Don't say any more," he shooshed her. "We'll start fighting again. Can't we just leave it at—we'll both try to be more sensitive to the other's position?"

"Yes," she smiled. "That sounds good. Fighting with you is too exhausting. I have to think too much to try and stay ahead of you."

"I don't want to fight."

"Me either. It's just that when I saw you with those girls, I almost went crazy. I don't know what I'd do if I ever lost you."

"You won't. Don't worry about it. Just keep loving me. And now I'd better get back to work."

"You didn't even get a chance to eat."

"That's love for you," he winked with a smile. "Can you live on love? I forget how that saying goes."

"I don't think so."

"Whew," he sighed as he raised his eyebrows. "I'll have to eat a big dinner. And for now I'll grab a candy bar on my way in."

She kissed his cheek and left.

He was a bit distracted the rest of the day. He thought about what he had said to Joanne, and at the same time he couldn't deny the physical stirrings that had been going on inside him lately. Sex was becoming more than just a three-letter word to him. It was difficult because when it came to sex, he knew that he and Joanne were not nearly on the same page. At least not any more. When they were younger, it hadn't been that much of an issue. They had always enjoyed each other's company and never ventured into forbidden pleasures. Though Cain respected her views and the fact that she was a year younger than he was, he couldn't help becoming more and more haunted by strange and yet unexplored desires in his soul. He hadn't discussed this with anyone yet for he still wasn't sure that what he was experiencing was normal. Matt would be the one to talk to, but as of that moment he wasn't ready to bare his soul. In the mean time, being with Joanne was driving him crazy in a way he had never experienced before. This was going to get worse before it got better.

Experiencing a sense of gloom, he walked back into the store. He bought a large candy bar, hoping its decadence would temporarily satisfy all his demons so he could get back on track and concentrate on the job at hand. So much on his mind. So many decisions to make. Which paths to follow. He had spent his whole life rushing his childhood so that he could be grown up, and now that adulthood was poised at his doorstep, he wished he could turn back time.

# CHAPTER 3

Matt had just walked in the door as the phone was ringing. He answered it as he and his grandfather exchanged confused glances. It was nearly midnight.

"Get Dad!" said Cain rather frantically.

"He's not here. What's up?"

"Shit," sighed Cain.

"What's wrong? Where are you?"

"Everything's wrong, and I'm at the police station."

"The police station! Cain!"

Robert needed to hear no more. He was up in a flash and grabbed the phone from Matt.

"What the hell is going on?" he demanded.

"I've been arrested . . . I need $100."

"What?!"

"Grandpa, please. Just come, and bring $100."

"You must be crazy."

"No," said Cain on the verge of an emotional outburst. "I'm not. I'm perfectly sane, and I want to come home. But I need someone to come and get me and bring $100."

"What happened?"

"It was a party. There was beer. Someone called the police."

"What police station?" asked Robert levelly.

"Deer Brook."

The only response Cain received was the receiver slamming down on the other end. Now there was really going to be hell to pay.

Cain walked numbly back to his chair next to Scott.

"My parents aren't home. My grandpa's coming."

"Ouch," sympathized Scott.

"I wish I was dead," he sighed as he slouched desperately in the chair.

"You may as well be once your grandfather gets a hold of you."

Cain rolled his eyes and then sat quietly awaiting his doom.

Robert didn't make him wait long. The two made unsettling eye contact the moment the old man entered the police station and walked up to the desk. Cain tried to belie the quaking in his soul with a confident, self-righteous facade. Robert didn't have to hide anything. He was stern and angry, and it was clearly evident. It took only a few minutes to take care of the details. No sense in delaying the inevitable.

"Jesus Christ," sighed Cain under his breath to Scott as he got up to face his greatest critic.

"Lord have mercy," smiled Scott.

Without a word, Robert led the way out the door and to his car.

"Are you drunk?" he asked as they each got in and closed the doors.

29

"No," answered Cain solemnly. "Not any more."

"Well, I hope you have a good story, because you have a court date set for about ten days from now. This time you're going to have to explain your nonsense to a judge. Your dad's not going to be able to get you off like he did in Lake Geneva."

"Where is my dad?"

"He and your mom are out for the evening—enjoying themselves. What a nice thing to come home to."

Cain sighed guiltily realizing his parents didn't deserve this but knowing there was nothing he could do to spare them.

"What about my money, Cain? I'm on a fixed income—$100 is a lot of money for me."

"You'll get it back at the hearing. The policeman explained it to us."

"I'll get it back Monday morning as soon as the bank opens," corrected the grandfather.

"Okay," agreed Cain trying to placate the old man in any way he could. "Grandpa . . ."

"Shut up. Just shut up. I don't want to talk to you any more until we get home."

Until we get home. Cain didn't want to have to talk to him any more at all. He prayed his parents would be home when they got there. Then Robert would be dismissed and Cain could deal with his much more rational father. This was not to be his night, however. There was no sign of his father's car as they opened the garage door and pulled in. *Shit!*

Matt, Sean, and Jim were watching TV when they walked in. All eyes were on him, and he gave them a helpless shrug.

"Get upstairs," ordered Robert before Cain could get any other ideas.

"What?!" asked Cain indignantly.

"You heard me. Get your ass upstairs. I'm not through with you yet."

Cain looked over at his brothers and then opted to obey his grandfather rather than anger him any further—all the while praying his parents would come home. Much to his dismay, Robert followed him up. Cain went to his room and tried to swing the door closed quickly behind him, but Robert caught it and let himself in. Then he slammed the door angrily. Various odds and ends around the room rattled accordingly. Cain knew he was in trouble but didn't realize the full scope of his dilemma until he turned to see his grandfather sliding his belt from around his waste. Cain looked at him in uncontrolled horror. Keeping a wary eye on his grandfather, he stepped back to put more distance between himself and the old man.

"What the hell?" he stammered as he bumped aimlessly into a desk chair.

"You shut up. I'm in control here. I'll do the talking. You've been asking for this for a long time now. If your father doesn't have the guts to beat your ass, I do."

"Stay away from me," said Cain as he continued to move slowly about the room in an effort to keep out of his grandfather's reach.

"I told you to shut up."

"I want my father. This is his job, not yours."

"Your father doesn't know how to deal with you. I've been telling him that for years. Now get over here."

Cain's heart was nearly pounding out of his chest, and he had to draw deep into his lungs for each breath. Large tears welled in his eyes. The old man's grip tightened relentlessly on the loose ends of the belt as he tapped the looped end menacingly against his knee.

"I'm sorry," said Cain softly, dropping the attitude.

"Get . . . over . . . here," commanded Robert. "It's too late for anything else. You should have thought of that sooner."

The door opened, and Cain collapsed in relief against the wall as he saw his father.

"What's going on?" asked Will.

"This is none of your concern," stated Robert without taking his eyes off his grandson.

"That's my son," declared Will. "This is my business."

"If you had seen to your business all along, your son would not get into so much trouble and we would not be standing here right now."

"Nonetheless, he is my son, and this is my business to see to as I please. You have no rights here. If punishment is needed, I'll see to it in my own way."

"There is no *if* about it, Will. Go ahead, ask you son what he was up to tonight."

"I intend to, but not until you've gone. This is between Cain and me. Good night, Dad."

Robert stepped up close to Cain and looked him straight in the eye.

"You skated through again. Your daddy has you spoiled rotten. One day, Cain Farrell, you'll get yourself in a mess that no one can get you out of. Then you'll pay. You wait and see."

Cain's blood ran cold through his veins as he looked his grandfather boldly in the eye. He managed to swallow around the lump in his throat as he stood his ground and waited to see what was going to happen next. To his great relief Robert turned and left the room.

"Thanks," he sighed to his father.

"Don't thank me yet," said Will, less than congenially. "I have yet to begin. Maybe we'd best sit down, and you're going to take me all the way from square one to the police station. The rest I've figured out myself. And when I've heard your story, unless it's one helluva saga, I'm going to make you wish you had never gotten up this morning.

Don't you **ever** put me in a position like that again with my father. Do you hear me?"

The cold glint in his father's eye was more fearful to him than was his grandfather's belt. The brief relief he had been feeling abandoned him and a whole new terror seized him. He thought of arguing that is was Robert who had picked the fight and set up the unhappy triangle they had found themselves in, but it didn't seem wise at that time to say anything. Instead he just mumbled a feeble, yes.

The retelling of the story didn't seem at all as daring and reckless as actually living the experience had been. On the contrary, as he told the story of that evening under the hostile and unyielding glare of his father's gaze, he felt stupid and irresponsible. Only a total idiot would have been part of that party. There were no adults present, the crowd was sizable, the music was way too loud, and the neighbors lived way too close. It was a fiasco headed for failure right from the start. What made him think he could get away with it? Why had he wanted to? He didn't even really like beer.

"God, I feel stupid," he said as he finished the story.

"God, you were stupid! How about I go out and get you a cold six pack, and you sit here and drink the whole thing until you puke your guts out and find out what drinking can really be like?"

"You don't have to do that. I already did throw up once—at the police station."

"Then how about I take off my belt and whale the living daylights out of you?"

Cain took a deep breath.

"That's up to you. I wouldn't like it, but I do deserve it. I would take it from you, but not from that old man."

Will closed his eyes and sighed as he let the blind anger escape his body.

"Christ, Cain," he said, "this is bad. This is not a little, innocent prank up in Lake Geneva. You're not going to get off so easy with the police this time. This could be a police record that could follow you around for a long time. What the hell is wrong with you?"

"I don't know," Cain said as he felt a fresh rush of tears threaten.

Will sat silent for a moment. Then he sighed wearily.

"Go to bed. We'll talk more in the morning. I need time to let this all sink in. Don't make any social plans for a good, long time. Your ass is in this house until your 21$^{st}$ birthday, the way I'm feeling right now; but we'll talk in the morning."

"Okay." That was all he could say. He was sure anything else would stick in his throat, so he didn't even attempt to say more.

"Good night."

Cain mustered the last bit of strength he could for that day and in a strained voice he said, "I'm sorry, Dad."

Will nodded at him, but said no more and left.

Cain awoke in the morning with a whole new sense of mortification and dread. Damn, why couldn't life be simple? He wanted to avoid his grandfather at all cost, but that was next to impossible. Then he still had to finish dealing with his father who he was sure would not be in any better of a mood than he had been the night before. And to top things off, his head was pounding with the remnants of a night of too much beer and festivities. He pulled his pillow over his head with the hope of delaying things as long as possible. His sabbatical was short-lived, however, because Jim soon stuck his head in the door of their room. Walking over to Cain, he pulled the pillow off his brother's face and smiled sarcastically.

"Dad wants to see you—NOW," he said then left.

"Shit," moaned Cain.

The gray November morning did nothing to elevate his mood or give him hope of better things to come. Pulling on a pair of sweat pants and a tee shirt, he stopped in the bathroom, took a couple aspirin, and then plodded downstairs to face his father.

He was right. Will's mood if anything had deteriorated overnight. He was cold, distant, and matter-of-fact. Cain wasn't used to this side of his father, and he didn't like it at all. It didn't take Will long to bring Cain's social life to a grinding halt for more than the next six weeks. No **nothing** until January 1—the day **after** New Year's Eve. Cain was in shock. He felt like someone had just dumped a bucket of ice water over his already battered head, but he said nothing. He knew better. His father was a straight shooter, a fair man. What he said was law. There were times when Cain could argue and at least have a say. The outcome rarely changed, but it felt good to at least get the protest off his chest and let himself be heard. This was definitely not one of those times, however. In spite of all his stupidity of the past day, Cain was smart enough to know that this was one time to just keep his mouth shut. His fate was sealed, and now he just had to absorb it all and hope he'd live till the first of the year. This would be the longest Christmas vacation ever!

Will was a man of few words, especially when he was angry. After he carefully spelled out all aspects of his punishment, he walked out of the family room where they had met. Cain stood still for a few minutes; still reeling as all the implications of his father's harsh limitations hit him. Six weeks is forever when you're seventeen. Finally, he took a deep breath and walked into the kitchen where most of his family was seated around the table for Sunday breakfast. He made a point of not directly meeting anyone's stare. He would have skipped breakfast altogether except that his father had told him to join the family, so join the family he did.

He loved his mother. She was his champion; she adored him, and he knew it. She was the best mother in the world—all of her children would agree. But she was a mother, so she began waiting on him and trying to ease the misery she knew he must be in. The problem was he was trying so desperately not to draw attention to himself, and she was totally defeating that purpose. He especially avoided looking in his grandfather's direction, but he could feel the weight of the old man's disapproving stare. His head was throbbing and his stomach didn't feel real great either, but he managed to choke down a bit of breakfast. Normally he ate enthusiastically, but this morning was not even close to normal. After eating a respectable amount, he excused himself, cleared away his dishes, and went upstairs to his room. The first day of house arrest had hardly begun, and already he was bored.

He decided to sit at his desk and try to do some homework, but he ended up staring out the window instead. He never heard Robert enter, so he jumped with a start as his grandfather walked up behind him and dropped the morning paper on the desk in front of him.

"I thought you might like to read the morning news," said Robert.

Cain glanced down at the local paper. The headline at the bottom of the front page jumped out at him: **UNDERAGE PARTY BROKEN UP . . . TEENS ARRESTED**.

"Jesus," he moaned as he looked at the damning review.

"Congratulations—front page and all," said Robert leaving the paper and walking out of the room.

Cain looked miserably at the paper. This just made the whole day complete. He didn't want to read it, but he had to find out what was said and if names were mentioned. With great distaste he began skimming the article. He was beginning to feel relief that they were all minors so no names had been published when he spotted the damning words *president of the Student Council at Deer Brook High School*. His name wasn't mentioned, but there was only one president of the Student Council at Deer Brook High School, and he was it. No one else's identity had been given away—just his. Pages of newsprint fluttered about the room as he threw the front section of the newspaper recklessly to the far wall.

"Whoa," said Matt walking in just in time to see the newspaper-sized confetti storm.

"DAMN!!!"

"You have a phone call," announced Matt.

"I don't want to talk to anybody."

"It's Scott."

Cain took a deep breath and tried to calm himself down. Then he reached over and picked up the phone.

"See the newspaper?" asked Scott.

"You could say," answered Cain looking at the carnage on his floor.

"I'm sorry, Cain. How do they find out stuff like that?"

"I don't know, but now everyone who matters knows I was at that party."

"How'd you make out with the old man?"

"It worked out."

"How about your dad?"

"That's another story, but I only have ten minutes. That's all I can spend on the phone at a time."

"He was mad, huhn?"

"Yours wasn't?"

"No, he was. I've been grounded for two weeks, no car or anything."

"Well, I can eat, sleep, and go to work and school. That's it until January 1."

"January 1!!! We're still a week away from Thanksgiving!"

"I'm screwed. I can't even make a phone call without asking."

"I'm sorry. I know that party was my idea. Not one of my better ideas either."

"I could've said no. Are we idiots or what? And I feel like shit today."

"Well," said Scott, "you did meet that girl, Carrie."

"Christ, don't ever tell Joanne about that. I was getting pretty drunk by then."

"What? You didn't even do anything. Quit beating yourself up. You're not married."

"I know, but she might not understand. I just rather she didn't know."

"No problem. She'll never hear it from me."

"Look, I gotta go. I'll see you tomorrow at school."

"Okay. Keep your chin up, buddy. Six weeks isn't forever."

"Says you," said Cain letting a small smile cross his lips.

As he hung up the phone, he noticed that Matt had reentered the room and was picking up the newspaper.

"I don't want to talk about it," said Cain getting up. "Here, I can do that."

"We don't need to talk if you don't want to," said Matt handing him the papers he had picked up. "I just wanted to see how you were. You were asleep when I came up last night, and you didn't say a word at breakfast."

"I feel like shit. How long does a hangover last anyway?"

"I don't know. Did you at least have fun last night?"

"Yeah, it was all right. Not all that sort of thing's cracked up to be though. I can live without ever going to another party like that—not counting the cops and all. That I can definitely live without. I did meet Carrie Willet though. Do you know her?"

"I know of her. Her dad's some sort of congressman or something. She goes to Cedar Crest High School."

"Yeah. She's pretty hot."

"Is she? What about Joanne?"

"As far as Joanne knows, you and I never had this conversation. Besides I didn't say I was interested in Carrie or anything. I was just commenting."

"I see. Did she like you?"

"I think so," smiled Cain. "She kind of hung out with me and Scott for most of the evening."

"Did she get arrested?!"

"No. She left just before the cops got there. She had to be home earlier than most of us. I just wondered if you knew her. I'll never see her again anyway."

"It's probably just as good," commented Matt taking notice of the look on his brother's face.

"Yeah, it probably is."

Just as he was getting used to the idea of all the trouble he was in, he was confronted with a whole new aspect of it when he went to school the next day. During homeroom he was given a signed hall pass to meet with the dean later that day.

"Did you get one of these?" he asked Scott when he met him out in the hall.

"Yeah, everyone got one. They got a list from the police."

"Shit. They can't do anything to us, can they? I mean, this didn't have anything to do with school."

"Except that we go to this school and the name of the school was mentioned in the paper along with the fact that the Student Council president was one of those arrested."

"Christ, what a mess."

"Lighten up. You're way too tense."

"I feel like my world's unraveling, and I don't like it."

"Well, it's not. You're going to live through this. It's not the end of the world."

Cain's meeting with the dean was scheduled for 2:00. It seemed like forever as the day stretched out before him. He agonized over the prospect of what was going to happen. It didn't even help to talk to those who had already been in. His situation was different, and he knew that. He felt bad enough about what happened, and he didn't want to have to keep confronting it. He reported to the office and was told to go inside. Dean Barber looked up at him with a stern expression as he stood at the door.

"Come in and have a seat."

Cain did as he was told. The dean finished writing on a file on his desk as Cain waited in mortification and dread. After what seemed an endless amount of time, the man finally put his pen down and looked up. It was another eternity before he spoke.

"Of all the people I've had to call before me today, you're by far the most disappointing."

Cain wanted to look down at the floor but forced himself to make eye contact.

"What do you have to say for yourself?"

Cain shrugged. "Nothing. It was stupid. I'm sorry."

"What were you thinking?"

"I wasn't thinking."

"Obviously not. Do you realize how you may have jeopardized you future?"

"That's all I've been realizing. I'm about to go crazy."

"Cain, you hold all the cards to your future. You're one of the select few in this world who literally can be anything you want to be. You have the brains and the ability to write your own ticket—whether it be baseball, law, engineering, or whatever else you choose. Scholarships are at your fingertips. The best schools are within your grasp. Don't get caught up in teenage rebellion and negative assertiveness—you have too much to lose."

"It wasn't like that," protested Cain. "I was just at a party, and I had a couple beers. It was as simple as that—stupid but simple. I'm sorry. I know I embarrassed the school and my family, but I just wasn't thinking. I know what you're saying, and I appreciate it. It's just that sometimes it's hard being who I am. Sometimes I just want to be like the other kids. It's a poor excuse, but it's the truth. I know I have a lot of talent and potential, and I'm grateful; but along with that goes a lot of responsibility and pressure. Every once in a while, I just want to be like everyone else and do something foolish and mindless."

"That's understandable," said the dean. "You're under a great deal of pressure, I know. But you have to realize that you and Matt and others like you serve as examples, role models if you will, for other students. They look up to you. Was Matt with you at all last night?"

"No."

"Would he have gone to that party if he had been?"

"No. Probably not. What are you getting at?"

"He seems to steer clear of things that get him in trouble."

"Why does everyone do that?!" complained Cain becoming agitated. "Why does everyone keep throwing Matt up in my face? We're not the same! We'll be the first ones to admit that. We look alike, that's all. We have two different brains. We function totally independent of each other!"

"All right, calm down. I didn't mean to start anything here. I was just trying to point out that he takes the time to stop and think, and maybe it would be good if you would try to do the same."

"Be a clone?"

"Come on, you know what I'm trying to say. You're purposely missing the point."

"Okay, I'm sorry. I'm sorry for everything. Am I in trouble?"

"There was talk about you resigning your office as Student Council president."

"What?!"

"I think I've got everyone calmed down, but that's what I've been getting at—you have to watch yourself or you'll end up shooting yourself in the foot. I don't think I need to explain, do I?"

"No," answered Cain softly. "Thank you for whatever it was you had to do. Nothing like this will happen again."

"I know. That's why I went out on a limb for you. I do think you need to write the school board a letter of apology and thank them for a second chance. I expect it on my desk first thing in the morning."

"No problem," sighed Cain.

"Okay, get back to class."

His steps were heavy on the way back to class. This thing was snowballing and growing to proportions that he didn't like at all. Now the school board was involved. His parents, the school administration, the school board, the courts—everyone who had any kind of control over his life was poised over him ready to pounce at his slightest misstep. What a mess.

After school when he went to his locker, Joanne and Matt were there waiting for him.

"Don't ask," he said dialing in the locker combination. "Everybody wants a piece of me. You'd think I robbed a bank or something."

"But everything's all right?" asked Matt.

"Everything's far from all right, but it could be worse."

"Come on," said Joanne trying to cheer him up, "let's the three of us go across the street and get something to eat. My treat."

"I can't, Joanne," complained Cain irritably. "I have to be home in a half-hour or my ass is grass. I don't have a life for the next six weeks."

"I'm sorry. I forgot. Besides, I'm mad at you."

"Get in line," quipped Cain as he put his coat on and closed his locker.

"Don't you even want to know why?"

"Can't we save it for another time when not so many people are mad at me? Then I can deal with it. Right now I'm not sure I can."

38

"I heard Carrie Willet was at that party on Saturday night and she was putting the make on you all night."

Cain shot a glare in Matt's direction. Matt held up his hands in innocent denial. *It wasn't me.*

"What the hell, Joanne?" This was obviously not the best time to have brought up the subject.

"I'm going to leave this one to you guys," said Matt closing his locker. "I'm going home. Keep your eye on the time, Brother."

"I'll see you at home," answered Cain without breaking his eye contact with Joanne.

"Cain . . . " stammered Joanne as Matt left them alone.

"Where the hell is this coming from? I didn't even know you knew Carrie Willet."

"I don't, but I heard that you were pretty cozy with her Saturday night, and I just wondered if it's the truth. I hear she's pretty and very spoiled. She gets what she wants. Does she want you?"

"Jesus Christ, all the shit that's going on in my life, and you have to start pulling this on me now. Who the hell have you been talking to anyway?"

"It doesn't matter."

"No, you're right, it doesn't matter," he said taking her by the arm and briskly walking toward the door. "I'm not in the mood for this right now. I don't want to fight with you. You of all people. Everyone else is on my back, why can't you ease off?"

"I just need to know. I'm sorry."

"No," said Cain emphatically as they walked into the cold afternoon. "The answer is no, I wasn't cozy with her at the party. I talked with her for a while, and that was it. I was at a party. I was socializing. I enjoy other people—I love you." He stopped her and leaned over and kissed her briefly but with feeling. "I love you."

She was amazed that the warm glow she was experiencing didn't melt the freshly fallen snow around her.

"I love you, too," she said. "I'm sorry but I can't help it. You're so gorgeous. Other girls are always talking about you."

"You're kind of cute yourself," he said deciding to lighten the situation.

"I'm serious."

"So am I. Carrie Willet can't hold a candle to you. That's an old cliché, but I'm too weary to be clever right now." He leaned down close to her ear. "I want to fuck you so bad I can hardly walk."

"You're such a gentleman!" she said jabbing him with her elbow. "And so romantic I can hardly walk."

That drew the first laugh out of him in two days.

"Hey, I'm always a gentleman," he grinned. "I'll work on romantic. Then will you change your mind about fucking me? Shit, I'll buy you flowers and candy and anything else you want!"

39

"Forget it, Romeo," frowned Joanne becoming serious again. "You know I don't like to be teased about this. I'm just not ready for sex. I thought we had an understanding."

"We do. It's just that I'm spending a good part of my life these days with a hard-on."

"You're such an adolescent," she said picking up her pace and walking ahead.

"What?" Cain thought a second and then hurried to catch up with her. "You're right, I am. That's all part of adolescence, haven't you heard?"

"Grow up, Cain," she admonished playfully. "Why don't you ask your brothers how they handle these things? They all seem to be coping."

"Yeah—they're probably all getting laid but me!"

She stopped, and he put on the breaks.

"I have a solution," she mused.

"What?"

She bent over and found a spot to put her books. As she did, she picked up a handful of the wet, slushy snow. Before he knew what was happening, she pulled on the waist of his jeans and deposited the snowball down the front of his pants.

"There, that ought to hold you for a while!"

"You bitch," he grinned playfully as the snowball neutralized his passion and melted down the insides of his thighs.

Joanne was laughing wildly and wisely off running. Cain dropped his books and was soon at her heels. It didn't take long for him to catch her and tackle her to the ground. They both rolled and struggled in the snow for a while, but she was no match for him and he soon was straddling her helpless body as he pinned her to the ground. She laughed and pleaded for mercy as he took a handful of snow and rubbed it in her face. As the snow melted in tiny droplets all over her pretty face, he felt a longing and a desire that was new to him and stronger than anything he had ever experienced before. He leaned over and kissed her long and passionately.

"Cain," she said sensing the intensity of his emotion. "That snowball was meant to cool you off."

"I just love you so much," he whispered. "I'm so confused right now. I'm not a kid any more, but I'm not a man either. Everything's out of whack. I'm sorry. I really do understand how you feel. I feel the same way. It just isn't always easy. But I won't pressure you, and I will be a gentleman."

He deftly hoisted himself to his feet and then helped her up. They walked back to collect their books, and he glanced at his watch.

"Shit!" He said. "My dad's going to call, and if I'm not home, I'm dead."

"Go ahead," she smiled. "I'll see you tomorrow."

He gave her a brief kiss and turned toward home. As he trotted along the street, he became aware of how wet and cold his pants were. His teeth were chattering as the cold wind danced around his wet legs. He was very thankful when his house came into view. *Please, God, don't let Dad have already called.*

The phone was ringing when he walked in. Finally a break; a prayer answered. Nora gave him a disapproving leer, however, as she picked up the receiver. She handed Cain the phone, and he talked momentarily with his father. Then hung up.

"What?" He asked his mother who still looked stern.

"You cut that kind of close, didn't you? Matt's been home for some time now. Haven't you learned your lesson?"

"Mom . . ."

"Cain," she cut in, "Dad's not kidding. Don't push it with him. I won't lie for you. If you're not home when he calls, that's what I'll tell him."

"I don't want you to lie for me. I never thought you would. I don't expect you to. I'm going upstairs."

As he walked past her, Sean came into the kitchen and looked at the front of Cain's pants.

"Couldn't make it to the bathroom in time?" he teased.

"Go to hell," said Cain not the least bit amused.

He walked around his stunned brother and continued to his room. His mother called after him, but he didn't stop or even look back.

"Bad day?" asked Sean.

"I guess," sighed Nora.

He went upstairs and was dismayed to see Matt in their room. He had wanted to be alone. The good mood he had experienced while he was with Joanne had worn off, and he felt depressed and unmotivated. Matt sensed his mood and made no remark about his wet pants. For that Cain was grateful. Without a word he put his books down, grabbed a clean pair of sweats, and headed for the bathroom and a hot shower. He was totally chilled to the bone by that time, and the bathroom was the only place where he could be alone just then.

As the hot water warmed him, he couldn't help but think about the dean's lecture, the letter he had to write to the school board, his father's continuing ire, and the court date that he faced. How could he have messed things up so bad? He had disappointed so many people who had had faith in him. Finally, he pressed his palms against the wall of the shower and leaned his head on his arms and cried like a baby. The hot water washed the tears away, but not the pain, the sense of being a failure. It was quite a few minutes before his tears were spent. Dejectedly, he turned off the shower and got out. Wrapping a towel around his middle, he leaned over the sink and turned on the cold water. He splashed it liberally on his face. Then he dried off, combed his hair, got dressed, and went back into his room. Matt looked up, but made no comment when he noticed the redness that the cold water couldn't wash out of his brother's eyes. Cain simply dropped onto his bed and after a few silent tears, fell asleep.

The morning of the hearing, Cain woke up before the alarm. The sickness in the pit of his stomach robbed him of any desire for breakfast or for even getting out of bed. He tossed and turned, but there was no way he was going back to sleep. Soon he just got up, showered, shaved, and dressed in a white shirt and tie. He grabbed his sport coat and went downstairs to the family room. He got the newspaper and sat down and tried to read, the whole time aware of every beat of his heart. Nora offered breakfast, but he declined for fear of throwing up. He enviously watched his brothers leave for school. Soon his handsome father came down dressed in a coat and tie.

"Good morning," greeted Will.

"Good morning, Dad."

"Are you ready for this?"

"Do I have a choice?"

Will smiled. "No, I guess not. Did you have breakfast?"

"Are you kidding? I think I'll pass on food until after this is all over—if I'm not in jail."

"You won't be in jail."

Nora wanted to join them, but Will convinced her it would be better if she stayed at home. The courthouse would be filled, emotions would be running high, and this was something he could handle on his own. He had checked with their lawyer to be sure that it wouldn't be detrimental to Cain's case if his mother wasn't there. The lawyer assured them things would be pretty routine—cut and dried. He was not expecting any problems. Now if Cain could only feel as confident.

At the courthouse Cain searched the room for Scott and was relieved when he found him. Somehow this trouble he was in was easier to take because he was able to share it with Scott. They'd been friends since kindergarten, and knowing he wasn't alone in all of this helped.

"How you holding up, Ace?" Scott asked when they got together.

"Not very well."

"Somehow I knew you wouldn't be. Come on, everyone's been telling us that this is not the best that could happen to us, but it's not the worst either. It'll all be over soon. You worry too much, Cain."

"I don't like being considered a screw-up."

"You're not being considered a screw-up. Look around. These are not the hard cases and losers of the school. You're in good company." He looked around the room. "Wow, school must be pretty empty today."

Cain couldn't help but smile.

Moments later he tensed up again though as the judge entered the courtroom. He was sure everyone could see him visibly shaking. His left knee was bouncing nervously as they sat. He wasn't even aware of it until Scott reached over and gently put his hand on Cain's knee. He immediately stopped.

"You're driving me crazy," whispered Scott.

"Sorry."

"You probably just need a stiff drink!"

The proceedings got underway with a stern lecture from the judge about the dangers of irresponsible drinking, breaking the trust of their parents, and having something like this on a record, which could follow them for life. It was not a short lecture, and he drove the point home—this kind of behavior would not be tolerated. He ended the hearing by placing them each under court supervision for a year, and they were each sentenced to forty hours community service. He did leave them with some encouragement before banging his gavel and dismissing them. They would meet back in this court in one year from this day. Each case would be considered individually. As long as the community service had been met and the defendant had not been brought before the court during that time, all charges would be dropped and the record would be destroyed. Cain almost collapsed with relief. Just one year of staying out of trouble with the police, and it would all be forgotten. Since he had never intended to be in trouble with the police in the first place, it shouldn't be so bad—he hoped.

He went home feeling a bit more optimistic about his future. Things didn't look nearly so bleak. Now all he had to do was make it to January 1 and get back on his father's good side. He smiled when he walked into the house and saw his mom. She gave a quiet prayer of thanks because it was obvious that everything had gone well. Will nodded in affirmation, and they all sat down to talk about the day.

# CHAPTER 4

Cain had had his share of the law. Seemingly ordinary passages of youth turned into legal disasters. It wasn't fair, but he had come to accept it as a fact of his life. Vowing that he had learned his lesson, he spent the next months being especially careful not to even get so much as a speeding ticket. He fulfilled his community service and cruised through the next six months without any problems. He should have known better than to relax his guard and think that the worst was behind him. He was like a magnet, attracting trouble from the least expected places. It seemed to come out of nowhere and attack him like a thief in the night. Just as he was beginning to think he was older and so much wiser, he stumbled into the biggest disaster of his life.

Cain lay on the floor on his stomach holding a pillow under his head. Carrie Willet knelt next to him artfully massaging his back. It was a warm, early May night. Senior year was coming to an end and college was around the corner. Best of all, it was nearly summer. Cain closed his eyes in ecstasy as Carrie worked out all the tightness that had invaded his back during a long day of work. Saturdays were always hectic at the grocery store, and he always seemed to get scheduled to work on Saturday.

Carrie was working herself, baby-sitting. The kids were small and long asleep for the night. She and Cain would have many hours of privacy before he would have to leave to avoid running into the people when they came home. This was not the first time they had met like this.

"Have you ever told anyone about us?" Carrie asked.

"No. There's never been any need. We have a no-strings arrangement, right?"

"Yes," answered Carrie. "You've never even told Matt?"

"Especially not Matt. I'm not sure he'd understand."

"Scott?"

"No." Cain turned on his side and propped himself up on his forearm. "What's this about?"

"I just worry about my parents ever finding out. God, I don't even want to think about it."

"Well, I don't want Joanne to find out either, so relax." He lay down again. "Get my left shoulder right by my neck."

She kneaded at the muscle, and he sighed with pleasure. She loved his body. It was lean and hard and very beautiful. Theirs was strictly a physical relationship. In fact, if it weren't for sex, they would have had nothing in common. In the few months they had been seeing each other, they had discovered that they liked each other okay, but neither would seek out the other as a serious prospect for a life partner.

Cain had been fascinated with her since the night they had met, but that was at the party when he had gotten arrested for underage drinking. She had gotten pushed into some dark recess in some obscure corner of his mind, but she had never left it. Joanne was adamant about waiting for sex at the same time his body was screaming for it. It was a conundrum that nearly made him crazy until he and Carrie had run into each other at a basketball game against their two schools. She approached him, but he was with Joanne, and he was mildly confused by how uncomfortable he felt introducing them. He couldn't deny the attraction. When she said good bye, she discreetly took his hand and pressed a small piece of paper into it. He immediately slipped it into his jacket pocket and didn't take it out until later when he was alone. It was her phone number with the words "CALL ME!" His heart raced wildly at the prospect; but he really did love Joanne, so he crumpled it and threw it away. Soon after, however, she was waiting for him when he came out of work one night. She knew all the right things to say and all the right buttons to push, and before he knew it, he was thinking with his hormones.

It all made sense. Without her parents' knowledge she was on the pill, she was looking for some daring excitement, and he needed an outlet before he went mad. At this point in her life she didn't believe in any serious commitment—a girl never knew who was out there still to be conquered. Besides, commitment is the number-one killer of spontaneity and excitement. After years of people telling him to think before he acts, here was someone telling him not to think—just feel and enjoy. He surrendered, and she opened doors in his mind and body that he never even dreamed existed. This was about the fourth or fifth time they'd been together, mostly while she was baby-sitting.

"Are you going to sleep?" she asked as she purposely pinched and dug into his muscle.

"Ow!" he protested as he propped himself up to his elbows. "Come on, I've had a rough day."

"Then you should have stayed home like a good boy and gone to bed. I don't have use for good boys—I only like bad boys."

"You do, do you?"

He swung around, grabbed her, and wrestled her to the ground. She shrieked with excitement and giggled with delight as she managed to put up a good fight. A few times she dug her long nails into his back and shoulders and left welts. It wasn't until she swiped at his face, though, that she caught him just right and drew blood.

"Damn!" he cried out in pain as he gave up the fight.

But she wasn't about to stop. She threw her arms around him and kissed him passionately. At first he tried to push her away, but soon his anger and pain gave in to his passion and he stopped struggling and kissed her back. She began to pull at his clothes, and then she started taking her clothes off. After she was sure she had him where she wanted him, she stopped kissing him and took him by the hand.

"Come on," she said leading him toward the bedroom.

He hesitated. They had never used the bedroom before, and he knew he didn't like the idea.

"Come on, pussy," she chided as she took off her bra, dropped it on the floor, and scampered to the bedroom.

He was at the point of no return; so, the flame burning brightly, the unsuspecting moth flew toward it. He quickly removed his clothing and moved to join her. In spite of the burning inside him, he couldn't get passed the idea that this was someone else's bed and he had no right to be in it; so gently he lifted her naked body and carefully put her on the floor on the plush carpeting. Now, undaunted, he proceeded to finish what she had begun. Although he was young and eager, it was a while before he was spent, and she encouraged him all the way. Then they both lay back on the soft carpeting and basked in the euphoria while they caught their breath. Soon Carrie sat up next to him as his chest still heaved for breath.

"You are so gorgeous," she said tracing zigzags on his washboard stomach.

"I hate when you say that," he said with a grin.

"Well, it's true. From head to toe. And there are two of you. That's almost obscene. Now we have to think of a way to explain those scratches on your face. You're clever, think of something."

"How about . . . " he began to ask as the last carefree seconds of his young life passed unnoticed.

"Shhhhh!!!" she said putting her fingers on his lips to quiet him.

"What's wrong?"

But even as he asked, he heard it—the garage door opener was humming. *SHIT!*

"They're home!" cried Carrie hysterically. "My God, they're home early! My parents!"

Cain was already up and getting his pants on. His heart was pounding in his throat as time blurred before his eyes. Carrie heard the garage door closing, and she knew there was no chance of her dressing, straightening the house, and getting rid of Cain before the Brownings caught them. She had to devise a plan to cover herself. She liked Cain, but she knew she had to sacrifice him. Her parents could never find out. She panicked at the thought, so her hysteria was not all contrived as she began to scream at the top of her lungs. Cain looked at her in horrified disbelief. Before he could react, she reached for a metal nail file that was laying on the night stand next to her and began slashing at her own body, cutting herself mercilessly with the file.

"What the hell?!" he cried as he pulled his jeans on and ran over to her.

"My parents!" She screamed hysterically. "My father can't know! Oh my God!! Oh my God!!!"

She started to slash herself again with the file, but he reached down and wrestled it from her.

"Stop it!!!" he cried.

Although he was confused, he was beginning to get an inkling of what was happening. He felt like he had just stepped into someone else's nightmare. But the nightmare was all his and it was just beginning.

"Get him away from me!!!" screamed Carrie in terrified hysteria as she pulled at the blankets in an effort to cover her naked, bleeding body. "Dear God, get him away from me!!!"

The Brownings burst into the room.

Time stopped for Cain at that moment. Everything froze into an unnatural setting as he began to fully realize what was happening to him. *Somebody wake me up!* But the nightmare continued. Suddenly, he looked up to see Mr. Browning extracting a gun from his dresser drawer. *CHRIST!*

"Hold on!" screamed Cain. "For God's sake, don't shoot! It's not what you think!"

"Drop the file!" ordered Mr. Browning visibly shaken.

Cain looked absently at the nail file he still held in his left hand and let it drop. He didn't even remember taking it from Carrie.

"Now move away from her," said Mr. Browning clutching the gun frantically. "Over there, by the wall."

"Okay, okay," said Cain, "I'm moving."

Cain did as he was told. The man was extremely nervous, and Cain feared he'd do something crazy. Looking down the barrel of what he assumed was a loaded gun was the most terrifying thing he'd ever done. It didn't take much to notice that Mr. Browning was an amateur when it came to guns, and that made everything all the worse.

Mrs. Browning ran to Carrie and brought the sobbing, hysterical teen a robe. As her husband continued to hold Cain at bay with the gun, she picked up the phone and called the police.

"No!" pleaded Cain. "It's not what you think. Tell them, Carrie! This has gone far enough. Tell them what happened!"

"Shut up!" said Mr. Browning waving the gun as his wife continued the phone call to the police. "We saw enough to know what happened. Turn around and put your hands on the wall. The police will be here in a minute. And don't try anything funny because this gun is loaded, and I'd like nothing better than to have an excuse to use it on you."

"Jesus," sighed Cain as he slowly turned and put his hands on the wall. "Carrie, please. This is getting out of hand. Tell them what happened."

Over his shoulder he could see Mrs. Browning shepherding Carrie out of the room. Carrie was still crying and acting very much the victim. It was obvious she was not planning on coming to his rescue in the near future.

"Can't I call my father?" Cain asked as Mr. Browning stood over him with the gun.

"We'll just let the police take care of that."

The wait, though only minutes, seemed endless. Soon they heard the police arrive, and a whole new panic overtook Cain. He felt hopelessly locked into a situation over which he had no control. The officer cautiously entered the bedroom with his gun drawn. *Jesus!* Cain had never felt so vulnerable in his whole life. He was standing wearing only a pair of unbuttoned and unzipped jeans with two loaded guns pointed in his direction. Mercifully, after assessing the situation, the policeman returned his gun to his holster and approached Mr. Browning.

"Okay, sir," he said to the still vigilant Browning, "put the gun down. I'll take over from here."

"We need to keep a gun on him," insisted Browning. "I think he raped her, or he was about to rape her. For sure he cut her with that file over there."

"It's all right. I can handle this, sir. Please put the gun down." He turned to Cain. "And you don't move a muscle."

Browning returned the gun to the dresser drawer, and the officer made a mental note to check on it later. Then he walked over to Cain who was still facing the wall with his hands propped against it. The officer kicked at Cain's bare feet to spread them, and he patted him down in a check for weapons. Then keeping an opened hand on Cain's back, he reached with the other hand and pulled Cain's wallet out of his back pocket in a search for identification.

"Those your clothes over there?"

"Yes," answered Cain looking over his shoulder.

"Get dressed," ordered the policeman handing him back his wallet. Then he read him his rights.

That was the moment Cain knew it would take nothing short of a miracle to ever get his life back to where it had been just a few short minutes ago.

The instant he finished tying his shoes and stood up, the officer skillfully clamped handcuffs on his right wrist and almost in one move pulled it behind his back. Then he grabbed his left wrist, swung it around his back, and locked it in the cuffs.

"Let's go."

At the police station they booked him and then let him make a frantic call to his father.

"Dad, I'm at Cedar Grove police station! I need you! Bring a lawyer!"

"Now what?" asked Will feeling the angry stirrings of déjà vu.

"Please hurry, Dad. This is serious. It's not like before. I'm scared."

"What's the charge?" asked Will becoming alarmed at his son's tone.

"Rape. I didn't do it, but no one's listening to me."

Will felt the air get sucked out of his lungs, and for a minute he felt like he was going to faint.

"Okay," he was finally able to say, "don't talk to anyone—no one. You understand?"

"Yes."

"You sound dazed. Are you sure you understand what I'm saying? Don't talk to anyone! Don't say anything! Don't sign anything! You haven't done any of that, have you?"

"No."

"Okay. Be sure you don't—no matter what they tell you. Wait for me. I might be a while because I have to get in touch with a lawyer. It's Saturday night—it might take a while. Just sit tight, I'll be there."

"Okay."

"Son?"

"Yeah, Dad?"

"It'll be okay. Try and relax. Don't talk to anyone. And I'll get there as soon as I can."

"Why is she doing this, Dad?" he asked as tears threatened.

"I don't know. We'll get to the bottom of it, though. I just need you to keep your wits about you and try not to worry. Trust me."

"I do."

"Okay. I'll see you as soon as I can possibly get there."

By the time he hung up, Cain was shaking uncontrollably. The officer on duty took pity on him.

"Come on," he said gently taking his arm. "You look like you need to sit down."

He led him to a small holding cell down the hall. Cain froze for a minute before he could actually make himself walk in. Before closing and locking the door, the policeman went to a Coke machine in the hallway, put some money in from out of his own pocket, and got a can of Coke. Cain was standing in the room in a state of shock.

"You might want this," said the officer putting the can on the table in the room.

"Thanks."

He squeezed his eyes shut in terror as the door closed behind him and locked. He had to almost force himself to breathe. He felt like he was being smothered—buried alive. There was nothing in the room except for the wooden table and a few chairs. Conscious of every nerve in his body, he walked across the room and looked out the small barred window. It only looked out into an alley, so it didn't matter much that it was really too dark to see anything. For a while he paced nervously. He was still shaking, and there was no way he would be able to sit still. He tramped aimlessly for some time trying to wear out his wide-awake nervous system. He hugged himself and fought the urge to cry. He kept walking, walking, walking. Finally he realized he was stirring himself into a wild frenzy rather than calming his nerves, so he went to the table and sat down. He held the cold can of pop up to his aching forehead and savored the coolness. He began to feel as if his father would never get there.

For the first time in his life, he knew what real desperation was. He had thought things were bad at other times, but nothing even came close to this. Popping the top, he drank some of the Coke. He could feel his body beginning to unwind—not relax, just become somewhat numb. It was a defense against the absolute terror he was experiencing. In spite of everything, he still kept hoping that somewhere out of the blue Carrie would come to her senses and set everything straight. It was a remote possibility, but it was the only thing keeping him from completely sinking into despair.

All the events of that evening began to pile up on him and seize him in the form of extreme weariness. His body ached, the damning scratches on his face burned, and his head was pounding. Folding his arms on the table, he leaned over and closed his eyes.

He didn't remember falling asleep, but the next thing he knew the door was opening behind him and his father was entering the room with a lawyer. It took Cain a few seconds to completely awaken and realize where he was and what was going on. He stood up and looked at his father, never so happy to see anyone in his life. Without even a moment's hesitation, they approached each other and embraced. Cain could stand no more, and he began to sob uncontrollably on Will's shoulder.

"That's the way," comforted Will patiently. "Get it all out. Then we'll talk. Take your time."

Cain clutched and grabbed on to his father as if his very life depended on it. He was frantic in spending his grief. Will held him fast and wished for a simpler time.

"I didn't do it!" he proclaimed over and over again.

"I know," said his father. "You could never do anything like that. Try to pull yourself together so you can tell us what happened."

Cain wiped his face, carefully avoiding the open scratches on his left cheek. It took a few minutes before he could bring his body under full control. He sat down and breathed deeply a few times while he tried to control the trembling that had seized him once again.

"Where's Mom?" he asked testing out his composure.

"She's at home. This is no place for her."

"Is she pretty upset?" he asked as a new wave of tears began streaming silently down his face.

"Cain, don't torture yourself. We'll talk about Mom later. This is Bruce Rothwell. He's a criminal lawyer, and a golf partner of mine. I've known him many years; you can trust him."

Cain looked up but couldn't speak. He nodded his head at the stranger who now had his future in his hands. Rothwell walked around and sat at the table across from Cain. Will stood in the background.

"Have you talked to the police?" Rothwell asked.

"No," answered Cain wiping his eyes with the backs of his hands. "I told them right from the beginning that I had a lawyer coming, so they put me in here to wait."

"Good. We'll have to do that before the night is over, but right now I want you to tell me the story from the very beginning. Don't leave anything out—even if you don't think it's important."

As Cain related the shameful story, he was glad his father, his hero, was standing behind him and he didn't have to see his face. He told it all, exactly as he remembered it, going back to the party where he had first met Carrie. Rothwell stopped him occasionally to ask a question or clear up a point, but otherwise he just let him talk as he recorded the conversation and took notes.

"I know you're tired," the attorney said, "but the police are really anxious to talk to you. They already have Carrie's statement. It's a good idea for you to get your side down on record before they get too used to her story. Besides, I don't think they'll let you get any sleep until they've had their chance at you. You may as well get it over with."

"They think I did it, don't they?"

"I'm afraid that's the direction they're leaning. Just tell the truth. And don't elaborate. Tell them only the bare facts. That's all they need to know."

"Okay," sighed Cain wearily.

"You all right?" asked Rothwell.

His eyes were swollen and red, his beard though not yet fully matured was way past the 5:00 shadow stage, and his head still throbbed. He looked up at the ceiling and pointed to it.

"That's up," he said. "I think."

Bruce and Will both smiled.

"That's the spirit," said Bruce. "Before we go, say good bye to your dad. They won't let him in with us, and we could be there a very long time. It's better if he goes home."

"No," protested Will. "I'll wait by the front desk."

"No, you'll go home. There's no more you can do here tonight. I'll call you as soon as I get home."

"Wait," said Cain in a whole new panic, as he began putting two and two together, "I can't stay here. Please tell me I can go home."

Will already knew what Bruce was about to say. They had spent a good deal of time before going to the police station trying to arrange bail only to be put off until Monday morning. Cain didn't like the news, but steeled himself against it, as he knew he had no choice and he was determined to act like a man. That's what the situation called for, and that's how he'd handle it.

"Go home, Dad. I'm okay. Go be with Mom. Tell her . . . I'm sorry. I'm so sorry."

Bruce walked with Will over to the door and rapped on it to get the attention of the police so they would unlock it. Cain sat at the table with his head in his hands.

"He's only eighteen," sighed Will softly.

"He'll be okay. They know that; they'll watch out after him. This isn't a hard core lock-up. Go home and get some rest."

At 5:00 AM Cain was still sitting with the police going over the facts of the night before. He was totally exhausted, needing his hand to hold up his head. His eyes blazed a bright blue as they always did when he was over-tired. It was getting harder and harder to keep his eyes opened, and he craved sleep even though it meant being locked in a jail cell. But the police wanted him to confess and clean up the whole thing. Sam Willet was hot, and he wanted this matter settled as soon as possible with the least amount of difficulty for his daughter. She had already been through enough. Throw the animal in jail and lose the key. Knowing that a trial would mean Carrie Willet would have to testify, the police were most interested in clearing this all up now with a signed confession. Cain was having none of it, however, so they were really getting nowhere.

"Gentlemen," said Bruce. "I think we're about talked out—at least for this session. My client has been through a lot, too, and he's not receiving the pampered treatment that Miss Willet is. He needs sleep. We'll sign the statement he has given you, but that's all. We can sit here for a week, and you'll get no confession. He simply didn't rape her."

They weren't happy, but they had to agree—there was no more to be gained by going over all this ground again. Frankly, everyone was getting tired. There was no point in continuing. It was a small victory, but Bruce smiled inwardly as he thanked his stars that he would not be the one to break the news to the forbearing Sam Willet. The man was a tyrant and used to getting his way. He was not going to be happy.

A police officer was summoned and took Cain by the arm and pulled him to his feet. Cain had to struggle to calm the terror that was rising in his chest. He was exhausted, but the reality of the situation was they were going to lock him in a cage. Though he had innocently brushed with the law before, he had never been locked up. He was thankful for being so tired; otherwise, he wasn't sure he could just turn himself over. After a few words of encouragement from Bruce, he left with the policeman.

The jail was mercifully quiet. The few people who were there, mostly drunks, were asleep. His eyes took in the whole, awful sight as he was taken to a cell. Nausea churned in his stomach as he walked in, and a chill ran up his spine as the door slammed into place and was locked. Seeking the refuse of sleep, he headed straight for the bed. It wasn't much—a mattress, a pillow, and a folded blanket at the foot. He kicked off his shoes, but he left his clothes on. Undressing would have been too much like moving in, and that was more than he was willing to concede. Unfolding the blanket, he pulled it up over himself. A tight fetal position was the opted-for sleeping style—at least until sleep took over and relaxed both body and mind.

Growing up in a large family, he was used to noise and able to sleep through most types of disturbances. Thus, the normal morning routine of the jail failed to break into his subconscious and wake him. He slept on, numb to the pain that consciousness would renew.

"Who's the cherub?" inquired a policewoman with a smile as she paused outside his cell.

"He's become an overnight celebrity in town," answered her colleague who was about to go off duty. "Don't you read the papers? If you did, you'd know he ain't no angel."

"The Willet rapist?"

"In the flesh."

"You're kidding," she said as they moved on. "Who's ever going to believe that he would have to rape anyone? The way I see it after looking at him, it's more likely girls would be tearing off their clothes and waiting in line."

"Best keep that theory to yourself. It's not bound to be a very popular approach around here or within the camps of the women's movement."

It seems hospitals and jails had one thing in common—neither was meant to provide its occupants with rest. Into only his third hour of sound sleep in the past 48 hours, Cain was awakened by a police officer and a technician. Each time he thought he had hit bottom, someone came along to pull the floor right out from under him sending him toppling to new depths. This visit was a prime example. They needed hair and fluid samples for evidence. Not to worry, this was routine in all rape cases. He vaguely remembered Bruce mentioning it to him before he left, but he'd managed to push it way out of mind. Not to worry.

He was thankful he was still so tired that this all seemed like a dream and, therefore, didn't have the bite of reality. After submitting to the humiliating procedure, he curled up facing the wall and dove back into the oblivion of mindless sleep. Not to worry.

They tried to wake him for lunch, but he sleepily brushed off all attempts by moving closer to the wall and pulling the pillow over his head. He wanted to will himself into a coma where no one could reach him again until Carrie came around and admitted she'd lied about the whole thing.

It was Bruce who was finally able to wake him when he came for a visit. Cain never heard the cell door open and then close and lock again. Bruce called to him a few times and then pulled the pillow from over his head. Cain stretched lazily and rolled to his back. He rubbed his eyes and blinked them a few times to try and chase the drowsiness from them. Bit by bit reality began revealing itself in huge, ugly doses.

"Shit," said Rothwell with a smile. "Your mother's here, but she'll die if she sees you like this."

"Bruce, I can't see her. Not now."

"You can, and you will," said the attorney getting very serious. "She needs to see you. She's been a basket case all night. She's worried out of her mind. I brought you clean clothes, a razor, toothbrush, and everything else you need to help you feel more human. I even talked them into letting you go down and shower. I'm going to call the guard, and then while I go out into the visiting room with your parents, you're going to bring yourself back to life and then get out there and convince your mother that everything will be okay. I don't care if you feel that way or not. She needs that from you right now. None of this was her doing. You didn't rape anyone; but you were playing with fire, and you should have known better. Your parents did nothing but love and trust you. You owe them for that. You understand?"

"Yeah. I'm sorry."

He had to admit that he felt much better after he cleaned up and changed his clothes. He still dreaded facing his mother, but he knew Bruce was right about his parents. This was all his doing, not theirs. Their lives were being turned upside down because of him. They had raised him better; he had let them down. That hurt him worse than anything else did. People were talking—about him, about them. There aren't many things lower than a rapist. What kind of parents are they anyway?

Gloom was descending on him and souring the freshness he had felt from the shower. He shook it off and told the police officer that he was ready. He was escorted out to the holding cell where he had waited for his father the night before. The door was open when they got there, but as soon as he entered, it was closed and locked. Nora began to cry when she saw him. Knowing he had to be strong for her, he was able to dam his own tears. He walked over to her and put his arms around her. He smelled of fresh soap and clean clothes as she hugged him close and cried into his chest. It was a while before either spoke.

"I'm sorry, Mom," he finally managed to say. "I didn't rape her."

As she drew back from him, she pulled herself together. Now she was ready to take on her parental role. She reached up and gently put her fingertips on his lips.

"Shhhhh," she said softly. "You don't even have to say it. I know. I always did know. We'll work it out. There has to be a way. You have the best lawyer. We'll work it out together. You have to believe that."

"I do," he lied.

"Did they give you anything for those scratches?" she asked.

"No, but they're okay."

"She got you pretty good. You would never hurt anybody."

"No, Mom, I wouldn't." He guided her to a chair and then knelt on one knee next to her so they were eye to eye. "Carrie and I were doing something we shouldn't have been doing. We have been for a while now. I knew you wouldn't have approved, so that's why I didn't tell you. I didn't tell anybody." She put her hands up over her ears as tears streamed down her face. He knew the gesture was symbolic rather than an attempt to shut him out, so he continued. "We had just had . . . sex . . . and we weren't dressed yet when the people came home. She panicked and cried rape because she didn't know what else to do. She's afraid of her father."

"She's a selfish, lying bitch!" declared Nora shamelessly.

Cain let a small smile cross his lips at his mother's statement.

"Yeah," he agreed, "she is. But the police and her father believe her. It worked for her. Unfortunately, it leaves me kind of hanging out to dry." He hesitated while he chose his words. "I don't know how this is all going to end up, Mom. The longer she waits to tell the truth, the least likely it is that anyone will believe her. And then, she may never tell the truth. Either way, I'm in a tight spot. I have to face that fact, and so do you. But I'm going to fight it. I'm not giving in. I'm not selling myself out. I came out here with every intention of convincing you it was all a big mistake that would soon be straightened out, but I can't do that. I don't really believe it, and I can't lie to you any more. This is going to be a long fight, but I'm up for it, and I'll never admit that I'm a rapist. I need you, Mom. I need you to believe in me, and stand by me no matter what. I'll be okay. You don't have to worry about me. I got myself into this, and I'll deal with whatever comes along. I just don't want you to be hurt or to worry."

She reached over and gently fingered a wispy lock of his sandy hair that was still slightly damp from his shower.

"I'll be fine," she said, now steady as a rock. "We'll all face this together, and we'll be there for each other. That's what our family's all about. Thank you for being honest with me. In spite of what everyone's telling me, deep inside I knew it wasn't all going to go away. Right now I just want to get you home. I want you out of here."

"Me, too," smiled Cain getting up from his knee and sitting in a chair.

Bruce explained to them all about the hearing downtown the next morning. He said it was very likely bail would be set, but it was bound to be sizable. Cain's heart sank as he was introduced to one more aspect of his folly. This was going to cost his parents more than grief and worry. Will assured Bruce and Cain that he could get his hands on the money.

"Our biggest problem," said Bruce, "is not that we're fighting a cunning and crafty young lady. That's bad enough in itself. But our biggest problem is her belligerent and powerful old man. He is going to fight us every step of the way."

"Whatever it takes, the story I told you is the truth—exactly the way it happened," insisted Cain. "I'm not changing that or settling for any less. I don't care who her old man is or what punches he pulls. I'm just taking it one step at a time. That's all I can do. Somehow I plan to keep my sanity through all this. That's more than I can say for Carrie. She has totally flipped. And the thing that scares me about that is it tends to make her story even more believable and me even more despicable. Not only did I rape her, but I've driven her to some kind of breakdown."

"You've been doing a lot of thinking, haven't you?" commented Bruce.

"There hasn't been a whole lot more to do. And I picked up a lot of vibes from the DA and the police last night. I know what they're thinking. That's why I'm telling you right now—that's my story, and I'm sticking with it."

"That's certainly your right," said Bruce. "And we'll talk more later when we know what our options are."

After they all left, Cain went back to the cell and kicked off his shoes. Then he sat on the bed, pulled his knees up to his chest, and leaned against the wall. He knew if he lay down he'd fall asleep immediately. He was still strung out and tired from the night before, but he wanted to avoid sleeping the day away. He knew he couldn't sleep endlessly, and he wanted to be tired when night came.

For the first time he allowed himself to think of Joanne. That hurt. It made him feel selfish and heartless. She was the real innocent victim in all of this. The last thing he wanted was for her to be hurt and embarrassed. There was no way to avoid that now. The story was out, and she had no choice but to deal with it. How can you love someone with your whole heart and soul and yet cause her so much pain? That must be what she was thinking about at that very minute. Facing her was going to be even harder than facing his mother was. That unpleasant thought took its place in the growing knot in the pit of his stomach.

The next morning he awoke eager to get things going but apprehensive about going before a judge as a hardened criminal of the lowest sort. The Lake Geneva incident never got to court and the underage drinking violation now seemed like a romp in the park. But this was way different. This was the one that could break his back. He was no longer fooling himself that Carrie would come to her senses and set things straight. He knew he was in this for the long haul, and he knew it was pretty much him against the world. At that moment, however, he couldn't afford to think too far ahead. He had to stay with the moment and move ahead minute by minute. Otherwise he knew he'd drown in a sea of utter futility.

They chained him up to take him down to the county courthouse for the bail hearing. He found that a most unbearable state. He wanted to tell them that it wasn't necessary; he'd go quietly and without a problem. But he knew they thought of him as an untrustworthy criminal, and chains were the way they dealt with such.

Much to his dismay the press was waiting outside the courthouse when they arrived. He doubted that reporters often made such a fuss over an ordinary rape case. After all, this was a big city, not unfamiliar with crimes of all sorts. But when the victim is the daughter of a powerful, local politician, the crime suddenly gains prominence and, therefore, so do the principals involved. This was one kind of prominence he could do without; but being as he had no choice, he accepted the role with as much dignity as he could muster.

The hearing was mercifully short but degrading and sobering. The finality of it all began to really hit him and sink in. This wasn't just a few insufferable days in jail. This was all just the beginning of a much longer and more difficult battle yet to come. Listening to the judge dispassionately reeling off the charges as lawyers for both sides pleaded the possibility of bail, Cain felt control of his life slipping away. He had the distinct impression of being on the outside looking in as his life was being laid out and debated in front of him. Occasionally, he had to remind himself that they were actually discussing him. He didn't recognize the hideous events and descriptions that were being bantered around by the prosecution. He wanted to scream out in protest, but Bruce had warned him not to speak unless spoken to. He had already made a mess of his life trying to bypass the good advice of his elders, so he kept his mouth shut.

In the end the judge granted bail. Cain reeled at the vast amount of money, and once again he was reminded of the extreme seriousness of the charges against him. An outbreak of sizable proportions erupted from the courtroom behind them. As Cain turned around, he came face to face with Sam Willet, Carrie's nonplused father. He was bellowing about the injustice of granting bail to someone who was capable of such a heinous crime. How would the judge explain it to the next girl who tried to say no to Cain Farrell? Cain's blood ran cold as he witnessed the man's wrath. Family members and friends rushed to escort the raving father from the courthouse as the judge pounded his gavel. Cain's heart banged against the walls of his chest.

Will had counted on the large bail and had arranged for the money. Once the bail was paid, the handcuffs were removed and for the first time in two days, Cain was able to move about freely—as long as he didn't violate any of the stringent terms of his bail. Now he could go home.

Home was another can of worms. At least in jail he didn't have to face the questioning stares of his family and friends. He didn't have to face the public with the "Scarlet Letter" Carrie had emblazoned on his face. Those scratches would be around for a while to attest to his stupidity and to draw the curious attention of anyone who saw them.

It was early afternoon when they arrived home. School wasn't out yet, so except for Robert the house was empty. Cain was in no mood to deal with his cantankerous, old grandfather, so he walked deliberately passed him on his way up to his room. Cain made a point of not making eye contact as Robert watched him walk by.

"This time you've really done us proud," said the elder Farrell.

Cain contemplated a major tirade, at last putting the old man in his place, but he was too aware of the presence of his parents. He had put them through enough; he would spare them the unnerving scene. Instead he ignored Robert and continued on his way upstairs.

When Matt got home from school, he ran straight upstairs to see his brother. Cain was sitting on his bed trying to read a book. Matt walked over to him and placing his hand under Cain's chin, turned his head to look at his scratched cheek.

"Ow," he said. "How are you?"

"I'm a wreck. Food gets caught in the middle of my throat when I try to eat, I have to be falling over on my feet before I can sleep, and I walk around with a splitting headache most of the time. I just got a call from George at the store, and they're very sorry but they have to let me go. It seems people have been calling in since this all came out, and as much as they'd like to stick by me, it just wouldn't be good for business. And if that wasn't enough good news for one person in a day, school called and they want to see me tomorrow with Mom and Dad. So now I'm getting expelled—one month before graduation. Life sucks, you know?"

"Did they actually say you're getting expelled?"

"No, but what else could it be?"

"It could be anything."

"Well, let's just say it's not going to be anything good. And I still have to face Joanne. I'm screwed. Just don't say you told me so, all right?"

"I wouldn't."

"Well, there's one bright spot in my day."

"What are you going to do?"

"I'm going to go through with this charade because I have absolutely no choice, and I'm going to pray that my life is destined to end some time in the next few months."

"Cain."

"I don't have a life any more, Matt. I'm screwed right up to my eyeballs. The law is in total control now."

"You haven't been found guilty yet."

"It's just a matter of time. You haven't seen Carrie's performance. She's good, man. She almost had me believing I did it."

Matt sighed dejectedly.

"What about Joanne?" he asked.

"Now that's a bridge I can't wait to cross. God. Do you think it's possible that my life is slated to end in the next few minutes?"

Matt smiled. "That's highly unlikely."

"Then I guess I'd better get my ass over there and get that over with. What do I say to her?"

"I don't know," sighed Matt. "She wasn't in school today, so I haven't seen her. I have no idea what frame of mind she's in."

Cain walked the four blocks to Joanne's house. He thought it best not to call first. She would probably refuse to see him, if her parents even let him talk to her. This way he'd take them all by surprise and stand more of a chance. Joanne's mother who normally was enthusiastic about his presence glared at him through the screen door.

"I don't believe you have the nerve to show up here," she said.

"I have to see Joanne."

"Joanne doesn't need to see you. She's spent the last two days trying to forget you exist. She couldn't face her friends at school so she stayed home today, and she and I went and returned her prom dress."

Hitting him in the head with a hammer would have been more humanitarian and would have caused less pain.

"Please. I have to see her."

"She's in the backyard," relented the mother. "I'll be right in the kitchen. Make it fast, and then I don't want to see you around here any more. If my husband catches you here, he'll have you horse whipped."

Cain sighed. One hurdle passed, now for the big one. He walked around the back of the house to the backyard. He spotted her before she saw him. She was sitting on the porch swing where they had spent many carefree hours. He was nearly to the stairs before she looked up and saw him. Quickly she got up and started for the house.

"Jo, wait!" he called frantically as he ran up to her and grabbed her arm.

"Don't touch me!" she screamed as she pulled away from him and an invisible dagger pierced his heart.

"Okay, okay," he agreed as he held his hands up in surrender. "Okay, just don't go in. I need you. I need to talk to you."

"Don't bother. It's all been in the newspapers and on TV. I'm up to date."

"No, you're not. You don't know what's going on inside of me. None of that's been in the newspapers. I love you, Joanne."

She forced a hysterical laugh, and the dagger tore through his heart.

"You're something else, you know that? You lie and cheat, and then when you get caught, you come to me and say 'I love you, Joanne.'

And you expect me to believe it. What a riot you are. How stupid do you think I am?"

"I don't think you're stupid at all."

"No? Then why do I feel so stupid?"

"I didn't rape her."

"Of course you didn't. Don't you think I know you well enough to know that? She's a lying bitch, but that's not the point, Cain. You can't deny you were seeing her, though, can you? And fucking her! That's the back-breaker. You were telling me how much you loved me, and then running off to her after I was safely home and in bed. I don't know how to tell you this, but that's not love. You have a hell of a lot to learn about love."

"I'm sorry," he said as tears threatened. "I didn't want to hurt you."

"What did you think would happen? For God's sake, Cain, you're an honor student and something like this had to happen before you could see the consequences of what you were doing?"

"Joanne . . ."

"Forget it, Cain. I hate you. I could never forgive you—not in a million years. You've made me a laughing stock at school. I feel like such a fool. I don't want to ever see you again. Don't call me. Don't come over. Don't even think about me anymore. I've burned all your pictures, and I'm going to pretend like I've never even met you."

"Okay, I know you're hurt. You can't say anything to me that I haven't already said to myself. Just promise me you'll give yourself some time. I won't bother you for a week or a month or however long it takes—just don't shut me out. I love you."

"I don't want to hear that! I don't want to hear it ever again from you—or from anyone for that matter! Love is highly overrated, and you of all people don't have a clue of what it's all about. And forgive me if I can't get all concerned about how much trouble you're in. You deserve everything you get as a result of this! I don't feel a bit sorry for you. You and Carrie Willet can go straight to hell for all I care!!!"

Tears streamed freely down her face as she spoke. Large tears spilled over Cain's dark lashes and onto the front of his shirt as he watched her lash out at him with a fury he had never dreamed possible. She reached up and soundly slapped him across the face right over the tender scratches. Then taken aback by her own hysteria, she threw her hand over her mouth and ran into the house.

He stood frozen to the spot, unable to move. His face throbbed, but it was the invisible dagger that rendered him helpless. He was sure he must have been bleeding all over the front of his shirt for the pain he felt. His eyes blurred with tears as he turned his anger inward on himself. She was right. What did he know about love? How could he have let his body rule his mind? He knew better; he really did. How did everything get so out of hand? He couldn't remember. He pressed his palms to his temples in an effort to calm the demons fighting for possession. Everything was wrong. How much further in despair could he sink?

Everything in the yard took on a surrealistic view through the tears in his eyes as he looked around the familiar sight for one last time. Finally, summoning strength he didn't know he had, he wiped his face with his hands and headed for home.

The next morning he enviously watched Jim and Matt get ready for school as he lay in bed trying to find some reason for getting up. The only thing he had to look forward to was the 9:30 meeting with school officials and his parents. He knew that was to be yet another painful experience, so his bed was his place of choice. He didn't know how much more rejection he could take. All of his emotions screamed in pain as he looked across at his nightstand at a framed, laughing picture of Joanne and himself on a happier day. He thought back to a mere week ago when he was still innocently bounding his way through life footloose and fancy-free, as they say. If only it was possible to turn back time.

His disposition didn't change as the morning progressed. His heart was full of foreboding as he traveled with his parents to his school to meet with the administration. This time it was not simply one dean that he was summoned before, but a panel of administrators all the way up to the principal. The meeting began amiably enough with everyone greeting each other with friendly handshakes and smiles, but Cain remained sullen—waiting for the ax to fall. The principal, Dr. Randmeier, didn't take long in getting to the point.

"Myself and my colleagues are deeply saddened that we have to meet here today under such circumstances. We're sorry for the tribulation you have all been put through, and we're sure that in the end, Cain, you will be able to prove your innocence. But . . . "

There it was . . . *but* . . . a three-letter word that could bring the most starry-eyed optimist to his or her knees. At this point Cain wasn't even close to being optimistic let alone starry-eyed, so his prayerful trust in a benevolent God once more took a lethal hit and sent him to the depths of despair. Blood raced hotly through his veins as his heart pounded with fury in his chest. He looked around the room, but he realized he wasn't seeing or hearing anything. It was as if he was in some sort of a muffled cocoon that was closing in around him and making it hard for him to breathe. He was fighting the urge to faint and he was trying to collect himself when he realized that all eyes were on him, waiting for an answer to a question he'd never heard.

"What?" he asked lamely.

"Do you understand?" The principal asked.

He took a moment to compose himself and sort through the events of the past few minutes as snatches of conversation began sinking in. He wasn't being expelled, *but* he wasn't welcomed back at school either. They thought it was best for him and for the school. After all, there was only a month left. He would be sent a schedule of his finals, and he could come back to take them. Certain teachers would be in touch with him by phone to discuss any assignments that needed to be completed for a final grade. That way he would still get a diploma. They had discussed it at length before this meeting, and all attending agreed that graduation and honors ceremonies would not be appropriate, nor would prom or other social functions related to the end of senior year. And of course he would have to resign as president of the Student Council. Cain looked around the room. His mother was softly crying. Will looked as though he'd been punched in the stomach. The others were waiting for some kind of agreement from him to soothe their consciences.

"Cain?" said Dr. Randmeier.

"No," answered Cain happy to observe he still had some dignity left. "No, I don't understand at all. Whatever happened to being innocent until proven guilty? I haven't even been officially charged with this bogus crime yet, and you have all passed judgment and found me guilty. You said yourself you were sure that in time it would all get cleared up."

"Well, in that case, we . . . "

"In that case nothing!" stormed Cain. "My whole life is crumbling right before my eyes, and there's not a damn thing I can do about it. I might have made a mistake, but I didn't do anything that merits the consequences I've been experiencing. In my wildest dreams I couldn't have imagined the chaos and bigotry I've been thrust into. Everyone's worried about appearances. Whether or not I actually committed this crime is not important. I DIDN'T RAPE THAT GIRL! I **DID NOT RAPE HER!!!**"

"We know you didn't," said Dean Barber with assurance.

"Then why are you doing this to me? You're stripping me down to the bone and then you're patting me on the back and saying, *Good luck, Cain. Go out and get 'em. We know you can do it.* How is this going to look if this does go to trial? My school, my employer, all the people who know me best are cutting me loose and setting me adrift. It's not exactly a strong show of confidence to put before a jury. I didn't do it, damn it; and I need help to prove it."

"We're truly sorry," said Dr. Randmeier as he let his eyes drop to the table in front of him.

"Fine," said Cain more angry than mortified. "Where do I sign the Student Council resignation?"

"Right here," someone said pushing a paper and pen in his direction.

He grabbed the pen in his left hand and scrawled out his signature. Then slamming the pen on the table, he got up.

"I want to go home," he said exiting the room before giving them the satisfaction of witnessing the tearful outburst that was threatening to explode behind his eyes. An errant tear escaped and rolled down his cheek as he walked through the outer office and on out the front door of the building. Will looked across the table at the men who had just crushed the last of his son's hopes and dreams. He sighed deeply before he spoke.

"That was rather a low blow," he said.

"We're sorry, Will," said the principal sincerely as the others tried not to look uncomfortable. "We have people to answer to."

"You realize what this does to any possibility of a baseball career and his scholarships?"

"Truly, I'm sorry," repeated Dr. Randmeier.

"Yeah," said Will getting up from his chair and reaching a hand out to Nora. "I'll send Matthew to clean out his locker. Don't let anyone else touch it until he does."

"We won't, but he's welcomed to come back and clean it out himself."

"I doubt he wants to ever come back here, and I'm not sure I want him to either. There's very little I can do these days to shield him from pain, but this I can do for him. Just don't let anyone touch any of his stuff until Matt gets a chance to do it himself. And now, gentlemen, I'm going to try and pick up the pieces."

Without another word or as much as a smile or a handshake, he left with Nora to find their son and try to give him something to believe in. That would not be an easy task.

Cain was standing off to the side of the car under a tree. He was leaning with his back and head resting against the large trunk.

"Here," said Will handing Nora the keys to his car. "I'll be right back. Wait here for us."

Feeling depressed and inadequate at the moment, Nora was more than agreeable.

Will walked up to Cain who continued to stare straight ahead into space as silent tears trailed down his cheeks.

"I don't want to live any more, Dad," he said solemnly. "There's nothing left to my life."

"I know it seems that way . . ."

"No, it **is** that way. Joanne, my job, school . . . and then there's the law still to contend with. I'm going to go to prison."

"Cain . . ."

"Don't say anything. It only makes it worse. It gets worse by the day, and I see no other ending. Carrie holds all the cards. There's no way I can prove my side of the story."

"You don't have to. They have to prove you did it."

"Dad, it's my word against hers. They have pictures of these scratches. I grabbed the file from her, so my fingerprints are on it. She was out of control, screaming hysterically. Joanne has a right to be pissed, but everybody else should be behind me, and they're not. How am I ever going to get a jury to believe me? And I know I'm going to be indicted in spite of what I said inside a while ago. This gets uglier all the time, and I just don't want to live any more. I don't know how much more I can take."

"I'm not going to insult your intelligence with platitudes and false promises, but don't give up yet. You have a lot of people behind you. Even the people who seem to have deserted you are actually behind you, they just have to cover themselves for appearances."

"I feel like a door mat." He wiped his face with his hands and tried to compose himself. "I wish these damned scratches would go away. At least then I wouldn't have a constant reminder every time I touch my face or look in a mirror."

Will smiled.

"How about some ice cream? We'll stop on our way home."

"I don't know. I'm not really in the mood."

"For ice cream?! Come on. It'll make Mom feel better."

Cain glanced toward the car where his mother was waiting.

"Okay," he said as he pushed off from the tree. "I'd do anything for her."

Will put his arm around him and together they walked to the car.

# CHAPTER 5

Cain spent the final weeks of May canceling his college plans. An indictment had come down, he pleaded not guilty at the arraignment, and then he set about dismantling the last part of his life that had remained untouched by Carrie Willet. The trial was set for early August, and he knew that even if by a miracle of the highest order he were acquitted, he would never be ready to leave for college on time. Expecting the worst all along, he was becoming desensitized to these setbacks. It was a monumental disappointment, but he was working on steeling himself against these things so that he would be spared a life of crying bitter tears. College would have to be on hold for a while. Hopefully, he could pick up where he left off after the holidays during the winter semester. For now he had to concentrate on keeping himself out of prison, and that would take all the energy he had.

Bruce had come to him with an offer from the state—plead guilty and do less time. Sam Willet was eager to get this over with. He was very discouraged when Cain pleaded not guilty, thus forcing a trial. Sam wanted his daughter spared a trial and was pressuring for a plea bargain. Cain, on the other hand, was hearing nothing of it. He looked forward to the time in court to get his story out. He would not go down without a fight. In fact, it made him happy to know that Carrie was uneasy about going to court. Finally she was feeling some of the fallout from her actions. Though he was pushing for his day in court, Cain knew it was a long shot. Carrie would still be viewed as the helpless victim and he the plundering animal. Bruce was banking on Cain's clean-cut good looks and obvious intelligence to at least sway the jury to some extent. He already knew that in spite of the charge of rape, he would not be opposed to a largely female jury. Cain had a winning way about him that was hard for many women to resist.

As graduation approached in early June, Cain braced himself for yet another hurdle to navigate. He felt that if he could just get past graduation and all the festivities attached to it, he could face his uncertain future with his past firmly laid to rest in yesterday. But for now he still had to get through the pain and disappointment of not being part of the formal closing of his boyhood school days. Matt and his parents were ready to stage a mini-demonstration of their own by not attending the graduation ceremony. But Cain convinced them that he would only feel worse than he did if Matt didn't take his rightful place at the head of the class and if his parents weren't there to beam with pride. Although the administration benevolently offered Cain an invitation to attend as part of the audience, he politely told them to *stick it!* He wouldn't be anywhere near that auditorium for people to gape at. He'd been through way too much humiliation and agony to willfully submit to that. At least he had the satisfaction of knowing that he had passed his finals with flying colors in spite of all adversity, and he would be receiving his diploma.

He also went down on record as being number 5 in his class, while Matt was number 7.

While the others were at the graduation ceremony, Cain sat around at loose ends. His older brothers and Molly were all home from college, and each had privately volunteered to stay home with him, but he would have none of it. He really felt like being alone, anyway. After they were gone a while, he began to feel restless, so he went out for a walk. Whether by design or just sheer habit, he soon found himself walking by Joanne's house. He hadn't seen her but that one time since his arrest. He had gotten her message loud and clear. He hoped that by staying away he would give her some time and she would change her mind about forgiving him. Maybe someday she could even love him again.

He had kept up on her through Matt's on-again-off-again girlfriend, Alexis. For instance, he knew that Joanne and her family were away this weekend on a family trip, so he knew it would be safe to walk passed her house. An old, comfortable feeling stirred in him as he did. It was elusive, though, and he knew it wasn't his to keep. Still, he was amazed that he could sense another time, and he wished beyond hope that he could go back. He walked around to the backyard of his youth. So many days and night were spent in that backyard. So much laughter and fun. He sat on the old porch swing where he and Joanne had laughed together and had professed undying love.

Time went by unnoticed as he stared himself into a trance. Pictures of the past flashed before him. He got to a point where he could almost feel Joanne sitting next to him. In fact, it was when he reached over to take her hand or to touch her knee that he was jolted back to reality. He sighed and wondered why he was torturing himself this way. This mental romp through the past could serve no useful purpose. It was time to collect his wits and go home before someone reported him for trespassing. That was all he needed.

When he got home, he felt stressed-out and on edge. He went upstairs and took one of the tranquilizers the doctor had prescribed for him for moments just like this. Then he sat down and concentrated on breathing deeply and trying to get a rein on his runaway nervous system. He felt electrified and charged with nervous energy and nowhere to put it to use. He forced his hands to stop drumming at an alarming rate, and finally his legs stopped bouncing as the effects of the drug began to wash over him. He laid his head back into his father's big easy chair and closed his eyes in an effort to chase the demons away for a while. He hated taking the pills, but there were times when the anxiety he experienced was too much to deal with. He felt his body becoming one with the over-sized chair as he cleared his mind. He wanted to sleep and not think about what was going on across town at that very minute. He hadn't thought it would bother him so much to miss graduation, but it was driving him crazy. Then somehow, he managed to lapse into a dreamless sleep, which was exactly what he needed.

Later that night during a small gathering of friends and relatives, Cain thought he had slipped away unnoticed; but Scott, who had dropped by, saw him leave and followed him out the back door. He saw Cain sitting on the back stairs, so he pulled up next to him.

"I know," said Scott, "you want to be alone, but, oh well, I'm here."

Cain smiled at him.

"I'm glad you're here."

"You should have been there today," protested Scott. "I'm still pissed off about that. Not that you really missed anything, but you deserved to be there."

"Well, it's over, and I wasn't there, so let's drop it."

"Okay," said Scott staring out into the night. "So what do you want to talk about?"

"Nothing," replied Cain, "that's why I came out here."

"That's right. What can I do for you? What can I do to put that mischievous sparkle back in your eye? Do you want me to go shoot the bitch?"

"No," said Cain smiling in spite of himself. "I'm okay."

"Are you really?"

"Yeah, for now anyway."

"How 'bout your grandpa? How's the old geezer been? A pain in the ass?"

"No, actually he quit talking to me some time ago, so I don't talk to him. That's fine with me. I certainly don't lose any sleep over it."

"Good." Scott hesitated a minute as he looked out over the dark lawn. "There's something I've been wanting to ask you. Why didn't you ever tell Matt or me what you were getting into with Carrie?"

Cain took a deep breath and exhaled.

"It's not exactly something you go around talking about. Not if you're a gentleman, anyway. Isn't that ironic? I considered myself a gentleman, and then I end up getting arrested for rape. Go figure. Do you think you could have stopped me?"

"I don't know," shrugged Scott. "Maybe. At least I could have tried."

"No, save your guilt or whatever it is you're feeling. Nobody could have dissuaded me. I thought I had it all figured out. And it was very pleasurable, though short-lived. She didn't want anything from me. We just totally used each other for the moment. Saying it out loud now, it sounds very depraved. It wasn't, though, not really. There was something I liked about being with her, but not enough to want to make it permanent—or to hurt Joanne the way I did. I never meant for that to happen. We were at different stages, Joanne and I. I had needs and curiosities she wasn't ready for, and I respected that. So I charged full speed ahead when Carrie made me an offer."

"You're too damned good looking for your own good."

"Come on, where's this coming from? My point is nobody could have stopped me. Maybe that's part of the reason why I never told you—I knew you'd hassle me over it. I didn't want to be bugged; I didn't want to be made guilty. So, you see, I have no one to blame but myself. And now I'm more sure than ever that I'm not going to get out of this."

"Don't say that."

"It's too late. They won't take her seriously even if she did suddenly tell the truth. But let's talk about something else. My nerves are rather fragile these days. What are you still doing here, anyway? You're parents must be having a big party."

"Yeah, they are. I have to go soon. I just wanted to be sure you were okay."

"Well, now that you've seen how super duper I am, why don't you get the hell out of here and go celebrate with your family?"

"Yeah, I will. Why don't you stop over a little later?"

"I'm not really good company these days."

"What? You think we care about that? My mom said to be sure and have you come by."

"Thanks, but I think I'll take a pass. There's some preliminary stuff for the trial going on tomorrow, so I think I'll get to bed early. I didn't sleep good last night, and it's been a long day. Thank your mom for me. I'll be over to see her, but under less formal circumstances."

"Okay. Can I go with you tomorrow? I can get out of work."

"No, I've got it covered. But thanks."

The next days and weeks were spent with endless meetings either in court or at Bruce's office. There was so much to cover, so much litigation. Summer had taken on a new meaning. Cain no longer cared to be with his friends. He stuck close to home. He was able to find a new job at a car dealership where he worked in the service department prepping cars for delivery after the sale and running cars for customer pick-up as well as doing other odd jobs and errands. It was mindless work, but it kept him busy and provided him with spending money. It also kept him out of the eye of the public so he would not have that to contend with. He worked as much overtime as they would give him, and he spent much of the rest of his time dealing with his legal problems. His parents tried to encourage him to get out and have fun with his friends, but life wasn't much fun for him anymore, and he preferred being alone. He spent a good deal of his free time reading law books and doing research on the Internet. He wanted to be as prepared as he could be for what lay ahead of him.

The first day of the trial approached with the quickness and the dread of an impending storm. Nothing could delay it or make it go away. Actually, Cain had gotten to a point where he was just as happy to get out of limbo and get on with the rest of his life—whatever that may be. He knew the trial would be emotional surgery without the benefit of anesthesia, and he just wanted it over with. Delaying things now was only adding to the agony. Bruce met with him often to go over the nuances of the proceedings. He was to remain as stoic as possible. It was imperative that he keep his emotions locked up inside him, no matter what **anyone** said. The jury should not be able to read his face whether it be approval or blind outrage he was experiencing. When Carrie Willet testified, he needed to look her straight in the eye and listen as a dispassionate observer. He could vent afterward when he was clearly out of the eye of the jury and the press. Since dispassion was not even close to one of Cain's attributes, he knew this would take some practice.

Finally, the preliminaries, including jury selection, were all out of the way, and the show was about to begin. Since the prosecution was up first, Cain had lots of opportunity right from the start to display his newfound aloofness. He was, indeed, every attorney's dream defendant: tall, good looking, impeccably dressed, looking like he just walked off the pages of *GQ*. He exuded intelligence and good breeding without appearing arrogant and over-confident. In fact, much to Bruce's delight, he was able to maintain the angelic innocence that had impressed the lawyer since the first night they met. That had to work in his favor. People, especially the jury, had to look at him and wonder how he ever could have committed the crime he was accused of. In spite of the evidence stacked against him, the prosecution would have to work a little harder to offset his striking appearance. And there was even more mystique about him because of his identical twin brother sitting in the courtroom behind him. What a magnificent pair they made. Bruce noticed the fascinated stares of nearly everyone in the courtroom. The DA also was aware of the movie star aura that had settled over the young defendant, and he knew that his battle would be somewhat tougher because of it.

Cain spent most of the first morning perched casually, though not slovenly, in his chair at the defense table. He folded his hands much as if in prayer over the lower half of his face with his chin resting on his thumbs. Watching blandly over his templed fingers, he died inside as he heard his character disseminated and thrown out on the floor in front of him for the prosecutor to step on and walk across at will.

"How're you holding up?" Bruce whispered to him just after the judge had declared a lunch recess.

"Like I'm going to throw up. How do I look?"

"Magnificent. Keep it up."

The press descended on them the minute they walked out of the courtroom. Why did Carrie have to be Sam Willet's daughter and cast him in such an infamous spotlight? If she were just a nobody, the press wouldn't care about the trial beyond a passing remark on page 8 or 10. Now because of her, he was front-page news, and he hated it. With as much dignity and poise as he could muster, he waded through the imposing cameras and microphones, totally ignoring all questions and comments.

Lunch proved to be an impossibility. His mouth was hopelessly dry, and his stomach was unreceptive to even the thought of sustenance. He managed to choke down a few bites in order to make his mother happy, but then he pushed his plate away with a pleading look in answer to her protests.

The afternoon was every bit as demoralizing and degrading. Cain found it harder and harder to maintain his composure, but he knew he didn't have a choice. He carefully masked the tension and rage he was experiencing behind a facade of an interested onlooker. As witnesses were called against him, Cain did as he was told and met each person's gaze with keen interest, but no attitude. Some of the early witnesses he knew as acquaintances who had seen Carrie and him together at the party when they met. He knew they were doing what they had to do, and he only hoped they didn't believe the outrageous charge against him. But none of that mattered now. Once in a while he would glance at the jury to see if he could read what they were thinking about him. Occasionally he'd look over to see one or more of them already looking at him. Then he'd let his gaze linger for a moment before casually looking back to the witness. It was to his greatest relief when the judge called it a day, and he could finally go home. What an ordeal, and he would have to repeat it again the next day and the next—each day getting closer to his own testimony and the final outcome of this whole fiasco.

Once he was home, he pealed off his coat, tie, and long-sleeved shirt. Then he went to the bathroom and splashed cold water on his face and tried to wash away the misery he was feeling. But the misery was reaching way down into the depths of his soul and would not be easily flushed down the drain. So, acquiescing, he dried his face and went back to his room and finished changing into a pair of sweats.

As the days wore on, the state called many more witnesses—the Brownings, doctors, technicians, and the police officers who were called to the scene—slowly but surely building up to their star witness, the victim herself. Cain hadn't seen her since the night he was arrested, and as each witness came and went, he knew he was getting closer to the moment he most dreaded with the exception of the reading of the verdict. The night before Carrie was to take the stand, Bruce had a meeting at his house with Cain. He had his wife bring them something to drink and then instructed her that they were not to be interrupted.

"You've been doing a great job up to now," he told Cain. "I just want to be sure you'll be able to pull this off tomorrow. This is the most crucial performance of your life. You already know what she's going to say, and she's going to swear under oath that it's all true. It's going to take a great deal of composure on your part to listen to that with the same lack of intensity that you've exhibited so far. For the first time since the trial began, your sexual conduct is going to be laid bare to the world. They're going to want her to be specific. And then I'll have a shot at her." He hesitated momentarily. "Is there anything you haven't told me? Anything at all? I don't want any surprises."

"There's nothing. I've told you everything. But when she's basing this whole case on a lie, isn't there a good chance there'll be some surprises? She could say anything she wants to."

"That's true, and I'll deal with it. I just want to make sure that she doesn't come up with some undeniable fact that I'm not ready for."

"I'm not intentionally leaving anything out."

"Are you ready for explicit details of your sex life, even if some of them aren't true?"

"Do I have a choice?"

"No, you don't. But the one thing in our favor is that she's going to deny any intercourse until that last time. You're probably the one who's going to have to spell out the details of earlier experiences."

"Jesus," he sighed as a sick feeling rolled through his stomach.

"We'll cross that bridge later. Right now, how about tomorrow?"

"I'll be okay as long as it's not possible to hear the hammering of my heart."

Bruce smiled. "As far as I know, that has never happened."


The next morning as Cain took his place at the defendant's table, he could barely swallow. He knew that the punishment had already far exceeded his crime, and the case had not even gone to the jury yet. And now he had to sit by and calmly watch Carrie Willet bury him with a lie that would almost surely sentence him to prison. And there was nothing he could do.

With a pound of the gavel, the judge set Cain's worst nightmare in motion. The prosecution called Carrie Willet to the stand. There was a rumbling in the seats behind him and a shuffling to turn to the door where Carrie was about to enter, but Cain kept his eyes riveted on the front of the courtroom. His foot began tapping almost uncontrollably as Bruce reached over and discreetly put a calming hand on top of his knee.

"Sorry," whispered Cain as he swallowed hard and tried to remain calm.

He continued staring ahead as he heard the doors close behind him and soon caught a glimpse of Carrie as she entered his field of vision and stepped up to the witness stand. There was no way he could delay it

71

any longer. He shifted his eyes to watch as she made a mockery of the whole judicial system and swore to tell the truth and nothing but the truth—so help her God. So help **her** God? What about him? There was no one to help him, and he had never felt so forsaken in his whole life.

As she took her seat, her eyes momentarily connected with his, almost by accident. She quickly looked away and stared down at her hands crossed in her lap. She looked nervous and upset, but Cain took no solace in that because what kind of a rape victim would she be if she sat there oozing confidence and poise? Before she even opened her mouth to utter her first lie, the jury had taken pity on her and her situation. They must be thinking him such a beast to put her through this horrible ordeal. His heart beat wildly and he felt like he was about to vomit as he willed himself to appear calm and look directly at her. She didn't return his look, but then what rape victim would sit and boldly stare down her attacker? So far her roles as villain **and** victim perfectly coincided to her distinct advantage. Once again he templed his fingers over his lips and concentrated with all his might on not screaming. Her voice quivered as she answered questions that one-by-one pounded nails into each of his hands and feet. As she approached the details of the actual "attack," she began to falter and lose her composure. It was very effective. The judge took mercy on her and called for a recess until after lunch. Cain sat leaden in his seat. He couldn't move. He wanted to cry, but that would never do. He watched numbly as the prosecutors and Carrie's father raced to her side—the damsel in distress. He could see the tears were genuine; it wasn't an act. She was so caught up in her lie that there was no other way out. It was of little comfort to him that she was totally distraught over what she had to do, but at least he knew he wasn't being sacrificed without a second thought. She sobbed as she leaned on her father and walked passed him. She didn't look at him; but her father did, and the look made his blood run cold. Cain rubbed his hands over his face wearily and sighed.

"I'm screwed," he said bluntly to Bruce.

"That was quite a performance," agreed Bruce, "but we're not through yet."

"Neither is she," said Cain. "There won't be a dry eye in the place by the time she finishes this afternoon. Jesus Christ himself could come in and testify for me after that, and it wouldn't do any good."

"So, what, you're giving up? You're going to jail without a fight?"

"I don't know what I want anymore."

"Let's get out of here for a while. Maybe some fresh air will help."

When Carrie resumed her testimony, he could no longer maintain his impartial air. He felt his throat tighten as she began to describe how he held her down. He did manage not to squirm uncomfortably in his chair, but he clamped his hands together in a nervous, gnawing knot. He clenched his jaw in order to hold back a desperate, woeful moan. He knew his mother and the rest of his family were sitting behind him listening to the horrible lie, and he wanted to die for causing them such humiliation. Reluctant but undeniable tears welled in his eyes. He managed to blink them back as he fought valiantly against her scathing accusation.

*How could you?!* screamed his eyes, but she never looked over to witness his anguish.

She was in enough pain of her own, and looking at him would have been unbearable for her. She knew exactly what she was doing to him, but that didn't mean she liked it. And once again the jury and many of the onlookers misread her guilt and desperation as the pain and agony of a spirit broken by a maniacal madman. Here he was the one they should all be pitying; he was the real victim, but everyone was watching the fragile shadow of the girl he used to know. They all wanted to comfort her and spare her this ordeal. He was the monster who abused her and then put her through a trial. He felt the animosity in the courtroom, a heavy mist that was settling on him and dampening what was left of his spirit. Just as he had reached a saturation point, the judge called it a day. Carrie still had not finished, but he felt she needed some time to compose herself and it was nearing the dinner hour.

"Are you all right?" asked Bruce as Cain stood numbly at his side.

"I can't believe I'm sitting here taking this. It's all like some kind of a joke. I can't believe the judicial system. I thought it was meant to protect the innocent, but everything's turned around and upside down. I'm the one being raped—right here in front of everyone, and they don't even realize it. They're too busy feeling sorry for Carrie. How can she do this? How does she look at herself in the mirror every day?"

"Well," said Bruce, "if it makes you feel any better, I can tell she's not enjoying it."

"That makes me feel much better. Thanks. I'll keep thinking about that when I'm in prison."

"Come on. Let's get you out of here."

"I feel like I'm at the tail end of a terminal disease. I only have a few more days of freedom left, don't I?"

"You're judge and jury now?"

"Don't I?" he repeated ignoring Bruce's attempt to derail his pessimism.

"We don't know that. Let's just take it one day at a time."

"Let's get the hell out of here."

He slept fitfully that night. He couldn't get the sight of Carrie out of his mind. She had taken him by surprise. He had expected her to be more composed, more in control. Instead she appeared very, very fragile. She looked thin and drawn with dark circles under her eyes. She looked way too much the part of the victim she was portraying. Her lie was working to her advantage, and that bothered him. He didn't know how he could ever defend himself against such a pathetic looking reminder of why they were all there. It was well past midnight before his mind would let him drift into an uneasy sleep.

He awoke the next morning feeling unrested and cranky. It was all he could do to drag himself from his bed. Going to court was getting more difficult with each passing day. Then as he and Bruce drove to court together, Bruce dropped a bombshell on him.

"I'm subpoenaing Joanne to testify in your defense," he announced.

"No!" Protested Cain. "No! No way."

"Yes. We need her. She's the only one who can testify to your behavior when it came to sex. She said no to you and you backed off. You never forced her to do anything she didn't want to do; you never were rough or ungentlemanly. That's a pretty strong factor in your favor."

"She's been through enough because of me. You can't put her on the stand. What about cross-examination? They're going to try and discredit her. They'll tear her to shreds."

"There's nothing to discredit, right?"

"Right, but you know how they are. They'll try to twist everything that she says. Please, Bruce, don't do this. There has to be another way."

"Well, there's not. She'll do fine. We need her. End of conversation. We're up against a brick wall here. You have to do something to fight back. Otherwise, you may as well just plead guilty and get it over with."

"I can't do that."

"Then at least give yourself a fighting chance. Joanne will get over it. She has nothing to hide; nothing to lose—unlike yourself."

The day had started off bad and only got worse. Carrie got into the most damaging part of her testimony, and there was hardly a dry eye in the courtroom. Cain's heart pounded and he was about to explode with outrage, but he maintained a calm facade as he listened to the fabricated events of that horrible night. He was there, yet he didn't recognize more than half of what she was saying. He was numb by the time she finally finished. She mercifully didn't make him out to be a sleazy degenerate, but she had to portray him as "crazed" and "out of character" because of the cuts on her breasts. She wished she had not done that to herself, but in the heat of her hysteria, she reacted with little or no thought. It left physical scars and caused her to have to accuse Cain of more than just rape—a circumstance that dramatically complicated the trouble he was in.

74

She never once looked at him in all the hours she spent on the stand. Even when asked to identify him as her assailant, she looked in his direction but never caught his eye. He wanted to make eye contact with her. He wanted to beg her with his eyes; he wanted to beseech her to end the agony he was in. But she never gave him the chance, and now she was being whisked away. He'd probably never see her again. If by some miracle his heart held up through the stress and trauma he was experiencing, he was now certain he'd be spending many years of his remaining youth behind bars. The jury was buying it, he was sure. And though she sought to make excuses for his behavior and to play down as much as she could, she ended up making more points for herself than for him. She had found it in her heart to forgive him and try to understand his depravity—what a wonderful, generous human being. He didn't deserve such an overwhelming act of human kindness.

He sighed deeply as people began leaving the courtroom for the day. Joanne, nobody, was going to be able to help him now. Carrie had dug a pit way too deep for him to climb out of.

"Uncle," he moaned as he eased himself back into his chair.

"What?" asked Bruce. "You want to change your plea?"

"The horse we're beating is way beyond dead. It's only making us look more foolish and sadistic than ever. Everybody's thinking I raped her and now I'm dragging her through the muck of this trial."

"So . . .?"

"So, I'm not sure I can go on any more. Every day seems more and more futile. I fucked the wrong girl; I may as well face it."

"I know what you're saying," said Bruce, "but come on. We've come this far. There's still a chance. Now that Carrie has testified, the DA is not likely to offer much in the line of a plea bargain; so why not play it out and take your chances? Don't underestimate yourself. You'll be a formidable witness. You're not some greasy stud dressed up in a coat and tie. You're intelligent, you come from a well-to-do, upstanding family, and you have a lot of charisma. Some people on that jury have to have noticed. There are seeds of doubt out there. We just have to believe that they'll take root somewhere where they'll do us some good. A few more days. If it turns out as you're imagining, you haven't lost anything. I know it doesn't look good, but let's stick with the game plan unless the DA comes to us with a plea for a lesser sentence. Then we'll have to talk and seriously consider your options. Okay?"

"Fine," sighed Cain. "I guess there's nothing to lose in waiting it out."

The prosecution closed its case the next day, and that at last left the proceedings to the defense. At least from here on out, most of the testimony in court would be favorable and easier for Cain to tolerate. He sat and listened as people got up and attested to his character and morality—none of which mattered at all. It was all a formality. What he was in the past was unimportant. What mattered most was what he was at that moment with Carrie, and she had already testified to his crazed and uncharacteristic behavior. Since his behavior had already been labeled as uncharacteristic, it didn't matter what his character was like to that point.

Joanne made a very convincing witness, although once again she was describing a time before the incident in question. Like Carrie, she never looked him in the eye. It was easy to see she was uncomfortable with her role, and she was still quite upset with him. When she finished, she left the stand and the courtroom, and he never had the chance to approach her and initiate conversation—not even to thank her for the gesture. It was clear to him that she wanted nothing to do with him. He hoped it wasn't quite so obvious to the jury.

Then finally, it was his turn. He listened to Bruce's coaching and buried his desperation. He had to appear confident without casting a disparaging light on Carrie whom the jury had already taken to heart. He told the truth: he didn't know why she would lie except that she was obsessively determined that her father not find out that she was no longer a virgin. In fact, it was well before he met her that she had fallen from that state. She had managed to hide the fact that she was sexually active and on the pill to that point. If she admitted the truth when the Brownings came home, her father would find out and she couldn't allow that. He didn't rape her, he said in conclusion. He could never do that to anyone. He didn't have to rape her; she made herself very available to him.

Bruce rested the case for the defense, and the prosecution was about to take over when the judge called a recess until the next day. Cain took a deep breath and hesitated a minute before getting up and joining his family.

"Don't say anything," he said as he approached them. "I don't want to hear about it. I don't want to talk about it. I just want to go home. Now."

He went home and changed into jeans and a tee shirt and then announced that he wasn't interested in dinner. Ignoring protests and offers of companionship, he left the house alone and began walking aimlessly. He needed to get out in the fresh air and shake off the stifling effects of the courthouse. Untold numbers of emotions and anxieties were doing battle for his attention, and he was trying hard to ignore them all. Instead, he focused on the beautiful summer evening that was emerging in the shadows of the sweltering day. A front had passed through, and the air had become drier and cooler as it breezed gently through the trees. He'd been so preoccupied with the trial that he'd had little time to take advantage of the glorious summer that was all too quickly nearing an end.

As he walked, he came upon a park where he had played with Molly and his brothers as they were growing up. It had been quite a few years since they had abandoned it for more adolescent ventures, but the memories were fresh and readily called to mind. He smiled nostalgically as he watched the current bevy of youngsters running and playing without a care as proud parents looked on. He sat on a bench out of the mainstream and watched from a distance. Although numb and weary, he was able to clear his mind and just watch with a passing interest.

He didn't know how long he had been sitting there when he became aware of the fact that he was no longer alone. Sitting up straighter in the bench, he turned slightly to his right to see Alexis standing near. She and Matt were pretty much broken up at this point. Theirs was not a solid relationship from the beginning, so it only made sense that they'd call it quits before they each went away to different colleges. Neither seemed especially distraught over the split.

"Hi," she smiled. "Would I be intruding if I sat for a while? Whether you admit it or not, you look like you could use some company."

Exhibiting the manners and breeding he had testified to earlier that day, he stood.

"Thanks," he grinned as they both sat down. "You're right. I was on the verge of drifting into a melancholy that would be hard to shake off. Where did you come from?"

"I was just passing nearby and thought I saw you."

"How'd you know I wasn't Matt?" His smile nearly melted her.

"I didn't. It was a lucky guess. Matt and I are friends, so it wasn't much of a risk on my part. How are you?"

"Oh," he sighed, "I've been better. Thanks for coming to the trial everyday. I truly appreciate the support."

"My pleasure. I wish there was more I could do."

"You're here. I thought I wanted to be alone, but I'm really glad you came over." He hesitated a minute. "How's Joanne?"

"She's fine, Cain. Don't worry about her."

"I didn't want her to have to testify, but Bruce said there was no other way."

"Well, she survived. You haven't talked to her at all?"

"Nope. I'm poison."

"Well, I think she's being a little ridiculous. I could see her being mad, and even freaking out at first; but come on."

Cain sighed and stared straight ahead at the dusky pinks and purples in the sky as he changed the subject.

"This could be the last free night of my life for a long time to come. I can't quite get that thought out of my head."

"What do you mean?"

"Well, the prosecution will probably finish up with their cross examination tomorrow, and then it goes to the jury."

"And they could come back with a not guilty verdict."

"You've been there. It's pretty open and shut. It's her word and the mountain of evidence against my word. Admit it, there must have been a fleeting second or two that you must have wondered if I hadn't actually done it."

"No, not even for a second."

"Well, you know me—those people on the jury don't. When the verdict comes in, it will be guilty, and they will probably take me away right then and there. So since this could be my last night of freedom, I don't want to sit here and talk about it. Are you about ready to leave for school?"

"Pretty much. I still have a few more things to get."

"I had to withdraw from Northwestern," he said barely managing to keep his voice even.

"I heard," she said hardly above a whisper.

"I had to give up a full scholarship to play baseball. That hurt."

"Well, Northwestern's been around for a long time. It'll still be there when this mess is all straightened out."

"That could be fifteen or twenty years from now."

"Cain . . ."

"You're right," he said, "I'm talking about it again. It's just that this fiasco of Carrie's has consumed my whole life. There is nothing more left to my life but what pertains to the trial. So no matter how hard I try not to talk about it or think about it, I always come back to it. It's all there is."

"How could one person cause so much devastation?"

Cain sighed and rubbed his face wearily.

"You know," continued Alexis with only the slightest levity, "you could just leave. Go somewhere far away and get lost."

"I'm way ahead of you," he answered. "I thought of that, and Matt and Scott had it all planned out, but my life would still be ruined. I'd never be able to come home again. They'd be watching my family and friends, checking phone calls. I'd have to completely cut all ties forever."

"You could go to Ireland and stay with you grandparents. They don't have jurisdiction there."

"They have ways. Besides I had to turn over my passport when I was indicted. Any more ideas?"

"No," she sighed sincerely. "I'm sorry. I wish I did."

"Then," he said slouching back on the bench and staring straight ahead into the sunset, "will you write to me while I'm in prison?"

Alexis choked up and couldn't answer right away. She took a minute to collect herself.

"Of course. You know I will."

"Thank you."

"It's the least I can do."

"No, I mean thank you for letting me face the reality of all of this without trying to fill me with false hope. I need that. Everyone else keeps throwing these empty hopes at me, as if hoping hard enough will make it come true. I have to be ready for the worst, because in my heart I know the worst is what's coming. My mother is going to be a basket case when she has to face the fact that she just can't wish and pray something into existence. That's what worries me. How is she going to handle this? There's not much happily-ever-after in real life. I know that. I'm psyching myself up for a shot right between the eyes. I know what I did was wrong, Alexis. I know I hurt Joanne so much. And I know I let my parents down, but it's just such a damn high price to have to pay for being a stupid jerk. That was my crime—I was stupid and I was a jerk. You shouldn't have to go to prison for that. But I don't see any way around it. Tomorrow at this time, I could . . ." He stopped midsentence and took a deep breath. "I think I need to walk. Do you mind?"

"Do you want to be alone?"

"Not especially. I mean, I thought I did, but now I'd rather be with you. Is this awkward for you—because of Matt and all?"

"No, I told you he and I are friends. That's all. We realized our relationship had run its course, and we're both going away to college. I have to admit, it's strange sitting here looking at you and telling myself that you're a totally different person. Same face, same mannerisms, different guy. It's very weird." She reached out for his hand. "Come on, we'll walk."

They strolled without any specific destination for some time. In fact, they did very little talking. Cain seemed to withdraw inside himself, and Alexis respected his privacy.

"My mom's probably got the Marines out looking for me," he finally said with a fond smile.

"Your mom's a mother right from the word go. And I mean that as a compliment. She's crazy about all you guys. Being an only child, I've always envied you guys."

"Oh, it gets pretty heavy at our house some times. It's not all what it seems. Jim and I still have trouble being in the same room together. And my grandpa doesn't even talk to me any more."

"That's got to hurt."

"It makes for some pretty tense family meals. Speaking of meals, I didn't eat tonight. I wasn't hungry before, but now I could go for a burger and some cheese fries. Do you have time, or do I have to eat alone?"

"No, I have time. Do you just want to go across the street?"

"They have the best cheese fries in town, and that's my specialty. I promise I won't even be maudlin and refer to it as my last meal."

"Good," she said, "I'd hate to have to slap you around."

He smiled, and she glimpsed the aura that was Cain. It was funny—he looked just like Matt, but she knew she'd never confuse them again.

It was getting dark as he walked her home. It was no use trying to stave off the inevitable. His morning court date was rushing toward them as the last moments of dusk waned. The next daylight to dawn would not be a welcomed sight. He pushed the thought from his mind as they stopped in front of her house.

"Want me to get the car and drive you home?" she asked.

"Nope. Thanks anyway, but it's not that far to walk. Somehow I keep thinking that if I don't go home, morning will never come. It's like the clock will start ticking again when I walk in the house. Pretty scary, huhn?"

"No, I kind of know what you mean. I'm glad I ran into you tonight. It's been fun."

"Yes, it has. Thank you. I appreciate the diversion."

"I wish I could do more. I'll be in court tomorrow."

Cain smiled uneasily. That's when she could resist him no longer. Putting her hands on his cheeks, she tiptoed up and kissed him on the lips. He felt a stirring inside him that had long been dormant. He wanted to take her in his arms and kiss her back until all other thoughts were driven from his mind, but foreboding loomed too large on his horizon and this was just too strange a set of circumstances he found himself in.

"I'm sorry," she apologized meekly.

"Don't be. It was nice—one of the nicest things anyone's done for me in a long time. I actually felt human again."

"Then I'm not sorry. And by the way, in case it crossed your mind, I was kissing you not Matt. Good night, I'll see you in the morning."

He watched her hurry up to her front door, and he wished he had the rest of his life to explore the possibilities that this evening presented. But he was already beginning to feel swallowed up by the night, and the demons that tormented him were draining all light-heartedness from his soul. It was time to go home and somehow prepare himself for the hell that the morrow could bring.

"Where've you been?" asked Matt as Cain walked in the door.

"Just out. I needed air . . . or something." He measured his next words. "Um, Matt, I ran into Alexis tonight. In fact, I spent most of the evening with her."

"Oh."

"That's all—oh?"

"What else should I say?"

"I don't know. Are you mad?"

"No. I've told you—that's over. We were never like you and Joanne. We had fun together, but neither of us had any illusions of it being a lifetime commitment. If you want to spend time with her, that's between you and her. What'd you do, or shouldn't I ask?"

"Just hung out. She talked, I listened; I talked, she listened; neither one of us talked, we just walked—and held hands. I almost felt human again."

"Then I'm glad. But Mom's a little frantic."

"I figured that, but I was suffocating. And I couldn't bear the idea of sitting down at the table with Grandpa. I wasn't in the mood for his bullshit. I've been meaning to ask you—did you see the boxes in our room that I packed up?"

"Yeah, what the hell is that?"

"My life. I've put some stuff away downstairs that'll keep. The things that are still upstairs are yours or whoever wants them—I'd rather it not be Jim, but at this point I don't really care. My clothes will fit you the best, so . . ."

"Wait, wait, wait," interrupted Matt. "What is this?"

"Don't make this harder than it is. We both know my days are numbered. I'm not going to need CD's, baseball equipment, or clothes."

"Cain . . ."

"Shut up, okay? Just shut up and say you'll take care of it for me."

"Okay. Fine. If I have to, but you'll probably just have to put it all back again."

"Stop it," said Cain sternly. "Make believe doesn't help."

"Okay," relented Matt. "I'll do it. You don't have to worry about it."

"Thanks," said Cain emphatically. Then he walked away to find his mother and reassure her that he was still among the living.

About 2:00 in the morning he sat down in the family room composing a letter to Joanne. He ached for missing her. He hadn't seen her since she testified, and it had been forever since he had spoken with her without Carrie Willet looming between them stifling the easy-going innocence they had once enjoyed together. He had finally admitted to himself that there was no future for him that included Joanne, but he felt a desperate need for some sort of closure.

> *Dear Joanne,*
>     *This is not a good night for me. Frankly, I'm scared. I know that tomorrow will not go well for me. I'm being realistic because I cannot afford to lull myself into a false security. The fall would be too catastrophic, and I may not survive it. But none of that is any of your*

*problem. I know you're thinking I'm only getting what I deserve, and perhaps you're right.*

*I'm writing because I'm hurting so desperately inside, Jo. You haven't really given me much of a chance to tell you how sorry I am, and I need to do that before I go away. I don't know if I'll ever see you again, and that's killing me. But what's worse is knowing how much you hate me. I'm sorry for all the lies and deceit. If only there was some way I could make you believe me. Maybe it will come in time. I'll be gone for a long time, so I won't be bothering you any more. I'll always think about you, though. I don't think I can ever love anyone else. I want you to know that you're the most wonderful thing that ever happened to me, and I'll never get over what I did to you.*

*I'm rambling. I'm sorry. My nerves are shot. I can't sleep, but I'm tired and unfocused. I never meant to hurt you. What went on had nothing to do with you. It was me being selfish and impatient and thinking I had the uncontrollable under control. I guess my arrogance alone justifies the mess I find myself in. You need to know that if I had it all to do again, it would be you that I would think of. I will never forget the look on your face.*

*I don't think I'm making sense. I don't think I'm saying this right. Why am I going on with this? I just can't finish. I can't say good bye for the last time. I can't bear the thought that I'll never see you again—that you'll never be the love of my life like I had always planned. I wish I were dead.*

Before signing it, he picked up the paper and crumpled it in his hand.

"It's kind of late, isn't it?" asked a voice from the door of the family room.

Startled, Cain looked up.

"Dad."

"Shouldn't you be in bed?"

"I can't sleep."

"What are you writing?"

"Nothing. Just doodling." He tossed the abandoned letter into a nearby wastebasket. "How come you're up?"

"I have a headache, and I got up to take aspirin. I saw the light on down here."

"Do you think tomorrow's going to be it, Dad?"

"I don't know. I suppose it could be, but I really think it'll go into the next day."

"You think they're going to find me guilty, don't you?"

"Cain, I don't know what to think. I know it looks bad, but I'm trying to keep a positive attitude. You should, too."

"I can't afford that. I can't afford to fool myself. You know that, don't you? I wish there was something I could believe in, but it's no use. I just wish it was over. I feel like I'm at the end of a painful terminal illness. I just wish it would get over. I'll deal with what I have to, but I can't stand this limbo much longer. Everyday is just delaying the inevitable. I'm not enjoying life anymore, so I may as well just get on with my screwed up future. More than anything else right now, I wish I could have some time with Joanne where she'd just listen to me. That's still so unresolved, but I hear she's seeing someone—so I guess she's moving on." He looked at his father and smiled. "I'm rambling. That seems to be one of the best things I do lately."

"You're tired."

"I am. Maybe I'll just lie on the couch and watch TV for a while. I'll sleep down here. I feel like a little kid, but I don't want to go up to bed in the dark. When the lights go out, the monsters all come haunting. They torment me, and I can't sleep. I just lie there in a cold sweat, praying for morning. I've never been so scared in my whole life. I feel like I'm being buried alive."

"How about if I sit down here with you for a while? My head is pounding, and I can't sleep anyway. We'll watch TV. That ought to put us both to sleep."

Cain smiled in spite of himself.

"Thanks, Dad. I'm trying my best to be a man about all this, but I'd appreciate the company—at least for a little while."

"Don't worry," assured Will, "I don't know if I could be as big a man about all of this as you're being."

Will sat down in his chair, and Cain stretched out on the couch. About a half-hour later, Nora came down. Will quickly motioned for her to be quiet as Cain was finally asleep. She looked over the couch at him.

"Shouldn't we wake him to go up to bed?" she whispered.

"No, he doesn't want to go up there. And I'm going to stay down here with him. Just be sure to wake us in time in the morning."

"Okay," she said softly as she unfolded a nearby quilt and gently laid it over her angelic-looking son. Tears sprang to her eyes. "We're going to lose him, aren't we, Will? They're going to take him from us."

"We don't know that for sure. Let's just wait and see how things go before we get all worked up over it. You go back to bed. I think I can finally relax and sleep; I just don't want to leave Cain alone."

"Okay," relented Nora. "Do you want a blanket?"

"Yeah, something light."

She went to the closet and brought back a light blanket and draped it over Will.

"Thanks," he smiled as she bent over and kissed him.

Morning got there before any of them was ready for it. Each day it got harder and harder to get up and go to the courthouse. This day was especially hard as the uncertain end drew near. There was no way to put it off, however, and nothing to do but face it. Cain was especially quiet. He was nervous about returning to the stand. The prosecution was going to be cross-examining him, and he knew it was going to be brutal. After all, they were convinced he was guilty, and they wanted to be sure to put him away for a long time. It would also put a fine feather in their cap where Sam Willet was concerned. Cain was keenly aware that Sam Willet was a man to be reckoned with. Watching Sam's behind-the-scenes maneuvering of the trial, Cain got some insight into why Carrie was so terrified of him. Still, Carrie was not facing a long prison term, and Cain could never forgive her for sacrificing him in the name of remaining Daddy's little sweetheart.

The proceedings turned out to be everything Cain had feared and more. He remained in control and stuck to his story, but the DA had a way of twisting the facts and adding nuances of meaning that made him sick inside. It was interesting to him to note that Carrie had not shown up in court except to testify. He wondered if the jury had noted it, too—and what they thought of it. He wanted her to at least be there and agonize over her guilt. But she was nowhere to be seen. Her overbearing father and the rest of her relatives were there, however. They didn't miss a minute, so she was well represented

Of little note to the jury, but just as disheartening to Cain, was Joanne's absence. She, too, had shown up only to testify, and that was it. He wished he could get her out of his heart. He had a lot of heavy-duty things to contend with and to take up his time, but she remained in the wings of his soul always reminding him of what he had lost. Somehow he knew this whole ordeal would be a lot easier to face if she were behind him offering her support.

When his testimony was over, the judge called a recess for lunch. Closing arguments were scheduled for after lunch, and then it was all up to the jury.

The thought of food sent Cain's stomach into a tailspin, and the hour and a half break was sheer agony. But the long afternoon finally got underway. Cain felt as though he were a rag doll of sorts that the two sides were doing a tug-of-war over. As he listened to the speeches, he could feel himself splitting in two, and he had to struggle to keep from spilling his insides all over. Nobody could know the soul-wrenching agony he was experiencing. He had to remain calm and that took phenomenal effort.

Then finally, mercifully it ended. Both sides rested, both sides made final arguments, both sides were ready to sit and wait for the jury to decide. Since it was near dinnertime, the judge instructed the jury to be back by 9:00 the following morning for their instructions from him.

Then they would be sent off to deliberate until they came up with a verdict.

Cain slumped, numb and withdrawn, back into his chair after the judge exited the courtroom. He put his hands over his face and tried to rub some life back into his countenance. Everyone else stood up and started toward the exits.

"How 'bout it?" said Bruce putting his hand supportively on his young client's back. "Let's go home."

"I can't move. I'm totally drained. I wish I was dead."

Scott snaked his way through the crowd until he reached Cain.

"Come on," he said taking his best friend by the arm and lifting him off the chair. "You and I are out of here. You can go, right?" He looked over at Bruce, who nodded approvingly.

"Go where?" Cain asked.

"To the beach," answered Scott. "If I ever saw anyone who was suffering from beach withdrawal, it's you. Come on. First, we'll slip passed the Gestapo, and then we'll put the bum's rush on the press. Matthew, change jackets with your brother."

Matt smiled and shook his head as he took his sport coat off.

"What the hell?" asked Cain still confused.

"They'll think you're Matt. Come on, this twin thing has to have some advantages. He can hang back a little and leave with the rest of your family. By the time they figure out they got the wrong guy, we'll be on our way. Come on, quick give me your jacket; they're working their way through the crowd. Lucky you guys wore two totally different jackets."

"They probably don't even know what jacket I had on."

"Don't kid yourself," said Scott helping him on with Matt's coat. "It's their job to know."

Wasting no time, they breezed passed the barrage of photographers and reporters who were now closing in on Matt and the rest of the family. Once outside they laughed and ran toward Scott's car as if they didn't have a care in the world.

"That was great," laughed Scott as they both collapsed against the front seat of his car.

"I wish I could run away from this whole mess as easily," said Cain.

"Canada awaits," tempted Scott.

"Don't even start. That's not an option."

"Okay. I promised you I wouldn't bring it up again, so forget I did," said Scott as they pulled out of the parking lot. "But we can at least try and forget about it all for a little while. I'll take you home to change. I have a change of clothes in the back of the car, and I told my mom I wouldn't be home till late; so let's get on with it Peter Pan!"

They parked the car near their favorite beach and got out and walked. The sun was beginning to set, but they still had plenty of daylight left. The first thing they did was sit down and take off their shoes. They both were wearing shorts, so there was no need to roll up pant legs.

"I feel like I don't have a care in the world when I come here," said Cain picking up some small stones and throwing them far out into Lake Michigan. "The rest of the world seems so far away."

"I know. That's why I knew we needed to come here tonight. You know, when this is all over—whether it's tomorrow, the next day, or . . . ten years from now, you and I are going to come back here and celebrate."

"It's going to be at least ten years from now, you know that, don't you?"

"Well, then we'll be old enough to bring champagne."

Cain smiled.

"God, I'd never get through this without you," he said as they began walking down the shore. "My family's great, but sometimes I feel so guilty over what I'm putting them through that it hurts too much to be around them. With you I can just be my idiotic self. Shit, I'm scared."

Scott reached down and scooped up a handful of water, threw it at Cain and commenced running down the beach with Cain at his heels. They ran until they were both ready to drop. Being young and in top shape, they soon recovered. They went to Scott's car for his volleyball and began a competitive game of one-on-one at a nearby net. A group of girls came up and after flirting a little with them, asked if they could join them.

"Sorry," said Scott hardly able to believe his own words, "not this time. This is a private game. Anyway, we're gay."

Cain laughed out loud at his friend's audacity. The girls smiled, too, as they knowingly walked on.

"Well," said Scott defending his statement, "we are. I haven't been this . . . gay . . . in a long time."

It soon became too dark to see the ball, so they stopped and sat on a bench for a while watching the waves roll carelessly up on the beach.

"Do you think those girls believed you—that we're gay?" Cain asked with a smile.

"Na. One look at me was a dead give-away. My eyes were popping out of my head, and I was drooling all over myself."

"It could've been because of me."

"Yeah, in your dreams. What do you want to do now?"

"Die."

"Come on, Farrell, work with me here. You're losing the moment."

"I'm sorry. I want to go down and wade in he water again for a little while. I don't know when I'll ever get back."

"Cain," scolded Scott.

"Humor me, huhn? If I'm wrong, I'll let you say you told me so—but I'm not wrong."

"Come on, we'll wade in the water all right. I'd drown your ass as well if you didn't have to ride home soaking wet in my car ruining my upholstery!"

On the way home they suddenly realized they hadn't eaten any dinner and decided to stop near home for something to eat.

"Thanks for tonight," said Cain as he picked at his food. "If I was gay, you'd certainly be the one I'd pick for my life partner." He smiled.

"Thanks," nodded Scott, "me, too, but let's keep this under our hats. I'm not sure my parents would understand at all."

Once again Cain smiled his warm, big-hearted smile.

"You know," said Scott, "you're the only person I know—including Matt—who actually would never need to talk. Your face says everything for you. You actually say more by not speaking. That's why you're such a bad poker player."

"I'm not that bad a poker player."

"Well, I guess not, but . . . oh, shit."

"What?" asked Cain turning to follow Scott's gaze and locking in on Joanne as she walked into the restaurant. "Crap."

"Who's that with her?"

"Her new boyfriend, I guess. I heard she's been seeing somebody. He's a senior."

"Whoop-dee-do. Of all the people to run into, why did it have to be her?"

"It's all right," sighed Cain. "Actually I've been wanting to talk to her, but I can never get passed her parents. Maybe this will be my chance."

"Are you crazy?! Screw her, Cain. She's a bitch. Sure she was hurt, but Christ, she bailed on you when you needed her most. That's not love. Love finds a way through the bad times. You're better off without her."

"I don't want to fight with you over this—especially not tonight. You don't understand. Nobody understands. I can't get her out of my system. I can't forgive myself for what I did to her; how can I expect her to forgive me? I just need to talk to her and see if there's hope that maybe someday she'll want to see me again. I'm grasping at straws, but that's all I have right now."

"Has she seen us?"

"I don't think so, but she just got up to go to the bathroom. I'll be right back."

"Cain . . ."

But it was useless. He was already out of his seat and on the way back to the small alcove where the bathrooms were. He stood in the small hallway and waited for her. When she came out, she was taken by surprise.

"Cain," she said stiffly. Then she became flustered. "I . . . I didn't see you."

"I wasn't sure whether you had or not. You've been doing a pretty good job of treating me like a nonentity."

"I . . ."

"Is that your new boyfriend?" He interrupted.

"Yes . . . that's Jason."

"I wanted to thank you for testifying at the trial."

"No problem. Is it over?"

"No. If it was, I wouldn't be standing here. I'm going to prison, Jo—maybe as soon as tomorrow."

"I don't know what to say," she shrugged. "But I've got to go. Jason'll be wondering where I am."

He put his hand out on the wall so his extended arm blocked her exit.

"I still love you, Joanne. I always will. If there was anything I could say or do to make up for how I hurt you, I would."

She stared down at his arm blocking her way. "I have to go, Cain. Good luck with the trial."

He took the hint and moved his arm, and she left. He couldn't move, though. He stood in numb silence as he pulled himself together. Scott noticed his mood as soon as he got back to the table.

"That didn't go well," he observed.

"No. Boy, I really set myself up for that one."

"Let's go," said Scott handing Cain his car keys. "Go out and wait in my car, and I'll go pay the bill."

"I'll go with you."

**"Go out and wait in my car,"** repeated Scott. "Go out that side door and you won't even have to walk passed her."

Cain took the keys and left.

Scott got up to pay the bill but made a side trip over to Joanne's table.

"You're a bitch, you know that?" He said to her.

"Hey," protested Jason as he stood up.

"Sit down," continued Scott. "This has nothing to do with you." He turned back to Joanne. "I do have to thank you though for being a bitch, because he's **way** better off without you. Once you showed your true colors, I never wanted to see the two of you together again. You can't be trusted to hang in for the long run."

"Me?!" she said indignantly. "What about him? Or are you forgetting what this mess he's in is all about?"

"I'm not forgetting anything. He's human after all. Everyone thinks of him as some kind of a god or a superman, but he's not. He screwed up. He admitted that—to you and to the whole world. But that's okay, Joanne. You keep it up, and don't ever go near him again. Leave him alone, and I know he'll get over you. Hell, he can have any girl in the world—he doesn't need your shit."

Not waiting for her reaction, nor that of Jason, Scott turned and went to pay the bill. When he got to the car, Cain was waiting in the passenger's seat.

"What took so long?"

"What?" asked Scott still distracted. "Oh, I don't know. A lot of people decided to leave at the same time, and I had to wait." He started the car and headed toward home. "I'm sorry we had to run into her."

"That's okay. It actually gave me the chance to say some things I've been wanting to say to her."

"Well, at least now you know to stop holding out hope."

"No, I still have hope. She just needs more time."

"Hey, genius, does she have to cut your heart out of your chest and hand it to you before you get the picture? She's a bitch who only cares about herself. Forget her."

"I told you I don't want to fight with you, so let's drop it. You have your opinion, and I have mine."

The rest of the way home they hardly said a word to each other. Soon Scott pulled up in front of the Farrells house.

"Thanks for tonight," said Cain sincerely. "It's just what I needed."

"Me, too. And, Cain, I'm sorry about Joanne. I promise I won't say any more about her. I'll see you in the morning."

"Yeah, I can't wait."

That night Cain slept on the couch again. He was restless and not only did he know he wouldn't be able to get comfortable in bed, but he didn't want to face the prospect of sleeping in his bed for what could be the last time. Once again he was bone-tired and mentally drained, but he couldn't sleep. He turned away offers by his family members to stay up with him. He had the TV; that was the most company he wanted to deal with at that time.

It wasn't long before sunrise when he finally fell asleep. As the rest of the family awoke one-by-one and went downstairs, he was caught up in a sleep that was fraught with nightmares and demons that offered him anything but rest. The pillows flung on the floor and the quilt wound around his body gave witness to the type of night he had spent.

Bruce and Scott arrived within minutes of each other. The mood in the house was extremely somber. Cain was still asleep in the family room.

"I guess we should wake Cain," sighed Nora. "We wanted to let him sleep as long as possible. I don't think he had a very good night."

"I'll get him," said Scott as the others poked at toast and coffee.

The minute Scott called to him and touched his shoulder, he jumped and sat up with a start.

"Holy shit, Cain!" reacted Scott as his heart pounded in his chest. "I've never seen you move so fast. I came in here to shag your skinny ass out of bed, and you nearly gave me heart failure."

"What time is it?" asked Cain as he rubbed his face.

"7:00. We have to leave in about an hour."

"I'm going up to take a shower," Cain said throwing the blanket aside. "Tell my mom if I even look at food, I'm going to throw up, so count me out for breakfast."

When he came back down about a half an hour later, he was groomed and as handsome as ever. His shirt matched the blue of his eyes and made them especially brilliant. His tie was draped around his neck, and he carried his sport coat.

"Good morning," greeted Bruce. "Man, I wish all of my clients went into court looking like you."

"Well, don't let it fool you," said Cain without a smile. "I only slept about two hours, and I feel worse than shit. I can hear my heart pounding in my ears—that can't be a good thing."

"Did you take a pill?" asked Nora.

"No, I didn't, Mom," he answered testily. "That's all I need. Those things make me feel like I'm on another planet. I need to be aware of what's going on. Besides there's something about the raw pain that keeps reminding me that I am alive, and I am awake, and this is not someone's idea of a sick joke."

He turned sharply and left the kitchen. Will angrily got up and started after him, but Nora caught his arm and held him back.

"He shouldn't talk to you like that," said Will.

"He rarely ever does," said Nora. "I think we need to give him a little leeway this morning. I'm fine."

"Let me go talk to him," said Scott getting up from the table.

When he found Cain, he was in the living room in front of a mirror trying in vain to tie his tie.

"You didn't really need to bite your mom's head off," said Scott from behind.

Cain looked up into the mirror and caught his friend's eye.

"Go to hell."

"Ow," said Scott. "Now me. You must have had a bad night."

"I had a night from hell! And you know what really stinks? The day promises only to get worse! I'm so tired I can't think straight, my head is pounding, and I can't get this fucking tie tied right. My hands are shaking so bad I can hardly hold on to it."

"Do you want help?"

"No. I'll do it. I can do this. I've sat there for over a week now listening to lies and watching my reputation get dragged through the gutter. I can see it through to a conclusion. I'm sorry I'm crabby. I don't mean to take it out on you or my mom, but I've got to keep an edge. I can't afford to breakdown now. If she even comes near me, I'm going to fall apart. I'm going to beg her to take me somewhere far away and keep me safe like she used to do when I was a little boy and I still believed she and my dad could fix anything. She understands."

"So do I," said Scott. "I guess we all just feel every bit as helpless as we actually are. We're just groping for some way to do any little thing to help."

"Just be here," said Cain. "That helps. And if my knees buckle, catch me."

"You got it."

Soon Will came in and announced it was time to go. Cain looked at Scott and raised his eyebrows helplessly. Scott helped him with his jacket and they started toward the door.

"Wait," said Cain going back to where the Irish setter was sleeping peacefully. He lifted his head and wagged his tail as Cain approached him and crouched down on one knee.

"You take care," he said stroking the dog's glistening coat. "You're the best dog in the whole world." The dog playfully licked his face as he reached over and hugged the beautiful animal's neck. Then he got up and continued on his way to meet his fate.

As they gathered in the courtroom waiting for things to begin, Cain tried to keep his mind occupied. Bruce told him how important it was for the jury to see him and have a last knockout impression of him to take into the jury room with them. At least he didn't have to say anything. He just had to stand around and look confident but not cocky; hopeful but not desperate; and as innocent as a slightly wayward angel. He kept busy by chatting idly with family members and friends. It all seemed almost bearable until he caught sight of the one thing that would be the most damaging to his case—the helpless victim. He heard the increased activity and excitement of the press. When he looked up, he caught sight of Carrie being shepherded in by her father and the rest of her family. She hadn't been in court this whole time, and Bruce was hopeful the jury had seen the last of her. But there she was taking her place in the front row right behind the prosecution table. At least she didn't look his way, and he didn't have to deal with direct contact even if it was just visual.

"My last prayer—up in smoke," he sighed. "I guess now we know whose side God is on."

"They had it planned," said Bruce. "We needed her to stay away for one more hour. It would have strengthened our case immensely. They knew that, and they weren't about to let it happen. It had nothing to do with God, so let Him off the hook."

The actual courtroom proceedings didn't take very long. The judge addressed the jury and spelled out exactly what they were supposed to do. He defined the case and the limits and reaches of the law. The jury listened carefully—sometimes looking at Cain, other times gazing over at Carrie. Then they left to begin their deliberation.

"Someone shoot me, will you?" sighed Cain after they were gone and the court was adjourned.

"Come on," said Bruce, "there's a room down the hall where we can wait. It's going to be a while."

The room was small, but comfortable. There was a TV and magazines as well a deck of cards, checkers, chess, and a few other board games. Cain divorced himself from the group and went to look out the window. The first thing he noticed were the bars that covered the window, and his blood ran cold as he looked through them to the street below. People were scurrying about tending to their daily lives totally oblivious to the fact that his life hung in the balance. Actually there was no balance about it. It teetered delicately ready to slide out of control with one word from twelve people he didn't even know.

Bruce left the others and walked over to him.

"I don't want to get gloomy, but I'd be remiss if I didn't remind you that if there's a guilty verdict, they'll take you into custody right then and there."

Cain drew in a deep breath and let it out.

"I know. That's all I've been able to think about. God, this is torture."

The waiting was unbearable. Knowing it could well be the last time he would be with Scott and his family for some time to come, he tried his best not to snap at them when they insisted he have something to eat for lunch. He also did his best to hide the pessimism that was eroding his soul. It was not an easy stunt to try and stay on an even keel since he also felt that it was necessary to steel himself against the guilty verdict that he knew was coming. Sometimes as much as he loved them, he had to separate himself from them and go off by himself. They all knew it and respected his privacy. He paced; he watched out the window; he sat with his head in his hands. The pressure and stress mounted with each passing hour even though Bruce told them the longer the jury was out, the better it was for them. A quick verdict was sure to go in Carrie's favor.

At 6:00 P.M., eight hours after they had gone into deliberation, the jury announced it had reached a verdict. The color drained from Cain's face, and he felt bolted to the spot where he was standing. Everything seemed out of sync and unreal. The bailiff explained that the Willets wanted to be present, so the verdict would not be read until they had been notified and had arrived back at the courtroom. Cain unrolled his shirtsleeves and buttoned them. Then he buttoned his collar and slid his tie back into place. He felt like his throat was closing up, and it was hard to swallow.

"You know this system is definitely torturous," he said as he looked in a small mirror on the wall and adjusted his tie. "Why don't they just come in and say, 'Farrell, your ass is guilty, now let's go'? Instead we have to sit here and wait for the Willets to come back. And then we have to all assemble back in that God-forsaken courtroom again and wait for the formalities to get underway. They've decided—don't I have a right to know what that is right away? Why all the bullshit—except to torture me? I'm going crazy; I can't stand much more of this."

"It'll be over soon," assured Bruce. "Hang in a little while longer."

He had no choice, so he paced nervously as he tapped his fingers on his legs. Then he stood by the window tapping on the sill. Scott walked over to him and gently put his own hand over Cain's to silence the nervous distraction. Cain turned to look at him.

"This doesn't help," explained Scott, "and frankly it's driving me crazy."

Cain exhaled a deep breath.

"I didn't even realize I was doing it. Sorry."

"It's okay. Try and relax. It'll all be over soon."

"Actually, that's not a whole lot of consolation—considering what *all over* implies. God, I feel sick."

There was little conversation over the next forty-five minutes while they waited for the Willets to return. Everyone was tense, and the uncertainty that pervaded the room was overpowering. Then finally came the awaited word—the Willets had just taken their places in the courtroom. Everything was ready.

Cain adjusted his tie once again as he took his seat at the defense table. He stared over at the empty jury box and tried to keep from fainting on the spot. Then suddenly a door opened and the jury began to file back to their places. He tried to read their faces, but there were too many ways to interpret what he saw. No way to know for sure. Then everyone stood for the judge.

As the next minutes elapsed with dialogue between the judge and the jury, Cain's knee bounced frantically under the table, a familiar sign that Cain was on the edge. Bruce was aware of it and discreetly reached down with a calming hand to steady it.

"Sorry," whispered Cain as he concentrated on sitting still.

Then he was told by the judge to stand. His heart banged in his chest, and he wasn't at all sure his legs would hold him, but he did as he was told. Bruce stood supportively next him. His family held their collective breath.

He wasn't sure how long it took the guilty verdict to register in his brain, but it echoed through his head at an alarming volume. In fact, it continued screaming in his brain and coupled with the surreal images that the courtroom had taken on, he was no longer aware of what was going on around him. Suddenly he became aware of a bailiff standing next to him.

"What?" he gasped as reality began taking shape.

"Empty your pockets on the table."

He took out his wallet, keys, and some change and put them on the table.

"Any jewelry?" asked the bailiff.

Cain pulled off his Irish Claddagh ring, and then reached up to his left ear and felt the small diamond stud earring he wore. As he took it off and put it on the table with his other things, he could hear his mother sobbing uncontrollably behind him. He turned to look at her.

"Can't I go to my mother?" he asked.

"You'll get to see her before they take you away," answered the bailiff. "Now your coat, tie, belt, and shoelaces."

"I'm not wearing shoelaces," he said absently as he glanced down at his loafers.

He put all the required clothing on the table in front of him.

"I'll take care of all of this," said Bruce as comfortingly as possible.

A second bailiff appeared with handcuffs as the first patted him down. As they turned him to clasp his hands behind him, he looked up and peered helplessly into Carrie's eyes. She was crying as her family was still in the process of congratulating each other and celebrating. They were jubilant and gushing to the press about the system and how it works—you just have to have faith. The other side of the courtroom still sat in stunned, unspeakable grief. Even though the odds were stacked against them from the beginning, there was always that outside chance, that ray of hope to cling to. In an instant that was taken from them, and now they had to try and cope with the dreadful reality that they wouldn't let themselves contemplate before.

When the cuffs were secure, the bailiffs took Cain's arms and began to lead him away.

"Bruce?!" He called out frantically.

"Go on. I'll be along in a minute."

He put Cain's belongings into the pocket of his sport coat, and then turned to the Farrells. Nora grabbed the coat from him and hugged it to her heart as tears spilled over her lashes.

"He's only eighteen, Bruce," she sobbed. "My God, he's only eighteen. That's my child."

He found Scott standing next to them in numb disbelief and took them all back to the room where they had waited for the verdict.

"He was right," said Scott as large tears streamed down his face. "I thought for sure the truth would win out and we'd all be saying, 'I told you so, you big dope!' Something's terribly wrong."

"Let me go down and talk to Cain for a bit," said Bruce. "Then you all can come down and see him."

The bailiffs took Cain to a holding cell, which was actually a small room with a toilet and a sink. They removed the handcuffs, and as soon as the door was closed and locked he bolted for the toilet and vomited until he thought everything inside him, including his internal organs, was going to come out. When Bruce came in, he found him still kneeling on the floor, hugging the toilet.

"Come on," the lawyer said as he took him by the shoulders and eased him back into a corner against the wall.

Bruce flushed the toilet and then wet a paper towel and cleaned his face off.

"She stole my life from me, Bruce," he said as the tears he had denied himself for so long began to burst forth.

"I know," said Bruce having a hard time fighting the lump in his throat. "We gave it our best shot."

"I am so fucking scared, I can't see straight!!!"

With that, he threw his head back against the wall and sobbed convulsively.

"Let it out," said Bruce. "You're entitled."

It was quite a while before he was spent and able to bring himself under control again. Bruce sat next to him and hugged him close. As his body slowly began to calm down, he heaved labored sighs of despair.

"I'm so tired," he cried. "I haven't slept for two nights. I knew this was coming, but you can never be completely prepared."

"I know," said Bruce, "but listen, as soon as I leave here I'm going to get my staff busy on appeals. We're not finished yet." He got up and wet a paper towel with cold water from the sink and handed it to Cain who immediately pressed it against his eyes.

"Thanks," he said. "My head is pounding. What's next? What are they going to do with me?"

"They'll drive you into the city to the county jail to await sentencing."

"Shit."

"You'll be held in protective custody there. I've already taken care of that before I came in here. Because of your age and all, they don't want to mix you with the population."

"Great. But sooner or later I'll have to mix with the population. What then?"

"Let's take one step at a time. We can make some requests as to what prison you'll be sent to. Let me work on it—I won't hang you out to dry. Did you hear the sentencing date?"

"I didn't hear a thing except my mother crying."

"Two weeks from today. We'll talk about that more later. I'll be down to see you—just hang on for me, huhn?"

"I'll try."

"That's good enough."

"What do you think I'll get? The plea bargain they offered was ten years. Christ, it has to be more than that."

"Let's don't get ahead of ourselves. I'm working on that, too. You need to trust me. Just do everything you're told. They'll be coming for you soon, but your family would like to come in first. Are you ready? Should I send for them?"

"Yeah, we may as well get this over with."

"You don't have to see them if you don't want."

"No. I want to. I just don't want to see the pain I've caused."

"I'll be right back."

Bruce went down to the room where the Farrells were waiting. Discreetly, he took Scott aside.

"Go down and see Cain before I send his family down there. I have to calm Nora down—I don't want him to see her like this. He's having enough trouble keeping it together. He's right down the hall. You'll see the guard outside the door. Give him whatever hope and good thoughts you can. He's having a hard time."

When the guard unlocked the door and Scott walked in, it took him a few seconds to find Cain since he was still sitting on the floor with his knees drawn up to his chest. Scott went over and sat down next to him.

"I'm sorry," he said. "I'd hoped against hope that it would turn out different. What can I do?"

"How's my mom?"

"It was a shock, but she'll be okay. How are you? You look a little ragged around the edges."

"That's an understatement. But I have to put up a good front for my mom. I'll take a few deep breaths and I'll be okay at least until she's gone. Did you talk to Matt?"

"Yeah, he's pretty shook up, but that's to be expected. You didn't think they'd all shrug it off and walk away, did you?"

"No. God, I've screwed up all their lives. How embarrassing must it be to have a convicted felon for a son and a brother? Scott, I'm too scared to try and think even a few minutes ahead. I mean I'm terrified. I don't have control over my life any more. And I'm going to be . . ."

He stopped mid-sentence.

"Listen," said Scott lining up directly in his gaze. "You have the best family in the world. They don't care about appearances or what other people think. And don't even mention Jim and your grandpa. They don't count—actually it serves them right if they are bugged by it.

And you're going to be fine. This is a major setback—I'm not trying to minimize it, but you're a survivor. You'll work it out and put it behind you one day. And I'll be there every step of the way with you. And when you finally come home, you and I are going to take off for the mountains for a super ski trip of a lifetime. I'll plan it all. I'll keep you up to date regularly so you have something to think about and look forward to. You understand? And no matter what you ever need or when, I'm here."

Cain reached over and hugged him close as hot tears burned down both their faces. No words were exchanged for some time—no words were needed. Scott was the first to make a move. He stood up and then reached a helping hand down to Cain. Cain grabbed it and pulled himself off the floor.

"Now," said Scott, "wash your face off and get ready for your parents. You don't want to freak out Nora."

"No, she's having a hard enough time because of me."

"She'll be fine. She's a tough lady. When they get here, I'm going to go."

"No," said Cain, "don't leave; not yet. Don't leave me alone here."

"I won't. I'll wait for your family. They'll want to spend some time with you, but I'll find out how to get in touch with you, and you'll be hearing from me. Don't worry."

"This is not real. This is not happening."

"She cried—Carrie—when they read the verdict, and her damn family was so busy congratulating themselves they never noticed or took the time to ask why. Any idiot could see those were not tears of joy. You got screwed royally, but she's in her own private hell. I don't know if that makes you feel any better or not, but she must have a conscience— no balls, though!"

A trace of a smile found its way to Cain's face. They heard the key in the door and knew that Bruce was back with Cain's family. They looked at each other for a long minute without a word.

"Thanks," said Cain. "Thanks for last night. I'm taking that with me."

"Good. Me, too. And when time gets hard, think about champagne on the beach and a foot of powder on the slopes."

"Keep talking like that and people will begin to think we're gay."

"Keep safe. I'll always be near."

They embraced. Then Scott gave him a light slap on the cheek with an open hand and winked before hurrying out the door.

Nora had handed Cain's coat to Molly and was making her way across the small room to her son. Without a word they grasped onto each other as if they could hold off the inevitable.

"She won. She always gets her way, Mom. We knew that, but I'm glad we at least tried. I'm going to be all right. I need you to believe that."

"I do," she said valiantly fighting a sobbing breakdown. "I do. You're a survivor. You deserve better. But Bruce said he's going to try and get you sent somewhere that won't be too bad, and you can even take college courses. We just have to believe."

She hadn't considered the fact that he had lost all ability to believe in anything, and he was determined to keep it that way. One by one he hugged members of his family. Tears were shed, and grief was thick in everybody's throat. This was a wake without a corpse.

He nearly panicked when they were told they must leave, but he managed to hold back. It would never do for him to expose the terror he was hiding. This ending had to pass on a hopeful note, even if they all had to put on the performance of a lifetime. Otherwise it would be so devastating that they may never be able to climb out of the depths of futility. Each was brave for the other, for that's what one does at a time when security and stability are threatened.

He died a little as he said good bye to each of his brothers and his sister, but it was Matt who nearly brought him to his knees. Besides the fact that they were so close, it was as if he were watching himself walk out of the cell and back out to freedom. He pledged his tearful undying love to his mother and begged her once again to forgive him, but it was his father he grabbed onto the most desperately. His father, his hero from his not-so-long-passed youth. But with the embrace they both understood that this was something that not even a hero could conquer. Will had to finally loosen the bond and bring the inevitable to fruition. It was time.

As soon as they left, a guard showed up at the door with a full set of chains.

"Jesus Christ!" said Cain as he backed away shaking his head. "No. No. There's no way. I can't do this, Bruce."

Bruce asked the guard to give them a minute. He walked over to Cain and took his face in his hands. Large tears already began rolling down the younger man's face.

"Look, you don't have a choice," Bruce said looking him straight in the eye. "You'll just make it harder on yourself. Go along with it now—as soon as I leave here, I'm going to my office to start work on an appeal. I already have my staff on it." He reached into his pocket and pulled out a small prescription bottle. "I had your dad bring these today just in case we needed them. Take one."

"No. I hate them. They make me feel like I'm even more in the middle of a nightmare than I am."

"They'll take the edge off."

"No. I just want to go home."

"You're not helping yourself, Cain. They're not going to be patient much longer."

"Okay. Just give me a minute. Tell me what happens now."

"One minute," said Bruce going over to the sink and getting a paper cup filled with water. "Take this pill. You're trembling all over. You're in the midst of your worst nightmare right now—this can't make it any worse."

Cain opted for the shelter of the drug and swallowed the pill. His hands were shaking uncontrollably, and he could barely talk. He hugged himself tightly as Bruce went on.

"I'll stay with you as long as I can, but that's just until you leave here. They'll drive you downtown in a squad car, and there's no negotiating the hardware. These next weeks are not going to be easy, but you will get through them. Once you get downtown, they're going to want to take their own set of pictures, prints, and all that. Then they'll give you clothes and box this stuff up to send home."

"Okay." Tears streamed down his face, but he was becoming more accepting of his fate. "Then what?"

"Then they'll put you in a cell somewhere where you'll be kept apart from the general population like I told you before. You'll wait there for the sentencing in two weeks."

"My grandpa wasn't here today. He wouldn't come to the trial at all, but I thought that maybe he'd come today. He told me I'm an embarrassment to him."

"Don't worry about him. He's the big loser."

"I'm a convicted felon. There's no more presuming. How am I ever going to get my life back together?"

"Let's take it one day at a time, huhn? You have a shitload of people who care about you. They're not embarrassed; they just love the hell out of you. Bank on that for now. Lean on those of us who care about you, and you'll see—in time you'll stand on your own again. For now allow yourself to grieve and hurt, but do everything you're told and keep your nose clean and you'll be fine. You'll see. Okay?"

Cain drew in a full capacity of air and gradually let it out. Bruce could see the drug was already having a calming affect.

"Okay. I'm just plain tired."

"Then how about we get this over with? It's been a long day. The sooner you get it over with, the sooner you can go to bed. I'm sending your prescriptions along. Ask for something if you have trouble sleeping or you feel you're coming unglued. Lean for a little while."

"Fine. Tell them I'm ready."

He closed his eyes as the guard dressed him in the heavy restraints. Right then and there he made a promise to himself that he would never give them his soul. They had his body, but his soul would always be free and always belong to only him. Somehow that proclamation of independence gave him a moral boost and allowed him to withstand the indignities of the system that had failed him.

Bruce didn't miss the transition. He saw a new resolve in Cain's eyes, a flash of the spirit which was uniquely his, and he made a mental note to call Will and Nora and let them know that this is indeed a remarkable young man they have raised.

During the long ride to the county jail, Cain put his head back on the seat of the police car and closed his eyes. Within minutes he was adrift in a dreamless, purging sleep. The Valium had done its job.

Upon arriving at the jail, however, he had a hard time waking up and shaking off the effects of the drug. He felt as though he was having an out-of-body experience as he was put through the paces of the indoctrination into the institution. It was a most unpleasant experience, so he was thankful for the semi-oblivion that the drug offered.

After having survived the process of being booked into the county jail, he dropped onto the less than desirable bed of the cell that they put him in. Wrapping the blanket around himself, he turned toward the wall and let go of the man he had become and cried himself to sleep like the boy he wished he still was. Mercifully sleep was only a nod away, so he was spared a long and exhausting cry.

In the morning he woke with a terrifying jolt as the booming horn signaling the start of a new day sounded throughout the jail. Cain sat up in bed trying to shake off the grogginess of drug-induced sleep and determine exactly where he was and how he got there. It took only a matter of seconds for the blissful hangover of sleep to wear off and despair to set in. He sat on the edge of his bed with his elbows propped on his knees and his forehead dropped into his palms. That's when he realized that he hadn't removed any clothing to sleep—not even his shoes.

# CHAPTER 6

The next days passed at an excruciatingly slow rate for Cain. Endless weeks and years filled with nothingness stretched out before him, and he was extremely depressed. There was little to keep his mind occupied, so he tended to dwell on the future. Bruce visited him almost daily, but he would not allow his family or friends to come to the jail. It was a long way from home and not in the best of neighborhoods, and he didn't want them traveling down there. Besides, his mood was not receptive to any attempts to comfort or encourage him. He saw the whole thing as an effort in futility for both him and his visitors. The only reason he saw Bruce was for the practical reasons of keeping abreast of his case.

At one meeting with his attorney on an afternoon less than a week before the sentencing hearing, he could tell Bruce was coming in with news that was less than good.

"When are you going to let your parents come down and see you?"

"Is that what this is all about?"

"What?"

"The look on your face. I can tell something's wrong. I have nothing to do but sit around and think about how much I don't have any more. I've become an expert on determining the quality of your news before you even give it to me."

"Did you get the books I brought you?"

"I read them—I'm a fast reader, and like I said . . . there's nothing else to do."

"I'll get more."

"Bruce. What's wrong?"

"Well, actually it's nothing that I'm the least surprised at, but I'd hoped we could have avoided it."

"Bruce, please."

"It's Sam Willet. He's not satisfied with a guilty verdict. He's fighting my efforts to get you sent to a medium security prison. He wants you to do hard time—as hard as possible. And he's pushing for a maximum sentence. He has a lot of influence and the sympathy of the court. He's calling in a lot of favors."

"Shit," sighed Cain dropping his head and running his hands through his hair."

"I'm not giving up yet, but I thought it only fair to warn you. I don't want you getting your hopes up because it doesn't look good."

Cain slouched back in his chair and picked absently at his thumbnail.

"He ought to worry less about me and more about getting to know his daughter," he said lifting his gaze to meet Bruce's. "Will they testify at the hearing?"

"Yeah," answered Bruce reluctantly.

"Then I guess I'd better get ready for the long haul."

"The judge is going to be looking for remorse from you. I don't want to tell you what to do, but it could help counteract some of Willet's bitterness. Judges are likely to be more lenient with defendants who are contrite."

"How can I do that, Bruce?! How can I admit guilt and throw myself on the mercy of the court?"

"I don't know. It's just my job to let you know your options. You need to make the final decision."

"I already have. I'll never admit that I raped her, let alone apologize for it. I'm innocent. They made a mistake."

"They don't want to hear that."

"I don't care."

"Well, think about it anyway. We have some time. We'll talk more later. I also have something else on my mind."

"And that would be—?"

"You parents. They need to see you. They're going through hell right now, and they need to see you. They've tried to be patient and give you some time, but they're hurting. They don't understand why you won't see them."

"I just . . ."

"Let's forget about you for a minute," interrupted Bruce. "Let's think about the real victims of this whole thing. You at least have some degree of guilt in getting yourself into all of this. After all, Carrie didn't just happen to pick you out of a crowd and say *he's the one*. But what about your parents? They had no say. In fact, they did everything they could in raising you to help you to avoid such pitfalls. You made choices contrary to what you knew they would approve. Your mom is more devastated by your refusal to see her than she is by the guilty verdict."

Cain buried his face in his hands and kneaded his aching forehead with his fingertips.

"Tell her I'm sorry," he said from behind his hands as tears sprang to his eyes and dropped into his open palms. "I'm so sorry. I want to see them, too, but it'll just make them feel worse. This is a terrible place. And I can't touch them. I can't really be with them."

"They know all that, and they're entitled to make their own decisions. You owe them that much."

Cain wiped the tears away with his open hands.

"Fine," he said as his emotions dammed in his throat and nearly choked him. He leaned back in his chair and tears ran freely down his face. "Tell them to come. I'll try to be upbeat. I can do that for them. You're right, I should have thought of that. I should have thought about them instead of myself. I'm sorry."

His hands were trembling and his knee was bouncing nervously as tears continued to stream down his face.

"Relax," said Bruce calmly. "Do you get out of that cell much?"

"Um, yeah, a little. For about an hour each day. There's this small yard—if that's what you want to call it. They bring meals to the cell, and then every whatever day I get out for a shower. But I'm always alone."

"That's because they want to keep you separated from the hard core."

"Yeah, Bruce, and what about next week when I get sent to who knows what God-forsaken hole? What then?"

"Wherever they send you we can request they keep you in protective custody."

"For fifteen or twenty years?!! No thanks. I'll take my chances with the savages. I'm not totally white bread, and I'm sure I'll learn a lot about taking care of myself."

"It's not going to be fifteen or twenty years. Not lock-up time. You won't even be gone ten."

"Is that taking the Willet Factor into account? The man seems to be in control."

"Yeah. No matter how much power he seems to have, he can't negotiate an unfair sentence. You do still have some rights."

"That's refreshing."

Bruce smiled. "I brought you something. I had to leave it up front, but they'll bring it back to you."

"What is it?"

"A box from home. There are a lot of odds and ends in it. I gave your family a list of things you're able to receive, and they filled it up. I'm not sure what all is there."

Cain sighed a deep breath, digesting this newest revelation. He was incredibly homesick, but he wasn't sure if this would help or make it worse.

"Thanks," he said in a voice that was barely audible.

"Just be prepared—as we speak, they're probably going through it. It all has to be searched before you get it. They'll probably even open the letters."

"Great. I checked my dignity and my right to privacy at the booking desk. I don't know if I'll ever get used to it, but I have come to expect it."

"Are you sleeping at night?"

"No, not really. I'm not used to being so inactive and confined. I don't get tired enough to sleep a whole night. And sometimes I fall asleep out of sheer boredom during the day. Then I'm definitely screwed at night. There's a track around that stupid yard, and I run laps around that until I can't stand any longer. But that only helps a little. The lights go out at 10:00, and I lay there for hours trying to sleep. I don't think

I've ever slept more than three hours at a time. And please don't tell me that I'll get used to it because that's a terrifying thought."

Again Bruce smiled at him.

"So it's okay if your parents come to visit you? I'm sure you can expect them tomorrow."

"Yes."

"What about Matt, Scott, and the others?"

"Why not? I don't like people seeing me like this, but it's going to get worse before it gets better."

When he went back to his cell, the box Bruce was talking about was there. It had been opened and its contents examined and tossed back in. Cain shook off the feeling of having been violated and sat on the bed to explore his prize. He crossed his legs Indian-style and pulled out a bag full of his favorite candy bars, some puzzle books, and a hand-held computer game and batteries. It was the contents of the bottom of the box that brought tears to his eyes. First, there was a white gift box filled with his mother's homemade chocolate chip cookies.

"Way to go, Mom," he said out loud as he sniffed back tears.

Then he reached in and pulled out the quilt from their family room that had been his security blanket the last nights before he left. He held it to his nose and drew in a long breath. Home. He could smell it. *I want to go home.* He hugged it close to him and let the tears come. Finally, he reached a trembling hand into the box for the last of its possessions. A packet of letters that miraculously had remained undefiled by the sensors. Somebody had a heart.

He couldn't read them, though, because by this time his vision was totally washed out with tears and despair was creeping in. Clutching the quilt, he eased himself down on his bed. He put the letters under his pillow for safe keeping, and then burying his face he sobbed muffled, hopeless tears until he fell asleep from pure exhaustion.

The next day his parents did indeed show up. When they unlocked his cell and told him that he had visitors—plural—he knew that this was the moment he had been dreading. He had to pull this off. He knew that seeing them was only going to make him feel more homesick and desperate about his plight. Then guilt took over and reminded him that he had to think about them, too. He knew he had to climb out of this major depression he was in, but he had no idea how to do it. He also knew his mother would see right through the act he was preparing for them. He was being pulled in numerous emotional directions, and none of them was particularly appealing.

As he spotted them through the heavy wire screen that separated them, he almost broke down; but he sucked in a huge dose of courage and sat down at the table opposite them. Unable to speak for a second or two, he extended his hand toward his mother—palm side flat against the screen. She placed hers on top of it.

"Please don't cry," he pleaded.

"I won't," she said though her eyes glistened.

"I'm sorry, Mom," he said. "I'm sorry I've been so selfish. Actually, I've been wallowing in a sea of self-pity. It's about time I grow up. I apologize to both of you. It won't happen again."

They talked small talk, mostly catching him up on things at home since he left. It was hard to avoid the topic of Matt getting ready to leave for the University of Illinois, less than a week after the sentencing.

"He's coming with Scott tomorrow," said Will. "Thanks for seeing him—he's having a hard time over all of this. It'll help him to see you."

Cain made a sarcastic laugh.

"I don't know how," he said, "but if it helps that's all I care. Did Bruce tell you about the sentence hearing?"

"Yes," said Nora. "It's not fair. This is all so unfair. And the frustrating thing is there's nothing we can do about it."

"Bruce said I could be remorseful, and that might help. But I don't think I can do that."

"You'd have to admit guilt," said Will.

"Yeah. Right now I'm between a rock and a hard place. As far as the law is concerned I'm guilty, and I'm just being stubborn if I don't show remorse. I've already dragged the poor girl through an ugly trial; the least I could do is apologize and say what a bad boy I've been. But I'm not bad, and I'm afraid I'd choke on the words. This system operates under the assumption that juries are flawless and never make mistakes. I guess they have to believe that or their consciences would never let them sleep at night. I don't know what to do. Is it cutting off my nose to spite my face if I don't play the game and try to talk myself out of a shorter prison term?" He rubbed his face wearily. "I haven't been able to think of anything else since I talked to Bruce yesterday. I wondered what you thought."

"This sounds like a cop out, Cain," said Will, "but that's something we can't really tell you. That's something you have to decide for yourself. I can tell you this—we're behind you no matter what you decide."

"I know," he sighed. "Right now I'm standing firm. Maybe I'll cave when the time comes, I don't know. Let's change the subject. Thanks for all the stuff yesterday. The cookies were the best, and thanks for the quilt. It's funny how seemingly insignificant things can become so important. That's my prized possession right now and for probably some time to come. Bruce said I'll probably leave here in a bus, but he'll collect my things and bring them on for me. So can I take it with me?"

"Of course," smiled Nora.

The night before the sentencing hearing Cain couldn't eat or sleep. He wished he could run off to the beach with Scott and forget all about it for a while, but that wasn't possible so all he could do was think and worry. He was glad the trial and the past two weeks were behind him. Now if he could only get through the next few days, all the uncertainties would be cleared up and he could begin to deal with cold, hard reality.

When he got to the courthouse in the morning, they allowed him to change into a coat and tie that his family had brought for him. After two weeks of lying around in the ill-fitting jail jumpsuit, it felt good to have "real" clothes on again. He reminded himself not to get too used to the feeling, however. At least now he could face the Willets and the media with a little of his dignity in tact.

When he entered the courtroom and took his seat at the defendant's table, his family was not allowed to go anywhere near him. There was no satisfying the urge for physical contact. The isolation he felt was harder to endure than anything else. He felt like he had an infectious disease.

After days of agonizing over whether or not to make a statement and what to say, he opted for letting Bruce speak for him—but not apologize for something he didn't do. He couldn't sell himself out, even if it meant less jail time. Bruce said his client was sorry for all the trouble both families and the court had been through because of his adolescent behavior and poor choices, but he maintains his innocence of the charges that he was convicted of. That was it in a nutshell.

The judge took a few minutes to mull the facts over; and then in a manner which suggested he wasn't buying Cain's innocence, he delivered his twelve-year sentence. Cain was stunned; he had expected much more. He could have gotten as much as thirty years, and he would have if Sam Willet had had his way. The mumbling of discontent from the Willet side of the courtroom suggested more than disappointment. Then the judge dropped the other shoe. The sentence was to be carried out at Maddox Correction Institution. Though not the most brutal prison in the state, it was one of the most severe maximum-security institutions and it was over two hours from Cain's home. That was their worst case scenario. Cain could feel the hands of Sam Willet tighten around his neck as the judge's gavel pounded and he left the bench.

"What the hell?" sighed Cain. "I'm confused. I was expecting at least 15."

"I don't think he's in accordance with the jury. He's trying to serve his conscience and Sam Willet," explained Bruce. "That's the only explanation."

Twelve years. Cain was numb. The sentence was like a swarm of locusts on the field of his youth. To an eighteen-year-old, twelve years was a lifetime. It was two-thirds of the life he had already spent. Forever. So even though he had expected more, this was no gift. This was the final kick in the teeth. He turned to his family as the law came to take him away. There were no hysterics this time, just quiet tears of unspeakable grief. He managed to wink at his mom before the bailiff turned him and led him away.

In his cell that night he lay back on his bed and stared up at the ceiling. Nothing particular went through his head; he just stared up at the bleakness that was the rest of his life. His dinner sat untouched. After the hearing Bruce had tried to convince him that he'd never serve the full twelve-year sentence. He wasn't hearing any of it though. It was as if now it all really had sunk in. The finality of it weighed on him until he could hardly bear it. He didn't even move when the lights went out, and he had no idea of what time it was when he finally fell asleep.

He never got to officially say good-bye to his family and Scott. At 4:30 the next morning without any warning, they woke him and told him he'd be joining the other inmates who were going to Maddox on the bus that was leaving in half an hour. They usually did transfers unannounced to avoid any chances of a planned jailbreak from the bus. His stomach took a dive. He was told to get dressed and then put everything he wasn't wearing into a box that Bruce would forward to him. Just as he was packing the last things in the box, they delivered breakfast to the cell.

He carefully folded the quilt and clutched it close to him. His security blanket. He was going to have to go through this on his own— cold turkey. As if it were made of china, he placed it in the box. He looked at the breakfast and took it to the small table in the cell. After a few less than enthusiastic bites, he put the fork down—unable to eat any more.

Sitting on the edge of the bed, he looked down to notice his knee bouncing out of control, a habit that was becoming most annoying. He took a deep breath and tried to calm down. This was scary. This was way too scary.

It was nearly 5:30 when they chained him hands, waist, and feet and put him on the bus with the rest of the county prisoners who were on their way to Maddox. He was the last one to get on, and all eyes landed on him as he boarded. A cacophony of catcalls and whistles erupted, and the guard screamed for quiet. A terrified chill ran through his body, but he betrayed no emotion as he took his seat. He already knew he must become a master of the poker face if he was to survive at all. He thought of Scott telling him that his face always betrayed his thoughts. He laid his head miserably back against the seat and watched out the window as the bus began its trek to Maddox. Suddenly he felt the guy sitting behind him breathing in his hair.

"Give us a kiss," the convict whispered huskily.

Cain's pulse quickened, but he said nothing. For all the guy knew, he was deaf.

"Hey, pretty boy," persisted the con, "I'm talking to you."

He could hardly hear his own voice for the pounding in his ears, but he remained unruffled.

"Get fucked," he said without moving his gaze from the window.

"Oooohooo," laughed the other prisoner as he sat back.

"Shut up!" admonished the guard on duty. "No talking."

Cain was thankful for the edict, and focused all his attention on the outside. This would be his last view of it for a long, long time. He drank in the free world as it rushed passed him with alarming disregard for his need to savor it. Then quite without meaning to, he fell asleep. He had not been sleeping well in jail, and the swaying of the bus was irresistible. He cursed himself when he woke up and realized that they were approaching the prison. He wanted to rub his eyes, but he couldn't move his hands from his waist. They'd been on the bus for over two hours, and his arms were stiff. He strained his neck to get a glimpse of the mammoth gray fortress that was to be his home for the next decade or more.

"Home, sweet, home," someone chimed from the back of the bus.

Cain's stomach took another turn, and he had to literally concentrate on not throwing up. He also made sure not to start bouncing his knees for that would rattle the chains and give him away for sure. As they got closer, he could see the massive double cyclone fences with rolls of razor barbed wire along the top. He fidgeted slightly in his seat at the thought of being confined to that one square mile of earth for the next twelve years. He watched with great anxiety as they pulled up to a back gate and were ritually admitted.

Booking-in was humiliating and degrading, but he was at least thankful to be able to turn in the ugly, orange, county jumpsuit for the gray sweats of the Admissions Unit of Maddox. It wasn't easy, but he did his best to ignore the large black letters D.O.C.—Department of Corrections—stenciled on the front and back of the sweatshirt and down the front and back of the left leg of the pants. They fit well and were comfortable, so that's all he cared at that time.

After more mug shots, fingerprinting, and some initial instructions, they were locked into four-man cells. On each bed was a collection of toiletries and other bare necessities of day-to-day living. Having established sleeping arrangements, Cain put his things away in his locker and proceeded to sit on the bed, trying to let these new surroundings take on some sort of realistic slant. He leaned against the cement wall with his knees drawn up to his chest. He was on a top bunk, which he was glad of because he was at eye level with the tiny, barred window. His cellmates were talking, but he mentally drifted outside the window and thought about how far away from home he was. Matt and Scott were supposed to visit him that afternoon. It was the last day home for both of them. They'd be leaving for college the next morning. He never got to say good-bye, and that bothered him. Now he couldn't have visitors, except Bruce, until he was transferred out of Admissions, which could be anywhere from two to four weeks depending on number of variables. For at least the tenth time that day, he looked down and stared longingly at the white mark his ring had left on his tanned finger. As incredible loneliness overwhelmed him, he became aware of how quiet the cell had suddenly become. He shifted his gaze back inside and was taken aback by the three pair of eyes trained on him.

"Well?' someone asked him.

"Well, what?" he asked.

"What are you in for?"

Cain looked back out the window and thought for a few seconds. Bruce had warned him not to talk openly about being there because of a rape conviction, nor should he bemoan his innocence to the inmates. He boldly met the inquisitive gazes of his cellmates.

"For being incredibly stupid."

"How old are you, anyway?"

He already had noticed that he was by far the youngest of anyone who had been booked in with him. These men he was celled with ranged from their middle twenties to nearly forty.

"Eighteen," he said without apology and happy that his six-foot height at least gave him some authority.

"Shit," sighed one of the other guys as he lay back on his bed, "who did you piss off?"

That night Cain slept on his stomach with his pillow propped under his head so he could see out the window. There wasn't much to see, but he could get a glimpse of a few stars. He thought about Sam Willet. Whom had he pissed off, indeed. *Whatever you do, don't mess with Sam Willet's little girl.* His eyes burned as tears forced their way passed them. It was all right to cry now. No one could see. Just do it quietly.

The next afternoon Bruce came to visit. Cain was happy to see him. He desperately needed some contact with home. The visiting arrangements were much better at Maddox than they had been at the county jail. There was no more annoying screen to distort and separate. A large table spanned the width of the room completely separating and cutting off the inmates from the free side. There was a 12-inch-high divider that ran the width of the table and discouraged any physical contact. That was one of the rules: no reaching across the table, no touching of any sort.

"Thank you for coming," said Cain as he sat down across from Bruce. "I wasn't sure anyone even knew I was gone."

"They contacted me yesterday after you were admitted here. How's it going?"

"Okay, I guess. I'm with three guys for the time being. At least I have someone to talk to—when I feel like talking. I've spent so much time alone the past few weeks, I'm kind of out of practice."

"I brought your things from County. I left them with a guard. They have to go through it all, and then they'll bring it to you."

"Thanks," he said as he absently rubbed the white ring of skin on his finger. "I could use my glasses. Since I only use them for reading, I left them behind. But all morning I've been filling out forms and reading and signing their crap, and I'm developing a massive headache. I thought applying for scholarships and getting into college was a major hassle, but that's nothing compared to the paperwork of incarceration. And there's something really unnerving about signing your name to a piece of paper which in effect says you no longer have any rights. How's my family? Did Matt get off to school?"

"I guess. I talked with them yesterday after I got word you'd been transferred. They were planning on leaving early today."

Cain rubbed his face, doing his best to deny the tears that were threatening.

"He's nervous," he said with a distracted smile. "His roommate sounds a little on the weird side. I've always been his roommate—and Jim, but he don't count."

"He'll be fine. It's always a little scary to leave home and start something new."

Their eyes met, and Bruce became painfully aware of the foolishness of his statement. No words needed to be spoken; Cain's eyes said it all.

"How do you like these clothes?" Cain asked trying to add a little levity to the moment. "Everything has fucking D.O.C. printed on it—just in case you forget where you are. And I have my choice of either this short-sleeve tee shirt because it gets kind of hot in here—they're not much on air conditioning or fresh air—or there's a nifty sweatshirt. I can't believe my life once revolved around brand names and designers. Would you tell my mom that I love her—my dad, too? I don't think I said it enough times. This place kind of makes you prioritize your life and realize what's important. I know I can't call, but can they write to me?"

"Yeah. And I'll give them your message, but I'm sure they already know it. You're a wonderful family. And don't worry, the time will go by before you know it until they can come to visit."

"This is a long way to drive for a visit. I think they send you far away on purpose—it cuts any ties. It makes it easier for them to control you."

"Maybe you're right."

"I know I'm right," said Cain in all seriousness. "I can feel it. Even after just a day, I can feel it."

The next day after lunch during a break from the orientation process, Cain chose to go back to his cell rather than go outside. He was feeling exceptionally homesick, and he hadn't slept well the night before. He was glad everyone had opted to go outside because he craved the quiet and he needed to be alone. He went from total isolation at the county jail to never being alone here. He sat on his bed with his legs crossed Indian-style and stared aimlessly out the window. He was too distracted to read, and he didn't want to sleep. He had already learned that taking a nap in jail meant many sleepless hours during the night after the lights go out at a ridiculously early hour. Suddenly he was aware of someone coming down the hall. He looked up to see a Catholic priest standing outside his cell.

"Hi," said the man. "I've been looking for you. They told me outside that you had stayed in. Anything wrong?"

"No," answered Cain less than warmly.

"Good. I'm glad to hear that. Would you mind if I came in? I won't stay long."

Cain shrugged his shoulders acknowledging that he had little control over who came or went. The priest looked down the hall and waved to the guard on duty. Seconds later the door automatically slid open. The priest entered and the door slid shut and locked again.

"I don't know that you were planning on it, but please don't get up. Stay right where you are. This is not a formal visit. I just wanted to introduce myself, so I guess I should do that. I'm Fr. Mike Curtin, but please call me Mike. I'm the chaplain here."

Cain regarded him suspiciously, not at all sure he was happy for the intrusion. It wasn't like him to be rude, but he was in too much pain to care. He turned his attention back outside the window.

"And you're . . . pissed," observed the priest. "I guess I picked a bad time. You should have said so when I first came up. I can take rejection. I'm used to it. I'll leave you alone. We can talk another time."

"No," said Cain looking back to his visitor. "I'm not pissed; I'm rude. I'm sorry. It's really not like me, but this place is not like me. Please stay. I can't even offer you a chair, though."

"That's okay. I can sit right here on the edge of this bed."

"Did you say you were looking for me?"

"Actually, yes. I have to admit I've been following your case on the news and in the papers."

"It was on the news here?" asked Cain incredulously.

"This is a small town. Not much goes on. We have to look to the bigger cities for our news. So anyway, when I heard you were coming here, I wanted to be sure to come and see you. You're very young and far from home."

"And not guilty," said Cain deciding this was someone he could vent with. "Or do you believe the fair maiden?"

"No, I really didn't make a judgment. I wasn't privy to the facts in the courtroom."

"That doesn't matter. The jury was there, and they still came back with the wrong verdict; but then I guess you hear that all the time, so why am I wasting my breath? But just for the record—I don't rape girls, and I definitely didn't rape Carrie Willet. The thought never even entered my mind."

"Okay," smiled the priest. "Enough said. I want to be your friend. And looking at you and knowing what I do about your background, I find it hard to believe her story. Truth be known, I was pulling for you the whole time."

Cain's eyes filled with tears as he leaned his head against the wall and bit back an outburst. He couldn't speak.

"I'm here," said Fr. Mike. "I'll help you through this. I know it isn't easy."

"I've got to stop doing this," said Cain softly as he wiped tears away with the back of his hands.

"Everyone cries here—even some of the biggest and toughest."

"Yeah, well, I'd better start getting tougher, or I'll get eaten alive. Shit, I just want to go home." As soon as he said it, he thought better of his choice of words. "I'm sorry."

"Why?" said Mike with a smile. "Because you want to go home?"

Cain smiled back at him.

"Thanks," he said.

"You're welcome," said the priest. "And you know what—one day you will go home. I guarantee it. And until then, I'll be around. I live on the grounds. You let me know if there's anything I can do, okay? Just let any of the guards know you want to see me. They know how to get me, and I'm kind of privileged like a lawyer when it comes to visiting rights and all that."

"Thanks. When you first came in, I thought I was going to get the Bible thrown at me or something. Repent, sinner."

"Oh my Gosh," laughed the priest. "No wonder you were so unreceptive. No. I'm guessing you're a little out of touch with God these days, and I don't want to push anything. That'll all come in time. But just for the heck of it, did you ever go to Church regularly?"

"I went to Catholic grade school. I used to be an altar boy till I went to high school."

"An altar boy. How did I guess? It must be that angelic aura of yours."

Cain laughed in spite of himself.

"I don't think angelic is quite the word," he said absently rubbing his empty ring finger.

The priest looked at the very white tan line.

"They took your ring," he said, knowing that such things were not allowed.

Cain looked at his finger and smiled sadly.

"Yeah," he said. "I can't quite get used to not having it. I have grandparents in Ireland, and they gave it to me for my Confirmation in eighth grade. I don't think I've taken it off since." He rubbed his forehead. "I have such a headache."

"You still have some free time left. How about we go out for a walk? It's a nice day, and it's kind of stuffy in here."

"I can't leave once I lock-in."

"I have some pull. Let's see what I can do."

In less than a minute, Cain was putting his shoes on to go out.

"Ow," he moaned as he jumped down off his bed. "I got a shot in the ass with a railroad spike this morning as part of my physical, and man that hurts."

The rest of the afternoon as he sat through endless lectures about the system at Maddox, he was glad that he had gotten out for a while. That night after dinner, he sat on his bed and wrote a letter to Scott while his cellmates played cards.

> *Dear Scott,*
>
> *Have you gotten settled at school? I guess things are still pretty new. Is it too early for me to ask about your classes? Any cool girls? No cool girls here, but then you know that.*
>
> *I'm going nuts. I had to sign over a power of attorney to the state. Now they really own my life. Plus, they now have the right to open all my mail and search any packages. But without it, I get no packages or mail, so I signed. I've been getting poked and prodded in the name of physical examination, and they've been picking my brain in the name of mental examination. Tomorrow I have an appointment with a shrink to discuss my anti-social behavior and my problem with women. That ought to be good. Wouldn't you like to be a fly on the wall?*
>
> *You know what's freaking me out the most? The people I'm socializing with and spending all my time with are murders, armed robbers, burglars, and real rapists! Why didn't I think about that before? I guess I was too busy adjusting to my new social status and being terrified of being taken so far away from home. It's hard to find anybody here that I can identify with. Everyone else seems to be finding someone to bond with. Oh, well, it's probably better if I just stick with*

*my books. I met the chaplain today, and he seems pretty cool. I feel better since I talked with him; I don't feel quite so alone. We spent part of the afternoon together, and I told him all about you and Matt. The best part is I think he's really interested—at first I thought it was just a 'let's be nice to the convict' act. But the more I talked with him, the more I felt he was sincere. He wants to meet you guys one time when you're here.*

*Life here is going to be really hard for me—at least for a while. In a week or so I'll get moved to A Unit. It's high security with practically no privileges. Sam Willet's wet dream for me. I can only have visitors on weekends during limited hours. The day starts at 6:00 with this freakin' obnoxious horn that blows to wake everyone, including the dead. Then there's breakfast, work, a little yard time, dinner, and lock-in right after dinner. The lights go out every night at 10:00—seven days a week, 165 days a year. That will be my life for at least the next two years. After that, with good behavior and a little luck, I'll get transferred to B Unit. That's even air conditioned in the summer and heated in the winter! More free time, few restrictions on visits, better food, TV, more movies, more and better everything. Do you think I can hold out two years? God, help me.*

*God, I miss home and you guys so much I can hardly stand it. Sometimes I just want to die for the loneliness—don't worry I'm not about to do anything stupid, and I know God won't do me the favor.*

*Well, I'd better go. Lights go out soon, and I have some reading to do before tomorrow. Do you believe it—we even get homework here? I read and then sign a little more of my life away each day. It's a slow, <u>painful</u> process. Write! Love, Cain*

The next morning he sat in on more lectures about his upcoming life. This one explained the uniform which consisted of a light blue denim shirt, jeans, and work boots. Period. Sweats could be worn in the cells, but anyone out of his cell had better be in uniform. In the summer, they were allowed to cut the sleeves off or completely out of the shirts, but that was the only exception. The part that bothered Cain the most was that A Unit inmates were called "white-stripers" because their jeans were specially made with a thick white stripe up the outsides from ankle to waist. It identified them as the hard-core and unprivileged.

As he listened, he could feel the chip on his shoulder growing to burdensome proportions. That had to go and he knew it—he just didn't know how. He listened as they babbled on about laundry, showers, and the fact that there was no hot water in the one-man cells of A Unit. At least the one-man cell part was something he considered a plus. A cart would come around about 9:00 P.M. and pass out hot water for washing and shaving before bed. That made sense—shave before bed and wake up with a 5:00 shadow. What a place. He shrugged it off as a laughable non-issue because there was no one there he cared to impress anyway.

That afternoon he had a meeting with a psychologist. Now this, he thought, would be interesting. He had no idea what to expect or how he was going to play it out. He decided to just show up and see what happened.

The man was middle-aged with a thin body and even thinner hair. He wore wire-rimmed spectacles, a white shirt and tie, and a cardigan vest, which Cain noticed right away was buttoned wrong. He met Cain at the door to his office and told him to come in and sit down. As he did, Cain did a quick scan of the small room. Lots of technical books, certificates in frames, family pictures.

"Now," said the man, "let me introduce myself. I'm Dr. Schwarts, with an 's'—at the end. We'll be meeting from time to time on a pretty regular basis as part of your rehabilitation. The Parole Board relies quite heavily on my report, so it's to your benefit to cooperate."

Cain regarded him warily as the chip on his shoulder got a teeny bit heavier. The man waited a bit for some verbal response from Cain. When there was none, he went on—not quite as confidently as he had in the beginning. He had thought because of Cain's age and inexperience with the law, he'd be an easy mark—eager to do what he could, anxious to please, and scared to death. But that wasn't the inmate he was now encountering. Already Cain had become adept at masking his fears and anxieties. Only certain people would be privy to that side of him, and this man certainly wasn't one.

"You don't seem to have much to say," commented Dr. Schwarts.

"I'm not sure what to say."

"I see. Why don't you start out by telling me a little about yourself."

"Isn't that all there in my file in front of you?"

"Well, yes, but I'd like to hear it from you."

"I don't want any trouble, and I know you can make trouble for me. I truly don't know what to tell you because I'm not what you think I am. You've already thrown the Parole Board up to me, and I'm smart enough to know that you were trying to intimidate me. Okay, I'm intimidated. I want to get out of here as soon as I can. I don't want to make you mad, but I don't know what to say to you either."

"Why don't you just start by telling me the truth."

"Nobody wants to hear the truth from me. I told the truth under oath in court."

"Oh brother," sighed the doctor. "If you knew how many times I've heard that."

"See, I'm confused. What do I do, make something up because that's what you want to hear? I can't. Not even in the interest of bullshitting my way out of here. I can't bring myself to say it. I can't admit to doing such an unspeakable thing."

"Then we're not going to get very far, are we? As long as you're in denial, we're at a standstill."

Cain laughed sarcastically.

"I'm not in denial—you are! You can't let yourself believe that an innocent person could be sent to prison. You can't let yourself believe it because then you'd be part of this whole sham we call justice."

As soon as the words came out, Cain knew had had said too much. He closed his eyes to center himself. Then he took a deep breath.

"I'm sorry," he said. "You're just doing your job. I'm majorly stressed out."

"That's easy to understand," said the doctor. "That's what I'm here for."

"Yeah, but we're not on the same page here. We're not even in the same book. And you know the funny thing? I could probably use a shrink right now, but you're just going to screw me up more and cause me more anxiety."

"Well, let's give it some time, huhn? We don't have to start right off with the main issue. Let's avoid that for a while and just kind of get to know one another. Let this be a refuge for you, and we'll see where it leads."

"That's fair enough. And you'll keep an open mind? That's all I ask. Forget all the pre-knowledge you have. You don't even know me."

Dr. Schwarts smiled amiably.

"Okay. We'll put the topic of rape on ice for a while. We still have a few minutes left before you have to leave, why don't your tell me about you family?"

That night at dinner a large inmate approached the table where Cain was sitting. He pulled the man who was sitting next to Cain out of his seat and handed him his tray.

"There you go," he said, "you're finished. Get lost."

Without an argument the man left. Then the second man took over the chair. Cain watched him and then turned back to his dinner.

"I'm Herb Lidell," the inmate said. "I've had my eye on you since we got here—since the bus, actually. I know your last name's Farrell. What's your first name?"

Cain's heart was pounding. He had been wanting to remain as anonymous as possible. This extra attention was unnerving him, especially since he knew it was leading to no good.

"Cain," he said blandly.

"Hey, I like that," said Lidell. "Yeah, I've been watching you. You got a great ass."

Cain had to struggle to swallow the food in his mouth, but he didn't let on that he was bothered. He didn't respond either.

"You obviously haven't been here before," continued Lidell undaunted. "You're just a baby. That's why I'm here. See, I've been in this pit before. In fact, this is my second time. So I know it's a jungle down in population. You're gonna need someone to look out for you."

He looked over at Cain with a big, toothy grin. Cain's mind raced to keep ahead of him.

"Thanks," he said. "But I think it would be better if I took care of myself."

"You're gonna have you hands full, boyo. You are by far the hottest thing to walk into this place in a long, long time." He shook his head and exhaled a lecherous breath. "You're just way too pretty. Way too pretty. They're going to be literally killing each other over you. I have pull around here. Guys know to stay out of my way. One word from me, and they'll all back off and leave you alone."

"I get the feeling, though," said Cain, "that this favor doesn't come cheap."

"Well," shrugged Lidell, "we can kind of take care of each other. A man has . . . needs . . . when he's locked up for a long time."

"I don't get off on that kind of thing," said Cain.

"Yeah, and I'll bet you've never tried it, either. You're way too young to have experienced the world. Stick with me, and I'll not only protect you, but I'll show you things the likes of what you've never seen before."

"Thanks anyway," said Cain smiling uneasily, "but that's just not my thing. I'll take my chances on my own."

"We'll see, we'll see. You'll be looking for me before long, don't worry. It's better to have one thing going with someone who's able to look out for you than to get used by everyone and anyone who takes a fancy to you. I'll wait—you're a prize worth waiting for."

He reached down and squeezed Cain's thigh, and then got up and left.

"Jesus," sighed Cain rubbing his face with both hands. He couldn't think of eating another bite.

When he got back to his cell, he couldn't shake the look and the feel of Herb Lidell. The thought of him sat like a rock inside his midsection. He lay on his bed and tried to read, but he couldn't concentrate. Later, after the lights went out and he lay listening to the sounds of men going through the paces of sleep, he was still haunted by the encounter. God, what had Carrie done to him? How was he ever going to handle this? It was bad enough he was locked up like an animal, but he was locked up with animals who were used to getting their way by snatching it at any cost. He knew this was not going to go away. The day was quickly approaching when he'd have to face it and deal with it.

The days were passing, and it was soon time to enter the population as a full-fledged convict. The only thing that remained was a meeting with a counselor. The counselor served as a liaison between the institution and the inmate.

When Cain walked into Victoria Doleman's office, he was somewhat taken by surprise. She was a handsome, well-groomed woman in her fifties. He didn't know what he had expected, but it wasn't her.

"Sit down," she told him somewhat abruptly. He did and eyed her skeptically as she scanned over his file in front of her. Then she looked up. "How are things going?"

"Well, I'm managing to get myself out of bed every morning. Right now that's still quite a feat."

"This isn't a country club."

"No," he sighed, "that it definitely is not."

"You committed a crime. You're a rapist. You can't expect much more."

He leaned forward and eyed her seriously, but not threateningly. "I'm going to say this one time, and I really don't want to have to say it again. I didn't rape anybody. I was set up and railroaded. I'm here; I don't like it, but I'll make the best of it. But don't ever call me a rapist again."

She stared at him for a long minute.

"All right," she agreed. "But there's something I need you to remember. Whether you're guilty or not, I'm an ally. I'm here to help you through these next twelve years—or however long you're here. I'm not the enemy. You're not a rapist; I'm not the enemy. Okay?"

"Okay," agreed Cain.

"But you do have enemies in high places."

"Sam Willet," said Cain perplexed that the man had even managed to follow him here.

"Yes. As I've been going over your file, something wasn't ringing true. First of all, your age and background. First time offender. You don't fit the profile of the norm here. Your test scores go off our charts, so I tried to get you into one of the better jobs, but I was stonewalled. Everywhere I turned, I was running up against the proverbial brick wall. So I started to do a little investigating, and I have some information that you may be interested in. I debated whether or not to tell you, but I think you have a right to know."

"Something about Sam Willet?"

"Yes. He and Warden Green are very good friends. They golf together regularly during the summer, and their families have socialized together. They're pretty thick."

"Sweet Jesus," sighed Cain.

"You're in for a rough ride, I'm afraid. There's nothing illegal about your being here. The court was perfectly in its rights to send you here. It's just that they usually try to cut someone of your circumstances a break and send them to a little less punitive place. And I wouldn't be surprised if the word hasn't already gone down to the guards to lean on you to make your stay even more distasteful. You need to watch your step. That's why I'm sharing this with you. And I think it would be in your best interest if no one knows you have access to this information. It'll give you one up on them if they don't know you're on to them. There's nothing you can do. Everything's above board. So just be forewarned."

"So what job did they stick me with?"

"The warehouse. It can be backbreaking, but it's good exercise. It'll help wear you out, so you'll sleep good at night. It's more the foreman I'm concerned about than the job. Nate Lewis. He's real hard core. Strict, demeaning, inflexible. A real hard-ass. He's been a guard here for almost twenty years. A real career man. Watch out for him. He can buy you a whole lot of trouble. I know you were assigned there on purpose so he can harass you—it's right up his alley. Don't play into his hands."

"Shit," sighed Cain under his breath. "When do I start."

"The day after tomorrow."

"I'm in the eye of the storm, huhn?"

"Yeah. I'll do what I can, but they're pretty much calling the shots. Not that you have a choice, but do you think you can handle it?"

"I'm getting pretty used to blows below the belt, and I'm still standing. I don't know, this whole prison thing is still not real to me. I keep thinking I'm going to wake up in a cold sweat in my own bed. All the implications are still revealing themselves. And now this news just really excites me."

"Maybe I shouldn't have told you."

"No. No, I'm glad you did. I need to know what I'm up against. I don't know the warden, but I wouldn't put anything passed Sam Willet. Nothing he does surprises me any more."

The next day he was issued a full set of prison blues, and he was told to pack up to be ready for the move. Okay, this is it. He had been gradually and painstakingly moving toward this moment for about three months, and now he was there—about to take the final step into madness, into the system which would swallow him up for the next twelve years. He noticed that his runaway fear and panic were abating. It wasn't that he was no longer afraid or ready to jump out of his skin, but he was getting a handle on it. He was controlling it rather than it controlling him. That was a plus. He knew he couldn't go on the way he had been without having a breakdown of some sort.

As he walked into the thirty-forth cell of the second tier of A Unit for the first time, he felt like he would never see the outside world again. And then the bars slid shut behind him. That sent every nerve in his body scrambling for a safe place. He had been locked up for nearly a month now, but this was different. There was something about this door closing on him that symbolized the finality of it all. Everything else was just a series of steps to the end of the plank. This was stepping off into the shark-infested waters.

He stood back looking around the tiny 5'x 9' cell and took in a few breaths to ward off the claustrophobia that was seizing him. After the numbness wore off, he unpacked his few possessions and clothes and made up his bed. He had to be locked-in for the rest of the day, and then in the morning his stretch at Maddox would officially begin.

He sat at the table in the cell and started to write a letter home, but he couldn't get passed the date. He felt antsy and unable to focus his concentration. He took out a deck of cards and absently began playing Solitaire. Just before lunch the horn blew, and inmates began returning to their cells for the count before lunch. Cain kept his back to the bars and continued playing his game. After everyone had passed, he got up and walked over to the bars. At Maddox inmates had to be standing at the bars and holding on with both hands for each of the four waking hours counts. Cain could see no logical reason for this other than it was some kind of exercise in control.

The guard began making his rounds down the hall with clipboard in hand. He was checking faces and the ID numbers stenciled above the pockets on the denim shirts. When he got to Cain, he first checked the nametag on the bars outside the cell. Then he shifted his eyes to Cain's face and lingered for a moment or two longer than usual. After talking to Mrs. Doleman, Cain couldn't shake the feeling that he was a marked man, and this guard was propagating that feeling. Cain didn't flinch, however. He stood his full height and met the man's challenging stare. The guard was the first to look away as he shifted his gaze to Cain's shirt pocket for the number. Then a check on the clipboard, and without a word he was on his way. Cain exhaled a nervous breath and stood holding the bars for support as the Jell-O that had been creeping into his legs turned to muscle and bone once again. He turned and went back to his game.

A few minutes later the doors slid open again except for Cain's, which remained locked tightly. He paid little attention until he heard a voice calling his name from the bars behind him. He swung around to see a young inmate of about twenty-one standing there.

"Cain Farrell," repeated the young man reading the name off the tag on the bars, "welcome. I'm Jon Harrison. I live next door. Nice to meet you."

He stuck his arm through the bars and offered Cain his hand. Best to humor him. Cain got up and went over to the bars and shook the man's hand.

"You locked-in?" Jon asked.

"For today," answered Cain.

"It's a bitch, ain't it? There's nothing I hate worse than being locked-in. We spend enough time in these sardine cans as it is."

"Do you have a job assignment?"

"The warehouse."

"Hey, me, too. It's not too bad an assignment as long as you stay out of Lewis's way. He's a real bastard." He leaned in closer to the cell and whispered, "A real prick."

Cain smiled. "I've heard. How long have you been here?"

"About three or four months. How old are you, anyway?"

"Eighteen."

"Jesus, what'd you do, rob a candy store?"

"No, not quite."

"Well, it doesn't matter. You gotta be better than the last guy who was in this cell. He was some kind of psycho."

"Hey, Harrison," called the guard from down the tier, "get your ass outta there. He's locked-in; you know better than to talk to him. Get to lunch, or I'll lock you in."

"Okay, okay," shouted Jon. Then he turned his attention back to Cain. "You're kinda like a leper when you're locked-in. No one's supposed to talk to you or acknowledge you in any way. But I'd better go—that screw would like nothing better than to lock my ass in. It makes 'em feel powerful. I'll catch you later."

"Yeah," said Cain as Jon turned and ran down the hall.

He didn't want to jump the gun, but maybe Jon Harrison was the person he was looking for to help dispel his unbearable loneliness. He'd have to see.

Cain learned that being locked into your cell made you the ultimate of outcasts. Not only was everyone instructed to ignore you, but neither the hot water cart nor the commissary cart, which sold various food items and pop, stopped outside the cell in the evening after dinner. At least at lunch and dinner they dropped off a tray at his food slot.

That night just before the lights went out, the guard on duty stopped outside his cell as he did the count for the night.

"So, did you like sitting on your ass all day?"

"No," answered Cain matter-of-factly.

"Good. Remember that. Because any time you step out of line, you'll be sent up here to lock-in for however long we decide: an hour, a day, a week. We usually lock newcomers in on the first day to show you

121

what an unpleasant experience it can be. Now either dry shave or use cold water, but don't show up unshaven in the morning."

"No problem."


The next morning Cain was still tying his boots as the door automatically slid opened. In a matter of seconds, Jon appeared and waited for him.

"Come on," hurried Jon. "The doors slam and lock thirty seconds after they open. If you're still inside, you're locked-in for the day."

"Shit," said Cain rushing his tying.

"You got your ID card and your privilege card?"

"Yeah," answered Cain patting his pocket and hurrying out the door not too many seconds too soon.

"They probably told you this in Admissions, but don't go anywhere without them. If you get caught, they'll lock you in and throw away the key."

"They really get off on locking us in, huhn?"

"Yeah," smiled Jon as they walked to breakfast. "Wait till you meet Lewis. I swear he gets a hard-on just thinking about dangling the possibility in front of you. He gets this mean smile." He lowered his voice gruffly as he mimicked Lewis. "*You wanna get your ass locked-in? Huhn? Huhn? You wanna play 'Who's the Boss' with me, asshole? Cause I'll be glad to show you!* He loves his authority."

# CHAPTER 7

The first thing Nora noticed when Cain walked into the visitors' room was the pack of cigarettes in his pocket. Her eyes dropped down to his shirt pocket and then back up as she did her best to hide the shock she was experiencing. It was the weekend before Thanksgiving. He had been at Maddox only about three months, but more and more she felt him slipping away. She hated the feeling of having to relinquish him to a society that had no good effects on him whatsoever.

Though she had tried to act nonchalant, Cain caught the slip of her eye, and he felt the weight of her disapproval. Still he opted not to be the first to bring it up. He had defiantly left the cigarettes in his pocket during this visit because he had felt it was time his parents knew this was a choice he had made and they had little to say about it. Will was the first to mention it.

"Cigarettes?" he said coming straight to the point.

"Yeah," said Cain sitting down across the table from them.

"Why?" asked Will.

"Why not, Dad? What else is there to do around here?"

"Surely you could find something to do besides smoke?" said Nora joining in the sparring match.

"Like what, Mom? There's nothing else to do here. They own every part of me. This is one thing I have some control over. Besides, cigarettes are used like money here. You can't even get into a decent card game without cigarettes."

"And since when are you such a big card player?" persisted Will.

"Since I got my ass locked in here and I found it's one of the few ways to pass the time. I don't want to talk about it any longer; I don't want to fight with you. You've come too far, and I see you too little to waste time arguing over a moot point. I'm not going to quit."

Later that day he sat with Jon in the large recreation room. It was cold and raining outside, so fresh air out in the yard was not an option. They sat at a table and pushed checkers around a board. Cain's heart definitely wasn't in the game.

"You know," commented Jon, "you really shouldn't have visitors. You spend every weekend after they leave in this big funk. You'd be better off if they just didn't come."

"Yeah, they're probably thinking the same thing," sighed Cain as he made a move. "I was crabby before they even got here. They spent two hours driving each way to see me, and then I was an asshole most of the time they were here. And I can't help it; I go into a major depression when they have to leave. And if that's not enough, every damn time I have a visit, I have to do a strip search when it's over. It's supposed to be random, but they get me every time."

"The long arm of your tormentor reaching into the prison system once again."

"Yeah, well, I'm getting sick of it, but I'd really go crazy if my family didn't come. And I'll go lock-in if I'm bothering you. I don't really like this stupid game anyway; someday I'll teach you how to play chess."

Just then Lidell approached them.

"I thought we were supposed to meet this afternoon," he said to Cain.

"I had visitors," said Cain trying to sound braver than he felt.

"I don't care," snarled Lidell. "This was not an invitation—it was a command performance. Face it, Farrell, I've been taking good care of you. If it wasn't for me, you'd be the sweetheart of every guy in this place. They've left you alone because of me. But now it's time to pay up, and I've been patient long enough."

Cain exhaled a burst of queasiness and dropped his face into his hands.

"Get lost, Lidell," said Jon. "This is a private game."

"I don't want to play no games. I just want to be sure I'm totally understood."

"You're totally understood," sighed Cain.

"Good. I'll be in touch."

He tousled Cain's hair and went on his way.

"Shit," said Cain as he ran his fingers through his hair to fix it.

"What are you going to do about him?"

"I don't know, but I feel sick. I don't want to talk about it."

"You'd better talk about it, buddy boy, because he means business. He's not going to just give up and go away just because you don't want to face it."

"Okay," said Cain becoming even testier, "so what do you suggest?"

"I already told you what I think—you gotta fight him. You gotta stand up to him—unless, of course, you want to spend the rest of your sentence being his personal love slave."

"SHUT UP!"

"I'm just trying to save your ass—literally."

"I'm no match for him! He's got nearly a hundred pounds on me, for God's sake!"

"So you construct yourself a piece—a shank. We've talked about this, genius."

"So we have, and I think I told you I could never do that. Christ, I could never stab someone with one of those things."

"And I could?" asked Jon incredulously. "That's why I'm a fucking burglar, for Christ's sake—I don't get into the weapons thing. I'm a coward—just sneak in when no one's home, take what I can get, and sneak out. But this is the jungle, Cain. It's every man for himself—

and every man had better have a weapon here. He's ready to strike; that's what this was all about. And he even has the balls to come over and all but announce the time and the place."

"Christ," mumbled Cain as he concentrated on keeping his stomach.

That night in his cell, Cain tried to forget about Lidell and concentrate on his books. During his months at Maddox, he had been reading avidly, and the joke with the librarian was that he'd read all the books in the library before half his sentence was served. He had applied for advanced college courses that he could take through the mail, but he kept getting his applications back rejected by the prison censors before they were even sent out in the mail. Victoria Doleman kept trying to get something pushed through for him, but even she was getting nowhere. Sam Willet had him buried alive.

He took out the book for the math class he was taking at Maddox, and he looked over his homework for the next day. The class was way too easy for him, but it got him out of the warehouse and Lewis's grip three afternoons a week for about an hour, and it forced him to think and keep his mind sharp. This night, however, his mind kept wandering out of control. In an effort to avoid thinking about Herb Lidell, he stumbled on the thought of the coming holiday—Thanksgiving—the first of countless holidays that he would spend away from home. Jon told him that they served a turkey dinner at Maddox, but if he was looking for anything like at home, he had better change his expectations right away. He thought about his brothers and Molly all coming home from school. He hadn't seen any of them since he left for Maddox. He never thought it was possible to miss anything as much as he missed his home and family.

Home was such a long way away both in time and distance, and the nightmare that was about to devour him was just too close. Finally, it just hurt too much to think anymore, so he curled up in a tight fetal position and tried to shut out the pain. Hopelessness pervading, he finally fell asleep. And while he slept, Herb Lidell entered his cell with the help of a guard, and with the stealth, power, and agility of a full-grown tiger proceeded to steal from him the last fragile remnants of innocence that had managed to survive the treachery of Carrie Willet.

Cain never had a chance. Taken by surprise, he was greatly overpowered. Lidell's brute force and heavy fists neutralized any struggle he was able to muster. Still disoriented and confused from the rude awakening, Cain cried out in terror. Lidell grabbed a fistful of his hair and smashed his face into the bars. Stars exploded in a painful show before his eyes. Lidell was saying something to him, but he couldn't hear what it was. His blood was pounding through his ears at a thunderous rate, blocking out external sound. He felt as if he were falling through a massive black hole in time, while wrestling with some demonic phantom of the night. Struggling against hope and depravity, he realized he was losing the fight. Panic and terror seized him as Lidell grabbed his arms and forced them through the bars where his unidentified assistant clamped handcuffs on them. Now he was totally helpless. Lying facedown on the bed with his arms cuffed through the bars, there was little he could do to defend himself. That's when Lidell sent him into total hysteria as he yanked the pillow from underneath him and put if over his head, muffling his cries, stifling his breathing, and distorting his reality. The taste of blood in his mouth was making him nauseous, and the closeness of the pillow against his nose and mouth sent him gasping for breath. His head was spinning, and he was afraid that he would pass out. But as his strength was ebbing and the fight was deserting his body, he wondered if oblivion might not be desirable in the light of what Lidell was about to do to him. The big man tore at his own clothes and at Cain's as he plundered on in the prison ritual of supremacy. Cain forced his mind out of the cell—far away—to the beach. It hadn't been that long since he had been there; he should still be able to achieve a total recall. Girls. Hot sun. Cool water. Good friends. Girls. Hot sun. Cool water. Good friends. Girls. Hot sun. Cool . . .

He cried unashamedly into his mattress as pain ripped through his body. He was nearly crushed by the bulk of his tormentor, which made breathing an even more difficult task. In spite of the discomfort, he was glad for the pillow over his head. Somehow it made him feel detached and removed from the ugliness. He knew there would be plenty of time to reckon with that later.

Finally, Lidell was spent and collapsed in a heaving mass on top of him. Cain let go of a muffled cry as the air was forced from his lungs. He wished he had the strength and energy to buck the hideous man off his back and onto the floor, but he had no choice except to endure the remainder of the humiliation and pray for Lidell's hasty retreat. Lidell was not a stay-around-kind-guy, so he at least obliged him that far. Cain cried softly into the mattress as Lidell rolled himself onto the floor. The hairs along his spine stood on end as he anticipated Lidell's next move. The hulking man didn't make him wait long. Fastening his pants, he reached down and snatched the pillow from over Cain's head and threw it across the cell. Then with excruciating roughness, he yanked Cain's head by a handful of hair. Tears streamed across his face a he stifled a first-class cry of agony. Lidell got right in his face.

"Don't **ever** make me do that again!!!" he snarled. "Rape is your game, not mine! From now on, you make yourself available to me whenever it is I want you! You got that?"

Cain stubbornly clenched his jaw as his bruised and bleeding face did little to assure Lidell that he had indeed won this war. The big man was not used to defiance, nor did he tolerate it well.

"How would you like to have another taste of those bars across your pretty face? And this time I'll make sure to break your nose."

"Okay," sighed Cain as Lidell nearly pulled the hair from his head.

"Okay, what? The bars?"

"No." Cain could barely speak through the torturous yanking of his hair.

"I'll get a warmer welcome the next time?"

"Yes."

Lidell let go of Cain's hair. Then he reached over and slapped him sharply across the bare backside. The pain was more than minimal as Cain bit back a cry.

"Good boy," grinned Lidell as Cain turned his face into the mattress to hide the fresh wave of tears that had escaped. "That's what I like to hear. It doesn't hurt so much if you relax, you know. But that's up to you because I'm going to have you one way or the other."

He gave a lecherous laugh and left the cell, leaving Cain naked, except for his tee shirt, and in agonizing pain—his arms still extended through the bars and cuffed at the wrists. Taking a few seconds to let reality crash around him, Cain turned his face back into the mattress and sobbed the mournful cry of the forsaken.

It was a good half-hour before his tears were finally spent and exhaustion began to take over. His body trembled from a combination of emotion and the cold. He wanted to sleep, but he was shivering uncontrollably. He kept his mind in the present—afraid of what might happen to it if he let it drift too far into the past. Suddenly he was jarred to his senses when someone touched his hands. His body stiffened and recoiled convulsively like a trapped animal awaiting his fate.

"Easy does it," laughed the insensitive guard. "I just came to unlock you here. You've had quite a night."

Cain tried to look up to see the guard who had betrayed him, but he was in too much pain to move and his eyes wouldn't really focus anyway. So he just lay there staring blankly, hoping sleep was not far off.

"Geez, you're shaking like a leaf," commented the guard. "How do you expect me to do this? Lay still."

Mercifully, the cuffs slid from his wrists. Pains shot through his arms as he gingerly eased them back into the cell and tucked them under his chest.

"Sweet dreams," chided the guard as he walked off.

Cain lay there shivering and trying not to cry any more. He wanted to get his pillow and pull his covers back on, but he couldn't move. So he concentrated on calming his soul to the best of his current ability. His teeth were chattering so violently that he was afraid they would break. He had to calm down; he needed his wits about him. This was real; this needed to be dealt with, but one step at a time. First, he had to calm down; then he had to get warm. One step at a time. Baby steps. Breathe in, breathe out. Don't think; just breathe.

Pretty soon when he suspected that the trembling of his body was not going to be quieted without the external comfort of warmth, he dared to move and reach for his blankets, which Lidell had shoved aside. Pulling them up, and seeking out the quilt in particular, he wrapped himself in a snug cocoon and waited to see what step he needed to take next. Soon in spite of the terror and loathing in his heart, the warmth of the blankets helped to relax him. The quilt had long since lost the smell of home that had comforted him at the county jail while waiting for transfer to Maddox, but it still had the feel of home; and at that minute, it was just what he needed. He was not alone—there was a family out there who loved him, and he would get through this. He just wasn't sure how at that minute.

He awoke in the morning to face the cold, hard facts of what had transpired over night. His pillow was still on the floor, and the pain that seized his body was debilitating. He decided it was best to just focus on getting up and functioning because thinking too hard was bound to cast him into a dangerous mine field of emotion. But how does one go about not thinking about such an obscenity? How was he ever going to find the strength of character and body to get out of bed and move on?

He could hear Jon calling to him from his cell next door, but he couldn't move; he couldn't answer. Jon continued to call frantically; he had heard the commotion the night before, and he had guessed at what had happened.

When the doors finally rolled open a short while later, Jon left his cell in a hurry and rushed to Cain. What he saw caused him to pull up in an abrupt stop and scramble his resources in an attempt to know what to do next. Cain was sitting on his bed in a dazed stupor. He was dressed for the day except for his boots. His mattress was bare, and the sheet that had been on it was in a heap on the floor at his feet. Even in a disheveled pile, it was easy to see that it was smattered with blood. The cuts and bruises on Cain's face were evidence that he did not go down without a fight. It was the vacant look in eyes, though, that worried Jon the most. Those ever-expressive eyes were blind to the world around him.

"Jesus," Jon sighed beneath his breath.

With little time to think before the doors would roll shut again and lock for the day, Jon did a quick check down the tier to see if the guard was watching. Seeing that the coast was clear, he ducked quickly into Cain's cell. Cain put both his hands up in front of him, holding Jon off.

"Don't touch me," he said deliberately. "Don't touch me."

"You gotta get out of here, Cain. Let me help you."

"I just can't get my boots on; I think my ribs might be broken. I don't know if I can move."

"Come on, before the doors close. For God's sake, don't stay in here—he might be back for you when he finds out you locked-in. Hurry, I'll help you with your boots."

Jon grabbed the boots with one hand and then extended the other to help. Reaching out with his left hand, Cain took a hold of Jon's outstretched hand and eased himself forward off the bed. He cried out in pain as he did, but he knew he had to hurry and leave the cell before the door locked on him.

Once in the hallway, he stopped and gave Jon a look. *Okay, I'm out here; now what do I do?*

"Hold onto the bars and lean against the wall," said Jon reading his mind. "I'll put the boots on for you; I'll be careful."

Cain stood in a state of suspended animation—suspended brain activity—mindless to what was going on around him as Jon guided his feet into the work boots and then tied them.

"Stupid-ass kid," mumbled Jon as he went about the task. "You gotta look out for yourself. I can't take care of you while I'm locked up, too. That's why you gotta arm yourself." He looked up at Cain whose mind was still a million miles away. He finished with the last boot and stood up. "Come on. We gotta get you to a doctor."

"No!" said Cain exhibiting some touch with reality. "No doctor. I'm fine."

"No you're not," argued Jon. "Your face is cut and bruised, and you can hardly move." He went to brush the hair from Cain's forehead, but Cain pulled his head away from the contact. "That knot on your forehead is the size of a baseball. You might have a concussion or something."

"I said I'm fine," insisted Cain with the same uncharacteristic detachment that he had been exhibiting all morning. "Let's go down to breakfast. You can go ahead if I'm holding you up."

"No, I'm staying right with you."

"Okay," said Cain, "but not a word to anybody. I can talk for myself."

"Okay," agreed Jon. "Is it too soon to ask what you plan to do?"

Cain looked over at him with all the seriousness and deadly passion of a rattlesnake.

"I'm going to kill the fucker if he ever comes near me again."

Knowing his exuberance wouldn't be appreciated at that moment, Jon hid the celebratory smile that was trying to break out on his face. He much preferred the anger and resolve that he saw slowly moving into Cain's vacant eyes. Reluctant inmate that he was, Cain had no choice but to get into the stream of life at Maddox and make his statement to all. In this case that meant standing up to Lidell and letting him know that obedient servitude was not his nature.

Jon was encouraged by the way Cain handled himself at breakfast. Though he ate little, he managed to hide the pain he was in and thus allay the curiosity of those around him. Luckily, everyone knew better than to ask any questions, so he was spared the ordeal of making up an explanation. Lidell walked passed them once and nailed Cain with a lethal stare. Jon was certain that Lidell was caught more than a little off guard when Cain met his stare and held it defiantly until the big man nearly walked into a support pole that was nearby. Had it not been suicidal to do so, everyone who witnessed it would have broken out into hysterical laughter. Instead, they bit back their grins and pretended not to have noticed. All except Cain, that is. The concentrated hatred never left his face—he never even gave a thought to a grin that had to be stifled. To him, nothing was funny about any of this. Jon watched him carefully. He couldn't quite put his finger on it, but he saw a new determination and resolve taking up residence amidst the bumps and bruises. In spite of the size factor, he knew he would not want to be Herb Lidell.

The visual confrontation seemed to have swung the momentum slightly in Cain's favor. It at least helped him to get up from the table and make the trip to the warehouse with a bit more spring in his step. Of course, Nate Lewis was not one to let a golden opportunity pass him by. He jumped right on Cain's frazzled nerves with both feet.

"I'm doing a random shakedown this morning," he told Cain. "Hit the wall."

"What?" questioned Cain defiantly. "I haven't seen anyone else getting frisked."

"Are you arguing with me, boy?" Lewis was a master at patronization. "Hit the wall, or I'll write you up and send you back to your cell."

A fate worse than death at this point. Reluctantly, Cain walked up to the wall and spread eagle with his hands opened flat against it. He bit back cries of pain as Lewis carelessly patted down his body, hitting every bruised and battered part. He remained facing the wall for a bit as he blinked back a few errant tears that had forced their way out. Not only was he in a great deal of physical pain, but he was emotionally repulsed by the feel of another person's hands on him. After Lidell, he never wanted anyone to touch him ever again. Having collected himself, he stepped back from the wall.

"Satisfied?" he asked Lewis.

"No. Tuck your shirt in. You know better."

Cain looked at him forlornly. *Have a heart.* Then he painstakingly shoved his shirttails into his pants.

"By the way," said Lewis, "what train did you walk in front of, anyway?"

No reply.

Lewis wasn't about to be put off so easily. "Have you explained those bruises to anyone? It looks like something serious has gone down."

"I fell out of bed. Nothing serious."

"Get to work," barked Lewis knowing when to quit. "You're wasting my time."

Cain gladly walked passed him and on into the warehouse. Lewis stepped in front of Jon to block his way.

"How does the other guy look?" asked the guard.

"I don't know what you're talking about," shrugged Jon in is cavalier manner. "He fell out of bed. He's young—I guess he needs sides on his bed. Do you want me on the wall for your random shakedown?"

"Get to work, smart-ass."

During a mid-morning smoke break Cain opted to separate himself from the others. He sat on a box and leaned against the wall for support. Soon Jon got up and walked over to him.

"You okay?" Jon asked.

"I'll live. There's no way I could sit over there on the floor, and besides I don't feel very social."

"That's understandable. But you look wiped out. Are you sure you're okay?"

"I don't know." He leaned his head wearily against the wall. "I don't know how many more boxes I can move and unload, and Lewis keeps sending more my way. I just want to take a strong painkiller and go to bed."

"Go over to the infirmary. Lewis has to give you a pass for there if you ask him."

"No. Too many questions. I have my class today the last hour of work, and after that I'm going straight up to lock-in and go to bed."

"You're sure you're going to make it till 2:15?"

"Do I have a choice?"

2:15 didn't arrive a minute too soon for Cain. He grabbed his books that he had brought back with him from the noon count and checked out of the warehouse to attend his class. As he walked into the classroom, his teacher gave him a look and raised his eyebrows asking a million silent questions. Cain offered no explanations, and the man knew better than to ask.

Sitting in the classroom offered him no real relief, but at least he didn't have to do any more manual work. He wasn't sure how many more boxes he could have lifted and unloaded. He found it hard to concentrate. His mind kept trailing off to Herb Lidell and how he was going to resolve this current dilemma in which he found himself. He could feel himself involuntarily falling deeper and deeper into the abyss of lost innocence with no real means of dragging himself out. It proved to be a waste of time for him to even be there, since he was totally unaware of anything that went on. When the class was over at 3:30, he remained in his desk, not at all sure he could get up.

"Can I do anything?" the teacher asked sincerely as the others began to leave.

"No," answered Cain. "Thanks."

"You weren't with me much today, but I'm sure you'll have no trouble filling in the blanks."

"I know. I'm sorry. It won't happen again."

"It's okay. I know how it is around here, and you look like you have more than a few things on your mind. Just stop in and see me if you have any trouble with the homework."

Cain woke up the morning of Thanksgiving Day in the deepest of depressions. Being alone this day was something he had been dreading for weeks. It was Thursday, so he wasn't allowed any visitors. He didn't know—maybe that wasn't so bad after all. He'd just end up feeling guilty about making them drive such a distance on a holiday when they should be home relaxing and enjoying each other's company. Then, too, there was the total letdown he always felt when his visits were over. That would only increase exponentially on a day like today. That having been established, he tried to turn his thoughts on a different path. Unfortunately, the only other path his thoughts traveled these days was the one that led to Herb Lidell, and that was a path riddled with land mines and pitfalls. Therefore, there was no hope in sight for his mood to lighten.

He got up and walked to the tiny window in his cell. It was a typical November day—gray and bleak—and the view from his room was as barren and forbidding as were his thoughts. There was nowhere for peace to be found. The only tiniest speck of good news in his life was the fact that he had seen and heard little from Lidell over the past four days since their unholy bonding. That in itself bore gloom. The longer it was that he didn't hear from Lidell, the closer it became until his next appearance. His body was recovering from the tough love that Lidell had inflicted on it, but his mind was caught in a revolving door of pain, fear, and anxiety. He knew very few hours of peaceful, refreshing sleep, and his waking moments were fraught with dread and hyper-agitation. His mind, which had always served as his great escape from the bars and restrictions that held him captive, was now turning on him and cutting off all avenues of retreat. There was nowhere to go anymore that didn't cause him stress and panic.

Jon tried to coax him out of the cell when the doors rolled opened that Thanksgiving morning, but he had reentered the cocoon of his mother's quilt, and he was firmly wedged into the corner of his bed where the bars and the cement wall met.

"This isn't good," warned Jon. "Come with me."

"I don't want to," mumbled Cain. "Besides, I'm not dressed."

"Okay. Then promise me that you'll get dressed and come down with me for lunch. Afterwards we can go to the gym or walk outside—whatever you want." He waited. No reply. "FARRELL!"

Cain nearly jumped out of his skin, regardless of the protective cocoon.

"Okay," he whined as his heart pounded. "Fine."

It actually felt good to be out in the fresh air as he and Jon walked out in the nearly deserted yard. It was cold and windy, but the wool pea coat and his upturned collar offered enough protection and warmth. His hands jammed in his pockets, he walked aimlessly as Jon babbled on about something or other. He didn't care—Jon was happy to have gotten him out of the cell, and he was feeling a temporary catharsis brought on by the cold, fresh air.

"Do you ski?" Cain asked from out of nowhere.

"No," laughed Jon taking heart in the fact that Cain was initiating conversation. "I'm a city boy. We never had the kind of money the kids out in the suburbs had—at least in the part of the city I'm from that was the case. Your family's pretty well off, isn't it?"

"We get by."

"I thought so. Just looking at you, anyone can tell you got breeding. That's probably what attracted Lidell to you in the first place—that and the fact that you look like Brad Pitt."

"What?!" said Cain with an incredulous laugh.

"Don't tell me that no one's ever told you that before. I read magazines and watch movies, and I noticed it right away. I bet the girls were all over you on the outside. I've even seen the way the women employees and guards gape at you. Man, I can't even imagine what that must be like."

"Yeah, well, that's what got me here, isn't it?"

"Yeah, I guess you're right."

"And as for the rest of it, you're full of shit. Nobody gapes at me."

"The hell they don't! I swear to God, Cain. You ought to climb out of your funk and start observing your surroundings a little more. You could probably have a lucrative, little business going—with all the women you want. You not only got shy, good looks, but you got class in a classless place. Boy, if that don't drive the females nuts, I don't know what will."

"Could we talk about something else?" asked Cain not at all bolstered by the adulation Jon was heaping on him. If anything, it was making him feel more uncomfortable.

"Okay," shrugged Jon as he went back to babbling to Cain's deaf ear.

That night Cain sat wrapped up in his quilt again as he waited for the lights to go out. He was thankful this excruciating day was over, but as always of late, he dreaded the dark for he knew that was when Lidell would be back. At least this time he was ready for him. His mind was set in acceptance of what he had to do, and his weapon of choice was finely crafted—thanks to the instruction of a few of the hard-core who he had somehow been able to befriend. Every night before he went to bed, he retrieved it from its ingenious hiding place and placed it deftly under his pillow. He had been assured by all in a position to know that he could make a move on Lidell without fear of prosecution in spite of the fact that Lidell had a guard or two in his hip pocket. The degradation and unholy activities that took place within Maddox not withstanding, there was a code among convicts that was not negotiable: Thou shalt not rat out any**one** for any**thing**. No matter what bad blood was between them or what atrocities took place, they always handled it themselves without getting The Man involved. A snitch always ended up ostracized or dead—no exceptions. Now all he had to do was wait out Lidell and see just how prison-savvy he had become.

He actually felt Lidell's presence before his door even opened later in the small hours of the morning. His heart began to pound, but he knew he had to stay calm and calculating. He stretched and moved as if waking from a sound sleep. As he did, he squinted through his lashes to see if the guard was standing watch. As best as he could tell, it was just Lidell. Slowly and inconspicuously he slid his left hand under his pillow and grasped the homemade weapon.

"You awake?" Lidell asked in his raspy voice.

"What?" asked Cain sleepily as if he were unaware of what was going on.

"It's time for lesson two in breaking you to the saddle. This time relax; it's not all that bad. In fact, you may find you like it." Lidell sat on the edge of his bed and began skillfully kneading Cain's shoulders. "There you go. Just relax and enjoy. How old are you, anyway?"

"Eighteen," answered Cain in a sleep-laden voice.

"God, you're too good to be true. We can have a most amazing relationship."

"Leave me alone," mumbled Cain hoping against hope that Lidell would oblige him.

"I thought we had an understanding from the last time. You didn't want a broken nose, and I didn't want a fucking struggle. Besides, you have no idea how many guys have their eyes on you. If I was to step back and make it open season on you, they'd all fuck you right out of your mind. I'm your guardian angel. I think I deserve something for that. Come on, I'll show you how good it can be."

"I said no," said Cain with attitude as Lidell pulled back the covers and began to reach into the waistband of Cain's sweats.

"What?"

"You heard me," asserted Cain as he sat up on the bed and brandished the razor-sharp weapon for the first time.

Lidell stood up to put some distance between them, but he wasn't showing much respect.

"What's this?" he laughed. "You think you're man enough to use that?"

"I know I am. Now get out of here."

Lidell laughed some more.

"You like it rough, huhn?" he said. "Okay. I could get into that. Did you like the handcuffs? I can bring them with me next time."

"GET OUT!" repeated Cain as he knelt up and readied himself for the attack.

Lidell was still not taking him seriously.

"Now," grinned the big man, "I'm gonna come over there, and you're going to be a good boy and give me that shank so I don't have to totally beat the shit out of you."

He made a move closer to the bed, and Cain swiped at him with the knife.

"Whoa!" laughed Lidell tauntingly. "You're a feisty son of a bitch. But I'll tell you this—you put that thing down right now, or I'm gonna break your arm when I take it away from you."

Cain stood his ground, showing no sign of backing down. Lidell kept laughing condescendingly as he took a step closer and reached for Cain's left arm. But Cain was athletic and in good shape, and in a heartbeat he slipped out of Lidell's reach and drove the knife soundly into Lidell's very fleshy thigh. The towering giant let out with a painful yell. Then with a menacing twist of his wrist, Cain yanked the knife from its mark. Lidell howled once again and dropped back against the opposite wall. With a menacing and crazed look on his face, Cain prepared to strike again.

"Jesus Christ!" stammered Lidell as he clutched at his bleeding leg.

"Come on!" said Cain, "Now that I've tasted blood, I'm ready to go for it again. I've thought of nothing else since your last visit. This knife may not be very big, but as you've already found out, it's fucking-ass sharp!"

"Hold on," said Lidell. "I got your message. No problem. I misjudged you, okay? I thought you were too pretty to have balls. I knew you were too good to be true? Didn't I say that?"

"Get out," snarled Cain not letting down his guard. "And don't come back because the next time I swear to God I'll aim for your heart or your throat. And tell anyone else who wants to try and do me to expect the same thing."

"Fine. Fine. Jesus Christ."

Lidell left the cell. Cain sat back on his heels, frozen to the spot, his hand shaking almost out of control. The door rolled shut, and he felt more secure; but it was several minutes before he was able to move as his heart wound down to a normal beat. Then he washed off the knife and tucked it back under his pillow for safe keeping—he had already learned that it was a deadly mistake to feel too confident and secure in the jungle that was Maddox. It would be some time before he would be comfortable enough to sleep unarmed. Still shaking from the confrontation, he went over to his table and lit a cigarette. As he smoked, he could feel his body wind down and relax. As distasteful as the whole experience had been, he had stood up and proclaimed his manhood to let everyone know he was not an easy mark. That made him feel good.

By dinner the next day, word had spread throughout Maddox that he was indeed a man to be reckoned with, and he was awarded the respect of his peers. That, coupled with his intelligence, good looks, and obvious breeding, earned him a folk hero reputation among his fellow inmates. The guards on the other hand kept an even more diligent eye on him. They knew it wasn't good to let someone rise above the ranks and enjoy too much popularity. But that was the kind of charisma that Cain had, and it was hard to counteract. Brains, beauty, and balls. The population had accepted him, now it would be up to the guards to see to it that Sam Willet was kept happy.

# CHAPTER 8

"Holy shit!" exclaimed Cain at breakfast one morning, "There's a women inmate over there!"

Jon followed his friend's incredulous gaze while the others they were eating with smiled knowingly.

"Oh her," said Jon.

"Oh her. That's all you have to say? That's a goddam woman!"

"Do you want to meet her?"

"What is this?"

Their tablemates grinned.

"Well, you had your big 2-0 birthday a few days ago, and you've been here over a year and a half now, but I'm just not sure if a college boy from the suburbs can handle the idea of Josie."

"Will you tell me what's going on? She's really a man, isn't she?"

"You **are** smarter than you look," laughed Jon as he briskly mussed Cain's hair. "But she doesn't like to be thought of or called a man."

"Why haven't I seen her before?"

"Because she just got back. She got out just before you came, and, BINGO, she's back again. I heard she just came down from Admissions yesterday."

"I thought they kept guys like that segregated."

"They do—except Josie. She loves it down here. The inmates love her. And the guards love watching all the shenanigans that go on around her. It kind of breaks up the monotony for everyone."

As if on cue, Josie looked their way and smiled with a delicate little wave. Then excusing herself from the group she was with, she approached them.

"I always get confused at times like this," said Jon as she sat down with them. "Is it appropriate to say, welcome back?"

"That's fine," said Josie looking directly at Cain. "Hi."

"Cain Farrell," introduced Jon, "meet Josie."

Cain smiled in his shy, disarming manner.

"Nice to meet you." He said as she continued to mesmerize him.

"Thank you," she giggled seductively. "I noticed you first thing this morning when you walked in, and I knew I was going to have to get to know you."

Cain watched her as she talked on and laughed and flirted. He wasn't sure at all what to make of her. She wore prison blues, but she had delicate features and not even a hint of a beard. Her hair was long and pulled back in a ponytail at her collar, and she wore very tastefully applied make-up. Had he met her under any other circumstances, he would not have even questioned her gender. She was very attractive, and Cain felt confused by the stirrings he felt in the pit of his stomach.

Over the next few days, she sought him out whenever she had the opportunity, which was during their free time and during meals. He had to keep reminding himself that she was actually a man; however, he did find himself carried away by her attention, and at times, he was lost in the smell of her perfume. This was a problem he had not expected to encounter at Maddox, and he wasn't sure exactly how to handle it.

"I like being with you," she said one afternoon as they sat over a chess game.

"I like being with you, too," he smiled. "You're the only one around here who can give me a run for my money at chess. The rest of them are hopeless."

"I'm glad," she said smiling demurely. "You know, you're just way too beautiful for a place like this, and too smart, too. I never thought I'd meet anyone like you here. When I look at you, I think I must have died and gone to heaven because you could only be an angel."

"Come on, Josie," he said, "it's your move. Concentrate on the game."

"Okay, okay, but it's not easy when I'm with you."

Just then Jon came up and broke the spell as he pulled up a chair. Josie wasn't particularly fond of Jon because of his sharp tongue and blunt manner. She sighed and purposely made a move that would allow Cain to win the game.

"What's this?" asked Cain. "You know better than that."

"Yeah, well, I have to go anyway. I have a book for you that I think you might like. I'll bring it down tomorrow."

"Hey, don't leave on my account," said Jon. "I didn't mean to break anything up."

"You didn't, don't worry," said Josie getting up from her chair. "Good bye, gorgeous."

She leaned over and kissed Cain on the forehead. He closed his eyes as he remembered days long past. Then without another word from either of them, she left.

"Whoa," said Jon. "What's this?"

"Nothing."

"Have you got something going on with her?"

"No."

"Watch yourself, friend. She can be real trouble."

"What's the matter—you jealous?" asked Cain with an impish grin that lit up his face.

"Come on, Cain, I'm not kidding around here. They use her as bait. That's why she's down here; she's a trap. And you're a perfect victim because of Sam Willet."

"She wouldn't do that to me."

"No. She's not part of it. It's the guards. They watch her like a hawk, and then they nail whoever they catch with her. They'll bust your ass to Solitary for months if they catch you fooling around with her."

"Well, then there's no problem because I don't plan on *fooling around with her.*"

"Just watch yourself. Don't forget what part of your anatomy got you in trouble before. You got caught with your pants down once, don't let it happen again."

"Don't worry, Jon," said Cain becoming angry, "I won't forget. And now I'm going up to lock-in. Excuse me."

He got up and started to storm away just as Fr. Mike was walking up to them.

"What's wrong?" asked the priest.

"Nothing," said Cain brushing passed him and continuing on his way.

The priest gave Jon a questioning glance. Jon shrugged ignorantly.

When Jon walked passed Cain's cell a short time later on his way to lock-in for the count before dinner, Cain was lying on his bed, facing the wall.

"So, are you going to pout now?" asked Jon as he threw in a twisted, empty cigarette package and hit Cain in the back.

"Go to hell," mumbled Cain as he pulled the pillow from under his head and planted it firmly over his head.

"Come on, asshole. I just don't want you getting in trouble over all of this."

"She likes to read," said Cain flinging the pillow across the cell and swinging his legs over the side of his bed until he was sitting up. "We talk about books; we play chess. What's the big deal?"

"Tell me you never thought about fucking her."

"No, for God's sake!"

"Yes, you have! I can see it in your eyes. You're wondering what it would be like. Maybe if it was dark enough and you closed your eyes . . ."

"Jesus Christ," sighed Cain with mounting frustration as he got up and walked across the cell.

"I gotta lock-in," said Jon and he walked away.

Cain walked over to the table and picked up his cigarettes. Lighting one, he tried to exhale his anger with the smoke. He walked over to the window and looked out. What a zoo this was. What a fucking, crazy zoo.

When the count was over and the doors rolled opened for dinner, Cain stood back to see if Jon would stop like always. He was relieved to see that he did.

"Come on, cowboy," Jon said. "I'm off my soap box. I won't say another word. It's your life."

At dinner things were back to normal and the conversation was light among their friends as it usually was. That is until Josie came up behind Cain and started massaging his shoulders.

"You are so damn sexy I can hardly stand it," she whispered discreetly in his ear.

Her breath dancing across his ear and the smell of her perfume nearly drove him wild. All sorts of demons were at war inside him as he looked up and ran head-on into Jon's knowing glare. He felt uneasy as if Jon was staring right into his soul. Cain was the first to look away.

"Not now, Josie," he said quietly as he reached back and gently removed her hands from his shoulders.

Jon got up and left. Cain glanced around the table and exhaled uncomfortably.

"I'll see you later," he announced as he got up to follow his friend.

He had to run, but he finally overtook Jon.

"You know," said Cain, "I already have a mother."

"Yeah," ranted Jon, " and it must be one hell of a frustrating job."

"What happened to not saying another word because it's my life? You're back on the soap box, Jon!"

"I said I wasn't going to say any more, but I don't have to sit there and watch you make a fool of yourself. *Not now, Josie*. When? Later?"

"I already told you, I don't want anything from her. It's too weird."

"And the rest of this isn't?"

"What's wrong? Are you jealous because she's paying more attention to me than she is to you?"

"Oh, yeah, right. That'll be the day."

"Well, that's how you're acting. What do you want me to do? Pretend she's not around?"

"For the last time—you're going to get busted. You're playing right into their hands, and that dumbfuck, Josie, is too stupid to realize that she's making it easy for them. Look around the next time you're with her. Every fucking screw has his eye on you two. They try to pretend they don't, but they're bad actors and it's way obvious. They're itching for you to bite. They have wet dreams about promotions and who's going to bring you down and serve you up to Sam Willet."

"Okay."

"Okay, nothing. Tell her to stop touching you and treating you like some kind of a toy, or they're going to start filling in the blanks and making things up. And enough people have seen what's going on."

"Okay."

"You've been here long enough to know that they're not beyond setting you up if it suits their purposes."

140

"What do you want me to say?" smiled Cain. "Okay. I'll tell her she has to stay an arm's length away. Is that good?"

"It's better, but you'd be better off telling her to get lost."

"But I like being with her. We have a lot of the same interests."

"Fine," said Jon as they got to their cells. "It's your ass. I'll see you in the morning."

"It's damn hot out," said Josie some months later as she and Cain walked out in the yard.

"Yeah," sighed Cain. "I can't believe that next month I'll be here for two years. What a goddam waste of life. Perfectly good years I'll never get back. And still a lot more to go."

"I can't imagine what it would be like to actually have something to live for on the outside. This is more home to me than any place I ever lived. Where's Jon?"

"He said he'll be out in a while."

Cain squinted into the hot July sunshine as he watched a baseball game taking place across the yard. His mind drifted back to a simpler time, and his body ached to get into the game.

"You like baseball?" Josie asked as she read the longing on his face.

"Yeah," he sighed. "I love baseball. I used to play—in school."

"Why don't you see if you can get in the game? I'm sure they could always use another player—especially if you're any good."

"I'm probably real rusty. It's been a long time."

"You know they have a team that travels. You have to be out of A Unit, though, in order to leave the grounds. No white-stripers allowed."

"Well, I'm hoping to be out of A Unit before too much longer. Just about this time next year, I'll be eligible for a transfer. So, who knows, maybe next year I'll play baseball again. Maybe I will."

Cain took off his shirt, which was soaked with perspiration from a hard day's work. The sun though very hot felt good on his bare skin. He was already bronzed from hours outdoors in the sun. His sun-streaked hair played lazily across his forehead as his intense blue-green eyes stole one more peek at the baseball game. Josie began to reach across and rub Cain's bare back. She felt his muscles stiffen almost immediately.

"I'm sorry," she said as she withdrew her hand. "Sometimes I just forget. You're incredibly gorgeous."

"I thought we had an understanding."

"We do. I'm sorry."

"You're a good friend, but I'm not comfortable with anything more than that."

"And Jon's probably right."

"It goes beyond what Jon says. It's just not me. But sometimes you confuse me, and . . ."

"Don't worry, I understand."

"There's a shady spot over there. Let's go sit down, and I'll go buy us some ice cream."

They found a premium spot in the shade, and Josie sat down to save their place. Cain threw his shirt on the ground next to her and went over to the commissary cart to buy the ice cream. As he turned to go back, he saw Josie engaged in heated discussion with another inmate. Quickly he returned to Josie.

"Farrell," said the ornery inmate, "tell this faggot to move over and make room. I want out of the sun, and there's plenty of room here for all of us."

"Get lost, Bentley," said Cain. "There's hardly enough shade for us, and we were here first."

"I'm not leaving, so move your sweet ass, fag boy," persisted Bentley.

Josie looked up helplessly at Cain. She saw his body harden as anger brewed.

"It's okay," she said hoping to avoid trouble. "I was about to go in anyway. Come on, Cain, walk me to the door."

"Yeah, Farrell, walk your whore to the door and whisper sweet nothings in her ear. What do you see in this freak, anyway? You could do better."

That was it. The buttons had been pushed. The rocket had been launched. There was no turning back. Cain dropped the ice cream bars on the ground and lunged at Bentley with the fury of a charging bull, taking him to the ground. They rolled savagely, each getting in solid punches. Other inmates gathered around, cheering and reveling in the action. Tears sprang to Josie's eyes as she grabbed Cain's shirt and stood up. Hugging his shirt close to her, she wished there were some way to get him out of there. But it was already too late. Guards came from all directions, elbowing and clawing their way through the gathering crowd.

Two of them grabbed Cain who was still kicking and struggling on pure adrenaline. They dragged him back away from Bentley who was older and showing signs of his age.

"Okay, Farrell," snarled a guard, "your choice—calm down or we beat the shit out of you."

Cain's spirit was not so easily tamed, so the guards cuffed him behind his back and led him away with Bentley. His nose was bleeding and running down his face, dropping into little rivulets on his bare chest.

By the time they got upstairs to the Captain of the Guard, Cain had calmed down. In the Captain's outside office, the guards removed the handcuffs and told him to sit down. Bentley was already seated across the office. Cain purposely avoided all eye contact and stared down at his hands. Blood continued to drip onto his chest. He sniffed it back, but to no avail. The Captain's secretary walked over to him with a handful of tissues.

He looked up at her with suspicious eyes. He had learned to never completely trust anyone at Maddox. He tentatively reached up and accepted the Kleenex.

"Thanks," he said as he dropped his head back and held the tissues up to his nose.

The secretary's intercom buzzed, and they were told to enter. They stood side-by-side in front of the Captain's desk—two sweating, bleeding statues. This was no court of law; they both knew that. They had no rights here; no one wanted to hear their stories. That was probably because there were no stories to tell; the Captain of the Guard knew that. No matter what bad blood or monstrous atrocities went down between inmates, it didn't even come close to the hatred they all felt toward the system that held them captive. They fought among themselves, they stole from one another, they preyed on the weak, but they **never** informed on one another. The inmates had their own system of justice by which they lived. They took care of their own, one way or another. The Captain of the Guard was there to punish, and each man was expected to take his punishment without a word, regardless of circumstances or degree of guilt. The worst offense inside the walls of Maddox was to "rat" on another inmate. Lives were taken because of finger pointing and cowardly whinings of innocence.

"This will be short, but I hope painful," said the Captain. "I want each of your privilege cards on my desk right now."

Bentley reached in his pocket and put the card symbolizing his small amount of freedom on the Captain's desk. The Captain shifted his eyes impatiently over to Cain.

"It's in my shirt—outside," he said without having to be asked.

"What the fuck, Farrell!" ranted the Captain. "Don't you know you're to have that card on your person every minute you're out of your cell?"

"It's hot. I took off my shirt. I didn't think."

"Get his shirt," the Captain ordered one of the guards. Then he turned back to the two inmates. "You'll have lots of time to think over the next two days—both of you—while you're doing hard labor on the Rock. And when you're not working, you're on high restriction in your cells. In other words, you're allowed to breathe—that's all."

Cain clenched his teeth as the punishment was announced, but he showed no signs of cowering. He stood his full height, his shoulders square. Reaching up with the back of his hand, he wiped at his nose, which was still bleeding a little.

"Do you need a doctor?" the Captain asked.

"No."

The Captain told one of the guards to escort Bentley back to his cell and see that he was put on restriction. Then he turned back and regarded Cain. There was something about the proud, young man before him that unnerved him. It was much easier dealing with violence than it was dealing with pride. He also sensed it would be better not to get into a verbal confrontation with him if he wanted to maintain an upper hand.

Moments later the guard returned and handed him his shirt. Cain fumbled through the pockets and found his privilege card. Keeping his reluctance internalized, he laid it on the desk in front of him.

"You realize I could send you down to Solitary for not having this on you?" said the Captain.

Cain eyed him through narrow, angry slits.

"It was hot," Cain said sullenly.

"Well, don't let it happen again."

*Get fucked!*

"Go back to your cell and get plenty of rest," said the Captain accurately reading the message in Cain's eyes and deciding it was best to end this discussion. "You're going to need it. And put your shirt on and tuck it in."

A guard followed him back to his cell for while he was on restriction, he wouldn't be allowed out of his cell without a guard. The switch was pulled so his cell door would not open with the rest, and they hung a large, red-lettered sign—RESTRICTED—on his door. That meant the commissary cart with cold drinks and snacks wouldn't stop, nor would the hot water cart. No one was allowed to even stop and talk to him without fear of reprisal from the Captain of the Guard. He was now an outcast in the society of outcasts. He took his shirt off and threw it angrily across the cell. Then he did the best he could to wash himself up. At least in mid July, the cold water felt good. He took off his boots and sat back on his bed against the wall with his knees drawn up to his chest. He was too angry to do anything else. He just sat and stared at the wall in front of him.

It was a while later when his door unexpectedly rolled opened. Cain turned his head to see what was going on. Victoria Doleman walked into the cell.

"Mind if I sit down?" she asked.

Cain shrugged. She sat on the stool next to his table and glanced at the untouched dinner. The cellblock was quiet since the other inmates were already down at dinner.

"You're dinner's getting cold."

"I'm not hungry."

"I see." She hesitated. "I heard about the trouble you're in."

"What do you want me to say?"

"You know this is not going to look good in your file when they review it for transfer to B Unit."

"I figured."

"Cain, I'm not here to scold you or make you feel worse."

"That's good."

"You're not being very cooperative."

"No. I don't feel very cooperative. I already know I'm an idiot. I don't need anyone else reminding me."

"That's not why I'm here."

"No? Then why are you here?" Sweat rolled down his temples and onto his cheeks. "If I were you, I'd be in my air-conditioned car driving as far away from this dump as possible. I'm not in the mood for a lecture."

"Come on, you know me better than that."

Another disinterested shrug.

"Is this thing over with you and Bentley?"

"Yeah. I don't even remember what it was about."

"I'm serious, Cain. It's not going to erupt again in the cafeteria or in the yard, is it?"

"No. Now go home. I'm ready to go to bed because they're getting me up early."

"It's going to be a very hard two days."

"Oh, I have no illusions along those lines."

"And you'll hold your temper—and your tongue?"

"Yes, ma'am. Now go home."

"I thought you'd be more receptive. I'm about the only person in the world, besides the guards, who can talk to you."

"I don't really . . . " He stopped before he said *give a shit.* After all, she was only doing her job.

"What's going on with you and Josie?"

He sighed, expelling some of the building steam that was about to blow the top of his head right off.

"I'm really getting tired of answering that question."

"Well?"

"I don't think that's any of your business—or anyone else's. That's my usual answer."

"I'm trying to keep you out of the big trouble that that relationship can bring you."

"Then you have nothing to worry about. Please. It's damn hot in here, and I feel like shit. I just want to strip off the rest of my clothes and go to bed."

"All right," she relented. "We'll talk later."

"Not about Josie," he said as he poked his left index finger emphatically in her direction.

"I'll see you later," she said as she got up and approached the door. "Just a few words of advice about tomorrow. Leave the attitude here. Swallow your pride and do what you're told. It won't be easy, but you'll survive, and it'll be over in two days."

"Fine," he said hoping to satisfy her so she'd leave.

She sighed and shook her head. Reaching across, she placed her opened hand gently on his cheek. He didn't miss the motherly look in her eye.

"Take care," she said. "And don't give them cause to punish you any further."

Guilt and loneliness overwhelmed him, and he couldn't respond. He wanted his own mother. He could only stare back at the wall ahead of him as she walked out. Seconds later the door rolled shut with an echoing bang.

In the morning when the guard woke him a half-hour earlier than usual, he was lying in a sea of perspiration. The air in the cell was oppressive and stale. He hated summer at Maddox more than any other time of the year. Trying to coax some life back into his body, he splashed cold water on his face. Then he dressed and prepared to take on the Rock. What a life.

There were four other men joining him and Bentley on the punishment detail. Each was seated at his own table for breakfast as the guard laid down the law of the day.

"There is to be **NO** talking at all during the day unless you're answering one of the guards," said Mueller, the guard in charge. "You're not to interact with one another for any reason. If you remember that and you work your ass off, you won't have a problem. Any one who screws up buys himself another day on the Rock. The quarry is down the road a bit, so we have to leave the prison grounds. There's a transport truck and chains waiting outside the door here, so finish eating and we'll be on our way."

When they had finished eating, Mueller was joined by a second guard, Marge Clintock, Large Marge as she was more commonly known among the inmates. She was a huge woman with broad shoulders and hips and a husky demeanor. She outweighed many of the men and could probably take most of them on in a hand-to-hand scuffle.

The two guards quickly frisked and cuffed the six inmates. Mueller then ordered them to climb up into the open-topped military transport truck. As Cain climbed in, he noticed that each person's place was marked by a pair of leg irons securely bolted to the floor by the center link of the chain. Trying not to think about it, he took his place and squinted up at the cloudless summer sky. Then Clintock came along and snapped the irons shut around each of his ankles. He was thankful for the high-top work boots he wore, for she was none too gentle.

"All right," said Mueller after everyone was secured, "rest assured that neither Clintock nor myself have keys to the hardware you're wearing. They are at the quarry. When we safely lock the stockade, you'll be unlocked."

Cain stared ahead between the heads of the two men sitting across from him. He tried to avoid the thought of an accident and being tethered to the truck by his ankles with no one able to release him. Marge Clintock sent the thought fleeing from his mind as she climbed onto the back of the truck and sent it rocking and rolling. Cain thought for sure that the whole truck was about to go over on its side as she dropped herself onto the bench in preparation for the ride. Mueller took his place in the cab at the driver's seat.

"Okay, boys," said Marge, "sit back and enjoy the ride."

The ride was bumpy across a dirt road. Though he couldn't move his feet very far apart, Cain was able to spread his knees so he could reach down with his hands and hold onto the seat between his legs. The truck kicked up a lot of dirt and dust as it wended its way across the thankfully not too far distance to the quarry.

Work on the Rock was hard, indeed, and Cain was thankful for his youth and fitness. There were large rocks and boulders that needed to be broken up and loaded onto waiting trucks. As the morning progressed and the sun became more and more unforgiving, Cain took off his shirt.

"Whoa," sighed Marge to Mueller from their shady digs over by the guard station, "he is just way too gorgeous. Way, way too gorgeous."

Mueller laughed. "Down, girl. He's a rapist, you know."

"Now that totally doesn't make sense. I would think if there was anyone in this world that would be a total failure as a rapist, it would be that young man. I mean, you'd think girls would just chase him around . . . begging."

Mueller laughed once again. "I guess you don't understand the true nature of rape."

"I guess not," she said dreamily eyeing Cain.

Sweat kept running down his face and into his eyes, so he took a bandanna out of his hip pocked, twisted it a few times, and tied it around his forehead under his shock of sandy hair. He was thankful for the break when it was announced at 10:00. There was no shade except over by the guard shack, so Cain gave up any hope of getting relief from the sun. Instead he walked over to where his shirt was and sat on the ground. He took out a cigarette and lit it. He was breathing heavily and his face was flushed from the hard work and sunshine as he put the cigarette in his mouth and took off his boot to empty out a stone. As he was about to put the boot back on, he saw the shiny shoes of the guard standing next to him. He looked up to see Marge Clintock smiling at him.

"Water?" She asked offering him a bottle of water.

"Thanks," he said taking the cigarette from his lips and laying it on the ground next to him.

As he reached for the bottle of water, she noticed the scraped knuckles on his dirty hands.

The water tasted more refreshing than anything he had ever drunk before. He saved a little to pour on the back of his neck. As he finished his cigarette, he scanned the area where the other men were scattered. A few of them looked half dead already, and he wondered how they were ever going to make it through the day. Bentley caught his gaze, and they locked onto each other for a few seconds. Neither one of them seemed to remember or care what their quarrel had been about.

After ten minutes rest they were ordered back to work. Cain noticed fatigue setting in as the morning progressed. His hands more than anything were taking a beating. Blisters were forming on his fingers and palms while the backs of his hands were scraped and cut. Sweat rolled down his back and chest, streaking his dirty skin and soaking the waste band of his jeans. The sun was relentless, and Cain made a mental note to bring one of his baseball caps the next day.

At noon they were all thankful when Mueller mercifully called a lunch break. Cain slipped his shirt on, but didn't button it. Just as he was about to walk over to where Mueller and the others were gathering, the guard stopped him.

"Farrell," he called, "you stay over there by yourself."

Cain looked over at the others and then to Mueller.

"Why?"

"Because I said so, and because I don't want no fights breaking out. It's kind of your thing lately, ain't it? I mean, that's why you're here. So sit your ass over there away from temptation."

Cain looked over at Bentley who gave him a puzzled shrug. There was no sense arguing. He knew he'd never win, and he couldn't talk to anyone anyway, so it wasn't worth the risk. He just didn't like being singled out.

Lunch consisted of two pieces of ham and a piece of cheese on two slices of less than fresh bread, three carrot sticks, and water. When Cain finished, he lit up a cigarette and daydreamed about beaches, sand, and girls in bikinis. Right that very minute under the same sun, people were actually enjoying such things. Propping his forearms on his raised knees, he stared into the rock-hard ground as a vision of a refreshing beach materialized before him. He could feel the fun he used to have. That feeling was still there inside him. He was so swept up by it that a bittersweet smile crossed his lips.

"Having a good time, are you?"

Cain jumped back to reality, his heart racing from the sudden, unexpected intrusion. He looked up to see Mueller standing over him.

"What?" he asked still feeling confused.

"You seem to be enjoying yourself. Maybe I'm not working you hard enough."

"I was daydreaming. That's not allowed?"

"Are you back-talking me, boy?"

"No," answered Cain looking down at the ground and stifling the string of obscenities that were ready to burst forth.

"Well, that's good, because I'm in charge, and you ain't nothing but shit. And don't you forget it."

"I won't," said Cain in an icy cold tone that stood out in contrast to the sweltering day. He looked up and caught Mueller right in the eye. "I won't ever forget that you said that to me. Don't worry."

Realizing he had lost control of the conversation, Mueller made a hasty retreat. Marge Clintock was laughing when he returned to the guard's shack.

"I'd have to say he won that round," she teased. "And I also wouldn't turn my back on him if I were you."

"Shut up."

After they got back to work after lunch, everyone was moving much slower. Cain caught sight of the man nearest him who had been struggling most of the day. As the man rocked unsteadily, Cain stopped to watch and be sure he was all right.

"Farrell," called Mueller, "get back to work—NOW!"

Not wanting to push his luck with Mueller, Cain hesitantly started back to work. It was only a matter of minutes later, though, that the man went down on one knee and fell forward. Cain dropped his hammer and ran to the man.

"Are you okay?" he asked as he helped him to sit down.

The man, who was nearly greenish in color, nodded his head.

"Farrell, you just bought yourself another day on the Rock," screamed Mueller.

"FUCK YOU!!! GET OVER HERE!!!" was Cain's irritated reply.

Marge Clintock kept a watchful eye on the others as Mueller ran to the fallen man.

"Move away from him," he told Cain.

"He needs help!"

"I can see that; move away from him."

Knowing that Mueller didn't trust them and wouldn't approach the man while he was there, Cain moved aside. He knew the guard up in the tower had a rifle, and he was always careful not to make the armed guards edgy or defensive. Nothing worried him more about being at Maddox than the thought that one of the armed guards would go off the deep end or panic during some inmate unrest and start shooting into a crowd.

Marge Clintock moved in to get the others back to work while Mueller tended to the sick man. Cain moved slowly, keeping a concerned eye on the man. Mueller got him up and helped him over to the guard shack where there was shade and cool water.

After he got the man taken care of, Mueller went back to Cain.

"I got you down to come back tomorrow and Friday, too," he said.

Cain kept working without looking up.

"You hear me?" Mueller asked.

"Yeah, I hear you."

"And you're not going to whine?"

Cain stopped and glared at him through weary, but willful eyes.

"No," he said. "You've made up your mind. You're an asshole, and I'd rather not waste my energy." Without waiting for a reply, he went back to work.

Once again Mueller was taken aback. He wasn't used to verbal chess, and it was not his strong suite.

"Watch your step, hotshot," he said as he walked away.

Cain let him have the last word and continued on as if he hadn't heard. Underneath his calm exterior, however, he was seething, but he was determined not to let Mueller know. There was nothing to be gained by unleashing the rampage that was rearing up inside him. He reminded himself over and over again that Mueller was baiting him and waiting for him to lose his temper. He was determined not to give him that satisfaction. Instead he attacked the rock with renewed venom, picturing Mueller's face at the center of the bull's eye of each strike. That gave him a great deal of pleasure and helped him deal with the anger and frustration he was feeling. Everyone would be so proud of him.

And then finally the excruciatingly long day came to an end. Cain nearly dropped to his knees in thanksgiving and could not even allow himself to think of two more days of this hell. He walked over to where his shirt was and put it on, not bothering to even button it. As he went to Mueller to be fitted with handcuffs for the trip back, the guard gave him a once-over look of disapproval.

"Button your shirt and tuck it in," he barked.

Cain scanned the group of inmates. Only two others had their shirts tucked in. It was obvious that he was playing Cinderella to Mueller's wicked stepmother. Without taking his eyes off Mueller's face, he buttoned the shirt, tucked it in, and presented his wrists for the cuffs. Mueller was happy for an excuse to be the first to break eye contact as he looked down and clamped on the cuffs. When he finished and looked up, Cain was still glaring at him.

"Get on the truck," the guard snapped.

When they got back to Maddox, they were allowed to take a shower, and each was given a navy blue jumpsuit to put on over his bare skin and told to slip his bare feet into his work boots. Then just as they had eaten breakfast, they were each seated at a different table in the cafeteria and served an early dinner. It was barely 4:30, but Cain was starving. The lunch he had eaten was hardly enough, and he knew this would be all he'd get until breakfast.

After they were finished, guards escorted each back to his cell. Mueller hooked up with Cain, much to Marge Clintock's and Cain's chagrin. All the way up to the cell, Mueller went on and on about the next day and how it was supposed to be even hotter and more humid.

His words were wasted on Cain, though, because he was way too exhausted to care. He couldn't wait to get to his cell and lay down. Each step was becoming an effort, especially considering his sockless, booted feet. When they got there, Mueller stepped aside and let Cain enter.

"Strip," the guard said matter-of-factly. "I need the coveralls back."

Cain let out a weary, cynical laugh.

"You never give up, do you?" He said and then undid the jumpsuit, slid it over his sun-sore shoulders and back, and let it drop to the floor.

Sliding his bare feet out of his work boots and each pant leg at the same time, he reached out with his left foot and kicked the jumpsuit out the door of the cell and into the hall where Mueller was standing. Then without putting on any clothes, he eased his naked body facedown onto his bed, caressing his pillow beneath his aching head. He only heard the cell door roll shut, after that he fell into an abyss of exhausted sleep.

His rest was to be short-lived, however, as Marge Clintock made her way up to the tier while the rest of the cellblock was out at dinner.

"What brings you up here?" the tier guard asked her.

"Cain Farrell. He's here, isn't he?"

"Yeah, he's here, but he's out cold. I've never seen anyone who can sleep like he can. I couldn't even wake him for the count."

She smiled. "He worked hard today. I hate to wake him, but I need to talk to him. What number's he in?"

"34, but I wouldn't count on having an intelligible two-sided conversation with him."

"Well, I have to try. This is the only opportunity I'll have before he goes back out to the Rock tomorrow."

"Are you shy? He don't have a stitch of clothes on."

An amused smile crossed her face.

"Now that has to be a dream come true!"

She walked down the tier until she came to his cell. The oppressive heat made her wonder how these men ever existed in A Unit during the summer. Looking in on him, she was overwhelmed by his innocent, good looks as he slept—still on his stomach, clutching his pillow. The pillowcase and the sheet underneath him were soaked with perspiration. His body glistened with moisture from head to toe, and his hair clung in soft ringlets to his forehead. She didn't have to ask why he didn't have any clothes on.

"Can't you get him a fan?" she asked the tier guard who had accompanied her.

"Our fans are few and far between. Besides, he's on restriction, so he don't get nothing. I'm not even sure you should be here talking to him."

"It won't take long," she said, "and it is important."

"Hey, Farrell," called the tier guard through the bars. "Wake up; you got a visitor."

Nothing.

"Come on," coaxed the guard running his nightstick back and forth along the bars only inches from Cain's head. That caused him to moan and stir. "Wake up. You got a visitor."

"What the hell," sighed Cain sleepily as he raised his head up. He had trouble keeping his eyes opened, and when they were opened he could barely focus. He propped himself up on his forearms. "What's wrong? It can't be morning."

He rubbed his face and squinted up at Clintock. Cursing under his breath, he dropped his head back on his pillow.

"Come on, now," said the tier guard, "is that any way to greet your visitor? You're not allowed many visitors, you'd better be nice to the ones you have." He smiled at Marge Clintock. "He's all yours."

She watched the other guard walk back down the hall. Then she turned back to Cain.

"Do you want to get dressed?"

"Yeah," he said as if the answer were so obvious the question need never have been asked.

She turned and walked a few steps down the hall while he got up and slipped on a pair of lightweight sweatpants. He went to the sink and splashed some cold water on his face. Then drying himself off with the towel, he walked over to the bars.

"What's up?" he asked.

"I wanted to talk to you about Mueller," she said coming back to the bars.

She couldn't stop her eyes from running the length of his body and back.

"You woke me up for that?" he said sitting on his bed Indian-style and leaning his bare back against the cool cement wall. "What time is it?"

"5:20."

"Christ," he sighed, his voice still heavy with sleep. He dropped his head back against the wall. "What about Mueller?"

"Do you know there's unofficial word out among the guards about you?"

"I've heard some sort of shit. Why?"

"Well, Mueller's out after a promotion at your expense. I just wanted to tell you to watch out for him. He's not going to let up. I just thought if you knew, it might help you to tolerate him a little more. I don't think it's fair that he holds all the cards, so I just wanted to come and warn you."

He was silent as his eyes searched her face.

"Okay," he said not comfortable with trusting her completely. "I'm warned."

"I'm not kidding," she insisted.

"No, I didn't think you were. I know his type. Is that all?"

She was a little miffed that he wasn't more appreciative and in her debt, so to speak.

"Just watch yourself," she said.

Just then the tier guard came down.

"The crew's coming back from dinner," he said. "I need to stand here and baby-sit so no one stops to talk to our boy here."

"Yeah," said Marge, "I need to get going anyway." She hesitated and winked at him. "I hope to see more of you in the future." She laughed and walked away. The innuendo did not go unnoticed by Cain or the guard.

"Boy, she likes you," laughed the other guard.

"You're all pigs," sneered Cain.

He was going to lie down again, but he decided to wait a few minutes to see if he could catch a glimpse of Jon and get his attention. He was down to his last half pack of cigarettes, and he wouldn't be able to get to the commissary to buy any until Saturday. That was nearly three days away.

As if he could read Cain's mind, Jon lingered outside Cain's cell just passed the guard so he could look in. He winked and smiled. Cain put his fingers to his mouth as if he was smoking, but he held no cigarette. Jon got the message.

"Come on, Harrison, move along," ordered the guard. "You don't want to get your ass locked-in, too."

"Oh, no, sir," mocked Jon with a smile and a nod of his head.

The next day on the Rock was every bit as bad as the first; actually it was worse because the day began with the cuts and blisters that had been cultivated the day before. Besides Cain and Bentley, there was only one other man. Mueller made Cain eat his lunch off to the side away from everyone else again, but Cain paid little mind to it. He spent the day being a model prisoner, and that aggravated Mueller more than anything did.

He also made a point of being distant with Clintock. Here he had no rights, and sexual harassment was just another fact of life over which he had no control. He still wasn't quite sure what her motives were in coming to him about Mueller, but he was sure he didn't need, nor did he want, her as a friend. He didn't like the idea of being indebted to anyone who expressed a desire to "see more of him" after walking in on him and catching him bare-assed and uncovered in bed. He wondered how long she had been standing outside his cell before they woke him up. The thought sent a chill up his spine in spite of the 94° temperature.

By the end of the day, he could barely hold on to the tools he was working with. His hands throbbed and burned with blisters and tiny cuts. He was tired, and he felt ornery. But more than anything, he was weary of the segregation. He wanted to be with his friends again. He wanted to talk with people. He wanted the commissary cart to stop at his cell in the evenings so he could buy cigarettes or a cold can of Coke. Everyone and everything was within his grasp, but totally off limits to him. Thinking of putting in another day of all this nonsense because of Mueller's whim turned his mood even blacker. He looked at Bentley who was all but lying on the ground with exhaustion and envied him the fact that he was about through with this detail. He could feel the frustration building up inside him, and he thought it best not to dwell on it. He made a mental note never to fight again, and then went on pounding at unyielding rock.

Finally it was time to quit. Handcuffs in place, Cain was maneuvering his way onto the truck when Mueller gave him a shove with the sole of his shoe. He fell forward, scraping his forearms and the sides of his cuffed hands on the floor of the truck. With the agility and quickness of a gazelle, he righted himself and turned on Mueller.

"You motherfucker!!!" he yelled in a rage. "Don't ever do that again!"

Mueller who had not expected open defiance fought to mask his surprise.

"Or else what?" he foolishly challenged.

"Or else . . ."

Marge Clintock quickly stepped between the two and cut Cain off.

"That's enough," she warned before he could finish his threat. "Sit down."

He hesitated as he glared at Mueller, but then he moved to his seat. She shackled his feet, and they were on their way. Cain hung onto the bench seat between his legs and hung his head down until his chin touched his chest. His shock of sandy, sun-streaked hair dropped down and shielded the top part of his face. As Marge Clintock looked over at him, she saw two or three angry tears drop down onto his shackled wrists. Bentley and the third man respected his privacy and stared out the back of the truck.

When they got back to the prison, Clintock waited with Cain while Mueller unlocked the other two men and took them inside. As she unchained his feet, he sat upright for the first time. His eyes were moist, and absent tears had left telltale tracks through the sweat and dirt on his face. She reached up to place a comforting hand on his cheek, but he pulled his head away from her.

"Don't," he said in an even, warning tone.

"Let's go," she said with authority as she attempted to cover up her embarrassment.

After he showered and ate in silence with the others, she walked with him up to his cell. She made attempts at conversation, but he barely spoke. When they got to his tier, the guard on duty gave him an assignment from the teacher of the class he was taking. She wanted to be sure Cain didn't fall behind while he was missing class.

When they got down to his cell, Cain went inside and put his papers on his table. Then he turned to Clintock. He was tired and miserable, but the expression on his face still loudly spoke his mind. *Get lost, pig!* She clearly understood, but raised a challenging eyebrow as she stood her ground. He started to unbutton the jumpsuit, but just as he got to the buttons below his waste, he turned and walked to the back of the cell. It didn't offer much privacy, but with his back to her, he slid out of the coveralls and pulled his sweat pants up over his narrow hips. Tying the drawstring on the sweats, he bent over and grabbed the coveralls that Clintock was waiting for. Angrily he whipped them at her and hit her square in her buxom-y chest. She got his message, but she shrugged her shoulders with a smile.

"I can't help myself," she laughed. "You have such a NICE ass!"

It wasn't until after she was gone that he saw the carton of cigarettes that Jon had tossed through his bars and onto his bed. That helped his state of mind somewhat. At least now he didn't have to worry about trying to make the end of his pack last until Saturday. He was bone tired, but he wanted to work on his assignments to keep up with his class. He knew if he tried to sleep first, he'd never wake up until morning and the work wouldn't get done.

He pulled out his stool and sat down at the table. Putting his glasses on, he leaned over the work and tried to concentrate. The stifling heat made it hard to breathe let alone focus his attention. He got up and wet a towel with cold water. Then wringing it out, he draped it over his bare shoulders and sat down.

Suddenly his door rolled opened. The rest of the tier was still at dinner. There was no reason for them to open his cell anyway. He swung around to check it out and got the shock of his life. The warden was approaching his cell followed closely by Sam Willet. Cain dropped his pen and stood up.

"Mind if we come in?" the warden asked as the guard came down the hall to officially stand guard over Cain's distinguished visitors.

Cain stood speechless and stunned as the two men entered the tiny cell; he felt imposed on, and he grew angrier by the second. Sam Willet was busy looking around at every inch of the cell. Cain watched him, seething at the thought of this man walking in on him. The exhaustion and frustration of the day helped whip him to a senseless frenzy, but his curiosity put his anger at bay for the time being.

"You remember Sam Willet," said the warden.

"You've grown," commented Sam.

"What the hell is going on?" asked Cain in an even, inhospitable tone as he took off his glasses and put them on his table.

"I needed to come here," said Sam. "My family has been in such a shambles for over two years because of you. I needed to come and see for myself that you were being punished enough."

Cain laughed and shook his head incredulously.

"Um, I think I want to see my lawyer," he said. "Is this legal?"

"Screw legality," stormed Willet. "You gave up your rights when you raped my daughter. She still has nightmares and emotional hang-ups from it. Do you have any idea what that must be like?!"

"Yes!!!" hollered Cain losing control and letting his frenetic rage take over. "I have more than an idea. I was eighteen years old. It happened right here. I think about it every night when I go to bed. I know more about rape than your daughter will ever know."

"Are you calling my daughter a liar?!"

"She lied about me! She put me here, and believe me because of it I have plenty of nightmares and emotional hang-ups myself!"

"Listen, Farrell, you're nothing but a two-bit rapist. I was hoping that by now you'd at least show a little remorse, and I could reconcile myself with what has happened. But I see you haven't changed a bit. Do you realize that I have the power to petition that you stay in this dump for the full twelve years you were sentenced to? This display of temper of yours could be the biggest mistake you've ever made!"

**"Wrong!!!"** yelled Cain charging at the red cloth Willet was waving. **"Fucking your daughter was the biggest mistake I ever made!!! Now get the hell out of here!!! I don't have to take this!!! GET HIM THE HELL OUT OF HERE!!!"**

The warden grabbed Willet by the arm and pulled him from the cell just as the guard, brandishing his nightstick, entered.

"Okay, Farrell," the guard said, "move back—to the window. Don't make any sudden moves. Just ease on back to the window, or I'll beat the shit out of you."

Cain was shaking with rage as he took a few small steps to the back of the cell by the window. The guard approached him as if he were a ferocious animal.

"Put your hand up and grab a bar on the window," he ordered.

Cain knew what was coming and wanted to scream at the top of his lungs. The guard quickly snapped one side of his handcuffs to Cain's wrist and the other side to a bar on the window. Even though he knew it wouldn't do any good, he wanted to yank and pull at the cuffs until he collapsed and didn't care anymore. He had had more than enough of this day. After the door was locked, Cain heard the guard asking after the well being of the warden and Sam Willet as they all walked away. Nobody seemed to care about him as bitter tears rushed from behind his eyes and a moan rose from his throat. He pressed his free hand over his mouth to hold back the sobs that were bursting forth as he stood staring out the window, feeling like the world had just ended.

Hours passed, and he didn't know how much longer he could stay on his feet. He had never been so tired, and it didn't help to have his bed so close by. He held onto the bars with both hands and laid his head on his arm. He was miserable and angry, and he couldn't stop the onslaught of tears that were burning down his face. His legs felt weak, and he wasn't sure how much longer they would support him. He was able to back up to the edge of his table and prop himself against it. It wasn't the most comfortable, but at least he had some support. He was just about to cave in when a guard finally came to set him free at about 10:00.

"Have you calmed down?" the guard asked.

Cain turned to look at him. His eyes were red and swollen, and he was very subdued.

"Yes," he answered through a sob in his throat.

As the guard unlocked Cain's wrist, he noticed the raw blisters and scrapes on his hands.

"This hasn't been your day, has it?"

"Just get out of here," he said softly.

"Sleep it off, you have an early day tomorrow."

"No shit," mumbled Cain as the guard left and locked the door.

He went to the sink and washed his face with cold water. His life was spinning out of control again. He could barely feel the ground beneath him as he made his way to the bed and lay down. His whole body ached, and his eyes burned from the bitter, angry tears he hadn't been able to hold back. He felt like he had sunk to a new depth of despair. He buried his face in his pillow and cried himself to sleep.

In the morning he was sitting on the edge of his bed when Mueller came up for him. The tier guard had awakened him earlier, and he went through the motions of washing, dressing, and brushing his teeth without even being aware of what he was doing. His eyes were bloodshot and red-rimmed, and the rest of his face wore the results of a night that was too hot, too short, and too stressful. His dreams had been nightmares that were intertwined and convoluted and, like most nightmares, made no sense. He felt anything but prepared for the day that lay ahead of him. He didn't want to fight with Mueller or put up with his abuse; he just wanted to get the day over. He was reserved and subdued when Mueller made his appearance.

"Come on, hero," said Mueller. "It's just you and me today."

Cain closed his eyes and prayed for strength. He said nothing as he stood up and waited for Mueller to unlock his door.

"Shit," said Mueller stepping aside to let him out, "you look like hell."

Cain gave him his best *fuck off* look, and walked wordlessly down the hall.

After breakfast Mueller chained Cain's feet and wrists and put him in the back seat of an official car. No need for the truck today.

"You're awful quiet today," said Mueller from over his shoulder as he drove to the quarry.

No answer.

"What is it?" asked Mueller. "Am I finally getting to you? Am I finally breaking that proud, stubborn spirit of yours?"

Cain was slouched back in the seat with his head leaning on the backrest. He stared aimlessly out the window and paid no attention to Mueller. He was trying desperately to rescue himself from the wreckage left behind by two days on the Rock and a visit from Sam Willet. He had no room for Mueller's taunts and jibes. He had to get himself back on track, but he had no idea of how to do it. His eyes burned, and already he felt exhausted. Somehow he had to get through this day.

He stood straight as Mueller unlocked him. Cain's composed and passive demeanor was somewhat throwing the guard off his game.

"There you go," said Mueller a little too enthusiastically. "That pile of rocks needs to be broken up and loaded onto the truck before we leave here tonight—even if we have to stay all night."

Cain looked at the huge pile of rocks and then back to Mueller. The guard shrugged.

"You're on your own," he continued. "Take as many breaks as you want for as long as you want, but we don't leave until this truck is loaded."

Cain surveyed the cloudless sky and then got to work. The pile of rocks was meant to be the mortal blow to his badly wounded spirit, but he was determined not to let that happen. He just prayed his strength and his raw hands would hold out and sustain him through the torturous day. He had to get his mind off Sam Willet and the horrendous meeting he had had with him the night before.

But it seemed that was all he could think about. He was afraid of the irreparable damage he may have done to his chances of an early parole. He should have learned by now that Sam Willet was hell-bent on his destruction and that he needn't offer him any fuel for his fire. The man was in control; what was Cain thinking of? But that was just it; he wasn't thinking. He was caught off guard after an exhausting and grueling day, and his emotions were running the show. The whole conversation flashed over and over again in front of him as he pounded rocks and tried in vain to forget.

He worked through most of the morning with only the briefest stops for water. He had not held back at all and yet the pile of rock seemed to be replenishing itself rather than diminishing. Finally Mueller called a break for lunch. Cain didn't want to stop, but the guard insisted. He even let him sit over in the shade provided by the guards' shack.

"Have you even said a word all day?" asked Mueller as Cain sat down and leaned back against the wall of the shack.

"No," said Cain uttering his first word of the day.

"What's up?" Mueller asked.

"What do you care? Besides, I thought silence was part of this whole fiasco."

"Yeah, well it's just you and me today, and I thought for sure I'd be getting a lot of grief from you."

Cain just looked at him in disgust and then went on eating his lunch. After he finished, he smoked a cigarette and got up to go back to work.

"You don't need to go back just yet. Relax a few minutes. You haven't had a break all day."

"You want me to get that pile done sometime before midnight?" asked Cain picking up a good-sized rock in his left hand and whipping it mercilessly at the truck in the distance. It hit its target with a pounding thud.

"Feel better now?" asked Mueller. Then he smiled. "I'm gonna have to write you up on damaging government property."

No smile from Cain. He was, however, secretly pleased and reassured that after over two years of not throwing a baseball he was right on target. He hadn't lost his touch—for all the good it would do him. He was amazed at how good it had felt to throw the rock and remember days when he was the king of the summer game. He realized he missed it even more than he had thought. Up to now the despair from the loss of that dream had kept him far away from any participation in the sport. But now as he worked, he remembered Josie telling him about the prison league and how he could be a part of it when he was in B Unit. Buoyed by the thought, he blocked out any possibility that this stint on the Rock was going to be a setback to his transfer out of A Unit. Instead he focused on next summer, and he decided to maybe join a pick-up game in the yard in the meantime.

That thought and the enthusiasm he gleaned from it got him through the early afternoon. At 3:30, however, he heard the horn blow at Maddox and he knew work was through for the day for everyone else. He looked at the pile of rock before him, and there was easily several hours more work ahead of him. Heat, humidity, and depression began taking their toll, and he had to stop. His face and unclothed upper body were moist and flushed bright red and covered with a film of dust and dirt. Sweat rolled and left streaks of mud. The top of his jeans were drenched in collected sweat, and though he wore heavy, cotton socks, his feet were sweaty and bore blisters much like those on his hands.

He couldn't let it get the better of him, and he forced himself to go on. By 6:00 he was beginning to see an end, but he wasn't sure how he'd ever get there. Youth and strength had long abandoned him, and he was working on pure willpower and determination. Even Mueller had to marvel at his spirit.

"Come on," said the guard a little after 6:00 as Cain kept dropping to one knee from exhaustion. "We can go back now. You've done enough."

"No!" said Cain stubbornly as he pulled away from Mueller's proffered hand and struggled to his feet once more. "I'm going to finish. This was a bum rap today, and we both know it; but I'm going to finish. I'm not going to have you coming around later and busting me for not finishing up. I'm almost through."

"I won't bust you for anything," assured Mueller as he once again tried to loosen the tool from Cain's grip and guide him toward the police car.

Cain became almost irrational as he struggled to pull away from Mueller.

"No! No, I don't trust you. Let me finish. This is what I get for trying to help a sick man; now let me finish."

Mueller sighed uncomfortably as he backed off. He knew Cain was right, and he was not pleased with himself at that moment. He was the one who had called all the shots and orchestrated this hell. Now he had no choice but to sit back and wait for it to be played out. Cain wouldn't let him cut short his folly and thereby soothe his conscience.

At 7:30, streaked in sweat and mud with exhausted tears burning in his eyes, Cain put the last of the rocks on the truck and dropped to his knees.

"Uncle," he said.

"Come on," said Mueller, "let's get out of here."

Cain laughed sarcastically as Mueller went through the ritual of putting on the chains.

"Where do you expect me to book to? I couldn't run anywhere if the devil himself were after me," he said wearily.

"It's just procedure," said Mueller.

"Yes, sir," mocked Cain with a grin.

"Come on, smart-ass, into the car. You just don't know when to keep your mouth shut, do you?"

"Before you complained I wasn't saying anything."

"That wasn't a complaint," said Mueller helping him into the car and shutting the door.

On the drive back Cain could barely keep his eyes opened. He put his head back against the seat and immediately fell into a state of semi-consciousness. Blurry visions filled his mind as his leaden eyelids succumbed to the exhaustion he felt. He was aware of Mueller's incessant chattering up in the front seat, but he had no idea what the irritating guard was saying. His body felt like it was filled with sand rather than muscle and bone as he became one with the car seat. The euphoria he experienced was short-lived, however, as Mueller was soon pulling at him to get out of the car.

"Get fucked," Cain moaned at him.

"End of the line," said Mueller. "We need to get you a shower and some food and lock you in for the night."

"Okay, okay," whined Cain still not totally awake as he yanked away from Mueller's grip and struggled to open his eyes.

The shower washed away some of the exhaustion with the dirt and sand, but he still ached with fatigue. Mueller gave him a few extra minutes in the shower as he stood with his hands on the wall and head bowed—letting the warm water flow over his back, soothing his aching muscles. Then with the towel wrapped loosely around his waist, he caught a clean jumpsuit that Mueller tossed to him.

"I called down to the kitchen, and they have dinner waiting for you," said Mueller as Cain got dressed. "They have people on duty all the time for guards who are on night duty. You have to behave yourself, though. These people are only used to dealing with guards; inmates make them nervous."

"Then don't take me down there," frowned Cain as he slipped his clean, bare feet into the dirty work boots. Mueller bent over and tied them for him. "Just take me back to my cell. I don't need to eat. God forbid I terrorize any civilians."

"No, I have to feed you."

"You make me sound like I'm two years old, or worse yet, an animal," complained Cain as he slogged across the locker room floor toward the door.

"You know what I mean. There're rules and regulations."

"Yeah, right," said Cain turning on him. "Like that was legal what you did to me today. How many hours was I out there? Twelve? Thirteen? I'm not stupid."

"You didn't say anything."

"Yeah, like that would've done me any good," said Cain.

"So, are you gonna turn me in?"

"Yeah, right," grunted Cain sarcastically. "Like this is grade school and you go to the principal to complain."

"You could go to your lawyer," said Mueller, testing the water.

"Relax. I'm not a crybaby. But don't ever underestimate me again . . . and don't ever call me shit again."

Cain was hungrier than he thought. Of course he hadn't eaten since noon, and it was now nearly 8:00 P.M. He put his weariness aside while he cleaned up the plate the cafeteria worker set in front of him. When he finished, he sat back in his chair to try and muster some strength. Suddenly the women tentatively approached him again with a plate of seconds. He looked her in the eye, and then shifted his gaze to Mueller.

"Go ahead," said the guard, "you're a growing boy."

161

"Thank you," he said accepting the plate. *See, we're not all Neanderthals.*

When Jon heard them coming down the tier, he jumped to his feet and went to the bars of his cell.

"Cain! Where the hell have you been?!"

Though he seemed to have gotten the upper hand on Mueller, Cain didn't want to press his luck so he said nothing. He merely looked at Jon.

"What's going on, Mueller?" insisted Jon. "He should have been back hours ago!"

"Shut up, Harrison," warned Mueller.

"Cain???"

Cain's expression screamed for understanding. *Just shut up and back off . . . we'll talk tomorrow.*

"What'd you do to him, Mueller?" Jon persisted.

"Nothing," the guard answered as Cain entered his cell. "He's fine, but you're really starting to annoy me."

Cain took off the coveralls and shoved them through the bars at Mueller.

"Get out of here," he said with an unmistakable hint of warning in his voice.

Mueller knew it was best not to push the issue with Cain. This was no scared, snot-nosed brat as he had once thought. Not only had he become street-smart, he was book-smart and that worried him more than anything did. Balling up the jumpsuit, he grunted and walked away.

Realizing more than ever that anyone could walk in on him at any time, Cain slipped on a pair of boxer shorts and eased himself onto his bed. He never believed the flimsy mattress and anemic pillow could feel so inviting. He didn't even notice the stifling heat. Once he closed his eyes, there was nothing that was going to wake him until he had slept himself out. He slept through the 9:45 count that night; the guard on duty gave up trying to wake him and just counted him present.

The next day was Saturday, and he slept through the morning horn and another count. Once again the duty guard was unable to get him to even stir, but he did remove the *RESTRICTED* sign from the front of his cell.

Jon stopped on his way to breakfast, but even he couldn't get a response from Cain. Smiling, he went on, figuring to see his friend later.

It was after 10:00 A.M. before he finally began to come back to life. He opened his eyes and felt relief wash over him as he realized it was Saturday and he was through with Mueller's detail. Feeling well rested and revived, he sat up and surveyed his ravaged hands. Then he walked to the window and looked out at the day. Reaching over to his table, he picked up his cigarettes and lit one. As he absently watched a baseball game out in the yard, a guard approached his cell.

"Get dressed," he said, "you have a visitor. I'll be back in five minutes to let you out."

Cain quickly went through the ritual of getting dressed and making himself presentable to visitors. He always liked visits, but today would be especially nice after spending the last three days restricted and incommunicado.

The guard returned his privilege card to him and unlocked the cell. Cain nearly flew down the halls on his way to the visitors' room. It felt good to be back to normal—or at least as normal as it got at Maddox. When he reached the door of the visitors' room, he quickly emptied his pockets as was procedure and let the guard frisk him. Then anxiously he returned his possessions to their rightful pockets, and the guard unlocked the door. He entered the room searching the crowd for a familiar face. That was when he froze in place. This familiar face was the last one he expected to ever see.

Jim caught sight of his tall, handsome, older brother before Cain saw him. He was amazed. Even though Matt was around to mirror Cain's growth and maturation, Jim couldn't get over how he was able to outshine his expectations. Only Cain could manage to look drop-dead good-looking and dashingly bred in the middle of a madhouse like Maddox. His clothes fit him perfectly; his hair fell seductively over his forehead and across his eyebrows; his eyes flashed just the right amount of self-assurance. He was even more exquisite and enviable than the day he had left home nearly two years ago—the last time Jim had seen him.

"What's up?" Cain asked tentatively as he approached his younger brother.

"Aren't you going to sit down?"

Cain stood silently for a long minute and then pulled up a chair across from his brother.

"Okay, I'm sitting. What's up?"

"I just came to see you."

Cain couldn't help but to laugh out loud.

"Am I on *Candid Camera* or something?"

"Cain, don't make this any harder than it already is."

"I'm sorry," said Cain sarcastically. "It's just that it's been two years without even so much as a card or letter from you, let alone an in-the-flesh-bigger-than-life sighting. Is your grandfather here?"

"No, but I am, and I'd like to set things straight between us."

Cain was taken aback.

"What's the catch?"

"No catch," said Jim. "I've grown up. We're brothers; we shouldn't fight the way we do—or did before you left."

Cain still couldn't believe what he was seeing and hearing.

"This is so out of left field," he said shaking his head. "Does Grandpa know you're here?"

"Yeah. I tried to get him to come, but . . ."

"No need to go on," laughed Cain. "That would have to be the conversion of the century. I'm not sure I even believe in God any more, let alone miracles."

"Cain, I'm sorry. I'm sorry for Grandpa, I'm sorry for my behavior, and I'm sorry for all of this." He gestured around the room. "You don't deserve any of it."

Cain leaned on the table and moved closer to Jim.

"All right," he said, "who are you, and what have you done with my brother?"

"You're not making this easy."

"No, I guess I'm not, but . . ."

"I understand things a lot better now than I did when I was younger. It's been too long since I've seen you. There was a time I thought I didn't care if I ever saw you again, but that's not true. Please, can we start fresh?"

Cain knitted his brows and stared intently at his brother.

"I'm at a loss for words."

"Well, that has to be a first," smiled Jim. "I'm not a kid any more, and I've missed you. It's that simple."

Cain sat back in his chair and tried to let this all sink in. He didn't know what to make of it, but he did know that it was time to drop the flippancy and make some sort of a sincere effort of his own.

"Thanks." He hesitated a minute while he collected his thoughts. "I've tried to pretend it didn't bother me, but if I was to be completely honest, it drove me crazy that we could never get along. And without getting into a discussion that could turn into an argument, I'm willing to take my share of the blame."

"Fair enough," said Jim. "Then we can be friends?"

"Yeah," Cain laughed, still incredulous. "This just blows my mind. I had no idea."

"I know. I took you by surprise, but I've been thinking about it for some time."

"Do Mom and Dad know you're here?"

"Actually, they do. They're here. They'll be up in a little while. They wanted to give us some time alone together first. Mom's ecstatic."

"No doubt," said Cain, still not sure how to talk to this brother.

"What happened to your hands?" Jim asked.

Cain looked at his throbbing hands.

"A little trouble I had to work off, but it's okay. How are things at home—just don't mention that old man to me."

Jim smiled as he went into a discussion of all the events that were of interest to Cain. They talked freely for a few minutes. Then Cain took over the conversation.

"Maybe you'll tell me . . . how's Joanne? No one else will even discuss her with me, and I find it as frustrating as hell."

"She's okay, I guess. I don't see her much, but I do see her once in a while."

"Does she ask about me?"

"She's dating someone else, Cain. Pretty seriously, I think. She never mentions you, but then she knows you and I never got along, so I wouldn't be the one she'd ask."

Cain exhaled the queasiness in his chest.

"God, if I could just get to her. If I could just talk to her."

"It's been a long time. Don't you think you should forget about her?"

"I'm still in love with her, Jim. Sometimes it just drives me crazy how much I love her. I want to jump out of my skin. How does she look?"

"Pretty much the same. She cut her hair. It's about chin length now. She's a little bit taller." He shrugged and then felt relief as he saw their parents walk up to them.

Cain lightly pounded his fist on the table, as he knew that was the end of all discussion about Joanne.

Later that day he went outside, still trying to dust out the cobwebs of the past three days. He couldn't figure out if he was angry with Mueller or if he felt sympathy for a grown man who was so driven to kiss-up to his superiors that he'd stoop to such levels. Anyway, it was over, and that was all he cared. He walked over to a large cyclone fence that separated the A Unit yard from that of B and C Units. On the other side a baseball game was going on between inmates at Maddox and a men's team from the outside. Cain was finding himself more and more attracted to baseball again; a passion that had been doused in cold water since his arrest and conviction. He loved the game; and even though he had long given up the dream of playing in the major leagues, he found he once again had a great longing to play. He wound his fingers through the wire openings in the fence as he lost himself on the other side. The difference in the two recreational areas was astounding. The B and C Units side had trees and benches, grass, picnic tables, and families. B and C Unit inmates could have visitors any day of the week, and their visitors could go outside with them. They weren't restricted to the stately table that stood sentry in the A Unit lounge. They could touch each other and even hug. Affectionate physical contact was one of the things Cain craved the most since coming to Maddox. Nobody touched him except to search or punish him.

The game was good, and he enjoyed watching it even though he felt like an orphan outside the candy shop. Players on both teams were skilled, and he recognized a challenge for his talent. Even though it would be a year before he would be up for a transfer, he felt uplifted—

like maybe there was some hope behind bars, something to look forward to.

"You should be over there playing ball."

Cain turned to see Josie who had walked up behind him.

"Next year, Josie," he said turning back to watch the game. "I have a year to make up for that debacle with Bentley."

"Actually that's what I wanted to talk to you about—Bentley, " said Josie unable to take her eyes off Cain's battered hands that were still clinging to the fence. "I'm sorry, Cain."

"Why?" asked Cain letting go of the fence and turning around to face her. "It wasn't your fault. I'm a big boy; I knew what I was doing."

"Well, I've never had anyone do anything like that for me." As soon as the words were out, she blushed an embarrassed scarlet. "I guess I shouldn't assume that you did it for me—you probably were just mad that Bentley made some cracks about your sexuality, but . . ."

"I did it for you," said Cain without hesitation. "I don't give a damn what Bentley or anyone else thinks about me. I thought I told you that. He had no right to talk about you or anyone else that way, though. I waited to see if you were going to do anything about it, and then I just saw red. I hope I didn't embarrass you. I thought about it later, and I wondered if you were mad."

"Mad?"

"I was kind of out of line. I mean, I let him go on about me and I didn't care, but I went after him when he wouldn't shut up about you. That was kind of condescending and kind of assuming you cared but couldn't take care of yourself. I forget you're not really a damsel in distress." He flashed a sincere smile.

"But I am, Cain. I would never stand up for myself that way. Most of my life I've been the brunt of people's sick jokes, and I've always just stood there and taken it." She gave a nervous giggle. "I am a freak; I know that, but I'm not nearly as secure about who I am as you are. You're one of the only people who doesn't make me feel like a freak." She dabbed at the tears that had sprung to her eyes. "You don't use me or abuse me—you're a real friend that I can be myself with. This is who I am. It's not a gimmick or an act. I don't know how I got different from everyone else, but I am. And all these years I've just put up with the cruelty of others, pretending I didn't care. I know they laugh at me, and it hurts."

"But why don't you do away with the makeup and the hair while you're here? You're out of your element here. At least on the outside, you can be with others like yourself."

"No, it's just as cruel on the outside. Maybe even worse. I've told you that I'm more at home here than anywhere. Here they might laugh and joke, but I am a unique and much sought after commodity; and I have a roof over my head and food on the table everyday. So I just keep adjusting the blinders. You offer me the chance to take them off, and I can't thank you enough for that—and for defending my honor. But even more, for making me feel like I have some honor to be defended."

Cain looked down at the fragile human being next to him. He had thought he knew about life and all kinds of lifestyles, but he was beginning to realize that there was still a lot to learn. He wondered if in the past back in high school he had laughed and joked about people like Josie. He couldn't remember, but he bet he probably had—back in the days when he was trying to understand his own sexuality. Looking at her now, he realized that Maddox did have something to teach him after all; and he was happy that somewhere along the line his parents had managed to sow the seed of tolerance. As it sprouted to maturity in him, it filled him with a feeling of satisfaction and good will.

"Come on," he said putting his arm around her, "I think I still owe you some ice cream."

# CHAPTER 9

"Why do they always play this **STUPID** song at Christmas?!" asked Cain irately as he slammed the cards he was holding down on the table.

Jon looked around the recreation room, unaware that music was even playing.

"What song?" he asked.

"*I'll be Home for Christmas*," answered Cain. "If they have to pipe in Christmas music, why do they have to play that song? They've gotta know that most of us won't be anywhere but here for Christmas."

"Think of this as home," quipped Jon as he leaned over and picked up the cards that had fallen on the floor.

"You're a jerk, you know that?" complained Cain unamused.

"Hey," scolded Jon. "Chill. You've been biting people's heads off all day. What's your problem?"

"It's less than a week before Christmas, this place is a pit, I'm twenty years old, and this is the third Christmas I'll be spending behind bars. How's that for starters?"

"That'd be fine, Cain, except all of those things were true yesterday, and you weren't this pissy. You sound like some old crone who hasn't had a good lay in . . . oh, now I get it."

"Shut up," frowned Cain pushing his chair away from the table and slouching moodily. "That's definitely not funny, so shut the hell up!"

"Okay," sighed Jon moving his chair a bit closer to where Cain had moved. "Why has this Christmas thing suddenly been getting to you more today than it has before? Come on, I know you too well. Something's up. You've been bitching all day at work, and now you're not even fit to be with. Spill your guts, Farrell. What's up?"

"Just lay off, will you?"

"Yeah, fine, I'll lay off, but then lose the attitude."

"Fine. I'm going to go lock-in. It's almost time for the count anyway."

Jon began to fume as he got up and followed after Cain.

"Do you realize how many times you do that?"

"Do what?" asked Cain.

"Run off to hide in your cell when you don't want to confront something. Face it. Talk about it. Maybe you'll feel better."

"Not now. Fuck off!"

Fr. Mike Curtin was across the room and saw what was going on.

"You guys are beginning to draw the attention of the guards," he said as he approached them. "Can I help before you both get busted?"

"Yeah, Father," said Jon. "See if you can talk some sense into him."

"I'm on my way upstairs," said Cain emphatically. "And I don't need anybody to talk sense into me."

Cain walked away and left Jon shaking his head at the priest.

"God, he can be infuriating!" said Jon.

"I've never seen you two fight before," smiled the priest.

"Oh, come on, we fight all the time. I've never known anybody so headstrong."

"What's wrong?"

"That's the thing. I don't know, but something sure is bothering him. He says it's the holidays, but it's more than that."

"Let me go see if I can talk to him."

"Is your insurance all paid up?"

Fr. Mike laughed patted Jon on the shoulder and left.

When Mike got up to the second tier, Cain was sitting on his bed, leaning against the wall, knees drawn to his chest, smoking a cigarette.

"Shit!" he said when he saw the priest. "I knew you'd come up here. You know, if you'd all just leave me alone, I'd be fine. I just need some space, and there is none here. No space. No privacy. I just want to be alone for a while."

"Okay," said Mike, "that's all you had to say. I just thought maybe you wanted to talk. You know where I am if you want me."

He turned and started down the tier. Cain drew a few angry breaths and ran his fingers through his hair. He turned on the bed and knelt by the bars.

"Mike!" he called through the cold steel. No response. "Mike! Damn it!!!"

But the priest had already exited the tier and was beyond the range of the angry, frustrated voice. But anger and frustration didn't even come close to what Cain was feeling. He took his stool and whatever else wasn't bolted down in the cell, and in an uncontrolled rage threw it all against the damnable bars that held him in. When the rest of the tier came back for the count, he was sitting on the floor in the corner by his window.

"What the hell?" said Jon as he stopped outside the cell.

"Get me something," pleaded Cain. "I don't care what it is, just get me something to get me through this night. I'll pay whatever it costs. You have connections, Jon."

"Cain?"

"Just do it!"

"I'm going to call Mike when I go down to dinner."

"You do that, but don't come back here without something to put me out for hours."

"Okay," said Jon in a worried tone. "Are you coming to dinner?"

"No. I just want oblivion. I don't want to look at that stupid-ass Christmas tree up on the catwalk or hear their stupid music or think."

When Fr. Mike came back up, Cain was still sitting on the floor amidst the shambles he had made out of his cell. He had just gotten control of the delirious sobs that had wracked his body. He had his head against the wall, his face red and tear-soaked.

"The guard won't let me in, Cain. He said you're out of control."

"Well, for once he's right."

"What's wrong? Please talk to me."

The priest sat on the floor outside the bars.

"I got a letter—in last night's mail. From my brother Jim." He stopped to shore up his composure. "She's getting married . . . Joanne . . . tomorrow. Nobody would tell me. Jim just found out."

"I'm sorry," said the priest sincerely. "I know how that must hurt."

"I never got a chance to talk to her—to ask her to wait for me— to give her another chance. I wrote letters, but they all came back. She always talked about getting married at Christmas because it's her favorite time of year and everything's so beautiful. But that was supposed to be her and me. How could she marry someone else now after all the plans we made? How could she marry someone else at all? There's still time, but I can't get to her—I'm locked up here. If I could just talk to her. I love her, Mike. I'll never love anyone else. I feel so dead inside."

"It wasn't meant to be."

"That doesn't help. She's only nineteen. She quit college to marry this guy who's like twenty-six or twenty-seven. He's a stockbroker or something. Even if she waited, what would she want with an ex-con?" He covered his face with his hands. "How many times am I going to have to pay for what I did with Carrie? My life is over."

"Now that's not true."

"I've been here for nearly 2½ years. That means I have 9½ left. That may as well be forever."

"Come on, nobody serves a full term. In a few more years you'll be eligible for parole."

"Nobody else fucked Sam Willet's daughter and got caught. He told me himself last summer he was going to see to it that I do all twelve years."

"He's powerful, Cain, but there are limits to even his power. You won't be here for twelve years."

"I don't care. I can't stand to be here for twelve more minutes. I'm feeling way claustrophobic, Mike. I'm ready to jump out of my skin."

"Okay, listen for a minute. This thing with Joanne . . . we've talked about it before. You've known for a long time that it was over. She told you that before you even left home."

"Yeah, but my life is on hold now, and somehow in my head, I have the rest of the world on hold, too. Things aren't supposed to change while I'm away. I want to go back home and take up right where I left off; and with Joanne, that means trying to convince her to love me again. I know I could do it if I had time. I can't stand being locked up any more. I can't stand not being able to come and go as I please. Where the hell is Jon, anyway?"

"Jon told me about your request, so I stopped by the infirmary on my way up here and got you some legal mindbenders. There's a sleeping pill for tonight and tranquilizers for the next few days if you need them. I have the sleeping pill, but I had to leave the rest with guard."

"Like I'm a fucking baby. Doesn't he have to come down to give me the sleeping pill?"

"No, I can do that, but first you have to get this cell cleaned up. That'll give you something to get your mind occupied. Then I'm going to get you something to eat; you're wasting away. After that if you want, you can take the sleeping pill and go to bed."

"How can I make anybody understand how much I love her; how much I need her?" he asked as fresh tears washed over his face. "I HAVE TO GET OUT OF THIS PLACE!"

"Come on, you know better than that. There's no way. YOU CAN'T LEAVE! Now get your head straight, and clean up this mess you made. We'll talk about Joanne later when you're in a more rational frame of mind. You have no choice but to pull yourself together."

"It's Christmas . . . I don't belong here . . . I **want** to go home. If somebody doesn't unlock that door soon, I'm going to lose my mind. These walls are closing in on me!"

The priest let out an exasperated sigh.

"Okay, forget the disaster you made out of this cell. Just come over here and take this pill. Sleep and we'll talk in the morning. Tomorrow's Saturday. I'll meet you down at breakfast, and we'll go out in the yard and walk."

"That's almost like going home," said Cain sarcastically.

"Cain," scolded the priest though he welcomed the sarcasm over the despair. "I'm doing the best I can. Work with me here, will you?"

Cain sat for a long minute with his head resting against the wall. He stared straight ahead toward Fr. Mike, but he was looking way beyond the bars and walls of Maddox. Then, sucking in a deep breath, he got up and retrieved his cigarettes and ashtray from his bed. Kicking books and papers and things out of his way, he went over to where the priest was still sitting and eased himself down on the floor opposite him. Mike waited while Cain lit the cigarette. The smoke seemed to reach

171

down to soothe and soften the edges of his pain as he inhaled and then exhaled it.

"I'm sorry," he said. "This whole thing just freaked me out, and it's Christmas and all."

"I understand."

"I'll always love her, Mike. I can't just give her up, even if she is married to someone else."

"Time has a way of working those things out."

"And we both know I have a lot of time to spare."

"Do you want this?" Mike held out the sleeping pill.

"Can I save it?"

"No. You have to take it now. We'd both be in a lot of trouble if you got caught with this in your cell."

"Keep it. I'll suffer." He shifted his eyes toward the bars and the priest and smiled slightly.

"Are you sure?" asked Mike relieved to see the smile.

"Yeah. Like you said, I have to pull myself together, and I'd rather do it myself than with drugs."

"Cain, I don't know if what Joanne is doing is right or not. Maybe she's using this guy to help her forget what she had with you, or maybe she really is in love with him. Either way, there's nothing you can do about it by tomorrow."

"You could call her for me."

"No. No, I won't do that. I won't interfere. She knows how to get in touch with you if she had wanted to. Instead, she chose not to . . . even going so far as to send your letters back. You have to respect that. You know I'm right."

"You're always right."

"No, not always, but I do try to give good advice . . . and my advice here is to let her go. It's not good for you in your position to obsess over her. Tomorrow she'll be someone else's wife." He nodded toward a picture on the floor by the bars that had been on Cain's table before his stormy battle against reality. "Is that her?"

Cain's eyes misted over as he resisted looking down at the photo. He took another drag on his cigarette, slowly exhaling the smoke. He didn't have to look; he knew.

"Yeah," he answered. "I took that just before this whole Carrie Willet thing blew up. She was laughing and driving me crazy with how beautiful and sexy she was. Every time I look at it, I remember she was looking at me when it was taken. I can't get her out of my mind."

"This might not be the right time to bring this up, but why on earth did you ever get involved with Carrie Willet when you were so crazy in love with such a wonderful girl?"

Cain rubbed his face.

"Sex. That sounds pretty shallow, doesn't it?"

"You're anything but a shallow individual."

"Well, it sounds shallow to me. I was seventeen and in a big hurry to grow up. Joanne's a year younger and she wasn't . . . ready. That was okay until Carrie kept coming around at opportune times and making herself very available. That's no excuse; I'm not blaming her. I was stupid, selfish, and very adolescent. It was just an outlet for me."

"Joanne didn't see it that way."

"No, not hardly. And then to make matters worse, she didn't find out about it until Carrie cried rape and it all hit the papers. I was in jail, and I couldn't even get to her myself to tell her before she read about it."

"Did she ever give you a chance to explain?"

"Yeah, I guess you could say that. She listened, but she had already made up her mind to hate me. I've asked myself a million times how I could have betrayed her that way. If I loved her . . . "

"Humanity's a mystery to us all. We all do dumb things we don't understand."

"I guess," he said. He absently fingered his hair away from his forehead, but it fell back in place. "And you don't get a chance to ever make up for some mistakes."

"And sometimes things that we think are the blunders of our lives end up being blessings in disguise. Just because you and Joanne were crazy about each other doesn't mean it would have lasted even if Carrie Willet hadn't come around. Love is always being tested—and I know this was a whopper of a test that your young love was subjected to, but it didn't persevere, did it? Don't torture yourself by holding this up as the love of a lifetime that you killed all by yourself. And don't think that there aren't other loves out there just waiting for a chance to bloom and grow into something lasting—especially now that you've learned this all too painful lesson."

"I know—as a convicted rapist I'm going to have to give out numbers to the girls who'll be just dying to be with me and plan a future."

"Oops, I'm detecting self pity. That's not going to help."

"So I should delude myself?"

"Did I say that?"

"That's what it amounts to."

"You're not a fortuneteller. And don't jump too far ahead of yourself. Take some time to get over this loss and to deal with your time here. Then see what happens when you're out and back in circulation."

"If I'm young enough to still care about being back in circulation." He crushed out the cigarette and flashed a small smile. "Self pity again—I just can't seem to help myself."

"This isn't just an act you're putting on for me, is it? Are you going to be all right?"

"Yeah," he sighed. "I just have to clean up this mess."

"And what about the picture?"

"It stays right where it's always been. I'm okay, but don't expect me to make some sort of miracle recovery. You said take it a day at a time, and I will; but right now I'm not ready to put the picture away."

"Fair enough. How about the pill? I have time to wait till you're ready to go to bed."

"No, I'm going to do this cold turkey. The last thing I need is to become dependent on pills. And thanks, Mike; it helps to talk to you. But I still love her—that's not going to go away for a long time."

"No, I don't guess it will. You know it's funny, but in spite of your actions to the contrary, maybe you were the one who was really in love all the time while Joanne was caught up in something less permanent."

"Yeah, or maybe it's just easier to keep on loving when you're not the one who was hurt so bad."

"Hmmm, brilliant observation, my young friend."


Although he slept better than he had expected, Cain woke up the next morning overcome with grief as he remembered that it was Joanne's wedding day. He was determined, however, not to lose control and become hysterical as he had the day before. He was sitting on his bed in a self-imposed funk when the doors slid open. In a matter of moments, Jon appeared just as he did every morning.

"Come one. Let's go."

"I'm not going to breakfast."

"You didn't eat dinner; you have to be starving."

"I got something off the cart last night."

"It's Saturday, for God's sake."

"No shit."

"Come on," said Jon taking a frantic look down the hall and hoping the guard wasn't watching. He took a step into Cain's cell, grabbed his work boots which were sitting nearby and then grabbed Cain by the arm and pulled him out the door. "I'm not going to let you lock-in all day and mourn over a bitch who doesn't have sense enough to know what's good for her!"

Cain struggled, but by the time he got to his feet, the doors had rolled shut and locked until the noon count.

"SHIT!" he cursed as he turned on Jon.

"Come on," coaxed Jon. "You'll thank me in the end."

"MY JEANS ARE IN THERE, YOU IDIOT!"

"What?!"

Jon looked more carefully at Cain. He was wearing a long-sleeved undershirt with a denim shirt over it, so Jon had assumed he was dressed for the day except for his boots. On closer inspection, however, he saw Cain was wearing navy sweats instead of his jeans with the white stripe on the sides.

174

"Christ!" freaked Cain. "I'm fucking locked out without my jeans. I'm going to get fucking busted, you fucking idiot!"

"Now calm down," said Jon. "There has to be a way to fix this. Where are your jeans?"

"In my locker. How long are your arms?"

"Okay, now just wait. I'll think of something."

"I just wanted to lock-in and be left alone, Jon. Now I'm going to end up in Solitary. That's a little more alone than I had in mind. You idiot—I can't believe you did that."

"Stop talking and let me think."

He went to his own cell and looked in, but there were no jeans within his reach.

"Who's the guard on duty? I didn't pay any attention this morning." Cain asked.

"Mueller," answered Jon reluctantly.

"Jesus, I'm screwed."

"Wait, maybe not. He owes you after last summer when he stiffed you out on the Rock."

"That was over five months ago! He's gotta know that nobody's going to listen to me if I threaten to lodge a complaint now. He'd love to bust my ass."

"Cain, he **owes** you. Call in the debt. Who knows, maybe he's a man of some honor."

"Well, he's going to be making rounds soon."

"Look, I'll go down and . . . "

"And, what? Tell him you were in my cell?"

"No, that'll never do. I'll tell him . . . I'll tell him . . . you were confused and thought you had jeans on, and couldn't he just be a nice guy and unlock your door for a few seconds while you correct the error."

"Why is it I come out of this looking like the fool?"

"I'd take the blame, but I don't know how to do it without implicating both of us, and that defeats the purpose."

"I could strangle you with my bare hands right now, you know that?"

"Yeah. I'm sorry. Really I am."

"Get your ass down to breakfast, and leave me alone. I'll figure this out myself."

"I'll stay and help you. I'm not going to let you take the blame alone. It's just that even if I tell him the truth, he'll still bust you too because I was in your cell."

"I know, I know, so get the hell out of here."

"You've got to hand it to me," smiled Jon opting for levity. "I gave you something else to think about this morning!"

"Leave, Jon, before I end up doing more time for murder."

Without another word Jon turned and hurried down the tier. Cain waited till he was gone and then walked down to the guard's station.

"Farrell," said Mueller, "what's going on?"

"I need you to let me back in my cell."

"The lock's been tripped."

"I know, and it can be untripped just as easily as it was tripped."

"Where are your stripes?"

"That's why I need to get back in."

"I'll bet this is going to be good. Why'd you leave knowing you weren't regulation?"

The guard picked up his book and prepared to write up a disciplinary report. Cain felt his knees grow weak, but he continued as if he hadn't even noticed.

"Just open the door and let me back in. I don't want to leave again; I'll lock-in all morning."

"You didn't answer my question."

"I know that. You screwed me over last summer, but I gritted my teeth and took it. Now can't you just unlock the damn door?"

"Last summer?" said Mueller feigning ignorance.

Cain sighed at the uselessness of the situation and presented his wrists.

"Just take me away; I don't even care any more."

Mueller reached over and flipped the switch that unlocked Cain's door.

"I'll give you thirty seconds to get in there."

"Fine," said Cain resisting the urge to say thank you.

"And, Farrell?"

Cain turned on his way back down the tier.

"Yeah?"

"The ball's in my court again—watch your back."

Without a word Cain turned back and jogged toward his cell. *I always watch my back in this place.*

After lunch Cain was notified that he had visitors. Angry that his family had kept the news of Joanne's wedding from him, he approached the visitors' room with mixed feelings. As he looked across the room and saw Matt and Scott, he stood for a minute measuring his emotions.

"He knows," said Matt quietly.

"Yep," agreed Scott.

"Well, if you two don't look like the cats that ate the canary," Cain said as he approached them and took his seat opposite them.

"What are you talking about?" asked Scott deciding to let Cain make the first move. *Maybe he didn't know.*

"Joanne's wedding today."

*He knew.*

"Oh."

"Oh, yeah," said Cain on the attack. "Why the hell didn't either of you tell me?"

"How'd you find out?" asked Matt.

"I got a Christmas card from Jim yesterday, and he sent a letter with it. He said he was sorry; he just found out when he got home from school for vacation. He hoped that by now I had gotten over her or at least gotten used to the idea of her marrying someone else. He thought I knew."

"I'm sorry," said Matt. "We didn't know how you'd take it, so we thought we'd wait till we saw you in person."

"Yeah," said Cain not satisfied with the explanation. "And how long have you known about this?"

Matt and Scott exchanged glances.

"I don't know," said Scott.

"For a while?" Cain pressed. "Since before the last time you were here for a visit?"

"Maybe," admitted Matt.

"What the hell, you guys? Were you even going to tell me today?"

"Yes," insisted Scott. "We tried before, but we knew how you felt, and we just couldn't do that."

"So you thought I'd never find out?"

"No, we knew we had to tell you," said Matt. "That's one of the reasons we're here."

"Well, thanks for waiting till the last minute. Thanks for nothing." He took out a cigarette and lit it. "Do Mom and Dad know?"

"Yeah."

"All the people I trust the most in the world."

He sat angry and rigid, smoking his cigarette. Scott and Matt were quiet, not daring to invade the hostile space between them and Cain.

Scott was the first to break the undeclared silence.

"Now what?" he asked.

"I don't know," said Cain. "I'm angry and confused."

"So now we're not friends any more?" asked Scott. "What about Matt, you're stuck with him. And tell me this: what difference would it have made if we had told you months ago instead of now? How would that have changed anything for you?"

"I could have written to her and tried to reason with her."

"Cain," said Scott, "you've tried writing her a million times, and your letters just come back. Surely you couldn't have forgotten."

"We all tried to tell you every time we came," said Matt, "but it was only because we knew you were helpless against the situation and you'd be hurt . . . well, the words just wouldn't come. So quit being a jerk, will you? Everybody was thinking of you. We're sorry. What else is there to say?"

"Nothing," sighed Cain. "I just feel like I've been kicked in the stomach."

"By us?" asked Scott.

"No. I just wish you wouldn't treat me like a child."

"That wasn't our intention," argued Matt.

"I know, but I have to be able to trust people to be honest with me. Otherwise I'll spend all my time worrying about what you're all not telling me. What am I going to find out next? If you're up front with me, I know there are no surprises around the corner."

"Okay," said Scott. "So how the hell are you?"

"Shitty," answered Cain without a smile, "just a breath this side of suicidal."

"Cain," said Scott, "Joanne's been lost to you for a long time. You know that."

"No," ranted Cain. "No, see that's where you're all wrong. You think I've been logical about this whole thing. My IQ has nothing to do with my heart and my idiotic daydreams and nightdreams. How do you make your heart stop feeling? I wish someone could tell me that. I have never given up hope that I'd win her back someday, and now my mind is blown."

"Cain . . ." said Matt.

"I'm screwed up," continued Cain. "I'm totally screwed up."

Scott sighed uneasily.

"What can we do?" he asked.

"Nothing," was Cain's blunt answer.

"Maybe . . ." started Scott.

"Nothing," repeated Cain not waiting for him to finish. "I have too much time on my hands here. All I do is think. The only challenge I have is how to pull off shit without getting into trouble."

"Like what kind of shit?" asked Scott with a grin as he moved to sidetrack Cain's moody frame of mind.

"Like none of your business," answered Cain with a scowl.

"You're getting a bit tiresome," said Matt.

"Leave," shrugged Cain.

Matt sighed and positioned his hands on the table to prepare to stand, but Scott reached over hand held him in place with the touch of his hand.

"He's kidding," said Scott.

Cain raised his eyebrows. *Call my bluff.*

"Do you want us to go?" asked Scott sincerely.

Cain sighed, no longer able to sustain his anger. "I'm not very good company, but no. I'll try to shake it off."

"You don't have to be good company," said Matt, "just don't take it out on us."

"I know; I'm sorry. It's this place, you know? There's no way I can let you know my mood until you get here and then it's too late. Like at home I'd throw a shoe or something at Matt when he walked in the bedroom," he smiled at his brother, "and that would be his clue to back off for a while."

"He's done that before," said Matt. "Nearly took out a window once."

"But you know what I mean?" asked Cain. "The last thing I want to do is take out my frustrations on you two. If I could have talked to you ahead of time, I probably would have told you to stay away this weekend because I wasn't fit to be with."

"Yeah, and we would have said, *fuck it, we're coming anyway.* So it wouldn't have mattered," said Scott. "But in the mean time let's don't even talk about Joanne."

Their visit buoyed Cain's spirits some, but his heart was heavy and his thoughts were full of Joanne. He listened to their talk and laughed at the right times, but he had to force his mind to stay on track and not be derailed by visions of Joanne in satin and lace. A few times he found himself smiling but not really comprehending much of anything that was being said. As much as he hated to see them leave, it was a relief not to have to keep up the charade any longer. He watched them walk out the door, and then he turned to face the dreaded strip search they always put him through. That turned his mood even blacker.

Dejected and feeling like the floor was dropping out from under him, he made his way back to his cell. Dropping on his bed, he lay on his back staring up at the ceiling. Desire burned in his chest and in his groin. He reached back over his head and grabbed the bars with both his hands. The futility of his situation nearly caused him to cry out in pain. He wanted to close his eyes and make love to Joanne in the only way that was available to him, but it was too early in the evening and the tier was still too busy with traffic that promised to intrude. This had to be hell. There was no other explanation for the frustration and grief he was feeling.

"Saturday night and no place to go?" said a voice from behind him.

Realizing he wasn't alone, he let go of the bars and jumped to a sitting position with a start. When he spotted Marge Clintock and a companion guard, he all but screamed out loud. He opted for silent, righteous indignation, however.

"Hi, angel face," she said undaunted. "It's been a while, huhn? This here's Ella. She's new, and when I heard she'd drawn this duty, I told her to be sure to look you up. Then I decided, oh hell, I'll bring her here myself—any excuse to look in on you. So how the hell've you been?"

He stared through the bars at them from under a thick fringe of sandy, blonde hair.

"I'm not in the mood for this," he frowned as he got up and went to his table for his cigarettes.

"No, you never are," sighed Marge. "I'll bet I could get you in the mood." She winked.

He was walking a thin line, and he knew it. He lit a cigarette and sat on his table with his feet on the stool. He was happy for the diversion of the cigarette to give him the chance to move out of her reach.

"Ella," she continued. "Isn't he everything I told you?"

Ella stood awash in amused embarrassment.

"Are you through?" asked Cain testily.

"No, not by a long shot. Some day I'm going to be on the other side of one of your famous strip searches. I go crazy just thinking about it. One day I'll be in the right place at the right time. I told Ella what a beautiful ass you have. It's too cold now; you keep all covered up—but, Ella, you have to be sure to check carefully in the summer." She grinned at Cain.

He watched her with measured patience, not saying a word. He hated when she got this way. She was making him pay for not falling at her feet with gratitude when she came to him about Mueller last summer. He had to be careful, though, not to anger her too much because he knew she could make life hell for him. It wasn't worth it, so he sat quietly smoking his cigarette as she went on humiliating him in the name of fair play.

"Why don't you come over here by the bars so I can massage your shoulders or rub your back or your thighs or something?"

"You'd best not ever touch me," he said icily warning her that she had gone too far.

That's when God took mercy on him and sent a redeemer.

"Is something wrong?" asked Fr. Mike as he approached the cell.

"No," said Cain relieved that he didn't have to assert himself any further with the guard. "Actually, they were just ready to leave."

"Yes, Father," smiled Marge. "Ella will be on duty tonight if you need anything, Farrell; and I'll be . . . around."

The two guards and the priest said their congenial good-byes, while Cain remained speechless still seated on the top of his table at the back of the cell.

"That was nice," said Mike as the two guards walked on down the hall.

"Yeah," answered Cain sarcastically.

"Still in a bad mood?"

"Let's just say she didn't help. Thanks for coming."

"I haven't been able to get you off my mind. At least your cell's still in one piece. That's progress."

Cain smiled in spite of himself.

"I feel like a zoo animal," he said picking up his ashtray and moving to the bars to be closer to the priest. They both sat on the floor opposite each other.

"What brought that on?"

"Isn't it obvious?"

"I hope I don't make you feel that way? The guard . . . "

"It's not you . . . it's Clintock. She has that effect on me."

"She really has you freaked out, hasn't she?"

"I don't like her. She makes me feel . . . I don't know. Just if ever you see her near me, rescue me."

"Like tonight?"

"Yeah."

"What's going on?"

"Nothing I want to talk about."

"Cain, if I'm reading you right, what she's doing is against the law."

"There are no laws here, Mike."

"Okay, but that doesn't mean she can get away with coming up here and . . . "

"Let's not talk about it anymore. I can handle her."

"Okay, if you're sure."

"I'm sure."

"How are you holding up?"

"Barely. This has been the longest day. I keep flashing back to a long time ago . . . another life ago. I can't help myself. I just don't know how to let go. Have you ever been in love, Mike?"

"No," smiled the priest. "I don't know if I'm ashamed to admit that or not."

"Why would you be ashamed?"

"Because here I am giving you advice, and I've never been there. Because I opted for the priesthood without ever having given the other alternative a try."

"Why? Other people have fallen in love and gotten married without ever having given the priesthood a try."

"I guess you're right there. I've had a few adolescent crushes, but I never got to the love stage."

"Well, it's not all it's cracked up to be, that's for sure."

"I always felt awkward and inadequate around girls."

"Good, you're better off. Would you do me a favor?"

"Sure."

"Would you call my parents tonight and tell them not to come tomorrow?"

"Why not?"

"It's too hard trying to pretend everything's okay. I can't sit there and talk small talk."

"You might change your mind by tomorrow."

"No. It's going to take way longer than tomorrow to get my head together. And I hate when people come so far, and I'm a bastard."

"Doesn't that come with the territory of being part of a family? I think you're parents can handle it."

"But I end up feeling guilty. God, I wish I could get stinking drunk."

"That wouldn't solve anything."

"Come on, Mike, no lectures."

"Sorry, I sometimes forget myself."

They both smiled.

"I just want to get hammered."

"Have you ever even been drunk before?"

"No," laughed Cain involuntarily. "At least not to where I just didn't care about anything any more."

"Well, you'd probably be a whole lot better off taking that sedative I brought you last night; it should still be down at the guards' station. It'll put you way out of your misery. And you won't wake up with a hangover."

"That I've had. Once. In high school. But I've never gotten really stinking drunk. Tonight would be the night for that. A pill just doesn't have the same impact."

Again they shared a smile.

"I guess you're right," said the priest.

"What about my parents? Will you call?"

"If that's what you want, of course. But what about Christmas? This'll be the last chance they'll get to see you—and you, them—before Christmas?"

"I know." Tears flooded his eyes. "What difference does it really make? Christmas is just another day to piss away here. They can't come that day, so what difference does it make what day they come? This prison thing is wearing real thin with me."

"You're mother'll be worried."

"She'll be even more worried if she sees me." He stared ahead and let his mind wander off. "I wonder what Joanne's doing right now. It's cold in here, isn't it?"

"It's freezing."

"It doesn't help that we're sitting on the floor. Maybe you should just go before you get pneumonia."

"I don't want to leave you just yet."

"I'm okay. Really. This is just something I have to work through. But please call my parents. Ask them to give me a week. I don't even think I want to get out of bed tomorrow." The far away look came back in his eye, and Mike knew that the conversation was switching gears again. "I wonder . . . if she's— She always— Maybe tonight—"

"You're torturing yourself."

"I'm torturing you. I'm sorry. Please go. I'm going to wrap myself up in as many blankets as I have and read for a while and then go to sleep."

"Do you want me to send your new friend Ella down with the sleeping pill? Maybe a little later?"

"No, that just delays the inevitable. It's over; she's married now. See, I said it; I'm on the road to recovery. Now will you get out of here? I'm starting to shiver uncontrollably, so I know you have to be cold."

"Okay," said Mike getting up off the floor. "I don't suppose I'll see you in Church tomorrow."

Cain looked at him through skeptic's eyes. No words were necessary.

"You can't blame a guy for trying," smiled Mike.


The next morning Cain went to breakfast with Jon, but after that he used schoolwork as an excuse to go back to his cell rather than go to the rec room with the others. Once back on the tier, he took off his boots and wrapped his quilt around himself and began reading, hoping for some sort of escape. His mind kept drifting, and he had to keep dragging himself out of the past. Too often he found himself staring blankly at the picture of Joanne on his table. The stabbing pain of reality nearly drove him to tears, but he was determined to get beyond that point and move on.

Just as he thought he had himself together, he thought about the holiday coming up. Homesickness overwhelmed him as he hugged the quilt closer against the cold draft in the cell. The longer he was segregated from society, the harder it was to imagine there was a world beyond the walls and barbed wire of Maddox. Weary from the effort of coping, he slid sideways along the wall until his head was cradled by the cool softness of his pillow. Wrapping the quilt even tighter around himself, he curled into a comforting fetal position and soon fell asleep.

It wasn't long before his peace was seized and arrested by a most frustrating and haunting nightmare:

*He could see Joanne off in the far distance. She was beautiful, and she waved to him. He started calling to her, screaming; but she didn't move. She just kept smiling and waving. He started running for all he was worth, continuing to call to her. Suddenly it was stifling hot, and he had to trudge his way through rocks and sand as the sun blistered the terrain and sapped his energy. He kept stumbling and clawing his way back up, all the time screaming for Joanne who never seemed to get any closer. His hands were scraped and bleeding.*

Suddenly it turned cold and started to snow. He kept screaming for Joanne, and she just kept waving as far away as when he had started his Odyssey. The cold winds bit into his exposed skin, and he was becoming numb and exhausted as he plowed his way through drifts and knee-high snow. Realizing he had been days on this trek and getting no closer to his destination, he started to cry out in futility. Tears ran down his face and froze his cheeks. His hair was already a mass of snow and ice. It was as if he was on a great, global treadmill and Joanne was suspended above the earth watching his fruitless struggle.

After a while when he had reached a point where he could almost go no further, the snow tapered off and there was green grass in the distance. He became rejuvenated, as he was able to pick up speed once again. Ice and snow melted from his body as a balmy sun buoyed his energy. Still, Joanne was no closer, and even the idyllic setting couldn't chase away the frustration and agony he felt. He sobbed hysterically as he kept running toward her, calling to her, begging her. He picked up speed as tears flowed freely down his face. Maybe he wasn't running fast enough, trying hard enough. He ran till he thought his lungs would burst, keeping the elusive Joanne in his sights. He kept pushing himself beyond human endurance, not giving up, until he ran full-speed into an invisible, unyielding glass wall. The crushing jolt sent him careening backwards while everything in his head went black, interrupted only by a myriad of streaking, shooting stars. He lay back in the grass as his wits settled about him. When he sat up, Joanne was still there, but she turned and began to walk away. *NOOOO!!! COME BACK!!! DON'T LEAVE!!! I'M COMING AS FAST AS I CAN!!! I CAN'T GET TO YOU ANY FASTER!!! DON'T LEAVE!!! I LOVE YOU!!! WAIT!!! JOANNE!!!!!!!!!!!!!!!!!!!!!!!!!!!!*

But she paid no attention to him. She kept walking, getting further and further away. He got up and ran to the wall, desperately searching for a way around it; but it was no use. He cried hysterically as he pressed against the glass in a futile effort to break through as he watched her become a speck on the horizon and then finally disappear.

He was beating frantically at the glass wall when a voice from reality finally was able to draw him from the abyss into which the nightmare had flung him. He opened his eyes and searched the cell, trying to distinguish fact from the surreal and then determine which state he was in. He sat up and looked at the guard on the other side of the bars who had unwittingly rescued him from a death caused by a lethal injection of hopelessness.

"You okay?" the guard asked.

"Yeah," he answered, his voice full of sleep and confusion. "What's wrong?"

"Nothing. You have visitors."

"DAMN!"

"That's a different reaction. That's usually good news."

"I know. Will you give me ten minutes to pull myself together before you open the door?"

"Sure."

The guard left, and Cain dropped back against the cell wall and tried to put together the scattered bits and pieces of his dream. Usually it was good to wake up from a nightmare and realize it wasn't real. This time, however, reality matched the agony of the nightmare, and there was no relief to be had. He sat for a few minutes trying to calm himself down. Then he dragged himself from the bed and, his hands still trembling, lit a cigarette. He stood by his window and looked out at the bleak snow-covered panorama. Finally he felt he could be civil, if not congenial, to visitors. He wondered who was there, but he had a feeling he knew and this was not going to be a particularly uplifting experience.

When he walked into the visitors' room, it only took seconds to confirm his suspicions. Taking a deep breath, he approached his parents, exchanged diluted greetings, and sat down across from them.

"Did you really think we would stay away at such a crucial time?" his father asked leaving no doubt that they had received Fr. Mike's phone call.

"Maybe it wouldn't have been so crucial, not to mention traumatic, if you had trusted me to be able to handle the news about Joanne right from the start. I could've had some time to get used to the idea."

"All right," said Will as Nora dropped her eyes, "it was a mistake. But what were you trying to do, punish us?"

"No—spare you. I'm in this fucking, pissed-off mood, and I was trying not to subject you to it. I was hoping you'd give me some time to figure out what I'm feeling."

"Well, obviously we couldn't do that, and you should've known we wouldn't stay away."

"Does what I want ever count for anything, Dad?"

"Of course."

"Then why are you here?"

"Cain," scolded Nora.

"You got Mike's phone call, didn't you?"

"Yes," answered Will, "but we couldn't let this go."

"But what about me?! I have so little freedom in my life—so little opportunity to make decisions on my own. I need more time; I thought you'd respect that."

"It's not that we don't respect your wishes . . . "

"Then what is it . . . because that's the way I see it."

"We felt we had to come and talk without letting any more time go by."

"I'm having trouble discussing this with you because I haven't come to terms with it myself. And don't, whatever you do, tell me it's all for the best. I don't believe it, and I definitely don't want to hear it."

"Okay. Fair enough."

"I hate that you keep things from me . . . like I'm some kind of a child or something."

"That's not the way it was," argued Will.

"Well, that's the way it seems, Dad. I feel like a fucking baby."

"Will you stop using that word in front of your mother."

"I tried to tell you not to come. I knew this was how it was going to be. I knew I was in no mood to be sociable and respectful." Tears sprang to his eyes, and he quickly covered his face with his hands.

"It's all right," said Nora's soothing voice. She wanted to jump across the wide table and take her child in her arms. She was on the verge of her own tearful breakdown. "We know how this is hurting you. We know it's hard, and we realize we made a mistake in not telling you sooner. We'll never do anything like that again, we promise. But, Cain, that's all past history. We can't change it. And we didn't mean to invade your privacy. We just wanted you to know how sorry we are. We wanted to tell you ourselves, and to see if there was anything we could do to help pick up the pieces. And it's nearly Christmas."

A fresh wave of tears burned through his closed eyelids and into his palms. *I want to come home.* It was a few minutes before he could find his voice again. Sniffing, he wiped his eyes with his opened hands.

"I love her, Mom."

"I know, sweetheart." Nora quickly wiped away her own tears.

"I've been spending every minute of the past three days trying to stop, but I don't know how. I'm sorry, I didn't mean to hurt you by asking you not to come, but you can see how I am—I'm a mess." He pulled himself together and sat up straight in the chair. Then he made a final sweep of his hand to dry up any tears still left on his face. "It's just best if we don't talk about Joanne. Tell me anything . . . what else is going on at home? Do you have your Christmas shopping done?"

They were able to continue without any more friction. Bygones had become bygones. Cain hung on to every piece of news that they brought. As much as he hadn't wanted them to come, he was heartbroken when it was time for them to leave. This was as close to a family holiday celebration as he was allowed—as much as he had been allowed for three Christmases now. He couldn't even hug them good-bye—no physical contact permitted. His spirits plunged, but he was determined to tread water until after they left. He knew his mother was already feeling his absence, and he didn't want to make this any harder on her than he had to. Now he remembered why else it was that he hadn't wanted them to come this particular weekend. Their leaving was agony for all of them. They were reminded all the more that he wouldn't be with them for the holidays, and he was made more acutely aware of what he was missing. It would've been better for all of them if they would've just left the door unopened since it only had to be slammed shut with finality in the end. But they did come, so they all had to play out their parts to the end, each trying to keep the others afloat.

As Cain sat dry-eyed in his chair and watched his parents leave, a wave of depression washed over him and dragged him under. *I'll be home for Christmas—if only in my dreams.* He waited a minute or two before he felt he could stand and successfully navigate his way through the certain strip search and then back to his cell. The last thing he wanted to do was take all his clothes off in the name of Sam Willet for some ambitious guard. It was cold, and he was tired and humorless. He didn't even dare hope that they'd spare him the indignity.

He checked in at the guard's table right outside the visitors' room door.

"Well, I'll be," grinned Marge Clintock, "if this ain't my lucky day. Weren't we just talking about this the other day? It says here that you're due for a strip." She turned to the other guard at the table with her. "I'll take care of this."

Cain stood woefully frozen to the spot. *This day is just getting better and better.* Where the hell was God whenever he needed a break? Clintock giddily walked into the small room where strip searches were carried out. Cain knew the room and the routine all too well. Forlornly, he pressed his feet into service and followed in her wake. His whole life he always felt very comfortable being naked—sometimes he even preferred it. And there was no room for modesty at Maddox. Guards were always using strip searches as a means of intimidation and punishment. Stripping had become more of a nuisance than anything else to Cain. He had even stripped for other female guards; but they were professional and all business, and he even found it kind of a novelty. But this was different. This he was not at all comfortable with.

"Hi, darlin'," she said as he walked into the room. "What luck, huhn? And I just recently came on duty."

He still said nothing as he emptied his pockets onto the table. His parents' leaving left him feeling dejected, and he just couldn't find any words. He looked at her as he put his foot up on the bench to untie his boot. The fire was out in his eyes, and she noticed it right away.

"You're taking all the fun out of this," she protested.

*Fuck you.* She read that loud and clear.

"Wait, wait, wait," she said putting her hand on his and stopping him from taking off his boot. "Something's going on with you. Something big, huhn? I like it better when you're all feisty and surly."

"Could we just get this over with?" he asked blandly.

"What's wrong?"

"Nothing I want to talk to you about. And if I need a shrink, I already have one."

187

"That's a little more like it." She smiled at him.

His eyes pleaded with her for mercy. *I'm in agony; let me get this over with.*

"Forget it," she relented. "I don't know what's going on with you, but it's totally killing the mood."

"Mood?" he asked. "What the hell? You want me to take off my clothes, or what?"

"No," she answered with a wince. "I can't believe I'm passing up yet another golden opportunity. We'll do it again some time when I don't feel like I'm totally taking advantage of you."

"Whatever," he said with a confused shrug.

"I feel like I'm raping you or something."

An amused laugh found it's way around the pain Cain was experiencing and caught him off guard as it burst forth.

"You're sick," he said as he tied his boot again.

"Yeah, maybe, but I'd better not be disappointed when I finally take my chance."

"Well, I'm certainly not going to lose sleep over it."

"Hey, tell me something," she said as he began returning items from the table to his pocket. "Word has it that you have an identical twin brother. Is that true?"

"I have to go," he said.

"I can't believe there are actually two of you!"

"No," said Cain sternly. "There's only one of me. And one of him. We're two different people."

"Of course," she said apologetically.

"Can I go?"

"Yeah, get your sweet ass out of here before I change my mind. It's my Christmas present to you."

"Look," said Cain digging his own grave, "don't do me any favors. It's not my most favorite thing to do, but I'll undress—just don't go thinking I owe you."

She looked at him for a long minute.

"Get out of here." He turned and started for the door. "Hey, Farrell."

"Yeah?"

"What's your brother's name?"

"Matthew. Why?"

"Just wondering. Merry Christmas."

He stood for a moment trying to figure her out. Then deciding it was an impossibility, he nodded and left to go back to his cell.

# CHAPTER 10

"Are you Cain Farrell?"

Cain abandoned the thought he was toying with and looked over at the man who had approached him. It was one of the first warmish days in mid April when spring seemed like it just might happen after all. He was outside by himself trying to clear out some cobwebs from the day's work and a life weary of this existence. Hands stuffed in the pockets of his unbuttoned pea coat, he was leaning against a wall enjoying the feel of the half-baked sun. His eyes locked onto the man suspiciously. He wasn't an inmate, nor was he a guard. This was interesting.

"Yeah."

"I thought so. Actually those guys over there told me you were." He stuck out his hand. "I'm Tom Benson. I coach the baseball team here."

"I see," said Cain hesitantly as he returned a brief handshake.

"I hear you're interested in baseball."

"I played in high school," answered Cain.

"Well, I have a few spots opened on the team. Fr. Curtin said you might be interested."

"He did, did he?"

"Yes. What position do you play?"

"First base."

"Lefty?"

"Natural."

"Perfect. Are you any good?"

Cain now regarded him with a slight, amused smile.

"I . . . can hold my own."

"Great! Why don't you come try out?"

"Mr. Benson, I'm a white-striper. No can do."

"Sure you can. Fr. Curtin said you're due to be transferred out of A Unit in a few months, and until then I can get permission for you to just play the home games on the B side of the fences. We have uniforms and everything. And we're not bad, either."

The thought intrigued him; he had to admit that.

"I don't know," he mused.

"Did you ever play anything after high school?"

"I came fresh from high school to here—do not pass GO . . . do not collect $200."

"That's okay—it's not like we're pros or anything. How 'bout it?"

"I don't know. I've been kind of thinking about it for a while now, but . . . "

"What's to think about?"

"I just need some time. Can I get in touch with you through Fr. Mike?"

"Yeah. Can you let me know soon? I need to start getting this team together. We start our games in a few weeks. April 27, to be exact."

"That's my birthday," smiled Cain.

"See, it's fate. That's a home game, too. How old are you, anyway?"

"I'll be twenty-one."

"You **are** young. Mind if I ask what you're in for? Fr. Curtin didn't mention it."

"Actually, I'd rather not talk about it."

"Okay. Will you get back to me in a day or two?"

"Yeah."

"Great." Tom patted Cain on the arm and walked away.

Cain stared out into the yard as the idea took seed in his brain. A persistent smile broke through his cautious reserve. Baseball.

It didn't take long for him to get in touch with Fr. Mike to tell him he was interested. The thought of it felt way too good to ignore. The night before he was supposed to meet with Tom Benson, he could barely sleep. He tried to remember back to a time when he was so excited about something; he couldn't. The nightmares and disappointments had blurred everything else out.

When work was over, he nearly ran all the way to the place he and Tom Benson had agreed to meet. He felt like it was his first day of school.

"How long has it been since you've played?" asked Tom as they walked toward the B Unit yard.

"Nearly three years," answered Cain remembering back. "A lifetime."

Tom smiled. "It's like riding a bike."

"We'll see," said Cain not quite so confident.

The team was gathered when they got to the practice field. Just like always, he was the youngest. The others were mostly between twenty-five and thirty. He felt like a bit of an outcast in his prison denims; the others all had civilian clothes on. But there was no way the Administration would let Cain leave A Unit without the telltale outfit. The team members eyed him curiously as they went about the routine of warming up.

"I swear, even the air seems clearer over here," he said.

"You ever been on this side?" Tom asked.

"Nope. I've just watched from the other side of the fences."

"Well, a few more months, and you'll be here for good."

"Yeah."

Cain looked around and was amazed at how different it was just crossing over a fence. Actually, it was two fences that separated them. There was a twenty-five-foot no-man's-land between them to discourage mingling. But on this side, one could almost forget he was in prison. Families were allowed, and their presence added a normalcy that he hadn't experienced since coming to Maddox. The air smelled fresh, the sun felt warm, and he planned to enjoy every minute he was free to spend there.

Tom introduced him to the team, and then suggested he take batting practice. Cain felt eager but nervous about picking up a bat again. It'd been so long. What if he had lost his touch? But as always he was able to mask his insecurities as he stepped up to the plate. He fouled off the first couple balls that were pitched to him, but it felt so good—so natural. It all came back to him quickly as he coordinated his hands, eyes, and concentration. Then after four pop fouls, he connected and sent the ball soaring to an unheard of distance. He couldn't contain himself. Raising his hands in the air, he let out a whoop of triumph. *God, that felt good!*

Tom rubbed his eyes in disbelief as the rest of the team conservatively stood in awe.

"Was that a fluke?" Tom asked.

"I hope not," smiled Cain. "I love this game."

During the rest of the practice, he proved he was a force to be reckoned with. He belted out one long drive after another, even when the pitcher was seriously trying to get him out. His base running was skillful and his fielding extraordinary. He felt a freedom and elation that he thought had been lost to him forever. There is nothing like being at the top of your game.

"Fr. Mike said you played some high school ball," marveled Tom as the practice came to a close. "I never dreamed you'd set my team here on its ear."

"I was scouted by professional teams while I was in high school, and I actually gave it serious thought."

"Well, I guess."

"But the world fell in on me, and I kind of lost heart for the game—and everything else—when I got arrested. Then one thing led to another, and bad turned to worse, and here I am. Until today I wasn't even sure I wanted to play again. But this was great, Tom, thank you."

"Thank **you**," said Tom. "I have a decent team, and with you on it, we actually stand a chance to win a trophy. We're not the majors or anything, but . . ."

"It's okay. That dream died a long time ago. I'm okay with it; and this is good."

"Well, I got permission for you to play home games here until you're transferred to B. Then you'll be able to travel with us. All that's left is for you to say it's what you want."

"It's what I want," smile Cain.

He was so excited to share his news with his family that he all but flew to the visitors' room on Saturday. Even the tiresome ritual of checking in didn't dampen his mood. He scanned the room for a familiar face. He saw Scott—every bit as good as family.

"What is with you?" asked Scott with a broad grin. "I can't remember the last time I saw you so up in the air."

"I'm playing baseball—on an organized team."

"Hey!"

"Yeah. The coach came to me this past week and talked to me about it. At first, I wasn't sure."

"Of course you weren't. You usually have to get bit in the ass before you're sure of anything."

"Can I tell the story?"

"Go ahead."

"Anyway, I've been practicing with them most of the week, and I'm still pretty good."

"No shit?"

"Scott."

"Sorry."

"They travel—off prison grounds. I can't go with them yet, but after my transfer goes through, I'll be able to. Our first game's on my birthday."

"I'll be here."

"It's a weekday."

"I'll work it out. You have to have a cheering section. Maybe I can drag some of your brothers along. We'll bring some champagne or something because you'll be legal."

"Not here I won't be."

"Then we'll bring grape juice. What the hell kind of a place is this anyway?"

"This is big, Scott."

"I know it. I know. And it couldn't have happened to a nicer guy. Enjoy. You deserve every minute of it. Before you know it, you'll be home."

"Whoa, that's jumping the gun a little. It's going to be longer than *before I know it.*"

"You'll see. But for right now, we'll be happy for this. We'll take it one day at a time."

"Thanks."

"For what? Coming and visiting your ass in here? It's nothing; I have nothing else to do anyway."

Cain smiled. There was something about Scott's visits that always made him feel good. Talking with Scott, he could really believe that this would all end one day. Scott seemed to be able to keep him focused, to keep him thinking about a life after Maddox. Sometimes he desperately needed that.

On Sunday afternoon he practiced with the team. Each practice he got more and more confident, and his skills became sharper and sharper. The extra exercise made him feel better; and he didn't know if it was his imagination or not, but he even seemed to sleep better at night. After dinner he was relaxing in his cell catching up on some reading, when a guard showed up at his door.

"Here's a pass," the guard said. "Fr. Curtin wants you in his office."

"Why?" asked Cain. He couldn't remember the last time he had been allowed out of his cell at night.

"I don't know. I was just told to get you."

Cain sat up and started putting his boots on. He didn't like this; it didn't feel right. He tucked in his shirt, grabbed the pass, and left. His heart rate increased with every step he took, so that by the time he reached the office, his heart was pounding against his ribs. His hand trembled as he reached for the doorknob to the outer office. Then confusion. Everything turned surreal. He recognized the image of his father, and Bruce? Was that Matt he caught sight of, or was it a mirror across the room? Nothing clicked. Nothing was making sense.

"What's going on?" he asked in a panic. "Something's wrong."

"Sit down," said Fr. Mike.

"I don't want to sit down! Something's wrong. Somebody tell me!!!"

His father emerged from the kaleidoscope of faces and shapes that were swirling by him.

"Cain . . . there's been an accident . . . "

"TELL ME!!!"

"Scott was in a very serious accident last night," his father managed to choke out. "He died a few hours ago."

Cain stood in disbelief. He started to tremble all over as the horrible realization doused out every last spark, flicker, or flame of happiness and enthusiasm in his soul. Tears flooded his eyes as he felt his legs go numb. Just before he would have collapsed on the floor, Mike lent a supportive arm and guided him to a couch where he eased himself down. He tried to let his father's words sink in, but somehow they just weren't real. He looked up at Will, a million questions in his eyes.

"No," Cain said amazingly calm. "He was just here yesterday. We talked for hours. He's coming back on my birthday for my first ball game."

"No," said Will as gently as possible. "He's not coming back . . . ever. Matt and I came right from the hospital to here."

Cain trembled as he let the words settle on him.

"Oh," he bravely choked out. "Please tell me it wasn't on his way home from here; please tell me it wasn't my fault."

"It wasn't your fault," reassured Will. "He probably told you he was home from school for his sister's birthday. He was out with friends last night, and a drunk driver broadsided the car he was a passenger in. He never regained consciousness. They pulled the life supports late this afternoon."

Cain sat in a dazed stupor. His hands were trembling and his eyes were misted over, but there was no emotional rage or bloodletting. He almost didn't seem to comprehend. Will looked helplessly over at Matt. The older twin went over to the couch and sat down next to his brother.

"Cain, look at me," he said. Cain shifted his weary, disbelieving eyes. "Cain, he's gone." Matt needed a few seconds to get control back. "Dad called me at school this morning because they knew there was no hope. They waited for me to come before they . . . " He stopped again and took a deep breath. "Anyway, I pretended I was you—I told him I loved him, and then I told him good bye. He was in a coma, Cain. I don't know if he heard me, but it was all I could think of to do for both of you. His family asked me to stay . . . he wasn't in any pain." Tears ran down his face. "I'm so sorry."

Incredible sadness weighed on his face and tears ran down his cheeks, but Cain remained composed. His hands trembled and he kept wringing them together as he nodded his head absently, trying to send a message that he understood what they were telling him.

"When's the funeral?" he asked.

"Nothing's been finalized, but probably Wednesday."

"I can't go. How fair is that? You should be beside your best friend when they lay him in the ground."

"I tried to get you some time to go," said Bruce. "I even offered to arrange and pay for a police escort, but they wouldn't even consider it. Immediate family only."

"You'll be with him in ways that count more," said Mike.

"A drunk driver? In the other car. He'd never drink and drive—or get in with someone who's been drinking."

"It was the other driver," said Bruce. "He's in jail."

"I wish that made it better."

"I know," comforted Bruce.

"He wasn't even hurt?"

"A few cuts and bruises."

"How is his family—Scott's?"

"Destroyed," said Matt. "But they thought of you right away. They're concerned about you."

"God, this is too much to try and take in. I don't remember not knowing him. He was just here yesterday."

"You were lucky to have such a good friend for so long," said Fr. Mike.

"Yeah, and how do I go on without him? He made sense of all the shit. He gave me a reason to go on." He stopped and looked at Matt. "Don't ever let anything happen to you."

"Okay," said Matt with a tearful smile.

As the evening progressed, Will felt uneasy about Cain and leaving him.

"He's too calm," said Will softly to Fr. Mike and Bruce as his two sons spoke across the room.

"It hasn't hit him yet," said Bruce. "He's in shock."

"Yeah, so how do I walk out of here and leave him to go lock into a cell all by himself?"

"I can go with him," said Mike. "They'll let me stay for a while anyway."

"How could something like this happen?" sighed Will as he ran his fingers through his hair. "I'm so worried about him, and there's nothing I can do. Thank God for you, Mike."

"I'll take good care of him, you know that."

"Thanks," said Will as tears threatened.

"I'm going to have to be getting him upstairs soon before the count and lights-out. You all have a long ride home, and it's been a trying day. Why don't you go—get some rest. I'll stay with Cain as long as they'll let me—which, if I use my influence, will be well into the night. I'll talk with him some more and see if I can't get him to open up."

"I can't thank you enough," said Will wearily.

Cain was distant and very into himself as he and Fr. Mike walked back to A Unit. They barely spoke. Once back at the cell, Mike locked-in with Cain.

"How can you stand to be in here if you don't have to be?" Cain asked as he sat on his bed and began taking off his boots.

"I'm not thinking of me right now. Besides I don't feel like sitting out in the hall with bars between us, so as long as they'll let me in— Are you tired?"

"I don't know; I'm numb."

"That's understandable. This was quite a shock. I'm just kind of used to you throwing things around and raging."

"This is different."

"You're right."

Mike sat on the stool as Cain sat on his bed, leaning against the wall with his legs folded Indian-style. He stared blankly ahead.

"We could pray," suggested Mike.

Cain regarded him skeptically.

"Don't look at me like that," Mike scolded. "This is the time when you need God. I think it's about time you stop blaming God for your problems and you start turning to Him for help and comfort. God didn't make you spend time with Carrie Willet any more than He made that man drink too much before getting behind the wheel of a car. Humans make their own choices, and God hangs around to pick up the pieces. And He's been getting a pretty raw deal from you lately."

Mike struck the nerve he was aiming for. Tears flooded Cain's eyes as he bit at his upper lip trying to hold back the agony that was welling inside him. His hands were trembling out of control.

"Come on," encouraged the priest. "He was your best friend. Grieve for him."

A few strangled sobs escaped his defenses, and he began to tremble violently as tears washed down his face. Still, he struggled for composure as if he could keep Scott alive if he could keep from breaking down. Persistent sobs wouldn't be denied, however, as he was slowly losing control.

"That's the way," prompted Mike as he moved over to sit on the bed next to him. "Let it out."

He placed his hand on Cain's shoulder and gently guided him down toward his bed and pillow. Not a second too soon, Cain buried his face in the pillow as soul-wrenching sobs of grief burst forth. He cried like he never remembered crying before. Sobs and spasms of grief wracked his body as he hugged the pillow to his face. The realization that his friend and confidant was lost to him forever was more than he could bear. A world without Scott in it was something completely foreign to him, something completely beyond his scope of understanding.

His energy was waning as the time for the count rolled around, but he was still lying facedown in a sea of misery when the guard came around. Cain wasn't even aware that the guard was there; Cain wasn't even aware of where he was at that moment.

"Come on, Farrell," said the guard, "you need to be up for the count."

"He's in no shape," said Fr. Mike, angry that the guard was being insistent on following the stupid rule. Most guards knew when to back off.

"He's supposed to be up so I can see his face."

"JUST COUNT HIM!" said Mike, his own emotions being tested.

"All right, all right, Father," relented the guard. "I'm sorry. I do have my orders, but I'll let it go this time."

"You're all heart," sighed the priest beneath his breath.

Cain's breathing gradually leveled off and became more normal. After a while he pushed the pillow aside and rolled to his side. The priest handed him a cold, wet washcloth.

"Thanks," he said, his voice heavy with the aftermath of spent grief. He sat up and wiped his face with the washcloth. "I don't know what I'm going to do. The few really good things in my life are disintegrating right before my eyes. I feel like everything's going to be gone before I get out."

"That won't happen. Some things are bound to change, but not everything."

"Who's going to be next? I'm scared to death."

"Cain . . . "

"I can't stand being cooped up here. How can I get through the next few days knowing what's going on at home? How can I not be there?"

"It'll be hard, but you'll find a way. You have no choice. You heard Bruce."

"Yeah, I heard Bruce. I'm a degenerate locked up in a cage who doesn't even deserve to be at his best friend's funeral."

"That's . . . "

"Don't talk to me. Just go home; I can tell I'm being a bastard."

"I can take it."

"I don't know if I can. I hate myself when I get like this. It's better if I'm alone—that way I'm not abusing anyone." He shook his head as his hands began to tremble again. "God, I just can't fathom this. I can't take it in. If it wasn't so awful, I'd be accusing someone of playing a joke on me."

It was well after 1:00 A.M. when Fr. Mike left. Cain spent most of that time on an emotional roller coaster. Once the priest left, Cain fell into a deep, dreamless sleep. The escape was so complete that he never even heard the wake-up horn that blared through the cellblock at 6:00 A.M. In fact, nothing penetrated his subconscious until well into the morning when he awoke on his own. At first he was disoriented and confused by the bright daylight and the quiet of the cellblock. Then everything settled on him at once: Scott was dead, and he had slept through Wake-up and missed the morning at work.

There was nothing he could do about either, so he dragged himself out of bed and went straight to the sink to douse his aching eyes with cold water. He dressed and made an attempt to shave. He was standing at his window staring blankly out into the bright morning when everyone began returning for the count before lunch. Jon stopped on his way to his own cell.

"Are you all right?" he asked from the hall. "I talked to Fr. Mike."

"I don't know how I am to tell you the truth," answered Cain without turning around.

"I tried to wake you this morning, but you weren't budging. You're coming to lunch, aren't you?"

"I'll go crazy if I stay in here much longer."

As they walked down to lunch together, Jon held back until the others had gone ahead and they were somewhat by themselves.

"Cain, I have to tell you, Lewis is pissed at you."

"Screw him."

"I know, but I just want to warn you. He's pissed because you didn't show up this morning and he's been going off half-cocked all morning. I know how you're feeling, and he's just looking for a fight, so watch yourself."

"I don't think I have any more emotion left in me. I don't care about anything."

"That's good. Let him bitch. And I'm sorry about Scott; I liked him."

"I so don't want to be here. We did everything together; we should be doing this together, too."

"I'm sorry. I don't know what else to say."

"I know. There is nothing else to say."

Lewis wasted no time in harassing Cain for not showing up to work that morning. Cain was prepared for him and not in the mood to be goaded. Not at first anyway.

"Well, well, well," sneered the guard. "If it isn't His Royal Highness. What've you been doing, laying in bed beating off all morning?"

The man was a crude moron. Cain knew it and walked passed him without comment.

"Hold it, hotshot," said Lewis grabbing a hold of Cain's arm. "Not so fast."

Cain stopped and glared down at Lewis's hand. *Don't touch me, asshole.* As he stood nearby, Jon saw that Cain was still filled with enough fire to burn down the warehouse; the revelation worried him. Lewis wisely let go.

"Grab some wall," the guard ordered. "I need to frisk your ass before I let you in."

"Come on, Lewis," complained Jon. "What the hell?"

"Mind your own business and get to work," warned Lewis. Jon hung back to keep an eye on Cain as Lewis turned back. "The wall, Mr. Farrell."

Cain sighed and put his hands on the wall.

"You can do better than that," said Lewis kicking his feet further apart.

Lewis was aware that Cain's mind was far from the task at hand, and that defeated the purpose of his inflicting the humiliation.

"Okay," he said setting out to regain the full attention of his young inmate, "let's just see how good a job you did while you were laying around in bed all morning."

As he moved to frisk down Cain's legs, he purposely reached way up into his groin—a practice that was used only on the most violent and untrustworthy of convicts.

"You faggot!" screamed Cain as he pulled away from the wall and spun around to confront Lewis.

Jon moved a little closer. Lewis was all smiles.

"What's better," he asked, "jackin' off in bed by yourself or raping a crying, helpless female?" That's when Jon moved in and grabbed Cain by the arm and jerked him away from Lewis. Lewis foolishly persisted. "Is that like the ultimate hard-on . . . rape? I wouldn't know because I have much more manners and breeding than that."

"Shut up, Lewis," said Jon shepherding Cain toward the inside of the warehouse. "Didn't your mommy ever teach you that it's not smart to play with fire? You're liable to end up getting burned."

"Hey, Farrell, Mr. Hotshot Rapist," called Lewis to Cain's back, "just for the record, I busted your ass this morning—I wrote you up for not showing up to work. One more, and your transfer to B Unit is a wet dream."

"Steady," mumbled Jon as they continued walking away. He could feel Cain tense beneath his grip. "Don't let him get to you. The man's a moron; he's not worth it."

"Farrell!" called Lewis trying once more to get a rise out of Cain.

Without turning around, Cain raised his left hand in the air and flashed his middle finger at Lewis. Then he did turn.

"Someday," he yelled back to Lewis so everyone around could hear, "I'm gonna fuck your fat ass, and then I'll be able to answer your jerking-off-or-rape question."

Hysterical laughter went off all around.

"Why the hell did I just say that?" Cain asked Jon as he turned back and continued walking.

"I don't know, but it was damn funny."

Jon laughed with everyone else, but it bothered him to notice that Cain hadn't even cracked a smile.

Lewis rushed over to where Cain had joined a trucker from the outside who had just delivered a trailer full of goods to be stored.

"You listen to me," he ranted at Cain as he waved a finger in his face, "you talk to me like that again, and I'll send you back to your two-bit cell and write you up right out of your transfer."

"Whatever," said Cain as he started to move boxes. "You do whatever it is that gives you a hard-on, because I just don't care any more. I don't care about anything—least of all, your bullshit."

"YOU THINK YOU DON'T CARE, HUHN?" screamed Lewis whipping himself into a rage. "WELL LET'S JUST SEE HOW MUCH YOU DON'T CARE!"

Convicts, the trucker, and guards alike were all watching the scenario unfold. Each was amazed at Lewis's obsession with picking a fight with Cain, and the way the tables were turning on him. Cain was getting under his skin much more than he was riling Cain. He persisted in his unwise taunting.

"What's this I hear about your mama out doing the streets to pay off you legal fees?"

Cain put down a box he was moving and gave Lewis a pathetic look. It was a cheap jailhouse trick to attack the integrity of someone's mother, wife, girlfriend, or sister. He wasn't dumb enough to get caught up in such adolescent drivel.

"You're an asshole," he mumbled as he picked up another box and began to move it.

"What is this, you're not man enough to stand up for your mother?!'"

Cain rolled his eyes wearily at the trucker at his side. Then he turned to Lewis.

"I'm assuming I'm every bit as much a man as you are—maybe more. But you're the only one who knows that for sure because **I've** never felt **your** balls."

Smiles all around, except for Cain and Lewis. The inmate walked around the red-faced guard as he took the box to where it was being stored.

"You got a smart mouth, you know that?" Lewis asked as he followed Cain. "But fuck, man, you're nothing but a pussy. Everyone here can see that. You don't have the balls to stand up for yourself."

Cain dropped the box and turned on Lewis. Jon tried to move through the small group that had gathered so he could get to Cain, but another guard held him back.

"Look," complained Cain coming face-to-face with Lewis, "all you've been doing is bitching about how I didn't work this morning; and now that I'm trying to get something done, you're following me around talking trash. Exactly what do you want? I'm not in the mood for your shit."

"Oh, you're not, are you? Well, good because I'm in the mood to throw a lot of shit your way. And if it bugs you, that's all the better. So what do you think about that, Mr. College-Boy-Hotshot-Rapist?"

Lewis who was inches shorter than Cain reached up and with both hands shoved him in the chest. Guards around the warehouse quickly tried getting the other inmates back to work, but nobody was moving. The guards removed their clubs and positioned themselves in front of the crowd that was assembled. Jon tried in vain to maneuver his way around so he could get to Cain, but guards kept everyone at bay.

The trucker was the closest one to Cain, but he backed off and kept his distance.

"Knock it off, Lewis," said Cain. "I don't want trouble."

"THEN WHY DON'T YOU DO WHAT YOU'RE SUPPOSED TO DO, WHEN YOU'RE SUPPOSED TO DO IT? HUHN?" He shoved him again. "INSTEAD OF LAYING AROUND IN BED ALL MORNING!"

"I OVERSLEPT!"

"NOBODY SLEEPS THROUGH THAT GOD-FORSAKEN HORN!"

"I DID!"

"NO, YOU DIDN'T! I THINK YOU JUST WANTED TO BE A PRIMADONA AND TAKE THE MORNING OFF! YOU THINK YOU'RE BETTER THAN EVERYONE ELSE! YOU THINK THESE GUYS CAN JUST PICK UP THE SLACK FOR YOU WHILE YOU TAKE SOME TIME OFF!"

"You're pathetic," sighed Cain shaking his head and turning to go back to work.

"DON'T WALK AWAY WHILE I'M TALKING TO YOU!"

Lewis reached out and grabbed Cain by the arm. Jon swore he could see the flash when Cain could finally take no more and exploded. Obviously others saw the fuse ignite also since a guard had already rushed to push the panic button in the warehouse just as Cain turned back to Lewis and sent a powerful left fist into the guard's face. Once the rage was turned loose, there was no way of calling it back, so Lewis flailed around helplessly, the victim of his own stupidity. Cain was out of control. All the frustration and emotion of the past two days fueled him with enough energy and rage to take on three men Lewis's size. Luckily for both of them the security squad arrived and spared Lewis serious injury. As it was, it took all four of the security officers to drag Cain away from Lewis.

He was crazed, though, and continued to fight and struggle with the strength of two men. They beat him with their clubs and wrestled him to the ground until finally they were able to cuff his hands and shackle his ankles. He was far from subdued, however, as they dragged him quickly from the warehouse.

He was cut and bleeding, but he struggled against the odds all the way. Soon they were at the top of a stairway. A guard sent a wooden club into his stomach, which doubled him over. It would have sent him to the ground if two of them weren't holding his arms. They had his attention. The guard grabbed a handful of his hair and lifted his head until he was looking down the stairway in front of him.

"Now," said the guard breathless from the whole ordeal, "you see those stairs? If you think we're going to let you take us down those stairs with you, you're crazy. So you either calm down and walk like a good boy, or we'll let go and you can break your own neck."

He was dizzy and confused, and blood was running into his eyes from a cut on his eyebrow, but he was regaining his wits and he knew he was no match for them. His legs felt like rubber and in some ways it seemed like they were no longer connected to the rest of his body. But he carefully stepped, praying they would hold on to him since he could not hold on for himself. He was disoriented and had no idea of where they were, but he was getting scared since they seemed to be moving deeper and deeper into the bowels of the prison. It was cold and dark and there was no one else to be seen but the five of them. Then he spotted the sign over a door they were about to enter SOLITARY UNIT.

"No," he cried dismally.

They dragged him along, causing the chains to pull and yank at his body. He felt lightheaded, and a few times he actually thought he was going to lose consciousness. The pain was intense, but he wasn't sure he was relieved when they finally reached their destination. They sat him in a chair and used a thick, leather belt around his arms and chest to strap him in. He was panting from breathlessness, and he could barely hold his head up.

"You've been a real pain in the ass, you know that?" the head guard told him. "Now sit still while we finish our work."

That's when he saw one of the other guards approach him with an electric clippers. He kicked and hollered in protest as they started shaving off his hair.

"You're just making it harder on yourself," the guard told him. "We certainly don't care how much scalp we cut when we do this. All we care is we get it done. You'll learn to fuck with us."

Cain knew the guard was right. There was no purpose to be served in struggling. Every time he moved the shears dug into his scalp. So he sat still, his whole body trembling, tears streaming freely down his face as he watched great clumps of his blond hair fall on his lap. Hair was all over. Some of it clung to the blood and sweat on his face; some got in his mouth and nose. This was an illegal practice, but a lot of good that did him. They cut as close to the scalp as was possible without a razor, leaving blonde stubble. Then suddenly as they finished, one of them dumped a bucket of water over his head to wash away the blood and hair. Feeling like he was drowning, he choked and coughed the unexpected water out of his nose and mouth. Now, not only was the temperature down there uncomfortably cold, but he was soaking wet.

This was no longer about him and Lewis. This had turned into an issue between him and the establishment, and he didn't like the turn it was taking. He hated them for shaving his head, and he wished so badly that he could get himself free to take them on. He felt ready to burst with anger and resentment all over again.

"There," said the head of the security squad as he squatted down right in front of him and looked him in the eye. "Now are you gonna be a good boy? We need to unchain you so you can strip before we lock you up and throw away the key."

In spite of his condition he had the presence of mind to be aware that he was about to knowingly do the stupidest thing he had ever done in his whole life. Looking the guard defiantly in the eye, he spat in his face. They had him right where they wanted him, but he wasn't about to just hand himself over to them.

The guard wiped his face with his shirtsleeve and then reached out and punched Cain square in the jaw. The stars were still swirling in his head as the four-man group accosted him—first unstrapping him from the chair, then pulling and ripping at his clothes. They literally tore or cut the clothes off his body with a scissors without removing the chains. He struggled and kicked for all he was worth, giving them a good fight and making them work twice as hard as they had expected.

The rest was a blur. How he got to the tiny padded cell, he had no idea. The first rational moment he had, he was chained naked on the floor of the cell pressed into a corner opposite the door. The other guards were leaving the cell making room for their leader who knelt on one knee in front of Cain.

"You spit at me again, and they'll be picking up your teeth all over the place," he warned, still breathless from the whole encounter. "You did this the fucking hard way, I hope you know. Now behave yourself, and maybe I'll be back later to unchain you. But you keep being a bastard and you'll do a couple months down here in chains, I swear to God."

Cain was staring blankly off in another direction. He couldn't have focused on the guard's face even if he had wanted to.

"You understand me?" the guard asked.

"Yes," mumbled Cain in a barely audible voice, still staring into space.

"I'd like nothing better than to kick the shit out of you, so don't tempt me."

Cain leaned his head against the wall and closed his eyes.

"That's more like it," crowed the guard.

Cain wanted to convey the message for him to *go to hell*, but his eyes were too tired and battered to speak. So he remained stoically propped against the wall, his eyes closed, letting his body language speak for him. The guard kicked him soundly in the hip and left. Cain swallowed a cry and tightened his tucked position. Chains bit into his body everywhere as he shivered from the cold. He was too exhausted and filled with pain to open his eyes and examine his new surroundings. Somehow he knew he wasn't going to like it, so why go through the effort? He just hugged himself tightly and pressed protectively into the corner as he tried to stay warm.

He must have fallen asleep because the next thing he knew, he was waking up in he blackest darkness he had ever experienced. For a minute it took his breath away and sent all his senses scrambling in search of some kind of familiarity as he tried to piece together the events of the day. If he could have raised his hand, he wouldn't have been able to see it in front of his face. He felt totally enveloped by the dark. His body shivered almost convulsively from the cold, and he could barely feel his feet. His face felt all distorted from swelling, and it throbbed. He remembered Scott. Hot tears burned through his swollen eyes and down his bruised cheeks. *Dear God, please tell me this is rock bottom—there's nothing left to lose.*

The darkness became the perfect medium for his reverie. He could plainly see Scott through the years as they grew up together, but it was that last night at the beach that kept coming back to him. He almost felt like he could reach out and touch him the way he did that night. One-on-one volleyball, chasing each other along the shore, flirting with girls, promising to meet back there with champagne. Tears streamed down his face as he broke down and cried for the loss of his friend. He didn't want to think about a lifeless body lying in a funeral home, but that was all he could think of. He hated the image, but he didn't know how to make it go away. How could it be? How is it that he'll never see Scott again, or receive his cheery letters?

His head hurt, and every cut and bruise he had was throbbing. It was hard to think. The events of the past two days were blurred into black haze of confusion, regret, sadness, and anger. He wanted a bed; in the worst way he wanted a bed.

Suddenly the light in the cell came on. He was totally blinded by it as he turned his head toward the wall for added protection from its intruding brightness. He heard the door open. He had no idea who was coming in, and at that point he didn't even care.

"Holy shit," sighed the doctor under his breath. He turned to the guard who had accompanied him. "Chains?"

"He asked for it," answered the guard in defense of the brutality.

The doctor knelt down next to Cain.

"I'm Dr. Samson," he said. "I'm not going to hurt you, but I want to check you over." He turned Cain's face toward his and winced at the swollen cuts and bruises. Cain was shivering uncontrollably. The doctor turned back to the guard. "He's in shock. Get me a pillow and a blanket—a large blanket. And don't argue with me, or I'm going straight to the warden and put in a complaint about this—it looks like someone got carried away with the club. I'd be curious to know how many of these cuts and bruises were administered **after** he was restrained in chains. Can you remove the chains before you leave?"

"I don't have the key. And it ain't my decision—or yours—to make. I have to wait for the boss to come back. And just for your information, chains or no chains, he fought like a grizzly bear until the very end when we dumped him in the cell."

"Christ," sighed the doctor. "Go get that blanket. Hurry."

Cain's left eye was nearly swollen shut, and there was blood all over his face and upper torso. Ugly bruises were becoming more and more evident every minute. He stared blankly, not really sure any more where he was or what was going on.

"I just want to sleep," he told the doctor.

"When I'm through, you can sleep, but first let me see where this blood is coming from. I have a nurse with me, and she's bringing some water and towels. Can you move your arms and legs okay?"

"I don't know; I'm cold."

"I know. I'm getting you a blanket." He started probing the cut in Cain's eyebrow. "Why the hell did you try to fight them? Never mind, I probably would've done the same thing."

The nurse appeared with the water and other supplies, and the doctor went about washing off the blood and cleaning him up.

"I don't think you need stitches over that eye, but I can't tape it up while you're shivering like this. Where the hell is that guard with the blanket?"

As if on cue the guard showed up at the door. The doctor snatched the blanket from him and wrapped it snugly around Cain.

"There," he said tucking it all around him to ensure maximum warmth, "that should help. Can you tell me if you have any sharp stabbing pains?"

"Nothing," he said absently, his head resting in the corner. "I want to go to sleep."

"I know. I'll be through soon. Let me see if I can put a couple butterfly bandages on that cut so it stops bleeding."

"My head hurts."

"I have a pain killer. There's a pillow here, do you want to try and lay down?"

"No, chains hurt too much. They dig in."

"Okay," said the doctor carefully applying the second butterfly strip over the cut on Cain's eyebrow. "But I have to move you because I want to check your ribs and the bruises and be sure there's no internal bleeding. Then I'll let you sleep. Okay?"

"Yeah, but I don't want to dream."

"Maybe you won't," smiled the doctor. "I'm going to disturb you for a minute though while I shift this blanket. Okay? I'm going to spread it on the floor so you can sit on it, and then we'll wrap it around you. That way I can check you out better, and you'll probably stay warmer, too."

The doctor took his time and made sure that Cain was all right. Then he gave him a pain pill.

"Did you see my mom?" he asked in confusion.

"No."

"She's going to worry."

"We'll tell her not to worry."

"Okay," he said still staring numbly into the air as silent tears streamed down his face. "How long do I have to stay here?"

"I don't know," answered the doctor. "That's up to the guards. Just promise me this: don't fight them any more. You can't win that battle. Just do what they say, and you'll get out a lot sooner without getting hurt any more. You got lucky this time. I know they battered the hell out of you, but there are no broken bones or internal bleeding. It's probably lucky your mom can't see you now; she'd never recognize you."

He packed up his things and adjusted the blanket around Cain.

"Is there anything else I can do for you?" the doctor asked.

"No. Thanks."

"I'm going to leave these pain pills with the guard. Just tell him if you want one."

The doctor left, and suddenly the lights went out. Cain gasped; that total darkness was going to take some getting used to. He'd have to think about that later, though, because now all he wanted to do was close his eyes and shut out all memory and pain for a while. The pill he had taken helped take the edge off. He knew the chains were still there and he couldn't move very much, but he could no longer feel them biting into his skin and rubbing it raw. His head began feeling light and airy. That was a relief. He closed his eyes, and he was gone.

He had totally lost track of time, so he had no idea what time— or even what day—it was when the lights came back on and nudged him awake. He guessed it hadn't been too many hours since the doctor had left, for he was still in the throes of the drug and he had a hard time coaxing his eyes opened. He opted to just leave them shut. Even when he heard the key in the door, he remained detached and unresponsive.

"Hey, you awake?" the lieutenant of the security squad asked.

"I guess so," said Cain groggily. "I doubt that you're a dream."

"No, but I could be your worst nightmare."

"Touché."

The guard carefully eyed the cuts and bruises as he went over and sat down next to Cain.

"So, hero, have you calmed down enough so I can take the chains off? You gonna be a good boy now?"

"I'm always good," said Cain sleepily resting his head back in the corner and closing his eyes again.

"That's a matter of opinion. Where'd you get the blanket?"

"From the doctor. I don't suppose you have any warm clothes for me to put on."

"You've got the blanket—don't push it."

"Just curious. Are you allowed to tell me what time it is?"

"It's just about 9:00 P.M."

"Same day?"

"Same day. Now how 'bout the chains? Ask me real nice, and I'll take them off."

"Nah," said Cain managing a slight smile. "I'm not good at begging."

"Then I'll leave them on."

"Fine. I don't care. Everything's a mess. Nothing matters. Actually, being dead sounds kind of inviting."

"What makes you think you'll be dead?"

"Can't move my hands—can't eat."

"Then I guess I'd better unchain you."

"Whatever."

The guard went about the job of unlocking and removing chains.

"How long do I have to stay here—about a month or two until my hair grows in and the bruises go away so you have no explaining to do?"

"Boy, you really don't know when to keep your mouth shut, do you?"

"It must be some post getting-the-hell-beat-our-of-me syndrome. I don't know what I'm saying." Cain rubbed his freed wrists. "Can I get some water? Your accommodations here stink."

The guard looked around the barren cell. There was nothing but padded walls and floor and a small toilet.

"We're hoping you'll be discouraged from wanting to come back."

"Mmm. Gotcha." He stretched his stiffened arms under the blanket.

"You know what? I'll see you and your bare ass in a month or so when we let you out of here, and then we'll see if you're still so cocky."

"I won't be," said Cain laying his head back against the wall. "Is that what you want to hear? I probably won't even be coherent any more. You'll win; I can tell you that now."

Thwarted, the guard stood speechless for a few seconds. Then he turned toward the door.

"I'll send some water down."

"Thanks."

And then the door closed and locked, and he was alone again. From the sound of things, it was going to be a while before he'd see another human.

A few minutes later a small glass of water was passed under the opening at the bottom of the door. Slowly and with much pain, he made his way across the short distance to the glass. It took only a few swallows to down the contents. He knew as long as he was in there they would leave him wanting for more. It was part of their psychological warfare. He rolled the glass back through the opening. Suddenly the lights went out. The blackness digested him whole as he sat for a moment trying to adjust to the change. Then he crawled around until he came upon the pillow. It at least felt good to be able to move again, even if it did hurt like hell. Carefully, he lay down and tucked the pillow under his weary, aching head. He pulled the blanket around himself, striving to cover his whole body. He was scared and alone, but he fought back tears, fearing once he started crying, he'd never be able to stop.

As might be expected, he slept fitfully, waking often trying to find a comfortable position. Dreams and nightmares punctuated the spans of time when he did find his sleep. More than once he woke up shivering uncontrollably because he had flung off the blanket in his sleep. By the time the lights came on again, he was near hysteria, not certain what was real in the blackness and what was nightmare.

He assumed it was morning, but there was no guarantee. He knew they would toy with his sanity by playing games with the lights. There would be no rhyme or reason or pattern to when the lights would be on or off. They wanted to confuse him, and he was too weary to try and beat them at the game. What difference did it make anyway? He wasn't going anywhere. Then he remembered Scott and stabbing pains pierced his wounded spirit.

Suddenly a tray was pushed under his door. A small box of cold cereal, dry toast, a carton of milk, and a glass of water—no utensils. He hadn't eaten in God-only-knew-how-many hours. This unappetizing breakfast would probably fill his big toe. He knew there was a camera mounted in the ceiling of the cell, and he guessed someone was on the other end enjoying his misery, but he was beyond caring. No utensils. As gracefully as possible, he navigated his way through the tasteless meal. Getting food passed his cut and swollen lips was a feat in itself. He couldn't bite the toast; he had to break off small pieces and put them in his mouth.

Soon after he finished and shoved the tray out into the hall, the light went out again. He nearly broke down and cried. There was nothing to see with the light on, but he felt more secure and in touch with reality in the light. He sat for hours in the dark, concentrating on keeping his mind from playing tricks on him and wishing he were dead. He had never been so cold in his life; and to make matters worse, time had stopped. He kept his body huddled in a tight knot as he clutched the blanket around him in an attempt to warm himself. If only he didn't have such a headache. If only his whole body wasn't screaming out in pain. If only he hadn't ever met Carrie Willet.

Then for no apparent reason, the light went on again. Maybe food was coming. It'd been a long time since breakfast, and he was definitely hungry. But then just as erratically as the light had come on, it went off about a half-hour later. No food, and now he was plunged back into darkness. He was cold; the blanket wasn't enough to ward off the damp chill. As the hours went by, not only did he give up on lunch, but also he had to fight off the hallucinations that were creeping into his brain. He began to imagine noises in the cell with him, and his frantic mind attributed them to mice and cockroaches, or maybe rats. He huddled tightly in the corner trying to stay warm, and he prayed that nothing was crawling on his blanket. His teeth chattered as he shook uncontrollably. Then the light went on.

As soon as his eyes adjusted, he searched the floor and walls for signs to give credence to his suspicions. But there was nothing. He took a few deep breaths to calm himself. Then some nameless, faceless benefactor pushed a food tray under the door. Gathering his wits, he examined dinner: macaroni and cheese, cooked carrots, two pieces of bread—no butter, and a glass of water. No utensils. Miserable tears of self-pity running down his cheeks, he attacked the tray voraciously. Barely had he finished and pushed the tray through the door slot when the light went out again.

"NO!" he cried frantically, anticipating many long hours of darkness.

He had to concentrate on not losing his composure. He didn't know how much more darkness he could take, and he had only just begun his sentence in Solitary. He couldn't let himself think of the days that stretched out before him. It was important to get through one minute at a time. He couldn't fall apart and let them win. As bad as he felt, he still had his pride.

Reasoning that one day had passed since he had been locked up down there, he realized that this was the night of Scott's wake. Tears that he didn't even know were threatening suddenly burst forth, and he sobbed out loud. It still wasn't real to him. He still couldn't imagine Scott without life. He had had very little experience with death, and this just hit too close to home to be comprehended. As much as he didn't want to see the shell that was Scott, he kind of needed to see it to make his grief complete. And now not only was he being denied this closure, he was being locked up and treated like an animal. His eyes burned and his head ached as he cried hysterically and then fell into a dreamless sleep.

As much as it didn't seem possible, the days did pass. He never saw or spoke with anyone. Magically, his two meals a day appeared under the door slot. The only other thing he was ever given was water, but he never saw or heard the guards who delivered any of it. He hadn't had a cigarette in days, and now that the numb shock of the whole experience was wearing off, his body was craving nicotine. It was only one more thing to drive him crazy.

His greatest fear was that they were going to forget him there—especially since he never saw or spoke to anyone. A few times he actually had to stop himself from hyperventilating as the thought consumed him. His heart raced, and panic welled inside him. He had no idea who actually knew he was there—or who even cared. He couldn't stop thinking about how easy it would be for them to just walk away, and leave him there buried alive.

There wasn't much else to do but think, and it seemed that only gruesome and depressing things entered his mind. He tried to keep his body from stagnating, but there wasn't much room to do anything but stand and stretch out a little. The majority of his time was still spent in the dark, which tended to magnify his fears. He thought he heard mice or cockroaches, or maybe both, but at first he concluded that it was important to convince himself that he was only imagining it. Then he realized that the reality of sharing his cell with rodents and bugs frightened him slightly less that the thought of hallucinating about their presence did. He had to keep his mind sharp. Once he let go, he wasn't sure he'd ever get it back.

One day a few hours after breakfast, the light went on and the key sounded in the door. He had his eyes squeezed shut and couldn't focus.

"Fr. Curtin was down here a while ago," announced the guard who had opened he door. "He comes down to check now and then. He said it's your birthday."

Cain frowned, almost as if he didn't understand. His eyes still weren't used to the light.

"Leave the blanket here," continued the guard, "and I'll give you ten, maybe fifteen, minutes with a razor, a toothbrush, and a bar of soap."

Cain got up and slowly started to leave the cell. He wasn't very far down the hall when he had to stop and hold on to the wall because he felt dizzy.

"You okay?" the guard asked.

"Yeah," he sighed groggily. "Just give me a minute."

"Take your time. We just have to go a little further."

"You didn't start counting my time yet, did you?"

"No," smiled the guard. "Hell, it's your birthday."

In the shower room he saw himself in the mirror for the first time since his fight with Lewis and the security squad. His eye and his lip were still somewhat swollen. He had a huge gash in his left eyebrow, and his lips were split in two or three places. The bruises covering his face and body were still pretty fresh and tender. He hardly recognized the image in the mirror; his hair was coming back in but was still little more than fuzz, and his beard was starting to become something of substance. The reflection was totally foreign to him.

His hand was slightly shaky as he attempted to shave the days'-growth beard, and he had to be careful of the cuts and bruises; but it felt good to get rid of the coarse facial hair. Then he brushed his teeth, which was the greatest pleasure. The hot water of the shower poured over his aching and chilled body and warmed him to the soul. It was also good to wash off some of the blood, which was still smeared and caked on him.

It all ended too soon, and he dried off and wrapped the towel around his midsection. He stood in front of the mirror and examined the cut in his eyebrow. Carefully he removed the butterfly strips, which had soaked loose in the shower.

"Do you have a Band-Aid or something?" he asked. "This is starting to bleed again."

The guard gave him two more butterfly Band-Aids which Cain carefully fingered back over the cut.

Then the guard held his hand out for the towel. Cain reluctantly gave it to him and walked back to the cell. He immediately grabbed the blanket and wrapped it around his shivering still-damp body. Without another word, the guard closed the door and locked it. The light stayed on. A birthday present.

He leaned against the wall and struggled with the realization that his brief stint on the outside was over and now he was doomed once more to loneliness and desolation. At least he knew that Mike came down occasionally, so he felt more secure about someone knowing where he was.

*Happy birthday.* He was twenty-one now—a man. If only he didn't feel like a dazed and frightened animal. His mind wandered back to past birthdays with Matt. He wondered how his brother would be spending this momentous birthday. Here was another right of passage that was taking place out in the real world and passing him by. You can never go back and have a twenty-first birthday again.

He remembered the first baseball game, and his mood plunged even lower. He had no idea how all of this was going to figure into the rest of his life, but he knew it wasn't going to be good. He guessed it was time to give up the baseball dream once and for all. He slid down the wall and huddled under the blanket to warm his legs and feet.

For a while he tried to keep track of the days, but it just got to be too much work. He kept losing count, and to be honest, he didn't really care. That was the main reason he gave up. What difference did it make? Why go to all the effort?

He didn't like the way he was starting to feel, but he didn't know how to stop the skid. He felt more and more remote and out of touch as the days continued to slip by. He felt like he was adrift in outerspace. The longer they held him down there, the more detached from the outside world he became. It was harder and harder to try and imagine daily routine going on anywhere. Sometimes he would talk out loud just to hear something. Sometimes he sang softly to himself just to break into the nothingness that surrounded him. His beard began to thicken again, and his hair felt less prickly and downier. But once again, who cared?

Then one day his nothing existence was interrupted by the sound of the key in the door. The light had been on all morning, so there was no intruding glare to interfere with his vision. Still, he squinted his eyes and didn't trust what he saw.

"Mike?" he asked skeptically.

"Hi," said the priest walking over and sitting down next to him.

"Don't get too close," said Cain weakly resting his head against the wall. "I remember the last time I showered, I just don't know when it was. But it was a long time ago."

"That's okay. It would take more than that to scare me away. How are you?"

"Alive."

"Well, I've come to take you out of here."

"I can't."

"Why not?"

"I'm . . . I don't know . . . I just can't."

"Well, let's talk for a few minutes. Then maybe you'll feel differently."

"I feel like if I step out of here I'm going to drop off the face of the earth."

"You've been here a long time—ten days."

"It feels like ten years. I've stopped relating to the outside. This is like a cocoon or something. I don't have to deal with anything." His voice was groggy and lethargic. "A lot of shit's going to come my way when I leave here. I'm not strong enough to deal with it now."

"That's why I'm here. I'll help. And it's not all bad . . . not as bad as you think."

"I don't think anymore."

"Come on, a shave and a hot shower will help. I'll give you a hand."

"I don't know if I can face what's out there. I know I'm in a lot of trouble. At first I used to cry and pray that they'd let me out. Now I think it's better if I just stay."

"I know what you're saying, but you have some things going for you on your side. They don't hold all the cards. Come on, I went to your cell and got you clean clothes. Cain, your parents are here."

He sat in stunned silence.

"Mike?" he finally said fingering the still-tender cut over his eye.

"They're prepared, Cain. I've talked with them. They're just so happy to be able to see you. And it's Thursday—not a weekend. You have some grounds for a lawsuit; the administration knows it. They're being very cooperative. So while you are in some trouble, they have trouble of their own; and they're willing to deal. Come on, I know you'll be interested. Can you stand?"

It was with a great deal of effort that he stood and maneuvered his way down the hall to the shower room. A couple of times he stopped and leaned against the wall for a breather.

"I feel wiped out," he sighed with a smile.

"Take your time," said Mike as he was about to leave him with the guard. "I'll be right down the hall waiting. You've lost a good bit of weight that you didn't have to lose in the first place. You'll feel better after you clean up and have something to eat. You okay for now?"

"Yeah."

Mike turned to the guard.

"Keep an eye on him," he warned.

After he had shaved, Cain studied his face in the mirror. The fading bruises were smudge marks on his forehead, his left cheekbone, and his chin. The cut over his left eye was still evident, but it was definitely healing. The cuts on his lips were pencil line openings. His hair had grown in to the point where it was lying down on his scalp in a soft mat. He guessed he didn't look too scary for his mother.

It felt good to put clothes on again, but he noticed right away that he had indeed lost weight. That wasn't going to go over good with Mom. He felt incredibly weak and off-balance. Out of sync. Relacing and tying his last boot, he announced to the guard that he was ready.

He was taken to a small room across the hall where he was stunned to see Mrs. Doleman and Bruce Rothwell sitting with Fr. Mike.

"Come, sit down," invited Victoria Doleman.

Bruce got up and gave him a fatherly hug.

"You okay?" he asked.

"I will be," sighed Cain as he feebly took a seat at the table where they were sitting. "What's going on?"

"Cain, what happened last week was a disaster—from all points," said Mrs. Doleman. "It should never have escalated to the extreme it did. What you did was wrong, but we have inmates who are willing to testify that Lewis instigated the confrontation by antagonizing you and even pushing and shoving you. The doctor who came down and cared for you reported that he believed many of the cuts and bruises you received were actually administered after you were chained up."

Now he understood why Bruce was there.

"Is that true?" she asked.

Cain rubbed his fingers along his jaw as vivid pictures flashed before him. He shifted his gaze over to his lawyer. Bruce nodded permission to answer.

"Yes." He had learned to answer questions without giving any unasked-for information.

"Okay," she went on. "We've had an investigation going on, lawyers checking into everybody's legal options, and a myriad of discussions taking place the whole time you've been locked up. This is the final conclusion we've reached. All we need is your agreement to it, and the book's closed."

Cain eyed her somewhat suspiciously, but he remained silent as she went on to explain.

"Lewis will not press criminal charges, so you're off the hook there. In return you won't press any charges against the security squad."

He made eye contact with Bruce again who once more sent a silent message of approval.

"What you did was grievously wrong, however," said Mrs. Doleman. "No matter what, you have to remain in control of your temper if you want the Parole Board to take you seriously one day down the road. Everyone, more in his own best interest than yours, agrees that you've been punished enough . . . except that they're pulling your transfer to B Unit . . . permanently. You'll spend the rest of your sentence in A."

The dagger found its mark, and Cain had to brace himself against the table to keep from falling over. It could be worse, he kept telling himself. Criminal charges from Lewis would certainly mean more prison time. It could be worse, but that didn't matter. The disappointment welled inside him threatening his fragile emotional well being.

"What do you think?" asked Victoria Doleman.

He looked at her, a shell of whom he was only two weeks ago. He knew he had no choice. He wished he felt better.

"Fine," he conceded.

"Okay," she smiled. "Bruce has the papers already drawn up and signed. All we need is your signature, and we'll put this all behind us."

*Except I'm doomed to A Unit*, he thought. He knew they'd have to come out ahead in the end. He wasn't sure he had the strength to hold the pen, let alone write his name in agreement to that horrific sentence. He managed the signature, and then rubbed his face wearily.

"What about Lewis?" he asked.

"What about him?" asked Mrs. Doleman.

"I don't see anything there about me being transferred to a different work station. Am I supposed to go back there like nothing happened and deal with his crap?"

Mrs. Doleman thought for a moment before she answered.

"He seemed to feel there'd be no problem with you going back there."

"What about me? What about what I think? What happened was not my fault. I was wrong, but I did not start that, and I tried to walk away from him—more than once."

"Well, you're going to lock-in until Monday, by then everyone will have had two weeks to let things cool down."

"You're totally missing the point, but forget it."

"Cain . . ."

"Forget it," he repeated testily. "I'm tired."

"Come on," said Mike, "enough business. You're parents are eagerly waiting up in my office. You have permission to meet up there—no table. I also had some lunch sent in for all of us."

B Unit offered open, free contact meeting with visitors. One-by-one the implications of his life sentence to A Unit were refreshing themselves in Cain's mind. It had been two-and-a-half years since he had been able to hug his mother, and after today it would be at least that long again.

Mike and Bruce accompanied him upstairs. They both reassured him that he had done the right thing in agreeing to an out-of-court settlement.

"Yeah, well, somebody had better talk to Lewis because we're going to get into it again," Cain said. "It's part of his agenda."

"I've already made a mental note of it," said Mike. "Now buck up for your mom, huhn? She's worried to death about you. And if it makes you feel any better, we also got permission for you to continue playing in the home baseball games. You just can't leave for away games."

"Well, I guess that's something anyway." He realized he sounded spoiled and ungrateful. "Thanks."

Soon they were up just outside of Fr. Mike's office. Cain stopped short of the closed door.

"You okay?" asked Bruce.

"Yeah. I just need a minute."

He carefully rubbed his healing face and took a deep breath. Then raising himself to his full height, he nodded he was ready. Mike opened the door. His parents were sitting in the outer office with the priest's secretary. They all turned in the direction of the just-opened door. Cain managed a smile as he walked in and took his mother in his arms.

"I'm okay," he reassured her as she cried softly into his chest.

After a brief moment she composed herself, but he held her close.

"Don't let go just yet," he said softly. "I'm okay, but I just want you to hold me."

"Sure, sweetheart," she answered hugging him tightly, painfully aware of the frailty of his usually firm body.

He stepped back and kissed her on the forehead.

"Can we sit down?" he asked feeling a bit wobbly.

"Sure," said Mike. "Everyone sit down and get comfortable."

"I'm going to let Bruce fill you in on all the crap that went on this morning," said Cain. "I don't want to talk about it, except to say there's nothing to worry about. I have to lock-in till Monday, and after that it's business as usual. It's open season on me as long as I have Sam Willet on my back, and there's nothing I can do about it. At least no more charges were filed, and I am grateful for that. Now, tell me what's been going on for the past ten days."

Nora reached over and took Cain's hand.

"Honey," she said holding it firmly in both of hers, "I'm so sorry about Scott. You know we loved him like one of our own."

"I know, Mom. He loved you, too. How's his family?"

"Devastated as you might guess, but they are holding up remarkably well. I talked with his mom just yesterday. She said to say hi to you, and to tell you she has some things of Scott's she knows he would like you to have. So she's saving them for you for when you come home."

Reality began taking concrete form again as tears began to burn behind his eyes.

"Okay," he managed to say. "And the funeral and everything went . . . okay?"

"Yes," answered Nora. "Matt was a pallbearer."

"I should have been there," said Cain rocking slightly in place.

"It was unfortunate that you couldn't be," said his mother reaching up to gently caress his bruised cheek. "But everyone who mattered knew and understood, and Scott didn't care any more. He's waiting for you in a better place."

"Why can't I get it through my head that he's gone? It's all I've been thinking about, yet something in me won't let me accept it."

"It's hard when you're so far removed," said Will.

"They have the guy who did it, right?"

"Right," answered Will. "This isn't his first arrest involving alcohol, so there's a good chance he'll get sent to prison."

"I'm so tired," Cain sighed as he slouched back on the couch and laid his head back. "How can I be tired? I haven't done anything for ten days."

"That'll do it," said Mike. "And you haven't been eating near the amount of food that you're used to. I sent for some sandwiches; they should be here in a few minutes."

Cain reached up and tried to rub some life into his face. His hand was trembling as he did. He had become used to the shakes he had been experiencing, but Nora noticed it right away.

"Are you okay, honey?" she asked with alarm.

"Yeah, Mom, I'm fine. It's nothing that a little rest and some good cafeteria food won't fix. At least I can look forward to three meals a day again."

"You haven't been eating three times a day?!" asked his mother.

"No," he smiled as he closed his eyes and tried to ignore the migraine that was whipping itself to a frenzy inside his head.

Nora shot a glance of motherly shock and concern to her husband.

"He'll live, Nora," said Will.

"No wonder you're so thin," said Nora rubbing his knee.

He still had his head back and his eyes closed, but managed to smile through the healing cracks in his lips.

"You know, Mom, if I wasn't so starved for affection, you'd probably be driving me crazy right now."

"Okay," conceded Nora. "I'll leave you alone. It's just that I've been so worried about you. I've been going crazy thinking about you being locked up all alone like that for so long. And I can't believe they cut off all your beautiful hair."

"Mom."

"Do you want to talk about it?"

"No." The smile was gone. "And you already know more than you need to."

"Okay," she smiled. "I'm being a mom again. I'm sorry."

"You'll feel better after you eat," said Mike aware of the trembling of Cain's hands.

"How long can I stay here?"

"Until the count before dinner. Are you okay with locking-in until Monday?"

"Yeah," answered Cain rubbing his face. His headache was raging. "I'm not feeling very good."

He got up and ran to the private bathroom across the room. Will got up and followed him.

"What's wrong with him?" asked Nora on the verge of tears. "What have they done to him?"

"He'll be okay, Nora," comforted Bruce. "He's had a rough couple weeks."

"That's right," said Mike. "He's been eating but not nearly what he's used to. They feed them a minimum diet down in Solitary. He hasn't even seen or talked to anyone in ten days, and he probably hasn't been sleeping well. He's young and healthy; he'll snap back."

In the bathroom Will handed Cain a few wet paper towels.

"Thanks," said Cain as he sat on the floor next to the toilet.

He had just thrown up convulsively until his sides ached. He pressed the cool, wet paper to his eyes. His hands were still shaking.

"Feel better?" asked Will.

"I will. I've been doing this a lot."

"Throwing up?" asked Will trying to hide his alarm.

"Yeah," said Cain feebly. "I've been getting headaches . . . from not eating enough, I think. They wouldn't give me anything . . . for the headaches." Tears flooded his eyes. "I'm sorry." He wiped his face with the paper towel. "Don't tell Mom, okay?" he sniffed back the outburst.

"How long would the headaches last?"

"I don't know. Hours. Days. I couldn't keep track of the time, but it would make me sick."

His hands trembled even more as he fought to bring himself under control.

"Why don't you let yourself go? I know it's been a terrible ten days. It's okay, we don't have to tell Mom."

Cain drew his knees up to his chest. The fetal position was becoming second nature. Silent tears spilled over his lashes and onto his cheeks.

"I tried to walk away from that fight. You know me, Dad. I wouldn't start that."

"Of course you wouldn't."

"He wouldn't let me. He knew I was the one who was going to get into trouble, not him. Then Security came, and they just kept hitting me and hitting me and hitting me. I almost passed out. I could hardly see. There was blood in my eyes . . . all over. They had me chained up, but I was so scared and I just kept fighting them. I don't even know why. I'll . . . I'll be okay in a minute."

"Take your time. How about if I go out and ask Mike if he has any aspirin for your headache? Do you think your stomach could handle it?"

"Yeah. Maybe it'll stop the pounding."

Will stepped out into the other room where everyone was looking at him expectantly. He sighed and shook his head helplessly.

"Is someone going to be looking out for him over the next few days?" he asked.

"Yeah, me," answered Mike.

"Good. It's going to take a while before he's able to come to terms with everything that's been going on. I just don't want him locked away somewhere without someone knowing what he's going through."

"I'll be up there all the time," said Mike reassuringly, "and you can come back over the weekend if you want."

"We will," said Will. "I don't know what we'd do without you, though. Do you have some aspirin? He has a splitting headache. I think that's why he's sick."

Will returned to Cain with the aspirin.

"Thanks," said Cain taking the three aspirin.

He remained on the floor for a few minutes longer.

"The room I was locked up in wasn't much bigger than this," he said absently.

Will looked around the small bathroom which barely held the two of the, and his heart broke.

"It's okay," he told his young son. "It's over now. When I went out for the aspirin, the food had arrived, and they were getting it set up. Maybe you'll feel better when you get something substantial to eat."

"I think you're right," Cain said holding out a trembling left hand to his father. "Could you give me a hand?"

"Sure," said Will. Offering a strong hand.

Cain splashed his face with cold water and rinsed out his mouth.

As he took his place at the table in Fr. Mike's office, he felt strangely apprehensive—almost like he had too much space and freedom. He noted the peculiarity and then tried to put it out of his mind. He tried to allay the fears of those in whose company he was by eating heartily, but he found out it was going to take some time to get his old appetite and eating habits back. Besides, his head was still splitting, and that chilled any desire he had for food. Still, he managed to get some food down, and he was happy to notice that the trembling in his hands was subsiding.

"This is really nice, Mike, thanks," he said. "If I didn't have such a headache, I'd probably clean up. This is real food—not cafeteria food."

The priest smiled. "Yeah, it's from a deli in town. I thought you and your visitors deserved a break. Are you feeling any better?"

"Yeah, a little. I'm starting to get acclimated again. It's going to take a while, though."

"Okay," said Nora pushing away from the table and going over to the couch, "come over here."

She was still young for her age and in good shape. She sat leaning against the arm of the couch and crossed her legs Indian-style. Putting a throw pillow on her lap, she motioned for her son to come lie on the couch. He smiled at her from the table.

"Come on," she repeated. "It's been a long time, but I haven't lost my touch."

Unable to resist such an invitation, Cain got up and joined his mother. He stretched his long body on the couch with his head on her pillow. Then she began her magic. With just the right touch, she began to massage his temples with her fingers. He had been prone to headaches all his life, and this was a ritual that went back to his childhood. He closed his eyes and lost himself in her soothing touch. She was careful to avoid the still-tender cut in his eyebrow as well as the remaining bruises. She could feel him relax beneath her touch. Taking advantage of the fact that he had his eyes closed, she allowed herself to look more closely at the cuts and bruises on her precious child. Her heart ached as she imagined what he had gone through. She looked down at the bruises on his wrists, which peeked out from under the cuffs of his shirt. Handcuffs. Tears filled her eyes as she continued rubbing his temples and forehead. She was glad he still had his eyes closed.

"Mom?" he said dreamily.

"Hmmm?"

"I love you," he answered as a small smile crossed his lips. His eyes remained closed.

A tear broke loose and rolled down her cheek. She looked helplessly over at Will then back at their son.

"I love you, too, baby," she smiled, leaning over and kissing his forehead.

The afternoon raced by.

"I have to go up soon," Cain announced as he walked over to the window and looked out. "Being here I could **almost** forget where I am if it wasn't for the bars on the windows. It's been a nice afternoon."

"Are you going to be okay?" asked Will.

"Yeah," answered Cain walking back over to his family and friends. "I'm fine. No need for anyone to worry." He held out his hand. "See. Steady as a rock."

Will glanced over at Nora, neither totally convinced, but each knowing there was nothing to be done about it.

There was a knock at the door. Cain jumped. Fr. Mike went over to answer it and found a guard on the other side. Nora fought back tears.

"Give him a few minutes," said the priest. "It's early yet."

The guard agreed and waited outside the door.

"Mom," said Cain taking his mother in his arms, "just hold me, okay? It's got to last for a long time. Just hold me. God, I wish I was going home with you."

"I'm going up with you," said Mike. "No arguments. I don't think it's a good idea for you to be alone with a guard for any length of time. Besides, it's something I want to do."

The good-byes were long and hard in spite of promises of his parents' return on the weekend. This was the closest they had been able to be in years, and now it was coming to a close. Mike took Cain by the arm and gently pried him from his mother.

"Come on," said the priest. "You don't want to be late."

He took his time walking to the second tier, speaking to Mike, pretending the guard wasn't there. He seemed to be taking everything in its stride until he walked into the cell and accidentally caught sight of the mail that had collected on his bed. He did a double take and turned to stone. Mike noticed the change in him immediately.

"What's wrong?" he asked.

With great effort Cain leaned over and retrieved the envelope with the familiar writing on it and stood staring blankly at it. Mike looked over at the envelope. It was from Scott.

"Dear God," sighed the priest.

Cain began to tremble with emotion.

"He must have written it right after he was here the last time. It's postmarked the same day . . ."

"Okay," said Mike switching gears to damage control, "just take it easy. This is one more thing you have to work through. I'm here; we'll do it together."

220

Mike cursed the major setback as he saw every pore in Cain's body ooze pain and frustration. A tear fell on the envelope as Cain steadfastly tried to hold it back.

"You know," he said choked with bitter tears, "I've stuck my chin out and took it all. I've dealt with and danced the fine lines of the gangs and the racial crap that goes on here; I somehow maintained my sanity and lived through rape and beatings and guard harassment; I had to sit by while the only girl I ever loved married someone else; I've watched the world go on without me. But this," he wiped his nose with the back of his hand, "I just can't deal with this."

Mike understood and for once was speechless. Cain walked over and placed the envelope reverently on his table.

"Aren't you going to read it?"

"No," said Cain as tears streamed down his face. "I can't. Not now."

"What can I do?"

"Nothing. There's nothing anyone can do. In fact, just go. There must be other people in this zoo who need you. You've been spending way too much time with me lately."

"Right now nobody needs me quite as much as you do."

"I don't know how to go on, Mike. I don't know how to claw my way out of this pit I'm in. Being with my parents this afternoon helped. It gave me something positive and good to focus on, but that was too short-lived.

"They had me chained up, and they kept kicking and beating me. Then they strapped me to a chair and cut all my hair off. And when I showed contempt for the indignity, they stripped me and threw me in a padded box and left me alone for ten days while I tried to make some sense out of the stupid-ass death of one of the most important people in my life. They kept me in the dark most of the time and made me eat with my hands instead of a fork. I was scared I was going to lose my mind. And now this letter. My life is out of control, and I have no idea what to do about it."

"Cain . . ."

"Mike, go. Go find someone you can help. I'm lost somewhere, and I— You could spend the whole night here, and it wouldn't matter. This is something I have to resolve myself—If it can be resolved."

"It can."

"Maybe. I don't know. But you've spent the whole day with me. If anything, you're making me feel selfish and guilty. I guess it's lucky I'm locked up, or I'd probably go out on a three-day binge. I know right now that that's what I want to do—drink my way to oblivion. Just put myself out and beyond caring. Please go. I'm grateful, but I'm just hurting too bad now to be able to relate to anyone."

"All right. Will you send for me if you change your mind? I don't care what time of the day or night."

"Yeah."

"You promise?"

"I promise."

"You're locked-in for three more days, so I'm coming back to see you."

"Okay. Thanks."

"You sure you don't want me to stay while you open your letter?"

"I'm sure. I know I can't deal with that now. I don't know when I'll be able to, but not for a while. I'm all cut up and bleeding inside. I have to find some way to let go of the past, but it's all I got. He used to make me feel that there was a life after this. Now I feel like I'm jumping off a cliff."

He wiped his tear-stained face with his hands. Without a word, the priest walked over to him and put his arms around him.

"You're trying too hard," comforted the priest. "You're trying too hard to be okay. You won't be okay for a while."

"I loved him, Mike," sobbed Cain as he slid down to his bed.

"I know you did. That's why it's going to take a while. Don't force it. It will get better, but don't force it. Let yourself grieve."

Cain was lying facedown on his bed with his head buried in his pillow. Mike looked up just as Jon returned for the afternoon count. He stopped and looked into Cain's cell. Mike shook him off and waved him on his way. Seeing Cain was in no mood for socializing, Jon nodded and went to his own cell. A guard walked up with Cain's dinner. The priest took it and set it on the table.

"Your dinner's here."

Cain rolled over.

"I'm not hungry," he said as he wiped his eyes.

"Are you sure? I'll stay while you eat."

"I had enough at your office. It's probably cold anyway; it always is when they bring it up here."

"Okay. It's on your table if you change your mind. I'm going to go. Jon's back; he walked by a minute ago. Your friends are worried about you."

"Thanks. For everything."

He got up and washed his face in cold water. The guard came down the hall for the count, and unlocked the door for Fr. Mike. The priest stopped outside the door as the guard locked it again.

"Any time—day or night."

"Okay."

A few minutes later the other doors rolled open for the inmates to leave for dinner. Cain sat on his bed, his back against the wall. He was in a semi-trance when Jon stopped outside.

"You okay?" his friend asked.

"I'm trying to be. I'm not doing a very good job of it, though."

"You look like shit. They beat the fucking shit out of you."

Cain gave a melancholy *no kidding* grin.

"You have a real way with words."

"How long do you have to lock-in?"

"Till Monday."

"Back to the warehouse?"

"Yep."

"Shit, Cain, I was hoping they'd transfer you."

"And uncomplicate my life?"

"Keep your chin up."

"Yeah. You'd better get your ass out of here before you get busted for talking to me."

"You know I don't care about that."

"Well go get your dinner then. I'll catch you later."

Jon left, and Cain dropped his head back against the wall. He pulled his quilt up over himself. At least he was warm and able to sleep in a bed again.


The next morning as soon as he was able to get away, Fr. Mike paid a visit to the warehouse and Nate Lewis. The guard eyed him skeptically.

"Ah," Lewis said with a smile, "wasn't it John the Baptist who smoothed the way for Jesus himself?"

"Come on, Nate, sarcasm really isn't your strong suite."

"That smart-ass kid is treated like some saint or savior or something. Do you know how many death threats I received warning me not to press charges against him?"

"He's well-liked."

"Couldn't prove it by me."

"I guess not."

"He beat me senseless."

"That's not what I heard. The way I heard it he got a few good punches in, but then you were rescued. He's a lefty, you know? You have to watch for that left jab. You look remarkably well—your bruises have all healed. That's more than I can say for your young adversary. Have you seen him?"

"No. I've made a point of steering clear of him until I have no choice."

"Well, he has cuts and bruises which are going to still require some time before they're completely healed."

"I hear they shaved his head."

"Yeah. But it's the bruises inside that I'm worried about. In time everything else is going to heal and get back to normal, but he's been through hell and it shows. He could use a break."

"Then you're in the wrong place because I can't wait to get his ass back here and make him wish he'd never been born. He's going to regret the day he ever decided to make an enemy out of me."

"Nate, he's young and in a lot of mental pain."

"What about me?! Huhn? Nobody cares about me."

"This isn't about you. I'm not going to get into this with you, but he has lots of reasons to feel frustrated and despondent. Just a little compassion—that's all I'm asking. He'll respond. He's not looking for trouble."

"The hell he ain't! Boy, he's got you snookered, don't he? He's got a smart mouth on him, and he don't think anything about shooting it off. He's a rapist, do you know that?"

"I know that's what he's in here for."

"Jesus Christ! No offense. Father, he's a two-bit con with a pretty face who thinks we're all going to fall at his feet because he's used to getting things his own way. You tell him to come back here with his tail between his legs, and he'd better keep his mouth shut. And he's going to pay for messing with me."

"He already has."

"No, that was play school compared to what I have in store. Come Monday his ass is mine, and I'm taking full advantage. And he'd best not even look at me sideways."

"In other words, you're going to be a hard-ass about this?"

"Father, this is a state prison. You don't survive if you're not a hard-ass."

"But we're not talking about your everyday criminal here. That's what I'm trying to tell you. There's no need for a problem. You just have to . . . ."

"He's a rapist, Father. That's one of the lowest forms of life there is. You don't have a daughter or a wife, but you must have a mother."

"Nate, you're seriously trying to tell me that you don't detect a difference between Cain Farrell and your run-of-the-mill convict?"

"What? Because he's educated and comes from a well-to-do family? That means he can't be a rapist?"

"I'm getting nowhere here."

"I'm sorry, Father, but that's right. He committed a crime, and he deserves everything he gets. And he better steer clear of me if he doesn't want to complicate his problems because I don't kiss up to anyone, even if he does have a silver spoon in his mouth."

"He's not wealthy; are you holding that against him?"

"He's a rapist—I'm holding that against him. And he hit me."

The priest sighed with exasperation.

"He needs a break, Nate. Treat him right and you won't be sorry."

"Like I didn't do that before? He's a rapist, for God's sake!"

224

"This isn't about him being a rapist!" said the priest returning the anger. "What I'm hearing is this is about him being good looking, intelligent, upper middle class, and having the balls to stand up to you. You set him up to punch you. There are any number of witnesses to that fact."

"Other rapists as well as robbers, murders, professional liars . . . should I go on?"

"Guards," said Fr. Mike. "Even guards testified that you goaded him into a fight. I'm not asking for special favors, Nate. I'm just asking you to give him half a chance. He's a great kid. He's experiencing a lot of stress right now. Can I come down with him on Monday, and the three of us will talk?"

"Father, this is a prison, not a Sunday School."

"You know Victoria Doleman will probably be down to see you sometime today, too."

"Oh, I don't doubt it. He's the crown prince around here. Hell, the inmates think he's the Second Coming of Jesus."

"That's because he's got a lot of savvy. He knows how to treat people."

"Well, you couldn't prove that by me, now could you?"

"He tutors inmates in his spare time. A lot of them have gotten their high school diplomas because of him. Some are even working on college courses."

"He's a snot-nosed hotshot who has no respect for authority."

"You're not making this easy."

"No. But it's easier than you think. All he has to do is come in here and keep his smart mouth shut and work his ass off. There's nothing hard about that, but he won't be able to do it. His mouth will get him in trouble every time. And you know what? I'm going to enjoy writing him up every chance I get until they laugh him right out of every parole hearing until he's served his full sentence. Won't Sam Willet and his family be happy about that?"

"Is that what this is all about—jumping into Sam Willet's hip pocket?"

"I don't know, but it's not a bad place to be."

"Well, as soon as you bring Sam Willet's name up, I know I'm wasting my time."

"He's a powerful enemy."

"So Cain Farrell has found out."

"Well, I certainly intend to stay on his good side. Too bad Farrell didn't use that world-class brain of his when it counted."

"It's hard fighting Sam Willet on his own. He could use a little help."

"Well, he's not getting it from me."

"You're a charmer, Nate. Thanks."

He turned to walk away.

225

"Hey," Lewis called after him, "tell your boy to keep his distance and remember who the boss is around here."

The priest waved him off and continued walking.

He spent the rest of the morning trying to get the cantankerous man out of his system. By early afternoon, when nothing else seemed to relieve his frustration, he headed first to the Administration Building and then to the cellblock.

"You're not dressed," he said to Cain as he walked up to the cell.

"And why should I get dressed?" Cain asked propping himself up on his elbow.

"Because," said Mike waving a recreation pass, "I went over and begged you two hours of freedom in the gym. You have until 3:00— before everyone else is off work."

"How'd you do that?" asked Cain as he sat up on his bed.

"It wasn't that difficult. Come on, get dressed. Time's awasting."

Cain quickly got up and began dressing.

"I haven't shaved."

"Yeah, you do look a bit scruffy, but I promise not to notice."

"I just don't want to get hassled."

"They're not going to hassle you, believe me. I'm going to go down and have the guard unlock your door."

The gym was fairly empty when they got there. They got a basketball court and immediately began a game of one-on-one. This was the first chance Cain had had to stretch out his muscles and bones in earnest. It felt good to run and jump, and he even found himself laughing. He took his shirt off and threw it over at the nearby bleachers. Mike couldn't help but to notice the shadows of bruises which covered most of his torso. Cain seemed so used to them that he didn't even appear to notice.

They played long and hard, each battling his own demons. The priest was the first to call it quits.

"I'm a good bit older than you," he smiled as he lumbered over toward the bleachers. "I probably won't be able to move tomorrow."

"I'm really out of shape from sitting on my ass for two weeks, but that really felt good. Thanks, Mike."

"My pleasure," answered the priest trying to choose the right moment to drop his bombshell. "Come over here a minute and sit down. I need to talk to you."

"What?" asked Cain growing serious as he took a towel and wiped himself down.

"I went to see Lewis this morning."

"And he was an asshole."

"Well, that's not exactly the way I was going to put it, but basically, yes."

226

"So what else is new?" asked Cain putting his shirt back on.

"You need to watch yourself with him, Cain."

"I will."

"No," reiterated the priest, "I mean **really** watch yourself. He used a buzzword today that I picked right up on. Parole. He's poised at the jugular and ready to strike."

Cain sat in stunned enlightenment.

"Shit," he said.

"Yeah, shit. He got your transfer revoked, and now he's already zooming ahead to parole. Because he's your boss, he'd be instrumental in your parole; but now this fiasco really puts all the cards on his side of the table. And the really bad news is he's already figured that out."

"Bruce already tried to get me a transfer out of the warehouse, but they won't budge on that."

"Right. So you really have no choice but to find some way to get along with him."

"For the next 2 ½ to 10 years."

"'Fraid so."

"That's like trying to get along with a barracuda."

"I know," smiled Fr. Mike sadly. "You can do it though if you keep in mind what's at stake."

"I'm not good at staying focused in the heat of passion."

"No, you're not, but you'll work on it."

"Can you believe my life has become so screwed up just because of knowing one girl? And before you remind me—as you're so good at doing—that I went further than just knowing her, a lot of guys do that all the time and they don't end up fucked out of their lives."

Fr. Mike could tell that Cain was becoming angry and frustrated again. That hadn't been his purpose in bringing him to the gym. He needed to talk to him about Lewis, but even more importantly he needed to calm him down.

"Maybe I should have told you this before we started our game. That's what you need to do, you know? Be active every chance you get. Knock yourself out on the court or the baseball field or the running track. When he starts getting on your case, store it up for your rec time. We still have a few minutes before we have to leave; do you want to go another round with me?"

"No," said Cain, "you'll probably have a heart attack."

Then he smiled knowingly as Mike picked up the towel and threw it at him.

That night he slept the best that he had in the two weeks since he learned of Scott's death. He had finally had a chance to really stretch and exercise his body; it helped to tire him out some. But even more importantly, he was able to ease some of the tension in his soul. He understood what Mike was getting at when he suggested exercise as an outlet for his emotions. It was advice he would not take lightly. Now if he could just mask his emotions and deny Lewis the advantage in their battle of the wills.

The weekend was a hard time to be locked up. During the week if an inmate was locked-in and missed work, it was not really a big deal even if he had to sacrifice his rec time in the afternoon. But on the weekend there was no work and a lot of rec time.

Cain woke up on Saturday feeling revived finally having had a good night's sleep but woeful of the many long, monotonous hours ahead of him that led to Monday. When he finally dragged himself from his bed, his eyes automatically searched out the letter from Scott, which was still sitting unopened on his table. He quickly looked away as he attempted to keep his spirits from totally disintegrating. Then for a lack of anything better to do, he washed up, brushed his teeth, and shaved.

As it turned out, it was lucky he did because he was hardly settled back on his bed with a book when the guard came down to tell him he had a visitor. A message from heaven. He wasted no time taking off his glasses and fumbling for his work boots. It was hard not to run all the way to the visitors' lounge, except that he kept in the back of his mind the more-than-likely possibility that he'd get sent back if he got caught. Luck hadn't exactly been with him of late.

He entered the visitors' lounge and began looking around for a familiar face, but he saw no one. At first he was confused, wondering who would have sent for him and then left. He was about to go check with the guard on duty when he saw her stand up. He was frozen to the spot momentarily. Alexis. He hadn't seen her since those last days of the trial. Actually the last time he really remembered seeing her was the evening they spent together just before the trial ended. He knew she had been at the trial to the end, but his mind overloaded when he tried to sort out the events of that last day.

Back then she was cute; now she was becoming beautiful. She smiled at him, and he was thawed from his position on the floor. Slowly, he walked over to her and, after she sat down again, took a chair across from her.

"I'm speechless," he admitted.

"Didn't your mom tell you I talked with her?"

"No. But then I haven't talked with my mom much lately."

"I know. I talked to her at Scott's funeral because I wanted to write to you, and she told me a little about the trouble you were in. Then she suggested when you could have visitors again that maybe I'd like to come with them. They dropped me off and pointed me in the right direction, and then they went off to run some errands so we could have some time alone together. They'll be here in a little while."

"You're looking good," he said making small talk.

"Cain, I'm sorry I haven't written or anything. I meant to, but . . . well, I really don't have any good excuse. I thought I did until I got here, and now I know there is no excuse. I haven't been a very good friend—especially after I promised you that night at the park that I'd keep in touch."

"Yeah, well, we all have good intentions."

She looked at him for a long minute.

"Are you okay?"

"You mean other than the fact that I'm totally screwed-up and my life is catapulting out of control?"

Neither of them smiled.

"I'm sorry," he apologized. "I'm not very good company these days. My parents should have known better than to bring you here."

"They told me it might be better if I waited, but I wanted to come now. I figure now is the time you need your friends. So I decided to take my chances. It's okay; I understand if you're out of sorts."

"I just sometimes have a tendency to emotionally beat up my visitors. I'll try to be on my best behavior." He flashed her a slight smile.

"Only you could have leftover cuts and bruises on your face and still look as sexy as hell," she commented smiling back at him.

"Well, I feel about as sexy as a stump, but thanks. Do you ever see Matt any more?"

"No. Just if I run into him at the store or somewhere."

"You were at Scott's funeral?"

"Yes. I saw all your brothers there and Molly."

He got a far away look in his eye as he fought back tears.

"I hear you and Jim are buds now," she said, changing the subject.

"Yeah, you see there is a God and there are miracles. Who'd've ever thought it?"

"Well, that's good. That's the way it should be? How about your grandpa?"

"Who?"

"Okay," she smiled, "I'm sorry."

"Alexis," he measured his words, "I don't know if this is the right thing to say or not—my social skills are kind of rusty—but I think about that kiss a lot. You know, that night at the park? You probably don't remember."

"I remember."

"Now that I think of it, that was probably a pretty stupid thing to say."

"No it wasn't. It's very sweet that you still remember."

"I can't forget it—it was the first and last kiss in the midst of a long dry spell. It kind of screams at me sometimes in the middle of the night." He rubbed his chin reflectively. "Um, how's Joanne?"

"She's okay. She seems happy; I don't know."

"What do you mean?"

"It's a strange relationship. He's a lot older; he has a lot of money, and she's his little princess. I think she's more in love with the idea of him and what he can do for her than she is in love with him. I wouldn't be surprised if she's still in love with you."

He laughed sarcastically.

"It's easy to see you weren't around when I tried to talk to her before I left. She definitely had moved on, even back then."

"How about you? Have you moved on?"

"To what? You don't move on in a place like this. You just kind of get stuck in idle. She's married; I at least can say that now. That's an accomplishment."

"She's crazy. I can't believe she just let you go like that. I know how much she loved you."

"No," said Cain modestly. "I'm damaged goods. Let's change the subject. Are you dating anyone?"

"Yeah, sort of."

He smiled warmly. "How do you *sort of* date someone?"

"I like him, and we have fun with each other; I'm just not in love with him. I'm not ready to fall in love."

"You're smart. It's not all it's cracked up to be."

"I used to think I was in love with your brother. You guys are so gorgeous. There were nights in high school where I couldn't sleep for thinking about him. Sometimes I used to fantasize about both of you."

She blushed. Cain grinned with amusement.

"At the same time?" he couldn't resist asking.

"Oh, yes." She blushed even more.

Cain couldn't remember the last time he had laughed out loud.

From out of nowhere, Jon suddenly pulled up a chair and sat next to him.

"Hey, you got sprung," he smiled rubbing his hand briskly on Cain's head.

"Yeah," smile Cain, "and you're intruding."

"I had to find out who this pretty lady is. You don't ever talk about anyone but . . . "

"Alexis, this is Jon." He purposely omitted last names. "He's sorry he can't stay."

"No, I can stay for a little while. Hi, Alexis. We don't get many classy ladies like you around here, so you have to excuse me for being nosy."

Alexis smiled coyly at him.

"What are you doing here, anyway?" asked Cain. "I didn't think you ever got visitors."

"I do. That was my brother or somebody who just left."

"You don't have a brother," reminded Cain.

"Well, it was somebody. I think a cousin. It doesn't matter; I like your visitor better."

Cain looked at Alexis and smiled. *You gotta love him.*

"So," continued Jon. "Exactly who are you, Alexis, and why haven't I heard about you before this?"

"She's a friend," answered Cain sparing Alexis the reply. "From home. I haven't seen her in almost three years, and my parents are due here soon. So . . ."

"Oh," smiled Jon. "Right. I . . . should go." He leaned toward Alexis. "Be gentle. He's been locked up by himself for a long time. And don't you like the new hairdo?"

"It's very dashing," answered Alexis with a grin.

"Dashing," repeated Jon. "You know, Cain, I've heard you called a lot of things, but I don't think dashing is one of them. Dashing. I like that. You know, come to think of it, Large Marge may have . . ."

"JON," interrupted Cain before his friend could embarrass him further. "Thanks for stopping. Sorry you have to be running along."

"Okay, I'd better be going. It was really nice meeting you, Alexis." He turned to Cain. "You have to lock-in again after this?"

"Till Monday."

"Then I'll see you upstairs. Can I bring you anything?"

"No. Thanks."

"Maybe I'll bring you some candy; you're getting way too skinny. Take care, Alexis. Make him laugh some more. He hasn't done enough of that lately."

He winked at her and was gone.

"What a character," she smiled.

"Yeah. He's only about three or four years older than me, but he thinks he's my mother."

Alexis smiled broader. "Who's Large Marge?"

"I don't believe he brought her up. She's a guard, a real pain in the ass."

"Does she think you're cute?"

"I don't know what she thinks, but she drives me crazy—and not in the way I would like to be driven crazy. Let's don't talk about her; it's really not a joking matter."

"I like Jon. I like that you have a friend like that here. It makes me feel a little better about you being here."

"Yeah, it's kind of weird, but here I can really be myself. Did you notice how he just walked up to me and started talking? He didn't squint and size me up and try to determine if I really was Cain. Or maybe was I Matt? Most people here don't even know about Matt, so I can be just like anybody else."

"Do you like that?"

"I hate being here, but, yes, it's kind of nice to be an individual for the first time in my life instead of one-of-two. My mom was always good about not dressing us alike when we were little, but I still always felt like some kind of freak show."

"Well, you and Matt are mirror images of each other. It's incredible."

"But you can't imagine what it's like going through life watching yourself come and go. Especially now. He comes to visit, and I find myself getting caught up in what he's wearing. The worst part is I can see exactly what I'd look like in the same thing. Denims and sweats for nearly three years is a little much, especially when there's no end in sight for the near future."

"Some people would kill for that chance."

"That's one way you get into this exclusive club."

Alexis smiled admiringly, and he felt his heart skip a beat.

"I can't believe how awkward I feel," he said, shifting slightly in his seat.

"Why?" she asked incredulously.

"I don't know," he shrugged. "I guess because I'm socially bankrupt. I haven't been this close to a woman I'm not related to in over 2½ years. Except for prison personnel."

"Large Marge?"

"Large Marge," he affirmed with a groan. "She scares me more than everyone else in this dump put together."

"Why?" laughed Alexis.

"She has way too much power over me, and she knows it. One word from her can cost me anything from extended lock-in time to busted parole. And she wants more from me than tail-between-the-legs-bad-doggy obedience. I can deal with that." He reached up and traced his finger across the cut over his left eye and smiled. "Sometimes not very well, but I can deal with it. She's much subtler but every bit as demanding. And I don't know why I'm telling you all this." He rubbed the back of his neck. "Please don't say anything to anyone—especially my family."

Alexis drank him in with a compassionate stare.

"Of course, I won't, but you are incredibly gorgeous," she said with an adoring smile, "so I guess I can't fault her there, but it's not fair that she can get away with being so manipulative."

"Well, so far I've been able to keep a step ahead of her by sheer wit. So what little is left of my dignity after Carrie Willet was through with it is still in tact."

"Good. She's probably more full of BS and hot air than anything else."

"Probably. My hormones are still alive and well, but they're not suicidal."

"I'm glad I came," she laughed.

"I am, too. My world has become so narrow that I sometimes have a hard time imagining anything beyond the barbed wire. It's good to have contact with the outside." He stared down at his hands and then back up into her eyes. "I've been trying to say all the right things so that you know how happy I am to see you, but so you don't feel obligated to come back. I know it's a long ride, and this is a morbidly depressing place. And you have a boyfriend who might not understand."

"Are you saying I shouldn't come any more?"

"No," he said with conviction as he patted his empty shirt pocket. "I've given up smoking—I figure I've gone two weeks without a cigarette, so I should just quit. Right now, though, I wish I had one."

"Well, I don't smoke, so I can't help you."

"Good. My lungs and my mother will be eternally grateful."

"Let's go back to what you were trying to say."

"I don't know, Alexis. I'm fucking confused. I'm trying to remain detached. When you spend your life bouncing around from day to day, continually banging into brick walls, you kind of grab on to any lifeline that anyone tosses in your direction."

"Well, that's good," she insisted. "You need that."

"No. That's a big responsibility, being someone's lifeline. It's not fair of me to do that to people. And the last thing I want is people feeling obligated to keep me afloat. So I'm telling you that's how it is with me. I'm really glad you're here, but there are no strings, no lifeline, attached."

"Okay," she agreed. "But if I really wanted to, I could come back some day?"

"Yeah," he smiled, suddenly wishing his parents would show up and rescue him from the edge of the passionate pit he could feel himself being sucked into.


Later that afternoon as everyone was returning for the count at 4:45, Jon stopped outside Cain's cell. Cain was lying on his bed, facing the wall.

"Hey, Romeo, what's up?"

"Shut up," answered Cain ill temperedly.

"Whoa, I thought you'd be in a good mood."

"Well, I'm not."

"You're not mad at me for . . . "

" . . . tromping on my visit? No. It has nothing to do with you."

"It's that girl, Alexis, isn't it?

"No," said Cain propping himself up on his elbow. "It's this place I'm trapped in. I hate it. And I'm ready to bite someone's head off, so it's better if you move on."

"You just need to get out more. One more day."

"Yeah, and then what? Eight hours a day with Lewis riding my ass? That's really something to look forward to."

"Okay, Cain, I have to go lock-in now. It's been a slice."

Cain grabbed his pillow and angrily shoved it under his head once again.

A while later after everyone else had gone down to dinner, Fr. Mike showed up outside of Cain's cell. He was carrying a large bag.

"Jon has a big mouth," grumbled Cain.

"Jon has nothing to do with this. I'm here with dinner. Italian. Specially packed. Guaranteed to be good and hot. If you're not interested, there's someone else down the tier who's locked-in; I'm sure he wouldn't turn it down. Can I come in?"

"Yes," answered Cain less than enthusiastically as the priest signaled for the guard to let him in.

Fr. Mike put the dinner out on the small table. Cain eyed it curiously.

"Hungry?" Mike asked.

"Actually, I am. I'm getting my appetite back. This is not prison food."

"No, it's not. And it is still quite hot."

They sat down together in the tiny cell and shared **the** best meal Cain had had since he left home.

"Cat got your tongue?" Mike asked borrowing the old cliché.

"What?"

"You've barely said a word since I got here."

"I'm sorry. This is really good."

"Did your parents come today? They had said they were coming."

"You didn't talk to Jon?"

"Well . . . "

"I knew it."

"I ran into him on my way up. He said you've been in better moods."

"He ought to mind his own business."

"Well, as long as we're on the subject, he said you had a beautiful visitor today. Does that in some way account for your mood?"

"She's a friend. We were never romantically involved. In fact, she dated my brother through much of high school. She made me feel things that I haven't experienced in a long time, but worst of all, she made me realize what I'm missing."

"That was hard."

"Yeah. She and Matt aren't seeing each other any more, so if I wanted I could date her. She kissed me once just before my trial was over. Nearly knocked me on my ass."

"So when is she coming back?"

"She's not. I told her not to."

"Why did you do that?"

"For about a million different reasons I don't want to go into."

"Okay."

"Now I have to figure out a way to convince myself that I don't need any of that shit. I live in a cage for God's sake. Animals in the zoo have more room than I do in here. Actually I don't think they even keep animals in cages any more."

"I can see this conversation going off in a direction we might want to avoid."

"What? We don't talk about it, and then I'm okay. Sorry. Because I think about it. I think about it all the time, and it's driving me crazy. Standing next to my bed, I can nearly touch the two side walls in here. From the bars it's about four healthy paces to the back wall. I just spent ten days in a room that's smaller than most people's bathrooms. I'm going crazy. It's spring. I want to be outside. I want to meet Alexis at that park again and see if that kiss was everything that I remember it to be. I want to go to Ireland and see my grandparents again. I'm twenty-one years old and spending the best years of my life in a goddam cage! And I don't deserve it. I want to be home."

"Okay, hold on now. You're not helping yourself. You've been confined for too long. You just have to get through one more day. One more day, and they'll let you out."

"That's what Jon said. But you're missing the point. They won't let me go home."

"Cain," sighed the priest, "we've been down this road a thousand times since you've been here. You're intelligent; you know there's nothing more to be done about that. I'm telling you this frustration you're feeling right now is because you've been locked up too long. Once you get out again, some of that will ease. Give it another day."

"I didn't even know how to talk to her today."

His hands were trembling again as he rubbed his face. He was obviously not taking comfort in the priest's well-meaning advice. Mike decided to take another approach.

"Why don't you open your letter?" he suggested. "You'll feel better."

"NO!"

Cain got up and walked away from the table. He went over to the bars and stared out at the empty hall. Grabbing onto the bars, he rested his forehead between two of them.

"No," he repeated more calmly as he stared straight ahead. "I'm sorry; I didn't mean to shout. I just know I can't open that letter yet. I feel like a goddam psycho; I didn't mean to yell at you."

"It's okay," said Mike. "I know you're under a lot of pressure."

"I don't know what I'd do without you, Mike," he said still staring through the bars. "Don't be mad at me."

"I'm not. I'm sorry I brought it up again. I should trust you to know when the time is right. I won't bring it up again."

"I'll read it—soon. He wrote it; I can't just ignore it. I just can't do it now."

"Come back here and sit down. You're torturing yourself over there; I know it."

"I'm going to lose my mind if I don't get out of here soon," he said turning around and going back to the table.

"You know I can't come tomorrow. It's Sunday, and my whole day is booked."

"I know. I'm a big boy; I'll handle it. Other people deserve and need your time more than I do. I'll be okay."

"I know you will."

"Don't worry, okay?"

"Deal."

"And thanks for this dinner."

"Well, I'm glad to see you eat and enjoy it. You've got to put that weight on you've lost."

He slept in on Sunday, pillow over his head to block out intruding light and the noises of the others getting up and going down to breakfast. His breakfast tray remained untouched in the opening of his cell door. He awoke close to noon, the relative quiet reminding him that everyone else was down in the gym or the rec room. He knew that dwelling on that fact was going to lead him down a road of resentment and depression, so he quickly shifted his attention.

He knew Matt was coming that afternoon, so he got up and went through the motions of starting the day. Then he walked over to his window and looked out. He had forgotten it was May. It was a beautiful, sunny day, so the yard was crowded with inmates soaking up the fresh air. Off in the distance he could see his baseball team playing a game. He should be there. Again, a dangerous topic to dwell on. He stood at the window, transfixed with the activity that was going on. He had a pretty good view of the game, so he stood and watched it. When his lunch came, he put the tray on his table and then ate standing up at the window. He was amazed that his spirits actually lifted as the day wore on. Jon and Mike were right: this was the last day he had to spend locked-in. Then he'd be able to get out and enjoy the warming weather, but best of all, he'd be able to get back to baseball. At least they didn't totally take that away from him. His nerves were becoming less jangled, and the synthetic jet lag he experienced from his unscheduled existence in solitary was passing. His psyche was coming back in tune with his mandated existence.

He was happy to be in pretty high spirits as he went down to meet Matt. Too often he was moody and out of sorts with people who had given up their time and driven a good distance to spend time with him. He hated that he was like that, but he didn't know how to stop himself. He walked into the small room to check in for his visit and was immediately nonplused by the presence of Marge Clintock.

"Hi, sweetie, long time no see," she grinned as he began to empty his pockets onto the table in front of her. "I like the new hairdo."

No comment.

"No cigarettes?" she asked as she gazed over his belongings.

"I quit."

"Good for you. I guess two weeks in Solitary has to be a big help. Now for my favorite part."

Without another word from her, he knew to raise his arms at his sides and slightly spread his legs. She patted down his body as she stared into his eyes. Boldly, he met her gaze and held it, silently communicating this had better be a routine shakedown.

"Okay, angel face," she said, "you're clean. Put your things back in your pockets. That's a pretty bad cut you have there on your lip."

She reached up to finger it, but he pulled back away from her. She was obviously not pleased.

"Go have a nice visit. We'll take care of business after."

So much for lightheartedness.

He walked into the visitor's lounge and sought out his brother.

"You look like you're about to explode," said Matt as Cain sat down.

"Na, I'm all right. Aren't you going to tell me how much you like my hair?"

"No, it looks like shit."

"Thank you. I knew I could count on you to tell me the truth."

"It doesn't really look all that bad. At least not everyone is staring at us." The smile faded from his face as he examined the ghosts of the nasty cuts and bruises his brother had suffered. "Are you okay? I've been nuts worrying about you."

"Yeah. It's been a bitching couple of weeks, but it's over. I survived. Now I just have to find some way to make sense out life without Scott in it. That'll take some time."

"No doubt. I feel better now that I've seen you."

"Guess who was here yesterday?"

"I already know."

"She is really hot, man. Are you sure you don't want to get something going with her again?"

"Yeah. There's nothing there any more—for either of us. Why don't you get something going with her? Write to her or something."

"I don't think that's exactly the kind of *pen* pal she had in mind."

Matt smiled the same infectious smile that belonged to Cain.

"I've just recently started seeing somebody from school. I've never felt this way about anyone."

"No shit."

"No shit. I want to bring her sometime to meet you, but I wanted to ask you first. She can't believe I have an identical twin, and she wants to see for herself."

"No! Not here. I don't want to meet anybody for the first time here—least of all, your girlfriend. I don't want anyone identifying me with this place."

"Come on, Cain. I've already told her the circumstances. She's on our side."

"I don't care. This is the single most humiliating experience of my life, and I don't need any more eyewitnesses. I'm . . ."

"Oh my Gosh!" said Marge Clintock as she walked up to them. "This is Matthew. Oh my Gosh! I can't believe my eyes!"

Matt looked confused and caught off guard; Cain rolled his eyes at him and rubbed his face in exasperation. She stood behind Cain with her hands on his shoulders.

"I'm Marge Clintock. Your brother has told me all about you. I can't believe two people can look so much alike. I'm so glad I got to finally meet you." She squeezed Cain's shoulders. "And I'll see you in a little while."

As fast as she had appeared, she was gone.

"What the hell?" laughed Matt.

Cain was as sober as ever.

"She's a bitch in heat."

"Oh, no," sighed Matt understanding his brother's innuendo.

"She's got me by the balls, and she's driving me crazy."

"What are you going to do?"

"I don't know, but rest assured I haven't told her all about you. I don't know how she found out about us, but one time she asked me your name. At the time it was best to placate her, so I told her. That's it. Now when I leave here, she's going to make me do a strip search."

"What?!"

"This place is a barrel of laughs."

"She can't do that."

"Want to come back and watch her?"

"Cain!"

"I've stripped for women guards before. There's really no choice. But the others are all so unisex and businesslike. This one I not only don't trust, but I resent being her private source of entertainment."

"Can't you complain to someone?"

"Right."

"What about Bruce?"

"Just let me handle this, all right? I can take care of myself. If nothing else I've become pretty streetwise here. I guess that's . . . good."

"How do you stand it?"

"I don't have a choice now, do I?"

"I guess not."

They talked for a while longer about things great and small, neither wanting to end the encounter. Soon, however, there was no delaying it.

"Well," sighed Cain, "you got things to do, and I guess it's about time I go give that . . . I hate to call her a lady . . . her thrill for the day." He winked at his brother. "Actually, she's been waiting a long time for this."

"You're okay with it?"

"It's all in a day's work," Cain smiled. "Hey, that's a thought for when I ever get out of here. I could always get a job as a stripper."

Matt shook his head and smiled.

"Don't tell Mom that," he said. "Even if you are just joking."

"It's just a thought," said Cain, "I'm always keeping my mind opened to different occupations this place is preparing me for when they're through with me. I've kind of already rejected bank robber, arsonist, and hit man, but I'm still considering pickpocket or cat burglar."

"You've been locked up by yourself too long," laughed Matt.

"Yeah, I guess," answered Cain, first smiling then letting the smile fade. "Seriously, take care of yourself. I don't know what I'd do if anything ever happened to you. This thing with Scott still hasn't completely sunk in."

"I know. That's going to take a while, but you'll be all right. He wouldn't want you to be anything but okay."

"I know; I finally figured that out. So I'm trying."

He stood and watched Matt leave until he was out of sight. Then it was time to deal with Clintock. He took a deep breath, hoping to clear out the sick feeling that had lodged in the center of his chest, and then he turned toward the guard station. She smiled broadly at him as he entered.

"Well, well, well," she said as she consulted a clipboard in her hand, "look here; it's your lucky day. It says you've been doing enough stripping in the past two weeks—sorry I missed it. Anyway, just let me pat down your beautiful ass with your clothes on and you can go."

He looked at her in disbelief, not liking the game they were playing at all. Then he laughed ironically.

"Why don't we just do this and get it over with?"

"As intriguing as that sounds," she said in a voice as rotund as her figure, "I have my orders. Besides, this way I can touch, and you do have a beautiful ass. There are benefits to both, and my patience will be rewarded one day. In the meantime, I can just keep anticipating. Now come on, spread your legs for me."

She made him feel cheap and superficial, and he hated her for that. All the way back to his cell, he fought the feeling of her hands on his body. That was almost worse for him than if he had had to endure a strip search by her. She was supposed to be feeling for weapons, drugs, or any other such contraband. Instead, she felt for muscle definition and body tone, working her hands down his body more like a masseuse than a correctional officer. There was no recourse for him but to suffer the indignity. At least to this point she seemed to know her limitations and stayed within them, though at times she came dangerously close. He worried about the day when she would overstep her bounds and start kneading and groping in forbidden territory. He knew he could never stand by idly and let her abuse him in that way. After all, that was how his confrontation with Lewis spawned; he didn't need another battle with another guard.

He walked back into his cell and eyed the unopened letter still situated on his table. Quickly he looked away and walked directly to his window. The cell door slammed behind him and sent a wave of resentment crashing into his back. He grabbed the bars on the window and watched with envy the activity that was happening outdoors.

The next morning he woke to the immediate realization that it was time to go back to work and face Lewis. He lingered in bed for a minute or two while he tried to gather as much calm as was possible. He knew it was going to take a lot of restraint to deal with the situation that he had left blazing out of control two weeks before. The whole mess had been left smoldering, waiting for him to come back and stoke it back into a raging inferno or douse it in cold water never more to rear up. Cain wasn't certain it was all quite so black or white. He was worried that there was no way he could put it to rest forever. He carried a live spark inside him, and therefore the threat of explosion was always imminent. He had to find some way to control the uncontrollable. Sighing miserably, already overwhelmed with doom, he dragged himself from his bed.

Looking in the mirror, he at least was happy that his appearance was becoming more normal. His hair was taking on the look of a typical buzz cut. The bruises and cuts, though still obvious, didn't stand out quite as much, and most of the soreness was gone.

Taking only minutes to get ready, he sat on the edge of his bed waiting for the count to be completed and the doors to be opened. When it all came to pass, he found he was unable to move. Jon stopped outside his door.

"You coming?" he asked.

"Do I have a choice?"

"Well I know you don't want to stay locked up."

"That's a fact," Cain said getting up. "Let's get this over with."

"Don't forget to leave your pride here. There's no room for it in that warehouse."

"Let's go," said Cain avoiding the issue.

He was pretty quiet during breakfast, choosing mostly to listen and reply with a slight smile every once in a while. He wondered if Lewis was giving this morning any thought, or if indifference was all part of being an asshole. All too soon it was time to put it all on the line.

As they approached the door of the warehouse, Lewis was waiting. Jon did his best to place himself between Cain and the guard and then just whisk himself and his friend through the door. Lewis had a different agenda. Cain came face-to-face with him and stared him down unashamedly. Not a good way to begin.

"You," said Lewis to Cain, "over there. Harrison, get to work."

"I will," said Jon. "I'll just wait for Cain."

"You'll just get to work right now, or I'll send you back up to lock-in."

Lewis returned his leer to Cain who reluctantly stepped aside to where Lewis had indicated. He nodded to Jon to go on in like he was told. Against his better judgment, Jon went ahead.

"This is going to be short and sweet," growled Lewis as Cain defiantly met his glare and raised it. "It's simple; from now until further notice, you are not allowed to speak in here—at all—except to say *yes, sir* or *no, sir* to me. That's it. I mean it; if I so much as see you open your mouth, I'll write you up and send you back to your cell. I don't care if they have to buy a new file cabinet just to keep all your yellow slips in. The Parole Board will laugh you right out of the hearing. But then that's not my problem, is it?" He waited but received no reply from Cain. "Let's practice: but then that's not my problem, is it?"

Cain stared him down.

"Come on, Farrell, you're a smart boy and you always seem to have something to say. If the Parole Board busts your parole, it's not my problem, is it?"

Cain stared at him for a long time and then thought it best to respond.

"No."

"No, SIR," demanded Lewis.

"No, sir," repeated Cain reluctantly.

"That's better. I'm the boss; don't you forget that. Don't ever forget that again. And I meant what I said about keeping your mouth shut and working your ass off. You don't talk to anybody, and nobody talks to you. Because if they do, they're going to get written up, too. I'm turning you into a regular Typhoid Mary. When we take our breaks, you find a nice quiet spot all by yourself. I've had your smart-ass mouth all the way up to the roots of my hair. So now I don't have to deal with it. The rules are simple; I think even you can figure them out. Any questions?"

He looked at Cain waiting for an answer.

"No," he finally said.

"NO, SIR. What the hell is so hard to remember about that?"

"No . . . sir," said Cain testily.

"Then get your ass in there and get busy. And be sure to check the attitude at the door from now on. Better yet, leave it in your cell."

Trying his best not to let his surly demeanor escape the tight hold he had on it, Cain sighed and then walked passed Lewis and on into the warehouse. Jon looked up from his work area. Cain exchanged glances with him, but did little to betray any emotion. Lewis had him in a real uncomfortable position, and he had to be careful not to provoke him into going off half-cocked and writing disciplinary referrals that would bury him at parole time.

He quietly checked the clipboard hanging on the wall for his work assignment. As he expected, it was a hefty order; he knew he could count on Lewis. Remembering his restlessness of the past two weeks, he went to work happy for the change of venue.

As he concentrated on hard work and exercise in order to alleviate his resentment and hatred of Lewis, the guard was making rounds of the warehouse making sure that everyone knew that Cain Farrell was a pariah to be avoided at all cost.

"You're an idiot," said Jon to the guard as Lewis approached him and the others working in his area.

"Talk like that will get you nothing but trouble," snarled Lewis.

"He's supposed to spend eight hours a day not talking or being talked to?!"

"He just spent two weeks of twenty-four hours a day incommunicado."

"This is nearly as bad," ranted Jon. "Besides meals there's only an hour of rec time after work. Then we lock into cells by ourselves for the night."

"Look, Harrison, I wasn't the one who broke the law and landed himself in prison, now was I? What did you think this was, a Kiddieland?"

"Fuck you," said Jon as he turned to get back to work.

"Sounds like you've been hanging around Farrell too long. His big mouth's what got him in trouble in the first place. You'd better watch yours."

"This is bogus," said someone standing near Jon, "and you know it. I think Farrell should get in touch with his lawyer first chance he gets."

"I think he should keep his ass out of trouble and be sure not to make me angry," said Lewis. "And I think the rest of you should keep your opinions to yourselves and get back to work."

Cain found it more of a nuisance to try and remember not to talk than it was to actually not talk. Not very much deep conversation took place during the workday anyway. At the morning break, he separated himself from the others. He felt strangely humiliated, which he supposed was all part of Lewis's plan, and he didn't want anyone else getting in trouble because of him. He sat on the floor with his back to everyone. He leaned against some boxes and ate an apple that he had brought with him from breakfast. He laid his head back against the box. He couldn't believe how tired he was; he wasn't used to manual labor after sitting around for so long. When the break was over, he tossed his apple core into a nearby dumpster and got back to work. Jon kept watching him wondering what was going on inside him. He seemed to be coping all right, but Jon knew Cain had a low threshold of tolerance.

When it was time for lunch, they met outside the door. Cain was happy for the break; Jon was happy to touch base with his friend to be sure he was not running on a short fuse. His friends found him in an unusually good mood. They were joking and laughing as they walked away toward the cafeteria. Lewis watched them from the door of the warehouse.

"That kid is way too popular for my liking," he said to a guard who was standing near by.

"Watch yourself with that one," said the other guard said. "He'll bring you a world of hurt. It's not a good idea to kick the ass of a favorite son. You're making a martyr out of him. The others will rally around him, and you know that's the last thing we want around here—especially with the hot, summer months approaching."

"What are you getting at? A riot?"

"They've started over less."

"No, never. I'm in control, don't worry."

"Isn't that what you were thinking two weeks ago when that kid put you on your back?"

Lewis snorted and walked away, trying to dismiss the words of doom.

At lunch the conversation of the warehouse crew was heated and attested little to Lewis's iron-claw control. Cain was especially uneasy with the turn things were taking since he was right at the center of it. All he ever wanted was to do his time and go home. How did things always seem to rocket out of control?

"Hold everything," he finally said. "Lewis is a fat son-of-a-bitch who's looking for promotion to God. We all know that. I don't want any more trouble. I don't want to become anyone's cause. I'm okay with his crap. Two more years and I come up for parole. I've already jeopardized that enough. I was stupid once and let him goad me into a confrontation. I've learned my lesson; count me out of anything you're planning."

"He won't stop here," one of the warehouse inmates said. "Once he knows he hasn't gotten under your skin, he'll find some other way to get your attention."

"Well, if that happens, I'll have to reassess my situation. But until then I'm going along with his absurdity, and I'd really appreciate it if you all would too. I want to go home."

Nothing more was said about it. It was really Cain's call to make, and the others were willing to respect his wishes . . . at least for now.

The afternoon went without incident. Cain found that he had drawn more into himself since the social aspect of work had been taken away from him. As he worked, he thought about the events of the past two weeks. He thought about Scott; he always thought about Scott. This was the longest stretch of time he had ever gone without being in touch with him. He wasn't sure how he could go on with such a void in his life. He only knew the choice wasn't his.

After work he nearly flew to baseball practice. Baseball was the one bright spot in his life at Maddox. His teammates cheered his appearance and let him know how much he had been missed. He couldn't get over how different he felt on that side of the fences. He actually felt like someone who had something to offer to the world. He felt whole, human. It was more than just baseball and the camaraderie of the team. He couldn't put his finger on it, but he knew he felt less of a degenerate once he walked through the final gate that separated him from B Unit.

And now at last he was finally totally freed from the confines of Solitary. He ran and played hard. He let go of the resentment and hatred that had consumed him over the weeks in Solitary and the ensuing days up in his cell. He took in deep breaths, which cleared out the musty dampness in his lungs. It felt good to finally be outside with the warm sun taking the last of the underground chill out of his bones. Even when practice was over, he didn't relapse for he knew tomorrow was another day and the baseball season was just beginning. He'd make it. There'd always be this big, gaping hole in his soul that was once filled with Scott, but he had more life to live and he couldn't go on the way he'd been over the past two weeks. He could feel the healing begin, almost as if being outdoors had purged him of the bitterness and regret and allowed his spirit to be free to mingle with the essence of Scott.

After dinner he went back to his cell to face the inevitable. There was no sense putting it off any longer, and he finally felt strong enough to take charge of the future. His hands began to tremble as he reached inside the envelope that had been carefully slit opened by whoever had censored his mail. It tore his heart out to think that a stranger had read this letter before him, but he couldn't dwell on that at this time. Tears automatically sprang to his eyes as he gazed on the familiar handwriting.

*Dear Cain,*

*I had to take a few minutes out to write to you while these feelings are still fresh in my mind. I don't know when I'll get back to see you, and I don't want to wait until I get time to write once I get back to school. I can't tell you how great it was being with you today. I saw a hint of that gleam in your eye that has been missing since the day you got arrested. I often wondered if I'd ever see that incredible lust for life of yours again. After today I know I will.*

*You and baseball belong together. You've tried to deny that for too long now. You're a natural at that game, and let's face it, your body was made to wear a baseball uniform and drive the girls crazy! I don't know how many girls at Maddox will reap the rewards of ogling you in a baseball uniform, but there are bound to be some now that you'll be permitted to enjoy some of the freedoms that B Unit will give you.*

*I'm so happy for you. Things are finally taking a turn and looking up for you, aren't they? And don't forget—I'm behind you all the way. It's been very hard for me these past almost three years. I've had to sit by helplessly and watch your world turn upside down, and I've missed you so much since you were snatched from my world. But now we're both able to see a light at the end of the tunnel. I've been working hard trying to keep your spirits up, but I can tell you now there've been many times when I've had a hard time believing this unjust punishment of yours would ever be over. But soon we'll be able to stand face-to-face again without that intrusive table between us. And two more years isn't all that . . . well, it isn't forever. Not anymore.*

*I feel better about you than I've ever felt since this whole nightmare began. I had to let you know that because I'm not sure I verbalized it while I was there this afternoon. It's been very difficult watching you go through this, but today I found glimpses of the old Cain, and it did my aching heart a world of good. We're going to see an end to all of this, and while we're waiting, the quality of your existence is improving. That makes me feel less guilty about being free. Hang on to these good feelings; I need to know that you're okay and happy.*

*In the meantime, I'll be at every game I can possibly make it to, but especially the one on your birthday. I haven't been able to get in touch with your brothers yet, but I probably will tomorrow. I have to run. I'm going out with friends tonight, and I still have to shower. I just had to tell you what a lift it gave me being with you today. It's probably the first time I've come home from that place that I haven't been in a depressed funk that took days to work off. Please hang on to the good feelings for the future, and don't let that spark go out. It looks awfully good on you! See you on the 27th. I can't wait!*

*Love,*
*Scott*

By the time he finished, he could barely read for the tears that welled in his eyes and ran down his face. He sat in a sea of mixed emotions, which at times threatened to pull him under. To think that Scott had written this only hours before the accident that took his life was almost more than Cain could deal with. Just as he was about to crash into an endless pit of misery and cry himself to sleep, he thought of Scott and how happy he was on that last day—happy because he, Cain, had finally begun to take his fate in his own hands. He imagined Scott looking down on him from that better place where all loving, devoted friends go, and he knew he had to carry on the legacy that Scott had left him in this letter. The last thing Scott would ever want would be for Cain to regress into an irreversible depression because of him. Now he just had to find some way to move on.

As he sniffed back bitter tears and struggled to hang on desperately to the last words of the once-in-a-lifetime friend he was so lucky to have had, he became aware of someone on the other side of the bars. He shifted his eyes to the outside.

"I'm sorry," said Fr. Mike suddenly realizing what he had walked up on. "I'll come back later, probably tomorrow."

"No," said Cain putting the letter carefully aside and then pulling up to his knees to call after the priest who had already begun his retreat. "Mike, please come back."

The priest turned around.

"I didn't mean to intrude. I had no idea."

"You're not intruding. Will you come in? If they'll let you."

"If you're sure."

"I'm sure. Please."

Mike went to the guard and asked him to let him into the cell. Cain took advantage of the minute or so that it took to get up and splash his face with cold water.

"Did you read the letter?" the priest asked as he sat down on the stool.

"Yeah, I did. I'm okay. I'll never get over missing him, but I'm okay."

"Good," said Fr. Mike somewhat taken aback.

"Do you want to read it?" Cain asked offering the letter.

"I'd like to very much, if you're willing to share it."

Cain stared in the opposite direction, out through the bars into the empty hall, as Mike read the letter.

"He was a very special person," said the priest as he put the letter back on the bed next to Cain. "A lot of people never have a friend like that. You're very lucky."

"I know. And I'm through beating myself up over it. He's gone. Nothing's going to change that, and the last thing he would want is for me to self-destruct."

"That's right."

"So, if it kills me, I'm going to be fine."

"That's good."

"I have my brothers."

"That's right," said Mike not wanting to get into the platitudes of friends yet to be met. "I dare say I couldn't have hoped for a better outlook from you."

"Surprised you, huhn?" Cain smiled.

"Totally."

"Well, he's right; I need to play baseball. I was being stubborn and feeling sorry for myself. Right now baseball is my whole life. All I can think about all day is practice. And I can't wait to play in a game."

"When will that be?"

"Saturday. They have a couple of away games during the week, but Saturday is a home game." He hesitated a minute. "Mike, I have a strong feeling I have you to thank for the fact that Maddox didn't completely pull the baseball carpet out from under me."

"Well, Victoria Doleman and Bruce and myself all applied a little pressure to their Achilles heel."

"Thank you. It's honestly the only thing I live for any more. The thought of putting on a uniform again and playing in front of a crowd . . . it sounds a little foolish, I guess."

"Not at all, Cain. Not at all. You've uncovered a passion that you tried to keep buried. Passions are what give us a reason to go on. And I'm going to be at that game on Saturday because I hear you're damn good."

"I'll try not to disappoint you," said Cain as he flashed a big smile.

The priest joined him in the lightness of the moment, but then let the smile fade from his own face.

"Cain, there's a reason why I came up here. I almost hate to bring it up."

"What?"

"I heard about the crap Lewis pulled on you. I purposely stayed away from there today because I knew I had to let you handle it, and I didn't want to make him any more defensive than he already was. I thought I should come up, though, to see how you are. I guess maybe that's why I'm so surprised to find you in the optimistic mood you're in."

"I'm not going to let him fuck with my head. If he wants to turn me into a social outcast, there's nothing I can do about it. It's really not all that bad—of course it's only been one day." He smiled.

Mike smiled back at him.

"Do you want me to talk to him?"

"No. Thanks, but no. As you said, I have to handle this on my own, and I have a lawyer if I need him."

"Okay, but if you change your mind, let me know. That's a pretty harsh punishment."

"I'll live. It gives me a lot of time to think."

"That could be dangerous," smiled Mike.

"No," said Cain returning the smile. "I'm going underground. Two years isn't forever. I don't want to sabotage my parole—if I haven't already done that."

"You are going to have to watch yourself. That's one reason I'm concerned about this thing with Lewis. He has you penned in, and I'm not sure how you're going to cope with that."

"I don't have a choice. He's the boss, as he always keeps reminding us. If it wasn't this, it'd be something else. He's not going to let me off the hook. And I'll do it because if I screw up again, I'll for sure add another year to my sentence. Like I said, I'm scared I may have already done that. But I keep hoping that there's enough time left that if I keep a low profile, I may be all right. So I'll go to his stinking warehouse everyday and play his stupid game. I don't care, as long as it makes him happy."

"And if you start coming unglued, you'll call me or Victoria or Bruce. You can demand to talk to any one of the three of us at any time."

"I know, and I will."

"You promise?"

"Thank you for being such a good friend. I'd never make it here without you."

"I've been praying that things would turn around for you; that you'd find a way. My prayers seem to have been answered."

"You mean God hasn't forgotten about me?"

"No. Never."

"I wouldn't blame Him if He had."

"He understands."

Cain picked up the letter and after carefully refolding it, he put it back in the envelope.

"This was rock-bottom," he said. "In that strip cell most of the time I wasn't sure which way was up, but I knew I had finally hit bottom and it was up to me to drag myself out of it. I'm starting to feel like I'm making a little headway."

"That sounds encouraging."

"Yeah. I feel encouraged. I hit two homeruns today at practice." He flashed a million-dollar smile.

"You did?"

"Yeah. Like out of the park. Not bad for my first day back."

"Not bad at all. I'm going to have to get over to that field and watch you. I talked with Tom Benson a while back to kind of explain why you weren't showing up to practice the past few weeks—I didn't know if anyone would bother to let him know. Anyway, he said you're an awesome baseball player. I was afraid he'd drop you from the team if you just all of a sudden quit showing up. But he said you have a spot on the team from now until you're released, and he'd wait as long as it took for them to let you out of Solitary."

A meek, unassuming smile found its way to his face. "That's what's keeping me going right now. There's something to finally get up for each day."

"You know," Mike said with a smile, "if I had a son, I'd want him to be just like you."

Cain laughed out loud. "God help you!"

# CHAPTER 11

Cain walked out of the locker room into the cool autumn afternoon. He had to step lively to get back to A Unit on time because he had lingered with his teammates until the last possible minute. The trophy stood bold and proud in the middle of the locker room, and he was as proud of it as he had ever been of any trophy that he had been a part of winning at any time of his life. But now reality was setting in with the cool duskiness of the Saturday afternoon. Baseball season was over. It was a long way till spring.

Cain had just finished his third year at Maddox and was facing his fourth struggle with the holidays behind bars. It didn't get any easier for him as time went on. Now that baseball was over, his spirits took an even deeper dive. He was able to read himself better, however; and as he forced himself to hurry back to A Unit, he recognized the dangerous path his emotions were traveling.

The elation of having won the championship was giving way to the urgency of getting back to A Unit on time. In the past he wouldn't have worried so much about it. *Screw them.* But he had been working on keeping a low profile in the hopes of making a case for himself with the Parole Board. He knew his efforts would have to be valiant in order to offset problems he had had in the past. Therefore, he picked up his step and soon began running to get back in time.

Word had spread through A Unit about the baseball championship, and guys he didn't even know were congratulating him at dinner. This amazed him for he didn't think these hard-core inmates even knew about the game let alone cared about the outcome of it. But he did enjoy a certain amount of celebrity, and it helped to soften the misery he felt over the completion of the baseball season.

"Were your parents at the game?" asked Jon at dinner.

"Yeah," answered Cain. "For all the good it does. I can't go near them or any other visitors. And the screws watch me, too. All I have to do is take a step out of my designated area, and what remains of my baseball career would go up in smoke. So we visit beforehand. It's not a big deal. I'm just happy they can be there."

"You know," smiled Jon, "you really have mellowed. The old Cain would have been raging and beating his head against a brick wall over how stupid the system was."

Cain laughed.

"You're probably right. But I just want to go home some day— even if I have to kiss ass to do it."

That night as he sat alone in his cell on yet another Saturday night, he could feel anxiety and frustration creeping into his soul. The baseball season hadn't been over for even twenty-four hours, and he was already suffering the side effects. Suddenly there was nothing to take the edge off his bleak existence. He was twenty-one years old, and he spent every night staring at concrete walls and bars until 10:00 when the lights go out—three hundred-sixty-five-days a year.

He thought about how over the past three years his oldest brother, his only sister, and Joanne had all gotten married while he sat in a prison cell staring through bars. While everyone else's life was moving on, he had no life. And in two more months it would be Thanksgiving, then Christmas. He couldn't even bear the thought of spending another holiday season behind bars. But seeing as there was no choice, he was going to have to find a way—once more.

On Monday after breakfast when he walked into the warehouse, Lewis was loaded for bear and waiting for him. Without warning or word of explanation the guard grabbed him by the front of the shirt and pushed him back the two or three steps into the wall.

"What the hell?!" said Cain in surprise.

"Shut up!" commanded the guard. He turned to Jon and the other inmates who had walked in with Cain. "Get to work! Now!"

He waited as they slowly moved on. Then he turned back to Cain.

"I want to know what the hell is going on," he said angrily. "And go ahead, you can talk to me as much as you want as long as you give me an explanation."

"I have no idea what you're talking about," insisted Cain. "And take your hands off of me."

"I'm in charge here. Don't forget it. I want to know about the riot that's being talked about on your behalf."

"What?!!! I don't have a clue what you're talking about. I don't know anything about any riot."

"I'm getting hate mail and death threats, and I don't like it. Call off your boys."

"I don't have any boys, and I don't know what you're talking about."

"Who's doing you, Farrell? Who's your boyfriend? That's probably who's behind this."

Cain glared at him, not even wanting to dignify the question with an answer. With the back of his hand he pushed Lewis's hands away from him and slid out of his grasp.

"Excuse me . . . Sir," he said feeling the need to put distance between himself and the guard.

At lunch he waited for Jon outside the door.

"What the hell was going on with Lewis?" Jon asked.

"That's what I wanted to ask you. He said something about death threats and a riot or something. And for some reason he thinks I'm at the heart of it."

Jon looked away as he borrowed some time.

"What's going on?" asked Cain, sensing his friend had information.

"There is a group," Jon sighed, "here at the warehouse. I've heard some rumblings. They're looking for a little action—things have been too quiet for too long. They're looking for a cause, and you're it."

"I don't want to be it!"

"You don't have a choice. These are hard-core, maniac types. You don't want to mess with them."

"Shit! Why me? How does this always happen to me? Do you believe I can get in trouble by just keeping my mouth shut and doing what I'm told?"

Jon laughed.

"Relax, maybe nothing'll come of it."

"No, that's not my luck," said Cain. "Something'll come of it, all right. Damn."

Within minutes of when everyone had returned from lunch and checked in, Lewis made a prophet out of Cain. He told Cain to stay where he was and called everyone else together just opposite him. The group stood curiously waiting to see what was on Lewis's mind. Cain stood in his spot of isolation knowing this wasn't going to be good for him.

"Okay," said Lewis once he was sure he had everyone's attention. He held out some papers that were filled with prison graffiti. "These have been finding their way onto my desk as of late. Those of you responsible know what it's all about, and those of you who aren't responsible don't need to worry about it. I'm not sure at this point who the guilty parties are. Let it suffice for me to say that I'm **extremely** unhappy about this shit, and I want it to stop. I'm in charge here, and how I chose to discipline unruly inmates is my business." He pulled out his pad of referral notices. "Therefore, Mr. Farrell, consider yourself written up and locked-in for the rest of the day."

He ripped off the yellow copy of the slip and held it out toward Cain who was standing in stunned disbelief as if he had just been slapped.

"And say one word," warned Lewis, "and I'll write you up for tomorrow, too. This, my *friends,* will go on every day until the crap stops. Your boy Farrell will sit on his ass in his cell while his file bulges with yellow slips, and you all will pick up the slack of his work. Good-bye, Mr. Farrell, get your ass locked-in. We'll see tomorrow if you get to stay here or not. That all depends on your friends."

Cain looked over at the group of faces that were staring at him. He didn't know for sure who was responsible, and he didn't care. It was Lewis he was angry with. He wanted to jump at him and choke the life out of him with his bare hands, but he already knew that would be a futile effort; so he choked down his pride and walked over and snatched the damning paper from Lewis. Shooting an *I told you so* look at Jon, he turned and left the warehouse.

With his jaw clenched in bitter anger, he stormed across the distance between the warehouse and the cellblock. He took the stairs to the second tier two at a time and slammed the paper down on the tier guard's table.

"Oh-oh," said the guard. "Bad day?"

"Just open the damn door," said Cain ill humoredly as he steamed down the tier toward his cell.

Once inside he wanted to punch something or tear the cell apart, but he had already been down that road, and he knew it would do little to satisfy what was bothering him. Instead he paced for a few minutes as he tried to work off the anger. Then he grabbed the book he was currently reading and lay on his bed. He stuck with it for nearly an hour but found it impossible to concentrate. Throwing the book on the floor, he turned toward the wall and stared at the cold concrete.

It was only minutes later when Lewis showed up. Aware that someone had walked down the tier and stopped outside his cell, Cain propped himself up on his elbow to look out. Seeing Lewis, he dropped back down on the bed, stuffing the pillow under his head.

"I dare say, I'm a lot happier confronting you with bars separating us." It was Lewis's attempt at levity. Cain continued to ignore him and stared at the wall. Lewis continued. "I'm sorry I had to do this."

"I'm sure you are," mumbled Cain to the wall. "For six months I've done everything you told me; I've put up with all your bullshit. Now this?"

"I had to do something to neutralize the situation down there. They care about you; they'll get in line."

"If you believe that, then you're an even bigger idiot than I thought." Cain sat up on the bed and leaned against the wall, crossing his legs Indian-style. "They don't care anything about me. They're looking for an excuse, and I'm handy. Just leave me the hell alone. I'm where I'm supposed to be. I have no choice but to be your pawn, but that doesn't mean I have to like it. So if you came here to soothe your conscience, forget it. You're using me, you asshole, just as much as they are. You have to save face, so I have to be sacrificed. Excuse me if I find that hard to swallow."

"You don't understand what it's like trying to keep things cool down there."

"No, you're right, I don't. Just leave me alone, and go do what you have to do."

He reached for the headphones that plugged into an outlet on the wall and put them on. Leaning his head against the wall, he closed his

eyes and listened to the music. *This conversation is ended, Screw.*
Lewis got the message and walked away.

When Jon came up for the count before dinner, he stopped at
Cain's cell.

"I think I'm getting to the bottom of all your trouble," he
boasted.

"Great," said Cain unable to help from sounding sarcastic.

"No, really. I told you I heard a few rumblings, so after you left
I went to the rumblers, and . . . um . . . it seems you're way more popular
than you thought. Jasper is about to get his high school diploma, thanks
to you and your tutoring, so he called in some favors, and they're ready
to tar and feather Lewis for you. I told them your situation, and I think
they're willing to back off if they know it's what you want. How'd you
ever get that snake interested in getting a diploma? He doesn't strike me
as the type who'd give a shit."

"Well, he is. Do you really think it's as simple as that?"

"That's the way it seems. Get a hold of him tomorrow before
work and see for yourself."

Happily Jon was right. Cain knew who to seek out and talk to,
and they were willing to back off since they had taken a stand for him.
Things were back to normal at the warehouse. It didn't take Lewis long
to notice that the heat was off, and he approached Cain one afternoon.
Cain was sitting off by himself during the afternoon break.

"I came by to thank you," said Lewis sitting on a box near Cain.

Cain didn't say a word. He was still forbidden to speak except
for *yes, sir* or *no, sir* and he usually opted to say nothing at all. He
wasn't sure what Lewis was getting at, but he really didn't care.

"I know you had something to do with calling off the unrest that
was going on earlier in the week. I'd like to think it was the pressure I
was applying, but I've been in this business a long time, and inmates
don't just back off after one warning. So thank you."

Cain stared intently out an open bay door as he watched a truck
backing into the slot. He refused to look at Lewis. Lewis wasn't
discouraged.

"I'm sorry I burned you with the yellow slip. I can't take it back
now, but as long as things go well, I can write commendations to put into
your file. They'll carry a lot of weight because they'll be the latter things
that were put in—they'll neutralize the yellow slips."

Cain turned his head and looked at his boss for the first time.
He was confused.

"Truce?" asked Lewis.

Cain nodded his head.

"And I want you to go back to normal. You don't have to
separate yourself any more. Maybe if we work at it, you and I could
even get along. You're a damn good worker."

254

"What about Sam Willet?" asked Cain. "And please don't insult my intelligence by pretending you don't know what I'm talking about."

"That's getting old," sighed Lewis. "Now get yourself over there with everyone else. There's still about five minutes left of break."

After work Cain and Jon went to the gym to play volleyball. It was on their way back to the cellblock for the count that Jon decided to tell Cain his news.

"You've been pretty preoccupied with Lewis this week, so I didn't feel the time was right to show you this." He handed Cain a folded piece of paper from his shirt pocket. "Actually, I don't know if there is a right time, but you have to find out sooner or later."

Cain looked at him quizzically as he took the paper and unfolded it. His expression hardened and his heart skipped a beat as he read the paper. He looked at Jon with incredible sadness in his eyes. Jon looked down at the floor.

"I'm sorry," Jon said. "I didn't know how I was ever going to be able to tell you."

The momentary sadness on Cain's face that was brought on by sudden shock softened to a sincere, heartwarming smile.

"You're sorry? This is great. This is great news. Getting transferred to B Unit is something we all hope for."

"I know, but you're supposed to already be there, and I should be joining you instead of leaving you behind."

"Well, it wasn't in the cards. But I'm happy for you; I'm just going to miss you like hell. Two weeks, huhn?"

"Yeah. I'll still be working in the warehouse though."

"That's true. But you'll have a different cafeteria and rec center. That's good; it's a step up from the junk we have here. And it says next year you'll be up for parole."

"And you're just a year after that."

"Yeah, but it'll be longer than that before they cut me loose from here. Sam Willet is probably already organizing his petitioners and picketers. Two weeks. Wow. That's great."

That night he cried himself to sleep for the loss of yet another friend.

His days with Jon were numbered just as they had been with Scott, only with Jon he knew the end was coming and each day became more difficult. Still he managed to stay happy for his friend's good fortune. He saved his grief for the hours when he was alone.

The day that Jon left he stopped outside Cain's cell. He had a large duffel bag, which held his clothes slung over his shoulder. In his arms he carried a cardboard box.

"Who'd ever believe that you could carry all your worldly possessions in one trip?"

"Yeah," smiled Cain as tears streamed down his face.

"Hey none of that," teased Jon.

"Yeah, I'm some hardened convict, huhn?"

"No, Farrell, you'll never be hardened—and that's good. And look, we're still going to be seeing each other."

"Yeah," agreed Cain without conviction.

"And I'm going to be coming to all your baseball games starting in the spring."

"Good," said Cain already knowing they wouldn't be able to get within ten feet of each other.

"Yeah, I'm finally going to be able to see just how good you really are."

"I won't let you down."

"I'm not worried about it. Well, I guess I'd better go; these things are getting heavy."

"Yeah. I'll see you around—at work on Monday."

Jon winked at him and left.

Cain turned his back and leaned on the bars as he let loose the tears that were welling inside him. Slowly he slid down the bars to the floor where he cried soul-wrenching sobs and felt totally abandoned.

Later that afternoon when he was told he had a visitor, he was surprised to see Matt waiting for him. He had just started his fourth and final year of college and didn't have much free time.

"What's up?" asked Matt. "You look tapped."

"Yeah," sighed Cain with a small smile. "It hasn't been the best day. But everything's okay. I'm surprised to see you."

"Well, I have something important to talk to you about."

"I'm all ears," smiled Cain leaning forward on the table that separated him from his brother.

"Remember I've told you about Melanie?"

"Yeah. 5'7', long hair, gorgeous figure, even more gorgeous face."

"Yeah," laughed Matt. "That's the one."

"What about her?"

"I'm going to ask her to marry me."

Cain straightened up in his chair as the news sunk in.

"Wow," he sighed.

"Yeah. I wanted you to know first. I think she's kind of expecting something at Christmas time, but I want to catch her off guard. So, I'm going to ask her tomorrow."

Cain couldn't speak for a long minute. His sense of security in the unchangeable past took another direct hit, and sent his emotions running for cover.

"I really love her, Cain. I've never felt this way before. I wish you knew her."

"I will," said Cain. "After I get home."

"I want you to be my best man."

"You're not planning on marrying until middle age?"

"You'll be out before then."

"No. Don't plan around me. Have Sean or Jake be your best man or stand in for me or something, but don't wait for me. It's nearly two years before I even come up for parole, and I'm not really counting on making it the first time around."

"I can't get married without you."

Cain rested his elbows on the table and templed his fingers over his mouth.

"Yes," he said, "you can. Sam Willet's going to keep me buried here for as long as he can, and I haven't done much to help myself. I've decided to fight back, though, and for six months or so I've been an angel."

Matt laughed.

"That hasn't been easy for you."

"No. It hasn't. But I want to come home—especially now that I can kind of see an end in sight. I just don't know if the new me is too little too late. You know what I mean?"

"Yeah, but you have to be positive."

"I know, but I can't be positive to the point where it clouds my realism. Losing touch with cold, hard reality is a sure way to go nuts in a place like this. I can't live in Never, Never Land. Although sometimes I think that's what I'm doing."

"What do you mean?"

"Like this news of yours. It's great; I'm so happy for you. But now I have to admit once again that there's a life out there that I'm not a part of, and I'm getting left behind. I'm twenty-one like you, but there's a part of me that's still eighteen and holding. I still see the world outside through my eighteen-year-old eyes because that's all I know. I can't visualize the house being painted or the furniture in our room being changed around now that Jim's moved out. I'm stuck in a time warp, and that scares the hell out of me for the future and how I'll ever adjust once I get out. And I'm sounding way too depressing after you've told me such great news. Does Mom know?"

"No, you're the only one I've told. Mom and Dad love her though."

"I'm sure they do, and I'm sure she's as wonderful as you say. You're lucky."

"I wish you'd let me bring her here. Along with her you're about the most important person in my life. She totally understands about what happened to you. She'd never be judgmental. Cain, it's important to me for you to know each other."

"Let me think about it. Let me give this new sister-in-law thing some time to sink in. There's time."

"Okay. That sounds fair enough."

257

Later that afternoon after Matt had left Cain started to go back to his cell to lock-in, but he knew he'd go crazy just sitting around thinking about how miserable he was, so he headed for the yard. It was a sunny, warm day, and he knew he wouldn't need a coat. He also was aware that there weren't many more days of this caliber left. He walked around, lost in himself when Josie ran up behind him and called to him.

"Hi," Cain said to her as he stopped and turned. "Where've you been? I haven't seen you in a long time."

"I know. I've just been keeping busy, I guess, and you've been pretty busy with baseball and all. I caught most of your games through the fence. It's not exactly the best seat in the house, but I could see okay. You're very good."

"Thanks. It made my summer to be able to play. And you're one of the main reasons I started playing baseball again."

"Well, I'm glad I could help. You definitely should be playing the sport. Hey, I saw you in the visitor's lounge with your brother. I really can't get over the two of you and how much you look alike. But is everything okay? You seem kind of out of it."

"I don't know. I mean, everything's okay and all, but . . . I guess I'm just feeling sorry for myself. I hate when I do that, but I don't seem to be able to help myself. Do you ever feel the world getting away on you?"

"No," answered Josie. "I think we've had this conversation before and we concluded that you and I are quite different in more ways than just the obvious. What's wrong?"

"Jon got transferred to B, and my brother just told me he's going to ask his girlfriend to marry him, and I'm still sitting around here on my ass—going nowhere. Same old story. I wouldn't have said anything, but you asked."

"Yeah, I did. And I'm glad you told me. You might think I'm strange, but I can be a good friend."

"I don't think you're strange, Josie. And I already know you can be a good friend. Thank you for that. I don't mean to be too busy to be your friend. My life is a train wreck. I wish I still smoked; I could use a cigarette right now."

"No, you don't need a cigarette. Come on, let's talk about something else."

"I can't talk about something else. There's really nothing else to talk about. There's really nothing else on my mind. It's like I'm obsessed." He sat for a minute, thinking. Then he smiled sadly at the empty air in front of him. "You know what I'd give a million dollars for right now?"

"A thick steak, baked potato oozing with butter and sour cream, and a hot fudge sundae with chocolate ice cream?" asked Josie describing her own fantasy.

"A woman," sighed Cain. "Someone soft to touch and to touch me. I want to hold a girl's hand again and feel her soft lips on my cheek, kissing my eyes. Joanne used to always finger the hair at my temples and her hand would brush across my ear. It used to drive me wild. Something so simple. I wonder if anyone will ever be able to love me . . . after she finds out about all this."

"I don't think you have to worry."

"I'm a goddam sex offender in the eyes of the law. Who could ever trust me enough to love me? There'd always be a lingering doubt."

"Why are you getting into this now? You're worrying about something that may never happen."

"What? Someone may never have doubts about me? Or someone may never want to love me?"

"Come on," scolded Josie. "You know what I mean. Don't try and figure out your whole future right now. Take it a step at a time. And quit thinking about girls. That's a dangerous pastime here. Unless of course you've changed your mind and you and I can . . ."

"Forget it," laughed Cain, thankful for Josie's flirtatious diversion. "Thanks, Josie. You're a better friend than you realize."

# CHAPTER 12

The next year passed with its share of turbulence and frustration. Matt graduated from college in the spring and got a high-paying job with a prestigious engineering firm. Late in the summer Jon was given an early parole. Because of overcrowding a lot of nonviolent offenders were being released a few months early. Cain was happy for his friend but sick with envy. He would have given anything to be getting out and going home. Not only did he have a year to wait, but also there would be no hope for early release for him since his was a violent crime. In fact, he'd be happy to get out on schedule. He tried not to think of Sam Willet and his determination to keep him behind bars as long as possible.

Then in September his grandfather died. The old man had lived with them for as long as Cain could remember, but they were never able to get along. He had hoped that one day after he got back home, they would be able to make some kind of peace; but that was no longer possible. He chalked up their differences to a personality clash and put the whole thing to rest with the old man, but he found it strange that he couldn't grieve. There was just nothing there. In fact, in some ways it was a relief not to have to worry about dealing with him when he finally did get home again. He could have gotten a leave to go to the funeral, but he would have had to be in restraining gear the whole time with a police escort. There was no way he was going to put himself through that humiliation for a grandfather who not only didn't love him but also was openly hostile to him.

And now he was dealing with Matt's wedding, which was coming up at the end of February, just a little more than a month away. He still hadn't met Melanie. He just couldn't bring himself to let Matt bring her to Maddox. His visitors had to go through metal detectors and their belongings were searched. They were treated much like criminals themselves. Cain felt bad enough that his family had to endure such humiliation. There was no way he wanted to meet Melanie under such circumstances. Matt was disappointed and even a little angry, but though he didn't like it, Cain was adamant. He felt totally outside the loop as it was, and not knowing Melanie made him feel even further removed. He and Matt took their relationship very seriously. They had spent nine months entwined around each other before they were born, and they were never quite able to move beyond that bond—even now as twenty-two-year-old adults.

Everything considered, he was able to keep his frustration in check because in less than a year he would be up for parole. Although he was doubtful about his chance the first time around, he couldn't help but to hang on to a shred of hope that he might slip through the system. He had been biting back all of his anger and channeling it toward the desired end—release. In the name of parole, he was ready to do anything. He and Lewis had been able to maintain their truce, and they had even come to respect one another. Bruce told him that that would be an enormous aid to his parole bid. Maybe they could even hope that Lewis would admit that he had misjudged Cain in the beginning. It was a long shot, but he needed to grasp any lifeline that was thrown his way. Even though the hearing would not come up before fall, Bruce, Victoria Doleman, and Fr. Mike were already busy laying the groundwork in the hopes of getting Cain back home where he belonged.

Since Jon had left A Unit, Cain had remained somewhat a loner. He picked up some in-house basketball or volleyball games now and then, but he didn't really pair up with anybody. Most of the inmates in A Unit were types who would only end up getting him in trouble if he associated too closely with them. After over four years he knew the game in A Unit and how to play it. It was a lonely existence, but he got through it by thinking about going home.

One problem he still hadn't solved was Marge Clintock. He had managed to avoid her much of the time, but she refused to give up. While other predators he had encountered and dealt with during his sentence at Maddox threatened his manhood and even his life, this one threatened his impending freedom.

"Do ladies get hard-ons?" someone asked from the basketball court as their game was coming to a close.

Cain laughed out loud.

"What are you talking about?" he asked.

The other inmate nodded in a direction behind Cain.

"You'd better put your shirt on," the man laughed.

Cain turned around to see Marge Clintock walking toward him. A woman with a purpose.

"Shit!" said Cain. "How long has she been here?"

"Since the shift change about twenty minutes ago. She had to put her eyes back in her fucking head before she could come over here. I know it's none of the rest of us she's coming after. You got yourself a girlfriend!"

"Farrell," she called out as she walked up to them.

The others laughed under their breaths and turned away in order to keep from drawing attention to themselves.

"What?" asked Cain trying to hide his disgust.

"I have a pass for you. It seems you have a visitor."

"A visitor? It's Monday."

"I know what day it is. I was just told to send you out for a visitor. I think it's your lawyer."

"What the hell? My lawyer doesn't just make social calls."

"Well, why don't you get your sweet ass out there and find out what's going on. Here's your pass."

He took the pass from her and hurried toward the door.

"Tuck in your shirt!" she called after him. "It's blocking my view."

Without turning around, he shot up his middle finger at her and sped out the door, buttoning and tucking in his shirt on the way, his friends laughing hysterically in the background. He wasted no time getting to the visitors' lounge where Bruce was waiting for him, horrifying thoughts and memories of Scott competing for his mind.

"What the hell's going on?" he asked Bruce as he all but crashed through the door, still stuffing his belongings into his pockets after the search by the guard. "What's wrong?"

"Relax," smiled Bruce. "Nothing's wrong."

"What? You had nothing else to do but take a ride down here on a cold and slushy winter afternoon?"

"Okay," said Bruce, "I do have a reason for being here, but it's nothing like you're thinking. Everybody's fine. There's no emergency. Okay?"

Cain took a deep breath to calm his nerves.

"Okay," he said as he sat down. "But why **are** you here? God, I wish I still smoked."

"Well, this isn't the best case scenario, but it could be a lot worse. I just found out this morning that Ken Blackburn has been sent to Maddox to serve his sentence."

"Who's . . ." He stopped as the name registered. "Crap." There was a long silence as he struggled with the news. "Is this another punishment from Sam Willet?"

"I honestly don't know, Cain. I just found out this morning, and I wanted to get here and let you know before you found out for yourself. The trial ended a couple of weeks ago, so he's probably still up in Admissions."

Cain's face was troubled and solemn.

"Now how do I deal with this?"

"Cain, the guy's an out-of-control drunk."

"Who killed my best friend!"

Bruce sighed, at a loss for words.

"I don't know what to tell you. Maybe you won't even run across him."

"The hell won't."

"Okay, even if you do, you need to be in control. He probably doesn't know who you are, so if there's a problem, it'll be your doing. It's that simple."

"Thanks, that helped."

"Come on, Cain. Think about it. He didn't know Scott; therefore, he doesn't know you."

"Unless, of course, this is a Sam Willet set-up."

"You're too paranoid about that man."

"Without reason?"

"He doesn't control everything."

"He's done a pretty damn good job at controlling my life for the past five or so years."

"Well, whatever, there's nothing I can do about this. I'm just here to keep you on your guard. I hope you haven't changed so much that I need to worry about you starting something with this guy."

Cain sat for a long time without a word.

"Cain," said Bruce, disappointed that he didn't get an immediate, desired response.

"Thanks for coming, Bruce. I know the ride is long and it's a really crappy day out there. I appreciate you letting me know."

"Talk to me, Farrell," said the lawyer. "I don't need to worry about you now, do I?"

"No," answered Cain matter-of-factly. "As much as I hate him, I want to go home more. I'm not going to do anything stupid. It wouldn't bring Scott back anyway."

Bruce sighed with relief.

"Okay. Then the trip was worth making."


For the rest of the day, Ken Blackburn was about all Cain could think about. He didn't even know what the man looked like, but he knew he was going to have a hard time being anywhere near him. He had had four DUI's and was not even supposed to be driving when he hit the car Scott was in. He was thirty-five years old and divorced twice. That was the extent of the knowledge that Cain had of him.

He wondered if he would be able to just go on day to day without trying to find out who he was. It would be better if he could; he wouldn't deny that. But he knew himself, and he knew he'd be eyeballing every new guy that came down from Admissions, wondering if he was the one. He also knew he could only operate in denial for so long before somehow their paths would cross, and Cain would find out who he was.

That night he had trouble falling asleep when the lights went out. He often lay awake in the dark unable to sleep at 10:00. He was young, and 10:00 was an unnatural time for bed on a daily basis. But this night he lay awake even longer, trying to get the thought of sharing the same air with Ken Blackburn out of his mind.


About a week later he was walking up to his cell after work when Fr. Mike caught up with him in the hall. Matching his step, the priest waited a minute before speaking.

"You've been quite a stranger lately," Mike said. "And now you're going upstairs instead of the gym or the rec room? What's up?"

"Nothing."

"Come on, Cain, I know you better than that. You've been spending more time alone since Jon left, but word's out that you're spending all your free time alone."

"Who's talking about me?"

"No one in particular—guards, inmates. I was asking about you since I hadn't seen you in a while, and I was told you're not socializing much these days."

Cain shrugged his shoulders indifferently as he walked on toward the cellblock.

"Something's wrong," insisted the priest.

"Nothing's wrong. I just want to go home."

"You've wanted to go home since the day I met you, but that never turned you into a recluse."

"Okay, fine. Do you know an inmate called Ken Blackburn?"

"Yeah, as a matter of fact, I do. He just got down from Admissions not long ago. He's in for . . ."

Mike stopped midsentence as he put the pieces of the puzzle together.

"God help us," he sighed.

"Bingo," said Cain not slowing a step.

"How did you know he was here?"

"Bruce was here to prepare me in case I ran into him since I knew his name. I don't want to run into him; I don't want to see him; I don't want to know who he is. Not right now, anyway."

"So you're locking yourself in all the time?"

"I'll kill him, Mike. I'll kill him with my bare hands."

"This isn't good."

"No, you're right. Who was the genius who arranged this? Sam Willet?"

"It could be coincidence."

"Come on, they had to know the connection between him and me. Isn't that part of their job?"

"There's not a direct link between you and him; it could have been arbitrary."

"I don't care. That's totally not important. What is important is that I can't trust myself to be in the same room with him right now. I got about six months till I come up for parole; I don't want my emotions screwing it up for me. I just thank God he wasn't assigned to the warehouse."

"So you're going to spend the next six months locked into your cell when you're not working?"

"I don't know how long it'll take, but if I have to—yes."

"Don't you go down to eat?"

"Yeah. I just stick with the same people and avoid looking around for new faces. There're hundreds of guys down there; I don't have to run into him."

"Let me help you."

"No! With all due respect, Father, butt out. I'm handling it."

"I could get you two together and be a mediator."

"Oh, that'd be just great," said Cain with a sarcastic shake of his head. "Then I'd have to kill you both."

The priest smiled, but Cain continued his quest up the open stairway to the second tier, Mike at his heels. Cain checked in with the guard, and Mike followed him down to the cell.

"I'm not going to come in."

"Good," said Cain. "I have no more to say about the situation, and frankly, I'm tired of talking about it."

"All right," relented the priest, "but think about what I said about meeting with him together with me. It could help immensely. You're going to run into him sooner or later, and that could be a great way to ease into it."

"Easing into it is impossible, and I want to avoid the whole thing as long as possible."

"You're not even curious?"

"No."

"Don't you think Scott would . . ."

"Mike . . . leave me alone."

The priest sighed.

"Okay," he said, "but you'll let me know if you change your mind."

"You'll be the first to know."

With a defeated nod and a slight wave of his hand, the priest walked away leaving Cain to wrestle with the problem on his own once again. Cain wasn't at all sure he was doing the right thing; all he knew was that this hurt real bad and he wasn't nearly ready to confront it.

Days went on, and he managed to avoid running into Ken Blackburn. He noticed, however, that it was taking a toll on what little peace of mind he had. Whenever he was out of his cell, he was edgy and irritable with the apprehension of finding himself face-to-face with this monster. He didn't know how he would react when he was finally faced with the inevitable. Unfortunately, the element of time was not on his side.

Barely a week later he was sitting in the recreation room involved in a poker game when one of the other players looked up from the game.

"Hello, Father," the man said.

Cain turned toward the priest, but never got passed the man at his side. His horrified gaze locked onto him as he sized him up. Anyone with half his intelligence would have figured out who it was. Then he glared over at the priest.

"You son of a bitch," he snarled as he put the cards down. "I'll never trust you again."

Angrily he got up, knocking the chair over as he did. This caught the attention of the guards.

"What's the problem?" the guard asked as he approached them.

"No problem," said Cain. "I was just leaving."

"Cain," called the priest, but the young man was already halfway across the room.

"You want me to go get him for you, Father?" the guard asked.

"No," said Mike. "I'll catch him later."

Cain raced back to his cell, trying to forget the previous minutes, but the face of Ken Blackburn was etched permanently on his mind. He knew he'd been robbed of the sublime ignorance in which he had been indulging himself over the past few weeks. He felt angry and betrayed. Nothing he could have done would have prepared him for that moment, but the unexpectedness of the encounter seemed to have thrown him off even more. He didn't have long to wait for Fr. Mike to follow him up.

"You'd better be alone," said Cain sitting on his bed and leaning against the bars so his back was to the priest.

"Oh, I'm alone," said the priest. "Don't you worry about that."

"That was a cheap shot," complained Cain.

"Maybe," admitted Mike, "but you acted rather childish, don't you think? I waited for you to make a move on your own, but I knew you never would. This is something that has to be faced by both of you. He's known about you for a while now. He came to me and asked me to help him locate you."

"I don't care," sneered Cain as he swung around to face the priest. "I asked you to butt out."

"Well, I'm sorry, but I couldn't make both of you happy."

"Well thanks for choosing his side."

"I'm not choosing anyone's side, Cain. This is an issue that needs to be dealt with. I can't believe you're acting like this."

"What? You didn't know how I felt?"

"No, but I thought you'd be a bigger man than this."

"Sticks and stones, Father?"

"Come on, you know what I mean."

"I know I'm pissed. And I can't believe you'd do this to me."

"He has needs, too."

"Well, you know what? I don't give a fuck about his needs."

The priest sighed as he measured his words.

"Fine," he said. "Then I'm wasting my time here. Why don't you get in touch with me when you do give a *fuck*? You know where to find me."

Having spoken his mind, the priest turned and walked away.

"SHIT!" growled Cain through clenched teeth.

That Saturday he sat in the visitors' lounge across the table from Matt and related the story to him.

"Have you seen him since?" Matt asked.

"No. I've been lying real low. Am I wrong? I mean, what would you do if it was Jake and you ran into the guy who killed him?"

"Hey, wait a minute. You and I may look alike, but we don't always think alike. You know that as well as I do. How can I answer that?"

"Well, try and imagine, will you? I need a little insight here."

"I think you already know the answer, and you're just looking for me to negate it and make you feel better. Jake and I have been friends a long time, and I would hate someone who did anything to him; but at the same time, what good is it doing? It's not bringing Scott back. It's costing you your relationship with Mike. You're revolving your life around avoiding this guy. And you're being eaten alive—I can see it."

Cain expelled a burst of queasy breath as he covered his face with his hands. After a long minute he slowly dragged his hands down his face.

"So you think I'm being a jerk?"

"I didn't say that."

"I got the message."

"Well you got it wrong. I understand how you're feeling. But you asked for insight, and I just tried to point out a few facts that maybe you haven't considered. You don't need to buy it if you don't want. And don't ask for my opinion if you really don't want to hear it."

"Okay, I'm sorry. This is just messing with my head something fierce."

"Well, don't let it. Cain, you don't have to be this guy's best friend. All you have to do is listen to him. Then tell him to go to hell."

Cain put his hands back over his face.

"I don't even know who I am anymore," he said through his palms.

"Come on," coaxed Matt, "you're getting to the end of this nightmare. Next year at this time you could be home. Don't give in to it now."

"I'm tired, Matt, and this is just one more kick in the teeth."

"I know. I'm not trying to second guess you and your pain, but maybe facing Ken Blackburn will help you to achieve some closure and relieve some of the anxiety of trying to avoid him. Just a thought."

Cain looked over at his brother. A large tear was perched on his lower, left eyelashes.

"It's almost a year."

"I know."

"Death is so final. I think about that sometimes. I'll never see him again—never. There's no going back like I once thought I could do.

I thought I'd get out of here and try to pick up the pieces where I left off. Now more than ever I realize that's not going to happen. You know when it's really going to hit me? When I finally get home, and he's not there."

"I'll be there."

Cain smiled. "Thank God. And changing the subject, I've been wanting to tell you it's not too late to make Jake your best man. You deserve a real best man who can be there with you. It's all right with me, really."

"I love Jake, but I don't want him for my best man; I want you. Before anyone else in the world, there was you. That's important to me."

"Thanks." He rubbed his face and sighed. "I don't know how I'll make it through that day."

"I still wish you would let me bring Melanie here."

"No."

"It just doesn't seem right that you don't know each other. I'm going to marry her in a few weeks."

"Are you having sex?"

Matt smiled the sly grin that they shared.

"What's that got to do with anything?"

Cain shrugged. "I'm jealous," he smiled.

"You're time's coming. I just know they're going to let you go next year."

"Well, you keep that good thought, but don't be too disappointed if it doesn't happen."

"You just did an artful job of changing the subject about Melanie coming here."

"There's no discussion on that subject. I thought I've been perfectly clear on that point."

"You let Alexis come."

"No, I didn't let Alexis come. She came on her own. I had no idea until I walked in and she was sitting here. And then it was too late."

"Then . . ."

"Forget it, Matt. I'll never forgive you if you pull something on me. If you're right, I'll be home in less than a year, and then we'll have the rest of our lives to be a real family again. Alexis has known me since we were kids. She knows this isn't me. I don't want this to be anybody's first impression of me. I've never met Dan's wife or Molly's husband."

"But that's different, and you know it."

"Are we going to fight about this?"

"No. We're not. I got the message."

Cain wrestled with the Ken Blackburn dilemma for the rest of the day and on into the night. He knew something had to happen soon or he would drive himself crazy.

In the morning he went down to breakfast, keeping mostly to himself, afraid to look around and inadvertently come face to face with his worst nightmare. In spite of the chilling weather he opted to go out for a walk and get some fresh air after breakfast was dismissed. He turned the collar of his pea coat up against the wind and stuffed his hands deep into his pockets. He wandered somewhat aimlessly within the limited area he had access to. His mind was a blur of pain, conscience, and frustration. Try as he might, he couldn't draw any good feelings to the surface. He was glad there was hardly anyone else outside. His heart was too heavy to deal with anyone else at that point.

He wasn't sure how, but he suddenly found himself standing at the outside entrance of the chapel with about fifteen minutes before the Catholic Mass was to begin. Across the other side of the fence, he could see B Unit inmates and their families walking toward their entrance. Even in the chapel he was segregated and made to feel an outcast. Now he knew why he never came here before. Something was drawing him inside, though, so using the excuse of needing to get out of the weather for a bit, he stepped in.

He hadn't been in a Church in so long—almost five years, since he had been arrested and felt totally abandoned by God and Supreme love. The chapel was small and quaint, very personal—except for the double chicken wire-type fences that separated A Unit inmates from everyone else. Actually there were only two other A Unit inmates beside himself. The B and C side was decidedly more crowded.

He stood in the doorway looking around. The confining fence even caged him off from the altar. There was a small opening for putting the hands through to receive Communion. He had heard a story about how some years back an A Unit inmate had gone berserk in the chapel during a service and wielding his homemade weapon made a hostage of one of the visitors and held off the authorities for a number of hours before finally giving up. The next day the fences went up. The irony of it all didn't escape him, and it repulsed him. Still, unable to help himself, he walked in and sat down in the very last pew, hands still stuffed into his pockets. Sighing deeply, he had no idea of why he was there or how long he planned to stay.

Fr. Mike spotted him shortly after taking the altar and beginning the Mass. He wasn't sure exactly what was going on; he had difficulty keeping his mind on the task at hand. He shifted his focus to the Divine and prayed to God that Cain would stay till after the Mass when they could talk.

Cain did stay, though he never moved from his initial position—an indifferent slouch, hands stuffed in pockets. He never stood or knelt; he passed on Communion. When the Mass ended and everyone began filing out, he remained.

Keeping one eye on the A Unit exit, Fr. Mike met the tiny group of worshipers as they left. Some stopped to chat which irritated him since he had other things on his mind, but he smiled graciously and exuded patience. Finally the last person left, and he was able to attend to his troubled, young inmate.

He stuck his head in the door of the Church.

"Promise me you won't move," he said. "I just want to go get out of these robes."

"I'm not going anywhere," said Cain without turning around to look at him.

Mike was back in a short while and placed himself in the pew with Cain. Still Cain had not broken his sullen stare to the front of the Church, not even to greet the priest.

"So," sighed Mike waiting for Cain to give him some hint of what was going on in his mind.

"This is what you've been wanting me to do?" responded Cain. "Come to Church in a cage every week?"

"The decor is not of my choosing."

"Still, this was one of the most degrading experiences of my life filled with degrading experiences. It ranks way up there with strip searches and cell shakedowns."

"Why did you stay?"

"That's what I've been asking myself. I don't know. I just know I didn't like it. I felt like an animal or something that everyone else needed to be protected from."

"Okay. What do you want me to say? I'm sorry. Would you look at me?"

For the first time Cain shifted his gaze and looked over at the priest.

"What's going on? Why are you here?"

"I wish I knew. That answers both your questions, by the way."

The priest sat quietly, trying to decide the best way to proceed. Cain turned his very divided attention back to the front of the Church.

"Cain . . ."

"Father," interrupted Cain, "I know I'm in Church, but I don't know any other way to adequately say this—I'm totally fucked-up over this whole thing, and I don't know what to do. I don't know where to turn or who to talk to. I don't know what's right. I don't know which way is up any more. I'm not sleeping, and I can't eat. I found myself here this morning out of desperation."

"I guess the first thing I have to ask is are you having trouble finding someone to talk to, or someone to talk to who agrees with you?"

"Damn it, Mike," frowned Cain as he pushed himself to an upright sitting position in the pew, "I knew I shouldn't have come."

"Now hold on," said the priest putting his hand on Cain's knee to discourage him from getting up. "Let's back up. Okay, you told me how you're feeling. Now I'm going to ask what I can do."

Cain looked up at the ceiling in a state of pure hopelessness. The pained expression on his face alerted the priest to the need for some extreme diplomacy and compassion.

"You'll feel better if you'll just talk to him. Just talk to him. He's not the monster you're holding in your heart. He's struggling with what he did, too. I'm sorry I blind-sided you the other day. I didn't want to betray your trust, but I knew you were never going to come terms with this by yourself. Cain, you can sit around for ten years waiting for some kind of peace in this matter, and it won't happen. Not without some kind of action from you. I'm sorry, but nobody can really help you here; it's all up to you."

"Shit," he sighed. Then he started to get up. "I got to get out of this Church. I keep swearing, and what's going on in my head is not conducive to Church."

"No, stay. God understands torment. Maybe this is just the place you need to be."

"Isn't there another service going on here or something?"

"Not for another hour. Relax, and tell me how I can help."

Cain dropped back in the pew.

"I don't know. I've just been thinking about Scott all the more since this has come up, and it's really starting to sink in that I'm never going to see him again. I guess that sometimes I kind of trick myself into thinking he's just away. And when that finality starts to reveal itself, it's almost too much to take in. I feel like I'd be betraying him if I even just met with Ken Blackburn."

"That's understandable."

"So what do I do about it? I **need** to hate him out of loyalty to Scott. And if I talk with him I might not be able to hate him any more. Then what have I done to Scott?"

"This isn't about Scott. He's beyond all this. This is about you and the bitterness that's eating you up. How long can you live with that?"

"Forever."

"Yeah? Then what are you doing here all tied up in knots?"

He began bouncing his knee, which was his nervous habit.

"How would this *meeting* happen—**if** I was to come?" asked Cain.

"We could meet in my office or anywhere else you'd like."

"I don't know, Mike. I just don't know if I'm ready. I talked to Matt about it for a good, long time yesterday."

"And what did he say?"

"He agrees with you—just not in so many words. He's more tactful than you."

For the first time the slightest smile crossed Cain's face.

"I don't want to rush you," Mike said. "You'll know when the time is right. Until then, promise me one thing."

"What's that?"

"Just keep an open mind. This guy is suffering for what he did."

"I guess I kind of want to hear that. Does that make me bad?"

"No. Of course you want him to be remorseful."

"No, I want him to hurt—bad. I want his life to be ruined. See, I think deep down I don't want to talk with him because I may in some way ease his mind and his conscience, and I don't want to do that. Nice, huhn?"

"It's understandable. But don't you think his life has been ruined?"

"I don't know. But if it has, good. I don't want to be the one to make him feel better. And I hate myself for that. I told you I'm a mess."

"Avoiding him isn't going to help."

"I know, but that's where I am right now."

"Okay. Uncle. I'll back off. You handle this your way. If you need me, you just let me know. But let's don't you and I fight any more."

"I'm sorry. I'm difficult, I know."

"You're intense. And that's sometimes self-defeating, but you'll work it out. I know you."

"And I'm not coming back to this stupid Church—don't you or God take offense, but you have to be some kind of masochist to subject yourself to the A side of this place. If I could sit on the other side, I might consider it."

The priest laughed.

"I guess I can't really blame you," he admitted. "Come on, I'll walk you back."

It kept haunting him though, like a sickly ghost, ever present but unseen. There was no way to avoid it. Ken Blackburn was there whether Cain liked it or not, and there was a chance that they'd run into each other with every corner turned. He was confused where his responsibility to Scott ended and his concern for his own peace of mind began. The truth was he'd know no peace of mind while he still felt responsibility to his friend. Knowing that Scott would gladly release him from this awesome burden didn't help. It was way more complicated than that.

He lay in bed that night staring at the ceiling waiting for the lights to go out. He couldn't get Scott out of his mind; he missed him like hell. How was he ever going to reconcile this whole thing? How was he ever going to move beyond the void that Ken Blackburn had cast him into? When was God ever going to stop punishing him?

"You're in bed early," said a female voice from behind him.

He recognized Marge Clintock's voice but didn't turn to face her. Neither did he answer her. She squatted down so her face was right next to his head on his pillow. She put her hand through the bars and began fingering his hair. With the speed of a frog snapping in a fly on its tongue, he reached over his head and grabbed her wrist.

"Don't," he said, still not turning toward her.

"You don't like that?" He could feel her breath on the top of his head.

"No."

"Come on, it's not that bad. You're too uptight. Relax."

No reply. He still hadn't moved to look at her.

"You're way too beautiful to be wasting away in here. I don't ever remember anyone quite like you being here before. You got class, you know?"

"I want to be alone."

"Yeah, you seem troubled. I bet I could make you forget all about it—at least for a while. How long has it been since you've had a woman?"

Now it was time to turn. He rolled to his side and propped himself on his elbow. His eyes were on fire.

"I've **never** had a woman, and I said I wanted to be left alone."

"Not so fast. Calm down." She eyed his bare chest and the glimpse of his sweat pants tied low on his hips beneath the disheveled blankets. "There's an empty cell down the hall. No one would bother us. You got to be horny as hell, and it's about time you had a real woman."

He paused long enough to bolster his dignity and quell his anger. The break in conversation also had the effect of underscoring his reply.

"The reason I'm here is because I fucked the wrong person . . . and I hardly ever make the same mistake twice."

He lowered himself back down onto his bed and turned away from her.

"You think you're so fucking smart!" she snarled.

"No," he raged lifting himself to a seated position and more than matching her anger, "I **know** I'm fucking smart, and thank God, I'm getting smarter by the day. I tried to tell you I wasn't in the mood for your shit, and I never will be. So go to hell, and leave me alone!"

"What's wrong, Mr. High and Mighty? You think you're too good for me? Remember, you're the one who's on the locked side of the bars."

"That reality never escapes me." His frustration was taking over. "What the hell do you want from me, anyway? Do you want to see me strip? Is that it?" He threw the covers back and got out of his bed. "That's a piece of cake. I've become so desensitized to a lack of privacy that I don't even think about it anymore. And all I have on are these sweats. Will that get you off my back?"

He grabbed at the drawstring just below his navel.

"Stop!" she demanded as he untied it.

He froze, and a sly smile played at the left corner of his mouth.

"What's wrong?" he said. "I thought this is what you've been waiting for? You've talked enough about it for a long time now. Or is that it? You're all talk. What would you have done if I had taken you up on your lust-filled offer of just a few minutes ago? You know, there's a name for a woman like that."

"Shut up and get back in bed."

"Yes, ma'am," he smiled feeling confident that he may have finally solved one of his nagging problems. Now if only everything else in his life could be so easily righted.

He stumbled through another week fighting with his conscience and at the same time managing to avoid Ken Blackburn. He knew this couldn't go on much longer, but he was no closer to dealing with the situation than he was in the beginning. If anything, things were more complicated.

Mike kept to his word and hadn't mentioned a word about it since their last argument. Thinking that was what he wanted, Cain was realizing that it only made him feel more isolated and on his own. Still he wasn't ready to debate the conundrum any further with the priest.

On Saturday when he went to the visitor's room, he searched for a familiar face but found none. Ready to leave and question the guard on duty, he caught the eye of a young man on the far side of the room. Something was familiar about the nod of his head and the recognition in his eye, but Cain still was confused as he walked toward him, realizing that this was his visitor. Just as he got to his chair, reality dawned. His gaped in disbelief as he sat down.

"Shut your mouth, Farrell. You're going to give me away."

"What the hell!" whispered Cain. "How'd you get in here?"

Jon Harrison had totally changed his looks. His hair was cut very close to his head, and he wore wire-rimmed glasses. A slight trace of a full beard covered his lower face. In all he looked very collegiate and sophisticated.

"I just walked in." He leaned closer and whispered. "I'm your brother Dan. I remember that he rarely comes to visit, so there was little chance anyone would realize I wasn't him. I have identification and everything."

"How?"

"I have my ways, and it's better if you don't know."

"You're not getting him in any trouble, are you?"

"He knows nothing about it, and I have a whole story concocted if I need it. Now relax. How the hell are you, anyway?"

"What if someone recognizes you? We'll both be screwed."

"You didn't even recognize me. Chill. The guard at the door was new—they always put the new ones at the door to kind of break

274

them in. And the guard in here is familiar, but I never had any kind of contact with him."

"I thought I'd never see you again," smiled Cain.

"You don't think I'd let their silly rules keep me away from you, did you? How do you like the look? I even got my ear pierced—like you."

"Very cosmopolitan," smiled Cain. "God, I've missed you."

"I've missed you, too. Who's been helping you out when you get in trouble?"

"Who says I've been in any trouble?"

"Cain, it's your middle name."

"Maybe," Cain smiled. "I've been doing a pretty fair job of keeping myself in line. I do have one problem that I'm not sure how to deal with."

"Ken Blackburn."

"How do you know about that?"

"The good Father. That's one reason I came now. You need a kick in the ass, and I've always been pretty good at fulfilling that role."

"What? Are you telling me you're ganging up with Mike against me?"

"Come on. Ganging up? We want what's best for you, and you're not always good at knowing what that is. Why are you running from this when you know it's going to catch up with you? There's nowhere to go, Farrell. Face it, get it over with, and move on with your life. Why are you dragging this out and torturing yourself? Other than the fact that you're good at torturing yourself."

"Did I say I miss you? I must be delirious."

"You miss me. Otherwise you wouldn't be in such a state over this whole Ken Blackburn thing. I'd've had it all under control by now."

"So what do I do?"

"You tell Mike that you'll meet with the fucker. You notice I didn't say that you **want** to meet with him—but you'll do it anyway. Then you just sit, keep your big mouth shut, and let him unburden himself or whatever it is he wants to do. When he's through, get up and say *whatever* and walk away. Boom, it's over."

Cain laughed in spite of himself as he propped his head up with his left hand. Then he became serious again.

"You make it sound so easy."

"It is easy, asshole. You're killing yourself inch by inch over this. Why?"

Now Cain put up both hands and rubbed his face.

"I don't know," he sighed.

"Cain, hello. You don't have a choice here. It chose you. It's a bitch, but it has to be dealt with. What you're doing is like pulling a tooth with a pliers when you could just go to the dentist and have it done and over with."

Cain stared down reflectively at his hands.

"Okay, fine," he said after a long pause. "Now that we've ripped me apart, what about you? Do you have a job and everything? Mike told me a little bit, but he hasn't heard from you in a while."

"Yeah, I have a little place of my own. After this, it's great—nobody looking over my shoulder watching my every move. And I have a real job—with a small import/export company. They're training me on the computer. I even like it, Farrell. See, your influence has rubbed off on me. You gave me some class. Not that I was exactly riff raff before, but now I want something more out of life. I'm getting older. And I definitely don't want to end up back here."

"You're taking a big chance showing up here."

"You're a good friend; and I may be egotistical, but I figure I may be the one person who can talk sense into you. And I don't give a damn about their stupid rules about us never having contact with each other again. You lost a friend, and I never really had one. We click. They can't make rules about that. We just have to be careful. I had planned on waiting till you got out before I went looking for you, but this couldn't wait. Give yourself a break. Quit beating yourself up over this and get it done. If I was still here, I would've dragged your ass to confront him a long time ago."

Cain smiled.

"Actually," continued Jon, "I told Mike that's what he should do, but he's being diplomatic. So when will you meet with him?"

"I need some time."

"You've had time, idiot. You're getting nowhere. Pick a day. Tomorrow? The next day? Come on, I want you to commit. And then I swear I'll kill you if you don't go through with it. How's that for pressure?"

"Jon . . ."

"You get in touch with Mike the minute you leave here, and you set something up. I'm not kidding. And then get down to the business of counting the days until you leave this pit. Now, when's it going to be?"

"All right. I'll see Mike later today and set something up for whenever it's convenient for him. Okay?"

"And you'll stick with it?"

"Yes. Anything to shut you up."

"You'd better go through with it."

"I will. I know you're right I'm turning this into a fiasco. I need to end it; nobody knows that more than I do."

"Okay. Tell me what else is going on in your life."

"Matt's getting married two weeks from today."

"How are you doing with that?"

"Not real good. The only thing keeping me afloat these days is the thought of possibly getting out of here next fall. I'm hoping for a hearing in August or September. Maybe I'll be home for the holidays."

"You will."

"No, I can't count on it too much. If it doesn't go through, I won't have to kill myself—I'll die of disappointment and frustration."

"Keep a good thought."

"It all depends on popular opinion, politics, overcrowding here. The law keeps changing. One minute you have to spend the majority of your sentence for a violent crime, and then the next they change it back to half. They don't know what the hell they're doing. I could be here three or four more years yet."

"Nobody's spending that much of their sentence."

"It's possible; that's why I can't dismiss it. And then there's the Willet Factor."

"Oh, that idiot."

"Yeah, well, he holds all the high cards."

"Well, shake it off. Keep a good thought. You'll—. Whoa," sighed Jon putting his hand up over his lower face more as a mask than a support.

"What's up?" asked Cain knowing better than to turn around and draw attention to them.

"Lewis just walked in. What the fuck is he doing here today? He doesn't usually work on the weekends."

"I don't know," said Cain with alarm. "Maybe he's filling in for someone. At any rate, you'd better get the hell out of here."

"As soon as you promise you'll get in touch with Mike as soon as you leave here."

"Okay, okay. Now book before Lewis recognizes you."

"That's probably a very good idea. I'm not going to take a chance and come back again unless you need me."

"I won't need you. At least not that bad."

"Okay. I'll be in touch through Mike. Take care."

"You, too."

Cain sat and watched as his friend left. He tried not to think of how much his life had been adversely affected because of Carrie Willet. There was no sense in dwelling on it, but a veil of loneliness dropped over him as he hesitated in his chair for an extra minute. He felt so isolated, so out of the flow, and six months seemed like forever.

Reluctantly keeping his promise, he set a course to Fr. Mike's office. He was somewhat taken aback by a new secretary sitting in the outside office.

"Where's Mrs. Solomon?" he asked none too politely.

"She's on vacation," answered the young woman. "Can I help you?"

Cain sized her up. She looked uncomfortable in these surroundings. She was probably from a temporary agency and not very happy with the assignment she had drawn.

"I need to see Mike. Now." He wasn't feeling overly gentile.

"He has someone in his office right now. Do you have an appointment?"

"I never have an appointment. I'll wait."

He walked over and sat down.

"It might be a while," she said trying to hide her nervousness.

"I got nowhere to go," he answered with a disarming smile that set her even more off balance.

"Okay," she smiled in return and went back to her work.

He sat for a while, and then paced restlessly, still not sure what he was going to say to Mike. Then he sat again trying to remain cool and on top of his dilemma. Finally the door opened, and an inmate walked out followed by Fr. Mike. The priest didn't see Cain, and went to the outer door with the other man, bidding him good bye.

"Father," said the secretary, "this man doesn't have an appointment, but . . ."

The priest switched his gaze around to the other side of the office.

"Cain," he smiled. "I'm glad to see you. Come in to my office. Hold all my calls, Sheila."

Cain gave her an *I-told-you-so* nod as he walked passed her desk. Then he stopped as he was about to walk through the doorway into Mike's office and looked back at her.

"Sheila," he said. "That's a pretty name." Then he proceeded into the office.

"You making time with my temp?" smiled Mike as he closed the door.

"Oh, no, Father. That could get me nothing but trouble. I just keep taking cold showers and praying that I get out of here before I go blind from the want of a woman. I don't know how you do it. Anyway, Sheila is a pretty name, and I was a little short with her when I first came in."

"You?" grinned the priest.

Cain nodded and then got serious.

"Okay, I'm here. What do we do next?"

"You're ready to meet with Blackburn?"

"No, but I'm willing to."

"Okay," said Mike enthusiastically. "Can I send for him now?"

"Let's get it over with. You don't have any Irish Whiskey around here, do you?"

Mike smiled as he picked up the phone and began the process of having Ken Blackburn sent to his office. Cain walked over to a barred window and peered out into the dismal, winter day. A million things raced through his mind, but he let them all go, not wishing to stop and seriously think about anything. He was still standing there when Sheila buzzed that Blackburn had arrived. Feeling his heart race out of control,

Cain remained consumed with the bleak countryside beyond the window. He couldn't move.

"Send him in," said Mike glancing at Cain's back and then getting up to open the door that led to the outer office.

The priest and the repentant alcoholic exchanged greetings, but Cain was welded to the spot. He still hadn't turned around. Mike motioned for Ken to sit down then turned his attention to the window.

"Are you going to join us, Cain?" he asked.

Knowing he had no choice, Cain turned toward the other two men.

"I guess I really don't need to introduce you two," Mike said as he expertly moved through the awkward moments at hand.

Ken Blackburn stood and extended his hand in friendship. Cain stared at him for a long minute. It was too soon. He didn't want to be there; he didn't want to be his friend; he didn't want to be friendly. Without returning the handshake, he walked over to the empty chair in the group and sat down. Mike sighed beneath his breath, knowing now for sure that this wouldn't be easy. Blackburn withdrew his hand and sat down again.

"This is about healing," said Mike. "You both have open wounds which need to be dealt with. We need to find some avenues of communication. Any suggestions?"

Cain sat silent and stubborn in his chair, an invisible wall of hatred and defiance firmly in place. He told Jon he'd meet with Blackburn; he never said he'd cooperate.

"Well," said Blackburn, "I just want to say for the record that I'm devastated by all of this. I've had drinking problems for a long time now, but I've never hurt anyone before. I still have trouble believing that I've killed someone. I live with that every minute of every day. I'm not a bad person, but I have used bad judgment. I'm sorry someone else had to pay for it."

Cain dropped his eyes; he wasn't sold. Mike could tell that right away, but he wasn't about to let him off the hook.

"Cain?" he invited.

Cain took a deep breath.

"I shouldn't have come. This is all wrong."

"No!" said Mike. "This needs to be faced. Don't you go pulling your famous disappearing act on me. Stay right where you are. Don't say anything if you don't want to, but you're not leaving."

Cain glared at him but didn't move.

"Ken," continued the priest quickly, "are you doing anything about your drinking problem?"

"Yeah, I'm seeing Dr. MacArthur, and I attend AA meetings."

Mike glanced at Cain who was obviously not impressed. He looked back to Blackburn.

"Father," said Ken as tears welled in his eyes, "I don't know what else to say. I've done some dumb things in my life, but this by far is the most destructive."

"WHAT ABOUT SCOTT?!" screamed Cain breaking his silence. "He doesn't have a life any more! He was an A student with his life on track. You're the one who should've died in that crash, for God's sake—not him! You should be dead!" Tears flowed down his cheeks in streams. "I loved him like a brother, and I'm having a hard time thinking about anything else right now except that he's dead and you're not." He brushed at his tears with his hands as he looked over at the priest. "I'm sorry, Mike, I told you this wasn't a good idea. I don't like doing this to someone; but I loved Scott for over fifteen years, and now he's gone forever. I can't say *it's all right; don't worry about it. I know it wasn't intentional, and you feel like shit over it.* It's not all right. I've lost a friend; but more important, my friend was cheated out of a promising life. He never had the chance to have a family and live out his dreams. This isn't about me. This is about someone who was robbed of life because of **his** irresponsibility. How is that ever going to be all right? How can I ever accept that?"

"I don't know," said the priest, "but you need to try. You need to accept the fact that there are no guarantees in life, and **nothing** is forever. People do dumb things and make mistakes—you should know that as well as anyone. You're confusing your grief with the fact that life goes on and we all have to find a way to deal with it. Instead of picking up the pieces, you're stomping them into even smaller pieces that can't be picked up. Let . . . go . . . Cain. If Scott were here, he'd be the first one to extend his hand to Ken, and you know it. He wants you to move on, to find peace, to forgive—not forget."

"How do you know?" asked Cain sincerely as his lower lip quivered and tears flowed freely. "How do you know he doesn't want me to get even somehow for him because he can't? How do you know he wouldn't hate me if he knew I made peace with his killer?"

"Cain, I knew him, but you knew him much better. Tell me he would want anything but the decent thing. He wasn't like that."

Cain squeezed his eyes shut, but bitter tears kept streaming down his face. He prayed for Scott to tell him what to do. After a minute he opened his eyes and for the first time looked over at Blackburn. Tears were flowing down his face, too, and Cain could see the pain was genuine.

"I'm sorry," the older man said, "I don't know what else to say. There are no other words. I'll never take another drink again, I swear. I can never get that night out of my mind."

"Did you see him?" sobbed Cain. "Was he in pain?"

"I saw him. He was unconscious. Peaceful."

Cain nodded his head as if this were something he needed to hear. Grief was never spent easily or quickly. He needed time to let it all sink in, maybe to even fully face it all for the first time. Tears flowed silently down his face over the next few minutes. No one said anything. Words he knew needed to be said stuck in his throat. How was he ever going to get through this? How could he get passed this huge roadblock he had come to? It took many tearful minutes before he could even attempt to speak again.

"I needed to be sure he didn't suffer." He said barely above a whisper. Then he proceeded with the determination of avenging his friend. "You make sure you don't **ever** take a drink again, and get your life together. At least then some sense may come of all this. You have a second chance that Scott never got, don't blow it, or so help me God, I'll find you and kill you with my bare hands. Please don't think I'm kidding."

"Don't worry," stammered Blackburn.

Cain nodded. Then with strength he knew could only have come from Scott, he held his hand out to Ken Blackburn.

Mike sighed with relief as the two men shook hands. Then Ken got up and walked to the door. Mike walked with him and thanked him. After Ken had left, Mike turned to Cain.

"That was no quick fix," said Cain firmly. "I just want you to know that."

"Well, thanks for throwing cold water all over my good spirits," said Mike.

"I'm sorry; I didn't mean to do that. I do feel better, and it'll be less awkward if I run into him somewhere."

"And you're glad you did it."

"Actually, I am."

"Well, then everything's cool. That's all we needed to accomplish. You don't have to be friends."

"Then why do I still feel sick inside?"

"Because this is a complicated matter. You're right when you say it wasn't a quick fix. It wasn't meant to be. You've confronted it, but now you have to learn how to live with it. That takes longer. Much longer. You did fine today. Scott would've been proud of you. It wasn't easy what you did."

Cain rubbed his face with his hands.

"God, I feel like I've been through the mill."

"You pretty much have. And now while I have you here, what about two weeks from now—Matt's wedding. What do you have planned for that day?"

"A good dose of cyanide and early to bed."

"That's what I was afraid of," smiled Mike. "I've cleared my calendar for that day. How 'bout we hang out?"

Cain smiled. "I'd like that, thanks. I wasn't cut out for this life. I'm not thick skinned enough."

"It's going to be a hard day to be locked behind bars."

"We've always done everything together—until high school graduation. They told me I couldn't be part of it—image and all that—but I could attend if I wanted."

"Did you?"

"Hell, no. I wouldn't give them the satisfaction. So he did that alone. And now this. I haven't even met Melanie."

"I know."

"Do you think I'm wrong?"

"I think you need to do what feels right."

"It does feel right, Mike. I'm not trying to be a spoiled brat about this. I don't want to put her through the ordeal of coming here, and I don't want to put myself through the ordeal of living through it. I don't get to make many decisions for myself these days, and this is important to me."

"Then stick with it. And you and I are on for that day?"

"Yeah. Thanks. Maybe I'll make it through after all. Just don't expect any miracles."

"With you," smiled Mike, "that's all I ever do expect!"

# CHAPTER 13

Cain held the paper in his hand as he hurried across the yard toward the Administration Building. It was a hot August day, and the only thing he looked forward to in this trip was the coolness of the air conditioners in the building. He showed his pass to the guard at the door and was admitted. As distracted as he was, he immediately noted the coolness that tried to soothe his body. Not able to enjoy it for his anxiety, he passed up the elevators—which he wasn't allowed to use anyway—and bolted up the stairs to the third floor. His heart pounding more from apprehension than fatigue, he entered Victoria Doleman's office.

"I got this," he said to the secretary as he pushed the paper at her.

"You don't even say hello?" smiled the secretary who had come to know him over the years.

"Hello. I'm sorry; I'm not thinking. This is bad news, I know. Could you tell her I'm here."

"I don't have to," said the secretary. " She told me to have you come in as soon as you got here."

"Do you know what this is about?"

"Maybe, but why don't you go in and find out for yourself. And smile—you just knock me out with that smile of yours."

Instead he expelled a burst of queasiness through his lips and knocked on the counselor's door. He opened the door and looked in. Victoria Doleman was sitting at her desk.

"Come in," she said lightheartedly.

"What's wrong?" asked Cain as he sat down across from her. "Something's wrong."

"Nothing's wrong." She shuffled through the papers on her desk.

"Any time you've called me up here it hasn't been for good news. I remember when my grandfather died."

"Cain," she said, "here."

She handed him a paper, which he quickly read. Then he reread it to be sure he got it right. He looked up at her in a mixture of disbelief and panic.

"Well, aren't you going to smile?" she asked with a large smile of her own.

"A date's been set for my parole hearing? Sweet Jesus."

"That's right. The first week in October. Just over a month away."

"But that's just the hearing. They can easily say no."

"That's true, but let's be optimistic for once, shall we? You have a good chance. The overcrowding's getting worse, and they're looking to parole a bunch of good behaviors."

"That's not me," laughed Cain, surprised that she didn't pick up on it.

"Sure it is. You've been an angel."

"What about the Solitary shit with Lewis?"

"That was a long time ago. Bruce, Mike, and I have been doing some legwork. I have a statement from Lewis stating that your behavior and your work have been exemplary. We have validation from several inmates that they've either received a high school diploma or are close to it because of you and your tutoring and study groups. I have your own college transcript . . . "

"That's impressive," interrupted Cain sarcastically.

"Straight A's?"

"In some rather lame courses."

"I have all the Administration's rejections of your requests to send out applications for upper level courses at some of the more prestigious universities that were ready to accept your correspondence work. It wasn't your fault; they held you back. But you still pursued the watered-down version and you excelled. I couldn't find anyone who would have a problem with you being paroled."

"Except Sam Willet."

"Bruce is checking out that avenue. It's true that's going to be tough road, but I have a pile of good stuff to offset it. Just a warning, if they let you go, it's liable to be highly restrictive parole—a lot of rules and guidelines."

"But I'll be at home—not some halfway house?"

"No. You'll be home."

"Then I don't care. I've dealt with this, I can handle that."

"That's what I wanted to hear."

"What about The Rock?" Cain asked still looking for trouble.

"That was even before Solitary."

"So?"

"It was minor. Trust me, will you? I've seen a lot of men through paroles before. You're in good shape."

"Okay," he sighed not all too positively.

"There is something I have to discuss with you."

"Ah, the blow below the belt. I knew there had to be one."

"It's not all that bad. It's not a low blow at all. In fact, I think it's good news."

"What?"

"I have a dean coming from the community college in your home district to talk to you. If we can get them to accept you for the winter semester, that would be a real feather in our cap."

"So why is he coming here? Isn't that a little unusual? I mean, usually you mail in your application, and they mail back their reply."

"Yes, but you've already been accepted—conditionally."

"Which means—"

"Which means I've already taken the liberty of contacting them and sending them your paperwork. They're very impressed."

"But—"

"But because of your conviction as a rapist, they want to interview you first before they make a final decision."

"And what if I don't even want to go to their goody-goody, fucked-up school?"

Victoria Doleman stifled an amused smile.

"Come on," she said, "it makes sense to go there. It's close to home, inexpensive, and low profile. Then after the dust settles and you're more acclimated, move on to bigger and better things. It would be a big plus to have their acceptance."

"When do I meet with him?"

"Tomorrow."

"I have a game after work. Could I meet him after the game? On the field where I'm more comfortable? In a baseball uniform rather than white-stripe prison blues."

She smiled.

"I don't see why not. He's coming in the late afternoon. We could catch the end of the game. It'll give him a chance to get to see another side of you."

"You need to set it up with A Unit. I have exactly forty-five minutes from the last out until I need to check in. The screw on the field phones in the end of the game to the tier boss, and my ass better be up there on time or else. One time I was three minutes late, and I had to lock-in instead of playing in the next game. I'm becoming a quick-shower-and-change-artist."

"Ouch," she grinned.

"Yeah, it's kind of like kindergarten."

"What about practice?"

"On practice days I have to leave at 4:30 to be back at 4:45 whether practice is over or not."

"Well, cheer up—you could be home by Christmas."

"Jesus," he sighed dropping back in his chair.

He spent the rest of that night and the next day trying to let it all sink in, afraid to count on it too much. It would be just like them to dangle freedom in front of him and then snap it back without a thought. Still, he was suddenly filled with an elation and excitement that he couldn't deny. It was just a matter of keeping it contained until everything was final.

He was thankful for baseball since that was his great love, and it occupied his whole being whenever he was involved in practice or a game. He was batting over .400, and his defense was as sharp as ever. He was by far the best player on the team—probably even in the league—and though he had had to give up his dream of playing in the majors, he got a great amount of satisfaction out of being able to participate and shine at this level.

He played as hard as ever, not giving a thought to Mrs. Doleman or the dean. He wasn't nervous about meeting with the dean—he was actually more angry than anything. Who did they think they were—coming out to see if they approve of him going to their school? Screw them—there were other schools.

When the game was over, he celebrated another victory with his teammates on the field. Then he brushed himself off and began searching the stands for Victoria Doleman and the dean. He hadn't even looked for them until now. When he spotted them, he walked toward the batter's box and waited. He didn't dare leave the field and approach the stands. That was strictly forbidden him as part of the agreement to let him play on the B side of the fences, much to the chagrin of more than a few young ladies who watched the games faithfully wishing to get more up-close-and-personal with him. His aloof unavailability made him all the more mysterious and seductive. He wasn't even aware of his matinee idol status.

He stood patiently as he watched Mrs. Doleman speak to one of the guards on duty. The guard then turned and motioned him to the sidelines where they all were standing. Brushing off the last remaining traces of a spectacular slide into second base, he stuck his glove under his arm and headed toward them as the guard neatly whisked all other spectators on their way as if he had some communicable disease they might catch. That was the first time he noticed the young woman standing with the dean and Mrs. Doleman.

"Dean Richards and Ms. Boston, let me introduce Cain Farrell," said Mrs. Doleman.

Looking rakishly handsome with just the right amount of dust smudged on his face, he held his hand out to them and nodded.

"Ms. Boston is a representative of the educator's association at the college," explained Victoria.

Cain shifted his gaze from the young woman to Victoria Doleman. *What the hell?* She gave him a curt, little smile. *I had no idea she was coming.*

"Nice game," commented the dean as Ms. Boston smiled and nodded agreement.

"Thank you," said Cain tersely. Victoria wished he'd lose the brooding skepticism.

"Can we sit over here on the bleachers?" the dean asked.

"Of course," said Victoria.

"Did you buy me some time?" Cain asked her as they walked over and sat down.

"It's all taken care of," she assured him. "I just have to call you in when we're finished. I hate for you to miss dinner, though."

"Don't worry about it. I have crackers and peanut butter up . . ." He resisted saying *in my cell,* " . . . upstairs."

"That's not much of a dinner for a strapping, young man," said the dean. "How tall are you?"

"6'2"." *What's that got to do with me going to your school?*

"I didn't realize this would be a bad time," Dean Richards said.

"It's not a bad time," said Cain on the verge of getting irritated. "It won't be the first meal I've missed. Actually you're probably doing me a favor. Now what is it you need to know from me?"

"Well," sighed the dean carefully selecting his words, "your academic record is outstanding. And you're certainly a gifted athlete—"

"But—" prompted Cain.

Victoria winced at his boldness, but then she knew he wasn't one to mince words.

"But frankly we're . . . uneasy . . . about having a convicted rapist on our campus. We need some reassurances before we okay your admittance."

"We have a number of women students and instructors," said Ms. Boston.

Cain took them both in with his dynamically expressive eyes which had the effect of slightly unnerving them both. Victoria quietly cringed as she waited for the next words from him.

"Can you do that?" he asked. "Can you deny me an education because I have a record?"

"Well, it's not so much that you have a record . . . but it's your sex offender status."

"I see. Other criminals are permitted to have an education, but sex offenders aren't?"

"Cain—" interrupted Victoria hoping to stop him before he angered the dean and lost his chance.

But he held his hand up to silence her. Then he stood up in front of the dean and Ms. Boston.

"Do I look like a sex offender?" he asked.

"Well, of course not," said the dean. "I mean, what does a sex offender look like?"

"Exactly," said Cain. "So how do you know that I'm a sex offender? Because some confused, neurotic, young girl said I was? And because the jury believed her as she sobbed on the stand?"

"I don't know," admitted the dean. "All I know is that I have a faculty and a student body to protect, and you're a dangerous threat to security."

"You don't know anything about me."

"Have you been getting some counseling while you're here? Is there anyone we can talk to about your rehabilitation?"

"Yeah," he said thoughtfully. "Yeah, there's someone you can talk to, but you see there's a major problem, sir—and ma'am—I'm being treated for a disease I don't have. I . . . didn't . . . rape . . . **anybody**. I never have, and I never will."

There was an appropriate silence after his emphatic statement. Victoria Doleman smiled inwardly. She felt Cain's true self was revealed when he so staunchly professed his innocence. While he had them at a loss for words, he continued.

"I meet with my therapist for fifteen minutes a week, and I've been doing that for five years. That's not really very much time, but this is a busy place for therapists. I don't know what he'll tell you, but he won't tell you that I ever admitted to him that I raped anyone—not that he hasn't been trying to get me to admit it. I'd rather be talking about what has happened to my head ever since that girl lied about me and what really happened; but for that to happen, he'd have to admit that I don't belong in this institution—and that doesn't serve their purposes at all here. They need to believe I'm guilty; otherwise, how could they sleep at night? I've spent five years in this zoo for something I never did, and my life will never be the same again. Now I'm asking you for a chance to help me to at least get back home again. You don't have to worry about any of your female personnel or students around me. I'm a little gun-shy when it comes to women these days, but I do know how to treat women with dignity and respect because that's the way I was raised."

"Well," sighed the dean, "you kind of have me at a loss here."

"You were hoping I'd beg—be remorseful and swear I'll never do it again if you'll just give me the chance? Would you feel better about my character then?"

"I don't know, I guess not."

"Good because that will never happen. Number one: I didn't do it; and number two: I have too much pride. I don't know what you were expecting when you came here today, but I won't beg. I will ask you to believe in me and trust that everything I've told you today is the absolute truth. I won't deny that you'd be doing me a large favor by accepting me; but if you don't feel it'll work out, there are other schools. And now I need to shower and change and get to my peanut butter and crackers. It's been nice meeting you both." He shook their hands. "Mrs. Doleman, will you please call upstairs and tell them I'll be on my way up in about fifteen minutes?"

Without another word he was gone and they were watching him walk off in the distance. Victoria Doleman smiled admirably. Then she waited for some reaction.

"Is he always so direct?" asked Dean Richards.

"Oh, yes," laughed the counselor. "But he's very sincere and genuine."

"Then you believe him?" asked Ms. Boston.

"Yes, I do," said Mrs. Doleman turning serious. "You saw him and talked to him. He's the kind of guy that women and girls follow around just hoping to get him to notice them."

"But rape is about control," argued Ms. Boston. "Just because a girl would flirt with him doesn't mean she wants anything more."

"I understand that, but that is not a rapist who was just standing before you. After five years of working with him, I'd bet my life on it. He's extremely sensitive and vulnerable and always respectful. He got involved with the wrong girl. He's been through some really rough times here, and he could use a break. That's my recommendation."

"He certainly has a great deal of potential," mused the dean.

"And he's going to run into brick walls everywhere he turns because of his record. Please don't throw another one up in front of him. Your approval doesn't insure his release, but it would be a great help. The Parole Board has the final say, however."

She spoke with them a little while longer, and then walked with them to the front gate that led out to the parking lot. They left her with the promise of giving careful consideration to what they had seen and learned of Cain Farrell that day, as well as what they already knew. They seemed positive and duly impressed. Now it was merely a matter of reporting back and working out the details.

With a light heart, she stopped down in the night kitchen and picked up a sandwich, chips, and a cold can of pop to offer her charge as she presented him with the improving outlook.

When she got to the tier, she saw that Marge Clintock was on duty. She knew of Cain's aversion to the bothersome guard and chuckled inwardly at his bad luck. It was a good thing she was not only bringing him hopeful news but also sustenance.

"Good evening, Marge. Could you please unlock Cain Farrell? I need to meet with him."

She presented the bag of food she carried since not even prison personnel were exempt from searches—especially in the cellblocks.

"I'll unlock him," Marge said, "but you're wasting your time. He's beyond communicating with."

"What are you talking about? I just left him a little over an hour ago, and he was fine."

"Well, he's not fine now. He came back here just about an hour ago in a real snit. I mean, I often get attitude from him, but this was major. I'll tell you, I gladly slammed that cell door shut on him."

"Did he say what was wrong?"

"No. He doesn't talk to me except to give me attitude. But by the time I did my 7:30 rounds, he was stripped down and in bed. He had his face buried in his pillow, but his body was racked with sobs and I'm sure he was crying."

"What?"

The counselor's face was twisted with concern. She couldn't think of anything that had transpired that would have caused him so much anguish.

"Yeah," continued Clintock. "I just got back from my 8:00 check, and he's out like a light. I don't think you'll be able to wake him."

"I need to see him," Mrs. Doleman said with increasing concern.

"I'll walk down with you and unlock him manually."

The counselor didn't want Marge Clintock intruding on her mission, but she was too troubled to argue. As soon as they left the air-conditioned comfort of the small guard's station, she was immediately assaulted by the smothering heat of the cellblock. Almost instantly her hairstyle and her clothing wilted. How did these men live like this? The noise level on the tier was somewhat subdued by the sweltering atmosphere, but there was still restless activity going on, and the amount of racket was far above the point of permitting serious relaxation.

With Marge Clintock in the lead, Victoria Doleman made her way down the tier, the smell of men living in squalid conditions burning her nostrils. Huge fans widely spaced down the tier whirred, offering relief only to those cells that were in direct proximity. She noticed that Cain's cell was one of those that was the furthest from the welcoming stirrings offered by the giant steel structures.

"See," said Marge as they stopped outside his cell and she fumbled through her keys.

Victoria's heart broke as she looked in on him. A single, bare light bulb blared like an unforgiving sun from the ceiling over his head— all lights were on a common switch that was pulled at 10:00. Wearing only a worn pair of cut-off sweat pants, he was laying on his stomach on top of the sheets. The pillowcase beneath his head and the sheet beneath his body were soaked in perspiration as was the waistband around the sweats. His body glistened with moisture from the stifling heat and humidity, and beads of sweat at his hairline were turning into rivulets that streamed across his face. He was in a deep sleep; his breathing was deep and labored, and it was obvious he wasn't enjoying a peaceful respite from his brutal world.

She looked to Marge Clintock with alarm.

"I told you," shrugged the guard.

"Did he have mail when he came back?" asked Mrs. Doleman searching for an answer to his distress.

"Yeah, but look—it's on his table unopened."

The counselor looked up. She was always amazed at how he was able to take such a drab environment and maintain a neat, intimate living space that reflected his character. But now the mail was scattered, as if thrown, across the small table, some of it having landed on the floor.

"Come on," said Mrs. Doleman impatiently, "let me in there."

"You're going to try to wake him?" asked Clintock as she unlocked the cell door. "You're taking your life in your hands."

"I'm fine," she said distractedly as she walked into the cell.

"I have to lock you in."

"Fine. I'll let you know when I'm ready to leave."

"You're sure you don't want me to wait and see how he is? He can be a real bastard when he wakes up."

"No," whined the counselor realizing why Cain couldn't tolerate the woman, "just get back to what you were doing. I'll be fine."

Finally the abrasive guard left. Putting her bag with his sandwich on the table, Victoria found a washcloth and dampened it with cold water. The whole time Cain had not stirred. She pulled up his stool and sat down next to him. Gently she called his name as she stroked his hair. Looking down on him, she couldn't help but think of her own son who was only slightly younger. He began to move about slightly and show signs of waking. Taking the washcloth, she patted his face, which was flushed from the heat. Then she remoistened it and sponged it across the back of his neck and his shoulders. Gradually he emerged from the blackness he had willed himself to and began opening his eyes. For a minute he was disoriented and confused. His eyes still showed the signs of the bitter tears he had cried into his pillow. Slowly he stretched out and then sat himself up to face her.

"What time is it?" he asked in a voice sill leaden with sleep.

"Nearly 8:30."

"At night?" he asked rubbing life back into his face.

"Yes. What's going on, Cain?"

Everything was coming back to him.

"Are they gone?" he asked.

"Yeah. That's why I came up here. Did something happen after you left me to put you in such a state?"

"Nothing except the crash of my morale."

"Why?" she asked, totally baffled.

He spotted the can of Coke next to the bag.

"Is that for me?"

"Yes, there's a sandwich there, too. Are you hungry?"

"No, but my mouth feels like cotton."

"Here," she said reaching over for the can of pop.

The can was sweaty and still relatively cool. Before opening it, he held it to his forehead and then rested it against each burning eye.

"Okay, now talk to me," coaxed the counselor.

He leaned back against the cement wall and let its coolness seep into his body. He took a long drink from the can and then dropped his head back against the wall. Large tears welled in his sunken eyes, and a 5:00+ shadow covered the bottom of his face. Victoria Doleman waited patiently.

"How am I ever going to leave here and go out into a world where everybody looks at me like they did?" A large tear spilled over his lashes and onto his chest. "I've always known it—there's been an awareness—but today for the first time I got a taste of the real world as a convicted felon. People are going to distrust me—even be afraid of me. I'm going to have to prove myself over and over—to everyone. I don't know if I have that kind of strength left in me."

"I see," she said, careful not to patronize him.

"I didn't want to adapt to this way of life, but I realized today that I have. Everybody here has a past. At first, I had a real hard time being viewed as untrustworthy and degenerate, but over time I came to just take it in stride."

"Well, can't the same be said for once you're out—it'll be hard at first, but then you'll adjust?"

"No." He was emphatic. "This is temporary—I've always known that. That—the outside—is forever. I'm a sleazy sex offender forever. Did you see how they looked at me? And they questioned my integrity. This little for-shit college is questioning whether I'm good enough to go there. It hit me like a ton of bricks. I didn't rape anybody. I didn't."

"I know," she said, not able to respond more adequately.

"I felt their disdain and suspiciousness, but I needed to make my pitch."

"And that you did—very eloquently."

"Yeah, well after I left you, I started to fall apart. I managed to keep myself together until I got back here. And then it was like a damn bursting inside me. I'm so tired of this rap, and today I realized in a real concrete way that it's never going to go away."

"Yes, but . . ."

"Mrs. Doleman, what woman could ever love me? How could I ever have kids when I know someday I'd have to tell them their father is a convicted rapist? How could I ever subject a family to the disgrace and humiliation?"

"Honey," she smiled as she reached across the space between them and put her hand on his knee, "you take it one day at a time. Give people a little credit. One of the reasons I came up here tonight was to tell you that I think you sold the college people."

"I don't care. This may all be a lesson in futility anyway. I'm acting like the Parole Board already said yes. That's one hurdle I have to negotiate first."

"There you go," she grinned. "Take it one day at a time. It's not so overwhelming that way."

"What are you still doing here anyway?" He asked. "You have a family."

"Oh, they're all grown up and can take care of themselves. They know and understand the demands of my job."

"Well, I don't want to be a demand of your job. Go home. It's too damn hot in here."

"That it is," she agreed, "but I'm not leaving until you eat the sandwich I brought."

"What kind is it?" he asked.

"Turkey, a little salt, lettuce, and mayo on wheat bread," she said handing him the bag.

A small smile found its way across his still-haggard face.

"See, I remember. Do you feel better now?"

He nodded as he took a bite of the sandwich.

"Do they ever move those fans around so that you get some air flow?"

"No," he laughed nearly choking on the food in his mouth.

"They should be able to adjust them now and again."

"I don't think I'm supposed to have one."

She looked out into the hall, and it did seem as if the two nearest his cell were each slightly turned away from his direction.

"Why didn't you ever say something to me?" she asked.

Again he laughed.

"Oh yeah, and get my ass kicked all over the damn cellblock."

"I guess you're right."

"I am right. And don't you go saying anything now because it'll have the same result. I've had enough cuts and bruises in this place to last me a lifetime, thanks."

"Okay," she agreed with a smile.

She sat with him and made small talk while he nearly inhaled the sandwich.

"I should have gotten you two," she observed.

"No, this is fine. Thanks."

"Well, there's a bag of chips there if you're still hungry. Do you think you'll be able to go back to sleep when the lights go out?"

"Yeah. Quit worrying about me and get home before it's time to come back again."

"Okay." She signaled to Marge Clintock that she was ready to leave.

The door rolled open automatically, and she exited the cell.

"Wish I was going with you," he smiled as the door rolled shut and locked.

"Me too. But it won't be long, you'll see." She started to leave but paused. "And, Cain, the ladies are going to be lined up at your door wanting to love you; it's just going to be a matter of you picking which one you want." Then with a wink she disappeared down the hall.

He smiled and promised himself not to dwell on it for he didn't share her optimism and he didn't want to sink back into the depths of despair.

He spent the next weeks trying not to think too much about the upcoming parole hearing. He had to appear before them and make the pitch of his life, and he didn't want to psyche himself out by dwelling on it too much. He'd been in touch with Bruce, Fr. Mike, and Mrs. Doleman—all giving him advice and letting him know what to expect at the hearing. There was one, big issue which they hadn't been able to resolve—remorse. They all knew that the Parole Board was going to be looking for remorse as a condition of parole.

"I can't say I'm sorry for something I didn't do," he said at a meeting with all of them during the week before the hearing.

"I can almost guarantee you they'll close the door in your face if you're not willing to apologize," said Victoria.

"Then I'll be here another seven years," he said stubbornly.

"You'd do that rather than grit your teeth and act repentant?" said Mike.

"You're suggesting I lie, Father?"

"Cain," said Bruce, "tell them what they want to hear. Kiss ass—do whatever."

"No. Even to get my ass out of here, I can't make myself admit to doing such a thing and then act sorry for it. They'd see through me in a minute. And they wouldn't see me as an innocent person who's having trouble lying about committing a crime—they'd see me as a conniving rapist trying to get his ass out of jail. Then they'd turn me down anyway."

"Well," admitted Victoria, "that's something you have to work out for yourself. There's nothing any of us can do about it for you. We helped you get the rest of your case together, but you're on your own there."

"Did Sam Willet get his petitions together?" Cain asked.

"Yes," said Bruce. "He has thousands of signatures."

"Christ," sighed Cain. "People I don't even know are signing my life away."

"That's a pretty routine part of all parole hearings," said Mrs. Doleman. "The victim's family always wants to make itself heard and be represented. It's a formality. Don't let it get you down."

"I'll try. Actually I'm more concerned about his unwritten pressure. His strong-arm techniques are impressive."

"Cain," said Bruce, "he's a powerful man, but he's not God. You have to trust in the system."

"Oh, yeah, I've had a lot of practice at that. Who would ever wonder why I'd be a cynic?"

"Okay," conceded Bruce, "you have a point, but I truly believe he reserves his influence for legal favors. For instance, he didn't tamper with the jury or the judge. And I don't believe he would try to unduly influence a Parole Board beyond his legal rights."

"But doesn't his reputation alone add subconscious influence?" asked Cain, refusing to be put off.

"Give yourself a break, will you?" laughed Mike. "You worried about Dean Richards and the college, but that came through for you. Now relax and just give it all you've got. Put Sam Willet out of your mind."

For the next few days he did just that. He concentrated on not concentrating on the hearing. He knew he'd drive himself crazy if he didn't. He also wouldn't let himself think about the possibility of going home. Not yet. He had had too many setbacks and rugs pulled out from under him to allow him such a frivolity. The devastation would be too much for him to handle. Although a seed of hope remained planted somewhere in the recesses of his mind, he kept it concealed and refused to nurture it until it became a reality.

As he had spent the previous days focusing on everything but the hearing, it was all he could focus on during the hours of the night before the Parole Board met. His mind whirled in every direction and totally consumed his ability to sleep. However, it was his sleepless condition that finally gave birth to his stance on the remorse issue. Suddenly it became clear to him what he needed to say in order to hopefully gain his freedom and yet still be able to maintain his pride and dignity. If it didn't work, he'd at least be able to live with the devastation because he hadn't sold himself out. That firmly established, he finally dozed off just over an hour before Wake-Up.

His restless night and lack of sleep didn't hamper him at all. He cruised through the day on pure adrenaline. He had asked that his well-meaning friends and advisors just leave him alone that day. This was something he had to do on his own, and he knew that their presence would only unnerve him and make him more edgy.

Then, finally, with a calm and confident composure, he met with the Parole Board. Clean-shaven and dressed impeccably, he was masterful in displaying just the right amount of self-confidence tempered with humility. Demeanor was one of his strongest weapons in combating the negativity of his crime and proving he was indeed ready to be sent back out into civilized society. After adeptly fielding their questions, he was asked to make a statement, which he knew was meant to include an apology and the promise to go forth and sin no more. He sat for a moment as he gathered all of his strengths and verbal skills. Then he began the speech of his life:

"Thank you for this opportunity to convince you that I am more than ready to leave here and go back home where I fully intend to live out a quiet existence. For weeks I have been wrestling with the issue of addressing you in a way which would be the most beneficial to my cause and yet wouldn't compromise my integrity. Then I decided that you would expect and deserve nothing less than my utmost honesty and sincerity—even at the risk of my freedom. My . . . victim . . . has no need to be afraid of my release, nor will there ever be any more victims for I've learned a lot through this nightmare. I've learned that the most important things in life are trust, patience, and the love of a devoted family. I've also learned that at eighteen I was not anywhere near being grown up like I thought I was. So in that respect, I owe my victim an apology—I should have known better. I should have had the strength of character to walk away from a situation that proved devastating to both of us. That's one of the biggest regrets and sorrows of my life. I take full responsibility for the nature of our relationship.

"Then I want to apologize to my parents for being so arrogant and so impatient as to take on the world in a way I knew they wouldn't approve of. I apologize to them for the financial burden I've caused, and I look forward to being able to get to work and pay them back. I apologize to my entire family for the embarrassment and humiliation my actions and incarceration here have caused them. I apologize to the world for being so incredibly stupid. There's no excuse for that, but I've more than paid for it; and now I want the opportunity to try and get my life back. I'll never take my freedom for granted, nor will I ever knowingly jeopardize it. I'm not good at begging, but . . ." He cursed the quiver that suddenly unsteadied his voice and the tears that began to burn behind his eyelids. ". . . please, let me go home."

There. It was done. Out of his hands.

He had accomplished his goal of getting through the hearing without mentioning the word *rape* or *rapist*. If nothing else he was determined to avoid that ignoble and unfair label.

Happy the workday had ended and feeling the need for fresh air, he headed straight for the yard as he left the hearing. The sun was warm and the air was cool, just what he needed. He avoided the company of others and moved off where he was at least somewhat alone. The hearing kept rerunning in his head. He wished he would have said more; he wanted to have said more; he definitely should have said more. Then another voice inside him told him there was really no more to say. Less was better than too much.

The queasiness in his stomach increased as the he realized that it was over and out of his control. Now there was nothing to do but wait. Victoria Doleman had told him that they usually handed down their decision within seventy-two hours. Three days. In three days he'd know if he was going home or be doomed to at least one more year at Maddox.

"How'd it go?" asked Josie approaching him and bringing him out of his stupor.

"Okay. No better. No worse. I wasn't able to read them at all—I don't know where they're at. I don't want to think about it."

"They'll let you go."

"I don't want to think about it any more, Josie. Do you have a cigarette?"

"Yes, but you don't want one of those. How long's it been?"

"Don't be my mother; just give me a damn cigarette!" He realized he was getting overbearing. "Please."

She reached in her pocket and gave him a cigarette. Just as he put it in his mouth and got ready to light it, Fr. Mike walked up from out of Cain's view and took if from him.

"You don't need this," he said breaking it and dropping it to the ground.

"Mike! Damn it!" complained Cain all but diving to the ground after it and trying to piece it back together.

"Will you excuse us, Josie?" asked the priest.

Josie looked over at Cain who gave his permission with a nod of his head.

"That was her cigarette," pouted Cain as Josie walked off.

"I don't care," said Mike. "Tell me about the hearing."

"They asked questions; I answered. I talked; they listened. There's nothing more to tell."

"Aside from trying to renew your smoking habit, are you okay?"

"Oh yeah, I'm great," he said sarcastically. "Isn't that why you're here? You expected me to be on top of the world about now. But I don't need a baby-sitter."

"I'm not here to baby-sit. Though you are acting like a spoiled brat."

Cain took a deep breath.

"I know," he sighed. "I'm sorry. But you did come to me. I've actually been trying to spare everyone my ill humor. You should know by now to stay away from me at times like this."

"Those are the times you need me the most."

"I guess." He took another cleansing breath. "Don't you ever get tired of always being right?"

"I'm not always right."

"It seems that way to me."

"Well, then you'd do good to listen to me, wouldn't you?"

"I do listen to you. I don't know what I'd do without you."

"That certainly is one of the nicest compliments I've gotten in a long time."

"It's true. You and Mrs. Doleman have helped me keep my head above water while I've been here. You don't think I've noticed?"

"I know you're appreciative—even though you have an odd way of showing it sometimes."

Cain gave him a heart-stopping grin—the first that he had shared with anyone that day.

The next three days went by in slow motion. Cain labored through each minute of each day trying to put the idea of freedom out of his mind. Of course, the harder he tried, the more he seemed to think about it. After dinner on Friday night when Victoria Doleman showed up at his cell door, he knew that time had come to face his future—whatever it would be.

"The Parole Board?" he said sitting up on his bed and laying his book aside. His face drained of color.

"I usually read these and then send them out in the next day's mail, but this one I wanted to deliver personally." She held it out to him. Her expression told him nothing.

Nervously he reached out and took it from her and then fumbled with it until he got it opened. Lots of mumble-jumble to sort through. His eyes quickly scanned it and tried to put it all together. It took a few seconds. Then the look of disbelief.

"December 11$^{th}$?!" he said having trouble containing himself. "I'm going home on December 11$^{th}$?!"

"That's what it says," smiled Mrs. Doleman.

"Oh my God! You're sure?"

"You read it yourself."

"I know, but I just want to be sure."

"You can be sure," she said. "There's one thing I want to be sure you didn't miss—and I did warn you of this. It says *Intense Restrictive Probation*. That's just a shade less than house arrest."

"But you said I'd be home, right?"

"That's right."

"Then I don't care."

"Good. Just be ready for a lot of rules and regulations to have to deal with. I'm not meaning to rain on your parade, but I want to be sure you're seeing this realistically. Do you want to call home and tell them the good news?"

He thought for a minute.

"They're coming tomorrow. I'd rather tell them in person."

"Okay. Two more months, my friend, and you're on your way home. Just in time for Christmas."

He nearly flew to the visitors' room the next day when his name was called. He could just imagine his mother's face when he told her. He hadn't known this much joy and excitement since before Carrie Willet had entered his life. It had been a long dry spell.

Of course every silver lining has its cloud. Cain's jubilant mood was eclipsed by the dominant presence of Marge Clintock at the check-in station. He was determined not to let her spoil his mood, though.

"Hello, gorgeous," she smiled.

"I haven't seen you in a while," he said as he began emptying his pockets. "Only once or twice since that night you so generously offered yourself outside my cell."

"Hey," she admonished wishing he hadn't brought it up, "that wasn't how it was, and you know it."

"Whatever."

"They were short staffed in B Unit, so I was working over there for a while," she went on as if he cared. "I just got back. And wasn't it just my luck to pull this duty today?"

"Could we just get on with this?" he asked impatiently. "My parents are out there."

"What's this?" she asked picking up the neatly folded parole notice which he had been carrying in his pocket and had laid on the table with his other belongings.

"None of your business," he said testily as he reached to grab it from her.

She pulled it back out of his reach.

"Honey," she said opening it up, "everything in this place is my business. You have no private business."

She read it over and felt her heart sink as she realized what it was and that he would soon be leaving. She looked up at him, wishing she hadn't pried.

"Congratulations," she said.

This time he successfully snatched the precious document from her and returned it to his shirt pocket.

"Are you through?" he asked sullenly.

"Until you come back through," she winked, unable to step out of her role as seductress.

Figuring he'd never totally understand her, he collected his few remaining possessions on the table and returned them to his pockets.

At the table across from his parents, he sat patiently as Nora asked the usual questions about his health and well being. He answered in his usual manner in spite of the bursting news he was concealing. Will was the first to sense something was not usual.

"What's up?" asked the older Farrell.

"This," answered Cain as he waved to a guard for assistance.

He would have rather done the honors himself, but he wasn't allowed to. When the guard approached them, Cain asked him to give the paper, which he had just retrieved from his pocket, to his parents. As per regulations the guard opened it and looked it over. Cain thought he would explode with anticipation. Finally the intermediary leaned over the wide table and handed the paper to the Farrells, the smile ever broadening on Cain's face. Will opened it, and together they read it. Nora threw a trembling hand over her mouth as if suppressing a gasp. Her emotion was not to be contained, however, as tears sprang to her eyes. Will looked up at his son and smiled in disbelief.

"How long have you known this?" he asked.

"Since last night. I could've called, but I wanted to see your faces. It's been worth the wait."

"Oh my God," said Nora finally able to speak. "December 11$^{th}$. I'm going to have to get your room ready—not that there's that much to do. It hasn't changed much . . . except now you'll have it to yourself since Matt's married and Jim has moved into Dan's old room. We'll have a wonderful Christmas this year. I just can't believe it."

"Okay," said Cain preparing the blow to bring everyone back to earth, "before you get too carried away, I need to ask you a favor."

"Anything, sweetheart," she agreed.

"Could we scale this all back? I don't know quite how to explain this to you, but as happy as I am to put this all behind me, I'm scared—no, I'm terrified—to come back home and try to pick up the pieces."

"Honey," soothed his mother, "there's nothing to be afraid of."

Will put his hand on Nora's arm to gently quiet her.

"Go on, son," said Will. "What's on your mind?"

"I'm so anxious to get back home—back to all of you—but I'm nearly paralyzed with fear at the prospect of becoming part of society again. I'm damaged goods; it's going to be a real uphill battle."

"Cain . . ."

"Mom," interrupted Cain. "I know what I'm talking about. People aren't going to trust me. I have to register with the local police as a sex offender. There are Web Sites . . . I'm not trying to ruin this moment. Maybe I should have waited a few weeks to bring this up—I just don't want you to go home and start preparing a big homecoming. I want it to be low-keyed. No party. No nothing."

"Well, just your brothers and sister."

"Mom, that's a party. I just want to walk into the house and take it all in a little at a time. I want to try and find myself within the familiar walls of that house before I try to take on anything or anyone else. They'll understand if you talk to them."

"But, sweetheart . . ."

"Mom, I need to walk before I try to run again. We have the rest of our lives—a day or two more won't make that much difference. Please try and understand."

"We do," said Will before Nora could lodge another protest. "We can wait until Christmas Eve to have our first formal family gathering."

"Thanks, Dad."

Cain had another shoe to drop, but he decided to wait until closer to his release date to go into it. This was enough for now.

After he had dealt with the highs and lows of that visit, he had to go and play whatever game it was he was playing with Marge Clintock.

This time she was waiting for him with a new determination. Luckily he didn't care.

"You're mother is very young looking and very pretty," she said making small talk as he started unlacing his boot.

"She's beautiful," corrected Cain not bothering to look up from what he was doing.

"Yeah," agreed Clintock. "And your dad is . . . well, you look like your dad."

Now he stopped and looked up.

"Could we cut the crap?" he asked. "This is business."

"Speak for yourself," she smiled with a shrug. "I'm thoroughly enjoying it."

"I'm glad somebody is," said Cain taking off his shirt and throwing it at her. "I'm paying for that night at my cell, aren't I?"

"I guess," she admitted. "I realized that night that I'd better find some way to put you in your place." She had to concentrate on not salivating all over herself as he stood in front of her, only a pair of well-fitting jeans and boxer shorts between her and her life's fantasy.

"I wasn't out of place that night," he said deftly sliding his jeans down his hips and thighs and then stepping out of them.

He caught them up in the toes of his left foot and tossed them up on the table in front of her. It was a move he had perfected over the past five years. He could tell that she was much more unnerved by the course of events than he was. Whether she liked it or not, he had the edge— clothes or no clothes.

"I was going to tattoo your first name on my ass," he said with a hear-stopping grin, "but I forget what it was."

He slid the boxers down. Her heart was pounding so wildly at that point that she nearly collapsed. She struggled to maintain some sort of composure. She knew now that this was a mistake, and she felt more exposed than he was. She struggled to maintain control of the situation.

"Not bad," she said way more matter-of-factly than she felt.

"Thank you. Can I have my clothes back now?"

"Not so fast. I need to check through them first. God, I wish I had a camera."

"It's illegal," he reminded her.

"Now that's just what I need—a convict telling me what's illegal."

"We're the authorities. My clothes?"

"Maybe I'll don the surgical gloves and do a digital search." She grinned.

"Don't touch me," he bit, ditching the humor but not giving her the edge back.

"Fine," she said realizing she was treading dangerous ground. She did a cursory check of his clothing. "You're clean."

"No shit," he said sarcastically.

"Get dressed, hotshot."

She watched him dress with almost as much relish as she had watched him undress. It took only a minute or two—it was easy to tell he was accustomed to the procedure.

"Marge," she said out-of-the-blue as he put his things back in his pockets.

"What?" he questioned.

"My first name. It's Marge. I wouldn't mind at all having it tattooed across that beautiful ass of yours."

His sense of humor was returning as he locked heavily onto her gaze.

"In your dreams—Marge."

He winked seductively then turned and walked out, leaving her a silly, embarrassed schoolgirl.

# CHAPTER 14

The countdown was on and freedom was an impending reality. Those last nights before his release, Cain found it almost impossible to sleep. So much was filling his head; so much was filling his heart. Everything was mixed up, and his emotions were a smattering of everything that it's possible to feel: hopes, dreams, doubts, fears. It took him hours in the night-lighted dark of the cellblock to finally calm all the sprites and demons that took life in him. Then once asleep, it was only a fitful rest at best. He couldn't wait until it was over and he could at least begin to live out the uncertain future charted before him. This last-minute waiting was agony.

On the last weekend before he left, he walked toward a final visit with his parents. He had asked them not to come since he'd be home only a few days after, but they insisted, so who was he to argue? Their fierce loyalty and constant companionship was the reason he still had his sanity and hopeful spirit. In spite of the cheerful anticipation of his joining them at home once again, he felt anxious about this last meeting with them. He had a second request of them concerning his homecoming that he had yet to reveal. He had tried to tell them during the past few visits, but the words just wouldn't come. They were so excited about him coming home that he just couldn't dampen their enthusiasm. It was obvious their perspective wasn't as convoluted and torturous as his. He had finally gotten his mother to understand his need for a no-nonsense arrival his first day home; he wasn't sure how she'd accept this second request. It didn't matter. It was something he needed to do. He didn't want to hurt them, but he had to make them face the reality had been facing for months now: leaving Maddox was a giant step right off the side of a cliff.

When he entered the visitors' room, they were both beaming. He smiled. How was he going to drop this bomb? He wished he hadn't been such a coward over the preceding weeks and it was already a known fact. He took his seat.

"Oh, my God," laughed Nora, "I can't even comprehend yet that this is our last visit. After so many weeks strung together, it often seemed endless. Now after today we have just one more trip to make. Well, Dad has one more trip. While he comes to pick you up, I'm going to stay home and cook a turkey dinner. You missed Thanksgiving at home, and I know your meal here wasn't that great. I didn't think you would mind that. It'll be just us and, of course, Jim."

"Well, actually," said Cain seeing his opening, "this is the last trip either of you has to make. You don't have to pick me up."

"Why?" asked Will more than a little confused.

"I told them to get me a bus ticket to Chicago. You can pick me up there if you want, or I'll take a train home."

"Dad doesn't mind coming to get you," said Nora. "Don't be silly."

"I'm not being silly, Mom. This is something I need to do."

"What's this all about?" asked Will.

"I can't begin to tell you how terrifying this all is for me. When I first came here, I thought the day I left was going to be the happiest day of my life. I lived with that illusion all the way up until this whole parole thing began taking shape. Don't get me wrong—I can't wait to get back home to you guys, but it goes way beyond that. I'm not coming home to become who I once was before I messed it all up with Carrie Willet. I'm coming home somebody completely different, and I'm not sure how that person is going to fit into the world outside of here. I'm as scared to go back home as I was to come here in the first place."

"What?" Nora couldn't comprehend.

"Yeah. I know it sounds strange, but it's the truth. I had to come into this hostile environment and learn how to protect myself and cope. I did that, and now I see the outside as just as hostile to someone like me. Like it or not, Mom, I'm a convicted felon—a sex offender, no less. The world is not going to open its arms to me."

"What's the bus ticket all about?" Will asked still not seeing the connection.

"I need to take that first step by myself. I need to force myself out into the world again, not riding on your coattails."

"But . . ."

"Please," he pleaded. "Try and understand. I'm hoping that as the miles go by and I get closer to home, I'll be able to find bits and pieces of myself along the way. I need some time—alone—to try and find out who I am now."

"Fair enough," said Will. "What time should I pick you up in the city?"

"Mrs. Doleman's making the arrangements, I'll have her call you."

"Okay. What else can we do for you?"

Cain smiled. "Nothing. And I do want to come home."

"We know."

"And you'll be glad to know I got the results of my physical yesterday, and at least physically I'm coming home in the same shape I arrived. I haven't contracted any deadly diseases or anything."

"That's a plus," laughed Will happy to get the conversation back on an up note.

Cain spent the next few days discreetly getting rid of the contraband in his cell. It was nothing too incriminating, but he still didn't want to get caught with it when they searched his belongings before he left. His homemade weapon which he had used against Herb Lidell and kept close for peace of mind in the early days had long since been disassembled and disposed of. But there were a few magazines, pictures, and the like that were against the rules and he kept under wraps. He also packed up a box of his books that he had read and wanted to leave for Josie. He had a special fondness for her, and he knew how she loved to read.

He realized more and more that there were men there whom he was actually going to miss. Besides Josie there were the men whom he had tutored and worked with over the years. Some of them were hardened, streetwise thugs and gangbangers, but they were interested in getting an education because they didn't want to be *stupid dumbfucks*. They were the main reason he was able to get rid of his weapon. He had all the protection and *big guns* he needed, and he didn't have to submit his body the way most did. Nightly he thanked God for his good mind.

On Tuesday after his last day of work, Lewis shook his hand and wished him well. That relationship had really come a long way. After dinner a guard brought him a canvas sea bag to pack his worldly possessions in. Guards who wouldn't be on duty the next day when he left came to say good bye. At one point while he was packing, he looked up to see Marge Clintock outside the cell. She flashed him her usual come-on smile. Shaking his head and upping her smile with one of his own, he went back to packing.

"Do you think if I hang out here long enough I could watch you get undressed for bed?"

"You've seen as much of me as you're ever going to see," he replied good-humoredly.

"That's what I was afraid of. You can't blame a girl for trying."

"God knows I don't know why, Clintock, but there's some perverted part of me that's going to miss you."

"Well, I'll be if that isn't the nicest thing anyone's said to me in a long time. How about if I go get my camera and you let me take one picture for old time's sake? You can leave your pants on. Just take off your shirt and unbutton and unzip the jeans. Then I'll cuff you, and you can give me one of those brooding, sultry looks of yours that drive me wild. My God, I could retire a very wealthy woman with a picture like that to market."

Not totally sure she was kidding, he shook his head and grinned at her.

"Now you're pushing it," he said good-naturedly.

"I guess that means no?"

"That means no," he affirmed.

"Well, at least I have the picture forever burned into my memory, and I can pull it up whenever I want. I'll keep if filed in my mental scrapbook right next to your strip search photo and the one of you sleeping so innocently without a stitch of clothes on after your first day on the Rock."

"You never quit, do you?" he grinned. "And I guess I'm getting out of here just in time because you're actually beginning to pique my libido."

"You know, that's my luck, Farrell. Damn, I just can't get lucky. But seriously, you're a good kid, and you've been a good sport in some rather indelicate incidents over the past years. I hope things start going your way now. You deserve a break."

"Well, now it's my turn to be shocked. Thank you."

"Just for the record, I looked up your case and read about it years ago when you did time on the Rock. There's no way you did what that little bitch accused you of. You have way too much breeding and class. Even I can see that." She winked. "Have a great life, and please be careful whose bed you share. There are a lot of scheming women out there, and you are just sooo hard to resist. Damn, I'm going to miss you!"

Before he could gather his wits to reply, she gave a little wave of her hand, blew him a kiss, and was gone. It took him more than a few seconds to regain his mental balance. She left him still not sure what to expect from her. Every time he thought he had her figured out, she threw him another curve.

There was almost no sleeping that night. For the moment he was able to put the future where it belonged, and his heart pounded with the immediate excitement and anticipation of going home. The next night he'd be sleeping in his own bed. How many nights had he cried himself to sleep for want of his own bed . . . and the warmth of his mother's arms around him once again? He thought of the seemingly little things which had been denied him and were now countable breaths away. But he also thought of bonds and relationships that he was leaving behind. This had been his entire existence for over five years. He couldn't walk away from it without some sense of loss, but he was going to be more than happy to try.

While emotions played tug-of-war with his conscious mind, he tossed and turned achieving only brief periods of semi-sleep. It turned into one of the longest nights of his young life. Then as is the case with typical sleepless nights, he was able to drift into a dreamless sleep toward morning, only to be awakened by the wake-up horn. The jarring sound brought him back to immediate consciousness, heart pounding wildly inside him. That wretched sound was one thing he would definitely **not** miss.

After a final meal in the less-than-appetizing cafeteria, there were hundreds of good-byes and well wishes. He took time out to hug Josie amidst resounding catcalls and whistles. Then while the others marched off to mundane work details, he headed back to his cell for the last time. As he entered and the door slammed shut behind him, he whooped out loud and threw a punch in the air to celebrate the last time he would ever hear that sound. Being locked behind bars was the most degrading thing of his life, and now it was finally over.

He stripped his bed and looked around for all last minute items that needed to be packed. Finally satisfied that he was indeed ready to leave, he walked over to the window and waited for his cherished moment of release. Holding onto the bars which always marred his view of the outside, he stared out into the morning that was just dawning. Snow was falling and covering the bleak panorama with a cozy coat of freshness. Watching Mother Nature ply her magic right before his eyes, he thought back to the frightened child he had been when he first set eyes on Maddox, now only to realize that he still wasn't a man fully grown. Not emotionally, anyway. This detour in his life had left a huge gap in the advancement of his emotional maturity. His life as he knew it had ended abruptly at eighteen, and now at twenty-three it was about to start again. Snowflakes drifted aimlessly without a care as he neared a major attack of panic at the thought. He felt like a trapeze artist swinging back and forth high above the big top, trying to find the courage to let go with both hands and grab onto the stationery perch that would get him back down to solid ground and end his nightmarish performance—all without the benefit of a safety net.

His heart fluttered restlessly, and his mind tried to envision what his home was like now. Over the past five years his grandfather had died, Dan, Molly, and Matt had gotten married, and Sean had moved into his own apartment—his girlfriend was living with him, but he made Cain swear not to tell their mother. Jim was the only one still home. It was hard to imagine that house not bustling with people. Less than a year ago the dog had died, so not even that old friend would be there to greet him. He had to keep reminding himself that this was another time; he was not stepping back into the past.

Just before he was totally overwhelmed with anxiety, a guard showed up outside his cell and manually unlocked it. He left the prison-issue things—except the clothes on his back—in a box on the floor and grabbed the sea bag with his personal belongings. Swinging it over his shoulder, he walked out of the cell. He stopped and turned around to scan his tiny domicile one last time. It was all too easy to remember how he had felt as he stood in that same doorway for the first time nearly five-and-a-half years before. Then with a sigh and ready to take on the world, he turned and followed the guard down the hall.

At the Processing Center he stripped off the last of his prison-issue and dumped it all in appropriate bins. Then he took the first of many showers to come in which he would attempt to wash the Maddox Correctional Facility out of his hair and skin. There was a final strip search, and then the guard gave him a box from his parents with civilian clothes in it. It was handy having an identical twin to insure taste and fit. He knew he would have to meet with his Parole Officer that day, so he had asked them to bring him dress clothes rather than jeans which he would have preferred. Real clothes.

He relished the feel of each item as he slipped it on his body: the gray pinstripe shirt, black dress pants, black shoes and socks, and a very expensive gray, black, and white pullover sweater. Matt really went all out. He stopped and enjoyed the crisp, new smell of everything as he put it on—something he had never even noticed before. He was glad to see senses, dulled by a drab and squalid existence, coming back to life. He felt good. Standing in front of the mirror and making the final adjustments to his hair, he had to admit he looked good. He was happy for the more formal look after viewing himself only in denim for over five years. He actually looked like an asset to society; perhaps in due time he'd feel like one too.

The last item left in the box was a stressed leather bomber jacket and leather gloves. Matt thought of everything. Grabbing the jacket, he stuffed the gloves in the pocket and then presented himself to the guard.

"Well," approved the guard, "there aren't many guys leave here looking like that. My compliments to your tailor. Now you can go to Mrs. Doleman's office for the last phase of checking out. I assume you know where it is."

"Yep."

"Okay then, you're on your way. Good luck."

"Thanks," he said and then made his way through the Administration Building looking for the first time like a responsible citizen rather than an inmate. That he definitely knew he liked.

"Magnificent," sighed Victoria Doleman as she took in the sight of him standing at her door. "Come in."

"I guess I'm ready," he sighed as he sat down across from her desk.

"I'd say you are," she smiled. "You just keep reminding yourself that you're twenty-three years old, you look like a high-priced fashion model, and you have a 140+ IQ. How can you go wrong?"

"If you say so," he grinned.

"I mean it, Cain. You have everything you need and more going for you. You'll overcome the rest. You'll see."

"I feel a little like a fish out of water."

"Well, that's certainly to be expected. Don't expect too much too soon. Let's start by officially changing your status of incarceration."

She put papers out in front of him, explaining each as she did. Little by little he signed his way back into the free world.

"In this envelope," she said, " is a check for the spending money you had left on the books and your last paycheck. It's not much, but it'll buy you a meal or two." She smiled. "And in this envelope is some cash—a little gift from Mike and me."

He looked up at her in surprise.

"It's only about $100, but you should have some cash on you since you're traveling on your own. You never know what may come up. And if you don't need it, buy yourself something you really want once you're home, and think of us. It's not a loan—it's something we want you to have."

"Thank you," he said taking the cash from the envelope and putting it into his pocket. "This means more to me than you know."

"Good. But now I'm afraid we have some unpleasant details to discuss."

"I'm not surprised," he said making her feel less guilty about putting a damper on his departure.

"On this paper is the name and address of your Parole Officer. You need to check in there by 6:00 tonight. They're keeping a tight grasp on your liberty. But you knew that, right?"

"Right."

"He's a jerk, Cain. I know him. I did everything I could to get you changed to someone else, but there was no negotiating it."

"It's okay."

"It's going to take all your patience and understanding to deal with him. I know you and how you respond to people like him, and I have to say I'm more than a little worried. One word from him and you're back here for the duration of your sentence. No trial, no lawyer, no nothing."

"Then I'll just have to kiss-ass, right?"

"Something you're not very good at. And there's no practicing—you do it or else. There's no room for pride when you're dealing with him. It'll be like walking through a heavily armed mine field."

"It sounds like a Sam Willet roadblock."

"Yeah, it does, but you don't have a choice."

"Ralph Meredithe," read Cain looking at the paper. "Okay."

"He has all the terms of your parole, and he'll have you sign a paper agreeing to them. I don't know what they are, but I know they'll be stiff. Just remember, sign the paper and live by it, or get busted back here. It's not very complicated and not very pleasant, but just keep remembering you'll be back home where you belong. You're way too beautiful and talented to be locked away in this place."

"I won't let you down, don't worry. I know you went out on a limb to get me out of here. You won't be sorry."

"Okay," she smiled. "And, maybe most important of all, here's your bus ticket to Chicago like you asked."

"Thank you," he said taking the most prized possession—the one thing that was going to put miles between him and Maddox. "Do I have time to go down and say good-bye to Mike?"

"Yes, you do. The bus leaves in about an hour. He told me not to let you go till he saw you—not that I'd even think you would. And I have a meeting, so I'm going to say good-bye now. You know where I am if you need me. Here's my card. Don't hesitate to call."

"I won't," he said putting the card with the rest of the papers she had given him and putting it all in his sea bag.

They both stood, and she walked around her desk.

"God's speed," she said wrapping her arms around him.

"Thank you—for everything," he answered, returning her embrace. "You've been the closest thing to a mom for me here, and you'll never know how much that means."

"That's the nicest compliment I've ever gotten." She kissed his cheek. "Now get out of here before I start to cry and ruin my make-up for my meeting."

Cain traveled the short distance to Fr. Mike's office. As he walked into the outer office, the priest was discussing some business with his secretary. Both stopped to look up when the door opened.

"I'm sorry," said the priest, "you'll have to make an appointment and come back another time. I'm expecting Cain Farrell."

"That'd be me," said Cain flashing his winning smile.

"So it would be," commented the priest returning the smile. He turned to his secretary. "Now does this look like an ex-con to you?"

"No, sir," she smiled. "Anything but."

"Well, there you go," said Mike, "I don't think anyone would ever guess unless you told them. That's my first piece of advice to you. Do you have a few minutes for an old friend?"

"Absolutely."

"Then let's go into my office for a bit."

Inside the office they both took a seat.

"Now, don't tell me—" said Mike. "—you're a mass of insecurities."

Cain smiled at his intuition.

"What am I going to do without you?" he asked.

"I'm assuming you do have telephones back there in the big city."

"Yeah, but it won't be the same."

"That's because you're not good at asking for help. That has to change. I'm not going to be around to know what's going on in your life and to anticipate when you're going to need me like I did here."

"So should I just commit suicide now and spare us both?"

"No," smiled Mike, "just promise me you'll pick up the phone and call once in a while—especially if you're having a rough time."

"No problem."

"Really?"

"Yeah. If I've learned nothing else, I've learned to cry uncle."

"Okay. I'm counting on that. And of course I'll be calling you."

"And you'll come to visit?"

"I'm looking forward to it. Just because you're not here any more doesn't mean we can't still be friends."

"Good. I'm a little short on friends these days."

"There'll be more. Take it one day at a time. And like I said— don't feel compelled to tattoo *CONVICTED FELON* across your forehead."

"The Parole Board will do that for me."

"Somewhat, yes; but you'll be able to enjoy some anonymity, and that's how you'll get your self-confidence back."

"I can't even remember far enough back to remember having any self-confidence."

"Oh, come on."

"Okay," Cain laughed. "I don't want to spend our last minutes together fighting. I had self-confidence, I still have **some**, and I'll get it all back in the end. How's that?"

"That's more like it. You're going to be fine. You'll be back in your element where you can thrive once again. I wish I could feel this confident about everyone we release from here."

"Well, I'd better go."

"Can I walk with you?"

"I was hoping you would."

It was such a strange sensation for him as they walked through the halls and toward the front gate how barred hallways were opened for him when he showed his papers. Before long he was entering areas that had been closed off to him for over five years. He tried to hang on to the metaphor of doors opening for him as he made his way out of the prison. Then there was the final locked passageway.

"This is it," said Mike as they waited for the guard to check their ID. "After this you're in free territory."

The gate opened and, shoring up his reserves, Cain took a deep breath and walked through. Straight ahead he could see the front door of the prison—the door that would take him outside the fences and barbed wire.

"Hold on," said Mike as they approached the front door. "This is as far as I go."

"What?" Cain tried to hide the panic in his voice.

"You need to take the next steps on your own. You're a free man now."

"You're throwing me out to the wolves?" smiled Cain sadly.

"You have to take the step sooner or later. The bus will be here in less than ten minutes. I think it's important that you have a little time on your own to try out the feel of your new status. Isn't that why you didn't want your dad to pick you up?"

"Yeah," he admitted.

"Then you understand."

"Yeah, I do. How do I ever thank you for everything you've been for me over these years?"

"Go back out into the world and knock 'em dead like I know you can. I'll know I've been a part of helping you to get there. You were a frightened, lonely child when I first met you. Now you're all grown up and ready to move on. There still may be some skeletons you need to deal with besides the Willets."

"Lidell?"

"Yes." He put a business card in Cain's hand. "Of course I'm always available to you, but I'm going to be far away. This is a friend of mine not too far from where you live. Call him when the demons kick up. He's a trained professional. Everyone needs help now and again."

Cain put the card in his pocket.

"Thanks," he said. "And thanks for this money from you and Mrs. Doleman."

"You're welcome. One last thing and then you'd better get your ass out to the bus stop."

He reached into his pocket and handed Cain a small white box. Cain took it carefully and opened it. Inside was a gold key chain with the word FAITH attached to it in large capital letters. On the circular key ring was a single key. Cain shifted his gaze the meet the priest's eyes.

"The most powerful word I know of in the English language," explained Fr. Mike. "Always remember that. And if things get a little rough now and then, reach in your pocket and grab a hold of it. It'll help you through when I can't be there for you. And by the way, that's a key to my house. You're always welcome."

"Shit," sighed Cain. "I don't know what to say."

"Don't say anything—it's probably best for both of us if you don't. Just get out there before you miss that bus."

"Yeah," said Cain feeling choked for words.

He unashamedly threw his arms around the priest and the two embraced.

"Thank you," sighed Cain barely above a whisper.

"You bet. Now get out of here—and don't look back."

Dabbing at a tear in his eye, Cain grabbed his sea bag, slung it over his shoulder, and walked briskly toward the exit. People were coming and going through the main entrance, and no one paid him any mind. It was as if he were anyone else.

He got to the bus stop with a few minutes to spare. About a mile down the road, he saw the gray, armored, school bus bringing in new inmates from the county jails. The memory and terror of that ride was still as fresh in him as the day he had made it. A slight shiver ran through his body, and he realized that as scared as he was now, he'd much rather be making this trip than that one.

And then as if to emphasize the contrast, the bus which would take him home appeared on the horizon. His heart thudded as he began to try and pull together all his emotions which had suddenly taken off in all directions. In quiet desperation he turned and looked back at the door where Mike had left him, but the priest was gone. He was on his own. As the bus moved closer, he said a silent prayer to the God he was not always faithful to but who he knew was always there. *Don't turn your back on me now.*

The bus stopped, and he hoisted the canvas bag up the stairs. After handing the driver his ticket, he realized that though he had nothing tattooed on his forehead, on this bus he was a marked man. It was obvious because of where he had gotten on and the fact that he carried a large, well-filled bag that he was fresh out of prison. The people on the bus knew it, and worst of all, he knew they knew. Summoning his tenacious pride, he made his way down the aisle toward a seat. Maybe it was his imagination, but it seemed ladies hugged their children and their purses a little closer and anyone alone in a seat discreetly moved toward the center putting out the invisible NO VACANCY sign. *Fuck you all!*

He found a seat in the back where he would be away from the curious stares of the other passengers. There was plenty of room on the only half-filled bus, so he pulled his bag in after him—half on the floor, half on the seat. Then as he had done on his way to Maddox on the bus, he looked out the window and devoured the wide-open spaces and the land of the free. At least this time he was not viewing it through jail bars on the window. In fact as he thought about it, he realized that this was the first time in over five years that he had looked at the world without interference from bars, wire mesh, or chainlink fences. The vastness of it all almost caused him to lose his breath as he experienced a kind of agoraphobia. When he first went to Maddox he had to deal with and get used to being so restricted and confined. He often had to fight severe claustrophobia. An ironic smile crossed his face as it became more apparent that he was now going to have to adjust to wide-opened spaces and making decisions on his own.

He had turned back in a moment of panic to look for Mike when the bus first approached him, but now that he was on it and heading toward home, he took Mike's advice and didn't look back at the hellhole he was leaving. If ever there was a time for looking ahead, it was now. He put his hand in his pocket and clutched his new key ring.

Then as often was the case, Scott jumped into his thoughts. This was the day they were supposed to drink champagne on the beach. Cain knew the snow flurries that were swirling around wouldn't have discouraged Scott from the promise of long ago. They had talked about it a lot when they were together. When things were the bleakest for Cain, it was the devil-may-care image of champagne on the beach that had gotten him through. Until Scott was killed. He knew a large part of his anxiety over his freedom was due to the fact that Scott wouldn't be there to walk him through the paces.

Then he thought about Joanne. That was another murky cesspool. Not only was she married, but she had recently had a baby. He knew he had no choice but to avoid her; now if he could just convince his heart. After having given her his heart in his youth, he had still not reclaimed it from her. He was even beginning to question if it was possible for him to take it back. It had been a long time since he'd seen her or heard from her, but his love for her still burned stubbornly inside him. He had questioned Victoria Doleman about how any woman could ever love him as a convicted rapist, but what he was even questioning more now was how he could ever fully love anyone but Joanne. If this long separation, her disdain for him, her marriage, and now her child didn't stomp out the smoldering fire within him, what ever would? That question was becoming more relevant as the bus traveled ever closer to his home.

He forced himself to stop thinking for a few therapeutic moments as he concentrated on the scenery. Gradually, fields and farmhouses began giving way to traffic and denser population. He glanced at his watch. A little over an hour and he'd be back in the heart of his beautiful city.

That peaceful thought on his mind, he laid his head back and closed his eyes. He dozed but only lightly. About every tenth bump or sway, he'd open his eyes to check his surroundings, looking for something familiar. Finally his patience was rewarded. Off in the far distance was the Chicago skyline just as bold and inspiring as it had been on the day five years ago when he watched it slip away from him. He straightened in his seat and sat forward so as to get a better angle. One would have thought that because of his fascination with the sight, he had never seen a big city before.

His heartbeat escalated as they got ever closer and soon the city and the bus became one. He could hardly keep himself in his seat as the bus wound and turned toward the depot where he would meet his dad. This was it—the rest of his life was truly beginning.

When he was finally able to get off the bus, he searched the small, waiting crowd of people, looking for his dad. Then he spotted Will threading his way through the group. Cain dropped his sea bag and ran to meet his father. The two came together in a rush of emotion and excitement and embraced. Both cried tears of overwhelming joy and anticipation. It was a long minute before they separated.

"I can't believe it," said Will. "Am I really holding you here—back home?"

"I'm home, Dad."

"Let me look at you. God, I've got my son back. And you look absolutely marvelous."

"I feel pretty good, too. Kind of like a new man."

"Good. Good, you deserve it. Let's go see your mother, okay? She hasn't slept for days, and she's been up since early this morning preparing a turkey dinner. I hope you're hungry."

"Yeah," he said thinking about it for the first time and realizing that he hadn't eaten anything since breakfast. "But there's something I have to take care of first."

"What's that?"

"I have to check in with my Parole Officer first. He knows I'm getting in town today, and he's expecting me before 6:00. His office is not too far from here, so I may as well get it over with before we head home."

"Okay," agreed Will feeling the effects of the mini-setback. "Let's go."

While his father waited in the car, Cain found his way up to Ralph Meredithe's office. The waiting room was not very large. There was some decor, but nothing fancy—nobody wanted to spend too much money for the comfort and enjoyment of ex-convicts. Two other men were sitting across the room. Cain approached the secretary.

"Well, hello," she flirted. "Can I help you?"

"Yeah," said Cain simply handing her his release papers. She was young and friendly, and at least she didn't look down her self-righteous nose at him.

"Ah, yes. You were just released this morning."

"That's right."

"I did your paperwork earlier." She smiled at him. "I was wondering what a Cain Harrigan Farrell would look like in the flesh. I love the name, and your DOC pictures, though impressive, don't really do you justice."

"How long do you think this will take?" he asked ignoring her flirtation. "I have somebody waiting."

"Oh," she said assuming, as he had hoped she would, that it must be his lady. "These guys are regulars. They'll be in and out in a few minutes. Have a seat; you'll definitely add a little class to this place."

He sat and waited with impatience born of an eagerness to get this over with and get home. His brain kept replaying Mrs. Doleman's warning about Meredithe. Soon the man who had been with Meredithe left. The other two who were waiting ahead of him must have earned gold stars for the week since they were in and out in just a little over five minutes each. Then Meredithe came to the door for the first time. He and Cain sized each other up in the instants that followed. He was a short, balding man with a generous waistline. Cain immediately envisioned him in an antique, French general's uniform with his hand tucked neatly into the opened buttons at his chest.

"Farrell, get your ass inside."

All his questions were answered in this one command. *The man really is an asshole.* Taking a second to calm his rearing temper, he slowly got to his feet. He glanced at the secretary who smiled sweetly. Without changing his brooding expression, he entered the inner office in front of the little general. Meredithe closed the door behind them and indicated a chair opposite his desk for Cain. Still without another word, he sat down and took Cain's file in hand. Many silent seconds passed. Cain had been part of the prison system long enough to know that Meredithe had already committed his file to memory and this silent intermission was meant to intimidate and manipulate. It actually had the opposite effect because Cain immediately realized that this obnoxious man had actually made the mistake of overlooking him as a seasoned product of the penal system and was instead thinking him a pushover because of his youth. His confidence level moved up a notch.

Finally Meredithe looked up at him with a scowl. Cain boldly met his glare.

"This is not a very impressive piece of work," said Meredithe. No comment from Cain. "You need to know right from the beginning that I think you should still be in prison. If it were up to me, rapists wouldn't be eligible for parole. As it is, I think you slipped through the cracks and got out way too early. What do you think of that?"

"You're entitled," shrugged Cain. "But I am out, aren't I?"

"Barely. You see, I'm going to allow you to breathe and . . . and that's about it." He gave a sarcastic, little laugh. He waited for a reaction from Cain. There was none, just an unflinching stare that was causing a bit of discomfort beneath Meredithe's collar. His smile disappeared as he went on. "You see, your clean-cut, schoolboy image doesn't fool me. I don't care where you live or what your IQ is, you're a rapist, and rapists are scum." Still no change in Cain's sullen expression. Meredithe played his next card. "Here are the conditions of your parole. You either sign it and live by it or go back to the slammer."

*Slammer? How quaint.*

He slid the piece of paper across his desk toward Cain. Cain picked it up and for the first time looked away from Meredithe as he read the paper:

> 1. I will obey the law at all times.
> 2. I will not travel more than fifty miles or leave the state without permission of the Parole Board.
> 3. I will carry my parole card evidencing my criminal status at all times.
> 4. I will work only at lawful occupations.
> 5. I will submit to medical treatment— psychological or physical—if ordered to do so by the Parole Board. This includes arbitrary drug testing.

6. I will not associate with anyone of questionable character, nor with anyone on parole or having a criminal record.

7. I will not correspond or visit with inmates of any correction facility without permission from the Parole Board.

8. I will totally abstain from all alcoholic beverages and narcotics of all kinds. I will not frequent places where they are sold, nor will I work in an establishment that sells liquor. (For the first time Cain broke eye contact with the paper and looked up at Meredithe. But he went immediately back to his reading.)

9. I will not change my residence, place of employment, or school without permission of the Parole Board.

10. I will report to the Parole Board through this office once a week until further notice.

11. I will not apply for a hunting license or handle firearms of any caliber.

12. I will not apply for a driver's license or buy a motor vehicle without permission of the Parole Board. (That got his attention.)

"I can't drive?!"

"Not right away. Behave yourself and we may change that later. For now that's my way of clipping your wings and keeping you close to home."

Refusing to be shaken, Cain went on reading.

13. I will not marry without the permission of the Parole Board, or without revealing my parole status to my intended.

14. I will not engage in sexual relations with anyone to whom I am not legally married. (He raised an eyebrow.)

15. I will be off the streets and in my own home by 11:00 P.M. and not leave my house before 6:00 A.M. without permission of the Parole Board. (He raised both eyebrows but made no verbal protest.)

"Do you have a pen?" Cain asked knowing this was not a negotiable contract and not wanting to give Meredithe the satisfaction of arguing or getting upset about it.

"Here you go," smiled Meredithe. "As you can see I'm keeping you on a very short leash, but it's really very generous considering you should still be in prison. The thing is if you try to move too fast or too far, I'm going to yank your chain, and it'll hurt."

He slid a pen toward Cain who took it in his left hand and signed the bottom of the document. Meredithe handed him a copy and put the original in his file.

"Next as an officer of the court, I have the authority to serve you with this, so consider yourself on notice."

"What is it?" asked Cain picking up the paper.

"It's a restraining order—an order of protection. You are not to see, talk to, or even be within 100 feet of Carrie Willet or any property owned by her family."

Now Cain laughed out loud.

"Shit!" he laughed. "The last person I want to see, talk to, or even be within 1,000 feet of is Carrie Willet. This is a joke. I should be the one issuing the restraining order."

"Well, it's not a joke. It's very serious."

"Of course it is," said Cain getting the edge back with a mock serious expression. "No problem."

This meeting wasn't taking the course Meredithe had intended, and it was he who was getting irritated. Cain Farrell was not at all the way he had expected him to be—a pathetic, remorseful, rich kid promising anything to stay out of jail. He thought by now he'd have him on his knees eating out of his hand. He was going to have to do some rethinking of the situation before their next visit. Now he was just eager to end the encounter before he suffered any more direct hits to his authority.

"Next I need to tell you I'll be calling your house regularly during the times you're supposed to be home, and by God you'd better be there. I'll want to talk to you—it won't do for someone else to just say you're there. I'll also be making unscheduled visits to your home, your work, and your school to be sure you're where you're supposed to be when you're supposed to be there. Don't fuck up. And I want to see you in this office every Friday some time between 9:00 A.M. and 5:00 P.M. starting next week since we've already met this week. If you don't show up, there will be a warrant for your arrest issued at 5:01 P.M. No booze, no women, no drugs, no guns. Any questions?"

"No questions."

"Fine. Then I'm sure I'll be talking to you and probably seeing you during the week. Keep your nose clean. Oh, and I nearly forgot. You need to get your ass to your local police department and register as a sex offender. Do it first thing tomorrow."

"Whatever," said Cain as he gathered up his copies of the papers that Meredithe had given him.

"Mrs. Doleman gave you your parole card, didn't she?"

"Yep."

"Good, that needs to be with you at all times."

"Bullshit item #3," said Cain referring to the list of Parole Restrictions.

Meredithe had to hide his amazement at the fact that Cain had accurately remembered and was able to immediately call to mind the number of the restriction to which he was referring.

"This is not bullshit, hotshot. This is what's going to keep your ass out of prison. That should make you happy. Just looking at you, I'm guessing you spent a lot of time face-down on the shower room floor."

He made a silly, little snicker.

Cain's deadpan expression burned right through him and chased the smile from his face.

"Whatever," shrugged Cain, not even the slightest rattled.

Didn't this fool know that guards made those kinds of remarks all the time, and he was more than immune to them? Water off a duck's back.

"Then I guess that's it for now."

"Good," said Cain taking his papers and heading toward the door. As he opened the door leading to the outer office, he stopped and turned back to Meredithe who had remained at his desk. "By the way, don't **ever** refer to me as an animal on a leash again. The metaphor is repulsive; and though they may have treated me like an animal, they didn't turn me into one."

Feeling like he had established himself as a force to be reckoned with, he continued his exit—firmly closing, though not slamming, the door behind him. He nodded a good-bye to the secretary and left the office to meet his father.

"How'd it go?" Will asked as Cain got into the car and closed the door.

"Pretty much the way I'd expected. I don't have much of a life, but at least I'm home. I'll show you this bullshit paper I got later. Right now I don't want to talk about it."

"Okay," said Will, "then let's go home."


The trip was a familiar one for Cain. He'd made it many times, but that was all a long time ago. Now in spite of the familiarity of the scenery, he felt strangely like an outsider—something he had been afraid of. Some things had been added to the landscape, while others had been taken away. People had come, and gone.

He and his father didn't speak, each experiencing his own combination of emotions; and the elder sensing and respecting the solitude with which his son had seemed to envelop himself. This was a more fragile moment than either of them had expected.

As they got closer to home, he spotted new mini-malls, service stations, and homes where empty parcels of land used to be. How could things have changed so much in just five years? *Life goes on* took on a whole new meaning to him. More than ever he realized that the past was gone for good and the present was going to be an adjustment.

Then they turned into their neighborhood, and nothing else seemed to matter. Christmas lights festively lit up most of the houses, and the external changes seemed minimal. The trees were already huge when he left and now they were bare, so there was little noticeable change there. Something stirred inside him giving hope that it hadn't died a slow death over the past five-and-a-half years. It was a good feeling, and he struggled to keep it treading water amidst all the anger and anxiety. That was when his dad made the turn onto their street and half-way down he spotted his house. The stirring inside kicked to life and spread to his outermost extremities. It was a warmth and excitement that he hadn't known since the moment that he had become aware of the fact that Carrie Willet had set him up for the fall and the biggest betrayal of his young life.

As they pulled into the driveway of the gray and white-trimmed Victorian house of his youth—his *other* life—the emotion, which was not only still alive but flourishing, found its way out of his soul in the form of large tears which streamed freely down his cheeks. All day, through the whole emotional roller coaster he had been riding, he had been able to control such an emotional display. A slight tear or two appeared as he said good-bye to Mike, a few threatened on the bus trip home, and more than just a few fell as he and his father were reunited; but this was different. This was more than just a burning of emotions behind his eyelids that produced tears. This was a whole, silent outburst of emotion that overflowed from within the very depths of him. There was no holding it back or controlling it just yet. With trembling hands he wiped at the steady stream. The car was stopped, but he couldn't move. He was glad that his mother didn't come running out of the house just then. He wasn't ready.

"I'm sorry," he said to his father. "I really wasn't expecting this. I just need a minute."

"It's okay," said Will reaching in the glove compartment and handing him some tissues. "Take your time."

"I'm really home," he said wiping his face and blowing his nose. "You have no idea how many times I've dreamed of this moment only to wake up in a cage."

"Not this time," smiled Will.

Cain made another swipe with the tissues at his tear-stained face and eyes. Then he pulled the visor down to check his look in the mirror.

"I don't want to upset Mom," he said.

"You couldn't upset Mom today if you tried."

"Then what are we waiting for?"

He went to the trunk to get his bag, but Will insisted on carrying it.

"Go say hello to your mother. I got this."

Cain smiled at him and then turned and ran toward the house and up the stairs. The front door was unlocked, so he went in. His mother, who had just spotted the car in the driveway, was rushing toward him. He grabbed her in his arms and swung her around as she cried out with delight.

"Let me look at you!" she cried as she reached up and took his face in both her hands. "And let me touch you! My God, you look wonderful! Absolutely wonderful!" She ran her hands up and down the outside of his arms, squeezing gently as she did. "And I can touch you!"

"Hi, Mom," he said with a heart-stopping smile.

She tiptoed up and kissed him.

"Just hold me," she said. "I've really missed you."

As he put his arms around her and hugged her, he noticed his brother for the first time.

"Matt," he said with surprise as he stepped back from their mother. He glanced to his left at the couch and saw a smiling young woman he recognized only from pictures.

"He wouldn't take no for an answer," explained a beaming Nora. "I knew you wouldn't care if he stopped by."

"Nice clothes," smiled Matt.

Cain sidestepped Nora and went to his brother. They held on to each other close and long. He had missed this affectionate contact more than he could ever begin to explain. Four feet is the closest he had been allowed to any of these people in more than five years. And even at that, there was no reaching across the distance to even touch hands.

"Come meet Melanie," said Matt. "She helped me shop."

Cain turned toward his sister-in-law who was awestruck.

"What do you think?" asked Nora as she proudly stepped between her twin sons, putting an arm around each.

"Absolutely remarkable," smiled Melanie, still not believing her eyes as she stood up to greet Cain. "Seeing pictures is one thing . . . but standing here now— "

Without a word Cain walked up to her and put his arms around her. The delicate feel of her and the soft smell of her perfume almost made him dizzy. Reminding himself that this was his brother's wife, he stepped back.

"I've been a jerk," he said. "I'm sorry. But this is how I wanted our first meeting to be. You wouldn't have liked the alternative."

"I'm a lot tougher than you think," she smiled, "but I understand how you felt. I've respected that, and I'm so glad we're finally all able to be together. It's just very strange to suddenly realize I don't really know who my husband is. I'm not sure I could pick him out if I didn't know what clothes he was wearing."

"Kind of gives a whole new meaning to the term *clothes make the man*, doesn't it?" grinned Cain. "But don't worry, we have standards—we don't share everything!" He winked at her, and she was captured by his charismatic spell, which she had heard so much about.

He walked around the room taking in every aspect of it, stopping to look at framed photographs and other mementos. He felt like a starving man set loose at a buffet table.

"Where's Jim?" he finally asked.

"Working," said Nora, "but he should be home soon."

"That's right, it's the middle of the week," remembered Cain.

"Why don't you sit down and relax?" suggested his mother. "What can I get for you?"

"Nothing, Mom. I'm fine. Actually, if you'll all excuse me, I want to go up and see my room and unpack my worldly possessions. Then I'm going to use a bathroom that actually has a door on it." He smiled and winked. "You guys have no idea what luxury really is!"

They all smiled as he took the canvas sea bag and headed up the stairs. Walking into his room again after so long sent another wave of nostalgia through him. Matt's bed, desk, and dresser were still there, but Jim's things had been moved out when he changed rooms. It seemed so large to him after existing in a 5' x 9' cell for over twelve hours each day. Everything remained just as he remembered leaving it.

Then he spotted the small jewelry tray on his dresser. On it rested his diamond earring and the Claddagh ring that he had left with Bruce before they had taken him into custody after the guilty verdict had been read. His eyes misted over as he remembered taking them off that last time. He already knew the ring would no longer fit, and as he held it in his fingers, he made a mental note to get it sized the first chance he got. Then he took the earring and smiled as it slipped into the long-vacant opening in his earlobe. He stared at his new *old* self in the mirror, and discovered he was feeling more and more comfortable with what he saw. Being back home was fitting him like a glove, and his *square peg* anxiety was gradually fading to the background. It seemed like it had been a lifetime since he had gotten up that morning. In many ways that's just what it had been.

# CHAPTER 15

After the excitement of the holidays and getting to know his family again, Cain began to settle into the routine of daily life outside Maddox Correctional Institution. Since he had been released, he had been working for a maintenance company doing work at night, which would allow him to go to school during the day. It also kept him away from the type of public scrutiny that he experienced at the grocery story where he was working at the time of his arrest. Because of his sex offender status, he wasn't allowed to work in any of the schools, but there was plenty of factory work. After working in the warehouse at Maddox for more than five years, he was used to manual labor. It kept his body in good shape, and his mind was free to wander where it pleased. He also liked it because they told him that when the weather got nicer, he could work outside with the landscaping.

The people he worked with were decent and down-to-earth. Some had histories of their own, but none quite the magnitude of Cain's. They accepted him as he was and didn't hold his criminal record against him. In fact, aside from an occasional, curious question or two about life behind bars, they never discussed it. His foreman was a fair man who realized Cain was far out of his element and thus tried to direct him toward more challenging work when it arose. He was amazed at Cain's lack of arrogance and at his willingness to do whatever job he was assigned, and do it well. He was more than glad to cooperate with the Parole Board and the restrictions on Cain's time and availability.

Ralph Meredithe was another story. He was determined that his lot in life was to extend punishment beyond the walls of the penal institution. There was no rehabilitating these men, and it was his job to keep them in line. He fulfilled that job by wielding an iron fist and showing very little mercy. For instance, he refused to extend Cain's curfew on New Year's Eve even until 1:00 A.M. so he could join family and friends at a party. No problem—his family and friends brought the party to him at home. He refused to even have a glass of champagne at midnight, for he didn't put it past Meredithe to show up at his house, syringe in hand, to do a blood-alcohol level test.

Cain grew to hate him and his intrusions into his life more every day. The man was a constant presence either in person with surprise visits or by phone. Cain had to wonder if Meredithe actually had a life of his own because he was constantly invading his. Will was worried about his young son's state of mind as the newness of being home was passing and his acceptance of the tight parole restrictions was beginning to wear thin. Meredithe's surveillance was close to being harassment, but it was unwise to complain. He held all the cards, so they could only hope that he'd grow tired of it himself and back off. However, at this point he was showing no signs of it.

School hadn't started yet, so Cain spent all of his time working or bouncing off the walls of his parents' house. He did a lot of walking since he wasn't able to drive. He didn't mind because he didn't want his parents' life disrupted any more than it already had been, and it was good exercise for a body that was ready to fly but had been denied wings.

One afternoon he was having something to eat at a local restaurant with some of the guys he worked with. He was laughing at some dumb joke when he looked up and saw Alexis walk in. Almost immediately she spotted him and stopped in her tracks. She smiled tentatively at him.

"Excuse me," he said to the men he was with as he got up.

As he approached her, she reached out and took his left hand. No wedding ring.

"I'm sorry," she smiled, "but I'm afraid you're one-of-two again, and that's the only way I can tell for sure which one you are. How are you, Cain?"

"I'm good," he grinned. "I'm home."

"Yes, I talked to your mom around Thanksgiving, and she was very excited. I'm happy for you. I'm happy for your whole family. So, what are you up to?"

"Right now I'm having dinner with some guys I work with. We have to clock-in in about a half-hour."

"Oh."

"What about you?"

"I'm meeting friends for dinner—over there. I guess I need to apologize to you once again."

"For what?"

"For not ever going back to visit you or writing. To be honest, I was confused the last time I saw you. I felt like you were holding me at arm's length, and you really didn't want me to keep in touch."

"It was a bad time for me. I was more than a little confused myself. I wanted you to come back—so much I almost ached for it—but I knew it was better if you didn't. I didn't want you coming because you felt obligated, and that's what I would have always been thinking. Then, too, I wasn't sure my hormones could stand regular visits from you."

She smiled.

"Don't you know me well enough to know that . . ."

"Alexis, it's over; let's don't rehash it. My life's complicated enough."

"Okay. You said you're working tonight. How about tomorrow night? I have my own apartment, and I'm a pretty fair cook. We have a lot of catching up to do."

The blood pulsed through his veins at an alarming rate. He'd been home for nearly a month now, and this was the first time that he was face-to-face with a real, live girl that was actually available to him.

"Um, I'm not working, but I turn into a pumpkin at 11:00."

She looked at him with a question on her face.

"Parole curfew," he explained. "The Department of Corrections still has me by one ankle."

"We could make it early."

"I can't drive."

"I can pick you up . . . unless, of course, you're trying to wiggle out of it."

"No, that's not it," he answered sincerely. "Are you sure you want to associate with me?"

"I'm not even going to dignify that with an answer. I'll call you at home and we'll make arrangements. Get back to your friends, and I'll see you tomorrow." She put her hand on his cheek, purposely brushing her finger across the diamond on his ear. "You look great. I'm looking forward to tomorrow." She tiptoed up and kissed his cheek. Then she was gone.

He nearly caved-in on the spot. Six years of involuntary celibacy, relying on fantasies and self-administered bouts of passion, had left him totally and helplessly susceptible to feminine charm. The feel of her hand on his cheek replayed in his mind before he turned to rejoin his friends.

The next day, being Saturday, he had plans with Matt during the day. He had finally begun getting paychecks he could spend, small though they were. He was slowly amassing a wardrobe again, and there were a few other things he wanted to pick up at the store. They liked to shop together whenever they had the chance because they found their tastes to be so similar that they often tended to buy the same things. That was something they both wanted to avoid at all cost, so shopping together was the guarantee. They always turned more than a few heads whenever they were out together.

"It's so good having you back again," said Matt as they waited for the waitress to bring them their lunch.

"There's something I've been wanting to talk to you about," said Cain broaching the subject delicately.

"What?"

"Alexis."

"Jones?"

"Yeah. I'm seeing her tonight."

"And you want me to—?"

"I don't know. I just wanted you to know. That's all."

"Haven't we been here before?"

"Humor me. Please."

"Cain, I told you before. That was high school. She and I have been over for a long time. I'm married now. I haven't even thought about her—except when you keep bringing her up."

"Okay. I just wanted to tell you."

"So you told me.  Now go out and enjoy yourself.  She's a great girl."

"Well, you of all people should know how I feel.  If she were Dan's or Sean's old girlfriend, it'd be different.  But with you I almost feel like it's incest.  It doesn't make sense, but that's not the point."

"I guess I know what you mean.  I'd feel the same if I was suddenly seeing Joanne.  Kind of like—is she looking at me and seeing you?"

"Right.  Can she get passed how I look and see who I am?"

"Who knows?  There's been enough time and water under the bridge."

"I just know I'm lonely and tired of being alone—and she's very beautiful.  That's not a very good combination."

"No, it's not."

"I keep telling myself I should call and cancel, but then the alternative is sitting home alone—again.  I've done enough alone time."

"Just be careful.  Meredithe has you by the balls.  Don't give him any ammunition."

"I know," sighed Cain rubbing his face miserably.  "I just want to have fun again."

On the way home, Cain had Matt take him to a long overdue appointment.  Dread and sadness overwhelmed him as they wound their way through the cemetery where Scott was buried.

"Thanks for doing this," said Cain staring blankly out the window into the gray, January afternoon.  "Without wheels I haven't had the chance to get here, and I didn't want just anyone with me when I came."

"No problem.  You should have said something sooner."

"There weren't many opportunities, and to be honest, I've been putting it off.  This is the hardest thing I've ever done—voluntarily."

Matt pulled over to the side of the road.

"You want me to wait here?"

"Yeah, it'll only be a few minutes."

"Right up there by the tree.  Take your time."

Cain trudged across the winter-hardened ground and then came upon the reality of his friend's death that had been denied him.  Trembling more from emotion than the bitter cold, he squatted down next to the tombstone and reached his hand out to touch it.  As tears blurred his vision and his lip quivered almost uncontrollably, he lightly traced the letters with his left fingertips.  From a bag he was carrying, he retrieved a bottle of champagne and placed it ceremoniously on the headstone.

"This is going to have to wait for another place and another time," he said softly.  "I can't drink it anyway, but even if I could I wouldn't want it without you here to share it with me.  I'm sorry I wasn't here that night—maybe you would've been out with me instead of where

326

you were. You don't know how many times I've tortured myself with that thought." He put his hand out flat on the ground above the casket, trying his hardest to imagine the lifeless body there below. "How am I supposed to go on without you? I'm not sure. I have my brothers, but they all have their own lives. My life is pretty nothing right now, but I'm not here about me.

"And, hey, how about me and Ken Blackburn ending up together at Maddox? Isn't that just my luck? I know you had a good laugh over that one. He's a goddam idiot, but he's not really a bad guy. I think he's sorry for what he did—that's the only way I could bring myself to be in the same room with him. I knew you'd understand that. You were a way better person than I am.

"Matt's waiting for me, so I'd better go. Rest well—and don't forget me, huhn? I can use any good words you can get in for me."

He lingered a few seconds longer and then stood up again. With his opened hands, he wiped the tears from his face and he sniffed back other tears that were threatening. With his back to his brother, he stared aimlessly across the cemetery, letting the cold revive him somewhat. Then with a last glance, he turned and walked away.

As they started the drive back toward home, he didn't say much. He just stared out the window, trying to get his thoughts together. Understanding what he was going through, Matt didn't interrupt him.

"Thank you for that," said Cain after about five minutes.

"No Problem."

They rode in silence for a few more minutes.

"Can I ask you one more thing?"

"What's that?" asked Matt.

"This is kind of an out-of-the-way place—can I drive this car—just for a few miles? I've been dying to get behind the wheel ever since I first laid eyes on it."

"Cain, you could get . . ."

"Please. I won't speed or anything. I haven't driven a car in nearly six years, and this is one, fine car."

Matt sighed.

"It's your ass," he said pulling over to the side.

Cain couldn't believe the performance and handling of the car. It was everything he had expected and then some. He also surprised himself that he was able to shift through the gears with only the slightest of hesitation. If felt good to be in control, and he couldn't get over how much he loved that car. He also couldn't get over the fact that he blew right through a stop sign. Luckily, they were in a somewhat remote area and there was very little traffic.

"Shit, Cain!"

"When the hell did they put a stop sign there?!"

"About two years ago!"

That's when Cain saw the flashing red lights in the rearview mirror.

"DAMN!"

He began to slow down and pull over. He looked over pleadingly at his identical twin. He didn't need to verbalize his request.

"You owe me your life!" said Matt quickly taking out his wallet and flipping it to Cain as he stopped the car. "I haven't even had a parking ticket in years!"

"Don't worry," said Cain just before he put the window down. "I'll give you my first born or whatever. I'll never forget this."

"Yeah, and just remember, I respect law enforcement officials— and I'm very polite."

"Of course you are," said Cain quickly taking off his baseball cap and tousling his hair as he watched in the side-view mirror as the police officer walked up to the car. "Now pull your hat down a little more, and for God's sake **don't** look directly at him unless you have to. Be natural."

"Easy for you to say."

The automatic window slid down, and Cain was face-to-face with the officer.

"Man, was that stupid of me or what?" said Cain as the policeman looked into the car.

"Can I see your license, please?" the officer asked.

"Sure," said Cain with an ease that Matt found remarkable, considering the stunt he was pulling off and the certain consequences if it all fell apart.

With candor and almost geekish politeness, Cain maneuvered his way through the agonizing minutes it took the policeman to write the ticket. More than once Matt rolled his eyes in disbelief at his brother's cornball attempt to placate the cop in order to get him on his way as soon as possible. What an act. He actually thanked the policeman and told him to have a good day as the cop handed him the ticket. Then he put the window up.

"Stupid, fucking screw!!!" he stormed once the police officer had walked away. Then he turned to Matt. "Were you polite enough?"

"I was so polite I wanted to throw up."

Cain smiled. He checked the rearview mirror, waiting for the cop to leave so he and Matt could change places again.

"Of course I'll pay for the ticket, and read the back because I think if you go to traffic school it won't count on your record."

"Excuse me. You mean if **you** go to traffic school, it won't count against me. And you bet your sweet ass you're going to traffic school."

"Okay, fine, I'll go."

The police car pulled around them and went on its way.

"You're damn right you will. And you'll ace traffic school."

"Okay. Relax."

"Now neither one of us has a driver's license!" said Matt as he put the ticket in his wallet and got out of the car to take back the driver's seat.

"Well, you probably should have known better than to let me drive. I have the worst luck."

"Cain, shut up because I swear to God if you don't, I'm going to break your neck! Now get in the car."

"Fine." He got back in the passenger's side. "One more thing, and then I swear I won't bring it up again."

"What?"

"Could we keep this between you and me? Don't tell Mom and Dad, or even Melanie. Besides the obvious, it's better if no one else knows, so then there's no way it could ever get back to Meredithe—especially since I still have to be you to see this thing all the way through. I mean, you can tell them **you** got the ticket if you want, but please don't tell them I did."

Matt sighed. "I could probably go to jail for all this, couldn't I?"

"Shit, relax, will you? I've got it all under control."

"What could go wrong, right?" Matt laughed.

"Right," said Cain with a prize-winning grin. Then he sobered. "You couldn't go to jail, but I could if Meredithe wanted to be a jerk. I'm sorry—this was all my fault. I'm the one who should have known better. Thanks, I really owe you, and I won't ever ask you to do anything like that again—I swear."

"Fine. We won't mention it at all unless we have to. Then I'll say it was me who got the ticket—because it was. All I have to say is it's a damn good thing we're far enough away from home that the police don't know you and—thanks to you—me. That could cause some raised eyebrows and big-time questions."

"True. That was a definite plus. See, my luck is not **all** bad."

That night as he went out to the car with Alexis when she picked him up, he couldn't believe how liberated he felt. He started to feel his world open up a little.

"This is the first time I've really been out since I've been home," he told her.

"No kidding?" she smiled.

"At least by myself—without a baby-sitter. I don't consider you a baby-sitter."

"Good," she grinned.

When they got to her apartment, he looked around as she hung up his coat.

"This is really nice," he commented.

"It's a little small, but it's home."

Cain thought about his cell at Maddox.

"It's a castle. And you don't have a roommate?"

"No. I'd rather have this small place to myself than have to deal with the hassles of living with someone. It works out well for me. Sit down. What can I get you to drink? Beer? Wine?"

"Coke'd be good. I'm not much of a drinker. I haven't had much opportunity over the past years to develop any drinking likes or dislikes, and I've found I haven't really missed it—which is good since Meredithe has that on my list of no-nos. You never know—a couple of drinks, and I'll probably start raping everyone in sight."

She laughed as she got him the Coke.

"You're just going to have to be patient with me because I'm not sure of everything you can and can't do. Just please tell me because the last thing I want you to do is get in any trouble because of me."

"There's a rule of thumb for that: if it seems like it's fun, I can't do it! And don't worry—if I get in any trouble it's because of me, not anybody else."

"But you're not going to get into any trouble. Right?"

He thought back to that afternoon in Matt's car.

"No, ma'am, I don't plan to. I've learned my lesson. My problem is I never plan to—trouble always just seems to be at my fingertips. And then it's like flypaper. My best bet is to just be a hermit. I've been sticking real close to home. I'm actually paranoid about venturing too far. I'm afraid of someone slapping cuffs on me if I look sideways." Again he thought about his encounter with the police that afternoon. "Even when I think I'm in a safe place, they come crawling out of the woodwork."

"Well, I hope you feel safe here. I checked the woodwork and under the furniture before you got here."

"Thanks," he smiled sincerely. "I know it sounds stupid, but—"

"It doesn't sound stupid at all. Just be comfortable here. I want to be a friend. I want to see you laugh again like you used to when we were kids."

"That's a tall order," he said with a seriousness that she was trying to dispel.

"We'll see."

They ate dinner and talked and looked at old pictures and talked some more. A fire blazed in the fireplace in the small living room, and he felt freer than he had felt in years. He closed his eyes, and he could almost forget he was under the watchful eye of the law and that his life dangled by a single, tenuous thread of freedom. He wanted to shut everything out but the moment he was in. Feeling very relaxed, he opened his eyes to see her watching him, a small, pleased smile on her face.

"A little self-hypnosis," he said apologetically. "I wasn't trying to ignore you."

"Are you happy?" she asked.

"Yeah."

"Then that's all that matters. Close your eyes again if you want. I don't mind; I love watching you. You're really very different from Matt."

A victorious, self-satisfied look softened his features.

"Really?"

"I'm sorry. That was really insensitive of me to compare you."

"No, not at all. I kind of needed that. When you look as much alike as Matt and I do, you kind of worry that . . . people . . . will start to think of you as one person."

"Did you worry about that with me?"

"It crossed my mind, yeah. You went with him for a long time."

"A long time ago."

"I know, but—"

She smiled sweetly.

"Don't worry about it," she said barely above a whisper. She knelt up on the couch next to him. "Does the Parole Board allow kissing between two consenting adults?"

"Um—" his heart took flight. "Kissing is acceptable."

"Then may I?"

She took his breath away as he felt like a very inexperienced teenager.

"Please," he said with a little laugh.

Seeming to know he was out of practice and even psychologically scarred by Carrie Willet, she kissed his forehead and his eyes with feathery wisps of tenderness. As she kissed his cheeks, she could feel his body awakening from years of social deprivation as he not-too-tentatively moved his arms to embrace her. When she got to his mouth, he was waiting eagerly and ready to kiss her back. She had applied just the right amount of seductive foreplay. He responded not with the savagery of a man who had been denied such pleasures for way too long, but with a gentle revitalization of his senses and a willingness to pick up where he had left off so many years ago. This was his first kiss as a full-grown man. And since there had been no bumbling, fumbling adolescent kisses evolving nonstop to this moment, it became a momentous occasion. How many men could actually pinpoint the exact kiss that opened the door to their manhood, leaving boyhood somewhere in the shadows? The bumbling and fumbling had been a brief part of his distant past. He had been becoming much more adept when his sexual advancement was drastically put on hold and then lethally terminated at the age of eighteen. Now at twenty-three, he was acutely aware of the vast ocean of difference between becoming adept and achieving mature proficiency. This was a kiss that would stay with him forever.

"Jesus," he sighed with what little breath he had left as Alexis sat back on her heels.

"Was that okay?" she asked softly.

"That was beyond every dream and fantasy I've contrived and tried to imagine."

"Wow," she smiled. "And let me tell you, you don't kiss like you've been out of circulation for nearly six years."

"You're nice to say so."

"I mean it," she said as she brushed at the hair at his temple. "You are so beautiful—inside and out."

"You can't believe how many times I thought of that kiss you gave me that night in the park. That was it for me—until now."

"How nice for me to be at the right place at the right time—twice."

He smiled somewhat self-consciously. "I guess I'm afraid I might . . . disappoint you." *There, I said it.*

"Oh, no," she protested sincerely.

"I haven't had all that much practice at it—even when I was . . . getting my feet wet."

"Don't worry. This evening was meant as a gesture of pure friendship. Then you sat there looking so goddamn sexy, I couldn't help myself. But the rest is up to you. I just don't want to take you anywhere you're not ready to go."

He realized he didn't really know where he wanted to go with all this. One would think that the first place a man who had been in prison for nearly six years would want to go would be to the bed of a warm and willing, young woman. But Carrie Willet and Herb Lidell were unwitting co-conspirators in the derailing of his sexual maturity and development, and they had each dumped cold water in the lap of his passion.

"People always tell me I'm intense," he said to her as he stared at the fire. Then he turned to look her in the eye. "Right now I'd give anything to be shallow and devil-may-care."

"No," she said. "You wouldn't want to be any different than you are. I wouldn't want you to be any different than you are."

"It isn't easy."

"I know. She really did a number on you, didn't she? Other than the obvious. I mean—inside."

"I feel a little disconnected, yeah. But it's not just Carrie. There're other things I need to work out."

"Joanne?"

"For one."

"Have you seen her yet—since you're home?"

"No. For years I thought that would be one of the first things I would do; but now that I'm here, it's not quite so clear. Not being able to drive hasn't made it any easier. I mean, you just don't say to someone: *hey, could you give me a ride over to my married ex-girlfriend's house? I'll call you when I'm ready to come home.*"

"No, I guess you're right."

"It's pretty complicated right now—my head. Sometimes I wonder if I'll ever get it all straightened out."

"I wish there was something I could do to help."

"You have," smiled Cain. "This night has been the best. I wish I never had to leave. I wish I could just stay here and shut out the rest of the world and just work on getting my head straight. You don't just come home from where I've been. You don't just leave it behind. Sometimes my parents don't understand that. They want so bad for everything to be like it was, but I'll never be like that again."

"But that doesn't have to be bad."

"No, it doesn't have to be. But right now it is. Except for you, my friends are either gone or I don't relate to them any more. The guys I work with are nice, but there's no one there I'd ever be good friends with. Besides, I'm free, but I'm not free—my time is pretty restricted, so there's not much time for building new friendships. I have these hideous nightmares . . . and why am I telling you all this?"

"Because you obviously needed to, and I'm more than happy to listen. Don't stop."

"No, because if I don't stop now, I'm going to ruin this evening. I've already said more than I should."

"It's all right . . . you need a friend . . ."

"Alexis," he interrupted. "Shut up. I need a diversion."

This time he initiated the long, tender kiss as he threaded his fingers through her strawberry hair and gently pulled her toward him. As he kissed her, he stopped thinking and let his body take over. There it was again—he hadn't mistaken it the first time. There was a definite quickening of his heartbeat and an undeniable stirring in the pit of his stomach. She took his hand and pressed it to her breast. It felt good . . . exciting . . . **normal**. Now what? He knew Alexis was ready to go as far as he wanted to take this—he just wasn't sure he was. They parted, and he looked at her pleadingly.

"The last time I kissed anyone like that, I ended up with a loaded gun pointed at my head."

"I know," she said sympathetically. "I'm so sorry, Cain. How does she live with herself and what she's done to you?"

"She probably doesn't give it a thought," he said. "Anyway, *Thou Shalt NOT Have SEX* is one of my Fifteen Commandments of Freedom. In fact, it's highlighted, underlined, and boldfaced. I think there are a number of asterisks around it too."

She smiled adoringly at his ability to bounce back.

"It makes sense," she said smiling. "How about some coffee and dessert?"

"Thanks," he said more for changing the subject and understanding where he was at than for the food.

333

That night he lay in bed trying to sort through all the different emotions that he had experienced that night. He concentrated on Alexis and how he had responded to her because he liked that. He liked that he felt comfortable with her, and she had made him feel like a man. He smiled when he thought of how at eighteen he had thought he was a man; only now did he realize what a child he really had been. And then the child was snatched from his home and thrown to the wolves at Maddox. He had to become a man quickly or he wouldn't have survived, but he never really felt like a man until tonight.

The phone rang and cut into his thoughts and feelings of well-being. It was Meredithe, he knew. He often called at all hours of the night to make sure Cain was home. So much for feeling like a man. He looked at the clock: 1:27.

"Damn it," he sighed under his breath. Then he lifted the receiver. "Yeah." So much for propriety.

"Good morning," said Meredithe in his condescending, cheerful tone.

"I'm home."

"But not asleep; you never answer the phone that quickly when you're asleep."

"Did I miss something where it says I had to be asleep?"

"No, smartass, I was just making an observation. You're awfully touchy."

"Well, I'm in bed. Does that count?"

"Alone?"

"So alone it hurts."

"Good. Romance your hand, and you'll stay out of trouble. You should be pretty good at that by now, anyway."

Cain hung up on him with out a word. Meredithe called back immediately. If his parents weren't sleeping, he would have let it ring. The man had found out what he had called for. There was no reason Cain had to put up with his crude degradation.

He reached over and picked up the phone in the middle of the first ring, but he didn't say a word. Fighting the urge to drop the receiver back on the cradle, he held it to his ear. Meredithe was not put off by the lack of response on the other end of the line.

"Do that to me again, and I'll slap your ass back in jail for a night or two for a refresher course!"

Cain listened but said nothing.

"Farrell!"

"Yeah?"

"Don't dick around with me, man. I am not someone you should dick around with."

"I wouldn't think of it . . . sir. I mean, nothing against you or anything, but it's just not my scene. Not to worry, I'll stick with my hand."

Cain didn't have to see Meredithe to know that he was red-faced and steaming. He knew it wasn't smart to irritate the man, but sometimes he just couldn't help himself—especially when Meredithe treated him like an impudent child. The man in him had no choice but to fight back.

"I'll have to look over your curfew," said Meredithe keeping a lid on his own temper but tightening the screws nonetheless. "Maybe I'll have to shorten it even more till you learn a little respect."

"You do that," said Cain, refusing to be tamed. "Is there anything else I can help you with, or can I got back to bed now?"

"I'll see you on Friday—and don't expect it to be a pleasant encounter."

"I never do," said Cain with a wince, wishing he could just keep his mouth shut.

This time Meredithe hung up without a word.

School started the next week, and Cain became really busy. He was taking sixteen credit hours plus he worked from 5:00-10:00 every night except Saturday and Sunday. His remaining waking hours were spent doing homework. He didn't care. It kept him busy, and it kept Meredithe off his back since the parole officer was satisfied that Cain was so busy that he didn't have time to get in trouble. He persisted in middle-of-the-night calls, however, as well as visits to his work—just in case. Cain knew it would be only a matter of time before Meredithe would show up at his school. It seemed there was no convincing the man that he wasn't interested in breaking parole or getting into any kind of trouble. Oh well, Cain was certainly used to scrutiny, and if Meredithe had nothing else to do with his time than chase a wild goose, he certainly didn't care. If fact, he was rather enjoying the idea that all of the running around and phoning that Meredithe did was producing no ammunition for the parole officer to use against him. The man thought he was being the guardian of the public, and Cain got a good laugh out of the foolish, little man's quixotic ventures. Meredithe, on the other hand, was sure he was being scammed, and it was only a matter of time before he caught Cain off guard in some compromising situation.

Cain kept to himself at school, taking advantage of breaks between classes to go to the library and work on his homework. As lonely as his life was, he wasn't interested in making new friends and trying to explain his limited existence. Instead, he opted to avoid social interaction. Besides he was three or four years older than most of the other students and almost totally removed from their social phase of development. There was no way he could relate to giggly discussions about movie stars or informal debates about the current music scene. A straight-A student, he was culturally deprived, and he knew it. Rather than display his ignorance with an awkward, passive demeanor, he avoided the situation altogether.

However, his standoffish unavailability only added to his allure. A person couldn't look like Cain Farrell and successfully fade into the woodwork. Given his criminal status, the more-than-willing-to-please attention of a good portion of the female population at the school was the last thing he needed. He wished he had thought ahead and bought a gold ring to wear on his left hand. Then no explanation would have been needed. He finally resorted to telling people he was engaged. That was probably better since a fiancée is less of a presence in one's life than a wife is. Unfortunately, a fiancée didn't deter the efforts by the males that he came in contact with. He had a certain charisma that attracted people to him despite his self-imposed inaccessibility. One look at him and people just knew this was someone they wanted to connect with. It was all part of his popularity in grammar school and high school and the reason for his success with many of the hardened and not-so-hardened inmates at Maddox. It became a full-time task to parry off inquiries into his private life, and it was really against his nature to be so sullenly reclusive. It was becoming more and more apparent what a huge hole had been blown through the vital organs of his emotional and social development—the fun he had missed in growing up while he was away at Maddox.

Not being one to lament for too long over that which he had no control, he strove to maintain as positive an outlook as possible and yet remain socially aloof and relatively unavailable. It wasn't much fun, but fun really had very little to do with his existence these days, so he was used to it.

Meredithe waited until the third week of school was well underway before making an appearance. Cain was not at all surprised to see him waiting in the hall when he walked out of his first class of the day; he wondered what had taken him so long.

"What a pleasant surprise," said Cain sarcastically as he walked up to Meredithe.

"Time for a parent/teacher conference," smiled Meredithe. "Let's go back inside."

"Oh, come on," complained Cain. "You could do that by phone."

"Yes, I could, but I'm not. I want you there, too. Now let's go."

"Could you at least wait till everyone else is out of there before you publicly humiliate me?"

"I'm not going to publicly humiliate you."

"You have your name for it; I have mine."

"Okay," said Meredithe, "I'll wait until everyone has left. Now come on."

Cain took a deep breath in an effort to shore up his patience, and then he followed the difficult, little general back into the classroom.

Sitting down in a desk in the back corner, Cain tried to blend in with the décor. Meredithe, on the other hand, walked up to the front of the room.

"Can I help you?" the teacher asked with a pleasant smile.

"Yes, you can," said Meredithe as Cain's heart temporarily stopped mid-beat, "but go ahead with your students first. We can wait." Cain's heart resumed its normal rhythm.

Cain tried to size up the instructor as he sat in his desk at the back of the room. She was young—probably in her middle thirties—and a bit dowdy, but she seemed pleasant enough. Her teaching style was mostly lecturing, so he hadn't had much interaction with her from the onset of the course. She seemed impatient with anyone who interrupted her with a question—hence the number of students waiting to talk to her after class—so he kept his questions to himself, opting rather to look them up on the Internet or in the library after class. Since none of his instructors had given any indication that they knew of his criminal record, he wondered if Dean Richards and/or Ms. Boston had forewarned any of them of his presence. It didn't take long before he found out.

The last question was finally answered, sending the last student on his way. Then it was Meredithe's turn to take center stage. From his seat in the back, Cain could tell that the parole officer was thoroughly enjoying his role as he proudly introduced himself, flashed his badge, and revealed his reason for being there. The teacher glanced up passed Meredithe to catch a glimpse of Cain. She hadn't known before—he could tell by the look.

"There has been some rumor among the staff," she said. "We're a small school—but I don't think anyone knows for sure if it's really true."

*Great, now everyone will know for sure.*

"Well, it's true," said Meredithe a little too merrily for Cain's liking. "And here he is in the flesh, Mr. Cain Harrigan Farrell, right in the middle of your class. Can I ask you, how do you feel about that?"

She looked back up at Cain. He was never one to bristle, so he met her gaze without the slightest hesitation or embarrassment.

"What was he in jail for?"

"What does that matter?!" protested Cain as he left his books on the desk and pounded up to join them.

"Rape," announced Meredithe before the debate could begin. Now there was no doubt in Cain's mind that the humiliation would be thorough.

"Jesus Christ," sighed Cain as he dropped into a desk at the front of the room.

Although valiantly trying to maintain an air of professionalism, the teacher couldn't hide the tiny gasp that escaped her lips.

"I see," she said as she recomposed herself.

"Do you have a problem with him being in your class?" Meredithe asked.

"It is a little frightening," she said, "I have to admit. But . . .," she inhaled a deep breath, ". . . I'm assuming he's paid his debt and he's ready to be a responsible citizen or he wouldn't be here in the first place. I'm a fair-minded person, so there shouldn't be a problem—unless Mr. Farrell wants to make it one."

"Okay," said Meredithe. "Then I don't foresee any problem since Mr. Farrell had indicated to me that he wants to be a good boy and keep his ass out of jail. Can I ask you to please fill out one of these reports at the end of each week and mail them back to me at my office in these self-addressed, stamped envelopes?"

"That's no problem," she smiled.

"Thank you very kindly," Meredithe's voice was dripping molasses. "And one more thing, one of the reasons I asked Farrell to be here was so that he could hear me tell you this . . . one disparaging word from you about his behavior, and his ass gets sent directly back to the joint. So you just let me know if he isn't a perfect gentleman at all times. My card's there with those papers I gave you."

As murderous anger reared up and kicked the humiliation aside, Cain got up, grabbed his books from his desk in the back, and exited the classroom without a word. He needed to put some distance between himself and Meredithe, but he knew he had better stay around for the verbal ass whipping he was about to get from his parole officer. He stormed about two doorways down the hall and then stopped. Pacing like a caged animal, he tried to relieve himself of the anger and resentment that was flooding his soul. He didn't have to wait long for Meredithe to catch up to him.

"What was that all about?!" ranted Meredithe. "You should have said good-bye; you should have kissed-ass. Didn't you hear me— one word from her, and you're back in the . . ."

". . . joint!" finished Cain. "Joint? What is this, the fifties? Nobody calls it the 'joint' anymore. A *joint* is something you smoke, for God's sake!"

"Look, Mr. Hotshot Cain Farrell, you show me some respect both in private and in front of other people, or I don't care what you call it now, your ass will be back behind bars before you know what hit you. You got that?!!!"

"Yeah, I got that!"

"Good. Now you go back and apologize for being so rude and say good-bye like a good boy."

Cain glared at him and had to concentrate on not throwing his books and then wrapping his hands tightly around the little general's neck until his eyes bulged out. The image clearly in his mind seemed to suffice for the moment. Gathering the shattered remnants of his pride, he turned on his heel and headed back to the classroom.

Meredithe spent the next two hours before Cain's next class dragging him to the offices of his other instructors, reliving the degradation of exposing his criminal status. His frustration and impatience with the activity was explosive within him, but he managed to keep it under control. One thing he had learned at Maddox was that there was no room for temper tantrums within the penal system. Such behavior was severely punished and, therefore, counterproductive.

"Cheer up, hero," said Meredithe as they walked toward Cain's next class to confront the last of his instructors. "Since we're spending so much time together today, I'm letting you off the hook for Friday."

"You're all heart," mumbled Cain finding it impossible to be excited about the news.

"Oops, your attitude is showing. You might want to do something about that before we go into the classroom—and before I say, *what the hell, come anyway.* It's no sweat off my back. What is it— another fifteen, twenty minutes out of my day?"

"Fine," relented Cain unenthusiastically. "Thank you."

"That's better, but you might want to work on it—just so you don't piss me off."

After the final trip to the academic confessional, Meredithe left and Cain got ready for his last class. His mind was on anything but school, but he had no choice other than to stay. He sat in the back of the room trying to figure out what the teacher was thinking of him now. He hated Meredithe even more for forcing him into the open and branding him a rapist. There was no need for that. He had done nothing to force Meredithe's hand—it was pure meanness and the flexing of authority. Cain tried to keep his mind on the class, but he couldn't. Grateful when it ended, he grabbed his books and left immediately, careful not to knock anyone over on his way out.

When he got home, he didn't even go into the house. Instead, he went to the garage, put his books on the workbench, and grabbed his baseball bat. It was February, but there was no snow on the ground and plenty of pent up anger in his soul. Nora watched him from the window as he headed with a purpose toward the park down the street. He never looked up to see her, and she wondered what was going on.

The park was deserted for which he was thankful. Standing on home plate, he picked up the largest stone he could find, tossed it in the air, and swung at it with all his might. The bat connected and sent the stone flying well out of the infield. He picked up another stone and repeated the motion. This purging of his soul went on for nearly an hour. There were plenty of stones behind home plate, and there was plenty of anger and resentment in his heart. He never even saw his father until Will walked up to him.

"It's kind of early in the year for baseball, isn't it?" asked Will.

"What are you doing home so early?" asked Cain as he whacked another stone into oblivion.

"Things were kind of slow today, so I left early."

"How'd you know I was here?" he asked continuing his ritual.

"Mom saw you leaving the garage."

"She worries too much."

"She's a damn good mother."

"No argument."

"Are you planning on going to work?"

"Yeah," answered Cain. "I have a little time yet. Why?"

A slight sigh of relief from Will. "I was just wondering. Are you going to tell me what's going on? This isn't exactly baseball weather."

Cain stopped and looked at his father.

"It's just been one of those days. Maybe coming home was a mistake."

He picked up another stone and sent it flying. The fury of his swing was not lost on Will.

"Whoa, whoa, whoa," said the father taking the bat from his son. "Let's have a seat over here."

They sat on the bleachers. Cain stared invisible holes into the ground and his mind was definitely far away.

"Son," said Will gently, "what happened?"

"Meredithe," said Cain still staring at the ground. "He really screwed me over today."

"How?"

"He showed up unannounced at school. Then he proceeded to drag me around the campus where he introduced himself to all my instructors and told them about my years at Maddox and why I was there."

"Oh," sighed Will miserably.

"They didn't know—a couple of them said they had no idea. I guess the dean who came to talk to me at Maddox decided to give me an even break, and he didn't make my record public knowledge. Now it is."

"I'm sorry, Cain."

"Not as sorry as I am. It wasn't fair. It just wasn't fair. I've done everything exactly the way he told me to. He had no reason to do that to me."

"You're right. That was a low blow."

"I hate him."

"I know, but you have to get along with him."

"I know. You should have seen how some of those people looked at me. I felt like the scum of the earth. And are they going to be able to be unbiased?"

"Cain—"

Cain wiped at a tear that had escaped.

"I'm not going to cry!" he said angrily as he got up and retrieved his bat. "I've cried too much in my life. I'm not some fucking baby!" He began smashing stones out into the horizon again. His father watched, unable to come up with words. Neither of them said anything for a few moments. "You want to know something, Dad? You want to know something funny—I don't think I could have sex with a girl right now even if Meredithe gave me his blessing. My head is so screwed-up right now. I'm this notorious rapist who's only had limited experience with one girl a very long time ago and who probably couldn't make it with a girl now if my life depended on it. And everyone's afraid I'm going to ravage the whole fucking campus . . . shit, the whole fucking town. Now that's a joke."

He smashed a stone harder than Will had seen him hit any others.

"Is this conjecture, or do you know it for a fact?" Will asked, trying to find direction.

"No, I don't know it for a fact. I'm forbidden to find out. I'm forbidden to fuck-ing breathe."

Another stone went sailing.

"I don't know what to tell you," sighed Will. "There's not much we can do here."

"It's Sam Willet." A thud of the bat and a large dirt ball was smashed to smithereens. "I know it's Sam Willet. From guys I've talked to, no one is nailed in as tight as I am. No one gets as much personal attention as I do. Meredithe would never get any free time, let alone sleep, if he checked up on everyone the way he does me." He stopped the compulsive batting practice and turned to his father. "You know, I'm starting to wish I had raped his daughter—at least then I'd deserve all this shit."

Will took in a deep breath of cold air. No argument he could come up with in his head seemed to make sense right then, so he said nothing. Instead, he felt a social impotence of his own. There should be something he could do to right this travesty, but Cain was right—they were up against a force that was too powerful and had too much law enforcement behind it.

"Let's go home," he said after a long minute of silence between them. "It's cold and it's getting dark. Mom has a good dinner ready for you before you go to work—you don't want to miss that."

Cain looked down at the dirt at his feet. There were still a lot of good stones to punish, but his gratitude for his parents won out. At that moment what he needed more than anything was a father who understood and didn't try to placate him and a mother who had a hot meal waiting after a hideous day at school and before a long night of hard work. He smiled for the first time that day that he could remember, and he and father walked home together.

He spent the next Saturday evening with Alexis. She picked him up in the late afternoon, and after a trip to the video store they went back to her apartment. He had talked to her on the phone quite a bit, but he hadn't seen her except for that one time.

"Well," she said, "what'll it be? Should we order pizza, or do you want to take a chance on pot luck from my refrigerator?"

"Pizza's good," he said. "I'll even buy—I just got paid."

"Hey," she said graciously accepting his offer, being careful not to insist on paying since she made quite a bit more money than he did, "what a deal—you're not only good-looking, but you got a pocketful of money. What more could a girl ask?"

He looked at her and smiled the heart-stopping grin that she could hardly resist.

"So," she continued, "what did you do today?"

"I have a paper due Monday, so I spent most of the day working on that. Computers have really changed in the past six years, you know?"

She smiled affectionately. "It's so much fun watching you rediscover the world."

"Well, I feel like an idiot—like I've been in a state of suspended animation or something. You don't think six years is all that long a time to be cut off from the world, but there are so many little things that just keep evolving almost unnoticed in daily living. Then when you haven't been a part of daily living for a period of time, you can feel very out-of-touch. Anyway, I've pretty much gotten the computer down again now, and I just have to put the finishing touches on my paper tomorrow."

"Do you ever have time to just have fun?" she asked sympathetically.

"Right here. Right now. I've been looking forward to this ever since you called the other day."

"I'm glad. If there's anybody I know who deserves to laugh a little, it's you. But it seems all you have time for is school, work, and homework."

"Meredithe's thrilled—it keeps me out of trouble," he smiled.

"Meredithe's a jerk."

"That goes without saying, but actually it's just as good for now because I'm walking on legal eggshells these days."

"I know, but you should be able to have some time to yourself to just have fun."

"I told you, I'm having fun right now."

"Thank you. That's a very nice compliment."

"You're my only real friend, you know that? Other than my family."

"What about Jon Harrison?"

"Meredithe put him off limits to me."

"You can't see him?"

"Or talk to him, or write to him."

"He's a good friend. That doesn't seem fair."

Cain laughed, though he didn't state the obvious for fear of becoming depressing.

"I keep in touch with him through Mike," he said. "Some year this parole thing will pass, and we'll get together again."

"Thank goodness for Mike."

"Yeah, I wish he wasn't so far away; and he's busy with his overworked schedule."

"What about people you work with?"

"They're really nice but mostly older, and they have way different lifestyles and interests than I do."

"That leaves me, I guess."

"That leaves you." He smiled again and nearly melted her on the spot. "Thank you for thinking about me and wanting me around. Some people don't—want to be around me."

"That's sad."

"But true. Thanks for being a good friend—someone I know I can count on to keep my life on an even keel."

"Then I guess it's not such a good idea for me to totally seduce you and ravage your perfectly gorgeous body right now?"

"I don't know if you're kidding or not," he grinned warmly, "but, no, it's not a good idea."

"I am kidding," she lied as her smile helped mask her disappointment.

"Good," he smiled. "Besides Meredithe, I still have some things to work through there."

"Then how 'bout you pick out which movie you want to watch and get it set up, and I'll go order the pizza. Have you reacquainted yourself with VCRs?"

"Yeah, that I can handle."

She kissed him benignly on the forehead and then went to the kitchen to order the pizza and get her disappointed heart back on track before it forced its way out onto her sleeve. A friend is . . . good.

# CHAPTER 16

School turned into a great source of escape for him. His mind was hard at work once again, and he could pretend he was almost any other normal person. Happily, none of his instructors ever brought up Ralph Meredithe; it was as if the nasty, little man had never been there. But then he was every teacher's dream—hard working, conscientious, and very talented. They would have been crazy to rock that boat. He still made a point of avoiding other students except for the briefest of polite conversations, but he enjoyed a certain amount of anonymous camaraderie and socialization. It had become a setting where he was successful on every front doing something that he really enjoyed, and it felt good to just be there.

He had been trying to get Meredithe to let him drive and get a car. He had saved up some money for a decent downpayment, and getting around on foot, bus, or the kindness of others was getting to be a hassle. Unlike his teachers who saw potential and nurtured it, Meredithe took delight in chastising him and reminding him how indebted he was to the Department of Corrections. After all, he'd only been home for three months. Who did he think he was—someone special?

"Just because you come from the suburbs and you got good grades doesn't mean shit," said Meredithe at one of their Friday meetings. "You're still a rapist. You strong-armed a trusting, young woman, scarred her body, and then had your way with her. We don't just forget those things because you got money, brains, and a pretty face. Guys like you think you're above the law and can get away with murder—or rape—because you got the good things in life. Well I'm here to tell you, you can't get away with squat. If it was up to me . . ."

"I'd still be back in the *joint*." Cain smiled deviously. He couldn't help himself.

"See what I mean?" bellowed Meredithe, more than a little embarrassed. "You got no respect. You think you're better than everyone else."

"Okay, okay," frowned Cain having heard more than enough. "I just thought I'd ask. The last thing I need is another lecture from you. I'll walk."

On the train on his way back home, he stared out the window trying to neutralize the effects of his visit with Meredithe. No matter how good his week had gone, there was always Friday to bring it all back into perspective. Sam Willet, through the office of Ralph Meredithe, was never going to let his debt to Carrie be paid. Sooner or later Cain would fulfill the terms of his sentence and be set free of the legal system altogether, but that could be up to six more years. Until then, the Willets would be turning legal screws to the max.

It usually took him the entire trip home to loosen the knot of hard-core reality that Meredithe tightly wadded and presented to him each week. And then it was anywhere from a couple of hours to days later before he was able to completely untangle the mess that always lodged itself in the center of his chest. Often on Friday nights he couldn't eat dinner because the invisible blockage didn't allow the passage of food and made him feel like he was going to vomit.

Nora had gotten used to his Friday bouts of depression and legally imposed anorexia, but she resisted the urge to mother him. She knew that would only make it worse, and though nothing had ever been said between them, she knew that he appreciated her non-interference. A mother hen would have definitely driven him over the edge.

On that Friday after his talk with Meredithe about being able to drive and get a car, he was particularly depressed. He didn't want a whole lot, and Meredithe's arguments never made much sense to him. He was always willing to listen to reason, but Meredithe's tack was always punitive—having nothing to do with reason. Though he didn't expect much, it was still a major disappointment when his expectations became reality. In an attempt to conceal his mood and thus spare his parents, he ate a hearty dinner—which wasn't all that hard since Nora was a great cook and always planned his special favorites for Fridays. Then he excused himself and went up and called Alexis.

"I know you have a date," he told her, "but can you spare me a few minutes?"

"It's Friday, Cain, I always plan in a little Meredithe damage control time. He said no to the license and car, didn't he?"

"Yeah. Shit."

"I'm sorry."

"I don't know why I expected anything other than what I got. But I did hope that maybe he would start to trust me and give me a break. Instead, he makes me feel like trash. Just because I'm from the suburbs doesn't make me better than anybody else. What an ass."

"I told you I shouldn't have made this date for tonight. And now I can't get a hold of him to. . ."

"Alexis . . .I'm going to work soon. I'm fine. I just wanted to let you know what he said."

"You're sure?"

"Yes, and now I'd better go get ready for work. I can't afford to be late—Meredithe calls there regularly to check up on me."

"How do you stand it?"

"No choice. And it is better than jail."

"Okay," she smiled. "Will I see you this weekend?"

"Maybe your date will have other plans."

"No, I don't think so."

"I'd tell you not to do anything I wouldn't do, but then you couldn't have any fun."

She laughed.

"I'm supposed to be cheering you up, but I think it's working the other way around."

"No, I do feel better. Thanks. I gotta run."

By denying him a driver's license and a car, Meredithe had placed Cain directly in the path of a speeding locomotive ready to derail his life and send him spinning out of control. Cain was totally unsuspecting that next week as he stood in the small bus shelter about a block from school on a cold, rainy March afternoon. Who'd ever believe you could get hit by a train while waiting at a bus stop?

At first the car drove passed him and then suddenly slowed down and pulled over to the curb. Cain paid it little mind; he was too busy trying to stay out of the cold mist that was swirling about him. He did take notice as the car slowly backed up, however. When it stopped directly opposite him, he became very curious; but even though he was only a matter of feet from the curb, he couldn't make out the driver because of the persistent rain. The passenger side window automatically opened.

"Hey, sailor," said a familiar female voice, "want a ride?"

He started feeling driven and confused—like when trying to put a name to a familiar tune. Squinting through the rain, he stayed in the shelter trying to grasp what was becoming apparent. That's when she leaned over closer to the passenger side, and he looked directly into the face of his lost, but hardly forgotten past.

"Joanne?" he said numbly. Then under his breath, "Shit."

"Get in," she called through the rain. "I'll drive you home."

"It's all right," he said feeling his body turning to jelly. "The bus'll be here soon."

"Cain, it's pouring. My car's dry. It's not out of my way. Now, get in."

He was losing his breath, and he felt as if he were under the effects of some powerful drug as he fumbled for the right words, the right thing to do. Flashes from the past were playing out in front of his eyes. Commonsense told him to run like hell, but as in all cases of the heart, commonsense takes a back seat. Therefore, he opened the door and took the front seat.

"Hi," she smiled as if there had never been any bad blood between them.

"How'd you know it was me?"

"Process of elimination. I know Matt works downtown, and you go to school. The bus is right by the school. It must be you. It wasn't really very hard. I've actually driven by before and seen you, but I didn't know if you'd want me to stop. I just couldn't drive by another time. There was too much left unsettled between us."

"I don't know. I thought you were perfectly clear. It took a while, but I got the message. Aren't you going to drive?"

"In a minute."

She reached over and smoothed raindrops from his cheek. He wondered if she could hear his heart pounding as he gently took her hand and put it back on the steering wheel. Why did women always have this compulsion to touch his face?

"I'm sorry. It's just that you are so exquisitely gorgeous and vulnerable looking." She answered his unspoken question.

Now he really felt uncomfortable. This was not only someone else's wife, but also the woman he had been in love with almost his whole life. *What the hell do I do now?*

"Jo, I really do have to be home soon, or I'll be late for work."

"Okay," she said putting the car in gear and pulling away from the curb. "How've you been?"

"Fine." *Stick to the point.*

"You look wonderful, but then you always did."

"You still wear the same perfume." *SHIT!*

"I'm surprised you remember. It's been a long time."

"Not **that** long." *SHIT! SHIT! SHIT!* "Um, how are your parents?" *That's more like it.*

"They're good. How about your family?"

"Good. Everyone's good. You heard my grandpa died?"

"Yeah. I'm sorry. Did you two ever settle your differences?"

"No. He was a bastard right up to the end."

"I'm sorry. I know how you felt about that whole situation."

"Hey, how about you getting married? That was a real . . ." *Jab below the belt . . . shot between the eyes . . . kick in the teeth . . . clothesline to the neck.* ". . . surprise."

"Yeah," she smiled coyly. "He's a great guy."

"You must love him a lot?" *Okay, are we almost home?*

"Yeah. Yeah, I do. He's older—thirty. He has his own business and does quite well."

"So, I've heard. I'm . . ." GOD *DAMN IT!* ". . . happy for you. And you have a baby." *Sinking fast!*

"Yeah. Brian. He's very cute."

"I'm sure." *Gasping for fresh air!* "I have two nieces and a nephew."

"That's wonderful."

"Yeah. They're great kids. Molly has a girl, and Dan has one of each."

"Your family is really growing—and it was big to start with."

"Yep. Well, here we are." *Praise God.* "Thanks for the ride."

"You're welcome. It's really been good talking to you."

"Yeah, you too." *I want to fuck you until I can't move—right here, right now—in this car.*

347

"Maybe I'll see you again soon."

"Yeah."

Thank goodness it was still raining because it gave him the excuse to slam the door quickly and run like hell to the house. Nora met him at the door.

"Who gave you a ride home? Someone from school?"

"Yeah. I can't talk right now, Mom. Maybe later."

Practically throwing his coat onto the hanger in the front closet, he grabbed his books and bounded up the stairs to his room at a record pace. Actually with the physical reaction that was racking his body, he was surprised he could walk at all. His door slammed, and Nora was left standing in a sea of confusion.

At work that night, Cain was happy for a job that depended mostly on a strong back rather than a quick mind. Although he had both, he knew his quick mind was shot to hell. He couldn't stop thinking about Joanne and how she had made him feel. He had always wondered if he saw her again whether his passion or his anger would win out. Now there was no question—he couldn't even remember why he had been angry. For the first time, he even felt he could put Carrie Willet and Herb Lidell in the back of his mind. All he could think about was how much he loved her—how much he had always loved her—and how much he wanted her. He refused to think about a husband and a baby. Seeing her again, smelling her perfume, was still too new. There was no room for rational thinking at this time. Maybe by not thinking about them he could will them out of existence.

What to do next? Where to go next? How could he see her again? Brian, that's what she said the baby's name was. *Shit, where did that come from?* He dropped absently against the wall. People didn't have babies without sex—and in this case a husband. *Shit!* Suddenly all he could think about was her baby and her husband. He was ready to scream out loud.

"You okay?" One of his friends asked.

He snapped out of the self-imposed stupor.

"Yeah, I'm fine. Just a little distracted."

"More than a little, I'd say. You were a million miles away."

"I'm sorry."

"It's okay. Just let me know if there's anything I can do to help."

At 10:00—his quitting time so he could be home by 11:00—he lied to the guy who usually drove him home and said his brother was picking him up. He needed some time to himself before he got home, and he figured the brisk walk would do him good. After living at Maddox, not much about the criminal element of society disturbed him, so he didn't mind that it was late and very dark. He was well versed in the art of taking care of himself.

348

As he walked toward home, his conscience and his libido were in constant battle. When did this conscience make an appearance? He never invited it. In fact, he did his best to ignore it. But this faceless baby and a husband kept creeping into places in his mind where there was really very little room for them. That made for quite an uncomfortable situation. Bottom line: she wasn't free to him. No matter how he tried to figure around it, the answer always came out the same. Joanne could never be his. They had run out of time to revive the innocent love affair of their school days, and the process was irreversible. He had been that close to her, smelled her perfume. Here was fate playing another dirty trick on him.

The reality of the whole thing hit harder and harder with each step he took until he nearly cried out in pain. Now what? He had to see Alexis.

As he turned down a block to head toward her apartment, he came across a small liquor store. He was a neophyte drinker to be sure, but at that moment he saw it as the only way to dull the pain he was feeling. He walked in, picked out a small bottle of John Jameson Irish Whiskey like he knew what he was doing, and prayed the cashier wouldn't card him. He was over twenty-one and legally able to purchase liquor, but he had no driver's license, and Meredithe had even seen to it that his state ID was stamped with the words **NO ALCOHOL** in boldface across the front. Good, old Meredithe didn't forget anything.

As he approached the cash register, he saw the sign: EVERYONE UNDER THIRTY-FIVE WILL BE CARDED. *SHIT!* It was becoming his favorite word. A million options began to flood his mind. He was clever. He had just spent almost six years pulling shit at Maddox. There had to be a way.

The clerk smiled and asked for the obligatory ID. Light bulbs flashed in his brain until he was nearly blinded with delight. He reached into his wallet and pulled out Matt's license, which he had just gotten back a few days before when he had finished traffic school. He hadn't seen Matt yet, so . . . he confidently handed the license over to the clerk who checked it, smiled, and returned it—no questions asked. As he put it away, he decided it was better not to mention this little transgression to his brother.

Having almost-legally purchased the Irish Whiskey, he set back out into the chilly night—on his way to Alexis's. When he got there, however, he hadn't counted on her not being home. *What the hell?* He knew she had to work the next day, so he sat on the floor outside her door, opened up the Irish Whiskey, and imbibed a mouthful of the panacea. It hit him in the back of his throat and the front of his brain all at once. He was glad he was sitting down and alone, since he definitely would have been rocked on his feet and he was choking and sputtering. What a kick. He had never had Irish Whiskey before, but it was at all of their family parties and he knew it was strong. It made him feel warm inside, manly. He liked pulling shit on Meredithe just the way he liked doing it at Maddox. It gave him a step up on those who thought they had him pinned down and hemmed in.

After three or four swallows, the whiskey began going down much smoother, albeit his head was feeling lighter. That was good. Lighter was good. Things were much too heavy these days, too complicated. *Where the hell is Alexis, anyway?* He looked at his watch and had to focus a little longer than usual to read it. 10:23. *Come on, it's going to be too late pretty soon.* But then he solved that problem by thinking he would suggest she take him home and they could talk there. *Then let Meredithe call if he wants! The stupid screw! Stupid Napoleon!* He took another swallow and noticed the hallway shift a little. *Whoa, that was weird! ALEXIS, WHERE THE HELL ARE YOU?!!!* He decided he had better pace himself a little and ease up on the whiskey. Unfortunately, as a more seasoned drinker would have known, by the time you decide to ease up on the drinking, it's already too late. Alcohol continues doing its thing to you long after the last swallow.

Now the hall did a total spin, and he put his hand flat on the floor to steady himself. He closed his eyes. That was a mistake. Not only did he feel dizzier, all he could see was Joanne's face. She hadn't changed much—her hair was a little shorter, darker. Her eyes and her smile were the same. It'd been so long since he had seen that smile directed at him. From what he could see in the car, her figure had remained as delicate as ever. He had had a few minutes of her in the flesh, and now she was back to being a vision as she had been for so many years. Untouchable.

He opened his eyes and blinked the view back into some sort of reality. But everything was fuzzy around the edges and wavy. He looked at his watch again. Moving his wrist and his head until the numbers stopped jumping around, he read it. 10:45. *Damn, I gotta get home.* There was still some presence of a sound mind. But as he tried to get up, he became painfully aware that the Irish Whiskey was now master of his body as well as a good portion of his mind. Everything began spinning again, only this time at carnival ride speed. He eased himself back against the door and concentrated on calming his not-always-reliable-stomach. *ALEXIS! JOANNE! SOMEBODY! WHERE THE HELL AM I, ANYWAY?* The hallway had taken on a surrealistic form that didn't look at all familiar to him. He had to close his eyes again— that's all he knew. He laid his head back against the door and drifted into a drunken half-sleep where nothing else seemed to matter.

It wasn't too many more minutes before Alexis and her friend came down the hall. Of course they spotted Cain immediately, and Alexis zeroed in on the bottle of Irish Whiskey with a fair amount missing, considering a neophyte drinker.

"Wow!" exclaimed her friend Linda. "Now I wouldn't mind coming home to that every night. Do you know him?"

"Yes," said Alexis without a smile as she looked down at her watch. "He has to be home."

She knelt down next to him and smoothed his hair away from his forehead. It flopped back in a silky fringe.

"Cain, honey, wake up. You have to get home."

"Joanne?" he asked groggily.

Her heart sank.

"No. Open your eyes; it's Alexis."

"Hell," said her friend, "tell him you're Joanne—tell him I'm Joanne!"

Alexis looked up at her and smiled patiently.

"You don't understand, Linda," said Alexis, "he's not just an ordinary guy."

"No kidding!"

"No, really. He could be in legal trouble if he doesn't get home **soon**. Help me try to get him inside."

"Gladly," smiled Linda.

"Where's Joanne?" he asked.

"I don't know," said Alexis. "You and I are going to have to talk about that, but not right now. Can you get up?"

"I'm not sure," he said. "I don't care."

"Yes, you do. Listen to me—it's after 11:00. We need to get you home."

"I'm home . . . I like it here. But I need to sleep . . . or throw up."

"Christ, Cain, come on, get up!"

She handed her friend the key, and she helped Cain fumble to his feet.

"Shit," he smiled. "I had too much to drink."

"No shit," grinned Alexis. "At least you're a happy drunk. What's this all about?"

"Joanne," said Cain as they stumbled into the apartment and closed the door.

"Fuck Joanne," frowned Alexis.

"I know—I wanted to."

Linda giggled.

"Did you see her?" Alexis asked.

"Yeah. She's still so beautiful . . . Perfume . . . I gotta throw up—everything's spinning."

"Okay, Romeo," said Alexis. "You know where the bathroom is. Do you need any help?"

"No, I can do it by myself."

Alexis and her friend exchanged smiles as he wove his way to the bathroom.

"God, he is adorable," sighed Linda. "Keep him here . . . tell him you're Joanne . . . take advantage of him! God, he is gorgeous!"

"I'd love to, but not under these circumstances. If I ever make it with him, he's going to be cold sober with his eyes wide opened. And he's **not** going to call me Joanne!"

"Who is he?"

"A friend. Someone I've known since high school. I used to date his twin brother."

"Dear God, there're two of him!"

"Identical," smiled Alexis. "Now excuse me, I have to call his home because he could be in a lot of trouble. Besides, I don't think you and I could get him there by ourselves. I'll have to get his dad or one of his brothers to help."

Will and Jim made it over to the apartment in record time. Alexis introduced them to Linda, and then led them to the couch where Cain was lying with a cold washcloth over his eyes.

"What's this all about?" Will asked Alexis.

"He keeps talking about Joanne. I don't know. Like I told you on the phone, I found him here about a half-hour ago. Meredithe hasn't called, has he?"

"No," said Will, "but he could call any time. There's no telling when. He doesn't always call, but if he does Nora's going to stall him and then call here right away. It's good news that we haven't heard from her."

"Well, let's hope he doesn't call at all tonight because there's no way Cain can talk to him."

"I could beat the shit out of him right here with my bare hands," snarled his father.

"Please try and understand, Will," she pleaded. "He still loves Joanne so much, and I think he saw her today. He's going to hate himself in the morning."

"He's going to hate himself well before morning. Nora's home making strong coffee right now. He has no choice but to talk to Meredithe if he calls."

Alexis sat on the couch next to Cain. Gently she took the washcloth from his eyes and began dabbing at his face with it.

"Come, dollface, your dad and Jim are here. You need to get home, or I'd let you sleep here."

"I need to go home," he said not really understanding or caring.

"That's right, Einstein," said Will pulling him to a seated position on the couch. "Here's your coat. Come on, we need to get your ass out of here." He turned to Alexis. "Thank you."

Alexis took Cain's face in her hands and kissed him lightly on the cheek.

"She's not worth it, sweetheart." She kissed his other cheek. "Sweet dreams."

The next morning as she was getting ready for work, he showed up at her door with flowers that he had bought at a nearby convenience store.

"You're the absolute last person I expected to see at my door this morning," she laughed as she let him in.

"I know. Please don't talk too loud." He frowned sweetly and put his hand to his forehead. "I have an early class, and I'm not allowed to cut classes—especially for a hangover." He presented the flowers. "These are for you. Can you ever forgive me?"

"I'll try," she smiled kissing his cheek. "Come on, I have coffee and a little time to spare."

"I'll pass on the coffee," he said sitting down at the table. "I want you to know I didn't come here drunk last night, nor did I have the intention of getting drunk."

"What happened?"

"I ran into Joanne—actually, she ran into me. Anyway, she gave me a ride home from school yesterday. I felt like I was in a time warp or something. She acted like nothing had ever happened between us. She smiled; she looked **so** good; she smelled so familiar. To this day I haven't been able to get that perfume out of my mind. Then she dropped me off and was gone."

"That's her style."

"Alexis."

"I'm sorry, go on."

"That's about it, except I couldn't get her out of my mind. All night at work I was nuts. When I got off, I decided to come here and talk to you. I thought I'd have one, stiff drink with you and then leave the bottle here and go home. I swear. I didn't come here stumbling drunk expecting you to take care of me. I was able to scam a clerk and buy the Irish Whiskey, but then you weren't home and I totally lost track of how many healthy slugs constitutes one, stiff drink. I feel so stupid. You had someone with you, didn't you?"

"Yeah, a friend from work. We had gone to a movie."

"I'm so sorry. What can I do to make it up to you?"

"Nothing aside from what you've already done. I feel bad I wasn't home."

"No, don't let me off the hook that easily. It's not your job to always be here in case I need you."

"Did Meredithe ever call?"

"No. Of course not—because I was so sober and wide awake after my dad got done with me that I couldn't sleep half the night anyway."

"I know your dad was really mad."

"God," said Cain with an ironic laugh, "he doesn't get mad very often, but when he does he doesn't hold back."

"Well it all turned out okay."

"Except for my ravaged body this morning. And I have a full day of classes."

"Your penance."

"I guess so."

"Let me go finish getting ready and I'll drop you off at school on my way to work."

"Did you say *fuck Joanne* last night?" he asked with a mischievous smile.

"Yes," she admitted with embarrassment.

"I thought so." He was still smiling that smile that drove her crazy. "I never heard you talk like that."

"I do . . . sometimes," she said defending herself. "And besides, I meant it—not literally the way you took it. But she's nothing but trouble for you. You've got to be able to see that. She's married, Cain, with a baby; and you're still nursing a teenage crush. Give it up. It's trouble under normal circumstances, and for you it's lethal. Just let Meredithe get wind of that situation and see what happens. There, you didn't ask what I thought, but I told you. Now I'm going to go get ready for work. I'll be right back."

She left him in a fit of confusion that his aching head wasn't prepared to deal with. Instead he folded his arms on the table and put his head down. He was tired and nauseous. His head was splitting, and he had no idea how he was ever going to make it through the day. He just couldn't sort out the Joanne thing right then.

They didn't talk much on the way to school. Cain put his head back on the seat and closed his eyes. Alexis took advantage and stole a few lingering glances whenever they came to a stop. She couldn't get over how attracted to him she was—even more so than she ever was to Matt when they were going together, so she ruled out looks alone. Despite the fact that Maddox had made him very streetwise and seasoned, there was a vulnerability and sensitivity about him that she found so undeniably sexy and irresistible that she could hardly bear it. Unfortunately, many females responded to him the same way, as she had evidenced with Linda the night before. The other thing she couldn't get over was how he hardly ever seemed to notice. She was always pointing it out to him in fun when they were together and girls were walking into walls to get a better look at him, but he always laughed and waved her off—called himself damaged goods. Damaged indeed. What woman in her right mind would want the chance to try her hand at repairing the damage and soothing the pain?

"Here we are," she said as she pulled into the parking lot as close to the buildings as she could get.

He opened his eyes.

"Oh, God," he moaned as the light nearly blinded him.

"Sorry I can't be more of a help."

"You've been a great help." This time he leaned over and kissed her cheek. "Thanks."

"I love you," she said before she could stop herself.

He made a playful click with his tongue and winked.

"I love you, too. Bye."

And he was gone, slamming the door on her moment. He had totally missed the depth of her meaning. The big, dumb, gorgeous ass. How could he be so smart and so dumb at the same time? She took a deep breath to try and calm her racing heart, and then she drove off to face a day just like any other day.

Joanne didn't let too many days pass before she showed up at the bus stop again. Cain couldn't believe his eyes and wasn't sure if he was happy to see her or not. It took a minute before he moved his feet to approach the car. Then, taking leave of his mind, he opened the passenger's door and got in.

"At first I wasn't sure if you were going to get in or not," she smiled.

"Neither was I."

"Why?" She was astounded. "We can be friends, can't we?"

"I don't get this, Jo . . . after all these years. You wouldn't even give me the time of day before I left."

"That was a long time ago," she shrugged as she pulled away from the curb. "I guess I'm trying to tell you I'm sorry. Can you forgive me?"

He took a deep breath and stared out the window for a minute. Then he asked her the question he had been wanting to ask for years.

"Why didn't you wait for me? You were supposed to have been in love with me."

She pulled over on the tree-lined, residential street and stopped the car. Now it was her turn to measure words.

"I was so hurt and, I guess, embarrassed. But most of all, I was too young to really understand love. Then not seeing you any more made it easier to deny what I had felt. Seeing you now, I can say that if you'd been around, you would have eventually worn me down."

"How the **fuck** do you think that makes me feel? I was locked up in a madhouse fighting daily for my life and my sanity. I HAD NO CHOICE!"

"I know." Tears were forming in her eyes.

"I sent letters for over a year, and you sent them all back—unopened."

"I know. I was too young."

"So was I! God, I had to grow up fast. So don't give me that shit."

"I was humiliated."

355

"And it was one, big ego trip for me!!! Joanne, I needed you. I was scared and lonely and desperately in love, and I needed you."

The tears were flowing freely down her face now as she tried to find some words that fit. Cain was on a roll as his soul was spilling over, so he continued.

"I kept telling myself you just needed time. In time you'd write. Or maybe even—best case scenario—in time you'd come visit. Or at the very least, in time I'd finally get home and be able to convince you how sorry I was and that we belong together. I mean, I'm twenty-three; you're twenty-two—it's not unreasonable to think I still had a chance to win you back. That dream stayed with me every minute of every day until I was beat right over the head with the news that you were getting married. You didn't waste any time, and I had nothing but time. I almost lost my mind that night. I was only gone—What was it, two years?—and you were already marrying someone else. You didn't let much fucking grass grow under your feet, did you?"

"I'm so sorry. What else can I say?"

"Nothing. You said it all when you said, 'I do.' There's nothing more to say. And I'm sorry, but I can't be your friend. That's just too weird, and I'm not a masochist."

"Then you still love me." It wasn't a question.

He looked in her soft, tear-stained eyes.

"Yeah. God help me, I'll probably always love you. Where does that leave us?"

"I still love you, too. I always have."

His face hardened as he reached for the door handle.

"FUCK YOU!"

"Wait!" she cried grabbing onto his arm. "Let me finish. Please stay." He settled back in the seat, his jaw clamped, his mind not much more opened. She went on. "You're right—I didn't give it enough time to come to terms with everything that had happened before I started dating Thomas. At that time I just wanted to hurt you like you had hurt me. He was older and rich and a very good catch. It sounded like a good idea."

"IT SOUNDED LIKE A GOOD IDEA?" He was incredulous. "Good God, Joanne, what have you done to us—to your husband and baby?!!"

"I don't know," she sobbed. "I just know when I saw you I knew I couldn't ignore it any more."

"Jesus Christ," he sighed softly like the prayer it was meant to be. "I don't know what to say."

"Don't say anything. You said it yourself—we need time. Let's don't rush anything this time. Let me give you something to think about."

Out of nowhere she put her hands on the sides of his head and pulled him toward her. Then as he totally gave himself up, they kissed with all the love and passion of their youth. It was everything he remembered and more. His heart pounded madly as he eased her toward him and they kissed again, this time with the love and passion of adults. How many years had he dreamt of this moment? Even before Carrie Willet. Joanne had always kept their relationship pristine, now she was taking his hand and putting it under her blouse. She was kissing him, inviting him to touch her. His head was swimming. She felt so soft and warm under his palm. The perfume was drawing him even deeper into the moment.

Just as his mind was groping for some way for them to move beyond the confines of the car and the daylight so they could finish this burning act, her hands reached inside his shirt and she accidentally scratched his skin with the diamonds on her wedding ring. He flinched, and the moment was interrupted.

"I'm sorry," she purred as she leaned forward and started to kiss the scratch on his ribs.

"What are you trying to do to me?" he laughed as he pulled her hand out to investigate the cause of his discomfort.

He saw the ring, and the moment was terminated. Suddenly the past and the present collided with astronomical force, and the resulting meteor shower fell down around them. Cain took a breath as he pulled away from her and sat back in his seat.

"What the hell am I doing?" he sighed.

"Something we should have done a long time ago."

"No. No, this isn't right. Christ, Joanne, you're married. You're the one who should be stopping me."

"I told you my marriage was a mistake."

"What, so you just throw it away?! That's what you did to us six years ago."

"I don't know what to do."

"I have to get home. I'll go back and get the bus."

"No. Don't leave. I'll take you home. We just need to take more time. There's no rush anymore."

They spoke little as she drove him home. He couldn't believe the tangled mess in his brain. What he thought he wanted . . . what was within his grasp . . . what was right . . . what was wrong . . . what to do.

"Cain," she said breaking into his thoughts as they pulled into his driveway, "marriages are reversible. This is not a hopeless situation."

"Right," he said blandly as he opened the door. "Thanks for the ride."

There was a double meaning to his statement, but at that moment he wasn't sure which one was from his heart. He was glad he didn't have to clarify it.

That night in bed he was on fire. During the afternoon and the night he had been able to keep busy enough with homework and his job

357

to keep thoughts of Joanne at a safe distance. In fact, he didn't want to think about any of it. But now everything was quiet. Too quiet. The feel of her and the smell of her was fresh on his mind and ate away at his attempts to sleep. He had never known such animal urgency as he had experienced that afternoon with her. The passionate force that overtook him both amazed and scared him. He was ready to start ripping at clothes, then throw her in the back seat of the car and start humping the life out of his passion, mindless of time, place, or circumstance. That voracious appetite left unsatisfied was now burning inside him. He knew very little of love, sex, and passion, and he wasn't sure he liked what he was learning. It was damned uncomfortable, that was for sure.

He decided it was best not to share any of that afternoon with Alexis or anyone else for that matter. He had to sort it all out first. How could he make anyone else understand when he didn't understand himself? And the last thing he needed was lectures and advice. For now he had to calm his desire, but he wasn't sure how long it would be before he would just have to have her. After all, he'd carried her vision with him through many lonely nights for many lonely years. He was good at satisfying his own passion, but he knew that was no longer enough now that she was within his reach and so willing to share his lust.

Thomas and Brian. He didn't like her giving a name to his major impediment. He didn't like it at all. It was much easier keeping them out of the picture—pretending they didn't exist—before they had names. At least she didn't show him pictures. How could this be? How could she finally want him, desire him, and yet be so off-limits? This was more agony than he had ever experienced over her. He thought about her as a principled teenager holding him at arm's length because she wasn't ready for sex. Now she was voracious and anything-goes. He couldn't help but to think that Joanne was another Carrie Willet victim— although he had to admit a large share in the guilt. Passion and love for her aside, it wasn't with good feelings that he finally found sleep that night.

She gave him little opportunity for sorting his feelings and coming up with some answers. The next day as he walked toward the bus stop, he spotted her sitting on the bench long before he saw her car parked well down the street. By the time he saw her, she was watching him, so there was no turning back.

"Hi," she smiled as he sat down next to her.

"How long have you been here?"

"About two hours. In spite of what you might think, I don't know your schedule."

"Don't you have a baby to take care of?" He was irritable after a poor night's sleep.

"I have a nanny."

He looked at her ringless left hand and lifted it slightly in the air.

"What the hell is this, Joanne?"

"I didn't want to scare you away again."

"And you thought taking off the ring was going to make all the difference?"

"I don't know," she shrugged miserably. "I just know I can't think of anything else but you."

"You know, my parole officer is like a goddam bloodhound or something—he shows up everywhere, all the time. And he knows my schedule. If he ever came around and found me spending time alone with you, my ass is grass—as they say."

"Then," she smiled coyly as she reached in her pocket, "how about this?"

She pulled her hand out and showed him a motel room key.

"WHAT THE HELL!"

"We have a couple hours."

"What are you trying to do to me?" he asked nearly out of his mind.

"I'm trying to make up for all the bad times you've had—especially the bad times I gave you. Tell me you don't love me, Cain, and I'll go away and you'll never see me again. I just need to hear you say it."

The pained expression on his face didn't even come close to revealing the pain and confusion inside him. He slouched back on the bench for a long, silent minute while she waited patiently. He searched his mind for something clever and witty to say, but it was obvious this was not the time for clever and witty.

"You can't say it, can you?" she finally said.

He sighed and looked helplessly up at the bright, spring sky.

"No."

She beamed. She knew it.

"Okay," she said.

"Okay, what?" he asked, not nearly as cheerful as she. "Where are we now but in more of a mess than ever?"

"Let's go to my spot," she held up the key, "and get to know each other again. Whatever happens, happens."

"And whatever doesn't, doesn't?"

"Yeah, okay." She was willing to compromise.

They drove to the motel which was in an out-of-the-way spot where they wouldn't have to worry about being discovered. Even as he walked into the room, he wasn't sure what he was doing there or where he was going to go with this. All he knew was that his body was beginning to take over and make decisions for him. This was as available as his dream of a lifetime was ever going to be. How many times at Maddox had he lain alone in bed playing out a drama like this in his head?

She already had her coat off and came over to take his from him. In a numb daze he let her take the jacket from his back.

"Joanne . . ."

"Sit down," she interrupted before he could throw cold water on the moment. "There are chairs; you don't have to sit on the bed if you don't want. We don't have to go near the bed."

Feeling somewhat reprieved, he sat down on a chair. She turned on some soft music and sat on the floor in front of him.

"You like your feet rubbed," she smiled. "See, I remember. How many hours did I spend rubbing your feet?"

She started taking off his shoes.

"Joanne," he protested.

"Now," she scolded. "We're getting to know each other again. I've thought about doing this a lot in the past while you were gone."

She finished taking off his shoes and began plying her magic. He leaned over and looked her in the eye.

"I've been away a long time—without a woman."

"So what are you saying?"

"I'm not a kid any more."

"I'm counting on that."

She reached up and unbuttoned her blouse and let it drop to the floor. He could scarcely breathe as he looked at the soft curves of her breasts above the lace of her bra. She knew she had him hooked as she reached back and undid the bra, dropping it to the floor. He should have been able to hear the voice of bad experiences calling him from the past, but his blood was pounding so hotly through his body that he couldn't hear anything. As she went back to rubbing his feet, it occurred to him that in the ten years he had spent loving her, he had never seen her without her clothes—except in his fantasies and his wildest dreams. Now he realized fantasies didn't even come close to measuring up to the real thing.

As she skillfully massaged his feet, any last traces of doubt he had about being able to successfully play out this drama to the conclusion were obliterated. She slipped his socks off, and then finished undressing herself."

"Are we getting to know each other again?" she smiled.

"I'd say," he said as he pulled his shirttails out of his jeans. "And then some."

"That's right. We've been in love for what—ten years?—and we've never done anything like this before. That has to be some sort of record."

He finished unbuttoning his shirt and pulled it off, then quickly peeled off his white tee shirt. She sat seductively on the floor looking like every prisoner's dream and admired his tight, washboard stomach. That she remembered. It was the rest of him she was waiting to see.

"You know," she sighed, "I don't know what I was so afraid of before—when we were kids. All I know is that I never got over the fact that I admired your gorgeous ass for so long and yet I never **really** saw it."

Now his heart was pounding out of control. He was a runaway train. He stood up, and she helped him to ease his jeans and boxer shorts down over his narrow hips and powerful, but not overly muscular thighs. Without taking her eyes off him, she reached in a drawer nearby and tossed him a condom. She had thought of everything.

"You are so beautiful," she sighed stripping him of his last thread of resistance.

He leaned over and lifted her out from among all their discarded clothes and carried her to the bed. That was the last rational thought he had for many minutes to come.

When he was with Carrie, he had been totally inexperienced and she skillfully led him and coaxed him along. Now, though no more experienced, he was a man. There had been lots of magazines and talk at Maddox, lots of fantasy and virtual reality during long, lonely nights alone in his cell. He knew what to do and how to do it, and he did it skillfully. It was like playing baseball—make all the right moves at the right time, and you're a winner. Better than baseball—there was no loser.

He drove into her with determination, purpose, and proficiency. The familiarity of her presence and his love for her, which he had carried with him all these years, dispelled any awkwardness he might have ever feared at this first performance in his return to the world of interactive sex. She was a willing costar, and he was driven to the brink of madness as he felt her respond wildly beneath him. Carrie had always been in control before; now there was no doubt he was in command, and he was taking Joanne to places they had never before been together. Fireworks went off in his head and throughout his entire body as he climaxed and cried out with emotion that could no longer be kept inside. He had felt and delighted in the culmination of Joanne's passion, so he breathlessly let his body wind down to a stop.

Propped up on his forearms over her and trying to catch his breath, he dared to open his eyes. She still had her eyes closed, and the dreamy smile on her face confirmed his prior assumption that he had indeed pleased her. He eased forward and kissed her, but already he could feel guilt creeping back into his soul, ruining the euphoria.

She opened her eyes and looked into his rather stern, unsmiling face. Her smile faded.

"What's wrong?" she asked still under the influence of the afterglow.

"Why the fuck didn't you wait for me?" he asked her for the second time in as many days. "You are so soft and so beautiful, but you're not mine any more. I have no business being here."

He carefully rolled off her and lay back on the bed for a minute to catch the remainder of his breath. Then he got up and began dressing. After the ecstasy they had just experienced, she was taken aback by his mood and wasn't prepared to answer.

"Cain . . ."

"I gotta go," he said curtly. "People are going to start missing me—I have to account for my time."

"Okay, I understand," she said as she crawled down to the end of the bed and started kissing his bare back. "Just promise me we'll get together again soon—like this."

"Joanne . . ."

"I want to tell him," she blurted before Cain could protest any further.

"NO! For God's sake, Jo!"

"Why not? And it'll make you feel better."

"No. It won't. Christ, it's been less than a week since we've seen each other again, and you're ready to give up your marriage already?"

"It's been ten years, Cain."

"I don't care. You rushed into that marriage, don't rush out of it." He pressed the open heels of his hands against his temples in frustration. "God!"

"Okay," she said soothingly, seeing he was getting way too upset. "Okay. Relax. Just promise me we can be together like this—soon." Now he was facing her as he pulled up his jeans and zipped them. She took his hand and pressed it against her bare breast. "Please."

He didn't pull away. In fact, he eased her back on the bed and kissed her long and sensuously. Then in a sea of misery, he sat back on his heels and looked down at her.

"You're the dream of my life, and the most beautiful thing I've ever seen. I've never loved anyone else but you. I'm not even sure I could love anyone else, but I can't make promises. Just leave it at that for now. Don't jeopardize your marriage any more than you already have, and don't rush us into something we're not ready for."

"I'm ready."

"Okay, then I'm not. I'm just getting used to being home again—it's been a big step for me. And now this. I waited all this time for a second chance with you. I've been obsessed with the idea. Totally obsessed. And now . . . I just don't know."

"But you're not saying good-bye?"

"No, I'm not saying good-bye. This is all just happening too fast."

She smiled in deep relief.

"Okay," she said putting her fingertips on his lips before he could say anymore to dampen her hope. "Let me get dressed, and I'll take you home."

He was glad no one else was home when he walked in the door. He needed some time to pull himself together before he was ready to face anyone else and act normal. But he did pick up the phone and call Alexis at work.

"I need somebody to talk to," he said when he heard her voice. "Tonight. After I'm through working. Can you meet me?"

"I'll pick you up. What's wrong? Meredithe?"

"No, nothing like that. I don't want to get into it now. I'll see you at 10:00."

"Okay," she agreed. "You're not in any trouble, are you?"

"No, but I desperately need a friend."

"Then I'll see you at 10:00."


He was glad when he saw Alexis waiting for him as he left work. His port in the ever intensifying storm.

"Do you want to go somewhere?" she asked as he got in the car and closed the door.

"No. This may take a while and I'm running out of time. Just go to my house, and we'll sit in the driveway in case Meredithe calls." He smiled. "I'm a classy date, huhn?"

"I've had worse."

"Thanks for this. I'm going crazy, and I don't know who else to talk to right now."

"It's Joanne, isn't it?"

"Shit, Alexis, I don't know what to do about her anymore."

"She's been around again?"

"Yeah—yesterday and then again today."

"She's persistent."

"I haven't exactly been chasing her away."

"Before I say any more and get you hopping mad at me, why don't you tell me why you called. I'll just drive my car and listen."

"I don't know what to say. I tried drinking her out of my head, and that totally didn't work."

"So—"

"I went with her today. To a motel room."

Alexis resisted the urge to drive off the road and into a ditch. Then she closed her eyes for as long as it was safe to do so while driving a car and fought to drive her emotions underground. A friend didn't fly into a jealous, heartbroken rage upon learning such devastating news. A friend listened objectively and then gave sound advice—if asked to do so. A friend definitely was supportive.

"Oh," was all she could manage to say.

"That's it—oh?"

363

"What do you want me to say, Cain—*Good going. Go for it. Fuck your married girlfriend and maybe your parole at the same time.*"

"You don't approve," he smiled, totally missing the real reason for her outburst.

She wasn't amused. All she could think about was when things were heating up between the two of them, he quickly backed off citing conditions of his parole and his new status in society as his reasoning. She respected that and dropped out of the hunt, giving him the time he said he needed. Now she wasn't sure if she was angrier with herself or with him. She couldn't even think about Joanne, *that conniving, little bitch.* She took a breath, trying to regain her "friend" stature.

"I'm sorry," she said flatly. "Go ahead."

"That's it."

"Did everything work?" She shot a sideways glance at him knowing he would understand her question.

He smiled. "No complaints."

She was glad they were pulling into his driveway because driving had become impossible. She just couldn't look at him for fear he'd see the tears in her eyes.

"I don't know what to say," she shrugged purposely looking out the driver's side window.

"I'll be back in a minute. I want to go in and let them know I'm home in case I get a call."

She watched him hurry to his house. She wanted to break down in miserable sobs, but that would have to wait. Right now she needed to recover. Quickly she wiped the tears from her eyes and forced herself to accept the cold facts that he was laying at her feet—Joanne was more in the picture than ever. She cursed herself for getting so involved with him since he'd been home; she had never planned on falling in love with him. She opened the window to let the cold night air revive her senses, and soon he was back in the car with her—too absorbed in someone else to realize what was going on with her.

"I don't know what to tell you," she said. "I guess I'm not sure if you just want to hear yourself say some of these things out loud, or if you want interaction from me."

"I don't know what I want. I don't know which way is up. I've never been so in heaven and in hell at the same time."

"Have you ever met Thomas?"

"No."

"He's a very nice man; he adores her and the baby."

"You're not being much of a help."

"Oh, I get it—you want my blessing. You're looking for someone to tell you it's okay no matter who you hurt along the way. You want me to celebrate with you because you got your sex life back on track, and you performed like a champion stud."

"No."

"Then what, Cain?"

"I don't know, but I wasn't expecting such hostility."

Alexis stared pensively out the front window of the car. He was right—she was acting more like a jealous lover than a caring friend. That would never do.

"I'm sorry," she said.

"I know how you feel, and, God knows, I know I'm wrong. That's the whole problem. What the hell do I do?"

"I can't tell you that," she said looking him square in the eye. "Besides, I think you already know."

"Okay," he conceded. Then he broke her heart with his sincerity. "Now tell me how. How do I walk away from something I've waited almost half my life for? I love her, Alexis, and I don't know how to stop—especially when she's always right there telling me she loves me."

"She turned her back on you when you needed her the most," said Alexis gently trying to remind him of Joanne's poor track record.

"I know." He dropped his head and studied his hands.

"I'm telling you this as a friend now—I'm not attacking or being hostile, just realistic: she's selfish, or she'd leave you alone. She knows she's not available, but she keeps coming around making herself irresistible. She's going to end up hurting you, Thomas, and even that little baby who has no say in any of this. She's torturing you; I can see it. And who knows what she's doing to her husband at home. All in the name of what makes Joanne happy this month. If she really loved you, she wouldn't drag you into this tawdry, little mess she's created. You said it yourself—she comes looking for you."

He covered his face with his hands and wearily rubbed his eyes, then the rest of his face. Will stuck his head out the door and called to Cain. Meredithe was on the phone.

"Damn it!" said Cain. He turned to Alexis. His voice was pleading. "Can you wait? He doesn't usually keep me long."

"Of course."

"Do you want to come in?"

"No, go ahead."

"Lock your doors; I'll be right back."

She smiled at his concern. Now if only he wasn't blind.

She sat and looked at the beautiful Queen Anne Victorian house with the wrap around porch. She had always loved that house. It was over one hundred years old, completely renovated and in mint condition. She wondered about the generations of people who had lived there before the Farrells. She wondered about people who would come in the future.

The future. That was a place she didn't really want to go right then. The present was too much of a jumble which left the view of the future hazy and way too uncertain. It was better to just let the future unfold minute by minute because if she looked too far ahead, all she could see was Cain tumbling passionately with Joanne—falling deeper and deeper into a spell he couldn't break.

She squeezed her eyes shut to dispel the image that was burning itself into the windshield of her car. She was relieved to see Cain coming back out of his house. Her heart pounded as she switched to her "friend" cap again.

"I'd like to say we could leave and I'd buy you a cup of coffee or ice cream or something," he said as he got in and closed the door, "but sometimes he calls back in ten minutes, or a half-hour, or an hour. Sometimes he doesn't call back at all. It's not usual, but there was a night when he called me four times in an hour and twice again before 6:00 A.M. He makes damn sure I have the message that I'd better not leave the house after 11:00."

"Isn't that harassment?"

"Who am I going to complain to who would care?"

"I guess you have a point."

"My mom says she'll make coffee, or we have Coke or something."

"No. Thanks. I'm fine."

"They don't know why we don't go inside, but I think this time it's better if we stay out here."

"Me, too."

She was careful not to sound too agreeable. She was thankful for the darkness for she wasn't sure what he would read on her face if he could see her in full light.

"I should let you go," he said to her. "I feel guilty about keeping you out this late, and then I can't even drive you home to see that you got there safely."

"There are nights when I'm out with my friends that I come home by myself much later than this. Besides, I don't think we're finished here."

"Stop loving Joanne! How does that sound?" he said. "And you thought I was stupid."

Even in the dark she didn't miss the pain that accompanied the dashing smile. She smiled back through pain of her own.

"I'm sorry if I hurt you tonight," she said. "I didn't mean to. I get carried away sometimes."

"No, you're right. Everything you said is right. That's why I called you. I needed someone I could trust who wouldn't let me rationalize the shit out of a totally srewed-up situation. Scott would have done that for me—and not as nicely as you have." He smiled again. "Matt or Sean, too, but I didn't want to put them in an awkward position with my parents—so I figure it's better if they don't know right now. You're my best friend, Alexis. Please don't hate me because of all this."

"Hey," she said feeling it would be acceptable to let him see her tears after such a touching declaration, "I could never hate you, honey.

You've become very . . . important . . . to me, too. I'm happy I can be here since Scott can't. And you're right about your brothers."

He sighed as if the weight of all his misery was crushing him. He stared blankly out the windshield.

"I've been trying to stop loving her for six years—almost to the day. What am I doing wrong?"

"Love is a funny thing," she said with new insight of her own. "It should make you happy, but too often that isn't the case. Maybe because we love the wrong person—or—the right person loves someone else."

He let her words take seed. She waited, giving him time to work through his thought.

"She said she doesn't really love her husband—she wants to leave him." He was staring holes through the windshield.

Alexis gasped, not realizing Joanne had gone that far off the deep end, but she recovered quickly to help him through the thoughts that were fighting to take form in his mind.

"This is not an admonition," she explained, "just something to think about: could you be happy with that?"

His stare had become so intense that he was nearly in a trance.

"I've been asking myself the same question," he said without breaking the spell. "I used to think nothing mattered as long as I got her back. I used to lay in bed at night and **ache** with the thought of taking her back and proving she was mine all along. For endless years of endless nights, that's all I thought about. The frustration of not being able to get to her almost drove me crazy. But I did good after I came back."

"Yes, you did," she encouraged. "You left her alone until she made the move and didn't give you the choice. She knows exactly what she's doing."

"Then I think, what can I offer her, anyway?"

"WHAT?!" said Alexis in disbelief.

He turned from the window for the first time and looked at her like she had been away on Mars.

"She has everything right now. I'll be twenty-four next month, and I'm an ex-convict, sex-offender, janitor working my way through a bachelor's degree. Even if Meredithe would let me, I couldn't even afford to support myself. They won't let me anywhere near an elementary or a high school—not even to watch a program or attend a family night open house."

"Okay," she said, "take a deep breath and give yourself a break. None of that will matter to anyone who **really** loves you. Because you're not really a sex-offender. It's all bogus."

"Yeah, but there are only a handful of people left who still believe that anymore. A lot of the old people who knew me and believed in me have moved on, so to most people I know now, I'm an ex-con who speaks little, if at all, about my crime or my recent past. So I have to prove myself all over again to most of society, and there will always be that lingering doubt when people look at me. I see it in their eyes all the time. My point: what kind of a life is that to offer anyone?"

"You're beautiful, talented, brilliant, sensitive, caring, genuine, unassuming . . . I could go on. My point: who cares about anything else?"

A grateful, almost shy, smile turned up the corners of his mouth. He reached across the back of the car seat and fingered a few locks of her hair.

"Thank you," he said softly. He eased her head toward him as he leaned forward and kissed her on the forehead. "And you'd better get going. It's getting late."

"Feel any better?" she asked as she steadied her voice and tried to sound normal in the wake of the pristine kiss.

"I have a lot to think about. It's clearer now but not any easier."

"Okay, sleep on it—and get that world-class brain of yours out of your lap and back up into your head where it belongs."

He smiled. "Lock the doors." Then he was gone.

# CHAPTER 17

He hadn't seen Joanne over the next few days. He wasn't sure if it was because he had been waiting till the last minute to run for the bus and therefore had missed her, or if she had mis-timed his last classes. Maybe she was busy. Maybe she was avoiding him. He forced the thought of all the options out of his mind, and tried to resume his life. One thing he had firmly promised himself—he would **not** go looking for her. He was having a hard enough time living with his renewed relationship with her, without going and looking for trouble. So he worked on shoring up his emotional and physical resolve during the respite she was giving him—whatever the reason.

"I have a favor to ask you," said Matt over the weekend when they were together.

"What's that?"

"Melanie has a friend. She's really nice, and quite pretty."

"Oh, no," said Cain rejecting Matt's proposal before he even made it.

"Wait, hear me out. She recently broke up with her boyfriend. She's invited to a wedding we're going to next Saturday . . ."

"All four of us!" Cain was incredulous. "How quaint. I'm way beyond *The Bobsey Twins Go on a Date*."

"Come on," frowned Matt. "She hasn't had time to get back into the dating scene, and she doesn't want to go to the wedding alone. And you could use a little female diversion."

*If you only knew.*

"Can I give her your number?" Matt asked when Cain didn't respond.

"You're forgetting one thing."

"What?"

"I'm not allowed to be a social being—I have to be in the house by 11:00 **every** night, no exceptions."

"I know. She knows about that."

"Oh great," laughed Cain ironically. "This is sounding more and more like something I'd love to do."

"So you're going to be a jerk about it?"

"Is that what I'm being?"

"Yeah—life-sized."

Cain sighed in frustration and looked away from his brother.

"She's a nice girl, Cain. She doesn't care about your record; she wants an escort to a wedding. You'll be with us; and if we're having a good time, we can go back to Mom's at 11:00—the pool table's there and everything."

"And what about this? What about if I don't even care about myself; what if there are people there who know who I am—where I've been? How is she going to feel about being there with me? See, I feel like I'm this social albatross around people's necks. I'd rather die than embarrass anyone like that—and you and Melanie, too. It's bad enough you have to look like me, let alone drag me around with you."

Now it was Matt's turn to feel frustration.

"Look," he said, "don't you think we've thought about that? Melanie and I don't care; we care about you, not other people. And Kristen—that's her name—knows your story and still wants to call you. It was only fair to both of you to be up front with her. She shrugged it off and said it sounded like fun. Come on, you have a pretty lady who doesn't care about your past and wants to get to know you. There won't be any awkward questions about how and when to tell her. She knows; she doesn't care. Get out and have a little fun. I mean, you've said you and Alexis aren't . . ."

"I know. We're not." *But I'm seeing Joanne.* "Let me think about it; I'll let you know tomorrow."

He had to admit the thought intrigued him. He needed to breathe some fresh air, and his all-work-and-very-little-play existence was beginning to take its toll. Maybe he'd even stop thinking about Joanne for a few hours, or at least a few minutes.

Just as he was about to talk himself into it, the Devil's Advocate made his intrusion into Cain's thought process. He hadn't been out in polite society for a long time—in fact, never as an adult. Would people understand if they should recognize who he was? No matter what family and friends said about not caring what others thought, they hadn't been put to the acid test—the scrutiny and criticism of the self-righteous. How could he put people he cared about in that precarious situation—in spite of what they say? Hadn't it been bad enough with him in prison? And what would this girl's family think if they knew she was going out—no matter how innocently and well chaperoned—with a convicted rapist, an ex-con? What if they were having a really good time and they all had to leave early because of his curfew? Talk about feeling like a grounded adolescent. And worst of all, what if little seeds of doubt sprouted and started choking out all her good intentions and she ended up being afraid of him?

He realized that even though he had started making some kind of a life for himself outside the walls of Maddox, he still had a long way to go. Walls and barbed wire still existed in his head, which in many ways was more confining than the real thing. Still, he was not one to run away from adversity. He knew the problem would not correct itself; he needed to make a valiant effort. The alternative was to not move forward, and that was definitely not acceptable.

The decision being made, he felt good. He even found himself mildly looking forward to it.

"I need you to go shopping with me," he told Alexis on Sunday night when she called him.

"Okay," she smiled. "What are we shopping for?"

"A suit for me. I usually go shopping with Matt so we don't buy the same thing, but I want a woman's opinion."

"Sounds intriguing. What's the occasion?"

"I have a date. Well, sort of."

"Oh." She was glad he couldn't see her face. "With who?"

"She's a friend of my sister-in-law—Melanie. It's not a real date. I've never really even met her."

"That sounds . . . interesting."

She fought to put a smile in her voice. Why couldn't she just tell him how she felt? She had tried so many times, but the words just wouldn't come. She had the sense he didn't feel the same, and she did have her pride. The steamy kisses of that first night after he had come home from Maddox had evolved into a beautiful, though platonic, friendship. Somehow friendship and sex didn't coexist for Cain. She guessed he was desperately attempting to replace Scott in his life—a role that he had already told her she was fulfilling. It hadn't dawned on him, though, that there were fringe benefits when his best friend just happened to be a willing, available woman. But, she needed it to be his idea, so she would be happy to be the harbor he ran to when he felt the need for emotional intimacy and shelter from the storms in his life.

This was a new aspect in her role as his harbor, however. She had to be happy for him as he was drifting toward someone else. With Joanne it was easy because she could scold him and be truthful about what a damaging situation that was. She could coax him back to the harbor, away from the siren on the rocks. But this was hard, and it had sneaked up on her without warning. She couldn't help but hear the enthusiasm in his voice as he told her the details and plans.

"So when did you want to go shopping?" she asked finally getting him to shut up about it all.

"I don't have very much time. I was thinking of asking Charlie if he could give me a night off without telling Meredithe. I don't know if he would, but I think he might."

"No," she said, "don't take a chance. With your luck Meredithe will call or make a visit to work that night. I have vacation time. Why don't I take a day next week when you're through with classes early? I could pick you up after your class, and we could go then."

She liked that idea because she knew that was when he usually met Joanne—this would give him one less opportunity. She was even happier when he agreed without a second thought to Joanne.

Joanne wasn't one to miss an opportunity, however, so it was no surprise when she was waiting for Cain on Monday after his last class. He could see the bus coming a way down the road.

"Hop in," she said. Then she smiled slyly. "I have another key. A different place this time. I thought it's best if we keep moving around."

"Sounds a little sleazy, doesn't it?" he said.

"You're the one who wants to keep it a secret still."

"It makes sense, Jo. But the bus is coming, and I have to get home. I have a lot of homework, and I have to work in a while."

"You don't even have an hour for me?"

"Not today."

"I already paid for a room."

"Did you ever think of asking me first? It's a little presumptuous just going out and getting a room, isn't it?"

"You liked it last time."

"That was last time. I haven't seen or heard from you in almost a week. And now you show up with a key, and I'm supposed to jump in and go along. Here's the bus."

"Wait, Cain. At least let me take you home."

He had to make a split second decision. His heart still in command, he got into the car.

"So," she said, "where do we go? This key is burning a hole in my pocket."

He rubbed his face, trying to give his will power a chance to surface.

"It's late, Joanne, and I have a lot of homework."

"Okay," she pouted as she pulled away from the curb and headed toward his home. "I was being over-anxious—not presumptuous. I just wanted to be with you so bad, and I haven't been able to get away until now. And I thought you'd probably kill me if I called your house."

"You're right," he smiled. "That's all I need."

"Then your parents don't know we're seeing each other?"

"No." Then a white lie. "Nobody does."

"Oh." She was a little disappointed. "You haven't even wanted to confide in Matt or a close friend?"

"Matt's too close to home, and I don't have many friends." He looked over at her with a sideways look. "Scott's gone, and my other friends have moved on with their lives."

She didn't miss his point, nor did she comment on it.

"So when can we get together again?" She asked changing the subject. "You're all I can think about."

He thought about Alexis and all the sense she had laid out before him. But he was in love, and even Alexis should know that the centers for love and commonsense were located in different parts of the body, operating independently of one another.

"I really do have a lot of work today, and tomorrow I have plans after school, so Wednesday or Thursday?"

"Wednesday," she beamed. "I'll meet you at the bus stop?"

"It's as good a spot as any," he shrugged. "You haven't said anything to anybody, have you?"

"Well just my one, really close girlfriend."

"I wish you hadn't," he frowned, though he was relieved she hadn't gone ahead and told her husband as she had said she was going to do.

"She's **very** discreet and completely trustworthy. I had to tell someone, or I would have burst with my feelings for you. I had to brag about you a little bit."

"Just keep one thing in mind—I'm dead if my Parole Officer gets a hold of this. He doesn't like me much, and he'd like nothing better than to bust my ass."

"Okay," she said remorsefully. "I'll be very careful, but you don't have to worry about Carol, really."

"You be sure," he said with dead seriousness. "I'm not real comfortable trusting my freedom to someone I don't even know."

"I'll tell her, okay?" she said soothingly. "Don't worry. I wouldn't do anything to hurt you."

For the rest of the day, an uncomfortable feeling kept creeping into his chest whenever he thought about Joanne brimming over with news of their love and wanting to share it. Why hadn't he thought to be more explicit with her about his situation and the consequences of what he was doing? There was something hauntingly familiar about this relationship that was taking seed in his mind, and he didn't like it. But this time he was in love. With Carrie Willet it had been pure lust and adventure, a coming of age. This was different. He had come back to reclaim what should have been his all along; he just needed some time to figure out the best way to do it. In the meantime he had to be sure he kept Joanne in control of matters.

He knew he could trust Alexis, but painfully aware of her disapproval, he thought it best not to bring it up when she picked him up at school the next morning to go shopping. However, when she asked, he valued her friendship too much to lie. He told her about his plans for the next day.

"No comment?" he said as she continued driving, her eyes riveted on the road.

"What more can I say to you? You don't listen anyway."

"I listen."

"Not very well," she laughed ironically.

"I don't feel like I can talk to you about this any more."

"No," she relented, "please don't feel that way. I'm here for you—okay?" Then she grinned mischievously. "And this time I promise to come visit you in prison."

"Christ," he sighed as the sick feeling flooded him again. "I mean, is this fair that I could actually go to jail for this?"

"Was it fair the last time?"

Alexis had a way of nailing things on the head.

"Let's don't talk about Joanne anymore, or I'm going to have to go home and throw up."

"Love is grand," laughed Alexis. She loved him more everyday, the big, dumb, gorgeous idiot.


Being alone with Joanne in the motel room on Wednesday drove all other thoughts from Cain's head. All he knew was he came alive in a way that was foreign to the rest of his existence. He couldn't get enough of her.

"Let's just stay here forever," he said as they lay in the bed, his arm around her, his body spent and yet deliciously alive.

"We have to eat sometime," she grinned.

"That's what room service is for. Besides, I like this a whole lot better than eating."

"You never were a voracious eater. That's why your body is so free of fat and flab." She rolled to her side and began kissing his shoulders and chest. "And I have a surprise."

"What?"

"Well, Thomas is going to be out of town all weekend—a convention or something. Sooooo, I thought I could get us a room on Saturday, and we could make love all day until you have to be home. Then I could pick you up Sunday morning for an early breakfast, and we could come back to the room and spend the rest of the day together—mostly in bed."

The proposition was inviting. But . . .

"I can't."

"Oh." She was duly disappointed. "Why not?"

"I'm going with Matt and Melanie to a wedding on Saturday."

She kissed down his chest seductively until she reached his navel. Then with the tip of her tongue, she traced little patterns on his stomach. It was truly a persuasive tactic.

"That shouldn't be too hard to get out of," she said knowing she was driving him crazy. "It's not a family thing, is it?"

More little patterns.

"No," he said barely able to speak.

"There you go. Just tell them you have too much homework or something."

The patterns were getting closer to the mark.

"I can't," he said ready to ease her back on the bed and relieve the fire she was igniting in him.

*I can't.* That wasn't at all the answer she was looking for or expecting. She stopped the tease, mid-pattern.

"I don't get it." She was all seriousness. "Why not?"

He wasn't sure he liked the way she had suddenly become so demanding, and the fire abated some. He pulled the pillows up against the headboard and eased himself to a semi-sitting position.

"I have a date," he said not caring to continue the verbal cat-and-mouse.

"With a girl?!"

"Those are the best kind," he smiled impishly.

"Cain!" Now she was sitting bolt upright. "What about **us**?!"

"What **about** us?"

"How could you make a date with someone else?"

"Excuse me, don't you have a husband out there somewhere in Never, Never Land?"

"That's different."

"It is?"

"Yes!" Her brow was furled in an angry pout.

"Do you know how it makes me feel laying in bed every night thinking of you home in bed with someone else?"

"Thomas and I haven't done **anything** in weeks."

"I'm not going to do **anything** Saturday night, so what's the problem?"

"Cain, it's not the same, and you know it! What are you trying to do, punish me for having a husband?"

"No. I'm just trying to have fun. She asked me to go, and I thought—why not?"

"Well," said Joanne not ready to give up, "we could have fun. All you have to do is break the date." She ran her finger playfully along the inside of his naked thigh. "Tell her something came . . . up."

He hated that he even considered it for a moment.

"No, I can't do that, and you'd better stop playing with me, or I'm going to lay you back and give you just what you're asking for?"

"What," she said more as a statement than a question as she reached for a vengeful, emotional dagger to strike back at him, "you're going to rape me?"

As soon as she had said it, she regretted it. His face had been playfully serious before; now it was deadly serious. She couldn't remember the last time she had seen that anger in his eyes directed toward her. Maybe never. She had always been in the driver's seat of their relationship—especially since Carrie Willet—but now he was in full command, and she hated herself. Without a word, he maneuvered out of the bed and started dressing.

"Cain . . ." she pleaded with tears in her eyes.

"Don't . . . say . . . anything," he said without even looking at her.

"Listen," she persisted as tears flowed. "I'm so sorry. I was just jealous . . . and angry. I wasn't thinking."

By this time Cain was pulling his sweater over his head and heading toward the chair for his shoes and socks. His mind was a blitzkrieg of emotion. He couldn't think straight; he couldn't believe the domino-effect collapse that his senses were experiencing. He had known the transition from convicted rapist to ardent lover had been too smooth. How arrogant of him to think he could achieve some form of normalcy. Then five words sent him into a tailspin. How stupid of him. STUPID!

"Get dressed, Joanne. I'm not walking out of here and leaving you alone. I may have spent a quarter of my life in a state penitentiary, but I'm not a total boor."

"If that's the case, then you need to take a minute to listen to me because I'm not ready to leave yet."

He interrupted the act of tying his shoes to look up at her. Unspeakable pain, not anger any more, veiled his face. She grabbed her over-sized sweater and pulled it on. This was not a time to try and distract him with sex.

"Hey," she said sitting on the floor at his feet, "I didn't mean to hurt you. I just can't stand the thought of you being with someone else."

"That's almost funny, you know?" he said with a frown.

"I know," she admitted. "But I'm not the one who started all this with us—way back."

"And I haven't been punished enough for that? Are you ever going to let me put it behind me?"

Now the anger was returning to his eyes as he got up and walked passed her to the mirror. He busied himself with fingering his hair into some sort of acceptable style.

"I'm sorry," she said nearing frustration. "I just keep saying the wrong things."

"Maybe that's not it," said Cain turning from the mirror and looking at her. "Maybe we just have too much history between us to try and make a go of things now."

"What are you saying?"

"I'm saying that you still haven't worked beyond the Carrie Willet thing, and I'm definitely fucked-up over your husband thing. Neither of which is a small issue."

"I know." She was nearing panic as she realized the direction the conversation was taking. "That's why we need more time."

"How much time do you think it's going to take, Jo? Because I've spent enough of my life clawing my way out of a quagmire of mistakes and regrets. The more time I spend with you, the more complicated I realize our situation is. I feel like I'm getting sucked into something that's causing me way more pain than pleasure."

"Just because I said the 'R' word?!"

He couldn't believe her. He had already forgotten she had made that blunder. That was something he could work through; the rest of it, however, was looming large on his horizon. Just like when he had gotten arrested, she couldn't see the big picture. She focused in on one aspect of it and then beat it to death. He just stared at her.

"Cain, I'm sorry. Come on, let's go back to bed, and I'll make it up to you. And I won't bring up **that** word or Carrie Willet or anything that causes you pain."

"Until the next time you get mad at me and need to lash out."

"You're not making this easy," she sighed.

"That's the whole point! It isn't easy. It's way too complicated, in fact."

"What we do in bed isn't complicated."

"**What** we do in bed doesn't have a thing to do with it! Damn it, Joanne! It's the fact that we're doing it, and we have no right to be. Not while things are all so tangled up between us."

"Oh, Christ, Cain! Since when did you become such a saint? You thought nothing of cheating on me in high school, and now . . ."

"Stop right there," he said with a note of finality. "*High school* is the key word there. If you can't see a difference between then and now, there's no sense in continuing this conversation. The way I see it, you're going to keep beating me up for that adolescent stupidity, and I don't need it. I've beaten myself up enough for it, and I've been through too much because of it. And now I'm wondering what the hell I'm doing. You make me think too much, Jo. And thinking totally devalues the benefits of sex."

"Then why the hell didn't you think more when you were with Carrie Willet?!"

"See what I mean?" he said without getting angry. "We're back to Carrie Willet."

"Okay," she said more as a way of ending the fatal discussion than as an agreement, "let me get dressed and we'll leave. I think we need a break right now. We'll work it out; it'll just take time."

Not wanting to inflict any more brutality on the dead horse their conversation had become, he wisely chose not to comment. Feeling a need to put some distance between them, he put on his coat.

"I'll be waiting outside."

On the way to the Farrells, she talked incessantly—almost as if something terrible would happen if she stopped. Cain stared out the side window, now and then adding only the slightest remark to remain polite. He wasn't sure what to do. He only knew this wasn't the way it was supposed to be; the way it had been in all his dreams.

"Okay?" she asked.

"Okay, what?" he answered, realizing he was way too distracted for the gravity of the situation.

"Thanks for taking this so seriously."

"I'm sorry," he frowned. "Just tell me what you said."

"I said I think we should wait a day before we see each other again."

"A day? You think everything's going to turn around in a day?"

"I'll pick you up Friday. We can just talk if you want."

"I can't do anything on Friday; I have to go into the city to meet with my parole officer. Then I work."

"Jesus, Cain, do you ever have time to just be you?"

"No, that's my life, and I got news for you—it's going to be my life for a long time to come."

"Fine, then I'll pick you up, we'll have lunch, and I'll take you in to the city—or better yet, we'll ride the train in together and have lunch downtown."

Cain sighed.

"No."

She looked at him as if he'd slapped her.

"That's something I need to do by myself," he continued. "It's not a walk in the park."

"I know, but I could go with you."

"I don't want him to know about you."

"Okay," she whined, "so I'll stay out of sight somewhere, and you'll meet me."

He looked at her for a long minute. Her blonde hair, her soft blues eyes, and the hint of pink on her cheeks. He must be crazy.

"Just come by one day next week," he sighed. "I don't care which one. We'll talk then."

Now it was she who was pensive.

"Is it this other girl—this friend of Melanie's?"

He dropped his head back against the seat.

"I haven't even met her, Jo. I can't think about this anymore. I feel like we've talked it to death for now. You can drop me off here if you want, and I'll walk the rest of the way. Then I'll see you next week—if you want—I'll leave it up to you. I'm sorry."

"This sounds like good-bye."

"Just stop the car and let me out. I said I'll see you next week."

"If I want. What about you?"

His laugh was frustration verbalized.

"That's what I've been trying to tell you—I don't know about me. I need some space. Please let me out."

"No," she relented. "Relax, I'll take you home. I won't bother you anymore."

He wanted to scream; but instead, he put his head back and closed his eyes for the remainder of the trip. There was no sense trying to reason with the unreasonable.

When he got home, he had homework he should have done, but both his mind and body were taxed to the maximum and he desperately needed an escape. Tactfully brushing off his mother's questions about how he had spent the early afternoon, he went up to catch an hour or two of power sleep before he had to be at work.

It was after work when Alexis called him that he began dissecting the remnants of the hours spent with Joanne that day. Somehow he knew he had to come to terms with that relationship, but he didn't know where to begin. He knew Alexis could help him sort through it, but in the end it was all up to him. Nobody could make a final decision and then live it out for him.

"I don't know what to tell you," Alexis wisely said after he had related an account of the day. "We've been through this before, and I'm not sure you're ready to listen to anyone but your heart."

"How do I stop that?"

"I don't know. If I did, I could make a million dollars selling my secret. You just have to ask yourself what's going to make **you** happy. You can't go back in time. Like it or not, Joanne got married and had a baby. That's the situation you need to deal with. And I don't know how wise it is to keep on seeing her the way you are. Things like that have a way of getting out."

"Shit," he sighed, "I have to break it off. That's becoming clearer by the day. I'm just not sure how to let go. It seems our relationship has done a full turn. Before we just always were together and we had fun without sex. Now we can hardly ever be together, and when we are, the sex is the only good part."

Alexis shuttered at the thought. If he only knew what he was doing to her.

"And you see this getting better in the near future?"

"No."

She knew how it hurt him to admit that, and her heart broke. But he was asking for her help and she had to continue.

"Sweetheart," she said softly, "you've been in love with a fantasy for six years now. You wouldn't be the first person to realize that fantasy rarely has anything to do with reality. In fact, only in the rarest of incidents can reality measure up. Just listening to you, I don't think this is one of those times."

Those were the words that stayed with him over the next few days. It was good that he didn't see Joanne because the fragile realization needed to take root and be nourished to some sort of vitality in order to maintain a life of its own. She always seemed to be able to trample the seedlings of his resolve.

Sunday was one of those glorious days in early spring where the sun shone warmly and tempted everyone to the outdoors to drink it in. Cain rode his bike over to the small lake near his house to meet Alexis for a walk.

As he rode, he thought about the cramped spaces he had roamed at Maddox on days like this. Now the wind was breezing past him, soft and warm. And it smelled good. There was nowhere to go at Maddox that didn't have the stale, rank smell of close confinement. He hadn't smelled fresh springtime in the air since before he had left, and then he had taken it for granted. His senses were all fine-tuned these days, and nothing got passed him unnoticed or unappreciated. Freedom was the most amazing gift.

Alexis didn't bring up Joanne. It wasn't a pleasant topic for either of them, and she felt Cain needed a break. But she did want to hear about the wedding.

"It was really nice," he smiled as they walked leisurely.

"And Kristen?"

He smiled reflectively.

"That was good."

"Good?" She didn't know if she liked that or not.

"It was nice being with someone who was simple and uncomplicated. And she is really pretty—but I don't even care about that anymore."

"I'm happy you had a good time. You deserve it."

"And they didn't even play *Jailhouse Rock*," he smiled. "That's one of the really big, irrational fears in my life—I'm going to be at a wedding or a party and that song's going to come blasting over the speakers, and everyone's going to turn and look at me."

"You're something else," she laughed. "Nobody but you would think about that."

"Don't make fun of me," he pouted playfully.

"I'm not," she smiled with adoration written all over her face. How could he miss it? "So are you going to see her again—Kristen?"

"I don't know," he said losing the smile. "It's really not fair to her until I do something about Joanne."

"I wasn't going to bring that up," Alexis said.

"I appreciate that, but the fact of the matter is I can't ignore it. I'm going to tell her—the next time I see her . . ."

". . . before she gets you in bed."

". . . before she gets me in bed." He smiled diffidently. "I'm not going to get that far; we'll talk at the bus stop or in her car. I know my limitations."

Alexis grinned.

"So, are you going to tell me what you're going to say, or would you rather not?"

"I'm going to tell her that I can't be with her any more. I don't want to ascribe blame, but this isn't ten years ago."

"Are you going to be able to say that?"

He was staring off across the lake. Tears perched on his eyelashes as he nodded.

"I have to. I'm driving myself crazy. I just wish it didn't hurt so bad."

She took a hold of his hand and squeezed it. Then she lifted it to her lips and kissed it.

"I wish it didn't either. With that face you should do nothing but smile and laugh and turn on the whole world. You've had enough hurt for a lifetime."

Now it was his turn to kiss her hand.

"Thanks. I'd never get through this without you."

"Hey," she said before her knees buckled from under her, "I have news."

"Good," smiled Cain. "It gets boring talking about me all the time."

"Honey, your life is anything but boring."

"So, what's your news?"

"Well . . . I have a date for dinner tomorrow night."

"Hey. All right." Enthusiasm; no sign of disappointment or jealousy. "Who is it?"

"He's one of our clients. He comes into the office once in a while, but I talk to him on the phone a lot. He's asked me out before, but even after Jared and I broke up—soon after you came home . . ." She looked up at him. No indication that he had put two-and-two together to get anything but two hundred-seventy-two. "Well anyway, I really haven't cared to date much lately. I've had a few dates, but nothing to really talk about. And then when he called the other day, I thought—why not?"

"Good," he said with the most genuine smile she had ever seen. "Does this mean he might be kind of special? You've never really talked about any of your other dates before."

"Yeah," she said with a little conviction, "he could be. But I don't know; I'm kind of hung up on somebody else."

Cain looked amused, like he had opened a new door in their friendship.

"Jared?"

"No, someone else, but that's another story. Maybe someday I'll tell it to you."

"Come on," he prompted, "I tell you everything."

"I know, but I choose to keep this one to myself for now."

"Do I know him?"

"Not now, Cain."

"I know it's not my brother."

"No," she laughed as he blundered through the trees in search of the forest. "I'll tell you someday. I just don't want to talk about it now. And a real friend would be cool enough to drop it."

"Okay, but it's going to bug me. How long do I have to wait?"

"I don't know." She laughed.

He looked down at her. Her green eyes were dancing with the secret as her long strawberry/vanilla locks were being stroked by the wind. Her creamy complexion had just the slightest dusting of powdered cinnamon freckles across the bridge of her nose. *How could any guy she was hung up on not want to sweep her off her feet and love her forever?*

"Does this guy know you have a thing for him?" He wasn't completely stupid.

"I thought we were dropping it."

"Humor me."

"I don't know; I don't think so."

"Well that explains it. I was just thinking he was some kind of an idiot, but you have to let him know, for God's sake."

"He is some kind of an idiot. And if he's too stupid to figure it out, then I'm not going to be the one to tell him."

"Do you want me to tell him?"

"No," she was nearing hysterical laughter. This was the most fun she had ever had toying with him. Then she became serious again. "I have my pride, Cain. I don't want to have to pry someone's eyes opened. I want a guy with his eyes wide opened who can't see anything but me."

She loved the look on his face as he seriously contemplated what she was saying.

"I guess you're right." He conceded.

"I know I'm right. Thank you for caring so much."

"He doesn't deserve you," he said with a sincerity and gentleness that almost took her breath.

Cain spent the next days keeping himself focused on the only possible path to follow with Joanne and at the same time dreading when he'd have to travel it with her. He knew what he had to do; he just didn't know if he could do it. When he was with her, all logic and reason was on vacation. Things had been building to a pitch, though, and there was no way out. He knew that for a fact. He had been over every possible avenue in his mind, and each one ended in an abrupt dead end—right off the side of a cliff. And he couldn't deny the knot that had taken up residence in the pit of his stomach. The only good thing was the love they shared in bed, and that was nothing to build a relationship on— especially when they had to tear another relationship apart before they could even begin the building process. Much of his life had been a huge uphill battle, and this was just one more mountain.

It all made perfect sense inside his head. Now if he could just get passed his desire and long-time love for her. For all the sense it made, it hurt like hell; and he knew it was going to get worse before it was over.

Everyday as he left school, he held his breath to see if she was waiting; but he had asked for time, and she seemed to be giving him some. Well, a little, anyway. On Wednesday, he turned the corner and saw her sitting on the bench at the bus stop. He mumbled some sort of prayerful plea for strength, and went on to see if there was still a God.

"Hi," she smiled as he walked up and sat down next to her. "I waited a week; I hope that was enough space. I couldn't stay away any longer."

"Could we go for a walk?" he asked. "There's a park right down the block. Maybe we could sit there. It's a little more out-of-the-way."

"Okay," she said taking note of his business-like composure. Her heart took nervous flight.

He took her hand as they walked and he held it tight. She took that as a good sign. But he didn't say a word. She took that as a bad sign. He reached in his pocket and felt the key chain that Mike had given him. Hoping to gain strength from it, he fingered it nervously. This was a death of sorts, and he faced it with no less trepidation than the real thing.

They found a bench in the warm sunlight. Cain was glad there was no one else around except for a few mothers and babies across the way at the playground. He still couldn't get used to the idea of Joanne being a wife and mother. He put his backpack on the ground and sat down next to her.

"So what've you been up to?" she asked, fearing she knew what he was about to say and trying to subvert him.

"Jo," he said totally ignoring the question, "I can't do this anymore." Tears flooded his eyes, but he forced himself to go on. "You were the first and the only love of my life, but I can't claim you as mine anymore. And I'm not blaming you. You had every right to move on, and I'm sorry if I've made you feel bad about that. I'm the one who screwed it all up. It's all my fault, and I hate myself for it—more at this minute than at any other time." Tears flowed freely down his face as he stared ahead and searched for the softest words he could find.

"Hey," she said as her own tears broke loose, "it's all right; it's fixable. I told you that. Don't worry; I'll take care of it all. I don't even have to mention your name. I'll just tell him I don't love him anymore, and I want to be on my own. We'll have to stay apart for a while, but then after a reasonable amount of time, you can enter the picture. That way no one will associate you with the divorce. It'll be like we just happened to get together after the fact. It'll work—I have it all figured out. You just have to trust me."

There was no sudden relief or congratulatory look on his face. The grief and tears were more intense if anything. She started to panic.

"I'm so sorry," was all he could say. "It's not fixable. It's in a million pieces. If I could do this in some way that didn't hurt, I would. I don't want to hurt you—I've done enough of that already."

"Exactly what are you saying, Cain?" she cried.

"In a few minutes, I'm going to get up and walk away, and that's going to close the chapter on you and me. I can't see you anymore."

"No!" she cried as her lip quivered. "You're the only one I've ever loved, too. I know that now. It's NOT too late."

"It is for me. I can't get passed these six years. I don't know, Joanne, I thought this was what I wanted." He wiped tears from his face. "Now I don't know what I want. These years that I've been away have been . . . rough, and I have a lot to still work through."

"Then you just need more time? We can do that."

"Damn it, you're not listening. I can't see you anymore. I can't see you anymore." He paused while the words sunk in. "I can't be with you and not belong to you, and I can't belong to you because the price is too high."

"I guess your date for the wedding was a lot more successful than you thought it would be," she lashed out.

He sighed in frustration. She had this way of exasperating him that was beyond all understanding. The *Low Fuel* light was flashing on the dashboard of his mind as he could feel the conversation passing its peak and slowly grinding down.

"There's no one else, Joanne. That's not it, and you know it." Fresh tears washed over his face. "We're hurting people by being together—even if they don't know it. I can't stop thinking about that. And even if you got a divorce, it would still always be there. There's a little boy who's not mine, and he's not going to disappear."

He was beginning to win the battle.

"Do you think you would ever change your mind?" she asked tearfully.

"No. I don't see it anyway. I'm sorry I ruined what could have been. There's a part of me that will always love you, and I'll never forgive myself for hurting you back then and again now. Go back home now, and try to make something of your marriage. It's not that bad—you've said that yourself—and you have a better chance to make it better with me out of the way. That little boy deserves a happy home with both his parents."

She reached over and hugged him close as she cried into his shoulder. Tears burned down his cheeks as he delayed the inevitable for just another minute.

"I love you," she sobbed still desperately clutching him.

"I love you, too," he answered through the tears. "You know I'm right, don't you?"

Unable to speak, she simply nodded against his shoulder. Now the absolute hardest part. He took her by the shoulders and pried her away from him. Then he leaned over and kissed her. He took his time because it had to last forever. She started crying harder, and he had to free himself from her clutching hands and arms. She was pleading and begging him to wait just a while longer. Never was it so hard for him to do something he knew was so right.

Once he was free of her grasp, he grabbed his backpack and took off running. He didn't like leaving her there like that, but he knew she was in a safe place with her car only a block away. Besides if he had stayed another second, he would have lost his nerve and caved in.

He never even looked back to see if she was still there. He just kept running and crying until his lungs were about to burst. He avoided the bus stop and anywhere he would come in too close contact with people. He desperately needed to pull himself together first. He realized there was nothing as painful as the death of a real, live, at-your-fingertips dream. He had experienced it in a literal sense when Scott died, and now this. This dream had clung gallantly to a fragile life for six, long years, and now he had just pulled the plug on the life support system. His breaking heart just wanted to die along with it.

# CHAPTER 18

As days turned into weeks, Cain was relieved that Joanne seemed to have accepted the fact of the demise of their relationship. A few times he thought he might have seen her car; but if it was her, she didn't stop, nor did she ever wait at the bench by the bus stop. More than once, he thought of trying to find her, but he was able to talk himself out of such lunacy. The head having been severed, it was best to just let the body go through the last of its knee-jerk reactions and spasmodic winding down. Then just bury the whole thing and move on.

He celebrated his twenty-fourth birthday on the 27th of April—the first birthday free of prison bars since he was eighteen. It was still hard not to be bitter over so much wasted time—so many lost years, but nothing was going to change that, so it was counterproductive to dwell on it. At least he had sense enough to realize that. He was overwhelming himself with the amount of commonsense he was acquiring with age.

Since his break-up with Joanne, he had been seeing Kristen on occasion. It was good to be with someone who didn't pose the kind of complexity and threat to his existence that Joanne did. He was determined to keep it casual, however, for he wasn't about to jump back into shark-infested waters. More commonsense. He'd had only one relationship in his life, but it had caused him so much pain that he wasn't sure he ever wanted to go that route again. Just keep things light. At the first sign of attachment, he would be gone. FAST. There was no way he wanted those fragile seeds germinating and taking root in his heart again.

Just as he seemed to be getting his equilibrium back after Joanne, he got blind-sided by the law, which sent his life spinning out of control once again. They caught him from out of nowhere and totally off guard. When Dean Richards entered his classroom—interrupting a class—and asked to see him, he had a bad feeling though he couldn't put a name to it or give it a reason for arising. When he walked out in the hall and saw two uniformed policemen, the feeling metastasized like some uncontrollable disease throughout his body. He frantically looked over at Dean Richards, who, like Judas, had already begun to hurry from the scene, trying to disperse the small crowd which was beginning to gather.

"What the fuck?" sighed Cain in disbelief.

While one policeman looked on, the other told him to put his hands on the wall and spread his legs. Reading him his rights, the policeman frisked him and cuffed his hands behind his back.

"Will someone tell me what's going on?!" he asked frantically.

But the officers were all about the business of taking him in; theirs was not to know or care why.

His mind raced all over the place in the back of the police car. He couldn't think of anything—as hard as he tried—that could even remotely result in his arrest. He panicked at the thought. He knew all too well how impossible it was to break loose of the law once it had its steel grasp on his life.

They put him through the booking process as intense claustrophobia and the feeling of being trapped seized him. He could scarcely breathe as he thought about how quickly his freedom had been snatched from him. And for what?

"Will somebody tell me what's going on?!" he asked hysterically. "I want to call my lawyer."

"As soon as I finish your prints, we'll oblige you," said the policeman who was fingerprinting him.

He'd been through all this before, and somehow it was more frightening the second time because he knew precisely where it led— even if he were innocent of any wrongdoing.

They put him in a small holding cell where he all but lost his mind from panic and uncertainty. For what seemed like an eternity, he paced like a caged lion just trapped from the wild. Then two plain-clothes officers entered. Good cop, bad cop—he'd been here before— different police station, same scenario.

"I want to call my lawyer," he demanded. "And I want to know why I'm here."

"You don't know?"

"NO!"

"Think back to last night. Haven't you learned that ladies don't like to have sex without their permission?"

"WHAT?!"

"You may as well admit it; the lady ID-ed you from our pictures this morning. She's still in the hospital."

"Jesus Christ," sighed Cain sinking back in his chair. That was it; he was seasoned; there'd be no more discussion without Bruce. "I need to see my lawyer. I won't have anything to say until then."

While he waited alone for Bruce in the chicken wire cage, he tried to think back to the night before; but the panic that had seized him was taking full control of his thought processes. He had to calm down; he had to think straight.

Hours passed, and he nearly lost his mind. They had him locked up again, and he had sworn he'd never let that happen. He kept trying to think back to the night before. He had been at work until 10:00, and then after that he was home—alone. *Shit!* What time were they talking about? His parents were out until nearly midnight, and Jim was still away at school. Why the hell hadn't Meredithe called him a zillion times that night? Had he talked to Alexis? No! He had gone straight home and then went to bed. This wasn't happening. He felt himself being buried alive.

When Bruce finally arrived, he had himself whipped into a frenzy. There was NO way in hell he was EVER going back to prison.

"I'm sorry you had to wait," explained Bruce as they sat down together at the table. "I was in court, and I just got your message. I got here as soon as I could."

"I'm supposed to be at work!" said Cain in a nervous fit. "My parents don't even know where I am. They wouldn't let me call them."

"They know now," said Bruce, "I talked to them before I came. Your dad's taking care of work. Now relax, and see if we can't clear this whole mess up."

In the end Bruce was able to give him some hope. There were some inconsistencies; and though the rape occurred during the hours Cain had spent alone, it had occurred on the north side of the city—a pretty good distance for a man who worked until 10:00 and didn't drive. He did have access to a car, though, since his mother's car was at home at the time. However, his parents could vouch that he was at home, in bed when they arrived around midnight. Thank God his mom always had a habit of coming in to say good night no matter what time it was. All in all, the timing was pretty tight, but not enough to rule him out as a suspect. Then his biggest break. The woman had told police that the rapist had a tattoo—on his wrist—a skull or something.

"You don't have any tattoos, anywhere, do you?" Bruce asked.

"No. That was one jailhouse ritual I never got into."

"Good. That'll help."

"That'll help?! That should be it!"

"Well, it's not. There are a few other things I have to check into. I think she said the rapist used a nail file," he looked up at Cain. *Sound familiar?* "But she said something about him being right-handed. I have to check that out. Bottom line—you're going to have to spend the night."

"NO! No way! I don't have a fucking tattoo! Get me out of here!"

"Just tonight. I should be able to straighten it all out tomorrow after the police can question the woman further."

"Bruce!"

"I tried, but they're not ready to let you go yet, and legally they can still hold you. Meredithe thinks it would be a good idea."

"WHAT?! He, WHAT?!"

"Relax, will you? There's nothing we can do about it."

"So where the hell's Meredithe coming from? In five months I haven't even looked sideways just to keep him happy. He can't even come to bat for me now?"

"Think about it. He's in Willet's hip pocket. It's his only recourse."

"What about me? WHAT ABOUT ME, BRUCE?! I've already done nearly six years on a bogus charge. How am I ever going to shake myself loose of Sam Willet?"

"We'll wind it up tomorrow, I promise you."

"Are you sure? What if this woman's running some game? I don't know—trying to protect someone or something? I'm not doing more time. I'll kill myself first, and I mean that."

"Listen, this is open-and-shut. The only thing that's complicating it is your prior conviction for the same crime and her ID of you. We still have a lot of options, but it all takes time. You're not locked into this one like you were the last time. Have you eaten today?"

"Not since breakfast."

Bruce took his time and spoke with the greatest of care. "I know this is bullshit for you, but trust me. I have something to work with here. Last time we were up against a solid brick wall. This will be over soon. Let me have them take you up so you get some dinner."

Cain dropped his face in his hands and let the inescapability of his situation sink in. He wanted dinner at home; he wanted to sleep in his own bed. He resisted the urge to sob hysterically and instead concentrated on steeling himself against the inevitable. He was going back into the jungle, so this was no time for weakness.

"I have finals coming up," he said putting his hands down and staring out into space.

"You'll be back before then."

"I've managed to get it all behind me at school and feel like anybody else. This is going to stir it all up again." A realization suddenly hit him. "Shit, they took me out of there in handcuffs. How do I go back?"

"One step at a time, okay? It's the old spilt milk thing. Go get something to eat, and then get some sleep. I'll see you tomorrow."

Cain wouldn't have minded so much if they would've just locked him in a cell, but they were institutionalizing him again. He had to give up his clothes and go through the demoralizing processing-in. At least this time he was used to it—even if he had thought it was all behind him.

Smelling like the objectionable disinfectant soap and his hair still wet from the shower, he walked grudgingly into the cell. Then the sound he hated worst of all—the bone-jarring crash of metal meeting metal as the door shut behind him—the steel jaws of the system. No one knew better than he did how those jaws could eat a person alive.

The cell was empty, but there was obviously another occupant. Cain knew the rules inside the steel jaws. Rule No. 1: THERE ARE NO RULES. EVERY MAN FOR HIMSELF. With that in mind, he considered asserting himself by tearing apart the made bed of his cellmate and taking it for himself, leaving the pile of sheets and blankets on the unoccupied bed. Practically everyone, to a man, that he knew at Maddox would have done just that. Not sure it was the wisest move, he opted for the manners and breeding which was more his nature and made up the empty bed for himself. Then taking off only his shoes—the dumbest move in a double cell would be to strip down—he lay down on the anemic mattress and jammed the lifeless pillow under his head. Truth be known, he was more tired than he was hungry. A few minutes later, a guard brought him some magazines and candy bars that Bruce had sent up for him. That was the last thing he remembered.

Cells weren't equipped with clocks, and they had taken his watch from him, so he had no idea what time it was when he woke up. His heart jumped into quick-start, however, as he turned and looked into the picket-fence grin of his hulking cellmate. He had never even heard him come into the cell. *Shit.* That's when he realized he should have definitely shown some jailhouse savvy and domination by stripping the guy's bed and taking it for himself. But he had been hoping for some first-time fish who would cower in a corner and leave him alone. No such luck. He should have known those miracles were reserved for others.

"Well, well, well," the nearly 300-pound inmate was beside himself with joy and was grinning ear-to-ear. He was sure he had been granted the first-time-fish miracle. And such a beautiful fish. "You finally woke up. I ain't never seed anyone could sleep like you. I was beginning to think you was dead or something."

Cain sat up on his bed opposite the massive brute. This was no time for basking in the afterglow of a sound sleep. The first thing he noticed was the tattoo on the man. It was a venomous snake, fangs bared and ready to strike. The nasty head was on the top of his right hand and the body coiled around his right arm like a huge spring and up over his right shoulder. Cain could only assume the tail was wound menacingly across his back. In his quick assessment of the situation, the next thing he noticed was that his magazines and candy were now in possession of the snake charmer. This was not acceptable. If he let that go, he'd be classified as an easy mark and in for all kinds of hurt. For the first time ever, he thanked God for his Maddox education. Without it, he would have ignored the fact that his cellmate had taken his things, figuring it wasn't worth the effort, and he would've ended up more than a little snake bit. Now, however, uninviting as it was, he knew what he had to do.

"That's my stuff you have over there," he said acknowledging that he had noticed.

"So it is," mused the snake charmer. "And good stuff, too. How lucky can I be to have such a drop-dead good-looking cellmate," he shook his head with oozing sexuality, "with probably **the** best ass I've ever seen **and** good candy and things."

*SHIT*! The situation was escalating. He'd better make a move soon; this charmer was way too big for him to deal with if he let him gain anymore momentum. One thing was in Cain's favor. It was becoming more and more obvious that his predator had totally misread and underestimated him. That was a fatal prison mistake, and Cain couldn't believe the man was making it.

"What'd you get arrested for?" the snake charmer asked. "Stealing your daddy's car and taking a joy ride?"

He started to laugh heartily, his excess pounds quivering with delight. Now Cain was certain the man had pegged him as an inexperienced fish ready for the taking. Still he said nothing and waited for his opportunity, which he knew was about to materialize. The charmer laughed and heaved until he was breathless.

"I have a great idea," the big man said as he sucked in spasmodic breaths. "How 'bout you take your clothes off, pretty boy, and give me a first-hand look at that nice, tight ass of yours? Then after I fuck to my heart's content, I'll give you one of your candy bars back— just for being a good boy."

It wasn't easy for Cain to contain the indignant fire that was burning within him, but he knew it was crucial not to give the man attitude and alert him to his great misconception. The element of surprise could trump fat, complacent, brute strength. He was confident; he just needed the right moment.

"Come on, come on," bellowed the snake charmer, no longer laughing but smiling lasciviously. "The clothes. We don't have all day—the guard'll be around soon. Pretty soon I'm gonna come over there and do it for you, and then you won't get no candy."

*Go ahead, asshole, move toward me.* Slowly and with just the right amount of humility and fear in his eyes, Cain began undoing the jumpsuit.

"I guess I should introduce myself," said the charmer with an excited leer. "I'm Snake."

*No shit.*

He reached his hand out mockingly to shake with Cain. The moment was here. In a quick fluid move honed by years of jailhouse experience, Cain took the proffered hand; but instead of shaking it, he swiftly jerked it backwards until the snake's head was nearly twisted from its body. Then he continued to apply pressure ready to break the wrist if he had to. This was no time to be shy or tentative. The more pressure he applied the further off the bed Snake rose until he was standing. Then just another quick move, and he had the large man pinned against the bars. Skillfully, as he continued inching toward the breaking point of the wrist, Cain took his other forearm and pressed it against Snake's neck, applying just enough pressure to the windpipe to convince the big man that he knew exactly what he was doing.

It was a most debilitating position no matter what the man's size. Cain knew this for a fact since one of the inmates he had tutored at Maddox had taught it to him as payment for the tutoring, but he insisted on demonstrating on Cain to show him just how "cool" it really worked.

It was as if he had needed to prove to Cain that this was a skill worthy of all the hours of time they had spent studying.

Snake was having no more illusions about his new cellmate. His eyes were bulging as he struggled for breath. He knew it wasn't going to take much more exertion on Cain's part and his hulking body was going to lose consciousness, but he was unable to speak. He was unable to do anything but listen.

"Look, motherfucker," snarled Cain reaching back for a language that he was sure Snake would relate to, "I ain't no fucking **boy**, okay? I was raised in a state prison, and there's no way I'm about to take any bullshit from you or anybody else. And you get this straight right now—I DON'T TURN ASS FOR **ANYBODY**. Now you grunt twice if you understand me and want to give my things back to me. Otherwise, motherfucker or snakefucker—whatever you are—I'll put you out like a light and take it back myself."

At this point his anger was climaxing, and he was functioning on pure adrenaline. He knew he'd put the snake to sleep if he had to. Survival of the fittest. He was back in the jungle.

Snake gawked at him, barely able to blink an eye. Still he managed two meager, gurgling grunts to indicate he would cooperate. More Maddox training: don't be lulled into a trap because of over-confidence. Therefore, Cain maintained the hold as if he were contemplating whether to release Snake or let him sleep it off on the floor. He was actually taller than Snake by a few inches, so it was easy to establish and hold eye contact; and with Cain, the eyes said it all. *Don't fuck with me, man.* Ever so gradually he loosened the pressure to Snake's windpipe, but he kept a firm grasp on the twisted hand. He stepped back slightly from the nose-to-nose contact he had established. Snake grabbed at his throat with his free hand as he coughed and struggled to suck air into his burning lungs. Cain lifted Snake's bent hand in the air and gave it a little shake before releasing it.

"Nice to meet you," he said purposely omitting his name. He didn't need this lunatic looking him up one day on the outside. "And never mind, I can get my stuff myself. Thanks anyway."

As the big man stood in obvious physical distress trying to recover, Cain walked away from him and retrieved his belongings. But he never took his eyes off his hulking rival. He was amazed how it had all come back to him. He performed flawlessly, making no mistakes. But he also knew he'd never be able to have another moment's sleep in this man's presence. Inmates often took advantage of a sleeping adversary to take revenge. He had learned that lesson at the knee of Herb Lidell. This time he had won a major battle, but the war wouldn't be over until he walked out of there for good.

Snake made a few groping steps toward his own bed and landed flat on it on his wide, padded butt, all the while rubbing his wrist. Cain glared at him, keeping up his guard and the attitude he had struggled to establish. Then he reached over and grabbed one of the candy bars. As Snake watched him with care, Cain flipped the candy bar across the short distance between them. Instinctively, Snake caught it.

"All you had to do was ask," said Cain.

Cain woke the next morning feeling unrested and crabby. He had slept very little during the night, and the sleep that he did have was fitful at best. Not only was he in new, hardly comfortable surroundings with a world of worry on his mind, but he didn't trust Snake. He left the cell for breakfast, but passed when it was their time to go down to the showers. At breakfast he tried to scope out who Snake's friends were, but he wasn't about to test their loyalty in the lethal setting of the shower room. More brutality and criminal behavior took place in the shower rooms of jails and prisons than any other similar square footage on earth. Besides, he had had one of their disinfectant showers the day before. He prayed Bruce would get him the hell out of there before he had to face the inevitable.

Snake seemed tamed enough, but paranoia was the backbone of the prison culture. Anyone who became complacent and self-satisfied was just asking to be brought down—especially when he was new and just establishing his position in the pecking order. The first time he was in the county jail before being sent off to Maddox, he was only eighteen and they kept him in isolation. Only now did he understand what a gift that really was. He couldn't even imagine being thrown into this environment without hard-core experience. At Maddox there was a little indoctrination before being mainstreamed. Here they just threw you to the wolves to be eaten alive if you didn't have survival skills.

When it was time for the morning exercise period, Cain waited to see what Snake was going to do, then he would do the opposite. He desperately needed to get away from that maniac for a while. He was glad when Snake opted to leave because that would give him three hours of solitude when he could maybe catch some quality sleep. If nothing else, he wouldn't have to be watching over his shoulder every second.

He was exhausted and felt like now he could relax. Setting his internal alarm for noon, he curled up with the pillow and he soon drifted off into a sleep that was much more substantial than what he had experienced during the night. His body and mind relaxed in spite of the unforgiving bed and his wretched situation.

He was able to deeply slumber through only an hour, however, when Ralph Meredithe showed up with a different agenda. The guard who let him in was none too quiet as he unlocked the cell door. Then he clanged it shut and locked it again, telling Meredithe to call down to him when he was ready to leave. Cain was beginning to climb out of the velvet pit he had willed his body into, but he wasn't coming around fast enough for Meredithe. Grabbing the pillow, the little general yanked it out from under Cain. That set off every alarm in Cain's body and sent him scrambling for his life. He jumped out of bed and almost before his eyes were opened, he had Meredithe pinned against the bars. It only took a second or two before he realized he wasn't dealing with the much larger Snake.

"JESUS CHRIST!" he bellowed at Meredithe. "What the hell are you trying to do?"

"What am **I** trying to do?!" sighed the little man collecting his dignity.

Cain stepped back to his bed and eased himself to a sitting position, his heart still thundering in his chest.

"You can't really be that stupid that you'd sneak up on someone in a zoo like this."

"I wasn't sneaking."

"Well, I sure as hell wasn't aware that you were here until I had you by the balls."

"Give me a break, Farrell. You're being a bit dramatic, aren't you?"

Cain smiled deviously. "You're just lucky I haven't gotten around to constructing a shank. You'd be bleeding like a stuffed pig—no pun intended." He slid back on the bed until he was leaning against the wall, and then he folded his legs Indian-style. "I didn't realize you made house calls here, too." Again the smile that drove Meredithe straight up the wall.

"Wipe that smile off your face, hotshot. You're in deep shit, and I'm pissed as hell."

"Well now that you bring it up," said Cain becoming menacingly serious, "I'm pretty pissed myself. What the hell am I doing here?"

"You never cease to amaze me," chuckled Meredithe. "You have to be the most arrogant son-of-a-bitch I've ever dealt with. You have that rich-white-boy-from-the-burbs-mentality—you think you can do whatever you please and everyone's supposed to turn their heads the other way because of who you are."

Cain measured the little man with his eyes as Meredithe made himself comfortable on Snake's bed. Why argue? The man was a moron. Besides there was something strikingly funny about Meredithe sitting on Snake's bed. All sorts of amusing images filled Cain's head, and the smirk returned to his face.

"See!" ranted Meredithe at the sight of Cain's levity. "You don't take anything serious!"

"Now that's where you're wrong," argued Cain maintaining a level demeanor. "I take this jail cell very serious, and I was just thinking that I wouldn't be sitting on that bed if I was you."

"Why?" sneered Meredithe with a fake pout. "The big, bad man's going to come back and beat me up?"

The smile broadened.

"Maybe," Cain answered. "But he's really more interested in turning a piece of ass."

"You . . . you . . .!!!"

Meredithe was enraged and couldn't come up with words to express his anger. He stood up and reaching his opened hand across his body prepared to strike. He was trembling with explosive anger, the kind that bubbles from a volcano. Cain replaced the smile with a squint-eyed look of his own as he momentarily quelled the white-hot anger that was coursing through his body.

"Go ahead, Ralph, take your best shot," he challenged levelly, "but you'd better make sure to put me out because if you don't, it's my turn next—and you ain't been to school, not the way I have."

Cain sat steeled with resolve, ready to take the blow if Meredithe was indeed more stupid than he looked. The volcano simmered down, wisely deciding to wait for another day to erupt. Struggling to maintain his authority and groping for a way to exit the standoff with some shred of dignity, Meredithe slowly lowered his hand.

Taking his victory in stride and not wishing to deal with the irritating, little general any longer, Cain grabbed his pillow and lay down—his back to Meredithe. *DO NOT DISTURB!*

"I'm not through with you!" ranted Meredithe still sputtering molten lava.

"I'm through with you, but go ahead. Just make it quick; I didn't get much sleep last night."

"Farrell," bubbled the volcano, "turn around and look at me—now—or I'm going back to my office and draw up a whole new set of parole regulations that'll have you all but under house arrest—that is if you even get out of this current mess."

Cain turned toward him, but it was not out of intimidation. Subjugation was the last thing on his list, which was more than obvious from the look on his face and the way he handled his body. He was in control.

"Look," he said struggling with his temper as he sat up on the bed, "you do what you have to do, but don't expect me to like it or start kissing ass. It's not my style. I don't even know why you're here—except to gloat, and that's really beginning to piss me off. This rap isn't going to stick because I was nowhere near the city or that lady, and with the advanced testing procedures they have now, it's only a matter of time until I can prove it. What's really making me mad is that I don't think you honestly believe I did it either, but you're taking advantage of the situation to flex some muscle. THAT'S REALLY MAKING ME MAD."

"Farrell . . ."

"Meredithe, go to hell. This jail thing is wearing very thin with me right now. I've already missed one night of work and two days of school. I'm just not in the mood for your shit."

"Okay, we'll see," threatened the cornered holder-of-the-keys. "I can think of all kinds of ways to punish you and get you back in line."

"You just take your parole regulations and shove 'em up you pompous ass—or better yet, I'll do it for you. Now get out of here."

Cain lay down and turned back toward the wall. That was it; he couldn't trust himself any further to deal with this man without wringing his neck.

"You'll be sorry," stammered Meredithe. He pressed his face to the bars. "GUARD!"

"Fuck you," said Cain not able to stifle the opportunity of getting in the last word.

He pulled the pillow over his head, and if Meredithe said any more before he left, it was lost on him.

That was the exact same position he was in when he woke up about an hour later—just before Snake was due back. He knew it was near lunchtime, and he cursed the slow-moving gears of the legal system. The longer he stayed, the more concerned he became about getting caught up in another losing battle. If he only knew what was going on. He was the one with the most at stake, and he was the only one who had no idea of what was transpiring.

He put the ominous thoughts out of his head as he prepared mentally for the return of his cellmate. If he stayed there much longer, he was going to have to use his ingenuity to create a weapon of self-defense. Just in case. He couldn't get complacent and bank on the assumption that Snake had been effectively charmed. Where the hell was Bruce, anyway?

At lunch he contemplated palming a plastic spoon to take back with him. It could be filed down into a pretty effective weapon. The guards watched pretty closely as inmates bussed their trays after eating, but Cain knew he could do it. He had become good at sleight-of-hand at Maddox, and though he was out of practice, it was a pretty easy maneuver. Still, he thought better of it for the moment; but he decided if he was still there at dinnertime, he'd definitely nab one. He was too tired already, so he knew he'd never be able to stay awake all night. The spoon would buy him some insurance toward a better night's sleep.

It was about 3:00 that afternoon when the guard came for him, telling him to bring everything with him because he was going home. *Finally!* Bruce was waiting for him after he had changed back into his own clothes. He was glad then that he hadn't taken the spoon because he would have had to find somewhere to get rid of it inconspicuously when all he wanted to do was get out of there. He emptied the large manila envelope that held his wallet and other things they had taken from him when he was arrested. Then checking it all over to be sure nothing was missing, he put everything away, and signed the release.

It felt good to be out of there and into the fresh air again. Every jail had the same stale, putrid smell, and he felt like it had permeated his

396

skin and clothing and was clinging to him like a cloud. He couldn't wait to get home and shower. But first things first.

"Just tell me everything's been cleared up; the charges have been dropped," he said to Bruce. "I don't want to hear anything else."

"Everything's cool," said Bruce. "All charges have been dropped. They caught guy who did it. He doesn't look anything like you except he's blonde. Tattoo gave him away."

"So I spent two days in jail and don't get so much as an 'Oops' or 'Sorry 'bout that'?"

"I know. I'm sorry about that if it counts for anything."

Cain grinned and rubbed his face.

"Shit, I'm exhausted. When you're celling with a guy named Snake, you don't sleep much."

Bruce laughed. "I guess not."

"I have just enough time to get home and shower and go to work. I hope I last until 10:00."

"Call in and take the day off. The DOC owes you that much."

"I can't afford to. I missed last night. Besides, even though the DOC might owe me, Meredithe will be out after my ass."

"He's part of the DOC."

"I know, but I'm afraid I rubbed his nose in a little prison shit, and he's really not very happy with me right now."

"He was in to see you?"

"This morning. The last thing I said to him was *fuck you* or *shove your parole regulations up your ass*. I might have even offered to help him do it."

"That wasn't very smart," said Bruce with a slight grin.

"I know. But it sure felt good." Cain smiled back at him. "So now I pay the piper—and tomorrow's Friday. Some day I'm going to learn to keep my mouth shut, but I'm not sure I'll live long enough!"

It was hard to go back to school the next day, but he had no choice other than to shore up his dignity and do it. He didn't owe anybody an explanation, and his dad had talked to the professors of the classes he had missed. Now it was just a matter of making up for lost time.

The trip to Meredithe's office was another story. He didn't know what to expect there, but he knew it wouldn't be pleasant. Reaching deep in his pockets for humility, all he found was anger and resentment. That wouldn't do. He walked from the train station trying to lose some bitterness, or at least push it way down inside where it wouldn't do him any more harm with Meredithe. He had had a good night's sleep in his own bed, and the morning at school had been uneventful. Now if he could just get through this weekly rite of punishment.

397

He hated this forced pilgrimage downtown every Friday. It was getting more than a little annoying. At first he saw it as a necessary evil of his freedom; now it was nothing but the extended arm of the law controlling and manipulating his life. What made him angrier was that he knew the arm belonged to the body of Sam Willet. It was a total waste of time that ate up most of his Friday afternoon between commuting downtown and sitting in Meredithe's outer office waiting his turn. He rarely, if ever, spent more than ten minutes face-to-face with Meredithe in mundane conversation about how the week had gone— most of which Meredithe already knew from on-site visits and phone calls. This man was way too present in his life, but there was no way of getting rid of him.

He realized his mind had wandered off on a dangerous side trip of self-pity, so he abruptly brought it back before any more damage could be done. As he walked toward Meredithe's office, he took in the sights of the city he loved best. That was what he needed to focus on—the only highpoint of his Friday visits. The city rejuvenated him and gave him sustenance to deal with the hateful, little man who pulled the strings of his life. At least there was a plus; for that he needed to be thankful.

By the time he got to Meredithe's office he had managed to swallow a healthful dose of humility, which he hoped would keep his put-upon attitude at bay. When he walked in, the secretary gave him a cheerful smile as always. He looked around the room of derelicts, con men, gangbangers, and the like. It was obvious Meredithe didn't handle any white-collar cases. He turned back to the secretary who was saying something about the weather. He smiled, and her day was complete.

"He'll be happy to see me today," Cain predicted knowing Meredithe probably couldn't wait to chew him up and spit him out.

She picked up the phone to let her boss know that Cain had arrived.

"You're right," she smiled with surprise. "In fact, he said don't even sit down—go straight in."

Groans from all the others ahead of him. He gave her a knowing grin, kind of like the one people would give a nurse just before she gives them a shot with an over-sized needle.

He didn't have to even open the door. Meredithe did the honors, which was a first since he usually sat on his throne behind his desk—the all-important despot.

"Get your ass in here!"

Cain turned back toward the secretary and shot her an *I told you so* smile. Then he walked passed Meredithe who immediately slammed the door. Cain stood in mock respect waiting for Meredithe to take his seat on the throne.

"I've been waiting for this all day," grinned Meredithe.

"I'm sure you had wet dreams all night in anticipation," said Cain easing himself into his chair. He hadn't meant for that to slip out, but it seemed so natural for the moment.

"You're a cocky son-of-a-bitch for the predicament you're in."

"Look," said Cain leaning forward in his chair but maintaining a level tone, "that's the second time in two days you've used that term with me, and I gotta tell you, I don't like it. You can call me whatever you like, but not only is my mother a lady, she doesn't have anything to do with the shit that goes on between you and me." He sat back in his chair but went on, giving Meredithe the message that there was no room for further discussion of the matter. "And what *predicament* am I in? I talked back to you after you barged in on me? Come on, you're surely thicker-skinned than that. I'm the one who sat on his ass in jail for two days over a bogus rap. You knew I didn't do that rape, and yet you recommended they hold me."

"She identified you! You're on parole for the same crime! It was open-and-shut."

"Everything's fucking *open-and-shut* with you. Do you have any gut feelings or instincts at all? Or are you just afraid to use them? I know I didn't spend time in jail on your say-so alone. I also know that no matter what you would've said, they still probably would have kept me. But would it have been so hard for you to have put in a word for me? What do I have to do to convince you that I don't want to go back to prison, that I want to put this all behind me and salvage some kind of a life for myself?"

Meredithe sat looking at him with an incredulous grin on his face. Inside, he was scrambling for a way to get control of the situation back. He sighed deeply. He was putting on a good show.

"One of the biggest mistakes of my career, not to mention my life, is to trust an ex-con—no matter how smooth talking he is. You're all alike, Farrell—50% bullshit, 50% planning your next move without getting caught."

Now it was Cain who was incredulous, but there was no ironic grin. He took a deep breath, putting on a show of his own, but he knew it was a study in futility. This system, at which Meredithe was in the driver's seat, was bigger than he was, and he had no recourse but to continue the ride. He shrugged his shoulders hopelessly.

"So what's my punishment?"

"How does electronic monitoring sound, Mr. Hotshot? You don't leave home except for work, school, church, and doctor appointments."

Cain looked down at his hands as he collected his emotions.

"You can do that to me just for talking back to you?" he asked quietly as he raised his eyes to look at Meredithe. But he already knew the answer.

"Of course I can.  Besides, it was a little more serious than just back talk.  You attacked me and you threatened me.  How about that for starters?"

Cain looked him straight in the eye and called him a pig without opening his mouth.

"So what do I do?" he asked opting not to get into a verbal battle.

"We get you fitted with a device right away.  I'd like to have it put around your neck like a dog collar, but we don't have any like that."  He laughed tauntingly.  "But I have to tell you, I didn't think it would be this easy.  I thought for sure that I'd have to send for help to drag you out of here kicking and screaming with rage.  Maybe I should offer you my alternative."

Cain was interested but didn't change his expression.  He sat stone-faced waiting for Meredithe to continue turning the screws.

"Well?  Are you interested or not?"

"Go ahead," muttered Cain.

"You could start by spit-polishing my shoes and telling me how nice I look today.  Then you could go on and on about how grateful you are that I didn't put you on house arrest.  And you can finish up by telling me how lucky you are to have a great guy like me as you parole officer.  Who knows, we might even work up to some literal ass-kissing—I think I might even enjoy that from an expert like you who I know must have had years of experience out at Maddox."  He laughed almost uncontrollably.

*Okay, you're used to trash talking.  Keep your head.*

"Do I get a choice, or do you decide?"  Cain asked.

"Oh, I decide.  But **if** you did have a choice, I'd be interested to know which you'd choose."

This is where Cain's quick wit and Maddox-trained irreverence usually reared up and demanded to be noticed, but he wasn't in the mood.  He was dead in the water—wind out of his sails.

"I don't know," he said with a shrug and little enthusiasm.  "I told you before, I'm not much good at kissing-ass—proverbial or, in spite of what you think you know, the real thing.  I don't think you'd be . . . satisfied."

Meredithe looked at him a bit bemused and taken aback.  The kid not only had spunk but convictions—not that he ever seriously expected him to prostitute himself in any form of the word, but he had expected indignant rantings and verbiage.  Instead, he got a quiet sort of dignity with a little twist.  His assessment stopped short of admiration.

"Get out of here," he said curtly.  "I'll see you next week."

Cain was confused.  He shrugged his shoulders and extended his hands, palms up.  *I don't get it.*

"Are you deaf?  Get your ass out of here before I change my mind . . . I'll see you next Friday—and stay out of trouble."

400

When he walked into the house, Nora picked up on is mood right away.

"Rough day?" she smiled.

"Yeah."

"I'm sorry, honey," she said kissing his cheek. "Was Meredithe impossible?"

"Meredithe's a jerk. But I don't want to talk about him. I'm going up to get changed for work."

"Okay, your dinner's just about ready."

He walked over and kissed her forehead and held her in his arms.

"Thanks, Mom."

"This is a difficult time, sweetheart. Don't lose heart."

"It's just hard, you know? They take me out of school, accuse me of raping some woman, make me sit around in a jail cell for two days, and then send me on my way without a word when the real rapist shows up. And there's nothing I can do but take it. I missed two days of school and a day's pay, not to mention added legal fees. Nobody offers to make up for any of that. It's just, *get your ass out of here.*"

"I just wish there was something I could do."

"There is, Mom, and you do it everyday—you're here, and I love you. And I'm sorry—I know this isn't easy for you. I've brought you a lot of pain. I know that. And you don't deserve it."

"I've always been a realist, Cain. My whole life. Somehow I've always known that there's no happily-ever-after in this life, but that doesn't mean it can't be good. You kind of take the good with the bad and make the best of it because we only get one chance at life. Maybe it was growing up in Ireland that gave me a better perspective—there are lots of struggles still going on there. People just kind of look at life differently there. I'm tough. I think I can take most anything life can give me—except if you were to give in to all this adversity in your life and let it destroy you. That would be more than I could take. You've always needed me more than your brothers or Molly, and that's given my life a special purpose—not pain."

The look on his face melted her heart as he took her hand and kissed it.

"I have to get ready for work," he winked. "Thanks, Mom."

She watched him leave the room—this man-child so abused by the world he was struggling so hard to understand and conquer. Being his mother was not for the weak of heart. The pain she bore for him was almost debilitating, but he would never know that. That was her secret. She needed to give him hope and confidence, not any more guilt or remorse than he was already experiencing. She had always been his beacon, his stabilizing force, and she took that role very seriously. There was only one chink in her armor, one thing that could bring her to her knees—knowing that one day she would have to step back and entrust his heart to the loving care of another woman. That would be her deepest sorrow. She had never verbalized that to anyone, not even Will, but she prepared herself daily for that inevitability. The beaming smile on her face the day of his wedding will be the ultimate acting performance of a lifetime. She knew she could do it, though, when the time came because she loved him far too much to be any other way. But for now she took heart in the fact that this was not an imminent reality. Right now he was depending on her to have a hearty dinner ready for him before he went to work, continuing a day which had already been too long.

Alexis had arranged with Cain to pick him up after work. She usually liked to be around on Fridays to pick up the pieces from his visits with Meredithe. After the week he had had, she knew this would be a particularly brutal Friday.

"How'd school go this morning?" she asked after he told her he didn't want to go anywhere but home.

"Okay. Better than I'd thought actually. A few people stared, but it's none of their business."

"That's the way."

"It wasn't in the papers, so I caught a break there."

"Are you sure you don't want to stop for ice cream or something? We have time."

"Nah, I'm tired."

"Tired or depressed?"

He covered his face with his hands.

"Meredithe?" asked Alexis, trying to get him to open up.

"He's such an asshole," he sighed as he dropped his hands into his lap. "But I can deal with him."

"What is it then? Something's not right. Is it Joanne?"

"No. I haven't seen her since we broke up."

She waited. Nothing.

"You don't want to talk about it?" she encouraged.

"I don't honestly know if I can," he admitted.

"Oh. I see. *Private Property, No Trespassing?*"

"I don't mean it to sound that way."

"I know you don't. And I don't want to barge in on anything too private. You just let me know if and when you're ready."

"That's the thing. I think if I don't get it out . . . if I don't verbalize it, it's going to take over and bury me."

She pulled up in his driveway and turned to him.

"Honey, what could be so terrible?"

"It's a feeling. Right here." He put his closed fist on his chest right below his throat. "I feel like I'm going to throw up most of the time."

"What could have brought that on?" she asked, knitting her eyebrows together.

"I know what brought it on. I just don't know how to deal with it."

"And you can't tell me?"

He drew in a deep breath.

"I don't know if you can understand. I don't know if anyone can understand. I don't know if that's a part of me I can expose—to anyone."

"Cain, this sounds serious, and you're scaring me. Can't you at least tell me what brought it on?"

He stared blankly out the front window of the car.

"Being back in jail. It dug up all kinds of crap I thought I'd buried pretty deep—but not deep enough, I guess."

"Honey . . ."

"Did you know that I know how to make a home-made weapon and then how to bury it into a man so quick and so clean that he'd be dead before he hit the floor?"

He turned toward her and nearly knocked her off balance with his stare. She had never seen him so intense, so determined. She didn't know what to say.

"He'd never know what hit him," he continued. "He'd just be . . . dead. Now there's something you don't learn at summer camp. But you need to know it at a place like Maddox, and other inmates need to know that you know."

He looked her in the eye, and she tried not to look scared to death.

"I'm sorry," he said as he turned away and leaned back against the seat.

"It's okay," she managed to say.

"People don't know the half of what goes on behind bars. I wasn't even nineteen yet when I saw a man get killed by other inmates— in the shower room, their favorite stalking ground. It was lucky Jon Harrison was with me because I don't know what I would've done otherwise. But he told me to act like I hadn't seen a thing and nonchalantly walk away—getting the hell out of there without drawing attention to myself. I don't know what the guy did to make them kill him—you don't ask questions. In fact, it's better if you don't know anything. I was shaking and I wanted to cry, but you never show weakness. All crying must be done in private. They prey on the weak. When I first got there, there was this guy who was older than me, but he was short and skinny. God, they harassed the hell out of him. I wanted to help him, but I was so scared and I didn't know what to do. I hated going down to shower because they gang raped him every time. I should have done something."

403

"You would've gotten hurt, too. You weren't prepared for that."

"I don't care. I never helped him. I should've helped him."

He turned to look at her. Tears were streaming down her face.

"I knew I shouldn't have said anything," he said wiping at the tears on her face with his fingertips. "I didn't mean to make you feel bad."

"It's okay—really. Maybe it'll help you. I'm okay."

"I've never told anybody any of this."

"Did anyone ever hurt you?" she asked with the deepest concern as fresh tears broke loose at the thought.

He was still facing her, but he stared passed her. Herb Lidell with his lecherous grin materialized outside the window. It was the same face that has haunted his nightmares for six years.

"Once," he was able to say, but he couldn't look at her nor could he go into detail. "That was when I learned the art of weaponry and murder. I didn't kill him, but I hurt him bad enough, and I made him think twice before ever messing with me again. I gained a lot of respect that night, but I paid way too high a price."

"I should have written to you while you were away like I said I would," she said wiping at the tears on her face. "You must have felt so alone. I can't believe I was so insensitive."

"Come on," he said with a grateful smile, "you had no way of knowing. I'm not telling you this to make you feel guilty or sorry for me. To tell you the truth, I don't know why I'm telling you. I've never been able to talk about it before."

"Good," she smiled as she wiped more of the tears away, "maybe it'll help somehow. I wasn't there for you then, but I can be here now."

"Just don't think anything bad about me, okay? I probably shouldn't have told you."

"Think anything bad about you?! Because you had to learn to protect yourself? And because Carrie Willet sent you to a crazy house?"

"It's just that I've been starting to kind of be able to shake off the *bad boy* image I've been carrying around inside me for so long now— even Meredithe was beginning to roll off my back. Once in a while I could even forget where I've been. But then those two days in jail really set me back, and I have to wonder if I'll ever be able to put it behind me. I don't feel good enough to be with . . . people. I have this whole dark side of me that doesn't relate at all . . . that's all corrupt and covert."

"You had fun at the wedding."

"Don't try to reason this away, Alexis, because I can come up with a valid argument for anything you want to say. I know. I've been over it in my head a million times. I'm like two people, neither of which fits into where I am right now."

"Have you thought of talking to someone professionally?"

"I've thought of everything. I just don't know what I want to do. I don't know if I want to dig it all up and rehash it. I don't know if I can."

Alexis was silent, wishing there was something to say.

"Just do me one favor," he said.

"Anything."

"Don't tell any of this to anybody."

"I wouldn't."

"My mom would die if she ever knew some of the things I just told you. She knew it was bad, but she has no idea how bad. Nobody does—but me." He dropped his head back against the seat. "I guess I'm going in; I'm really tired."

"What are you doing this weekend?"

"Not much. Studying and making up some assignments that I missed while I was sitting on my ass in jail. Finals are next week."

"After that you'll have some free time."

"Well, I'm taking two courses in summer school. So I'll have classes on Monday and Wednesday nights. That way I can work a full forty-hour week."

"Cain, honey," she sighed, "why don't you stop driving yourself and take some time off for living? It's summer—beach time, baseball season. School will still be there, and you're young—you have time."

"It's just two courses."

"Just two courses in summer school is a lot—especially the way you attack school." She reached across and lightly brushed at the hair on his forehead. "You should be playing baseball; that's what you love."

"No," he said definitively. "I've buried that dream; I told you that."

"I know. You think you're too old."

"I **am** too old to just be starting out, and I don't want to have this discussion."

"Find a team to play on for fun. It doesn't have to be professional."

"I don't have time."

"You won't take time. Why are you punishing yourself—isn't the Department of Corrections punishing you enough? You're out of prison, Cain; it's okay now to have some fun."

"I gotta go," he said putting a definite end to the night. "Thanks for the ride. I'll talk to you."

Without giving her a chance to respond, he got out of the car and slammed the door. Out of frustration he did the same thing to the front door of his home.

"Bad night?" asked Will who was nearby.

"Yeah, sort of."

"You want to talk?"

"No. I definitely have done enough talking for one night. I'm just going up to bed. Where's Mom?"

"In the family room."

After saying good night to his parents, he went up to his room to officially rid himself of the day. He still felt more relaxed and secure in smaller spaces—as long as they didn't have bars. Stripping off all his clothes except his boxers, he crawled into bed and relaxed into the thickness of the mattress. Sandwiching his head between his two pillows, he effectively shut out the world and slept. Mercifully, neither Ralph Meredithe nor Herb Lidell invaded his peace.

It was just past noon the next day when Alexis showed up at the Farrell's. She was wearing nice fitting jeans and a tee shirt, which showed off her willowy figure. Her strawberry-blonde locks were bound up in a ponytail and bounced freely from the back of her baseball cap. She was surprised when Sean opened the door.

"Alexis!" He seemed equally surprised. "Come in. I'm here doing laundry—our machine's broken at the apartment. My parents are out shopping, and Cain's still in bed—it must be nice to have nothing else to do but hang around in bed all day."

"He works hard, Sean. He deserves it."

"Only about twelve, fourteen hours a day," smiled Sean.

"Do you cook, too?" she asked with a grin.

"Of course I do. We share that job, but I leave the cleaning to Brianne."

"When are you going to marry that girl?"

"Ow," frowned Sean. He had the same impish smile that Cain and Matt had. "We don't say the 'M' word. Not for a while anyway—the longer the better."

"You haven't changed a bit! You're just as much a rogue as you've ever been."

"I'll take that as a compliment. You want me to go drag my brother's lazy ass out of bed?"

"No, I'll do it, but I think he's mad at me, so I may be back sooner than you think."

"Well, I don't know how close you two are, so maybe I don't have to tell you, but he sleeps like he's dead. You call him and call him and shake him, but he doesn't budge. So you shake him a little harder, and all of a sudden he jumps on you and grabs you around the throat and tells you that **you** scared **him** to death."

Alexis laughed.

"Well, we're not that close," she said, "so thanks for the warning."

She went up and knocked at his door, but there was no answer. She knocked again. Still nothing. Slowly, she opened the door and looked in. She had never been up to his room since they were teenagers and she was going out with Matt. The room was comfortable when the three brothers shared it, and now it was downright large. There was plenty of room for his desk, dresser, entertainment stand, bed, and a loveseat. It was tastefully decorated, definitely masculine, and pretty much what she would have expected from him. It was very erotic for her to be looking into this private part of his world at such a vulnerable moment. He was sound asleep on his stomach with his sheet twisted around his midsection, one bare leg exposed to the thigh. The look on his face was so peaceful and innocent, it was hard to believe all the pain and turmoil that lay beneath the surface. She wanted to cry for loving him so much. He looked like something from out of a most delicious dream.

Pushing fantasies aside, she called softly to him. He stirred but was a long way from consciousness. Calling to him again, this time a little louder, she knelt down next to his bed. He stretched his long body and turned, moving away from the call back to reality. Then she threw caution to the wind and kissed the back of his bare shoulder and neck. He'd never know. He twisted his body toward her and made a slight contented moan as if he liked it and wanted more. She knew she'd never be able to explain what the hell she was doing if she continued and he woke up, so she put her hand on his back and rubbed it briskly as she called his name. He remained on his stomach but pulled his body up till he rested on his forearms. Rubbing the last traces of unconsciousness from his face, he turned and looked at her.

"Lex?" he said sleepily.

"Yeah," she smiled adoringly. She loved when he called her that because no one else ever did, and that made it very private. "Good Morning, or I should say, Good Afternoon."

"What's up?" His voice was so seductively sodden with sleep that she could hardly stand to be so near him.

"Well, you have to get up and get dressed because we're going to the Cubs Game. I went this morning and got us tickets."

"You got what?!" he said untangling the sheet and sitting up on the bed. Now he was awake.

"My friend has season tickets and couldn't go at the last minute, so she called me to see if I wanted them. So I went over and picked them up. The game's at 3:00, so let's go."

He sat on the bed, sheet draped across his lap, and looked at her.

"What's wrong?" she asked. "Are you still mad at me?"

"No, and I wasn't mad. But you have a date tonight."

"I broke it."

"Alexis."

"I'd rather do this."

"Alexis."

"It's too late; I already broke it. But we made it for next week, so does that make you feel better?"

He smiled.

"Okay."

He threw the sheet back and climbed out of bed. She looked at his boxers and grinned broadly.

"Hearts?" she said with raised eyebrows.

He kissed her on top of the head.

"A Valentine present from my sister."

He went into the bathroom.

"Are these seats any good?" he asked after he flushed the toilet and opened the door.

She could hear him brushing his teeth. She got off the floor and sat on the edge of his bed, running her hands across the sheets, which were still warm from his body heat.

"Not bad, I guess, but I really don't know for sure. It doesn't matter; we'll have fun. One thing, though."

"What?" he asked walking back into the room, shaving cream on the lower half of his face, razor in his left hand.

"Only happy thoughts and lots of laughs—no heavy talk. Okay?"

He winked.

"You're the best."

She waited while he finished his morning ritual in the bathroom. Picking up his pillow, she held it reverently in her lap, resisting the urge to hug it close to her heart. He came back into the room looking so trim and sexy that she could hardly stand it. The waist of the boxers hung precariously low on his hips. There was no body fat for the elastic to grab onto. Her heart pounded madly out of control as she struggled to maintain the same nonchalant air he exhibited. He had no idea what he was doing to her. She found that both refreshing and disconcerting. He was unpretentious, but he'd never tease her if he knew her true feelings. It was obvious he still thought of her only as his good buddy. She cursed her pride and struggled for composure.

"I'll go wait downstairs," she volunteered finally able to get some words out. Her voice didn't sound natural to her; she hoped he hadn't noticed—she knew he was too dense.

He picked up the pillow, which had started the night before on top of his head but spent the later part of the night on the floor, and threw it at her.

"Hang on. I'll only be a minute."

He walked over to his dresser and opened the second drawer. As he took out a clean pair of boxers, she knew what was happening next and she feared she was going to lose consciousness. She clamped her jaw shut because she was sure her heart was ready to jump out of her throat at any time. He had his back to her as the boxers slid down his legs with the greatest of ease. No self-conscious fibers in this boy's body. She wanted to close her eyes as indescribable ecstasy washed over her, but she couldn't lose that moment. She felt guilty getting such titillating pleasure from a gesture that he viewed with such innocence. Fresh boxers in place, he walked to his closet.

"Now that I'm awake, tell me again where you got these tickets," he said.

"Um," she said stalling for time as she scurried to get all her faculties functioning at somewhat of a normal capacity, "my friend from work. She and her husband have season tickets." She gasped for a quick breath as he eased his jeans up over his hips. "Um, we talked yesterday about them going to the game, and I said it sounded like fun. Then she called this morning to say something came up, and could I use the tickets. Of course I thought of you right away, and here I am."

"I'd planned on doing laundry today," he smiled as he pulled his tee shirt over his head, "but this sounds like much more fun."

"Lucky thing," said Alexis, "because Sean's here doing laundry. That's how I got in."

"For someone who has his own apartment and wants to be so independent, he sure spends enough time here doing his laundry." He turned to the mirror over his dresser and fingered his hair back into place after its assault by the tee shirt. "He just comes over to eat our food. I think the laundry's just an excuse."

She smiled, feeling much more relaxed now that he was fully clothed. His feet were still bare, though, and she even found that provocative. Grabbing his shoes and socks, he sat down on the bed next to her. Then, his sea-blue eyes blazing with a sincerity that almost made her collapse, he turned and looked her in the eye.

"But before we go," he said, "are you sure about this date thing? I feel bad."

"Don't. The whole idea is to make you feel good. You're going to have fun today if it kills me. We rescheduled the date. It was for dinner and a movie that will still be around next week. This is what I want to do. Okay?"

"Okay."

He started putting his socks on. She was more comfortable when he wasn't looking at her like that.

"Are you sure you're not still mad about last night?" She had to ask.

"Alexis—no heavy talk. Your own decree."

"Does that mean, yes, but we'll talk about it later?"

"It means, I'm sorry if I acted like a jerk." He tied his shoes. Then he sat up and looked at her again. She nearly caved in as he kissed her lightly on the cheek. "Truly I am."

A smile filled her soul—he never would have kissed Scott. She had to pick up every small crumb wherever it landed.

# CHAPTER 19

For once Cain was looking forward to his Friday pilgrimage into the city. Today there was an up side; he was meeting Fr. Mike for lunch. They had spoken often on the phone, but this was their first meeting since Cain had been back home. What could be better for a hot, end-of-the-summer day than lunch on Navy Pier with a trusted friend?

"It's been too long," said Mike as they embraced and then walked along the pier. "I should have gotten here sooner, but you know how busy I am."

"Really?" smiled Cain. "I thought you'd have lots of time on your hands now that I'm gone."

"Well, I have noticed a lessening of my workload in the past eight months, but not enough to allow for a visit out of town."

"Meredithe refuses to give in and let me drive, or I'd have been down to see you."

"He's a difficult man, isn't he?"

"That's a very nice way to put it, Mike. I could never be a priest."

"You behave yourself with him, though?" smiled Mike.

"I try. He makes it very hard. But today I'll be on my best behavior because I'm hitting him up big time."

"What do you mean?"

"I just finished summer school, and my fall classes will complete the requirements for my associate's degree. I want to apply at Northwestern again. I had to turn down a scholarship and walk out on that dream a long time ago. Maybe this time it'll work out. I have to pretend not to want it too bad, though, or he'll turn me down flat. He really hates me."

"Don't let him discourage you. And worst of all, don't let him bait you into cooperating with your own destruction. You can be good at that."

"I know." No smile as thought about Joanne. "But I am growing up."

"That's good to hear. I mean, you're already what—twenty-four?"

"Don't worry, I still have a long way to go."

"Well, just practice humility in the name of making your dream come true, and let him know you need him."

"What worries me is Sam Willet. He still thinks I'm an animal, and he doesn't want to see me going anywhere with my life. And Meredithe is his yes-man, or in my case—his no-man. But even if by some miracle he let's me and I do get in, I still have to find some way to pay for it. Northwestern's damned expensive."

"There are ways—especially with your talents. Don't let that discourage you. Once you get passed Meredithe and Willet, the rest will be a piece of cake for you."

They found a table at an outdoor cafe and sat down.

"The view here is indescribable," said Mike as they ordered something cold to drink.

"I love the city. Scott and I—"

"That's still an open wound, isn't it?" said the priest when Cain couldn't go on.

"Yeah. We had so many plans for now."

"Are you making new friends? Somebody will come along to fill that void."

"Alexis kind of has—and my brothers. I'm not ready to open myself up to anybody else."

"Are you dating anyone?"

"This girl, Kristen. Did I tell you about her?"

"The one you went to the wedding with?"

"Yeah. She's very pretty and fun to be with, but I'm keeping things light. After Joanne I see no advantage whatsoever to being in love. It's highly overrated, and it hurts way too much."

The waitress brought their drinks. Mike eyed him warily and told the waitress they wanted to wait a while before ordering.

"What about your parents? They certainly have a beautiful love."

"Yeah, but that doesn't happen for everybody."

"Matt's not happy?"

"Mike, all I know is I hurt too much to even want to consider it. And besides, I can't even really take a girl out. I have to either double date or say, *Let's go out—you drive.* It's kind of awkward, not to mention a little hard on the ego."

"She doesn't understand that?"

"Yeah, she understands—that's not the point. I have trouble understanding it sometimes. **I'm** the one who has a problem with it. I'm not in prison anymore, but my life definitely isn't my own. Like, Alexis kept after me earlier in the summer to play baseball because she knows how much I love it, but nobody understands I still have a ball and chain around my ankle. I have very little time I can call my own; and when I do, I can't just jump in a car and get to where I have to be. And then I have to be back home by 11:00—not just go home, but **be in the house** by 11:00. That's another point Meredithe won't budge on. So my social life is crap. And he calls often to check on me, so I'm not comfortable pushing it even by a few minutes—which is exactly his intent. It was almost easier to be in prison—there the bars and razor wire were constant reminders that I couldn't do what I wanted to do. Now I see a whole world stretched out in front of me, but I can only move in tight little circles—mostly just chasing my own tail."

"You always have a way of nailing things down and leaving me very little to say."

"No, you always know what to say. That's why your friendship is so important to me."

It seemed like a good moment to take a break in the conversation to look over the menu before the waitress came back. After they decided and ordered, Cain was the first to speak.

"How's Jon? Please tell me you've heard from him, and everything's still good."

"Actually, I have, and he's doing very well. You were a good influence on him. He wants to come and see you, but he knows the bind you're in here and how much trouble he could cause you, so he'll stay away for now and be content to keep in touch through me. He even has a pretty steady girlfriend, and he's still going to school at night."

Cain smiled sincerely.

"I really miss him, you know?"

"There'll be a time you can be together again. But wait until you can do it legally. You have too much at stake right now to risk a meeting."

"My life is a lesson in patience."

"I know that," smiled the priest.

"Too bad I didn't know it back when I first met Carrie Willet. It sure would have saved me a whole lot of grief."

"Are you still totally pissed at God?" Mike asked.

"Who?"

"Come on, now," frowned Mike. "You can't still be blaming God for your troubles?"

"I never did blame God. I know I'm perfectly able to screw up my life all by myself. I just don't relate to religion. That's another part of me that's just sort of cold and dead."

"Beyond repair?"

"I don't know. I believe in God. I'm just not sure He believes in me. My mother's pissed at me because I don't go to Church anymore. She still has that Old Country, Irish-Catholic faith. She's sure I'm going to hell, and I'm not certain she's wrong. But even for her, I can't reconcile that part of my life. Maybe some day."

"Hopefully, you have plenty of time. None of us knows for sure."

"Nobody knows that better than me. But . . . do you want me to be fake or pretend? Wouldn't it be hypocritical to feel the way I do and go to Church just to keep everybody happy? Shouldn't I feel something inside?"

"Yes, but maybe if you went to Church you'd find a transformation taking place over a period of time. How can you expect God to come back into your life if you're not open to Him, if you don't give yourself a chance?"

"I don't need a lecture, Mike. I get enough from my mom."

"Okay," laughed the priest. "You're right, that's not what I came here for."

After they ate, they walked down the pier and sat down and watched the boats out on the lake. They talked about old times, and Mike filled Cain in on news of men he had known at Maddox.

All too soon it was time for Cain to leave for his meeting with Meredithe. He said good-bye to Mike with a lingering, almost desperate, hug, and then he turned and walked toward Meredithe's office. It was very hard for him to take leave of this man with whom he was able to connect so completely. Mike was one of the few people he knew who could understand and relate to where he was coming from—to where he had been and what he had experienced. Even Meredithe with all his big talk and pseudo-savvy had no real idea of what life was like behind bars. He didn't have to hide anything from Mike because Mike was there through it all—holding his hand and giving him the strength he needed to get from day to day. How could he ever repay a man who knew his total despair and had been his only strength when there just didn't seem to be anything left to live for? Go back to Church? *Is that You whispering in my ear, God?* Shaking it off, he continued his quest.

He had left a message on Alexis's answering machine before he left for work that night. Instead of meeting him at work like she usually did, he wanted her to meet him at the park near his house. He left specific instructions for her to be there no sooner than 10:15 because he didn't want her waiting there before he got there. If in some case he wasn't there, she was to wait in her car with the doors locked only for five minutes and then leave if he still wasn't there. *What was he up to?*

When she pulled up, she saw him sitting on a bench near the parking lot. She wasn't sure what this all meant; therefore, she couldn't call up any specific emotion to feel. Anxiety and apprehension just kind of took over and escalated as she approached him.

"Sit down," he said sounding pretty normal. He was slouched back with his long legs stretched out in front of him, crossed at the ankles.

"What's wrong?" she asked.

"Nothing. I just needed to clear my head a little, and I love being outside at night. Do you know that for nearly six years I was never outside past 4:30 in the afternoon? I used to stand by my window sometimes and look out and try to remember what it was like. There were lots of floodlights around, so it was nearly impossible to ever see stars, but I did see the moon once in a while. Now I can't get enough of it. Especially after a hot day like today. There's a natural coolness and winding down to the day. I don't want to go in yet until I have to."

He was staring out passed her into the darkness of the night.

"Honey, how'd it go with Meredithe today? Did you ask him about Northwestern?"

"Yeah, I did."

"And—" She was growing impatient with his vagueness.

"And I can apply. What a guy, huhn?"

"You had me worried," she sighed with relief. "At first I thought he said no."

"He would've had a real fight on his hands if he had. You know I was reading in the paper today that the parole system in our state is too lax, and they're trying to bring it up to speed. Some guys just call in to their parole officers once a week, and that's all the supervision they get. And I have to beg to go to school. But I don't want to talk about that anymore."

"What do you want to talk about?" she asked, feeling more relaxed.

"You."

"Me?"

"Yeah. I have something for you, and I decided to give it to you today because this is an anniversary of sorts for us."

"It is?"

"Yeah, see I knew you wouldn't remember. This is one of those things that's etched forever in my mind only."

"What is it?" she asked finding it hard to believe anything about him wouldn't be etched in her mind forever as well.

"It was six years ago today that I ran into you in this very park—just before my trial ended. We talked and we walked and we ate cheese fries from across the street. Then I walked you home . . . and you kissed me. I thought about that night a lot while I was away. It got me through some lonely times."

"Yeah, and then I never wrote to you like I promised."

"It's okay," he smiled. "You were here at that moment when I was about to bottom out, and you're here now. I don't know what I'd do without you. So I want you to have this."

He took out a small box and handed it to her. Inside was a beautiful, delicate, antique pendant on a fragile, silver chain.

"Cain," she sighed in awe. "This is exquisite."

"It was my grandmother's—my father's mother. After she died, my dad gave us all a piece of her jewelry. He told us guys we should put it away for the woman we marry." Then he pulled the dream right out from under her. "But I'm not ever getting married. I'm not even going to ever fall in love again. But you're my best friend, and I want you to have it. Thank you for that night six years ago, and thank you for all the days and nights since. I hope that whoever you marry understands our friendship because—I already said it—I don't know what I'd do without you. Try it on."

Her hands were trembling as she opened the clasp and put the delicate, silver chain around her neck.

"How does it look?" she asked still somewhat breathless.

"Beautiful, just like you. You suit each other."

Tears ran down her face. She wanted to tell him that she couldn't accept such a treasure, but there was no way she wanted anyone else to have it—ever. She recognized the opportunity to admit her undying love for him, but she was so afraid of scaring him off and ruining their friendship. She was never so touched but so miserable at the same time.

"What about Kristen?" she finally managed to say. "Something might come of that one day. You haven't given it enough time."

"No. I'm already thinking I've been seeing too much of her. She called me *honey* the other day."

"I call you *honey* all the time," smiled Alexis through her tears.

"I know, but that's different. My mom calls me *honey*, too."

"I'll take that as a compliment."

"Yeah, that's the way it was meant. I don't like when Kristen says it, though. It's like she's getting too comfortable. I'm not over Joanne yet—I don't know if I ever will be. I still go crazy thinking about her. It's all I can do to keep from going after her."

"But you haven't?"

"No. And I won't, don't worry."

"Have you and Kristen ever . . . ?"

"Fucked?" he said finishing her sentence.

She laughed inside in spite of her fear of his answer. He really had a way of getting to the point.

"That's not exactly the way I was going to put it, but yeah."

"I'm sorry," he said. "That was pretty crude."

"That's okay. And you don't have to answer. It's really none of my business."

"You can ask me anything. And the answer's no, we haven't. To tell you the truth, I'm still a little scared of sex—especially with Meredithe and the law breathing down my neck. And I had one female turn on me. That was enough for a lifetime I don't trust many people these days."

"If it wasn't for that, do you think you probably would be . . . having . . . sex . . . with her?"

He shifted his gaze to look directly into her eyes. It was obvious he was caught more than a little off guard.

"I'm sorry!" she apologized, totally astounded that she had verbalized the question that had been screaming in her mind. "That was out of line."

"I'd answer that, but I really don't know."

"We'd better get you home," Alexis said anxious to change the subject. Then she turned to him. "This is the most amazing gift that I've

415

ever received. I'll treasure it always . . . but if you ever decide it was a mistake and you should have waited, I'll understand."

"I'd never take it back from you. I remember my grandma wearing it even though she died when I was still pretty young. She'd be honored to know that you have it. I told my mom and dad I was giving it to you, and they both think it's a wise choice."

"Thank you."

They got up and started walking toward her car.

"Hey, there's one thing, though. All we've been talking about is me, and I wanted to ask you about your mystery man."

"What mystery man?"

"The one you told me about a while back. The guy you're hung up on but he doesn't know it."

"Oh," she laughed a little uncomfortably.

"Is he still in the picture?"

"Oh, yeah, more than ever."

"You're still not going to tell me who he is?"

"No. I almost did a few minutes ago, but I'm just not ready. I'm really confused, and believe me, you can't help."

"How do you know?"

"Don't worry, I know. Come on, we have just enough time to get an order of cheese fries and a few Cokes across the street and get to your house before 11:00. Thank you for remembering this anniversary. It's now etched in my mind forever. I'll meet you here for cheese fries and Cokes every year."

"Even if that mystery man finally comes out of his coma?"

"Yes," she laughed.

"Is that guy blind?"

"I don't think so—just a little thick-headed."

They went back to his house, and Alexis went in with him. Will had already gone up to bed, but Nora was reading in the living room.

"Hi," she smiled when they walked in, always relieved that Cain was in on time. "What have you two been up to?"

"Hanging out," answered Cain. "Burping and telling dirty jokes. The usual."

Nora shifted her gaze to Alexis who smiled demurely back at her. *You gotta love him.*

"Matthew called, and he wants you to call him right away."

"Okay, I'll be right back," said Cain. Then he pointed a finger at them. "And don't talk about me; I hate that." He started to go to the kitchen phone, but stopped and turned back to them. "Show Mom the necklace, Lex."

Then he left the room. Alexis brushed her long, soft curls back from her shoulders so Nora could get a good view of the beautiful necklace. She was beaming with the excitement of owning it. Nora recognized the glow right away. In fact, she had been aware for some time now that Alexis was in love with Cain. She was just amazed that her son couldn't see it. This was the young woman who was going to break her heart. She knew it as well as she knew anything. It was just a matter of when Cain with all his brilliance of mind was going to figure it out.

"It was meant for you," said Nora with a loving smile.

"It's so beautiful," said Alexis as she put her hand up to her neck to touch the pendant. "I just feel bad—it should stay in the family."

"You're family," assured Nora, "and you're not going anywhere, are you?"

"No."

"Well, there you go—it'll stay in the family."

"Thank you," said Alexis warmly.

"No, thank **you**—for being such a good friend to my son. Life is harder for him than most people, and you're the one bright spot in it. I hope he tells you how much you mean to him."

"He does," smiled Alexis.

"Not enough, I'm sure," said Nora with a telling smile, "but he'll figure it out."

"He's a very special person."

"That he is," agreed Nora. "He's just had this problem his whole life with coming up with five every time he puts two and two together. He's smart enough to know that it's not right, but it takes him forever to search out the right answer. And that has caused him, and the rest of us who love him, a lot of heartache. So anyone who loves him—in any capacity—has to be prepared for that. You've heard of the old expression about loving someone so much it hurts? That's what it means to love Cain, but your rewards far outweigh the pain."

"He adores you," said Alexis, "and now I know why."

"Thank you, and I'm glad you're so much a part of his life. I'm getting older, and it's nice to have someone to lean on. Will is a wonderful person, but men don't understand quite the way we do."

It was about three weeks later on a Saturday morning when Cain called Alexis and sent her into the biggest tailspin she had experienced since knowing him. She hadn't seen him or talked to him for a few days because she had been out of town on business. She was going to call him while she was away, but her heart needed a respite from the emotional calisthenics he put her through.

"It's not even 10:00," she said looking over at her clock.

"Did I wake you?"

"No, but you're never up before noon on Saturday."

"I know. I can't sleep. I'm in love!"

She stifled a gasp, and it took her a while to respond.

"Are you there?" he asked.

"Yes, I'm here. What's this all about?"

"I'm coming over. I'm riding my bike. See you in about fifteen minutes."

He hung up and left her thrashing around in water over her head, groping for something to grab on to in order to stay afloat. She leaves him on his own for two days, and he's in love?! The man who is never going to love again?! A queasiness rose up within her. She knew she wasn't going to like this visit at all.

When he got there, he was bursting with more enthusiasm than she had seen from him since they were kids. She forced herself to smile.

"You're not going to believe this!" he said as if he had discovered a cure for cancer.

"Why don't you sit down and tell me about it."

"She's in my psych class. I noticed her the first day, but who wouldn't? She's beautiful. She's Italian, so she has long, dark hair and the brownest eyes I've ever seen."

Alexis suddenly felt very pale and plain as he bubbled on.

"Anyway, I noticed her right away, and then she started sitting next to me."

"Well, you're so homely and unattractive, it's a wonder she would even give you a second look, let alone want to sit by you."

"Come on, Alexis, let me finish."

"Okay, I'm sorry."

"Yesterday she asked me if I wanted to go down for coffee with her after class. It was just lucky we both had some free time before our next classes."

"That was lucky—since you hardly ever have free time."

She was hoping she didn't sound as cynical as she felt, but he was too excited to notice even if she did.

"Yeah," he said. "Her name's Dania, and she's an interior design student."

"How nice for her."

He finally picked up on her tone.

"What's wrong?" he asked.

"Nothing. Go ahead."

"Well, that's basically it."

"On the phone you said, **love**, Cain. Not too many weeks ago you were telling me that you wanted nothing to do with that hateful emotion. What happened to the torch you're carrying for Joanne?"

"I don't know, but I haven't felt like this in a long time— probably since back in school when things were good with Joanne and me. And lately I've been noticing I haven't been thinking nearly as much about Joanne as I used to. But . . . I have a huge favor to ask you."

"What?"

"Don't say it like that—there's something in it for you, too."

"This sounds good—let's hear it."

"I thought you would be happier than you are."

"I'm sorry," she sighed, trying to conjure up a little enthusiasm in the face of total despair. "It's been a long two days, and I didn't get in until late last night—that's why I didn't call you. What's this favor you want to ask me?"

"I want to ask her out, but she doesn't know anything about me. I feel stupid asking her to drive. So I got this great idea. You could ask your mystery man out, and we could double. It would be a perfect opportunity for you to approach him."

"NO!"

"Alexis, the guy's a slow-start—he needs a little push. He's going to get away if you don't make a move on him pretty soon. This is the onset of the new millennium—it's permissible for girls to ask guys out. In fact, we rather like it. Maybe he's afraid to ask you. Maybe you're way too pretty and sexy and intimidating."

"Pretty and sexy are debatable, but intimidating?!"

"Maybe for him. He's probably afraid of rejection."

Her smile was oozing adoration. Even when he was breaking her heart, she couldn't help but love him.

"No," she said, "I can't ask him."

"Alexis, I'm desperate. I don't want to ask Matt because he and I are just way too weird sometimes, especially with someone who doesn't know us. One of us needs to dye his hair and go out and get plastic surgery or something. And Sean's tied up for the next few weeks. Please. I'll do anything."

"Anything?" she grinned.

"Well, almost anything. What are you thinking about?"

"Nothing. I'm just teasing you. I love doing that."

"I know. But please be serious for now. I have to get this worked out. I haven't wanted anything this bad in a long time. And I want you to ask that guy out, so you'll be happy too. I'm not just thinking of myself."

"I know you're not, and I love you for it; but I can't ask him. I think it might already be too late."

"Why?" frowned Cain with serious concern.

"I think there might be someone else."

"What?! Does this guy know you, or is it someone you've just seen but haven't met?"

"He knows me."

"How can he know you, and not want to be with you?"

She smiled and tenderly put her hand on his cheek. Then she lightly kissed his other cheek.

"It doesn't matter. I won't ask him, but for you I'll find someone else."

"But now I feel like crap."

"Why? There are other guys."

"I know, but this was supposed to be about both of us—not just me."

"Well things aren't happening for both us right now. So let's concentrate on you."

He sighed and sat back on the couch sincerely disturbed.

"I'll figure something else out."

"No," she insisted. "There's this guy at the office—his name is Cole. Isn't that a cool name? Almost as cool as Cain!" He smiled and nearly made her lose her line of thought. "Anyway, he asked me out once, but I turned him down. Maybe I could make up for it now. Who knows, maybe he could be the man of my dreams and I don't even know it because I haven't given him a chance."

"Yeah, but I know how much it hurts to love someone who doesn't love you back."

"That it does," she sighed. "But you said you're starting to get over Joanne, so it is possible. Let me do this for you. Just promise me one thing."

"Anything."

"If . . . this turns into something . . . special, you won't forget about me."

Tears filled her eyes.

"Hey," he said with the most sincerity she had ever seen from him, "that will never happen. I could never care for anyone who couldn't accept you as part of my life."

"Well, you know . . . I get scared sometimes when I think about it. Sometimes it's hard for a woman to accept another woman as her man's best friend. Actually she should be your best friend."

He was looking at her in the most bewildered way. Alexis knew the look. He was trying to make two plus two equal five, and it wasn't working. She immediately hated herself for luring him from the elated mood he had been in when he came over. It truly hadn't been her intention. She quickly wiped the tears from her eyes. This was getting way too intense.

"I'm sorry," she said. "I just don't know what I'd do if I lost you."

He looked at her in a state of total confusion, his addition still not adding up. He reached over and took her in his arms. She couldn't believe how gentle he was, how much care he took with her. She had never before felt so protected and safe.

"What's this all about?" he asked. "I only just met this girl. I don't even know if she wants to go out with me now, let alone if a time comes when I have to tell her I'm a convicted felon. You're talking like I'm getting married and moving to China or something."

"I'm sorry," she said cuddling into his shoulder and feeling the warmth of his body on her face. "I guess since you've been home, I've become way too possessive of you. And I don't want anyone to ever hurt you again."

"Alexis," he smiled and kissed her on top of the head, "it's a date. Okay? I haven't even asked her; maybe she won't even say yes."

"She'll say yes," said Alexis as she moved away and looked up at him. "Don't you have any mirrors in your house?"

"I hope I would be more to her than just looks."

"You will be, but that's where it starts. You're such a babe in the woods when it comes to woman."

"Well, I haven't had much practice. I'm still kind of stuck at eighteen."

"Just be careful," she said taking care to be a concerned friend and not a jealous lover. "Remember what you told me about not trusting girls after Carrie Willet. That makes sense in your position. Just as there are men who will take advantage of a date situation by expecting and demanding sex, there are women who will do the Carrie Willet thing just for revenge or any of a million other reasons."

"Okay, Mom," he smiled.

"I'll go along with this scheme of yours, but just remember, I will beat her ass if she pulls any shit on you whatsoever! And don't smile at me like that, or I'm going to have to beat your ass, too!"

"Yes, ma'am!"

"This isn't going to be easy," said Alexis. "We have to come up with a double date that fits in with all your time and place restrictions. For example, it's not a good idea to go out to a bar until 1:00 or 2:00 in the morning."

"Right," agreed Cain.

"We could go to the zoo and then to dinner. That would get us home early, and it would be benign enough for a first date."

"Except I don't do zoos, Alexis. It hits a little too close to home."

"Sorry. I wasn't thinking. Give me a little time to think about this; I'll come up with something. I'm pretty good at this. What are you doing tomorrow? I'll call you."

"I'm golfing with Matt and Sean. We have a 7:00 tee time."

"In the morning?!"

"Of course."

"It's the weekend, what happened to sleeping in? Oh, I forgot—you're in love."

"Are you making fun of me?"

"I wouldn't dream of it," she laughed. "Now get out of here because I have about a million things to do, and I don't get anything done when you're around."

"Okay. You'll think of something and call me tomorrow?"

"Yes. Unless of course **you** can think of something first."

"All right, I'll think, too. Oh, and by the way . . . about this mystery guy . . . I think he's someone I know because otherwise you'd tell me. It's just a matter of time before I figure it out."

"Okay, Holmes," she said opening the door and gently guiding him through it. "Just don't hurt your brain too much."

"Am I right?" he asked with a mischievous grin.

"Good-bye, Cain." A final nudge and she closed the door after him.

She leaned against the closed door that separated them and shed the false cheerfulness she had displayed for his benefit. From deep inside she could feel the reality of what he had told her taking root amidst all her beautiful hopes and dreams, choking them out. Then the million things she had to do materialized in the form of hopeless tears, which burst forth and didn't subside until at least a million had been shed.

"I made a few calls, and I was able to get four tickets to the Bears game next Sunday," she told him when she called the next evening.

"Perfect!" he said. "How much do I owe you—I'll pay for all of them."

"Nothing. I got them through work. And I talked to Cole . . ."

"You have his phone number?"

"Yes. Why?"

"I don't know. I didn't think you knew him that well."

"Well, I do. And he can go, so now you just have to arrange things with Miss What's-her-name."

"Dania."

"Dania," she repeated.

"You're acting kind of weird about this. Is everything okay?"

"Yes, everything's fine. I just hope you know this is way above and beyond the call of friendship."

"I do. Really I do. I owe you, sweetheart."

She couldn't see him, but she knew him well enough to know he winked and then broke out in one of his *How-can-you-ever-be-mad-at-me* grins.

On the morning of the game, Alexis steeled herself against spending a whole day with Cain while he fawned over Dania. She did everything short of helping herself to a stiff drink from the bottle of Irish Whiskey that Cain had left at her house. Cole was a nice guy, and she knew that under different circumstances she could have fun with him; but this was going to be agony.

To make matters worse Dania turned out to be every bit as beautiful as Cain had said, and she seemed thoroughly enthralled with him. Alexis made a point of concentrating on the game and on Cole so she wouldn't have to watch them. She couldn't believe how smooth

Cain was for someone who was supposedly out of practice. She was always telling him that he should have more fun, but now she was wishing he wasn't enjoying himself as much as he seemed to be. She cursed herself more than once for agreeing to this fiasco, but there was no recourse except to see it through. She also hoped that Cole wasn't able to see through her act and sense what a miserable time she was having. After all, he was an innocent player in this charade, and she didn't want for it to spoil his good time.

When Dania excused herself to go to the restroom and Cole went to buy a beer, Alexis and Cain found themselves alone for the first time.

"Well, I don't have to ask if you're having a good time," smiled Alexis.

He leaned over and kissed her cheek. Alexis amused herself with the thought of what people around them might be thinking since they obviously weren't a couple.

"I am, Lex, thanks. I'll make this up to you some day, I swear."

"I'm having a good time, too." Then the lie: "I'm glad you brought it up."

"I just didn't think you knew Cole so well."

"What do you mean?"

Cain shrugged. "I don't know . . . you had his phone number at home, and he just seems kind of . . . cozy."

Alexis wondered if it was just her imagination or if she actually did see a flash of Kelly green in his normally sea-blue, Irish eyes. Her heartbeat quickened a little, but she cautioned herself not to jump to conclusions that would cause her more heartbreak than ever.

"We work together," she said. "We've just never gone out before."

"Does he call you *honey* at work, too?"

"No," she answered, stifling a grin since he was dead serious. "But I told you about that. People use that word more now. It's a term of endearment, but it doesn't really mean anything."

She wasn't prepared for the look on his ever-expressive face. He didn't just shrug off her answer as a fact of life that he'd been out of touch with. He was disturbed, hurt.

"Oh," he said as if he had just learned there was no Santa Claus.

He was completely absorbed, wrestling with some problem.

"What about you?" he finally said shifting his intense eyes to meet hers.

She was so touched that she couldn't answer for a few seconds. That gave her time to prepare her answer. She realized this was one of the things she loved most about him. For all his suave maturity and impeccable sense of style, he still possessed a childlike innocence and wonder. She wanted to throw her arms around his neck and reassure him of the truth—he was the only person she called *honey*; the only person she wanted to call *honey*. Instead, she opted for a lie to protect her own interests. She was beginning to realize of late that she was free-falling without a parachute where he was concerned, and she knew the landing would be brutal—especially now with Dania in the picture.

"I guess I'm pretty much like everyone else," she shrugged. "I don't know. I never really thought about it."

He didn't respond, but she knew that wasn't the answer he wanted to hear. Cain left little room for doubt about his feelings when he looked you in the eye. She figured he must be a lousy poker player. She felt a little guilty, but she had to start looking out for herself.

After the game they went to a restaurant near home for pizza. They had just ordered and were discussing the game when without warning everything turned inside out. Cain had been a light-hearted part of the conversation when he arbitrarily looked up and collided at lightning-speed with his destructive past.

"Shit," he mumbled as his face drained of color and froze in horror.

His companions followed his icy stare, but Alexis was the only one to recognize and grasp the gravity of what was transpiring. Carrie Willet was easily recognizable, although much more the worse for wear than Cain. While Cain was muscularly fit and trim, she had gained about twenty pounds. Except for moments like this, he beamed and became more irresistible with each new day; she on the other hand looked drab and used-up. Alexis couldn't get over the change in her. She looked more like she had been the one who had spent nearly six years of her life locked up in prison. But then prisons imposed by the mind are often far more detrimental than the real thing.

Carrie had just walked in with friends, and she had spotted Cain too—or at least she thought it was Cain. The look on his face confirmed that she was confronting the right twin.

"Let's get out of here," said Alexis.

"Hold on," said Cain taking her hand and holding her in place. "We were here first. Let her leave."

"Cain, she's the one with the court order."

"I don't care. We're not leaving."

"Who is that?" asked Dania.

"A lying, conniving bitch," answered Cain. "And we're going to go on having a good time and pretend she isn't here."

"That's going to be hard," said Alexis, "because she's on the way over."

"Christ, what's wrong with her?" whined Cain.

She walked up to their table and stood motionless. She was right there. All Cain had to do was reach up and his hands would easily be encircling her neck. Then a squeeze and a jerk, and all his dreams would come true.

"Can I talk to you?" she finally managed to say.

"Go ahead," invited Cain. "Actually, I'm all ears. I can't wait to hear what you have to say."

"Outside." She glanced over at Alexis. "Alone."

"Carrie," the irony in Cain's laugh struck her right between the eyes, "there is nowhere on earth—or anywhere else for that matter—that I ever want to be alone with you again. I may have been naive and gullible when I was eighteen, but I've been to school and I'm a whole lot wiser now."

"I know," she said, her voice breaking and tears forming in her sunken eyes. "I know what I did to you, and what it cost you. I just want to tell you how sorry I am."

"I don't want to hear that, Carrie. I just want you to get the hell away from me before the police show up. You're putting me in a lot of jeopardy right now—again. You do whatever it is you have to do to soothe your conscience, but leave me out of it."

Tears ran down her face.

"I'm so sorry," she said. "I wish there was something I could do."

"Why don't you go have this conversation with your old man," frowned Cain. "Get the bastard off my back."

"I can't," she cried. "I've tried over and over, but I can't."

"Then there's no sense in us discussing it. And I'd really appreciate it if you'd get—what is it?—a hundred feet away from me right now."

"Cain," she begged.

"Carrie, I'm with friends right now, and they don't want to hear any more of this nonsense; and frankly, neither do I. And Gosh, I'm sorry I couldn't wipe the slate and make you feel better."

She took a deep breath as she realized she was wasting her time. Then without another word, she turned and left. Cain turned his back to her, but Alexis sighed with relief as Carrie and her friends left the restaurant. Cain looked over at Alexis. *Son of a bitch!*

"I'm really sorry," he apologized to Cole and Dania. "I suppose I owe you some kind of an explanation, but I don't really think I can talk about it right now."

"Then we won't," said Dania.

Alexis wished she didn't like Dania so much. She had been prepared to hate her, but instead she found herself liking her more and more as the day went on. Happily, they were able to move on, and Carrie Willet hadn't been able to cast a pall over yet another of Cain's moments.

He wasn't able to stop thinking about her, however. While he smiled his dazzling smile and laughed his infectious laugh, he couldn't shake the sight of her and he couldn't stop wondering what trouble was going to come his way because of this encounter. Sam Willet was a relentless adversary and Cain had just unmercifully spurned his daughter.

Usually a very demonstrative person, he kept this uncomfortable feeling under raps.

Alexis glimpsed it, however. Maybe it was because she was aware of what was at stake; but if that fact had evaded her, she hadn't missed the uneasy looks Cain stole her way every now and then. She wondered if he'd ever find peace while living in that town, but for some time to come, he really had no choice. It was hard to believe that such blatant injustice could take place within the legal limits of society. Like Cain, she was also wondering if Carrie would go home crying to her powerful daddy. Alexis could just imagine her right that minute dreaming up some diabolical spin on this latest episode in her fragile life. Well, there had been plenty of witnesses to the contrary; but Alexis was troubled by the fact that it was so easy for Carrie and Cain to inadvertently run into each other. What if the next time witnesses were scarce? She forced herself out from under the gloomy cloud that was settling over her.

In spite of her heroic acting job, Cole hadn't missed Alexis's unspoken adoration of Cain Farrell. It was when they were on their way home that he decided to bring it up to her.

"What is it between you two?" Cole asked her after they had dropped Dania and then Cain off.

"What do you mean?"

"I don't know—there's just an electricity there. I'm just curious why you were both out with other people."

"I explained the situation to you when I asked you to join us today. He's a dear friend, I was doing him a favor, and I thought you and I could have fun at the same time."

"Well, he's a lucky guy. I wish you'd look at me like that. And then there's the beautiful Dania—not any more beautiful than you, however. If he didn't look like a movie star or someone who had just walked out of a magazine, I'd think he had discovered the secret to everlasting happiness."

"He's a far way from everlasting happiness. And there's far more to him than just gorgeous looks."

"I know. I liked him. It was easy to see how people could be drawn to his personality as well as his looks. So are you just going to sit back and let Dania move in?"

Alexis smiled demurely.

"He's a good friend," she said emphatically. "In spite of how he looks and acts, he's going through a very hard time right now."

"I know," admitted Cole. "That . . . woman . . . was Carrie Willet, wasn't she?"

Alexis looked at him in amazement.

"You knew?"

"Not all along. His name was familiar to me, but I couldn't figure out why. Then when she showed up and I heard her first name and

426

got the drift of their conversation, I put it all together. It was pretty big news back then, even in my town."

"Thank you for not saying anything. Dania doesn't know—or at least I don't think so—but then I didn't think you did either."

"Well, she's a few years younger, so even if she lived here then, she probably wasn't that aware."

"You'd be surprised," she smiled. "You don't look like Cain Farrell, with an identical twin and your picture splashed all over the newspapers and TV, without drawing the attention of just about every female over the age of seven. He received flowers, cards, letters, trinkets, you name it, from adoring groupies during the trial. Of course, he got his share of hate mail, too. He saw very little of any of it because his lawyer set it up so he intercepted most of it. Then he had his staff go through it all to see if there were any bits or pieces that could be used in his defense. But I was at the trial every day, and I can tell you they had to set up barriers to hold the crowds—mostly female—back."

"Well, I hope Dania didn't get in on any of that."

Alexis shrugged as they pulled up in front of her apartment building.

"If he wants to keep seeing her, he's going to have to tell her sooner or later. Thank you for coming with me today and for being such a good sport."

"It was my pleasure," he smiled.

"Could I ask you up for a night cap without leading you on to think it's more than just a gesture of gratitude?"

"That would be nice. And don't worry, I know your heart walked out the door a few minutes ago when we dropped Cain off."

Well, Cole could add; now what was the matter with Cain?!

She knew there would be a message from Cain on her answering machine. She just didn't know if it would be a frantic call over Carrie Willet or a starry-eyed call over Dania. At any rate, she opted not to listen to her messages until later when she was alone.

She was more than a little disappointed that he didn't try calling her back—especially after she listened to the messages and he had indeed left her word to call him ASAP. She went to bed that night thinking about what Cole had said about sitting back and letting Dania move in. She firmly believed she had no control over that. That was Cain's move to make, and since he seemed to be moving in Dania's direction, maybe it was time for her to reclaim her heart and move on. She knew some day she'd laugh at all this—it just hurt too much right now.

Her resolve was firm and in tact until 10:00 the next night when she decided to drive over to meet him after work. Feeling weak and miserable, she waited outside the door he always come out of. Her heart reacted with the same hysteria it always did when she saw him, and she knew it was going to take a whole lot more will power than she had invested thus far.

He spotted her car, and ran toward it.

"Hi," he smiled. "This is a nice surprise. What happened to you last night? Did you get my message?"

Looking into his beautifully innocent face, she suddenly realized there was no way she could ever let him belong to anyone else. No, she wasn't going to just sit back and let Dania move in. But she was going to do it her way. There had to be a way she could make him realize that their unique friendship was just the beginning of what could be a very beautiful relationship, and she had to start right then. She had already wasted enough precious time. For all she knew he hadn't called her back the night before because he was busy on the phone with Dania. The thought of it drove her to action.

"Yes, I got your message, but not until kind of late after Cole left, so I thought I'd come here tonight in person instead."

"Cole was at your apartment last night?"

"Yeah," she answered trying to keep cool. "I wanted to thank him for being so nice and helping us out with your date with Dania."

The corners of his mouth turned up in an amused smile. She didn't detect jealousy, but at least he stuck to the subject instead of brushing it off to gush about Dania.

"How did you thank him, Alexis?"

She bopped his nose with her index finger. "It's none of your business, my dear. Let's just say, he said *you're welcome* before he left."

"Alexis!"

"What?" she asked remaining coy. "Aren't I allowed to have a life?"

"Well, yeah, but I thought you didn't even like him that much."

"That was before I went out with him. Actually, I think he's very nice."

She wanted to start driving, but she was enjoying the look on his face too much.

"He is nice," he conceded. "But I don't think he's your type."

"What?" Had she seen it? Was the tiniest flash of green in his eyes again?

"Yeah. I mean, don't get me wrong, he's a really great guy, but he looks like the type that would wear white socks and black dress shoes with shorts."

"And that's not my type?"

"No. And what about this mystery guy? He must be your type if you're hung up on him."

"The mystery guy's a jerk. I figure if he's too dumb to notice me, then I don't want him."

"Maybe you just haven't given him enough time."

"Cain, it's getting close to a year. How long does it take? And other people who have been with me when he's around have guessed my feelings for him. So either he's very stupid or just totally uninterested. In either case, I'm wasting my time. So he can just go jump in the lake."

"Just like that?"

"Just like that."

He knitted his brows together as he thought about it. She put the car in gear and began driving toward his house. They were quiet for the next few minutes: Cain struggling with simple math in his head, and Alexis praying for miracles. Cain tried to figure out why it disturbed him so much that Alexis was giving up on this guy. He didn't even know who he was. He was beginning to realize, however, that while she was loving in vain, she remained unattached. There was something he liked about that. Now if she was giving up, that meant she was ready to find someone to be with, someone to love. For the first time he stopped to wonder where that would leave him. No, he wasn't sure at all that he liked this idea.

"So, you're going to start seeing Cole?"

"Maybe. We got along quite well yesterday, don't you think?"

"I guess, but then I wasn't with you at your apartment while you were thanking him."

"No," she said loving the way the conversation was going, "you weren't."

"Did you have sex with him?"

"How about we talk about Dania? I think she's very nice and just as pretty as you said she was."

"I don't want to talk about Dania." He was becoming irritated. "Stop playing games, Lex. Did you have sex with Cole last night?"

"I'm not sure you have a right to ask me that. Who do you think you are?"

"You asked me if I was having sex with Kristen."

"That was different," she pouted.

"Oh." He wasn't convinced.

She pulled into his driveway and stopped.

"I care about you," he said.

"I care about you, too."

"Then why won't you tell me? You keep shutting me out when it comes to guys. You won't tell me who this other guy is, and now this. I tell you everything."

"Why is it so important for you to know?"

"I don't know. It just . . . is."

"Well, it's just as important for me not to tell you. I'm sorry I asked you about Kristen. I even told you that at the time. Remember? I said it was really none of my business."

He sat and stared at her, dead serious. She knew he was angry.

"Thanks for picking me up," he said.

Then he opened the door and got out. She would have liked it better if he had slammed the door behind him, but he didn't. Then without looking back, he went into the house. She exhaled a long breath through her lips. That certainly hadn't ended up exactly how she had planned it. She waited a few minutes hoping he would come back out, but she knew how stubborn he was. She put the car in reverse and left.

After a few cordial words with his parents, he said good night and went upstairs. He was glad he had gotten his homework done before he went to work, because he definitely wasn't in the mood now. He had never known a girl who could aggravate him the way Alexis could. Why was she acting this way?

Taking off his clothes and literally throwing them across the room, he got into bed. However, sleep was a long way off. He was far too agitated to be open to the type of relaxation that leads to peaceful oblivion. Staring through the dark, he tried to figure out what was happening to his relationship with Alexis. Why was she being so stubborn? Why did he care so much? What difference did it really make if she was having sex with Cole? They're both adults. And the other guy . . . well, he deserves to lose her. What an idiot! And why did it matter who he was? **BUT** . . . why was she being like this? Why couldn't she tell him? She didn't have to go into detail. He'd never expect that from her, but they were best friends—she should be able to trust him with her secrets.

He tossed and turned, trying to get comfortable, wishing he could stop thinking. He wasn't solving anything. He was just frustrating himself with an inability to fall asleep. This exercise in futility continued for over an hour. He reached over and picked up the phone. It only rang once before she answered. She must have been having the same problem sleeping he was.

"Alexis, I don't understand, but I also don't have a right to make demands on your privacy. I'm sorry. I just don't want you to be hurt. Be patient with me—I'm still stumbling through polite society. It takes a while to shed six years of lunacy. I've only recently gotten used to sleeping in total darkness and silence again, so it stands to reason that more complicated things will take a little longer."

"Listen to me, okay?" she said. "I don't want to fight with you over this. I value our friendship way too much. But I see it becoming more and more of an issue, so I need to talk to you. But I don't want to do it over the phone. I've just been laying here thinking about it. I haven't been totally honest with you, and I guess it's time I should be. I'm just kind of scared."

"Of me?!"

"No. You're the dearest, gentlest man I've ever known. Just go to sleep, and I'll talk to you . . . soon."

"Okay," he said knowing he really had no other choice.

"Hey," she smiled as she changed the subject, "you mean they don't turn the lights out at Maddox?"

"Not completely. There are night lights so they can see what's going on in the cells all the time, and then as if that's not enough, they come by on their rounds and shine their flashlights in your face all night."

"And it's noisy?"

"Beyond belief. Inmates banter back and forth with each other after the lights go out—all their funky jive-talk and rappin'. Then there's the moaners making love to their hands, and the other guys yelling at them to shut up. It's all part of the jailhouse culture. Can't put your pillow over your head to try and block it all out, either. The guards want to know who's sleeping in your bed. They don't want to take any chances it may be a dummy and you're off clawing your way out of their establishment."

"How did you stand it?"

"I got used to it. Then it was weird to be home where everything was dark and quiet and private. I think I've finally gotten acclimated to that again, but other things are taking longer. I'm sorry I gave you a hard time tonight."

"No," she said wishing she could hug him, "I'm sorry. So let's drop it, okay?"

"Okay."

"What about Dania? Did she have a good time at the game?"

"Yeah, she did."

"You don't sound real enthused . . . at least not like you did the other day—when you were in love."

"I don't know," he sighed. "Today at school she was all cling-y and possessive. It kind of freaked me out, you know?"

"Yeah," said Alexis thinking about her own decision to reveal her feelings for him.

"Why do girls do that?"

"It's not just girls who do it," she protested. "But in your case, you're just way too beautiful to be true. And you're a nice guy on top of it. She's just trying to solidify things before you can get away."

"I'm not going anywhere. I just want to take more time. I'm like scared of commitment right now. I don't even know her that well yet. And she knows nothing about me—and there's a lot to know there."

"That's a fact," laughed Alexis. "But it's getting late, and we both need to be up early. Thanks for calling. I feel much better now. I don't like when we fight."

"Me either. I'll see you."

He switched off the cordless phone and set it on the floor near his bed. Then almost before he knew it, he was asleep.

Alexis wasn't nearly as lucky. This being in love was the hardest thing she'd ever done. Every time she was ready to charge ahead, he'd say something that made her think twice and question the wisdom of her timing.  At the same time, hesitation could cost her dearly. It was some time before her tossing and turning evolved into sleep.

With Cain's naturally inquisitive and eager mind, she was surprised over the next few weeks that he never pressed her into having the discussion that she had more than hinted that they have.  He had come down off Cloud Nine where Dania was concerned, so she felt somewhat reprieved.  He still saw Dania on occasion, but Alexis could tell it was not the end-all of relationships that Cain had thought it might be in the beginning.  She guessed Dania had been just a little too anxious to rope him in and claim him for her own.  A fatal mistake where Cain was concerned, and another reason why Alexis put off baring her own soul.  Happily, he didn't press the issue; in fact, she wondered if he even remembered it.

She even began wondering if this wasn't the champion of lost causes.  Maybe Cain Farrell was an elusive butterfly, a beautiful, free spirit who could never be possessed.  Maybe he had become too jaded and battered by his past to trust anyone with his heart.  He certainly turned to stone at the first indication that a woman had any thoughts of him and happily-ever-after.  Even Joanne had gotten the boot when she had tried to claim him for her own.

At any rate, Alexis knew it would be a mortal mistake to try and make him understand what she was truly feeling.  Now if she could only convince her heart it was best to move on.

"Have you given up on your mystery man?"  Cain asked her one autumn Saturday as they stopped along the bike path to rest and enjoy the scenery.

"Yeah, pretty much," she said with a sad smile.  "He's hopeless."

"He's crazy," smiled Cain.

"Whatever," she shrugged.  "He's not interested.  I have a date with Cole tonight."

"Isn't this the second time in two weeks?"

"Yeah.  Is that some kind of a record or something?"

"No.  There's just something about him."

"I thought we've been through this: I'm the one who's dating him—not you.  Therefore, it doesn't matter what you think."

"Okay, okay.  But he's not your type.  He could never make you happy."

"Well, that's pretty prophetic.  On what do you base your opinion?  You hardly know him."

"It's just a feeling."

"Kindly keep your feelings to yourself.  I know how you feel, and you don't know what you're talking about.  Let's face it, Cain, you're no authority when it comes to matters of the heart."

"Ouch," he smiled.

"I'm sorry, but it's true. And don't even think for a minute that I couldn't love a guy who would wear white socks and black, dress shoes with shorts if he was crazy about me."

Cain looked wounded.

"Okay," he frowned. "Relax."

He waited a few seconds.

"Is he?" he asked.

"What?"

"Crazy about you?"

"I think he might be," she said modestly as she turned her eyes away from his disconcerting gaze.

He watched her for a minute, not sure how he felt about that news.

"We better go," he said dashing her hopes that he might finally come to his senses and tell her that he loved her.

"Yep," she sighed.


When they got back to her apartment, he went up with her.

"I'll be right back," she said as she dropped her mail on the table. "I have to go to the bathroom."

"Not before me!" he laughed as he grabbed her around the waist and playfully threw her on the couch and out of the path to the bathroom.

"You're such a gentleman!" she called after him as he went into the bathroom and closed the door.

She went over and started opening her mail.

He came out of the bathroom after a few minutes, ready to continue their playful bantering. But the smile vanished from his face when he saw her tucked in a tight fetal position on the couch. Large tears were running down her porcelain cheeks. She held a letter limply in her hand.

"Alexis?" he said as he went to her and sat next to her.

"My friend from college . . . Diane."

"The one with cancer?"

"Yeah." The words were not coming easily. "She died."

"What?! I thought she was doing so well?"

"She was. She just suddenly took a turn for the worse. Last week. This is from her mother."

Cain was sincerely distressed. He took her in his arms and held her close.

"I'm sorry," he said as tears welled in his own eyes.

Losing herself in the gentleness of his arms, she sobbed into his shoulder. He held her, stroking her hair and letting her spend her grief. He was no stranger to agony, and he knew there were no words that made sense at a time like this. He kissed her head, wishing he could make the pain go away. This was a whole new role for him, but one that he fell into rather naturally.

After a few minutes, her crying subsided and she sat back. He had never seen her looking so frail. Though beautiful and delicate, she was still robust and not at all fragile.

"I know what you need," he said getting up and first getting her some tissue.

Then he went into the kitchen and got out his aging bottle of Irish Whiskey that hadn't been touched since his one and only attempt at drinking his troubles into oblivion. He poured a small amount into a glass.

"Drink this," he told her as he handed it to her.

She managed a slight smile from under her tears.

"After I saw what it did to you, I'm not sure I want to."

"You're not going to have as much as I did," he assured her.

She took a small drink and screwed up her face.

"How do you drink that stuff?"

"I don't as a rule," he said, "but trust me, the more you drink, the easier it goes down."

"And you're an authority?"

"Trust me," he winked.

She smiled and took another drink.

"My date!" she suddenly remembered. "I have to call Cole; I wouldn't be much company tonight."

He watched her as she made the call. He couldn't help but to think how beautiful she was in spite of the fact that her eyes were puffy and red, and her face was drained of some of its natural glow. He drank her in as she smiled politely and explained to Cole, absently twirling a strawberry blond curl around her finger. Then she hung up and turned back to him.

"I'm staying here tonight," he announced.

"No, Cain, no. Meredithe will have your head."

"I don't care. I'm not leaving you alone tonight. He probably won't call anyway."

"But what if he does?"

"I don't care. He can go to hell."

"Well, we'll talk about it later," she said too spent to argue.

"I'll be a perfect gentleman. I'll sleep on the couch."

"That's not what I'm worried about, and you know it. I'd never forgive myself if you got into trouble because of me."

"Why does everyone always feel so capable of getting me into trouble? I do it all by myself. Look, my eyes are wide open—I'm stone sober. I don't want to leave you alone."

"Thank you for that, anyway," she said laying her head on his shoulder. "But we'll probably have a big fight as it gets closer to 11:00."

He wrapped her in his arms, and she put her arm on his chest. Her perfume was intoxicating. He struggled to think back if he had ever really noticed it before. Of course he had been aware of it, but he always had some other urgent thing on his mind. Suddenly, it seemed as though there was nothing else in the world but the two of them. He kissed the top of her head, and she cuddled in even closer to him. She sensed a change in him—it was something in the way he was holding her and drawing her toward him.

She raised her face to look up at him. He looked as if he was seeing her for the first time. She lost her breath at the incredible sexuality he exuded. Before she had a chance to think about what was going on, he leaned toward her and kissed her. At first he was tentative, almost like he wasn't quite sure what was going on. In reality, he wasn't. He had never felt like this before. Never. Not with Carrie; not with Joanne. Not even with Alexis on that first night they were together at her apartment after he had been paroled. This was different. He wanted to enfold her and keep her safe and drive away her pain. He never wanted to see her cry again. He never wanted to let her go again.

His kiss took on the intensity of the explosion of emotion he was experiencing. He realized she was kissing him back just as ardently, and it encouraged him to continue exploring this new, uncharted sensation. All these months, he had been leaning on her for support, depending on her to see him through the storms of his life. Now he was realizing he wanted to take care of her. He was ready to stand on his own two feet and become an equal partner in this relationship. He wanted way more than friendship.

They slid back on the couch until they were lying down. In the following minutes, their friendship evolved into a warm and loving trust that is reserved for only the luckiest of lovers. At first, he was afraid of taking advantage of her vulnerability, but she was responding readily to his every move and encouraging him to go on. With articles of clothing strewn all over the small living room, he adeptly lifted her from the couch and carried her to the bedroom.

She hung on to him—kissing his neck, loving the taste of his skin, the smell of his body. If only this moment could last a lifetime. As he laid her on the bed, she was afraid to open her eyes for fear it would all be a dream and vanish in an instant. But when she felt the warmth of his body as he came down on her, he sent her to heights that she knew were too intense, too explosive to belong to the abstractness of the dreamworld. They were good together; they both felt it. Each was totally aware of the other, which only served to heighten the pleasure for both of them.

Then as the fireworks were settling around them and euphoria wrapped them in warmth and love, Cain found the strength to raise himself to his forearms. He looked at her—not exactly sure how to feel—and definitely not wanting to spoil the beauty of what they had just experienced. Euphoria was giving way to reality, and he was now faced with dealing with an unexpected turn of events.

"This is the first time you've done this, isn't it?" he asked her gently.

She smiled and nodded. "I hope I didn't disappoint you."

"No," he sighed with a dreamy smile as he fingered her soft curls that floated across the pillow. "Not at all. You're beautiful. Did I hurt you?"

"No," she whispered. "I've been waiting all my life for Prince Charming. Imagine my surprise when I realized it was you."

"I love you," he said.

"Please don't say that unless you mean it. You don't owe me that."

"I love you," he repeated. "It was a first for me, too—I've never made love before. Believe me, there's a great difference between fucking and making love. I wouldn't have believed it until this very minute."

Tears filled her eyes.

"Do you know how long I've waited to hear that?—How long I've been in love with you?"

"Why didn't you tell me?"

"You weren't ready to hear it. I knew that."

"Are you sure I didn't hurt you?"

"Yes " she assured him as she took his handsome face in her hands. "I'm fine. Better than fine. Do you really love me—more than just a friend?"

"Yeah, I do. I've been very confused lately, and now I know that's why. I don't know when my feelings exactly began to change, but I know I didn't like seeing you with Cole. It was driving me crazy. Now I don't want anyone to ever touch you again but me."

"Can I still call you *honey?*" she smiled.

"Yeah," he grinned, "you'd better." He rolled slightly toward her and kissed her. "And now I'm going to make you some dinner. What have you got in there?"

He got up and set to work in the kitchen finding something to prepare. She wanted to help, but he wouldn't let her. Instead, he assigned her the job of building a fire in the fireplace to ward off the autumn chill. She sat curled up on the couch, her grieving heart wrapped in the warmth of this new love.

"The fire's all started," she called in to him. "Are you sure I can't help?"

"I'm sure. Actually, this is my specialty. I can't believe you have everything I need."

"Am I allowed to know what it is?"

"In a minute. I'm almost through."

He was busy putting things on the dining room table, which was actually part of the living room. Then he called her over. Grilled cheese sandwiches, potato chips, and tomato soup. She smiled broadly.

"Madam," he said holding her chair for her.

"Thank you," she said taking her seat. "Does your mother know you're such an accomplished chef?"

"Actually, my mother begs me not to use the kitchen."

Alexis laughed. "Then I guess it's better if I don't go into my kitchen right now."

"I'll clean it up," he assured. "And speaking of my mother, after we're through eating, I'd better call her to tell her I'm not coming home tonight."

Alexis's heart skipped a beat. What a beautiful end to a not-so-perfect day—lying beside him through what could be a very long night. But she knew she couldn't let him do that. Like it or not, he was still married to the legal system and there was too much at stake to risk a simple case of infidelity at this time. She didn't want to break the spell just yet, so she saved the discussion for later.

After dinner, she was sent back to the couch to wait while he cleaned everything up. She could hear him in the kitchen, and she knew the tiny room would never be the same again. She smiled, hoping she'd be able to find at least half of the things he was now in the midst of putting away. She stared into the fire, thinking of Diane and thanking God for this wonderful diversion of Cain Farrell with all his sexy innocence and genuiness.

When he finished in the kitchen, he came and sat next to her. He was wearing only a pair of jeans and a tee shirt. Pulling his bare feet up on the couch, he crossed his legs Indian-style.

"You okay?" he asked taking her hand in his.

"Yes. Thank you. I don't know what I would have done without you tonight."

"Thank **you**," he said lifting her hand to his lips and kissing it. "I thought I knew what loving and sex was all about—until today. Then I realized I didn't know anything about any of it at all. What I'm feeling right now is way beyond anything I've ever felt before—or even imagined . . . It's funny, but I guess something good did come of all this Carrie Willet shit after all. Otherwise you probably would have always stayed my brother's ex-girlfriend who I'd run into at the grocery store every now-and-then and reminisce with about old times."

"You paid a pretty high price, though."

"I know, but that just makes it all the more worthwhile. I'm finally seeing a return on my investment. Holding your hand like this and the love I'm feeling helps to make those years a little less futile and totally wasted. For the first time, I'm starting to feel like maybe I can put it behind me—at least it's not consuming me."

She reached over with her free hand and put it on top of their conjoined hands. Lightly, she ran her fingers across his hand. She recalled her one-and-only visit with him at Maddox—just after he had been released from Solitary. She could still see the cuts and bruises on his face, his lips; his beautiful hair shaved to a stubble; his spirit badly wounded. The image firmly in place, she moved her fingers to gently caress his wrist where the ugly black bruises from the handcuffs had been. The reality of the brutality he had suffered had sent a chill through her at the time, but it was this virtual jaunt into the past that had an even more devastating effect on her. In fact, tears burned in her eyes. Completely misunderstanding the reason for her tears, he took her in his arms.

"I wish there was something I could do to make this easier for you," he said, "but I know how much it can hurt."

"You are making it easier for me. You're so unselfish, and I'm so lucky. But, sweetheart, please don't stay here tonight—as much as I want you to." Tears streamed down her face. "Please go home where you're supposed to be. I don't want us to give Meredithe or anyone else a reason to ever hurt you again. There's no way he can find out about us having sex, but it's too easy for him to discover you're not home. I'll be a wreck all night worrying about it."

"Alexis . . ."

"Please," she begged as she began to cry even harder. "Come back as early as you want in the morning. 6:00 is fine. I'll even pick you up. And I'll fix you breakfast."

"Lex," he said wiping at the tears on her face, "I don't want him controlling my life any more. I can't stand it. I'm twenty-four years old, not twelve. And I've been home almost a year."

"I know. Believe me, I know how frustrating it is for you. I've been holding your hand through it all this past year. I've been here; I've seen it. And I'm sorry, honey, but I can live with a nasty, little man manipulating your life. But if you ever got sent back . . ." She couldn't even say the words. "Please go home tonight. I won't rest a minute if you don't."

He still held her hand in his left hand. With his right hand he rubbed his face. It was more than a few seconds before he said anything.

"I'm not even man enough to be able to stay here with you when you need me."

"No," she scolded, "no, you get that out of your head right now! I know what you want to do, and I know what you have to do—and they have nothing to do with each other. And it definitely has nothing to do with your manhood or virility or how sexy and beautiful and considerate and loving and—did I mention sexy—you are. Didn't your grandpa always used to say you weren't happy unless you were dancing with the devil?"

"Yeah, he did. Used to drive me crazy."

"There's some truth to that, Cain. There's a recklessness about you that defies men like Sam Willet and Ralph Meredithe to step in and do something about it. And you already know, they gladly will."

He sat staring intently at the fire—all kinds of things running through his head.

"Let go of the devil," she challenged. "The dance can be just as exciting with someone else."

He shifted his stare to look at her.

"With you?"

"Definitely with me. But within the law—please. I'm begging you."

He took a deep breath.

"You're sure you'll be all right?"

"I'll be fine. I think about you every waking moment."

"You could stay at my house—I just don't think my mom would be too high on letting us sleep together." His face beamed with a mischievous grin.

"I'll be fine. I'll call you if I need you—how's that?"

"Promise?"

"Yeah. I do have one more favor to ask you."

"Anything."

"Maybe you'd better wait and hear it first."

"What?"

"Will you go to Church with me tomorrow morning—if you get back here early enough?"

"It'll fall down if I walk in."

"No it won't. I want to go . . . I guess to pray for Diane . . . but I really don't want to go alone."

"I don't have a very good relationship with God these days."

"So?"

"So, what time do you want to go?"

"There are lots of different Masses we could go to. How about we see what time you get back here? You like to sleep-in on the weekends."

"Are you kidding? I probably won't sleep ten minutes tonight. I'll be here in time. And don't forget that thing you said about breakfast. I'm going to need a good breakfast if I'm going to take on religion again."

"Okay," she grinned. "One more thing."

"Yeah."

"What's two plus two?"

"What?" he asked in total confusion.

"Never mind," she laughed as she knelt up on the couch and kissed him on the cheek. "I love you."

# CHAPTER 20

The late October air was crisp but delightfully tempered by the bright sun. Cain walked the three miles to Matt and Melanie's apartment. He still hadn't gotten over the wonderful feeling of open spaces and freedom from prison bars and barbed wire fences. It had been nearly a year since he had been back home, and he still couldn't get enough of it. He could walk for miles without giving it a second thought, so screw Meredithe and his stupid parole restrictions. He couldn't believe how much tolerance he had amassed for that hateful, little man. Maturity; it must finally be dawning! And this morning, nothing could get him down. Everything was just too perfect.

He knocked on the door and waited for an answer. Matt was surprised to see him; he hadn't called first.

"Hey, come in," the older twin said as he stepped aside. He was wearing only a pair of jeans.

"Did I wake you?" asked Cain as he walked in.

"No, actually I've been up awhile, but it's a little early for you, isn't it?"

"Not today. I've got news."

"Well, have a seat," said Matt padding bare-footed to the kitchen. "Want a cup of coffee?"

"Yeah. Thanks. Is Melanie here?"

"No. She met her mom for breakfast and their monthly hair appointment. She's been gone awhile." He put two mugs of coffee on the table. "So what's this news?"

Cain put an envelope on the table.

"I got this yesterday. I was going to call, but I wanted to tell you in person."

"Northwestern," said Matt reading the return address on the envelope as he picked it up and withdrew the letter from it.

He looked over at his brother. Cain was beaming.

"I've seen this look before," smiled Matt. "A very long time ago."

"Read it," said Cain.

Matt's smile broadened as he read the letter.

"A grant and an opportunity for a job in research."

"Maybe my ship has finally come in."

"I'd say," grinned Matt. "This is pretty impressive. And I can't think of anyone who deserves it more."

"Thanks."

"Did you tell Alexis?"

"Yeah, I saw her last night after work."

"What's with you two, anyway?"

"What do you mean?"

"I don't know," said Matt. "I've just been trying to figure that relationship out. You're different lately, and I've been wondering if it has anything to do with her."

"Am I different better or worse?"

"Better," smiled Matt. "You couldn't get much worse."

"Thanks."

"Seriously, you're more relaxed or something. I know you've always said she's just a friend, but you spend an awful lot of time with her, and she is very beautiful."

"In other words, if you spend enough time with someone who's warm and very beautiful, sooner or later you have to come to your senses and fall in love with her?"

"Something like that."

"She's the best, Matt. Thank goodness she had the good sense to dump you after high school."

"Hey—it was mutual! But I'm glad, too. It turned out best for all of us, didn't it?"

"Yeah. That's a fact. I never knew I could ever love anyone like that."

"Well, I guess we could say your life is looking up."

"I almost can't believe it."

Just then the beeper that Matt had clipped on the waistband of his jeans went off.

"Do you sleep with that thing, too?" Cain asked as his brother checked the message.

"No," frowned Matt as the page registered, "we're in the middle of this big project. Let me call and see what's going on."

"It sucks to be a big, important engineer, huhn?" teased Cain.

Matt went to the phone and made his call. Cain walked to the window and watched the activity that was taking place four stories below. Saturday morning was in full swing, and everyone had places to go and things to do.

"I have to leave," said Matt pulling a tee shirt over his head. "But this won't take long. I was kind of hoping we could get in nine holes of golf this afternoon since the weather's so perfect. Want to hang around and call to see if you can get us a tee time? I'll only be about an hour."

"Sure."

"Unless of course you want to go wake up Alexis and see if she has a better offer."

"She's not a late sleeper. I already talked to her this morning before she left to spend the day shopping with her friend Linda."

"Okay, then." Matt put his shoes on and tied them. "Call Sean and Dan or Jim and see if they want join us."

"Melanie won't mind?"

"No. I already told her I might call you. I'll be back from this work thing before noon. Make yourself comfortable."

Matt grabbed a few odds and ends, said good-bye, and left. Cain went to the phone and called his brothers. Then after arranging a tee time for them, he lay on the couch and put on the TV. He always loved Saturday morning cartoons when he was a kid, and he was rarely up early enough any more to catch them. Feeling nostalgia wash over him, he became totally engrossed in the pleasurable experience. Life was good once again, and he could feel Maddox slipping another notch further into the past.

Sometime during the course of the next hour, the early hour of his rising caught up with him, and he fell sound asleep on the couch. He never even heard the door open when Melanie came in. She raised an amused eyebrow when she saw the cartoons bounding all over the TV screen. She had never known Matt to partake of that Saturday morning ritual, and she found it rather endearing. Putting her things down and taking off her jacket, she went over and knelt next to the couch. Matt had never been a particularly sound sleeper, and she was surprised he hadn't awakened by now. Playing with the hair on his forehead hardly had any affect on him, so she leaned over and started kissing his eyes and biting playfully on his ear. He stirred and began stretching back to life, but it wasn't until she started rubbing his back under his shirt and then the small of his back beneath the waistband of his jeans that Cain actually opened his eyes. It took him a few seconds to get passed the familiar face in an unfamiliar role. Things started falling into place, and he smiled with amusement as he realized what had happened.

"Melanie?" he said with his mischievous smile bringing his face to life.

The moment she looked into his impish eyes, she realized her mistake.

"Cain?!!" she blushed. "Oh my God, I'm so sorry!"

"Don't be," grinned Cain sitting himself up on the couch. "My brother's a lucky man."

"I'm so embarrassed," she said still blushing prettily. "I thought you were Matt. I've been feeling pretty cocky lately about being able to tell you two apart, but I guess I'm not as good as I thought I was. That was the weirdest sensation when I realized you weren't him. I'm sorry."

"Hey, it was my pleasure," smiled Cain with his heart-stopping grin. "And I won't even put you on the spot by asking you who has the better ass!"

"Oh my God," she repeated as the realization renewed itself. "I've never been so embarrassed."

"Well, don't be," said Cain as he kissed her on the forehead. "It's the most fun I've ever had being mistaken for Matt. He had to go in to work, by the way. He should be back shortly."

On Monday he sat in the library at school between classes pouring over research for a paper he was writing. He mostly kept to himself at school. His time at Maddox was still too recent, and he wasn't comfortable getting into it with new acquaintances. He had discovered with the few casual encounters he had had that it was too much effort to be friendly and yet steer around that seven-year nightmare of his life. He still ran into Dania on occasion; but she was not only beautiful but smart, and she soon got the idea that he really wasn't interested in taking their relationship any further. Therefore, taking a lesson from Maddox, he avoided people and spent most of his time alone in school.

On this day, however, that habit set him up for a close encounter of the most horrendous kind, for which he was totally unprepared. He was so involved in his work that he never even looked up when Carrie Willet sat down across from him. Not at all sure what she was going to say, she sat patiently waiting for him to notice her. It took longer than she had thought as he paged through books and scribbled notes with his left hand. For a while she thought he would never stop. But then reaching a natural stopping point and needing to change the focus of his eyes and stretch his body some, he sat back in his chair and looked up, right into her eyes.

"Jesus Christ, Carrie!" he said as his heart leapt into full panic mode. "What the hell are you doing here?"

"I need to talk to you, and I knew you wouldn't see me unless I could take you by surprise."

"Well, I'm surprised, but I still don't want to talk."

"Please," she begged. "This is important to me."

"Does your brain ever function on any other level than first-person? What about me and what I want? Huhn? I'm the one who's been through all the shit. I could go back to prison just for sitting here talking to you."

"I know that."

"Then why the hell are you here?! Why won't you just leave me alone?!"

"Because I'm a total wreck. This hasn't been a holiday for me either, you know."

"Excuse me if I don't shed any tears. How'd you find me here, anyway?"

"My friend goes to school here, and she says she sees you. I asked her to watch you and kind of get your schedule down."

"Christ," he sighed running his fingers through his hair and pressing his palms on his temples as if his brain was about to explode.

He sat forward on the table, picking through his brain and remembering back to when he was eighteen. That was the way he got involved with her in the first place. She'd follow him around until he was alone and vulnerable, and then she'd make him offers that were way too difficult for a virile, inexperienced teenager to walk away from. She knew just how to rope him in then, and here she was tracking him down again. He was more than a little afraid of the power she had over his life.

"Could we go outside where we could be alone for a while?" she asked.

If they hadn't have been in a library, he would have roared with sarcastic laughter.

"You have to be kidding, right?" he said with an incredulous smile instead.

"No. I really need to tell you things, and I don't want to do it here."

"There's that first-person again. The world doesn't revolve around you, Carrie—no matter what your daddy says."

"I know that," she said on the verge of tears. "I'm here about you."

"It's too late. You should have been here for me way back when we heard that garage door open. You deserted me then and cut me loose to fend for myself. It's been hell, but I'm doing okay now."

"Good," she smiled nervously as she sat wringing her hands. "I'm glad."

"No," he said adamantly. "Don't be glad. Just leave."

"Please, Cain. My life is a shambles—It has been since you were arrested. I should have told the truth then, but it's too late now. I need to tell you how sorry I am."

"While you let the rest of the world go on believing I could do such a horrible thing to you."

"I'm so sorry. I don't sleep at night. I haven't had a good night's sleep since this happened. I'm seeing a psychiatrist and I'm on medication, but it's not helping."

"Because you're living a lie, Carrie. Have you ever thought of that? The shrink can't help you if he doesn't know what your real problem is?"

"I can't tell the truth. It will ruin my father's career."

"Bullshit. Besides, what about my life and what you've done to me?"

"That's why I'm in the state I'm in. I can't stop thinking about that. I just wanted you to know that I'm a wreck, too. My life is a disaster. Please tell me you can forgive me."

"That's a tall order that I'm not really up to right now. I'm not a bad person, but I'm not that good."

"At least say you'll accept my apology."

"Carrie, I have a reoccurring nightmare that I really am raping you, and I have my hands wrapped tightly around your neck. Do you want to compare sleepless night? I wake up in a cold sweat with my heart beating out of my chest. And then I cry because I think I must be a terrible person to harbor thoughts that would give birth to such a hideous nightmare. I've considered therapy, too, but my family and friends are

444

getting me through it. And right now you're setting my progress back light-years."

Tears flowed down her face.

"What can I do? I've tried to tell my parents the truth; I just can't. I can't tell anybody."

"Leave me alone. Just get the fuck out of my life for good. You put me in hell, and somehow I survived. Now just leave me alone because you're nothing but trouble for me."

"Cain, please . . ."

"I felt deserted by you and God alike when this happened to me, and it hardened places in me that are only just now beginning to soften again. I've managed to come to some sort of understanding and reconciliation with God, but you're going to take some time yet. Maybe someday it'll happen—I just can't guarantee it. That's the best I can do."

"Okay," she conceded. "If it helps, I wish I could go back and change it all. I'm not a bad person either. I was just so scared, and before I could think, things had gone too far and I didn't know how to go back. I know it was worse for you, but a minute hasn't gone by that I haven't thought about you and hated myself for what I did. I haven't been able to be intimate with anyone since that night. I become emotionally hysterical if a man even tries to kiss me. Of course everyone thinks it's because I was raped as a teenager, but I know the truth."

Cain dropped his face into his opened hands and tried to rub the pain and confusion out of it. This was excruciating.

"Thank you for listening to me," she went on. "I won't bother you any more. I've interfered in your life enough."

He watched her get up and walk away. As much as he wanted to be able to stop her and tell her what she wanted—needed—to hear, he couldn't move or speak. His anger and hatred were still a knotted and twisted mass inside him. He closed his books and gathered his things; this study period had come to an abrupt end.

He wished Alexis was home, but she was at work; so when he got home, he dropped his books on the table and went to find his mother.

"Could you sit down for a minute," he said when he found her cleaning in the family room. "I need a major dose of your Celtic wisdom."

"What is it, honey?" she asked with concern as she came over and sat across from him.

He was visibly shaken and distressed. He had sat through his last class just after Carrie's visit, but he couldn't tell anyone what it was about. He was there only in body, and then only because he didn't want to have to deal with Meredithe because he had skipped a class. Now he looked over at his mother, not sure where to begin.

"I got kind of blind-sided today, and it's thrown me emotionally off balance," he finally told her.

"What happened?"

"Carrie showed up at school—out of nowhere. I looked up, and there she was."

"You stayed and talked to her?"

"Yeah. It was in the middle of the library with people all around. Besides I didn't have time to think of what to do."

"What did she want?"

"Forgiveness. Understanding."

"Oh." Nora was pensive as if she had expected as much.

"I ran into her once before a while back, but we were in the middle of a restaurant and I was full of anger and bravado, and it was easy to bitch her out and tell her to get lost. Today was different. Today it was just her and me, and I could see what all this has done to her. I guess I was just always thinking she was using the situation to manipulate her old man and everyone else into feeling sorry for her. But in a lot of ways she's far worse off from all of this than I am. I'm at least moving on; she's not. She's still all tangled up in that lie, and it's ruining her life. Then I probably just made it all worse."

"What do you mean?"

"I couldn't say it—I couldn't tell her that I forgive her, that everything's all right. Is that bad of me?"

"That's a big step for you to take—especially with no forewarning. I have to admit, I've been praying that someday you'll find it in your heart to forgive her. I think that's the only way you'll ever be able to put it all behind you once and for all. You can't find true peace while you're harboring hatred in your heart. But I've also known that it wasn't something that would come soon or easy. Maybe this is the answer to my prayer. She's forcing you to confront an issue which you have buried inside you. How long might you leave it there otherwise? Maybe this is your final struggle with this whole ugly chapter of your life. But don't expect it to be easy."

"I can't lie, Mom."

"I know that. But you need to search your heart. You need to determine what good is being served by you holding on to your hatred, and then you need to find a way to let go."

"Why didn't you ever tell me this before?"

"Because it had to come from you. For the first time I feel you're open to it—at least open to giving it some thought. God works in our lives in strange ways." She smiled warmly. "See? That's the first time in a long time that I've mentioned God that you haven't rolled your beautiful eyes at me."

He smiled back.

"You and Alexis have been going to Church on Sundays lately," she went on. "I've hesitated to bring it up because I was afraid of scaring you off. And before you put on your cynical *I'm-just-doing-it-for-Alexis* look, let me say that just maybe there's a remote possibility that God is finding a way back into you heart. And if that's true, then anything's possible. Even forgiving Carrie."

He buried his face in his hands as silent tears found their way through his squeezed-tight eyelids.

"She said such awful things about me and swore to it in court," he cried into his hands. "She sat back while they sent me away to that place—far away from everyone and everything I love. More people know me as a rapist than as who I really am. I can't vote, drive a car, or be out of the house passed 11:00 at night. I spent the last years of my best friend's life locked away from him. I can't go and visit my grandparents in Ireland. How do I forget all that?"

"Honey," said Nora, "you don't forget it. You just have to let it die a natural death. I know it's hard with the parole restrictions because they're still a part of your life."

"They're my whole life, Mom. And I'm getting pretty sick of it. How can I let Carrie off the hook while I'm still firmly impaled on it?"

"I don't know, sweetheart. I guess that's where the size of your heart comes into play. And the size of your character."

"You're not making this easy," he said as he leaned back and rested his weary head on the back of the couch.

"When did I ever say it would be easy?"

"Why does my life keep getting derailed every time I think I have it on track."

"Cain, nobody's life is ever completely on track all the time. You've had it tougher than most, but there'll always be setbacks."

"So what do I do?"

"Oh, my sweet child, that's entirely up to you. No one can tell you that. You have to feel it; it has to come from your heart."

"I can't call her, or, God forbid, I'll get myself arrested. But even if I could, I know I can't tell her what she needs to hear. I can't tell her it's okay—because it's not. How do you stop hating someone?"

"Pray," said Nora softly. "It sounds corny, but it's the only way I know. Reacquaint yourself with God and leave yourself open to Him. He'll find a way for you."

"Well, right now I don't feel anything but pissed off," sighed Cain as he got up. He kissed his mother on the forehead. "I'm going to go lay down before work. Thanks for listening, Mom."

Nora smiled forlornly as she watched him walk off.

"You have some work yet to do there, Lord," she sighed under her breath as she got back to her cleaning.

That night Alexis picked him up as had become their habit. As soon as he got in the car, she knew something was up. He kissed her absently.

"Okay," she said, "what's wrong?"

"Is it that obvious?" he asked.

447

"Cain, you're anything but a closed book."

He smiled.

"I ran into Carrie today—or rather I should say, she made it her business to run into me."

"What?!"

"I was working on my paper at school, and I looked up and there she was. I don't even know how she got there. She just appeared for all I know."

"She had to have known you'd be there. That just couldn't have been a coincidence."

"That's right. She had it planned. Could we stop at your place on the way home? I need a hit from my bottle of Irish Whiskey."

"Cain."

"Please, humor me. This has been a hell of a day. I'm about to explode. I have less than an hour, and I just need to unwind."

"With Irish Whiskey?"

"Come on, Alexis, it's not like I do it every day. I can't remember the last time I had a drink, and I am twenty-four years old."

"Fine," she conceded as she put the car in gear and headed toward her apartment. "One drink."

"Please don't be my mother. I already have one."

"Okay," she laughed, "but you have to tell me what Carrie said."

"When we get to your place. Right now I want to know how your day was—we already know about mine."

They went back to her apartment where she lit a few candles. Cain went to the kitchen and retrieved his bottle.

"Do you want some?" he asked.

"No," she answered, "I still have to drive you home, and besides that stuff is a little too much for me."

"I'll tell you what," he said putting his glass with the medicinal dose of whiskey on the table and then sitting down next to Alexis. "I'll just forget about the drink if we can make love nonstop until about 10:57."

"Sweetheart, as inviting a proposition as that is, it's not really all that long until 10:57, and . . ."

"I'll make it the best half-hour of your life!"

"You didn't let me finish . . . and I want to hear about Carrie. So quit trying to change the subject."

"We can talk about Carrie at my house after."

He started kissing her neck and her ear.

"Cain, I can't think about anything else right now. What happened? Is everything all right?"

"Hell, I don't know," he sighed as he moved away from her and reached for his glass. "She's been like sitting on my brain, right between my eyes all night. I've been doing my best not to think about her."

448

"Did she threaten you in any way?"

"No. I think that's the problem." He took a swallow of the whiskey and laid his head back on the couch. "She was remorseful, contrite, you-name-it. I wish I had had a tape recorder." Then he took a bigger swallow from his glass, nearly drained it, and looked her in the eye. "She wants me to forgive her. She said she's emotionally destroyed by what she did."

"Will she tell everyone the truth?"

"Now that's the sucker punch. No. She can't—she's tried, but the words won't come. I'm just supposed to say I forgive her and make her feel better."

"What'd you say?"

"In a nutshell—fuck off." He waited for a reaction from her, but she remained silent. "I'm a jerk, huhn?"

"No," she said putting her arm on the back of the couch and fingering the hair at his collar. "That's pretty presumptuous of her when she can't even offer you anything."

Cain inhaled a deep breath and let it out slowly.

"When I told my mom, she started in on how she thinks it's something I need to do—for me. And I don't know that she's wrong. I just don't know how to go about it. I don't think I could get the words out of my mouth."

"You still need time."

"Well, I've got it since Carrie left and said she wouldn't bother me any more—and I'm certainly not in a position to go looking for her. Her old man would have me back in jail before I could even get a word out. And she'd be sitting there crying wolf again. I may be stupid, but I'm not that bad off."

Alexis kept rubbing the back of his neck as she stared at the candles.

"Aren't you going to argue with me?" he asked looking a trifle wounded.

"No, I don't think so," she teased. "Am I supposed to?"

"Well, yeah. I mean, you're not going to send me home thinking I'm stupid, are you?"

"I wish I didn't have to send you home at all."

"I know," he said knocking down the rest of his drink. "Someday I'll be an adult who's in charge of my own life. But I told you—I don't give a damn about Meredithe any more. I'll stay."

"You'd better give a damn," she scolded. "You've been away from steel bars too long and you're forgetting what it was like."

"No!" he said emphatically. "That will never happen. I'll never forget what that was like. Why do you think I can't bargain with Carrie? There's this whole big, dead lump of memory lodged inside me. She did that to me, and I'm having a real problem getting passed it."

"Okay," she soothed. "Let's don't talk about it any more right now. We still have a little time left, and I don't want to waste it on Carrie Willet."

"There's still enough time for me to drive everything else from your mind—everything but me."

"You're pretty cocky," she grinned.

He turned toward her and turned her heart to Jell-O with his prize-winning smile.

"No," he said. "I just love you so much. You make me feel like I can do anything I set my mind to."

"You **can** do anything you set your mind to."

"Then what are we waiting for?" he asked as he laid her back on the couch with a kiss, the potency of which she could not resist.

It was some time before either of them paid attention to anything but each other. They moved from the couch to the floor and became totally absorbed in the love they were making. It was Alexis who first became aware of the lateness of the hour. Cain was lying on his stomach in an exhausted heap as Alexis sat next to him lightly running her long fingers down his back.

"Oh my God, Cain, it's after 11:00!!!" she all but screamed as her eye caught the clock.

"Shit, Alexis, you're going to give me a heart attack!" said Cain trying to keep his jump-started heart in his chest where it belonged. He raised himself to his elbows and double-checked the clock. "I told you I don't care."

"Let's go!" she said frantically as she began getting dressed.

"Relax," he told her as he tried to coax her back down next to him.

"Meredithe," she said.

"I don't give a fuck about Meredithe."

"Well, I do," she argued. "He can take you away from me. He can ruin all this. I've never been so happy; I don't want it ruined. Please, sweetheart, if not for yourself, do it for me."

"You drive a hard bargain," he sighed as he reached less than enthusiastically for his clothes.

Alexis's car had hardly stopped in the Farrell's driveway when Will opened the door of the house and stepped out on the porch.

"GET YOUR ASS IN HERE!" he hollered out to Cain.

Cain dropped his head back on the seat of the car.

"Why do I feel like I'm ten years old?" he sighed.

"They've been through a lot. They worry about you."

"**I've** been through a lot, Alexis. They had no choice but to come along for the ride, and I'm sorry about that, but **I'm** the one who lived it. **I'm** the one who went through it. And I'm so damn sick of the whole thing, I can't even begin to tell you."

450

"I know," she soothed.

"Now I have to go in and get my ass chewed by my dad? Jesus, I'm a man, for God's sake. Nobody will let me be a fucking man." He turned and looked at her. "Except you."

She smiled.

"You're a most amazing man, and I love you very much. Now go on in and get this over with. Do you want me to come with you? This is partly my fault."

"NO! Christ, this is humiliating enough. Just go home and I'll call you."

He lingered defiantly as he kissed her long and seductively.

"Lock the doors," he said as he got out. "You have your cell phone?"

"Yes," she smiled, loving his concern.

"Okay. I'll call you in a little bit—as soon as Will is through venting. I love you."

Again delaying his entry, he stood on the driveway and watched her drive off. Then he took a deep breath of the cold, autumn, night air and walked toward the house.

"Where the hell have you been?" asked Will angrily.

Cain looked over at the couch where his mother was sitting. She was as white as a ghost.

"What's going on?" he asked as he dropped his jacket on a nearby chair.

"It's 11:25," said Will. "Meredithe has called—twice."

"Shit," snarled Cain between his clenched teeth.

"He's calling back at 11:30, and if you don't answer the phone, he's putting out a warrant on you!"

"Screw him!"

"Screw him?!" said Will still in a rage. "You don't care if you go back to prison?!"

"I care. I'm just sick of this shit."

"That's not an option! He holds the cards, Cain! You know the rules! And what about your mother and me? Do you have any idea what we've been through in the last twenty-five minutes?"

Cain stopped and took a breath to try and quell his rising anger.

"I don't want to fight with you, Dad. I'm sorry. I was with Alexis, and I didn't want to leave."

"Bring her over here!"

"We wanted to be alone!"

"So you're willing to put everything on the line—the deal you have going with Northwestern, your relationship with Alexis, everything—just to thumb your nose at Meredithe? He's pissed, Cain."

"I don't doubt that he is. I'll take care of it. I'm sorry you got involved. I didn't mean to upset you."

"What are you going to do?" asked Will.

"I'll deal with him. Don't worry. If he were going to do anything, he would've done it by now. I'm home now; he'll calm down after he has his turn kicking my ass."

He went over to the couch and leaned over and kissed his mother.

"I'm sorry, Mom. I didn't mean to worry you. Everything's okay. I love you."

"Don't let your frustration take over," she said. "You have a beautiful, young woman to share your love with, and a promising future ahead. Don't self-destruct."

"I won't," he promised. The phone rang. "I've got it."

He took the stairs two at a time since he wanted this conversation to be private. He lifted the receiver in the middle of the third ring.

"Farrell?"

"Yeah, I'm home."

"Well, isn't that nice? Tomorrow. 2:00. My office. Be there. And be even one minute late, and I'll slap your ass back in jail for ninety days—I swear to God I will."

Meredithe hung up. Cain was furious.

"FUCK!" he screamed throwing the cordless phone across the room.

He paced the room aimlessly as he concentrated on controlling his temper and not making a war zone out of his bedroom. After a few minutes he calmed down enough to retrieve the phone and check that it wasn't broken. Miraculously it was all in one piece and working properly. He punched in Alexis's number.

"Hi," he said calming down even more at the sound of her voice.

"What happened?" she asked with concern.

"Meredithe called twice while I was at your place."

"Dear God."

"Yeah, well I avoided being arrested by five minutes. He's quite pissed, to say the least. That's something I'm really good at, Alexis. Why do I do that? Why do I play right into his hands?"

"What'd he say?"

"He wants to see me tomorrow at 2:00. Just what I want to do—screw away another couple hours of my life traveling down there. I have so much homework to do. I was planning on staying at the library after my last class, and I have an appointment with one of my professors who's helping me with a project I'm working on. Now I'll have to cancel that to go down and get chewed out by him. SHIT! What a goddam waste of time I don't have!"

"I'm sorry. I feel responsible."

"Don't be crazy. I knew what I was doing. Besides, you're the only bright spot in this whole day. I'd be nuts without you. In fact, I'm going to go to bed right now and dream about making love to you all night."

"Want me to go with you tomorrow?" she smiled. "I could get off work at noon."

"No. Thanks. I don't want you anywhere near that snake or his office. It's not exactly the classiest place to be, and I can already tell you I won't be in the best of moods. The last thing I want to do is take out my frustration on you."

"Well, if you change your mind, you know where to find me."

"Thanks, Lex, I don't know where I'd be without you. You know, one thing that keeps nagging at me is the proximity of all this to my Carrie Willet encounter this morning."

"You think he knows?"

"I don't know. But I'd guess no. I think if she had told anyone, they would've slapped me in irons and hauled me off hours ago. They wouldn't want to take any chances. But I'm not going to think about it. I'm going to think about you instead—and this incredible night we spent. Thank you for loving me. Especially knowing what it entails."

"You're welcome," she smiled as tears filled her eyes. "But it's not that hard, you know. Keep your chin up. This is just a minor setback. From now on we'll be much more careful. Promise me you'll grit your teeth tomorrow and not make a bad situation worse because of attitude."

"That's the least I can do. It'll be okay. It's just a pain in the ass. Meredithe needs to flex some muscle."

"Well, go to sleep now. You have a full day tomorrow. And don't worry—some day life will get easier—I'll see to it."

The next day Cain spent the train ride into the city trying to talk himself into being contrite and passive. After all, it was his fault. He wasn't home when he was supposed to be. It was that simple. He didn't need to make Meredithe any angrier because the price was too high. The frustration at having to make the extra trip downtown that week kept interfering with his self-imposed brainwashing, however.

When he arrived at the building, he went up to Meredithe's office but stalled around outside the door until two minutes before 2:00—allowing for any discrepancy between clocks and yet not arriving any sooner than he had to. He had statements of his own to make.

Meredithe's secretary smiled and flirted in her usual way when he came in. She was always trying to interest him in getting together for lunch or something, but even before Alexis he wasn't interested. And now she may as well have been invisible for all the notice he took of her.

"He's here," she said as she pressed the intercom to Meredithe's office. Then she looked up at Cain, standing tall and resolute. "He said you should have a seat."

A little surprised at the stay of execution, he sat down and grabbed a magazine. It didn't take long for his perceptive mind to pick up on the game Meredithe was playing with him. Everyone else was getting called in before him—even guys who came in well after he did. He looked at his watch. 2:20. He went back to his reading. 2:35. *What the hell?!* He looked up at the secretary who was drinking him in with her eyes. He shifted uneasily in his chair, which was not getting any more comfortable. At 2:55 he nearly lost his cool and almost began taking the small, outer office apart, which was one of his signature ways of dealing with frustration and anger. He was being punished and he knew it, but that didn't mean he resented it any less. He had schoolwork he should be doing and he had to be at work at 5:00. He wondered how long Meredithe was going to leave him sitting there. At 4:00 he was incensed and ready to throw all caution to the wind and create a scene the likes of which that office had never seen. Meredithe appeared at the door to his office just in time to curb that mounting impulse.

"Farrell," he said gaining Cain's attention, "go home. I'll see you Friday. And don't miss your curfew ever again!"

Then he turned and walked back into his office.

"WHAT?!!" snarled Cain, ready to explode. In two long strides he was at Meredithe's door and bursting through it into his office. "WHAT THE SHIT, YOU FUCKING LITTLE COCKSUCKER!!!"

Meredithe turned and laughed.

"Well, I see you haven't forgotten any of your raunchy, jailhouse lingo," he said. "You kiss your mother with that mouth?"

"You had me come all the way down here to sit in your office for two hours?!"

"Yep. You violated parole, hotshot. The way I see it, I did you a favor. You could be sitting in jail right now awaiting a one-way trip back to Maddox."

"God damn it!" ranted Cain, "I canceled an important appointment with a professor and I have tons of schoolwork I should be doing, and I'm sitting here for nothing?"

"That's absolutely right," said Meredithe dispensing with the humor. "Don't fuck with me. I told you that before."

"I have to be at work at 5:00, and it's ten after four now."

"Then you'd better get moving. Just in case you don't make it, I'll call and tell them you'll be a little late and to dock your pay accordingly. Now get out of my office and be home on time from now on."

Deciding whether or not to launch his tirade, Cain stood his ground and stared Meredithe down. He had the verbal skills to see the man and raise him, but the maturity that had been shaping his character of late was coaxing him toward the commonsense path of least resistance. What good would it do? And Meredithe was right—he was reverting back to his Maddox mentality, and he didn't like that at all. If there was anything he wanted to drive out of his soul, it was those six years. Deciding not to induce the anger that was waiting to be born of the pregnant pause and the two hours of sitting around and waiting for nothing, he let his eyes tell Meredithe exactly where to go and what to do when he got there. Then he took his leave of the whole infuriating situation.

Once outside he opted to turn toward the beach rather than the train station. He was going to be late for work anyway, and Meredithe was calling ahead for him. What better time to play hooky for a while? First, however, he stopped at a pay phone to call his mom. She was probably already starting to wonder why he hadn't come home yet to get ready for work. Then he braved the chilly October weather to take his pent-up anger and frustration to die a natural death at the beach.

He was thankful for the sun because the wind was brisk at the lakefront. Substantial waves crashed up on the shore as he sat on a bench and watched. He always had to laugh at people from out of town who questioned him about his fascination with the beach. *What beaches do you have in Chicago?* The Great Lakes were definitely not lakes in the common sense of the word; they were inland seas with much of the beauty and majesty of the ocean itself. There was a spot further north that he particularly loved where the waves crashed and broke on the huge rocks that served as a breakwater, sending sprays of water high into the air in a most awesome spectacle. In especially high winds—which Chicago often had—the spray would wash over Lake Shore Drive causing all sorts of driving hazards. No, Lake Michigan was no little fishing hole. This lake knew beauty and danger and, most of all, passion.

As he watched the waves crash on the beach as if they were trying to achieve limits that would allow them to experience another aspect of the world only to slide gently back to their rightful place in nature, he thought about his own life. His father had always been his tower of strength. His mother, she was his gentle, guiding light trying her best to steer him around the rocks in his life. His brothers and Molly were his staunch supporters and lifelong friends. And Alexis. Alexis was the love of his life who made sense of the chaos that sometimes consumed him and who loved him in spite of himself.

For the first time in nearly a decade, it felt good to be inside his skin looking out at the world. But was he ever going to be able to move beyond the Carrie Willet ordeal? That still was looming larger than life on his horizon, too often blocking the sun that was trying to break through. The Don Quixote in him wanted to strike back and take his lumps no matter what the odds, but he was coming to realize that that mentality may be more destructive than beneficial. Passivity was not his nature. He was much like the lake that lay before him. He possessed an awesome beauty, which often lulled others into underestimating the storms that could rise up from beneath his surface, making him a force to be reckoned with.

But this was one storm that could destroy his newfound contentment if he didn't find some way to calm it. That was a tall order, however. At least he was beginning to find ways to control it. He was learning there was no room for temper tantrums when dealing with Meredithe, and cutting off his nose most definitely only served to spite his face. This wasn't going to go away, so he had to learn to live with it. There was no way he was going to risk the love of a beautiful woman and the promise of a lucrative education and career on a game he had no chance of winning. He was headstrong and passionate, not stupid.

Not wanting to overextend his precarious romp in defiant independence, he gathered in his slouched body and his rambling thoughts and got ready to leave. As he began walking back to catch his train, he stopped and looked back at the beach. A hazy vision of days long passed played out before his eyes. This was the one place he could connect with Scott and the teenagers they once were. The world was theirs and the promise was limitless, but who cared? There'd be time for the world later. They were young with scores of years still ahead of them, nothing but time. Smiling ruefully, he blinked back a few errant tears and quickly turned back to hurry and catch the next train home.

"I've been waiting all day just to hear your voice," he said into the phone when Alexis answered.

"Where are you?" she asked glancing over at the clock.

"At home. I just changed, and I'm leaving for work."

"Cain, it's 6:30."

"I know. It's a long story. I just had to hear your voice before I left."

"What's wrong?"

"Nothing."

"What about Meredithe?"

"Everything's okay. I'll tell you all about it later. Just tell me you love me."

"Why? Something's wrong, I know it."

"No, I swear. I just love you so damn much, and it's been a fucking weird day. That's all."

"Okay," she teased, "I guess I do love you—a little anyway. How's that?"

"I guess it'll have to do," he sighed.

"Hey," she said sensing he wasn't totally in the mood for teasing, "I love you more than I ever thought I could love anyone. You are the most gorgeous, beautiful thing in my life."

"Even if I am a convicted felon?"

"Honey . . ."

"I can't step out of that role. I'm stuck with it, and I . . . hate sticking you with it too."

"The law can call you whatever it wants to. I know who you really are; that's what matters to me. Are you going to be in trouble for not being to work on time?"

"No. Meredithe's the one who kept my ass so long, and he's the one who'd be mad. He called Charlie to let him know I'd be late."

"How about if I come over and drive you? I want to hear what he said."

"No. You just got home yourself. Relax. Jim's going out, and he's dropping me off. But you'll pick me up at 10:00, okay?"

"I can't wait. But only if you promise—no fooling around like last night."

"You didn't like it?"

"I didn't like what happened to you because of it. So promise me."

"Don't worry, I'm cured. Meredithe has a unique brand of torture. I gotta go. I'll see you at 10:00."

Nora woke up during the night and saw Cain's light was still on. She gently knocked on his door and he told her to come in. He was sitting at his desk, glasses on, books piled high, pen in hand. He looked dog-tired as her heart broke for him.

"I couldn't believe you were still up," she said, "it's after 1:00."

"I wasted all that time with Meredithe, and I have to have this done by tomorrow . . . today."

"Your class is early tomorrow."

"8:00." He took off his glasses and rubbed his face. "I'm almost through."

"You always look so intelligent with your glasses on," she smiled.

"I **am** intelligent, Mom; I'm just not very smart."

"Don't be so hard on yourself. Can I get you something?"

"No. Thanks."

"Are you feeling any better than when you first got home from downtown?" She stood behind him and massaged his shoulders.

"I always feel better when I'm home," he smiled as he relaxed beneath her kneading fingers. "I was wrong last night, I know that. I'm going to work on using my head more often. The Department of Corrections owns me for a long time yet; I'm finally coming to terms with that." He rubbed his weary eyes. "I just wish I could drive and keep normal hours. Those are the two hardest things for me."

"I know." She kissed his cheek from behind. "After the holidays you'll be at Northwestern and you'll be working your new job. Things will look better then. And who knows, maybe Meredithe will ease up, too."

"He's so pissed at me right now, that I'm not expecting anything from him for a very long time. I want to ask Alexis to marry me, but I

457

have to go through him first." The dagger pierced her heart as he went on talking. "I was hoping to mention it to him soon, but now that's not a very good idea."

"Give him a few weeks, and he'll be more receptive," she said, smiling through tears as she continued rubbing his neck and shoulders. She was glad he couldn't see her.

"Maybe," he said unconvinced. "What do you think about that—me and Alexis?"

"Oh," she sighed, "I've always known someone would come along and win your heart, and I can't think of anyone I'd rather see you with than Alexis. She's beautiful and intelligent and she adores you. You're a perfect match. How can I be anything but thrilled? I was your first love, but I've always known I wouldn't be your last. You deserve a warm, loving relationship with someone who can fulfill all your needs and desires. I couldn't be happier for you."

He reached over his shoulders and took her hands in his and kissed them.

"I love you, Mom."

"I love you too, baby," she said leaning over and kissing his cheek once more. "And Meredithe will ease up. Don't worry. Just give him a little time."

"I hope you're right."

"I am. And now you'd better get finished with your homework or you'll be walking in your sleep all day tomorrow."

"Mom," he said turning in his chair to look at her, "Alexis could never take your place with me."

"Oh, Honey," she smiled through tears, "I know that. I didn't mean for it to sound that way. Alexis and I don't have to compete for you. We already love each other, and we both love you. We're all very lucky. Now get back to work—it's getting close to 2:00. I'll have to be dragging you out of bed in the morning, and that's not exactly one of my favorite jobs!"

"Okay," he smiled.

Once again Cain spent most of the trip into the city on Friday trying to allay his frustrations and to talk himself into a passive state of mind. He knew Meredithe was mad at him, and there was no sense in exacerbating that situation. He would just sit quietly and listen as Meredithe vented. Then he'd leave, tail tucked firmly between his legs. But then he always had good intentions . . . until he walked in the door of the office.

This week Meredithe was particularly pompous, buoyed by Cain's faux pas earlier in the week. Cain didn't wait long this time before he was admitted to the little general's private office. Feeling Meredithe's smug grin burning into the back of his neck, Cain walked passed the man at the opened door and approached the desk. Exhibiting prison-bred protocol, he stood and waited for Meredithe to mount his chair, shimmy up to his desk, and nod him permission to sit.

"So," sighed Meredithe authoritatively, "after having you to the woodshed on Tuesday, it seems you've been behaving yourself since. Am I right?"

"You're always right," answered Cain less than respectfully.

"Don't forget that. And don't be a smart-ass. You know how I hate that."

Cain just stared at him, his good intentions already beginning to crumble at the foundation.

"Let's try again—have you been behaving yourself?"

"Yes."

"Well, that's good for you because you have no idea how badly I want to ship you back to Maddox to finish your sentence. I'd probably be a big hero if I did; I bet over half the population there has been missing your ass since you left."

Cain managed to achieve the mental count of eight before his patience ran out and toppled his precarious house of good intentions.

"Why do you do that?" he bitched. "Why do you fucking act like you fucking know everything that fucking goes on in that fucking madhouse?!"

"Do you want to say that word one more time?"

"Fucking! And why is it you always fucking get off on harping about the homosexual activity behind bars? You're just a little too fucking obsessed with that, don't you fucking think?!"

"Farrell!"

"Have you even ever been in a prison?" said Cain ignoring the red-faced Meredithe. "I don't mean in the Admin Building, but deep down into the bowels of the Big Time. Do you even know what you're talking about?!"

"Farrell!!"

"I took care of my ass, don't worry about that; but they'd put you down in a minute because you think you're so almighty, fucking hot shit. You wouldn't last an hour down in the population. You've got *ASSHOLE* written all over you, and they know exactly what to do with assholes!"

"And you're nothing but a two-bit, smart-ass, ex-con. And you don't think I have power, do you?! You don't think I could pick up a pen and your ass would be back behind bars?!"

"No, I'm not stupid. I know you could do that. But your power is limited, man. Take off the gloves, Meredithe. Leave your pen and silver badge on your desk and get down and dirty with the hard core. Then come back and talk to me about turning ass and the population fighting over you. Come back when you fucking know what you're talking about because right now you don't have a clue."

"Well, I'll tell you what, how 'bout I get busy right now and start the paperwork? You could be back with all your friends in no time."

"For what? For missing a curfew by less than a half-hour? For saying *fucking* too many times in your office? Come on, you insult my intelligence. No judge is going to send me back to an overcrowded prison for such bullshit."

"You willing to bet your freedom on it?"

Cain stared holes through him.

"Yeah, I am. I got too much going for me down the road that you're going to have to overcome. I don't think you can do it. I'm just asking for a little respect from you."

"Yeah, right. Are you forgetting what you went to prison for? And you want respect?"

"Don't even go there," warned Cain with a menacing flash in his eye. "I'm going to say this one, last time—I'm not a rapist. I did not rape Carrie Willet or anyone else. An ugly lie put me behind bars. And somewhere deep inside, I think you know it. And that's why I want you to start working on some other paperwork. I want to drive, and I want to be able to keep normal hours. Next month I'll be home a year with no problems. I think it's time you show a little good faith and cut me some slack. Otherwise, I'm getting my lawyer involved. I think I've been patient for way too long."

"Is that a threat?"

"No," sighed Cain rubbing his face. "Come on. Why are you holding me back? Even if you do believe I'm some perverted socio-path, it's been a year. Do you really think rapes are only committed between the hours of 11:00 P.M. and 6:00 A.M.? Or only by guys who drive cars?"

"It was a date rape."

"Well, then, hey . . . I've been dating regularly since I've been home, and no one's complaining. Come on, Meredithe, I deserve a break. I did six years for a crime I didn't commit, and I've played your silly game for nearly a year. Are you that afraid of Sam Willet that you don't even have balls any more?"

"We're not here to discuss my manhood. And while we're on the subject, let's back up a little and talk about your social life. Whenever I've asked you about it before, you've told me that you weren't dating—that you were actually a little gun-shy when it came to girls and you were laying low."

"I lied," shrugged Cain. "It's not the only benign scam I've pulled on you. No matter what you and the Department of Corrections think, my social life is my business, and I definitely didn't want you poking your nose around in it. Don't worry I've been a perfect gentleman. You'd approve."

"And how many lucky, young ladies are we talking about?"

"Three," answered Cain without hesitation. He didn't count Joanne.

"And how many of them have you had sex with?"

"I'm not allowed," said Cain with a smirk. "Don't tell me you forgot."

"I didn't forget, but this is a disturbing revelation."

"Come on, Ralph, you didn't expect me to become a monk? And there was nothing on that paper that said I couldn't date."

"No, but you lied. I don't like that."

"Not really. For a while I **was** gun-shy and I **did** lay low. It took me a while before I started to feel human again."

"How many girls have you fucked, Farrell? You never answered my question."

"None."

It wasn't a lie; he had never gotten that far with Kristen or Dania, and he had never considered the intimate moments he had spent with Alexis as anything less pure and beautiful than making love. And since he hadn't included Joanne in his original count of three, he wasn't even lying about that. He had become a master at twisting the truth and skirting around undesirable issues. It was all part of his Maddox training.

"Wow," said Meredithe not buying any of it, "I bet you must be horny as hell."

"Life's a bitch," smiled Cain slyly.

"And are any or all of these young ladies currently being dazzled by your irresistible charms?"

Cain thought for a minute; then he decided, why not?

"One," he answered.

"And you're not fucking her?"

"I love her," answered Cain side-stepping the question.

"I see. And she . . ."

". . . loves me."

"Does she know about you and your not-so-brilliant past?"

"She was at my trial every day. I've known her since we were kids."

Meredithe took a deep breath and became pensive in order to buy himself some time. He hadn't been prepared for this turn in their conversation.

"So . . . where does that leave us?" Meredithe finally asked.

"I don't know where it leaves you, but it leaves me deliriously happy and wanting to move on with my life. Have we come full circle in this conversation?"

"I guess. Give me some time to take this all in. I'll have some sort of answer for you next week."

"Okay," sighed Cain a bit disappointed but not hopeless. Then a touch of sincere humility. "Thanks."

"Okay," answered Meredithe. "Now get out of here. You've already taken up too much of my time!"

Cain smiled slightly, wondering if maybe he and the little general had somehow managed to stumble onto some kind of understanding of each other that bordered however loosely on mutual regard. At any rate, his ride home on the train was somewhat more peaceful and relaxing than it had ever been, and he had been able to hold onto the tiniest thread of hope for the future coexistence of his criminal status and his need for a normal life.

On Sunday afternoon Cain went over to Alexis's apartment to watch the Bears game. Alexis was delicate and feminine, and yet she loved sports and understood most of them enough to be an able companion for any armchair quarterback or other sport's buff.

"I can't believe that some guy didn't come along and swoop you up a long time ago," he said to her as they sat on the couch together.

"They tried," she smiled, "but I told them I was waiting for you—of course, I didn't know it was you at the time, so I just said Prince Charming."

He looked at her with a half smile on his face, wondering if she was kidding him or not.

"They?" he questioned.

"Probably at least two or three."

"At least?"

"At least," she confirmed.

"Then I guess I'm lucky I came along when I did."

"I would have held out and waited."

"You would have?"

"Of course. I wasn't about to settle."

"What'd I ever do to get this lucky?"

"I don't know," she laughed. "You're so ugly and everything. I guess I just took pity on you because I knew no one else would ever want you!"

He dove over on top of her and began tickling her ribs with his experienced fingers; he knew just the spot that would drive her wild with uncontrolled laughter. She struggled to get free of him, but it was no use. The harder she fought, the more determined he was to drive her crazy. Pretty soon he was about to burst with the love that he felt for her, and he gradually stopped teasing her. As her laughing subsided, she gasped for breath. That's when he could resist her no longer, and he leaned forward and kissed her long and artfully on the lips. Every kiss, every caress, every act of love awakened desires in his soul that he never even dreamed existed. Gone were the days of worrying that past nightmares had permanently left their mark on his passion. Gone were the days of agonizing over Joanne's unrequited love. Nothing else mattered any

462

more. Nothing, except Alexis. She was his world, his reason for getting up every morning.

She reached up and put her hands on the sides of his face as he looked down at her. As she did, it struck her that he could look so much like Matt and yet be such a totally different individual. There were times back when she first started realizing she was falling in love with him that she was struck by the total weirdness of the situation, and she wondered if she would be able to separate her feelings for two such amazingly identical human beings, both of whom she had had a relationship with.

But looking into Cain's face, being beguiled by his vulnerable sexiness and open sincerity, she understood the mystique and total uniqueness of the personality. Even twins as identical as Cain and Matt could enjoy singularity in the psyche. She truly doubted that they could ever unintentionally deceive her as long as she had a few moments to glimpse beyond the gorgeous exterior.

"I had a thought I wanted to run passed you," she said as she gently pushed him aside and wiggled back to a seated position.

"About what?" he asked a bit disconcerted that their play was ending.

"About Carrie Willet."

"Come on, Alexis," he frowned. "That's the last thing I want to talk about."

"That's obvious," she said, "since you've been avoiding it since you ran into her the other day."

"What? I told you what happened."

"I know, but don't you think you need to talk a little more about what you're going to do about her?"

"No, because I'm not going to do anything about her. I'm going to pretend she doesn't exist as much as I'm possibly able."

"Do you think that's wise?"

"Alexis, why are you doing this? Why are you ruining a perfectly good day? We don't have that much time to spend together. Why do you want to spoil that?"

"I don't want to spoil it, I just think you need to confront this issue and resolve it."

"It's resolved!" he said heatedly. "I don't want anything to do with her."

"Even though you know that she's been destroyed by this whole debacle of hers and she needs some sort of understanding from you?"

"What is this?" he said angrily, getting up and putting distance between them. "What is it with you and my mother? What do you two see that I'm totally missing?"

"Cain . . ."

"You don't know what you're talking about. See, nobody gets it. Not you. Not my parents. Not even Ralph Meredithe who works within the system. She **lied** about me. It was in the newspapers, on TV, and in open court for everyone to devour. By the time she was finished, I was a crazed maniac who used my body as a weapon on a poor, defenseless girl who kept screaming *no* and tried to get away from me. She even added the bizarre twist of the nail file gouging and disfiguring her body just to dig me in deeper." He pointed out the window at the other end of the room. "There are people out there who believe that about me! Lots of them! Do you have any idea of the guilt I carry around about subjecting my family to all of that? I put them in such a despicable light. My wonderful family who never did anything but love me."

"Cain," she said trying to calm him down and reason with him, but he wouldn't let her.

"And while we're on the subject—you can't even imagine how I feel about what I've done to Matt. He has to even look like me and be mistaken for me all the time! How fair is that? But you know what? Whenever I start beating myself up inside, which is often, I stop and save the best for Carrie. Because no matter what, no matter how much blame I put on myself, I can't forget that she was the one who brought it all to life. She was the one who turned it all upside down and inside out and put it out there for the world to judge. Worst case, had she not screamed rape—Joanne would have found out and we would have broken up. I can even stretch it to say my parents would have been more than a little pissed. You figure it out, Alexis. It's nearly seven years since this all happened, and I'm still suffering consequences from it while she's still being pampered as the helpless victim."

"She's suffering consequences," argued Alexis. "I've seen her, and you even admitted it yourself."

"Alexis, I was locked away from my home and everyone I love for 5½ years. I spent my twenty-first birthday naked and beat senseless in a freezing, cold cell in Solitary. I was in that same God-foresaken cell and condition the day they buried my best friend. I missed the weddings of my brothers and sister. I MISSED MATT'S WEDDING. I'll never get over that. My family's planning a trip to Ireland in the spring for my grandparent's 60th anniversary, and I can't go. Do you know how long it's been since I've even seen my grandparents? And let's go back—I missed my senior prom and high school graduation, my baseball scholarship. Carrie Willet has trampled on every important event in my life to date. And now I'm almost twenty-five years old, and I have a baby-sitter. There's no room inside me for anything else."

"What about me? You say you love me. That wasn't there before, and you found room for it."

He turned toward the window in frustration and stared out. She wasn't getting it. He was certain now more than ever that nobody would ever understand his torment. He didn't care if Carrie was suffering. She at least did it to herself—she has no one else to blame. She was in control, and she blew it. And he hated her for being so weak.

"I gotta go," he said grabbing his coat from a nearby chair.

"No!" said Alexis getting up and going over to him. "Don't leave like this."

"I'm not in the mood for the game," he said pulling away from her. "I just want to go home. I have homework I should be doing."

"So you're going to walk out on me?"

"Yeah. For now. There's nothing more to say."

"There's plenty more to say."

"No," he argued, visibly struggling to keep his voice and his emotions in check, "there's not. I'll call you."

"At least let me get my coat and drive you home," she said as huge tears perched on her lashes.

"No, I'm walking. I need the fresh air. I'll call you."

Without another word or so much as a peck on the cheek, he left. She stood in a sea of exasperation and regret as she stared at the closed door. Then she ran to the window and caught sight of him as he jogged at a healthy pace down the street and all too soon out of her sight. She turned to the phone and called his home to warn them of the mood he was in.

When he walked in, his tear-stained face confirmed Alexis's phone warning. Without a word, he uncharacteristically dropped his jacket on a chair instead of hanging it up and bounded toward the stairs.

"Cain," called Will.

"I know she called," yelled Cain over his shoulder as he started up the stairs. "I don't want to talk about it."

He went into the bathroom and turned on the water. Will looked over at Nora and felt the all-too-familiar heaviness of heart that they had shared too often over these past nearly seven years. Sighing deeply, he got up.

"I'll go," he said.

When he got upstairs, Cain was still in the bathroom. He had just finished washing his face and was grabbing for a towel. But as Will stood in the doorway and waited, Cain pressed the towel to his face and cried fresh tears into it. Will waited patiently for a few minutes.

"Damn it!" said Cain as he threw the towel in the sink. "Why did I ever say anything? Why did I tell anyone I saw Carrie? She just keeps ruining my life over and over. I keep thinking I'm getting passed it all, and then she comes along."

"She lives here, son. Isn't it likely you're going to run into her?"

"Yeah," said Cain walking passed his father and going into his room, "especially when she keeps making it her business to be wherever I am. She has me served with an order of protection, and then she keeps flaunting herself around me."

"You can put an end to all of this."

"Don't you start, Dad. I just had a fight with Alexis, and I'm not up to another one." He gnashed his teeth together and kicked his wastebasket across the room. "NOBODY UNDERSTANDS!"

"Did you ever stop feeling sorry for yourself long enough to think that maybe, just maybe, it's you who doesn't understand—it's you who hasn't gotten it yet?"

"Is that what you think? I'm feeling sorry for myself?"

"Aren't you?"

"I don't want to talk about it."

"Well, that's certainly the way to deal with it. And how about answering my original question?"

"Dad, let me off the hook here," he pleaded as he wiped his nose with the back of his hand and fresh tears formed in his eyes.

"If it'd help, I'd be glad to."

"Okay! Okay! You all win—everything's cool with Carrie! I don't care any more! I know she was just young and scared and I happened to be in the wrong place at the wrong time! It's all okay! There!"

"Now mean it."

"That's the place I can't get to, Dad. That lie is still out there bigger than life. I don't know, maybe I am being selfish or feeling sorry for myself, but I know what I feel, and saying the words doesn't change it."

"So what do you need? A public apology?"

Cain thought for a minute.

"I don't know," he said wearily. "Maybe. I guess I need her to take some sort of responsibility beyond covert, little whisperings to me."

"Even if she came out tomorrow and made a public statement to the press, that's not going to change anything as far as Maddox and everything goes."

"I know. But it might change the way some people look at me—her old man for one. And it might bring some vindication for you—that you didn't raise a rapist. And maybe people won't look at Alexis like she's some sort of head case because she loves a rapist. It might bring an end to the black cloud that I bring into everybody's life. And before you say a word, I know you don't care, and I know Alexis doesn't care, but I care. I care so much it hurts."

"Okay," said Will not able to argue. "You're going to have to work this one out. What about Alexis? She's really upset."

"I'll call her, but not right now. I need some time. If I call her now, I'll just start another fight. I'm going to sit up here and watch the rest of the game."

"Mom and I are watching it downstairs."

"No, I need to be alone. I'm not fit to be with people right now."

"Okay," smiled Will. "I'll be downstairs."

466

"Thanks, Dad."

The game was on his TV, but Cain's mind was everywhere else. He especially couldn't think about anything except Alexis, but there was still that knot inside him that he knew he had to loosen before he could trust himself to be able to talk to her without getting defensive and ornery. Sometime during the fourth quarter, he gave it all up and fell asleep.

When he woke up a few hours later, he distinctly smelled food. In fact, it was probably the smell of it that finally reached through the barrier and coaxed him awake. As he stretched and opened his eyes, he saw the filmy, dreamlike vision of Alexis sitting on his love seat. He blinked and pulled himself to his elbow to try and decipher if she was real or an apparition of his waking mind.

"Hi," she smiled confirming that she was indeed really there. "I could sit here all day and watch you sleep. But now that you're awake, if you want me to leave, I will. However, I brought food, and I don't leave without it."

"In that case you'd better stay because I'm starving." He sat up on the bed and rubbed his face. "What time is it?"

"Just about six. I called, and your mom said you were sleeping. I'd heard somewhere that the way to a man's heart is through his stomach, so I stopped and picked up some chicken and fried mushrooms and other things you like."

"You found your way to my heart a long time ago."

"Well, I wasn't sure I was still there."

"You're still there," he said kneeling on the floor in front of her. "Cain . . ."

He put the fingertips of his left hand on her lips and then leaned forward and kissed her.

"Don't say anything. Okay? I'm sorry I walked out on you before. You see, I just don't know my way out of this whole mess . . . yet. I will figure it out, I promise you; but until then, let's don't talk about it."

"Okay," she agreed with a small smile. "I won't bring it up at all; and if you suddenly feel you need to talk about it, you bring it up."

"Okay," he said not breaking eye contact with her.

"Why are you looking at me like that?"

"Because you're so beautiful and I love you so much. And you brought food. Is it still hot?"

"Yep. I haven't been here that long."

"Well, then, let's eat."

467

# CHAPTER 21

Days passed, and the holidays neared. Outwardly, things got back to normal in Cain's life. Meredithe was still being obstinate about Cain's requests to drive and extend his curfew, but he was showing signs of relenting, especially alluding to January just before Cain would start school and his new research job at Northwestern. It was enough to keep Cain amiable in the man's presence and patient as he continued walking, taking buses, and accepting rides from others.

On the inside, however, Carrie Willet would not vacate the residency she had taken up in Cain's mind, and she was a nagging tenant at best. He began having more nightmares and bizarre dreams about her. He said nothing to anyone because he just wasn't ready to get into that aspect of his so-called criminal rehabilitation. Why did she ever have to come around again? Hadn't she done enough harm seven years ago? Now she was stirring up all sorts of emotions he had kept buried and had hoped to never have to confront. The more he wrestled with the whole thing, the further it was driving him away from the desired end he had hoped to achieve: the forgiveness he knew would set him free. He hated her more every day.

In the flesh, he had no more contact with her. He hadn't even seen her since that day in the library. All of his dealings with her had been metaphysical, which in many ways was more disturbing and destructive to his morale. He buried himself in his schoolwork in an effort to force her from his mind. And on days when that didn't work, he'd put on sweats and go for long runs in the ever-chilling, late fall air. If nothing else, his grades couldn't get any higher and his body continued to be lean and hard.

But it was just after Thanksgiving that his life took a turn that sent him reeling and grasping for anything to grab on to in order to remain steadfast and in control. It all started one night when he was at work trying to troubleshoot a computer program that regulated the heat in the building. He was so involved in what he was doing that he never heard Charlie, his boss, walk into the room.

"Um, Cain," said Charlie, "you have a visitor."

"What?!" said Cain more than a little confused as he turned toward Charlie.

His eyes skimmed right over his boss and came to a screeching halt on Sam Willet.

"What the hell?" said Cain barely able to speak.

"Can we talk?" Willet asked.

"Gosh, Sam, you know there's practically no one on earth I'd rather sit down and talk to, but I'm working."

"This won't take long, and I won't cause any trouble."

"Cain," said Charlie, "I know who this is, and if you don't want to talk to him, I'll show him out. Or I'll call the police."

468

"Please," said Willet in a quiet manner that was not at all in character.

"It's okay, Charlie," said Cain. "I can handle this. I'll take my break now."

"Do you want me to stay?" asked Charlie.

"No. Thanks. I'll call you if I need you. Just close the door when you leave."

Charlie hesitated a minute giving Sam Willet another leery look. Then he left, closing the door behind him. Cain nodded to a table and chairs across the room.

"The accommodations are better here than they were the last time we met," said Cain as he walked over to the table. Sam Willet followed. "State prisons are not the best places to entertain."

"I don't blame you for being less than happy to see me, but will you please just let me talk?"

"Go ahead."

"I know you saw my daughter a few weeks ago when she came to your school."

"Do I need a lawyer? I'm not saying any more without one."

"Good, then maybe you'll just listen. No, you don't need a lawyer. I told you I'm not here to make trouble." He rubbed his face as he struggled to find words. "Carrie . . . told . . . me."

"Carrie told you what?" asked Cain cautiously as his heart began beating out of control.

"The truth. Soon after she talked to you. She told me and her mother everything."

"Everything?" asked Cain not certain of what was happening. *What game was Carrie playing now?*

"She lied from the beginning. She made it all up so her mother and I wouldn't find out what she was really up to. She even went so far as to cut herself with the nail file to be more convincing."

"Jesus Christ," sighed Cain as he felt the blood drain from his head.

"At first I thought maybe you were somehow threatening her, or maybe after all this time she thought you'd been punished enough . . . I don't know. She persisted though. She told us all the details. It was your testimony exactly—and she wasn't in court when you testified. There was no way she could've known all that. I don't know what to say."

"You do believe her then?"

"Yes."

Cain let out a gasp of disbelief.

"That leaves us with a whole new set of problems," continued Sam. "You see, I could never let her admit the truth officially. She swore under oath that she was telling the truth. I don't know if they

469

would open up that whole can of worms and prosecute her, but I can't let her take that chance."

"Of course not," said Cain sarcastically.

"People wouldn't understand if she came out publicly now. They'd be dubious, as I was when she first told me. The public has a habit of hearing the facts and coming up with their own conclusions. I can't subject her to that. There's something I haven't told you . . . two days ago her mother and I checked Carrie into a hospital where she'll get the help and the rest that she needs."

"Where does that leave me?"

"Is that all you can think of is yourself?"

"I'm sorry, Sam, but yeah. You're daughter did me a great injustice, which you're telling me now has to remain our little secret. I'm sure whatever hospital you checked her into is plush and accommodating, unlike a state prison. And you see, people are not going to look at me as just a scumbag rapist anymore, but also as the scumbag rapist who drove the fair maiden to a mental hospital. She owes me something."

"How about this?" asked Sam Willet as he put a cashier's check on the table in front of Cain. "I liquidated some assets—many assets— and we want you to have this."

Cain's eyes nearly bugged from his head.

"That's a check for $150,000!"

"I know it's not worth the six years of your life that you were locked up, but with the advice of a good investment broker, you can pay your legal fees and still have a nice nest egg to insure yourself a very comfortable old age. There is a catch."

"I'm not surprised."

"All I'm asking is that you quietly get your life back on track, and leave my daughter alone to try and get hers together. I covered my tracks with the money, so no one can trace it back to me. You, of course, would tell family and close friends, but no press or law suits. I'll deny it if it ever comes down to that, and Carrie is in no shape to confirm or admit to anything."

"So you want to buy me off?"

"No. I don't have to give you a dime. I didn't have to come here to tell you any of this. I could have sat on it, but I do feel we owe you something. It was a terrible thing Carrie did to you. I'm just trying in my own way to make up for it. I can't do anything about your criminal record, but I'll do what I can to get it buried as deep as possible. And, as I'm sure you already know, I do have some influence, and therefore, I've already seen to it that Ralph Meredithe will be notified that you have fulfilled your parole obligations and he's to cut you loose. I'm sure he'll call you and make it official."

Now he had Cain's full attention. The money was one thing, but Sam Willet was literally handing him his life back. All of the harsh restrictions would be gone. He could live just like any other person.

"I feel bad because I know I've made these past seven years harder on you than they had to be," Sam confessed. "I interfered with your life as much as I could to make you as uncomfortable as possible. I couldn't help it—that was my daughter, and God help me, I believed her. I'm sorry. I know it's inadequate, but I don't know what else to say."

Cain's head was spinning with the reality that was being heaped upon him in doses almost too big to take in at one time. He watched Sam Willet's mouth moving and he heard the words he was saying, but he was sure he would wake up at any minute and discover this had all been a dream. Large tears flooded his eyes and perched on his eyelashes as he bit his lip to stave off a breakdown.

"You'll be able to end my parole?"

"I already have it in the works. I'll do whatever I can, except go public."

Tears rolled down Cain's face as he got up and walked over to the window to look out. He didn't want to let Sam Willet see him cry, and there was no way he could hold it back.

"I think of the magnitude of Carrie's lie everyday," Sam said to Cain's back. "I was at Maddox that day, so I have at least a little bit of an idea of what you went through and the agony your family must have felt. I know your life is still not easy. I've thrown up roadblocks wherever I could. I wish there was some way to take it all back. Carrie and I are going to have to live with what we did to you forever. That's what she just can't deal with right now." Tears of his own burned behind his eyes. "Her life hasn't been the same since that night, and she's just gotten progressively worse. In her own way she tried to tell me way back at the beginning. She said she didn't want to press charges; she just wanted to drop the whole thing. Of course, I thought she was crazy, and there was no way I could even consider that. All I could think of was hurting you any way I could.

"I know your life has been hell, but at least you've always known you were innocent. Carrie's been dealing with oppressive guilt, and it's going to be a long time yet before she'll be able to reconcile any of that and move on. She's paying a price."

Cain continued staring out the window. He couldn't say anything. Tears ran freely down his cheeks, but he wasn't sure if they were for himself or for Carrie. All he knew was that this was the last way he had ever expected to be spending this evening.

"I don't want your money," he finally was able to say, "I just want my life back. I want Meredithe off my back."

"It's being taken care of; I promise you. And I want you to take the money. You deserve it, and it does help me to feel at least a little better. I don't want it back."

Cain turned from the window and looked at him. Sam Willet was a shell of the man who had been menacing him all these years. It was obvious that he had been under a great deal of stress and he wasn't

471

handling it well.  He had never seen that look on his own parents. Somehow, no matter how bad things got, they always managed to hold up and keep things going.  They were devastated, he knew, but they never showed it.  Maybe the difference was having a clear conscience and being guiltless.  He guessed that as long as he had been forced to play a part in this whole fiasco, he was glad to have been the victim rather than the tormentor.  He wiped at his face with his hands.

"I don't know what to say," he finally admitted.  "This is all happening too fast. I'm still expecting to fall out of bed and rudely wake up."

"There's nothing more to say," said Sam.  "Just take the check and move on with your life.  I realize the criminal record is still a roadblock, but you have so much going for you that you'll manage just fine.  I'm not so sure about Carrie, but her mother and I are going to do all that we can for her.  Maybe if we'd been there a little more in the past, none of this would have happened.  Someday when you have children of your own, you may understand me a little more.  Take care."

Cain watched numbly as the older man walked out the door.  A moment later Charlie appeared.

"Is everything all right?" he asked anxiously.

"Yeah," said Cain vacantly.  "Yeah.  But, Charlie, I gotta leave. I promise you I'll get this computer thing taken care of first thing tomorrow, but right now I don't think I can concentrate on much of anything."

"Sure, Cain, but what if Mr. Meredithe calls?"

"Tell him to go to hell!  Just tell him to go to fucking hell!"


A friend from work dropped him off at Alexis's apartment a few minutes later.  He was wired and anxious to share his news.

"Cain!" she said more than a little surprised to see him.  "I thought I was supposed to pick you up at 10:00?'

"Get your coat, Alexis, we're going to my house."

"What's going on?"

"Just get your coat.  Come on, come on."

"I'm confused."

"Of course, you are.  I'll explain."  He took her keys from her. "I'll drive."

"No," she insisted.  "What if we get stopped?"

"Lex, it's only a few miles; but if we get stopped, I've got friends in high places.  Come on."

"Can't you tell me what's going on?" she asked when they got in the car and began to drive.

"Yeah, but I need my parents to be there.  This is something for all of us to share together."

He practically jumped from the car before it came to a full stop, and then he ran to grab Alexis's hand and nearly pulled her behind him into the house. His parents were as surprised as Alexis had been. She merely looked at them and shrugged as if Cain had lost his mind. Once they had taken their coats off, Cain reached in his pocket and put the check on the table in front of them all.

"Where . . . the . . . hell . . . did . . . you . . . get . . . that?!" asked Will as the women stared in disbelief.

"That's my name on there," said Cain excitedly.

"I see that," said his father. "WHERE DID IT COME FROM?"

"Sam Willet paid me a visit tonight at work." Without warning his eyes filled with emotional tears. "She told him the truth. Carrie told him what really happened."

Nora threw her hand up to her mouth as a small gasp escaped. Then she dropped to the couch, as her legs would no longer support her. Will stood in stunned disbelief.

"My God," sighed Alexis as tears sprung to her eyes. "My God, Cain!"

She threw her arms around him and held him close.

Cain related the whole story to them, careful not to leave anything out.

"It's not perfect," he concluded, "but it's damned acceptable. I'm free. Please tell me I'm not dreaming."

More than a few tears fell over the next few minutes as emotions ran high. Nobody spoke; each tried to take in the information and understand what was happening.

"I'm not sure about this money," said Cain breaking the momentary silence. "I don't want to feel like I've been bought."

Will took a few seconds to put together his thoughts.

"Don't look at it that way," he said. "They owe you; you deserve every penny of it. Willet was right about investing it. That money will go a long way if you take care of it. They're leaving you with a felony conviction you don't deserve. I don't think it's going to matter that much any more since you have some pretty influential people at Northwestern on your side and ready to back you up and attest to the work you can do. And since you never committed the crime, you always have the option of invoking tonight's bizarre chain of events in proclaiming your innocence. He's not buying your silence; he's simply saying he won't go public with it, nor would he admit to anything if you did. I guess the question is, is that enough for you? Can you live with that? Or . . . do you want to give the money back and go to the officials with this information?"

"It wouldn't do any good. He as much as told me he'd lie. He was careful to seek me out at work and get me alone where there would be no witnesses."

"That's right," agreed Will. "So he's not buying anything from you. Taking the money or giving it back doesn't change a single thing except the financial aspect of your future. Keep it. You deserve it."

"The main reason I'd keep it is to pay you back for the money you paid to Bruce. That's been weighing heavy on my mind since the beginning. I know it was a whole lot."

Will smiled, feeling content in having raised a sincere human being. He had always known, as Sam Willet was only now finding out, that that's something that even money can't buy. Through all the difficulties of this debacle, he always knew that he couldn't have asked for a better son and that with faith and determination they'd get through anything.

"We can talk about that," he said. "Later. Right now, I just want to concentrate on this good feeling that I haven't known for seven years."

Cain went over and hugged him warmly.

"Thanks, Dad. I don't know how I could have gotten through all this without you to grab onto."

"This is the answer to our prayers," smiled Nora knowingly. She put her hand over her mouth. "Oops, did I just say that?"

Cain beamed as he went over and took her in his arms.

"Mom, I don't know what I'd ever do without you and your prayers. Don't give up on me."

Then he looked over at Alexis who had been sitting quietly on the couch, silent tears flowing nonstop down her face. When he went to her and took her in his arms, she squeezed him and cried shamelessly on his shoulder.

"It's okay," he told her softly. "It's over."

"I can't believe it," she cried.

"I'm not quite there myself," he admitted, "but I feel damn good. We can have that party now, Mom. The one you wanted to have last year when I came home. Now I'm ready."

They sat and shared in the golden glow of the happy circumstances. The winter solstice had passed and the sun would be increasingly present in their lives.

"It's getting late," said Cain after a while. Then he made his announcement. "I'm going up to get my books and some clothes, and I'm going home with Alexis. I'm not sending her back by herself late at night any more."

"Do you think that's wise?" asked Will. "Nothing's been made official yet?"

"I know," admitted Cain. "But I'm not moving out. It's just for tonight, and I don't think Meredithe will call. It might not be official, but he knows. Sam Willet didn't put this all together just today. It's been in the works for a while. I'm betting that I'm actually the last one to find out. Don't worry. If he calls, either don't answer or tell him I'm coming in tomorrow and we'll talk about it then. Right now, I've been handed a new lease on life and I'm in love—that's all I can think about."

Will looked over at Alexis who gave him a shy, little shrug indicating that she knew nothing about this but she wasn't about to argue with Cain either. Will smiled, guessing he really couldn't blame his son and at the same time realizing it was time to step out of the role of guardian and fierce protector.

"We'll check the Caller ID, and we just won't answer," he said with a wink. "You can deal with it on your own."

"Thanks, Dad," beamed Cain. Then he went to his mother and kissed her. "I love you, Mom."

That night his mind was primed for anything but sleep, and Alexis got caught up in the euphoria and his childlike excitement. This time when they got back to her apartment, he didn't even mention the bottle of Irish Whiskey. He was too caught up in a natural high. He didn't want to dull it or in any way numb the effects. He was, however, bursting with desire and love for his Alexis, and he wasted little time with small talk or even large talk, for that matter. They took off their coats, and he immediately took her hand and led her to the bedroom.

"Don't say anything," he told her. "I can't say another word until I wrap myself around you and release all of this emotion that's been building up inside me. I love you so much. You're my whole world."

Although he could hardly contain the joy of his newfound freedom coupled with his love for her, he took his time and skillfully brought her along until her desire matched his and they shared the wild excitement that was born of it.

"I love seeing you so happy," she told him as she propped herself up on her side and looked down at him. "I haven't seen you quite like this since we were kids. There was always that little corner of sadness that I never could quite touch, but it was there nonetheless."

"I haven't felt like this since before I knew Carrie Willet. In fact, Lex, I don't think I've ever felt like this—I've never been a free man and in love with you at the same time. The only thing that could make it better is if I had never met Carrie Willet at all, but I'm realistic enough not to dwell on that regret and to concentrate instead on all the good things I have now." He put his hand up and gently touched her cheek. "I'm glad I didn't miss you along the way. And now I have at least some kind of a future to offer you."

"I don't care about any of that."

"I know. That's part of why I love you so much. But I care about it. You deserve better than to be associated with a rapist ex-con. Maybe now that it's not being thrown in my face and in my path everywhere I turn, it'll start to fade into the background. God—you and all this—it's almost too good to be true."

"It's about time something started going right for you," she smiled.

They spent the rest of the night wrapped in the warmth and intimacy of each other's naked body, enveloped in the blissful sweetness of contented, refreshing sleep. In spite of the unfamiliar bed and circumstances, Cain couldn't remember when he had had a more relaxing sleep. God was in his heaven, and all was right with the world.

After his classes the next day, Cain wasted no time in catching a train to the city to confront Ralph Meredithe with his newfound independence. All through the amazing and bizarre occurrences of the night before, he kept feeling the nagging reminder that all he had to go on at this point was the unsubstantiated word of Sam Willet. It was like having a check for a million dollars written out in his name but bearing no signature. Now it was time to be sure the bank was going to cash it.

He knew Meredithe didn't schedule command performances of his parolees this early in the day on Wednesdays, so he wasn't surprised to see no one in the outside waiting room. The secretary, however, was taken by surprise when he walked in. Cain gave her no time to recover.

"Is he in?" he asked bluntly.

"Yes, but . . ."

"Thanks," said Cain walking passed her and opening the door to Meredithe's inner sanctuary.

Meredithe looked up.

"I've been expecting you," he said from his file cabinet across the room.

"I'll bet you have," said Cain taking a seat across from the desk. There was no subordinate code of conduct followed this day. "And that better mean you have papers already drawn up for me to sign."

"As a matter of fact, I do. Actually, I was going to call you later, but I had a feeling you'd beat me to the punch."

"Did you call my house last night?"

"No. Were you there?"

Cain smiled but made no reply.

"You know," said Meredithe with a smile of his own, "it's that know-it-all grin of yours that I'm going to miss the most." Meredithe fumbled through some papers on his desk. "Here you go. Sign here and here."

"Is your secretary a notary?"

"Yes."

"Get her in here. Sam Willet may not be able to do anything about my criminal history, but I'm not having someone come along someday and jerk this termination of parole out from under me."

"You guys crack me up," laughed Meredithe. "You all come out of prison thinking you're some kind of store-front lawyers."

"When you've been through that system, you learn to look out for your rights, especially in my case. Just call her in and let's get this over with."

The secretary entered with her stamp as Meredithe had requested. Cain took the pen in his left hand ready to sign, but first he sagely took the time to carefully read over the papers. Meredithe grinned.

"You don't trust me a bit, do you?" he said.

"Not a bit," answered Cain as he wrote his name on the document and passed it over to the secretary.

As she went about notarizing it, Meredithe pushed a large envelope across the desk to Cain.

"Everything you need is in there—as soon as we put these notarized papers in. If you look, there's even a valid Illinois driver's license. No test, no nothing. A little gift from the state. That ought to be enough to give you a hard-on. The only thing is you'll have to make a trip to the DMV for a picture—we didn't think you'd want us to use your mug shot."

"You're all heart, Ralph," said Cain as he accepted his notarized copy of the papers from the secretary and put them in his envelope.

"Then I guess this is good-bye."

"You betcha," said Cain standing up. "I'm going to go home and see what I can do about this hard-on you just gave me."

Meredithe grinned admirably and shook his head.

"I got to admit, I'm going to miss that quick, irreverent wit of yours."

"Have a great life," said Cain as he started walking toward the door.

"Farrell," called Meredithe. Cain stopped and turned around. "You're just going to leave without demanding an apology or anything?"

"I wasn't expecting one, to tell you the truth, so don't trouble yourself. I got what I came for."

"In that case would you come back here and give me five minutes or so?"

Cain stood and skeptically eyed him for a few seconds. Then he went back and sat down.

"My job is not to make judgments, but rather to carry out the judgments of the courts. I'm not making excuses or anything, that's just the way it is. But I know I was instrumental in making your life more difficult than it had to be, and for that I want to say that I'm sorry. Especially in the beginning I thought you were a spoiled, suburban brat who got caught manhandling a defenseless, young lady. Sam Willet gave me the chance to help keep you in your place after you left Maddox; and as a man, I was more than happy to help avenge the young lady. I was wrong. I'm sorry. Are you surprised?"

Cain laughed, a tiny bit of sarcasm lingering. "I'm still a little blown away by all of this, but yes, I guess I am. Just like you've always had me figured for a degenerate, I've always had you figured for a prick. So, I guess I kind of owe you an apology, too."

Meredithe laughed good-naturedly.

"Well, I guess now you can say we're even," he said.

"Kind of," said Cain. "But I'm still walking out of here a rapist."

"That's true, but you'll be fine. I have no doubt. Look how well you've done against the odds."

Cain stood up, ready to leave.

"I'll just be glad to have you off my ass," he said. Then he smiled and put out his hand. "Take care. I wish I could say I'll miss you."

"Likewise," smiled Meredithe as he returned the handshake.


Things were good; things were very good; things were wonderful. Then what, Cain wondered, kept nagging at his peace of mind, not quite letting him enjoy life the way he felt he should be? At first the answer eluded him, but the more restless nights he spent grappling with it, the clearer it became. He knew what he had to do, but it definitely wasn't something he was looking forward to.

"I'm going to see Carrie tomorrow after school," he announced to Alexis one night.

"Oh," she said, not able to hide her surprise. "Do you think that's wise?"

"I don't know, but I have to do it. I kept thinking that it's all over now, so why do I still have this . . . feeling inside me? Then I realized it isn't all over. There's still one more closed door that I have to open. Do you understand?"

"Of course I do. I've been telling you that all along—me and your mom."

"Well, you're right," sighed Cain staring blankly into the distance. "I tried to ignore it, but it won't go away. So I called Sam this afternoon and told him I want to see Carrie. Once I assured him my motives are pure, he set it up. He'll probably be there hovering, but I'll deal with that."

"Good, I'm glad. You'll feel better once you get that behind you."

"All kinds of things have been going through my head. Meredithe accused me of being a storefront lawyer the other day. The truth is you don't get dragged through the legal system without picking up at least a working knowledge of the law, and I read a lot of law books in the library at Maddox. I couldn't shake the feeling I was being bought, and I started figuring a way I could get Carrie back in court to clear my name."

"Cain . . ."

"Don't worry. It was just a thought. I've seen my face in the newspapers and on the 10:00 news enough for a lifetime. Pursuing my rights would only stir up that mess again. It's kind of calmed down and faded into the background now. I'd be nuts to dredge it all up—and then there are no guarantees."

"I think you're wise. Things are going good for you."

"Well, and then believe it or not, I thought of Carrie. She's been through enough, too. I realize that what I've needed all along is for her to tell the truth, and she did that—even if it was only to a select few. The important people know. Now I have to leave her in peace to try and make some sense of it all. But first I have to let her know that it's okay—that I'm okay. After that she's on her own."

Alexis smiled affectionately.

"You're a special person, you know that?"

"I'm an ass, Alexis. Look how long it took me to come to this?"

"Sweetheart, you said it yourself, she totally turned your life upside down and inside out. It would have been unnatural for you not to harbor resentment and hatred. There are a lot of people who would never be able to let go. Don't sell yourself short."

"Well, I'll be glad when it's over, that's all I know."

"Do you want me to come with you?"

"I thought of that, and actually I'd like nothing more, but this is something I have to do by myself. I could never do it, though, if I didn't know you'd be waiting here for me when I'm through."

"You sure know the right things to say," smiled Alexis warmly.

"Well, let's hope that holds up tomorrow."


When he pulled up in the parking lot of the hospital, he couldn't help but to be overcome with the feeling of how much it was like a prison in a glamorous disguise. There was no barbed wire, but there was a functional, though decorative, fence enclosing the many serene and beautifully landscaped acres. Instead of bars, some windows bore ornamental wrought iron scrollwork. And then there was the fact that those inside weren't free to just walk out at will. It was exclusive but a prison nonetheless. He wasn't sure if that made him feel any better or not. He was slowly beginning to understand that there are many different kinds of punishment and hell-laden existences. He had always pictured Carrie as having pushed him out of her mind as she went about her charm-filled life. Now that he was learning that wasn't the case, he wasn't getting the satisfaction he would have expected. There was no real joy for him in retribution.

He sat in the car for a few minutes as all these emotions mingled with others and he tried to make sense of it all. That's when he realized there was no sense to be had in this whole convoluted mess. This was an anomaly which defied rational thinking and commonsense. The best thing to do would be to dig a deep hole, bury it, and move on—he in his way, Carrie in hers. He did know one thing for certain—this was the last time he ever wanted to see or hear from the Willet family. Taking a deep breath, he left the car to seal this final chapter of his errant youth.

479

When he got to her room, the door was open and both her parents were there. He had hoped to find her alone, but somehow he knew he wouldn't. And as he looked at it now, it was probably just as good to have witnesses to everything that was about to take place. Carrie's instability was his undoing seven years ago, and he had learned from that experience, albeit the hard way.

Taking hold of all the courage he could muster, he knocked lightly on the open door. Carrie jumped nervously and told him to come in. She looked even paler and her eyes were more sunken than the last time he had seen her. The red puffiness around her eyes told him she had spent more than a fair amount of time crying. He presented the flowers that he carried.

"Thank you," she smiled as she accepted them. "This is way too generous."

"Let's don't get started that way, Carrie," he said trying to keep his voice level. "Let's don't ascribe blame—even to ourselves."

He looked over at her mother whom he hadn't seen since his trial. She, too, looked as though the years had taken their toll. The irony of it all hit him square between the eyes. All these years he was sure they had all been basking in the light of the conquering heroes—having rid the world of a villainous rapist. But now they all looked downtrodden and lifeless.

"Please, sit down," said Mrs. Willet.

There was an empty chair in their circle. He was reluctant to take it, but he knew he couldn't play out this final act standing over them looking down.

"Before we go any further," said Mrs. Willet, "we all owe you a great apology. The words sound so insignificant in light of everything that has gone on over the past seven years, but let's face it, there are no words to ever make up for all you've been through."

"I really don't want to go into all that," said Cain. "Nothing can change it, and by looking back we're only going to make it harder on ourselves to move forward."

"That's very noble of you," said Carrie's mother.

"No," insisted Cain. "I'm not trying to be noble or anything of the sort. I'm just trying to get my life back, and I've learned there's no good to be had from beating the dead horse of the past. I'm moving passed that, and I don't want to look back. I've been dealing with this for a long time, and I've finally discovered what I hope is the last piece of my puzzle. That's why I'm here. You see, Carrie and I are not all that different. We're both trying to make the person everyone thinks we are fit into the skin of the person we really are. The difference is I've been facing and dealing with reality, while Carrie hasn't. Who knows, maybe that's the last piece of her puzzle, too. I'm here from a purely selfish point of view, but if it ends up benefiting Carrie, too, then all the better."

Tears had already begun to stream down Carrie's face.

"I'm so sorry," she said, her hands trembling noticeably. "I panicked. I didn't set out to hurt you."

"I know that," said Cain.

"And I tried." She looked somewhat frantically from her mother to her father and then back to Cain. "I tried to tell the truth—once. They took me to a hospital, and I asked where you were. The social worker told me you were in jail, and I shouldn't worry because you couldn't hurt me anymore. Then she said they had to do an exam to get evidence, and take pictures. She said it wouldn't be pleasant, but it would be over soon, and it would help make sure that you could never do this to another girl. That's when it all hit me. That's when I realized what I had done. I was only eighteen, and I don't know what I was thinking; but I didn't think it would ever snowball into the hell it became. I tried to take it back. I got hysterical, and I told them I lied, but no one would listen to me. They called it post traumatic response or something like that. They said women often do that more as a way of not having to face it than anything else. They pointed out the cuts from the nail file and some bruises I had gotten while we were wrestling earlier. Then I tried to say I didn't want to press charges. I just wanted to forget the whole thing." She turned to her father. "Remember, Daddy?"

"Yes," answered Sam softly as that night played over in his mind. "We thought you were just so frightened of him and you feared more retribution."

"Everyone kept telling me to be strong," she sobbed. "They said I was safe. They were going to be sure that you'd be locked up for a long time. They kept telling me how brave I was, and how I was making sure that some other girl wasn't going to have to go through this. I was eighteen; I didn't know what else to do. Then when I saw how serious this all was, I got scared I was going to get in trouble if I kept insisting and finally made anyone start to believe me. I mean, I lied to the police, I signed things that weren't true. I realized I was in too far, and it killed me inside. I'm so sorry, Cain. I just didn't know how to get out of it; I didn't know what else to do."

Cain sat dry-eyed and pensive as the reality of the later events of that night crystallized before his eyes. Then he somehow found the hardest words he had ever spoken in his life.

"It's okay." Once those words were out, the rest followed naturally. "It's really okay. It's over. I'm okay now, and I hope you will be too."

She was crying uncontrollably, and her mother reached over to put a supportive arm around her. Sam was lost on a stormy sea of memory and regret. Cain got up and approached her. He knelt down on one knee and took her hands in his.

"Did you hear me, Carrie?"

She looked into his eyes and nodded her head.

"I'm okay. My life is good, better than good. You're not responsible for me any longer. And I'm not blaming you anymore."

"Please don't hate me," she sobbed.

"No. I don't. There's no room in my life anymore for that. I came here for myself, but if I can help you too, then all the better. We were both young and out of our league, but let it all go now. Beating yourself up isn't going to change anything that's already happened. Start over. There's time to make a future. That's what I'm off to do right now. It's probably best if we don't see each other anymore." He lifted her hands, which he still held, and kissed them. "Peace."

Then he stood and walked out of the room, happy to put distance between himself and that unhappy situation.

When he got to his car, he realized his hands were shaking and he knew he couldn't go home just yet. He needed some time to bring himself back to calm. So what better place to head than the beach? He started the car and drove to the beach where he had spent that last night with Scott. He always went there when he wanted to feel close to his friend; the cemetery was too—dead.

It was cold and snow flurries were swirling around him. Having just gone over all that ancient history with Carrie made him feel strangely disconnected. It had been nearly a year to the day that he had walked out of Maddox and come home. And now the final chapter had been written. How bizarre it all was.

He picked up a flat board that he found lying in the sand. Then after collecting a handful of good-sized stones, he commenced with batting practice. No one else was around, which made him all the happier as he sent the stones soaring out into the lake.

"You were there, weren't you?" Cain said out loud to Scott. "I could feel it. You know that she finally admitted she lied." Now tears flooded his eyes as he attempted to continue to send the stones to their watery resting-places. "I can't believe this day has finally come. Now if I could just have you back. That's the hardest thing of all. I want to see your face right now. I even want to hear you laughing at me and telling me that you told me so." Now the tears won out and he could no longer see. He dropped his makeshift bat and sacrificial stones. "Damn I miss you, Scott. Damn it anyway."

The deserted beach was a perfect spot for the ghostly images of the past that played out in his mind. He laughed through his tears as he thought about how he always ran to the beach to refresh himself and renew his spirit. The last time he had come he was more involved with the power and beauty of the setting. Now he was looking to put the past to rest; this was a symbolic bloodletting. His childhood with all it's joy and pain had finally reached an excruciatingly long conclusion, and he finally felt free to become the man he had always wanted to be. He knew this would be the last time he needed to come to this place of lost memories and unfulfilled dreams. This was a time for looking ahead. As much as he loved this place, there was a lot of pain and regret still to be found here if he looked too hard for it, and there was no room in his life for that anymore. There were other beaches where he could enjoy the wonders of the lakeshore without confronting the agony of the past. This beach belonged to another time; a time he was more than willing to walk away from.

Still it was hard to get up and make that final exit. There had been so many good times here, and Scott was really here. But even that had to be put in its own perspective. No matter what his intentions, he always ended up dwelling in remorse and guilt when he came here. Scott would never stand still for that. As he stood there trying to focus through his tears, he could feel Scott setting him free and telling him to move on. It was time, and they'd meet again some day. The more his tears clouded his vision, the clearer it became that he needed to put one foot in front of the other and turn his back on this pain.

As he walked away and felt the sand turn to concrete beneath his feet, he wiped his tears with his coat sleeves. This time he didn't stop and look back, for he knew if he did he'd never be able to leave, so he walked through the swhirling snow with the insistent wind, which he knew was Scott, pushing at his back.

Ironically enough, even his car was parked facing away. When he got in out of the cold, he made some last dabs at his tears and sniffed back the last remaining threats of an emotional outburst. He forced himself into the present and the elation of the promise that lay before him. He thought of Alexis and how she was his future now. How lucky could a guy get? As he backed his car out of the space, he glanced back over his shoulder to be sure the way was clear. As he did he glimpsed the beach out of the corner of his eye; he smiled and turned his sight forward. *Thank you, Scott.*

That night he sat with Alexis at her apartment. The flicker of the fire blazing in the fireplace danced with the soft glow of the lights from the Christmas tree they had just decorated, and he had never felt so at peace in his adult life. He had his arm around her and his stocking feet up on the coffee table in front of them. He leaned over and kissed her affectionately on the head.

"You're really happy now, aren't you?" she smiled as she cuddled in closer to him. "I can sense it."

"There's nothing left in my way anymore. I've lived with being a convicted felon for so long that that doesn't bother me now that all the other obstacles have been removed and the world has been set in motion again. Oh, yeah, and I got so caught up last night in telling you that I was going to see Carrie today that I forgot to tell you that Jon Harrison called me yesterday."

"He did?!"

"Yeah, what a great surprise. I had called Mike to tell him about all this stuff with Carrie, and he told Jon. I'm not on parole anymore, so it's okay for us to see each other."

"How is he?'

"He's good. He hooked up with a good woman, and he seems happy to be a law-abiding citizen. He keeps telling me it was my influence, so maybe Maddox wasn't a complete loss for me. But anyway, I got my friend back. We're getting together next week."

Alexis smiled.

"You don't know how good that makes me feel," she said. "You're lucky enough to have your brothers, but you need friends, too. Someone to take up where Scott had to leave off. I've sensed that loneliness in you."

"I guess you're right because it sure felt good to talk to him. I've purposely avoided making any friends because my parole status didn't leave me any choice but to go into my past. Now there's no need to dredge that up at all. Alexis, I feel so . . . normal."

She smiled broadly and knelt up on the couch. Then straddling his lap, she sat facing him. She put her hands on his face and beamed at him.

"Sweetheart," she said, "you are anything but normal. You are the most beautiful, exceptional man I have ever known."

"Coming from someone who once dated my very successful, identical twin brother, that's quite a compliment," he teased.

"You betcha," she smiled, coining one of his phrases.

"You know," he said becoming serious, "if it hadn't've been for you and my family, I would've self-destructed a long time ago. And my family loved me in spite of myself—I've always known that and been grateful for it. But you showed me that I was someone who could be loved by choice, not just because I was born to it. You knew what you were getting into right from the beginning, and it didn't matter to you. You're the one person in my life who chose to take on my problems. You don't know what that means to me. And I'm happy for myself that those problems have been greatly diminished, but I'm even happier that I won't be tainting your life with them any longer. Any other woman wouldn't have stuck it out like you did when the going got rough."

"Well, I'm not just any other woman," she smiled, taking note of his referral to her as a woman.

"No, you definitely are not. And I want to spend the rest of my life making you happy and showing you how much I love you for standing by me when it would've been much easier to run. I want to marry you, Lex. Please tell me you will."

Her face softened into a mixture of wonderment and delight. Tears sprang to her eyes as she thought back to everything she had been through with him and how hopeless she had felt.

"It would be the greatest joy of my life—you're the greatest joy of my life."

"Then you will, right?"

"Absolutely."

"Shit," he sighed with an amazed smile, "how did I get so lucky?" He pulled her close and kissed her passionately, savoring every second of this blissful moment. "Now, if you get off my lap, I have something for you."

"It's still a couple weeks till Christmas," she smiled as she climbed back to her side of the couch.

"This isn't a Christmas present," he said getting up and going over to his jacket.

"What is it?"

"It's a . . . I don't know. I just love you so damn much I had to get it."

Alexis twittered with glee and anticipation as he fumbled through his jacket.

"I don't have anything for you, though," she confessed.

"You've given me everything I need."

He turned and for the first time she saw the tiny box in his hand. She lost her breath as her heart pounded with excitement. This was the first time they had actually talked about marriage and they hadn't even looked at rings at all, so she held her heart back from jumping to overly grand conclusions.

"What's this?" she asked accepting the box from him.

"Something I thought you'd like."

She opened it and time froze as she looked down at the beautiful 1-carat ruby solitaire engagement ring. It was set in platinum and flanked by two small diamonds. It was just the one she had always wanted, but she didn't remember ever telling him.

"How did you know?" she said as tears ran down her cheeks and her hands trembled from the weight of the promise of the tiny box.

"You never made a point of it, but I've seen you look at it when we've been out. Then I asked your mom to be sure." He took the box from her. "I think it's even the right size. One day while I was here, I took one of the many rings you always wear on that finger. Then I got it back before you could miss it." He took the ring out of the box. "Is it okay if I try it on you? This is your last chance to kick my ass out and send me on my way."

She couldn't speak through the emotion she was experiencing, so she simply held out her left hand. It was shaking so uncontrollably that Cain had to hold it still in order to put the ring on. As he had suspected, it fit perfectly. She tried to look down at it but her eyes were too filled with tears. She put her trembling hands on the sides of his head and pulled his face toward her. Then crying and laughing and hugging him, she kissed him over and over.

"Thank you," she sobbed. "Thank you for loving me this way. I've loved you for so long, but I always thought I'd have to watch you give someone else a beautiful ring like this."

"No," he smiled as he brushed her tears with his fingertips, "I'm way smarter than that. Just a little slower than most, that's all. I think I've even figured out who your mystery man is—you know the idiot who was too dumb to know how you felt about him and you wouldn't tell him because you wanted him to figure it out first?"

"Oh, him."

"Yeah. It was me, right?"

"Cain Farrell," she smiled adoringly, "you definitely are much smarter than you look."

"Yeah," he joked. "I do have a brain, you know. I'm not just window dressing like everyone tries to make me out to be."

"Okay, if you're so smart, I have one more test for you."

"Anything. Go ahead."

She looked down at her beautiful ring now that her eyes had cleared, and she was filled with a love for him that she had never even imagined before.

"Okay, but no pencil and paper or anything—just your world-class brain."

"Okay."

"What's 2 + 2?"

He looked at her in total confusion. God, how she loved him.

"You asked me this once before," he said, "What's up?"

"Come on," she insisted. "No stalling. Unless, of course, you don't know the answer."

"Four," he finally said hesitantly as if there were a trick answer.

"Oh, yes!" she laughed as she took him in her arms and held him close. "Wait till we tell your mom!"